Inductions Dangerous

John Bellen

Copyright © 2023 James Thorne.

All rights reserved.

ISBN: 9781068814518

Table of Contents

Incognition 1
The Art Lover 27
The Sundering Seas 62
Thirteenth Night 82
A Lesson in Politics 115
Misericord at Dawn 149
One Soft to Petrograd 176
The Old Ally 206
The Heart of Betrayal 241
Fallen to Earth 263
The Rhine Maidens 289
Secret House 330
Under the Willows 356

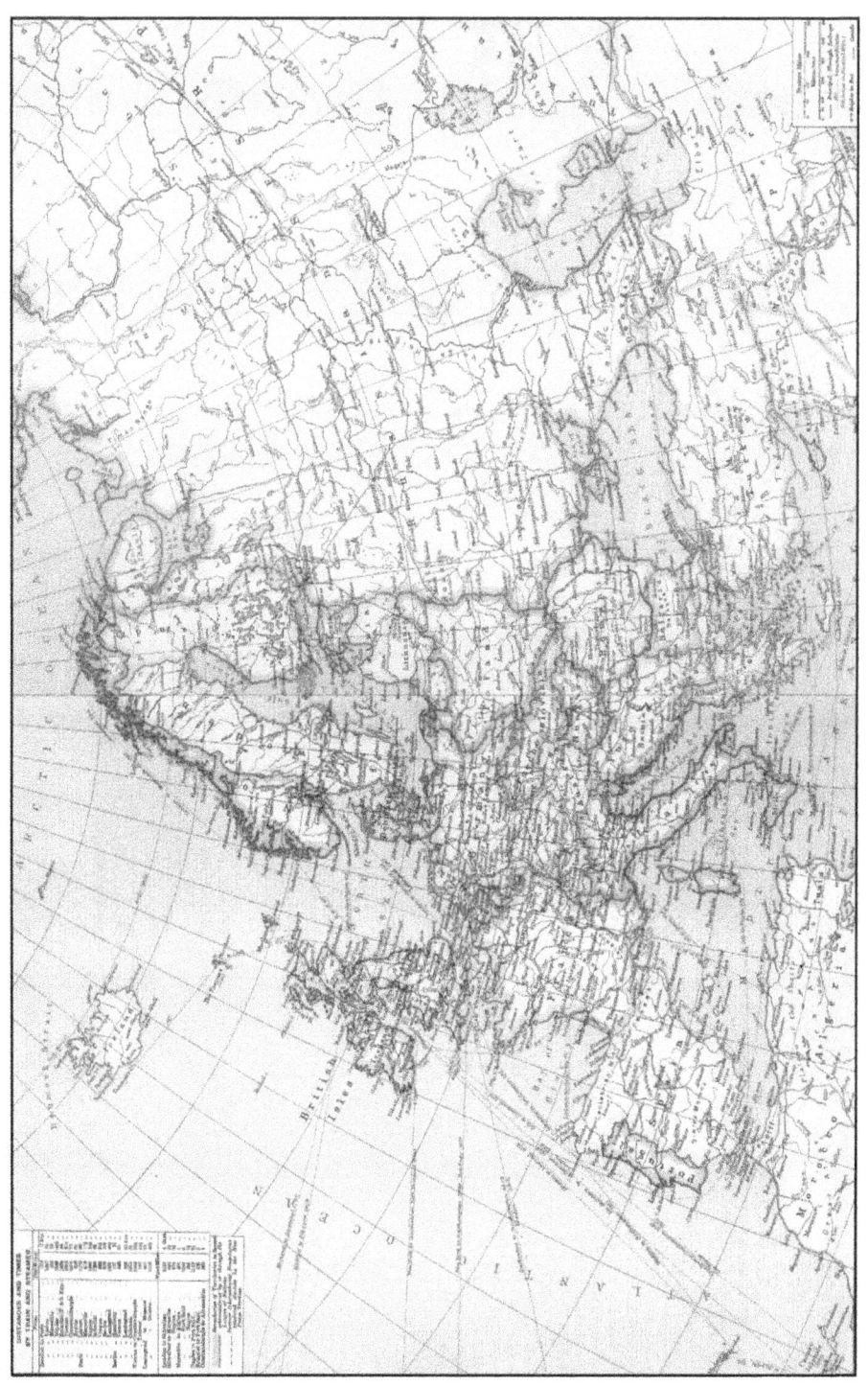

Europe 1920 ~ 1936

Incognition

No one paid much attention to the man who stepped from Cologne's Central Railway Station into the mellow September sunshine of the Bannhofstrasse. Though he wore an English suit of good quality, and gestured for a taxi with the random authority of a military officer, pedestrians on the pavements walked past him, rather than around him; to do the latter would have meant that they had taken notice of him. A motor-taxi did stop at his signal, just as a porter in the station had assisted him with his two suitcases. But they heeded him as simply another member of the public, a person of no special significance. His hold on their memories was so slight that he could have been anything to an observer, or nothing.

He was of an indeterminate age, and stood an average height, perhaps an inch more or an inch less. His shape was what might have been termed medium, neither stocky nor slender. His hair was of the vaguely dusty hue which could have been interpreted as dull blond by some, brown by others, while most would have sought an adjective in between. Even his eyes fit many possible descriptions: were they a blue pale enough to be green, a green sharp enough to be hazel, or a hazel deep enough to be brown?

Most people were spared these decisions, since they soon forgot the man anyway.

The ride from the station to the Domplatz was a short one, and though this was the newcomer's first visit to Cologne, he may have travelled the route five hundred times for the interest he apparently displayed. The taxi stopped at the entrance to the Hotel Excelsior, which had been, from just after the Armistice, the General Headquarters of the British occupation forces in the German Rhineland. The stranger presented himself at the desk in the elegant lobby.

"Yes sir." The corporal on duty managed to combine respectful attention and slightly disdainful boredom in that successful manner NCOs of Britain's regular army had been doing for centuries.

"Major Smith, to see Captain Osborne."

The corporal examined Smith's identity card with a detail unsuspected in his mien.

"Up the staircase, sir, to the second floor, then turn left at the landing," the corporal said, as the major scribbled his signature in a ledger-like visitors' book.

Incognition

"Room 216."

The hotel was a busy place, men, in uniform and in mufti, coming and going; except for the fact that no women could be seen, it could have been mistaken for assembly rooms, a government department, or even what the Excelsior once had been: an expensive hotel. Yet Smith was not deceived. A British military headquarters always seemed the same to him, no matter what its guise or location.

"Major Smith, sir."

Osborne's clerk introduced the visitor into his chief's room with a minimum of words. The captain, who had been writing at his desk, rose, and the two officers shook hands. Osborne was a spare man who carried more weight in his capacity as assistant provost marshal of Cologne than he did on his bones. His moustache may very well have been grown simply to provide ballast. It was appropriate that his uniform was that of the Somerset Light Infantry.

"You've come straight from the station, Major?" Smith mentioned that he had left his bags in the care of the corporal in the lobby. "You'd probably enjoy some refreshment. What do we have, Hoggett?" Osborne peered past Smith to the clerk, who was standing in the doorway.

"I'll see what's about, sir," responded Hoggett, closing the office door behind him as he left.

"Since you didn't even give yourself time to find lodgings, Major, I assume you'd like to get right into business."

"At your convenience, Captain."

"I'm still a bit vague was to why the War Office despatched you at all, sir," Osborne commented, as he resumed his seat behind the desk. He offered Smith a cigarette from the box at his elbow, then lit one for himself.

"It's a matter of routine, really," replied Smith blandly. "I'm in no way to supersede you in the investigation you've begun. Nor do I have any authority in the Zone of Occupation, or over you as APM. It's due to Major Warner's being in charge of counterespionage in the Army of the Rhine that I'm here at all."

"Ah, the brass hats are afraid I'll discover something hush-hush, what?" There was the hint of a modest smile under Osborne's moustache.

"I think they're rather hoping that you *will* discover something," responded Smith, blowing out smoke gently. "Things at the War Office have been a little slow since the Armistice, I gather."

Osborne chuckled as Lance-Corporal Hoggett intruded with a tray full of tea things. He apologised for the plate of plain biscuits that comprised the solid half of the refreshments, but Smith expressed gratitude nonetheless. When the officers were alone again, Osborne poured the tea and reclined in his chair.

"How much do you know, sir?"

Inductions Dangerous

Smith, who once claimed that he knew just enough about everything to appear usefully intelligent but not enough to be intelligently useful, decided that his host was speaking about the matter at hand, and answered accordingly.

"Start at the beginning, Captain. I've heard none of it from your point of view." Smith tasted his tea. It was typical British Army tea: bland and ordinary, delicious and welcoming.

"Right then." Osborne removed a note-book from a desk drawer and flipped back the cover. "I received a call at my billet just before midnight on Friday, the 15th."

"I thought telephone service in Cologne had been shut down upon occupation, except for British Army offices."

"And certain quarters. As APM, I qualify." Smith nodded and Osborne continued. "The body of a British officer had been found in the Osterallee, not far from here. I arrived on the scene about twenty minutes later, and found several of my men and some German police already present. The dead man was Major Charles Warner. I'd worked with him on more than one occasion. He had been stabbed just to the right of the middle of his back." Osborne used his hand to indicate the wound's position. "I was informed later by a surgeon that such an injury would have been instantly fatal."

"The work of somebody who knew what he was about?" Smith suggested quietly.

"I think so, as do the German detectives on the case. The time of death was probably thirteen or fourteen minutes to twelve."

"So exact."

"A German constable saw the man we're treating as our main — only — suspect, crouching over the body." The captain consulted his notes. "Wachtmeister Adolf Höhne was walking his beat when he observed a man rifling the clothes of a prostrate form. The suspect fled as Höhne approached. The policeman naturally gave first priority to the victim, Warner, but he was already dead. The suspect had vanished by that time."

"Was Höhne able to give an adequate description?"

"Rather. The Osterallee is well-lit at that point."

Smith drank some more tea as Osborne described how the victim had been walking home from his office in the Dom Hotel after a typically long day. He had been seen leaving the Dom a quarter-hour before and, according to the sergeant and sentries on duty, had appeared normal and untroubled.

"Did Warner have enemies?" Smith asked at length.

"I've spoken to his colleagues and friends and they've been able to suggest no one," replied the APM. He nodded. "I myself know — knew — Major Warner as a fine fellow, very fair, generous; a bit of a bore, but modest and good-humoured. My men are still checking into any possible motive for his murder. There seem only two."

Smith remained silent, except for the crunch of a biscuit in his mouth.

"There have been a few assaults on British troops in our zone, all in Cologne," said Osborne, stubbing out his cigarette with gentle force. "It's never been serious: former field-greys out on a spree. They usually pick those in mufti. That's why there's now a rule about having to wear either a great coat or forage cap with civilian dress: the offending Huns sometimes pleaded ignorance that their victim was an English soldier. But Warner was in uniform, and a quick thrust in the back hardly seems like a Hun out for fun."

Germans seemed to have had a ball with that sort of antic during the War, thought Smith. Still, he could see Osborne's point. He finished his tea.

"And the other motive?"

"The purpose of your visit to the Rhineland, I suspect, Major." Osborne closed his note-book and regarded Smith with mock wariness. "The documents Warner was carrying."

"Yes, they were reported to London by Colonel Mackenzie."

"You've seen them, then?"

"They were described to me."

"I'm no expert in intelligence matters, sir," said Osborne, "but as soon as I examined them, I realised they'd be sending someone who was."

The captain's implication was quite right: what had been discovered on Warner's body was of considerable interest in intelligence circles. It was why Smith was in Cologne; Osborne was correct about that, too.

As soon as he had arrived on the murder scene and had identified Warner, Osborne had contacted the victim's superior, despite the late hour. Lieutenant Colonel Alaister Mackenzie was the GSO2 — general staff officer second grade — in charge of intelligence in the British occupation forces. Apprised of what had been found in Warner's pockets, Mackenzie telegraphed London. From there, the news came to the attention of C.

Smith had been staying at the Metropolitan, his principal club, looking forward to enjoying the last fortnight of his leave, but dreading the undetermined future of his career afterward. The name on the invitation he received was an alias, one of many C had used during his career, and it was not until he entered the house in Kensington to which he had been directed that he suspected he had been summoned on Government business. And it was not until he walked into the C's room on the first floor that realised who had sent for him.

Even when not in uniform, it was obvious that the chief of the Secret Service was an officer of the naval rather than military variety. He was short in stature but stocky, plainly powerful — a monitor, rather than a battleship — and resembled Punch, with his nutcracker combination of prominent nose and chin. His hands were rough and leathery, his hair thick, stiff and white. Though he had spent the last twenty years on shore stations, thirty previous years at sea had left their marks. His face was red and lined, and his eyes were narrow, as if still staring into a salty wind or over a blinding calm.

The major sat in one of the slightly frayed armchairs ranged before the sailor's big desk. This was the man's private office, moved from quarters in Ashley Mansions, where it had been located before the War, and when Smith had last seen him. It was a pleasantly cramped room, being filled with a table, chairs and numerous filing cabinets. On the wall at one end was a large portrait of a young man, a subaltern in the Coldstream Guards; C's only son, killed in the War.

C began the conversation with a number of pleasant reminiscences, cheerful and jolly, all the while regarding Smith through his rimless eyeglass.

"Something's surfaced in the Rhineland," the Secret Service chief said eventually, "something quite important, and I've no one I can send to report on it from an intelligence viewpoint. When I heard you were closing on the end of your holiday cruise, and the War Office hadn't charted you a new course yet, I thought I'd see if you wanted to sail over to Germany for me, like the old days. How's your Hunnish?"

Smith had smiled. C's tale had struck him as rather too neat. He was informed that Major Warner had died the previous night. It seemed unlikely that C had received this news, heard of Smith's nearly completed leave, found where he was staying and asked him over, all in the hours of a morning. Besides, C could have relied upon Colonel Mackenzie to provide a report along the lines required. Smith suspected that the intelligence chief had had his eye on him for a while, and had been awaiting an opportunity to invite his former subordinate back into the Secret Service. The prospect implied by this theory intrigued Smith.

"Tell me, my boy," C said, as he led the way to his suite's dining room, where a fine meal was being laid out. "They used to call you 'the most unrecognised man in the Empire'. Do you think that still applies?"

"I don't believe we've met. I'm Colonel Mackenzie."

Smith reflected that he had indeed made the previous acquaintance of his host. Fifteen years before, both officers had been subalterns, serving in the War Office. They had been posted to different section of the Operations Directorate, but had met often. He did not refresh the colonel's memory.

Incognition

The British Army of the Rhine's Intelligence Branch was housed in the Dom Hotel, not far from the city's cathedral and the Excelsior. Smith had located Mackenzie in a large, third storey flat, poring over maps spread out on a lengthy, oblong table in the suite's dining room.

"You'll want to read the documents poor Warner was carrying when he was killed." Mackenzie stood to his full, and impressive, height. His squarish head, heavy lids over dark eyes, and bushy moustache, gave an illusion of heft that he did not carry. Smith mused that Osborne and this officer of the Black Watch were probably not far removed from each other in the matter of pounds, but they looked a hundredweight apart. "I have them here."

Mackenzie strode to another room, which served as his office, and opened a safe there. He allowed Smith the use of his desk to peruse the papers, while he himself went back to his maps. After a quarter of an hour, Smith returned the documents to the colonel.

"Explosive stuff, I think you'll agree," Mackenzie said.

"Yes sir."

The documents all seemed to be from the French Army, and detailed various aspects of its attempt to foster separatism in the Rhineland. As such, they would hardly have surprised the British, who were well aware of France's policies in this regard. But these particular papers, many of them originals, a few Roneos, the rest carbon copies, concerned the undermining, indeed, the covert destruction, of British authority in the Rhine region. Expense reports, lists of agents and sympathisers, tactics and strategy memoranda pointed to a co-ordinated criminal attack upon British forces in Germany by her erstwhile ally. There was even the copy of a letter, signed by a French officer, mentioning planned assaults, and worse, while quoting what were admitted to be lies uttered by French officials to their English counterparts.

"Did you know that Warner had this intelligence, sir?"

"No." Mackenzie's answer was unflinching but plainly displeased. He replaced the documents in his safe. "As the head of counterespionage, Warner's primary duties included watching German political movements, especially Rhineland separatism, since it would have significance for the occupation. We know the French are involved in the matter, but learning just how deeply, and how far they are prepared to go, is quite different."

"What might the discovery of these papers lead to?"

"How much do you know about the Rhineland, Major?"

"Some," Smith said unhelpfully. He suspected that the colonel was referring to political and, perhaps, social aspects of this western part of Germany, and not topography, geology or cultural history. Smith was actually well-informed on Rhenish geology.

Inductions Dangerous

Mackenzie sorted through the maps on the table, gesturing for Smith to join him. Before them was a large-scale map of Germany's Rhineland Province, the Zones of British, French and American Occupation denoted by different colours.

"When the Great War ended four years ago, France hoped to annex all of this area," the colonel's big hand waved over the map, "but neither we, nor the Americans, thought that a good idea. We didn't like the notion of such an enlarged France, and the U.S. thought it might only embitter Germany further. So the French, realising that outright conquest was not on, settled for the prospect of a client state, its economy controlled from Paris, its territory a buffer against future German aggression."

"How have these efforts proved, sir?" Smith wanted to know.

"Stillborn, mostly." Mackenzie leaned heavily on the palms of his hands. "Rhinelanders don't particularly care for being under the charge of a lot of Prussians, but better that than marching to a French beat. France, however, isn't really concerned with what the natives want, as long as they can find a handful of them to support as figureheads in a puppet government."

"Their plans aren't restricted to their own area, I assume." Smith indicated the green-shaded portion of the map.

"Correct. They want it all. His Majesty's Government is opposed to such French aggrandisement." Mackenzie stood erect and, removing his cigarette case from within his tunic, offered his visitor one of the contents before lighting his own. "A chap from the Inter-Allied High Commission spelled it out quite forcefully for me last week. Twelve per cent of Germany's coal, eighty per cent of its iron ore, fifteen per cent of its rail transport, thirty per cent of its textile manufactures, all in the Rhineland — not to mention two-thirds of the Reich's vineyards." Mackenzie inhaled from his cigarette, leaving Smith to wonder which of the resources mentioned the Scot thought most important.

"The gain of all these items by France, either directly or otherwise, and the equivalent loss to Germany, along with what would be France's new strategic position, would make the it the strongest power in Europe."

Smith could well understand that such a prospect was not palatable to HMG. Though the British and French had been allies in the Great War, relations between the two countries had cooled in the aftermath. Their interests, now that Germany was no longer viewed with anxiety, had diverged, and Paris had made it clear that it saw Britain as a rival in the Near East, the Levant, and elsewhere.

"In light of the state of affairs between our two nations," Mackenzie said, "evidence of French attempts to destroy our authority in the Rhineland, especially through blatant criminal action, might lead to a fatal schism."

Smith nodded but remarked, "Then the French must be viewed as prime suspects in Major Warner's murder..."

Lodging was difficult to find in Cologne. Smith discovered that there were plenty of hotels, but they all seemed to be full. It was the mark, Osborne had confirmed, causing Smith to think of some sort of sign or symbol that had been blazoned over the doorways of inns throughout the city. The currency, the captain explained — the German mark — had been worth twenty-one to the pound sterling in 1914. Now, hundreds of thousands were required to equal one sovereign. And the next day, the mark would be worth even less. Inflation had destroyed Germany's economy, and was raging like the Spanish 'flu epidemic of a few years before.

Consequently, Cologne was flooded with consumers, British consumers, come from home with a pocket full of shillings which would buy more than they could ship back to England. Smith saw evidence of it as he walked through the warm early evening: clothing, furniture, automobiles, paintings, food — everything — could be had for pennies. Osborne echoed the sentiments of his fellows on the GHQ staff when he called this swarm of 'damned civilians' a lot of 'vampires'. But the men, even the officers, of the British Army were not immune to the fever of purchase.

As he passed a wine shop in the Hohestrasse, and observed a gentleman, obviously English, directing sales clerks placing crates of bottles into the back of a horse-drawn wagon, Smith wondered if the results of such behaviour were as bad as the covetousness itself. Would it have been better for the German shopkeepers if their merchandise had gone unsold? Certainly few of the natives could afford much of it. Letting a grand piano, for example, go for five-and-three was preferable to selling it not at all, if one needed money for food.

And money was what Germany needed. The country wore a down-at-heels look, the buildings as much as the people wearing the post-War years shabbily. Children, especially, looked unhealthy, dressed in ragged clothes and standing inactive and staring.

Hotel rooms were at a premium. Osborne had suggested the Saint Adelheim, a small guest-house in the Stettinstrasse. He had hopes for the establishment, for they had the reputation for renting only to possessors of the pink identity card, issued by GHQ. This document meant that a visitor was allowed to exist in the British Zone. Many other hotels gave out rooms regardless of evidence — or lack thereof — of official approval.

The Saint Adelheim was a tall inn of pale, aged stucco with behind it, a small but attractive beer garden, sparsely used. There were lodgings available. The manager even permitted Smith to sign for his account and pay the amount owed later, thus obviating the need to carry a satchel filled with paper marks.

Inductions Dangerous

The sun was low when Smith, having washed and changed his shirt, walked into the garden, a green lawn with trees which provided shade during the height of the day. Now, a thick yellow light bathed the city, and all was pleasantly warm. Smith had his choice of table, and sat at one by the wall. As he ordered his meal, his mind was already composing the report that he would send to C.

He found that his thoughts comprised more questions than statements. How had Major Warner obtained the documents for which he may have died? How had his killer known that he had them? Was the deadly assault even connected with intelligence matters? And despite the papers casting such an ill light upon the French, were they the only ones with a motive for murder?

Smith sat back in his chair and mentally underlined the two words: 'the French'.

The next morning, Smith was woken by the breakfast-waiter, who entered his room bearing a wide, toothy grin and a tray filled with eggs and sausages, both foods poor specimens of their kind. But the coffee was real. The waiter arranged the tray on the bed, then raised the price of the room, printed in beige chalk on the slate hanging above the headboard.

As Osborne had explained to Smith, every British officer venturing forth in mufti in Cologne had either to wear his great coat or his peaked forage cap. It was too warm for a great coat, Smith decided, and wearing any military headgear with a civilian suit would have bordered on silly. He therefore arrived at the Hotel Excelsior in his normal khaki undress uniform, just as the clock in the lobby showed nine.

Smith found Osborne waiting for him in his office.

"I hope you don't think I'm trying to do your job, Captain," Smith said, as the two retraced their path down the staircase and out the front doors of the General Headquarters.

"I've been assistant provost-marshal in Cologne for three years, Major," said Osborne. "I can tell when someone is poaching. What you've done so far is no more than to ask for a licence to do some shooting in my wood." They crossed the Domplatz, beginning to fill with its daily quota of pedestrians, some with destinations, others just wandering. "Besides, you have information I don't — information I'm not allowed to have. If the same questions give different answers to you, then all I ask is that you share the results."

Smith wondered what Osborne's reaction would have been if he realised that Smith had been despatched to Cologne with fewer facts about the situation than anybody else involved possessed.

Just down the corridor from Colonel Mackenzie's office in the Dom Hotel were the two rooms occupied by one of his sections, that responsible for counterespionage in the British Zone. It had been run, until the end of the previous week, by Major Warner. The new, temporary, head was Warner's deputy, an officer named Humphreys, now working alone in the room he had previously shared with the dead man. He wore on the breast of his tunic the 1914-15 Star's ribbon; Smith inferred from this, and the fact that Humphreys was still only a lieutenant, that he had spent much of the Great War in the ranks, probably enlisting at the outset as an enthusiastic boy.

"Enemies?" Humphreys was sitting behind a table to one side, leaving vacant the desk once occupied by his late chief. "As I mentioned to Mr Osborne, sir, the major was conscientious in his duties, so he probably did make a few enemies." The lieutenant was only a few years younger than Osborne, clean-shaven, with a bright face and sharp, eager eyes: a look of unfinished adolescence. "But I truly can't think of anybody who would want to kill him."

"Communists, monarchists, separatists, anarchists, nationalists..." Smith listed. "None of these groups resented Mr Warner's efforts?"

Humphreys smiled, like a schoolboy asked an obvious question by a master.

"Of course, Major. But, to be honest, the average German is a sportsman about things like that — at least with us. The sort the average Hun hates is other Huns. Monarchists hate the Socialists, Communists hate the Freikorps; and of course they all hate the French. They might annoy us, taunt us, bait us, even hit us from time to time; killing us on principle is unlikely."

"If not on principle, what about in particular?" Smith said.

"Mr Warner had no professional or personal foes of whom I'm aware; not who would kill him." Humphreys was immovable on the subject.

"What about his habits? His friends and acquaintances?"

"Major Warner and I worked well together, sir, but I cannot say that we socialised a great deal. His routine was simple. He worked late most days, ate lunch at a... Sergeant!"

An NCO of the Intelligence Police had entered the room which, except for Humphreys and his visitors, was deserted. As the sergeant, who had obvious just returned from a journey, set down his army-issued attaché case and dropped his cap on a table, the lieutenant haled him.

"Branigan, what was that tavern Mr Warner favoured so much?"

"Oh, the Sieben Glocken, sir, near the Rathaus."

"That's right," confirmed Humphreys. "He went there almost every day for luncheon. I don't think you'll find the major's routine to hold many secrets, gentlemen."

"It's true." Osborne turned to Smith. "From my investigations, I've discovered that Warner could have been O.C. Laundry for all the motives for murder his duties generated. He was unmarried, with no girlfriend, local or otherwise—"

"Begging your pardon, sir," Sergeant Branigan said suddenly, standing beside the lieutenant's desk, "but I couldn't help hearing; I hope you're not suggesting that Major Warner had been doing anything improper..."

"Mr Warner was very well-respected, gentlemen," Humphreys pointed out. "The sergeant here served with him for four years."

"What do you make of the documents that Major Warner was carrying when he was killed, Sergeant?" Smith regarded the NCO.

"Them I don't understand, sir," Branigan replied, rubbing is closely-shaven cleft chin. "Mr Warner was a private man, but about private things, if you know what I mean, sir. Those papers were work, and I can't understand him keeping them secret."

"They were highly important papers, Branigan," Humphreys said gently.

"Work was work, sir," the sergeant reminded his superior. "Mr Warner involved us all in it."

"That's true," Humphreys conceded, nodding. "Branigan and I haven't been told much about the documents, other than that the major was carrying them and they are significant. It's certainly not like Mr Warner to keep us uninformed. It's possible that he wouldn't have divulged their exact nature, but to keep their very existence hidden...? It would have been pointless. All the NCOs in this section have years of intelligence and security experience. Yet there must have been a reason..."

After a moment's silence, Smith spoke, asking, "What sort of liaison did Mr Warner have with our allies? The Belgians, the French?"

"An active sort," responded Humphreys. "The major, myself, the NCOs, we're always on the move. Sergeant Branigan is just now back from visiting his colleagues in Solingen; Major Warner went to Mainz on Tuesday to speak with his French opposite number and returned on Wednesday; I'm scheduled to interview the president of the Allied Disarmament Committee in Dusseldorf this week-end, and the Belgians after that. Liaison is constant; none of us, British, French or Belgian, could do a decent job without sharing information."

Smith understood this. Civilians often thought that intelligence gathering was accomplished by the wearing of disguises and the meeting of low spies in dirty taverns. More information was collected simply by reading periodicals and exchanging reports.

"Thank you for your time, Lieutenant, Sergeant," said Osborne. He and Smith rose. "If anyone in your section recalls anything that might have a bearing on this case, please let me know."

"Of course," Humphreys promised.

The APM led Smith from the Dom, exiting through the rear of the building.

Incognition

He explained that he found this a quicker route to the square, and thus to the Excelsior. The pair passed through a close lane, under its single street lamp, the electric bulb of which was broken, and into a wider avenue: the Osterallee.

"Did Warner leave work by this way?" Smith noticed the Germans walking to and fro along the thoroughfare.

"Yes, every night," replied Osborne. "I pieced together the route he took Friday evening, and learned that he habitually took the same path. It would have been easy for someone to anticipate his stroll down the Osterallee, and when he would be there."

The two officers emerged into the Domplatz, the great cathedral looming over them.

"If we assume that Major Warner came by the documents in his possession during his trips to Mainz — something which is by no means certain — he would have needed a source," said Smith.

"Of course," Osborne concurred. "I doubt that he would have resorted to burgling the French GHQ. Someone must have provided them. But what—?" The APM halted in the centre of the square, causing several Germans walking close by to bump into him. They excused themselves roughly and continued on around the two Englishmen. "Your premise is that the French have the best motive for killing Warner: in order to retrieve the documents. If that's true, then they too would have guessed that he'd have a source — a well-placed French source."

Smith would have preferred the term 'deduced' rather than 'guessed' but he nodded nonetheless.

"Are you able to research recent French deaths in their zone?" he asked. "Probably in Mainz, but not necessarily attributable to murder."

"The contacts I've made with my French opposite number are quite informal. I'll see what he can tell me."

Smith and Osborne resumed their walk, but the former was troubled. Though he did not show it, he was bothered by what the APM might discover had happened in Mainz. He was also bothered by what he might not discover.

"Can I get you something, Major?"

Smith glanced up. Lance-Corporal Hoggett, Osborne's dutiful clerk, was standing in the doorway of his chief's office. Smith considered the open window, and the low angle of the sun outside, then consulted his watch. It was late, he suddenly realised; late enough for even conscientious men such as Hoggett to think of quitting work for the day.

"If you could set the kettle to boiling, Corporal, I'll finish the process," said Smith.

Inductions Dangerous

"Not to worry, sir. I'll get you some tea before I go."

Smith returned his attention to the papers on the desktop before him. These were copies of the much-discussed documents found on Warner's corpse. The originals had been sent to London, but Colonel Mackenzie had been allowed to duplicate them for study in Cologne. He had loaned them to Smith, and Osborne had provided the use of his desk, office and, if need be, clerk, since the APM was to be absent for most of this day.

Smith rubbed his eyes. They had been staring at printed and written French for hours. The documents were an eclectic group. They all dealt with French intrigue in the Rhineland, but each item's significance varied greatly. One memorandum was so innocuous as to deal with the manufacture of a number of red, white and green flags for the proposed 'Rhenish Republic'. Another report detailed receipts to German agents of the French Army's intelligence bureau.

The most interesting, and damaging, article, Smith opined, was an undated letter, or, rather, a copy of a copy of a letter. It was addressed to a Colonel Sembat, and signed by a Commandant de Coppet. It gave direct evidence of French criminality and duplicity toward the British in regard to Rhineland policy.

It will be remembered that the possibility of assaults against British officers and administrators — and even more violent attacks — was proposed. It may become necessary to implement these designs in the future.

However, please be advised that at the meeting on the 7th, we assured the English representatives that there is 'no contact, official or otherwise, between French and local German bureaucrats which could be construed as encouraging Rhineland separation.

Smith was wondering from what source that passage's quote had come when Osborne entered the room, carrying a tray laden with cups, saucers, utensils and pots.

"You haven't been demoted, have you?" Smith asked.

Osborne could not tell if his new acquaintance's concern was real or humorous, but decided for generosity's sake to treat it as the latter.

"I sent Hoggett home," he said simply. "Have you been at those papers all day?"

"No, only since the morning. Who is de Coppet?"

"Who?" Osborne set to preparing two cups of tea. "Oh, wait a minute. He's to do with the SR... I think he heads it in the French occupation forces."

"The local secret service chief..." said Smith, almost to himself. "Do you know of any meeting on the 7th, perhaps of this month, between British and

13

Incognition

French representatives?"

The APM was thoughtful as he handed his acquaintance a filled cup.

"I think there may have been one last month. At least, I seem to recall a meeting here in Cologne early in August. Colonel Mackenzie probably attended; I remember him asking me to be especially vigilant as regards threats against the French. And... Yes, Colonel Labelle was here for it; he's the director of the French occupation forces' Second Bureau."

"A conference of intelligence officers?" ventured Smith.

"You're most likely correct about that," Osborne said, as he lit a cigarette, "because Major Jorgensen, the American G-2, was in town then as well."

After a swallow of tea, Smith said, "And Colonel Sembat: do you recognise that name?"

"No, not him, I'm afraid." Osborne sat in a chair by the window, cheerfully brushing aside Smith's offer of his own spot behind the desk. "Here's another name that might interest you: Pierre Bouchez."

Smith regarded Osborne with a vacant expression, which gave the latter no clue as to the major's thoughts. Osborne grinned.

"You wanted to know about any deaths among the French in their Zone. Bouchez was a clerk in the Second Bureau at French GHQ, until he was stabbed to death Saturday night."

"He might very well have had access to intelligence documents," Smith mused, as he sorted the papers before him into the envelopes from which they had been taken. "Has your opposite number in Mainz any clues in the case?"

Osborne shook his head and leaned back. His weight appeared to make little impression on the chair's upholstery.

"No, none. Bouchez was killed while returning to his billet after a late night on the town. There were no witnesses. The crime was well-planned, in a deserted lane, a dark corner..."

"It seems the assassin took the time over Bouchez that he couldn't with Warner," observed Smith, comparing the two murders' settings. "Was the Frenchman's death instantaneous?"

"Quite professional." Osborne gestured with his cigarette. "The methods point to Bouchez's killer being Warner's, too."

"And that's the puzzling bit," Smith remarked, with no other explanation.

Cologne was taking on the aspects of a British garrison town, Smith noted, as he walked from the Excelsior to his rooms at the Saint Adelheim. This had been started less by the initial occupation of the Rhineland a month after the Armistice than by the allowing of spouses and children to join the troops in 1920. In the cool and pleasing twilight, Smith was saluted by a number of soldiers strolling the streets with their wives.

Other signs of permanence followed. Sports facilities, always evidence of British intent to stay a while, were constructed, and competitions and games of all sorts had become regular features of Cologne life. As well, a daily newspaper was now published for the edification, or at least the entertainment, of officers and men.

The distance from the Excelsior to the Saint Adelheim was not great, and it was certainly plausible that others, coincidentally walking from the Domplatz to the Stettinstrasse, would parallel Smith's own progress. But as he paused by the window of a cosy tavern, he knew that his instincts were not wrong. He did not believe the man reflected in the glass and visibly a German, who stopped when he did and moved when he did, was unconnected to him.

The man following him was good at physical surveillance, the Briton judged, but not very good. He was dressed without fastidiousness, was rounded in shape and a little shorter than average. A well-worn hat with a frayed brim kept the face largely from view.

When he reached his hotel, Smith saw that his shadow took up a position in a deep doorway across the street from him. Though the Saint Adelheim had its beer garden behind, there was no exit in its tall brick wall, making the portal under surveillance the only way in or out. Smith dallied in his room for a few minutes, refreshing himself, then repaired to the garden for a leisurely meal. Afterward, though it was only about ten o'clock, he ascended once more to his room, drew the curtains and turned out the lights. He changed from his uniform in the dark, donning a suit of mufti.

"Yes sir, er..." The night porter glanced up from his newspaper as Smith approached the front desk in the lobby. It was clear that the hotel employee did not remember this man's name, and indeed did not recognise him at all.

"There is a rather sinister character loitering across the street," said Smith, in English. "He followed me here. I want you to summon the police and have him investigated."

The porter surreptitiously peered through a window and observed a shape in the doorway opposite. He was a bit disturbed at this mystery. It did not do to have the gentleman — British, and who no doubt paid promptly and tipped well — displeased with the hotel's service. He pushed a button under his desk, in response to which a boy, attired in the establishment's worn livery, appeared through a door. The porter wrote a note and, giving it to the page, instructed him to take it to the police station.

It did not take long for a pair of German constables, in their green, military-style uniforms and streamlined shakos, to arrive. As they confronted the man in the doorway, invisible in the night despite the street lamps, Smith slipped through the hotel's front entrance. He hid himself in the mouth of an alley and saw the constables salute and move on. The man about whom they had been summoned remained in his dim spot; Smith's belief was confirmed.

It was less than half an hour later that the mystery man stepped from his hiding place, lit a pipe and, with a final glance at the darkened windows of Smith's hotel room, strolled away. Smith now followed him.

The Englishman was confident in his ability to be ignored. Indeed, he went unnoticed as he stalked his quarry through the city; unseen by the man in front of him and unminded by others whom he passed on the nocturnal streets. Smith felt that he could have tracked the stranger by smell alone, the tobacco in his pipe was so distinctive, though not unpleasant.

The Hotel Waterloo was near the Severnplatz; not the best part of town, Smith judged, and a district not frequented by British soldiery. It was an old, unkempt building, in a seedy-looking street, the kind patronised perhaps by less successful commercial travellers. Smith's quarry went through the front door, retrieved his room key from the night porter and climbed the staircase.

An interesting development, thought Smith, as he watched, in his turn, from a deep doorway across the street.

The next morning, once more in uniform, Smith walked toward the cathedral square under bulging grey skies. Despite his many years in parts of the world known for their sparse moisture, he had never lost his affection for wet weather, and he was not displeased by the threatening clouds. At a greengrocer's stall, where Smith paused to buy an apple — he might have had every piece of fruit on sale for less than two crowns, if the apple had not been the only appetising item — the proprietor held forth on the possibility of precipitation, perhaps on the widely-held assumption that Britons loved to discuss weather. Smith, though he said little, felt that this was probably a misconception.

"Is it raining yet?" Colonel Mackenzie wanted to know when Smith entered his room in the Dom Hotel. The Scotsman's hooded eyes enlarged, searchingly, as he looked out the window. "There's a meet tonight at the Merheim race course, and I never do well in the rain."

For a moment, Smith thought that the colonel was implying that he regularly ran in competition, but then decided that he was actually referring to bets he placed on horses.

"Do you know a German called Grob, sir? Most likely a police officer."

"It sounds familiar." Mackenzie withdrew himself from the open window and moved to a bank of tall, wooden filing cabinets that lined one wall of his room. "How did you come by that name?"

Smith encapsulated the previous night's activities.

"After the stranger went up to his room, I bribed the night porter to let me see the register."

"Why do you think he's with the police?" Mackenzie's large fingers nimbly flipped through the cards in a little drawer.

"He wasn't moved on by the constables summoned to the Saint Adelheim, who, in fact, saluted."

"Very good." The colonel smiled as he pulled a card, covered with typewriting, from his index. "You sound like a natural at this cloak and dagger business, Smith."

"I read Sherlock Holmes stories as a boy."

Mackenzie regarded the major warily but said, "I think this may be your man."

"Helmut Grob, a kriminalassistent of the Berlin Police Praesidium's Section IA." Smith glanced up from the card he had been handed. "Kriminalassistent — assistant detective; that approximates to a detective constable in our police service, I believe."

"You didn't learn that from Conan Doyle..."

"No sir. Fosdick's *European Police Systems*. It states here that Grob served Section V during the War. That was the Berlin Police's Political Branch. What's Section IA?"

"The same," replied the Highlander. "After the War, Germany's new republican government abolished the political police. Then they realised that they had more enemies than the old kaiser had had, and less power with which to handle them, so they brought Section V back under a new name. The Cologne police authorities must have called in experienced help when Warner was killed. What Grob hoped to accomplish by following you, I don't know."

"Perhaps you could assist me in another matter, sir."

The colonel gestured to an empty chair across the table from his, just as a bang of thunder invaded the room. The sound rolled, as if from one side of the Rhine to the other and back again, and was followed immediately by the much more gentle sound of falling rain.

"Damn." Mackenzie shut the window half-way. "And I'd had a tip on the third race."

"I was hoping to learn something about a meeting you attended on the 7th of August," Smith stated, taking his seat. "I understand some French officers journeyed up from Mainz for the occasion."

"That's right. We met in this room, in fact: Warner, myself, Colonel Labelle and Commandant de Coppet, the head of the SR at Mainz." Mackenzie walked to the switch on the wall near the door, and illuminated the room with dull yellow electric light. Until then, Smith had not realised how dim the day had become. "You're familiar with the French set-up, aren't you?"

Smith knew that the French Army's General Staff was divided into several departments, the second of which was responsible for military intelligence. Unlike Britain's Secret Service, which, despite its official designation of MI6, was run by the thoroughly civilian Foreign Office, France's organ for collecting covert information abroad, the Service de Renseignments, was a branch of the Second Bureau.

"Was anything extraordinary discussed?" Smith wanted to know.

"It was one of a series of irregularly held conferences to talk about intelligence and security concerns common to the French and ourselves," Mackenzie replied. "To be honest, it was more boring than most of the others. I assume you're asking because of the date referred to in de Coppet's letter, the one found on Warner's body."

"Yes sir."

"I think de Coppet must have been trying to please his bosses. The letter is addressed to Sembat, the ultimate head of the SR in the War Ministry in Paris. You see," Mackenzie sat down across from Smith, smiling, "de Coppet is a bit of an intriguer, a bit of a politician, like most officers in the French Army. Labelle, on the other hand, is relatively honest and straightforward. He realised that Warner and I wanted to know about French support for separatists in the Rhineland. Labelle told us that statements prepared by staff political officers were all well and good for politicians, but not for soldiers. He'd confirmed a number of things about French policy that we'd already deduced. He didn't go into details, of course, but he didn't deny the obvious."

"But he didn't admit to the worst things implied in the documents Warner was carrying, did he?" asked Smith. "Activities such as assaults on British personnel?"

"No," answered Mackenzie reluctantly, folding his big hands before him, "though it's perfectly possible that he doesn't know what's being done by his own people."

A gust of cool wind blew through the half-open window, raising the curtains in billowing waves and scattering a mist of precipitation across the table.

"I hope I've been of some help," Mackenzie said, reluctantly shutting the window completely.

"Yes sir," responded Smith slowly. "Things are becoming clearer."

By noon, the day's weather had settled into a fine imitation of a London rain. The clouds had consolidated after their initial burst of a few hours before, and wet and dreary was the forecast. When he repaired to a small restaurant off the Hohestrasse, Smith sat by a large window, so that he could enjoy the sights of the downpour more. He ordered a large glass of kolsch, the local beer, while he waited and watched British soldiers — officers and other ranks — visit the many shops.

The smell of his expected guest was strong: the aroma of damp wool warmed by a building's interior heat, mixed with a unique tobacco blend. Smith turned from the window to see the stranger from the night before approaching his table.

"Major Smith?" Helmut Grob held out a calling card, on the front of which was printed no more than Smith's name and regiment. "This is you?"

"That's right." Smith, standing, extended his hand, and Grob shook it tentatively. "Please, sit down."

A waiter took Grob's hat and coat, and the policeman slowly lowered himself into a chair opposite his host's. Neither man was unaware that of the many occupied tables in the dining room, theirs was the only one shared by two nationalities. Segregation was almost as complete as if decreed by law.

"You wrote on the back of your card 'Der Schwarzritter, noon' and nothing else, so," Grob said, with a slight spread of his hands, "here I am."

"I'm told that the trout, followed by the venison, is quite good here," said Smith in German to the waiter, as the latter returned to take their orders. The servant's confirmation was phrased in a guarded past tense. Smith chose to be optimistic. "Excellent. And the same for my guest." Phrasing his offer thus, the Briton informed Grob that he need not worry about paying. After a moment's hesitation, perhaps to consider the bare alternative of a link or two of dubious sausage in a cheap tavern, the policeman nodded, and the waiter departed happily.

"You've been following me, Assistant Detective," the army officer said, continuing to speak the local tongue. Grob's protruding eyes lowered their shutter-like lids momentarily, then opened again.

"I don't suppose I can deny it," he responded. "You, in turn, must have followed me, since your invitation came to my hotel. You're a better hunter than I."

"Most people — and animals — don't notice me at all, Mr Grob. Your interest is in the Warner murder?"

Grob nodded and pursed his naturally pouty lips.

"Germany has many challenges now, Major," said he: "the British, the French and Belgian occupation forces; separatists, Spartacists, monarchists, Socialists; Poles, White Russians, Red Russians... The Soviet secret police, the Cheka, have opened a residence in Berlin to take advantage of it all. They seek to weaken Germany further, to foment revolution. They even use nationalism for their own ends, declaring that the first act of a Bolshevik Germany would be to wage war against France. It is all a most appalling mess."

Incognition

"And with your experience in political policing, you were sent to see how Warner's death might affect the situation," concluded Smith. "Why follow me?"

"I thought you might have been sent to head the investigation into your countryman's death," answered Grob. "British interests do not coincide with German, so you would not have felt obliged to tell us the results of your inquiries."

"You were hoping to learn things from my movements. What *have* you learned?"

"From you, Major? Nothing. You have given me no opportunity. But from other sources? That the French are the most likely suspects in the crime."

"You would say that," Smith pointed out. "France is Germany's worst foe."

"We have many enemies," countered the detective, "but France is our most implacable. Do you think that they would not stoop to murder to gain their ends? Commandant de Coppet, who is, I believe, connected with their secret service, is quite amoral."

Smith thought it ironic to hear a German accuse another nationality of lacking scruples. But then, he reminded himself, as he took another drink of beer, many Germans did not even feel that they had lost the late War.

In an obliquely related vein, the Englishman said, "Tell me about the state of forgery in Germany today, Grob..."

"Some days, it's like the bloody Klondike must have been, or San Francisco, during California's gold rush..."

Captain Osborne stood near the doors of a rather jazz cabaret in the Stappelhaus district of Cologne, near the waterfront. It was out-of-bounds to British servicemen and at eleven o'clock, it should have been closed for half an hour already. Osborne's military policemen and some of the local constabulary were ushering an international crowd, protesting in two languages (three, if one took into account the Americans found there), from the bright, tawdry, smoky interior and into black marias waiting stolidly outside in the rain.

"There are dozens of these places all over Cologne," Osborne said to Smith, who was standing nonchalantly beside him. "Illegal fraternisation, after-hours drinking..." He sighed. "Most of them are harmless and, as long as the problems don't become chronic, we turn a more or less blind eye. But we keep a watch on the ones around here, and in the Buttermarkt area. A night out there can turn ugly."

A private of the Army Service Corps, propelled by a Red-Cap corporal, stopped suddenly in front of the assistant provost marshal and begged, a little tipsily, for clemency.

"She's British, sir, as true-blue as you or me," he claimed, in the dialect of deep, dark Manchester. He pointed to a stunningly beautiful blond in a nurse's uniform. "I admit I was out a bit late, sir, but I wasn't fratting."

Osborne turned his head to peer at the shapely ankles just visible beneath the hem of the young woman's skirt. Smith did the same. So did the police of both nationalities.

"Entschuldigung, fraulein," Osborne said, grinning and tipping his cap. He turned to the private. "Next time, get her silk stockings, instead of cotton." His men, chuckling, moved the two offenders out of the building.

The APM cast about the cabaret, from its small stage to the deserted tables and overturned chairs to the lieutenant presenting the owner with a notice of closure. He shook his head whimsically.

"Now, Major, you wanted to know about forgeries..."

The Rhine River valley was just as beautiful in 1922 as it had been when Smith had journeyed down its length ten years previously. There was, of course, little reason for it to have changed. Its cultivated hills, filled with vines, and its cliffs, topped with castles, some ruined, some inhabited, had not altered in a millennium. To have done so in a decade was unlikely.

A week after he had witnessed the raid on the Stappelhaus cabaret, Smith was travelling up the river with Colonel Mackenzie, away from the industrial north to the more agricultural, beautiful south. Along the left bank their train steamed, past the many towns and villages, halting briefly at Coblenz, in the American sector, before moving on, toward the French occupation forces' headquarters at Mainz.

Mackenzie, seated opposite Smith in the otherwise empty compartment, had remarked that one could always determine when one entered the French Zone. As the train rolled to a gentle stop at Mainz's railway station, the major understood. The building itself was bedecked with tricoloured flags — not those of Germany, but of France — and French soldiers, some wearing blue side-caps, others the distinctive 'Adrian' helmets, were on duty at the gates. During the short taxi ride to Ehrenbreitstein, the fortress which served as the Gallic GHQ, Smith observed in practice the regulation declaring that every German citizen passing a French officer had to uncover his head in an enforced sign of respect. He also noted that many residents of Mainz chose to go about hatless.

The French presence in their sector was much more marked than was the British in theirs, and combined characteristics of colonial overlordship with those of military mastery. In Cologne, the British acted much of the time almost as tourists — wealthy tourists — while here, the French swaggered as if in a newly-conquered province.

"My dear Mackenzie!"

Incognition

Colonel Maxim Labelle, chief of the Second Bureau of the French Rhine Army's General Staff, welcomed his British counterpart with open arms, literally. His expressive face widened with a big smile, his dark and generous moustache spreading to accommodate it. He embraced Mackenzie and kissed him on both cheeks. When the Scotsman introduced Smith, the latter forestalled any such greeting with a quick extension of the hand. Tobacco, coffee and tea were offered in abundance, and pastries to fill the gap made by the hours since luncheon.

The three settled comfortably into easy chairs to one side of the office, which was so spacious and so well-appointed that Smith guessed that its furniture and decoration had not come from the previous occupant's Prussian tastes. After the two colonels had lit their cigars, and Smith his cigarette, Labelle spoke of the matter at hand.

"Mackenzie informs me, Major, that you have some questions concerning a meeting he and I attended last month."

"Yes sir." Smith's tea was from China but he drank it nonetheless. "I was hoping that you could tell me who knew that Rhineland separation was to have been discussed."

After a moment's thought, Labelle answered, "Myself, Commandant de Coppet, who is in charge of the SR under me, my secretary and my political officer, Captain Beullac." Labelle gestured smoothly and easily as he spoke, in spite of the tightness of his tailored uniform. "It was not to be a secret, nor was it a significant part of the programme."

"Rhenish separatism always seems to be on the agenda these days," observed Mackenzie.

Labelle gave a laugh of the sort used to indicate sympathetic agreement.

"And the prepared statement, denying any contact between French and local German officials regarding separatism," added Smith, pausing to drink from his cup (very fine Dresden porcelain, he noted). "Who would have been aware of its exact wording?"

Mackenzie, with whom Smith had discussed his planned tack, was interested in Labelle's response. The French colonel was surprised that his guests were aware of the statement's existence but was not concerned about it. He ran a hand along the top of his head, tracing the part down the middle of his oiled hair.

"Beullac, my political officer, was responsible for writing it. He devised it just before the meeting, and, no doubt, his own secretary typed it. My superiors wanted to give some bland, obviously false statement to Colonel Mackenzie and Major Warner. I have more respect for their intelligence, and did not use it." He grinned. "Why do you ask?"

"Labelle, we need to know if this is Commandant de Coppet's signature." Mackenzie set his cigar in an ashtray and withdrew from his tunic's breast pocket a folded piece of paper. He handed it to the Frenchman. It was a copy of the letter found upon Warner's corpse.

Labelle frowned, lines appearing like window blinds upon his previously clear brow. He excused himself and, walking to his ornate desk (eighteenth century, Smith estimated), made an inter-office call on his telephone. Even before he had resumed his seat, the room's door opened and an officer in the uniform of a chasseur regiment entered smartly.

"Commandant de Coppet," Labelle said, simply, nonchalantly, to Smith.

The head of the local French secret service was a small, angular man, whose manner was indicative of economy and thrift in every facet. The thin moustache and pointed van dyke were so tidy that they might have been fake addenda attached to the expressionless face as one piece. He regarded Smith with flinty eyes. Labelle handed him the letter.

"Is that your signature?" The colonel asked his subordinate in English.

After his eyes had progressed up the letter to examine its contents then returned to the neatly written name at the bottom, de Coppet shook his head and said in French, "No. It's a close facsimile but not the genuine article. I do not recognise this letter, either." He gave the paper back to his superior, who in turn handed it to Mackenzie. "And, as far as I can recall, no conversation such as that quoted took place."

"You wouldn't remember those words, Commandant," said Smith, also in French, "because you didn't use them. Only someone who thought you had uttered them at the meeting on the 7th of August, but didn't know you hadn't, would have included them in that forged letter, for verisimilitude."

"Verisimilitude?" Labelle was questioning the context of the term, not its meaning.

"The person who provided the information for the text of this forgery also provided information which would have made it look all the more genuine. So a statement was added which the forgers believed you, Colonel Labelle, had used at the conference with Colonel Mackenzie and Major Warner. They were not to know that you had not used it. That suggests that this letter — and the other documents found on Warner — are fakes." Smith set aside his empty cup and saucer.

The SR chief turned to his superior, who inhaled some cigar smoke. Both Frenchmen knew the identity of the only person who could both have been aware of the prepared denial quoted in the letter *and* not realised that Labelle had not uttered it.

Labelle rose and, smiling politely, said to his guests, "I'm sorry, gentlemen, but you must excuse me for the time being. If you'll pause in my outer office, my clerk will arrange lodgings for you. We will speak again, over breakfast."

The Britons were unsurprised at the sudden termination of the interview and accommodatingly left the room. Labelle looked at de Coppet.

"Bring me Beullac."

"So Beullac has been arrested?"

Helmut Grob packed some soft, mossy tobacco into the deep bowl of his wooden pipe as he leaned on the deck railing of the little passenger steamer that was easing down the Rhine on its current. Though the late summer twilight was warm, the policeman wore his dented felt hat low over his face, and his overcoat close around him, as if expecting to be trapped in a cold downpour. Despite the peaceful evening and the beautiful scenery, caught between the set sun and the risen moon, Major Smith and he were the only people on the deck.

"Yes," replied the Englishman, dragging on a cigarette. "I suspect that the French would have preferred to deal with him in secret, but after the conversation they shared with Colonel Mackenzie and me in Mainz yesterday morning, that wasn't possible."

"Mmm." Grob straightened with sudden recollection and pulled a page of foolscap, folded lengthways, from inside his coat. "Following the information you provided me last week, my colleagues kept Captain Beullac under close supervision. Fortunately, he is much less alert than you," Grob's bulbous eyes briefly stared at Smith, "and led them to a number of suspicious individuals. About half have been arrested."

Grob paused to watch a flight of small birds wheel in the orange-purple sky over the boat, then skim across the smooth water.

"Several have already been most helpful in the way of providing information. Your theory was correct: the forgeries were created by the Bolshevik Cheka and forwarded, probably through their station in Berlin, to their people in Cologne."

Smith threw away his cigarette and breathed in the heavy fragrance of river-at-nightfall.

"You've arrested about half of Beullac's associates, you say..."

"The rest are identified, as far as they can be, on the list." Grob tapped with his pipe stem the list Smith now held. "Some are diplomatists with immunity, others are citizens of foreign countries, the rest have fled. But we've collected names — sometimes more than one per person — addresses and descriptions." The German chewed on his pipe for a moment, then asked, "Why did you trust me, Major? How did you know I'd give you this information once my men had collected it?"

Inductions Dangerous

"What would you have gained by doing otherwise?" Smith queried in return. "We're not too concerned about the ones you've arrested: you'll deal with that lot. Those who've got away may surface again, in which case we'll be as ready for them as we can be." The Briton pocketed the list. "We've both gained, and nobody was cheated."

"Except the French," Grob stated.

"It was their traitor who started it all," Smith pointed out.

Neither man spoke further, but leaned on the railing and watched lights spring up in the houses on the Rhine's right bank.

A few days later, Smith arrived in England. He deposited his bags at the his club, in St. James's (even in this sedate district, London was busier and noisier than he remembered it), then took a cab to Kensington. The house at 1 Melbury Road dated from the late nineteenth century, was large and brick, with big windows, having been built as the home of an artist. Now, it was the headquarters of the Secret Service.

"Good work in Germany, my boy," were C's first words to Smith, delivered with a beaming smile in his office. But then he indicated the closed folder on his highly reflective desktop, and, pushing a monocle into his eye, added, "Something I don't understand from your report, though, is what aroused your suspicions in the first place. You had definite ideas about Warner's death from the start. Why?"

"It was the light outside the Dom Hotel, sir," Smith answered.

C's impressive white eyebrows rose.

"Warner habitually left his work through the rear door of the hotel, where the only street lamp was broken," explained the major, as if not really interested in his own words. "At night, it would have been a very dark passage, yet the killer, who must have studied Warner's routine, chose to act along a well-illuminated street, patrolled regularly by police."

"Ah." C dropped his eyeglass, a smile again shining on his weathered face. "The murder occurred at the worst spot for it."

"But the best spot to be caught pretending to rifle the victim's body for documents. In fact, the killer, hoping to incriminate the French, was placing forged papers on the body, along with several genuine items. The real articles, as well as the models for the fakes, had been provided by Captain Beullac. For his purposes, the killer *had* to be 'interrupted' at his work by the police. Otherwise, people might wonder why, if Warner had been killed for the documents, they hadn't been taken."

"And the perpetrators?" C's face grew grim, like an approaching storm at sea. "The Russian Cheka?"

"Yes, hoping to cause a rift between us and the French. Even a minor row would have been helpful if the Bolsheviks were trying to foster revolution in Germany." Smith paused, then added, "The actual killer seems to have been a member or an agent of the Cheka."

"Unknown to us…"

"Yes sir. But I have high hopes that we'll become acquainted some day."

"Excellent work, my boy, excellent work," said C. "HMG is especially pleased that they'll be able to pretend that the plans the French had for wrecking our authority in the Rhineland were no more than forgeries designed by the Russians."

"Yes, now that those intentions are known, the French probably consider themselves lucky to be able to blame them all on the Cheka."

"And, consequently, our two countries have avoided a very dangerous rift." C was pleased as he stood and slapped his hands together behind his back. "You'll stay for dinner, of course? I have a proposition to put before you. The War Office hasn't press-ganged you into anything definite, have they?"

"No sir." Indeed, Smith feared a long spell on half-pay was his immediate prospect. But C smiled again.

"Excellent, excellent…"

Inductions Dangerous

The Art Lover

"You wouldn't think it to look at him, but that chap once blew himself up in order to sink a German transport ship."

C indicated a man sitting at a desk, writing. As he resembled nothing so much as an overgrown schoolboy toiling at sums, and seemed to be physically intact, Major Linus Smith felt bound to agree with the first part of his chief's statement. As C limped away from the open door before which he had paused, he resumed the elucidation from which he had digressed.

"Headquarters has changed rather a lot since you were part of it ten years ago, my boy. Our tiny squadron is now almost a fleet! Well, at least a flotilla!" C moved rapidly for a man with a wooden leg, using his stick and the rolling gait a sailor tended to acquire during years at sea. "The staff are given what we call 'cover' designations, corresponding to positions which they would hold were they not in the Secret Service. Because of their duties, and the hours they must work, each must be seen to have some berth in the bureaucracy, though nothing too definite. One may be a GSO in a War Office directorate, another listed as a Board of Trade clerk — just as you were listed as a member of MO5 during your time before the War."

None of the rooms into which C led Smith's attention was marked with either a name or a number. This was not due simply to the obvious need for discretion; the Headquarters of the Secret Service, neither the building nor its membership, was so large that such references were required.

C halted on the landing of the main staircase and smiled at the pretty woman ascending. She returned his cheerful salute and, as she walked winsomely away down a corridor, the chief put up his eyeglass and watched in appreciation.

"You field operators need a bit more cleverness," he continued at last.

C thudded down the staircase, his false limb almost bouncing him from one step to the next. He spoke as he descended, his words punctuated by the beat of his progress, making him sound as if he were suffering a bout of hiccoughs.

"You may be summoned at a moment's notice; you may not have an assignment for weeks, or even longer. When you do, it may last an hour, a month, or more. Each operator must have a 'cover' that takes this into account, yet which fits his individual circumstances."

By-passing the first storey, where the tour had begun, the pair reached the

The Art Lover

ground floor. C had a word for everyone they met, and each of his staff smiled freely when he saw him. The chief commented upon each person encountered after they had moved on, and each remark emphasised a complimentary quality.

"Where was I?" C wondered, as they left behind another cluttered room. "Oh, yes, operators must have 'covers' to fit them. For instance, I've just signed on a young chap from the RAF, officially 'seconded to the F.O. for special staff duties', to be precise, Air Ministry liaison. That will disguise a multitude of sins." C stopped and rapped on a closed door with the polished head of his teak stick. "Nerve centre of the whole place, my boy."

As C did not embellish this short, cryptic claim, Smith was left puzzled until he heard the flush of a water-closet from behind the door.

"We've decided to attach you to the Foreign Office's Historical Section," C said. "Frankly, I didn't know there was such an animal. But with your knowledge, it's a natural choice. Not only will people familiar with you believe such a posting, but you may be sent anywhere in the world to confirm a report, research a past event, what have you. Perfect camouflage for a roving commission."

At the far end of the house, by a little door that led obliquely into the walled back garden, was another staircase, smaller and narrower than the principal, central one. C's climb of the steps was slow, but in a series of jerks, he achieved the first floor without interrupting his monologue.

"We have a few part-timers as well, working for us when and where they can. You may remember some of them from the old days. They're usually without obvious government affiliation, individuals who are paid small retaining fees, or simply their expenses."

C bustled into his own chambers, the 'quarter-deck'. He waved happily at the secretaries in the anteroom as he and Smith passed through.

"And, finally, there is the Special Duties List of service personnel," he concluded, once more in his own office, "but you know all about that."

C laid his stick, a souvenir from the Malay coast of his early sea-faring days, across his desk in its far corner, and opened the French windows to the balcony. The October air was chilly, and accounted for the drabness of the garden below. But it was also bracing, and as he joined C at the white-painted balustrade, Smith felt refreshed.

"Well, my boy, you've had your ocean-trials long ago." The old naval officer placed his red, rough hands on the railing before them, and regarded the younger man at his side. "I think you can plunge right into sea-duty."

Though Smith had worked with the Secret Service before, in both London and Russia, times had changed, and he required some peculiar training. This had comprised only two weeks, but it had been a detailed and exhaustive, if not exhausting, fortnight. His tuition had been primarily administrative, and had included the organisation's structure, its methods of reporting, its finances. He had received instruction in the current ciphers and had spent long hours in the Registry, familiarising himself with what was known of rival services and their personnel.

"Whenever you like, sir," he said.

C turned from his newest subordinate, apparently gazing at Holland House, just visible over the roofs of intervening buildings and through the golden leaves of autumnal trees. But his youthful eyes, China blue, like those of a child's doll, twinkled, and his jutting chin stuck out all the further.

"First rate!" C led the way back into his office, which was being warmed by a modest but steady fire, and motioned for Smith to join him. When the balcony doors were shut, C had his guest sit. The sailor grinned. "How's your Russian?"

Six days later the sun was just rising behind a dark sheet of overcast as Smith's train crossed the Polish frontier and stopped at Zagorelovo station, fifty yards inside Russia. The small collection of engine, tender, goods van and passenger carriage could indeed have been termed 'Smith's', for, apart from the crew, he was the only person aboard. Despite the treaty ending the war the two countries had waged a couple of years previously, relations were strained between Poland and Russia; few citizens of the former wished to travel to the latter, and fewer still of the latter were allowed to travel at all.

Smith stood in the corridor of the carriage and wiped at the condensation covering the inside of a window's cracked pane. The resulting view was the first he had had of Russia since departing from Sebastopol in June of 1920. It was a discouraging sight.

Under the three or four dim station lights, several members of the Border Troops stood apathetically on the platform, swathed in great coats that fell to their knees, rifles with fixed bayonets untidily slung over their shoulders and peaked caps worn low over their unshaven faces. Each looked like a disappointed tout grumbling behind a brothel. Some of them smoked the crumpled remains of cigarettes that appeared as if they had been reclaimed from a street gutter, and one spat expertly onto the frozen boards at his feet.

The Bolshevik logic of its soldiers existing in such a state of slovenliness was, Smith realised, irrefutable. When the imperial government had fallen, the less advanced portions of the populace — and a goodly number of those who should have known better — took it as proof that rules, formerly applied from above, no longer obtained. In military bodies, hygiene, fastidiousness and discipline were manifest evidence of those old regulations. Therefore, their opposites were viewed as signs of revolutionary triumph.

The Art Lover

Smith retreated from the window as he observed a pair of the border guards hurriedly hand their diminutive cigarettes to comrades, unsling their firearms and advance upon the carriage's entrance, preceded by a third individual, whose type Smith recognised.

The Englishman appeared to be relaxing in his compartment, reading a book, when the door was opened without invitation.

"My name is Glazenapp, State Political Administration." The man thus suddenly revealed spoke Russian. "Let me see your documentation."

Dressed in a long leather coat, with a cap of the same material, this was the local representative of the GPU. Despite the organisation's official birth earlier in the year, no one who dealt with it believed it to be anything other than the Cheka re-named. Indeed, the clothing, manners, even the expression, were familiar to Smith from encounters he had had with the Bolsheviks' secret police during the civil war. Down to the Mauser pistol in its wooden holster under the belted waist of the man's coat, little had changed.

Smith was neither hurried nor leisurely in giving up the requested papers, returning his attention to his book while the documents were examined.

"Geoffrey Scovell?" Glazenapp's small eyes regarded the Englishman, and his voice switched to an adequate version of the latter's language. "You are expected. Come with me, please."

Had he entered Russia under his real name, Smith may not have received such courtesy. The members of the British military mission who had served with the White forces in southern Russia a few years previously had taken no pains to hide their identities, and so Major Linus Smith, attached to the Intelligence Section of the Army of the Caucasus's general staff, was probably the subject of a file or two in the GPU's Moscow headquarters. However, it was not Smith, nor even an officer of His Majesty's armed forces, whom Glazenapp now escorted to the customs shed.

"You will be joining the British Agency in Moscow?" The secret policeman, having ordered Smith to remove the contents of his two pieces of baggage, now assented to their return.

"That's right," answered the Englishman. "I must list everything that will be needed, and arrange an accounting. The British tax-payer hates to have his money squandered."

"I see."

In fact, the GPU officer sounded dubious that a capitalist country's government cared whether it wasted the people's treasure. To be honest, Smith was himself incredulous from time to time.

He glanced about. The principal room of the customs house resembled most of its kind, though with more dirt. The table on which his belongings had been laid for inspection seemed never to have been given more than a perfunctory cleaning, and that not for some time, while the floor beneath was not swept. Another soldier of the Border Troops, this one quite unimpressed with the GPU man, as he was with the foreigner, sat in a wobbly chair, scraping at the grime on the stock of his rifle with a filthy fingernail. Even the expected advantage of warmth in the shed was a disappointment: the stove in the corner of the room was not lit, and Smith's breath was nearly visible in the air.

"What of the train to Moscow?" he inquired.

Glazenapp barked a name, and a harried individual in several unmatching layers of clothes hastened through an interior door.

"The next train for Moscow, comrade..."

The man, whom Smith guessed was the stationmaster, or, perhaps, this being the new Russia, the president of the committee which had absorbed the stationmaster's duties and now spent its time discussing them, stammered.

"Midnight, comrade..." he said, as though offering a feasible suggestion. "There may be one before then, but that is the soonest that is scheduled..."

The GPU officer shook his head, as if dismissing the possibility of any rail traffic passing through, or near, Zagorelovo within the next sixteen hours. Smith decided that Glazenapp probably knew more about time-tables than any mere Transport Commissariat functionary.

"Midnight," the leather-clad official declared definitively.

Smith pulled tight the straps that bound his suitcases and said, "I don't suppose there is a restaurant or refreshment room open at this hour..." The expressions on the Russians' faces caused him to amend his query. "A restaurant or refreshment room at all, for that matter?"

"Are you feeling better?"

The countenance of the British official agent — for such was the title of His Majesty's semi-diplomatic representative in Moscow — was as solicitous as his question. Indeed, it would have taken a strong imagination to picture Basil Broster being anything but kind and generous, for certainly no record existed of him as less than completely sympathetic.

"Much better," Smith replied, "thank you."

He sank into the depths of a cavernous armchair upholstered in a faded floral pattern, the wooden structure groaning comfortably under his weight. Broster, pouring tea into a pair of cups from a steaming pot his secretary had provided minutes before, smiled tentatively at the response, as if thinking that there was still many things left to do for his guest. Setting a cup and saucer on the little, ornately-carved table at Smith's elbow, Broster then sat opposite his visitor, across the hearth of a glowing fireplace.

The Art Lover

"Excellent."

Broster's grin, making his full face appear more plump, grew surer. He was unremarkable-looking, a bit overweight, shorter than average, with thinning, dust-hued hair that darkened with the oil that kept it flat. This was to the detriment of his head, as it merely emphasised the size of his large ears. In his satisfactorily-tailored suit, from an inexpensive establishment in the Edgware Road, Broster did not resemble the British Empire's principal envoy to a foreign power.

"I especially appreciated the bath," commented Smith. The hot water for his ablutions had been brought to the big iron tub in the old-fashioned way, pail by pail, carried by servants from the boiler in the basement. This was in spite of the pipes that had been laid decades before throughout the building, and the taps that should have allowed the water therein to flow. That precious commodity was supplied only to parts of Moscow these days, and then intermittently, and never heated. "The last time I felt so dirty and sooty was in a war," he added, after a drink of tea.

"Well," said Broster, sipping from his own cup, "the Russians are, I think, doing their best. It was only in 1920 that fighting ceased throughout most of the land."

"Perhaps, but the same may be said of the Poles — more so, since their country had been a battlefield for six years — but they at least have found razors and soap for their soldiers."

"True, Poland has been through a great deal, but the Bolsheviks are conducting a great experiment, economic, social and political, and provision must be made for this, Mr Scovell." Broster pursed his full lips and nodded, as though stating a fact with which the world was quite familiar.

Smith put his cup to his mouth once more. His host, though from the Consular Service, was, due to his past postings, experienced in diplomacy, and no one at the Foreign Office, a hotbed of cynicism if there was one in His Majesty's Government, had ever considered him naïve. But Smith could not help wondering if a man who invariably sympathised with those among whom he was stationed was the best person for this prominent position in the new Bolshevik republic.

Certainly, Broster had established reasonably amiable relations with the country's leadership since he had arrived in Moscow. This had, after all, been the purpose of his mission. Smith, who always liked to know something about the people with whom he would be working, had read Broster's reports; they were full of conferences, meetings, dinners and informal talks with the top Communists. He invited them often to the house he had rented in Chistye Prudy, and, when asked, the Russians always came.

If Broster's house were anything like his office, it must indeed have been welcoming. The room in which Smith was now relaxing was rather like a study, filled with — but not cluttered by — an attractive collection of furniture. It was in the 'empire' style so favoured by the former Russian aristocracy, though none of the pieces exactly matched another. The paintings on the walls were probably all originals; Smith was unfamiliar with them, but believed they were of the native school.

"May I get you something further to eat, Mr Scovell? I could ring for some sandwiches..." Broster half-rose before Smith urged him to resume his seat. The diplomatist's fleshy face displayed an almost pitiful fear of doing too little for his guest.

"No, thank you," Smith said, and held up a hand to forestall further attempts on his behalf. "I at last feel as if I've made up the deficiency between the frontier and here."

Smith had not gone without nourishment during the fifty-two hours it had taken him to journey from the borders of Russia to its capital. Indeed, those in authority had tried, to an extent, to fill the void. The GPU officer at Zagorelovo had provided a kind of breakfast and a sort of luncheon at the small house in which he was lodged. The former consisted largely of bread tasting like sour sawdust, and the latter of borscht lacking either beetroots or clean water. Smith had at last resorted to the emergency rations that he always carried when travelling.

"There were no restaurants operating at the towns between? Minsk, for instance?" asked Broster, his eyebrows forcing his smooth forehead to wrinkle. "Or did the train not stop there?"

"Oh, yes, it halted at Minsk," Smith assured his host. He drained his cup and set it aside. "I was, in fact, five hours in Minsk, and so was able to tour the city at my leisure."

"And found nowhere to eat?" Broster took from the mantelpiece a plain silver box and offered his visitor the contents. Finished now with his tea, Smith accepted a cigarette, lighting it with a burning splinter from the open grate. The fire's fuel, he had noticed, comprised not cut and split logs but what appeared to be scraps from a carpenter's refuse pile. It nonetheless burned well, and floated a pleasant aroma around the room.

"There were several 'communal eating houses', all more or less conveniently situated," responded Smith, exhaling smoke. It dissipated lazily in the air above his chair. "Their title is the most appealing thing about them, and I decided to risk my health upon abstinence, instead."

"Oh, dear..." Broster shook his head slowly.

Smith had dined at worse tables than those he had found at Minsk, though such events had been dictated by necessity or duty. Besides, he was not in Russia as Linus Smith, major, Royal Fusiliers, but as Geoffrey Scovell, an emissary of the Treasury, and as such, it behoved him to be less adventuresome in his actions. It was a good excuse, at any rate.

"It is part of the experiment, you see, Mr Scovell," explained Broster, though without a maximum of conviction. "Restaurants charged prices that not all Russians could afford. The new eating houses make all opportunities for public dining equal."

Smith drew on his cigarette again and wondered why standards were always lowered in order to achieve equality.

"I must admit," Broster went on, "that when I arrived in Russia this summer, I too chose not to eat in Minsk when I passed through it. The smell, you see, was not encouraging." He blinked several times in recollection. "There was a typhus outbreak in the city at the time, and the authorities' ability to dispose of the dead had not kept pace with the need."

While Smith smoked, he and his host spoke of innocuous subjects, local cuisine, the state of housing in Moscow, the availability of merchandise and, of course, the weather. Outside, the snow fell steadily, in spite of the temperature being not far below freezing. The sun was a pale circle behind a sheet of clouds.

"Now, Mr Broster, why don't you tell me about this chap, Misolov?" Smith tossed the remnant of his cigarette into the flames of the fireplace and settled back in his chair again.

"Yes, the reason you are here." Broster nodded vigorously, the extra flesh of his face half a second behind the action. "Are you familiar with my career at all, Mr Scovell?"

"I know that you were consul here in Moscow before the revolution." Smith guessed that this was the salient point.

"That's right. In the post, I made the acquaintance of a great many Russian businessmen, the successful merchant class being the aristocracy of this city, rather than the nobility, as in Saint Petersburg." Broster gestured, as if introducing someone. "Anatole Misolov was a member of that upper class, a man whose family had been rich for generations, deriving their wealth from jam, I believe."

"There always seems to be money in sweets," observed Smith. "You saw Misolov ten — ten? — ten days ago now?"

The other man rolled his eyes toward the plastered ceiling.

"Closer to a fortnight it'd be."

Smith did not resent the correction. He himself believed greatly in accurate details.

"When was this? Under what circumstances?"

"It was at a dinner party I attended with some government ministers," answered the diplomatist. "What startled me was not that Misolov was in such company, for he wasn't, not really. No, he was working for them — as a chauffeur!"

"That must have been a surprising sight."

"Indeed. Though," recovering from his re-enactment of how he felt at the time, Broster frowned, "I suppose it shouldn't have been such a shock. In his glory, Misolov's great interest had been automobiles, and with his affluence, he had been in a position to indulge it."

"He was knowledgeable in mechanics and internal combustion engines?" queried Smith.

"Precisely, Mr Scovell. I think that expertise may have saved him during the turmoil of the revolution; he may have been taken on as a driver because of it."

"It may also have amused some of his new masters to have one of Moscow's formerly wealthy residents performing work that would be greasy and grimy," Smith suggested.

"Yes, that had occurred to me, as well..."

The diplomatist appeared embarrassed for the Bolsheviks and their petty actions. Smith guessed that his host, like himself, had never considered humiliation or degradation to be a punishment that civilised people would inflict.

"Where did this take place?" he wanted to know.

"The dinner was in the dacha country, just outside the city." Broster paused and, regarding his visitor a little quizzically, inquired if he were aware of the word's meaning.

"Dacha? Yes, a house, rural in character, though it may actually be situated among metropolitan suburbs. They are — or were, I suppose — retreats for their better-off owners on Saturday-to-Mondays."

"Quite right." If Broster was surprised by Smith's possession of the facts, he hid it behind a smile. "Though even the poorer of the middle classes liked to have some kind of hut, if they could, dachas were, for the most part, quite beautiful villas, rarely ostentatious, and even homely, in their ways." He sighed and stated, "The majority are dilapidated now; a number have been occupied by government officials and their associates."

"It didn't take long for a new élite to form," Smith noted, dryly.

"It is at least a more broadly based gentry, if one at all, I think you'll agree," said Broster, almost pouting, and sounding as if he had been personally hurt by the jibe.

Smith considered that, as it was easier to become an oppressor than either rich or titled, his host was, in likelihood, correct. He kept the opinion to himself,

The Art Lover

however, and steered the conversation back to its original direction.

"Were you able to speak to Misolov?"

Broster shook his head, saying, "No. It would have been as awkward as attempting to strike a conversation with another man's valet at a country house weekend in England." Smith recognised the truth in this. In Russia, it may have been dangerous, as well. Broster continued: "I did confirm that Misolov was working for the commissar of Foreign Trade, a man named Grek." The diplomatist's eyes widened and he said, "I really had no idea that the Secret Service would be interested in Misolov, or Grek, when I reported these facts to London."

"As the minister responsible for Russia's trade with other countries, Grek would possess information that would be valuable to departments headed by HMG," Smith explained simply, "and someone who regularly drives him, and his colleagues, to and from meetings, conferences, lectures, even just his everyday work, would be in an excellent position to learn things."

"Oh... I see... Yes..." Broster's round visage became contemplative, a short finger tapping his equally round chin.

"Furthermore, Grek, holding the portfolio that he does, would be a member of the Council of Labour and Defence, wouldn't he?"

"Yes, yes, he would," confirmed the diplomatist, acknowledging sheepishly that he had missed the obvious. His finger ceased its movements as he remembered something more. "And he works closely with Khuseff, the council's president."

This was intelligence of which the Secret Service had not been aware. Smith, the perusal of the Registry at Headquarters still fresh in his mind, recognised the new name. Constantine Khuseff was one of the most powerful Bolsheviks in the economic sphere, if not *the* most powerful. That made him significant in every aspect of Russian life. An agent with daily access to such individuals would be a potential treasury of information.

"Mr Broster, is there a way you can put me in touch with Misolov?" Smith inquired.

The envoy coloured, his wide ears turning pink.

"I would very much prefer if I were not directly involved in these activities, Mr Scovell," he said, hesitantly. "My dealings with the Bolsheviks are still in their infancy, as it were; I am still trying to win their trust." Smith thought that as the declared aim of the new Russian government was the violent overthrow of every other régime on Earth, it should have been the foreigners' trust that was sought. Broster put in: "I understand that this must make me most uncooperative..."

"Not at all." Smith's response was in a kind tone, as he had sympathy for his host's position. Despite what cynics may have claimed about diplomacy, it was as honest a profession as any and, when practised by a gentleman, was often at variance with methods employed by secret services. "Would it damage your efforts if you were to provide proof to Misolov that I am not an *agent provocateur*?"

Again, Broster's face contorted with emotional discomfort, and he told Smith that even a letter with his signature at the bottom, if it fell into the wrong hands, could be disastrous for Anglo-Russian relations.

"Something without your name, then," ventured Smith, almost enjoying the game. "A reminder of a shared conversation or incident, which would lend your authority — inferred only by someone such as Misolov — to an indication that I was genuine, but would lead nowhere, were anyone else to examine it."

For a moment, Broster's thick countenance continued to struggle with the ideas behind it. Then it cleared, and even brightened.

"Yes, yes, I think that may do, Mr Scovell," the envoy said happily. "In the meantime, if you think it will help, I can supply what I know of Grek's itinerary. I've dealt with him quite a bit and am familiar with some of his routine. The chances of finding Misolov will be better if you know where to find his employer."

Smith smiled and responded, "Mr Broster, we may make a secret operator of you yet," and had the fun of seeing the other man's expression of horror.

Smith had known Moscow before the revolution. He had spent the first of his two visits to tsarist Russia in Moscow, perfecting his knowledge of the local language. During the Great War, he had been posted to the Secret Service station in Petrograd, and his duties took him from Finland to Rumania, from the Prypet Marshes to the Danube River. He had been in St Petersburg on the very day the insurrection that would topple the tsar had broken out. But he had not seen Moscow since 1909.

Whereas Petrograd — for most of its history 'Saint Petersburg' and the principal city of the empire — had been built as the European metropolis of a western-gazing state, Moscow had grown organically for seven centuries, a true Russian centre and, in many ways, a semi-oriental place.

The snow that had fallen Tuesday, while Smith had warmed himself by the fire in Broster's office, remained unmoved two days later. In the streets, the thick, wet precipitation had been trammelled by cart and automobile tires, human feet and horses' hooves, crushed into a grey slush that had made the naturally indifferent surfaces — rounded cobbles set into sand — much worse. The resultant quagmire had by Thursday seemed to have rendered the few motor-cars in the city immobile. It was due to this inconvenience that Smith was able to meet Anatole Misolov.

The Kuznetsky Most had been Moscow's Bond Street, albeit a narrow version, and the best sort of shops had lined the thoroughfare either side. During the old régime, it had been one of the very few streets paved with asphalt. This was now cracked and holed, unrepaired beneath the churned snow, and all the luxury establishments, once filled with silks and furs, jewellery and fine food, were gone.

This did not signify that all the buildings were empty, however. Between rows of glassless, boarded-over windows, could be found businesses offering badly arranged merchandise, items of too good a quality to have been owned by the individuals now selling it. These were the 'loot' shops, displaying what had been the property of the aristocracy, the wealthy, or simply the hard-working who had at last managed to afford a life's dream. These regrettable establishments were permitted under the Bolsheviks' New Economic Policy, limited capitalism meant to invigorate a country that Communism was failing to revive. They, and the official stores, outlets for state-run production, were now the only commercial life in the Kuznetsky Most.

Armed with Broster's description of Misolov, and where he might be found, Smith surreptitiously searched the street. The once noisy thoroughfare was not crowded, and people seemed to use it as little more than a passage between two points. These trudgers through the deep, unshovelled snow pulled ragged coats about them with fraying gloves; those who had galoshes wore them, but most feet were shod with shoes, no proof against either cold or damp. Any attempt at fashion had long since vanished in the face of necessity.

As he passed corners, Smith peered down the lanes that intersected with the once-bustling market street. These were crooked, unappealing places, and when the light of the short day faded, their darkness would be unrelieved. They had not the lamps that the better streets boasted, though these afforded few advantages now, as most seemed to be missing vital parts.

Not far down one of these seedy side-streets was a motor-car, of an indefinite make. It sagged, listing in the porridge-like snow, and, from the exertions of the man dressed as its driver, it was clear that the vehicle was stuck fast. Though individuals looked on, they were most disinclined to help, lounging against crumbling brick walls or in dirty doorways with folded arms and sneering faces.

"Do you need some assistance, comrade?"

The automobile's chauffeur, vainly pushing against the vehicle, glanced up, surprised. He saw a nondescript man, dressed in old but serviceable winter clothes, boots and a battered peaked cap, smiling and indicating with a nod the stranded machine.

Anatole Misolov brushed from his hands clumps of snow and flakes of rust, both heavy on the car's fender, and answered, "I do, yes, thank you, comrade. I made the mistake of pulling in here while the commissar visited one of the shops."

Smith recognised Misolov. Broster's description had not been detailed, but it had been accurate. The square face, baggy skin that had once covered a better-fed frame, the wide nose with the nostrils that flared broadly when they inhaled; all were telling characteristics. In particular, the staring eyes that had sunk back into the pale face were identifiable.

The Englishman took up a position in back of the automobile, suggesting that the driver get behind the steering wheel to urge the engine forward. Misolov clapped his hands together and complied quickly.

"Well?" Smith straightened before putting a shoulder to his task and gazed about him at the amused audience of loafers. "You heard what the man told me. The commissar probably won't be pleased to learn of so many 'workers' who refused to help shift his car."

It was not so much that the vehicle belonged to a government official that caused movement among those watching, as the intimation that he might 'learn' something about them, that caused a change in the audience. A moment later, with a number of volunteers lending muscle to the task, the automobile was free of its slushy fetters and moving under its own power.

"Thank you, comrades," Misolov said to the crowd as it broke up again. His machine had come to rest on a patch of dirt sheltered by drooping eaves, and thus relatively free from snow and sludge. Misolov turned to Smith and repeated his words of gratitude, this time in the singular.

"I'm glad to help," Smith assured the Russian. With his body shielding the action from observers — though the by-standers, deprived of their amusement, were no longer interested — he handed a small, folded sheet of paper to the chauffeur, who took it out of reflex. "You dropped this as you were getting into the motor-car."

Misolov blinked at the page, but when he raised his colourless face to protest, Smith had turned. With his hands in his pockets and his shoulders hunched, he was already walking away.

No more snow fell that day, though the temperature did, and the ruts, holes and ridges into which Thursday's viscous sludge had been moulded by feet and wheels hardened by Friday morning. That night, Anatole Misolov's ankles ached from more than an hour's mis-steps. He had nearly twice dropped his bag of food, meagre as it was, as he stumbled in the ill-lit streets. The powdery bread and the stale dumplings in the paper sack could not be claimed a good meal, but it was the only one his family would get this night, and he did not wish to lose it.

"Misolov..."

The Russian was startled, and almost let his burden fall a third time. Since he had read the note the strange Samaritan had given him the day before, Misolov had been half-expecting to see the man again, yet he was not prepared for the sudden greeting. He gazed about. The street down which he had been slowly walking was dark, most of the sparsely-spaced lamps being broken, and the dusk having faded some time before. One or two other pedestrians had passed him, but they had been solely concerned with getting home, and out of the open cold.

"Where are you?" Misolov whispered.

"In the doorway to your left."

Even aware of the stranger's location, the Russian could not see him. With a final glance about, Misolov slipped into the recessed entrance of the building before which he had halted. A good place for a clandestine rendezvous, it was an empty townhouse, not yet taken over by new tenants. Misolov wrinkled his nose: someone had had a use for the space, however; it had been turned into a urinal, as was obvious, despite the cold.

"Do you have the note you were given?"

"No. I destroyed it."

"Good. Do you know from whom it came?"

"Yes, I think so. It read of an English motor-car for sale at the Slovansky Bazaar years ago." Misolov shook his head. "There were never any vehicles offered there. But I once inspected an automobile near there that I wanted to buy. It had been German, but I was with a certain English friend... You come from him?"

"No. But you know now that he's vouched for me, and that I'm not an agent of the GPU." There was a pause. "Do you know why I wanted to speak with you?"

Misolov chuckled, though more than he had intended. The cold had seeped through the thin layers of his garments, in spite of their quantity. He was beginning to stammer.

"A message from an old acquaintance, written in a kind of code; a stranger, a foreigner perhaps, despite sounding like a Russian, who wants to talk to me where no one will see..." Misolov was clearly not slow to deal with evidence.

"As a chauffeur for a government minister, you no doubt hear a great many things that your superiors would prefer to go no further."

"Yes, I suppose that's true," Misolov confirmed, rubbing his nose against the stench of his surroundings.

"I would prefer they go further."

"I see." The Russian's teeth started to chatter. He wondered if it were due entirely to the frigid air.

"We would be in a position to pay for the information, or even just to retain your services against future activity."

Misolov instinctively cast about. He saw no one in the dark and silent street. It was certain that no one could see him.

"I would need to know more," he said haltingly, "and then I would need to think about it."

"Of course."

"Why don't you come to my house?" Misolov snorted and corrected his invitation. "Or, rather, the place where I and my family live. Since you've stopped me on my way home, you must know where it is."

"I do, but..." Doubt crept into the speaker's voice. "Are you sure you want me to join you there?"

The Russian scoffed at such caution and seemed almost jolly as he said, "It is better if I don't hide any associations I have, Mister..."

"Nasonov."

"Come next Tuesday, Mr Nasonov. Shall we say two o'clock?" Misolov breathed on his free hand and switched to it the bag of food, thrusting the other into a pocket.

"Why Tuesday? It's Thursday yet."

"Commissar Grek keeps me very busy," was the reply, "not just driving, but in running errands. I'm his factotum." The tone could have been mistaken for one of whimsy. "But Tuesdays, he has me drop him off in the Angelskaya, and pick him up there three or four hours later. The interval is my own."

"What's in the Angelskaya that interests the commissar so much?"

"A weekly art auction," answered Misolov: "paintings and sculpture from the aristocracy put up for sale. The money goes to the people."

"To the government?"

"Yes." Misolov's voice was flat.

"Very well, I'll call on you then." The stranger made to move from the doorway, but he hesitated. "You'd better have these." The man stripped off his gloves, leather, and lined with fleece, and placed them in the Russian's stiff fingers. An instant later, Misolov was alone, and the blackness hid the footprints that may have shown that he had been otherwise.

The British official agent lived in almost isolated splendour. The house he had taken was large for a single man, even with servants, a kind of suburban mansion, on a boulevard that was attractive in any season. Conifers lined the street, though the verdure of their boughs was almost hidden by thick and heavy burdens of snow. Only before Basil Broster's home had the wooden pavements' white covering been disturbed, though the frozen pond at the far end of the street had been discovered by some children, who slid about on the ice, their worn shoes providing no traction.

"How did he appear to you?"

Broster stood close to the fire that blazed in his sitting room's grate. Here, proper logs were used and their heat was strong and fragrant, just enough to keep the exterior cold at bay. Broster's full face was pink, his large ears red, and he enjoyed the flames behind him as only a man could have done who had just come in from outside.

"Mildly emaciated, though not really unhealthy," Smith answered. He sipped at his sherry, indifferent stuff, probably purchased locally. He had been offered a cocktail but had declined, to his host's obvious relief. Broster confessed not only to preferring the traditional pre-prandial drinks but also to having no idea as to how to make a cocktail — or to knowing the contents thereof, for that matter. "His attitude was...cynical, I suppose one could describe."

"Mm, I wouldn't be surprised. He had a strong amount of that element when I knew him at the best of times. And the note?" Broster's eyebrows rose searchingly. "It was valuable?"

Smith said, "It achieved exactly what I'd hoped."

"I must say that I am glad you will be visiting Misolov next Tuesday, of all days," the diplomatist admitted. He took a seat on the satiny-surfaced sofa across from Smith's chair. The drawing room was furnished similarly to his office in Povarskaya Street, filled with articles of the same style and hung with Russian art. Smith thought the house a better setting for such items than the ordinary, generically European mission building.

"Why is that?" Smith queried.

"I will be busy, and since I'm meeting again with the president of the Council of Labour and Defence, I won't be associated with any attempt at espionage." Broster's expression changed. "I realise that sounds quite selfish, Mr Scovell, even cowardly..."

"Not at all," Smith responded truthfully. He drank some wine. "We each have our own duties to perform, Mr Broster, and diplomacy brings its own dangers. Your actions are open for all to see. Besides which, the Bolsheviks don't respect international courtesies."

"I suppose that's a fact," Broster stated, sighing. Even someone as forgiving as he remembered, with discomfort at least, the violation of the British Embassy by the Cheka in 1918, and the consequent murder of the naval attaché.

"Speaking of this council," Smith said, frowning, "shouldn't Grek, as a member, be attending these meetings with you and Khuseff?"

"No, I don't think so." Broster walked to the sideboard which, though it was hardly a small version of its kind, was almost literally overshadowed by a huge oil painting of what Smith assumed to be a subject from Russian history or legend. "Khuseff, as president, is the real power on the council. The other members are not precisely men of straw, but their positions under him are more consultative than executive." Broster lifted a decanter of sherry, silently offering more to his guest. The latter politely refused, whereupon his host refilled his own glass. "I've been conferring with Khuseff on a weekly basis, primarily regarding compensation to British firms whose assets have been confiscated. The fellow usually appears with a secretary and three or four clerks. Mr Olson, one of my own clerks, supports me." The diplomatist may have been forgiven if he cavalierly drank some more wine after this statement. He obviously felt that he and his subordinate were, in business matters, a match for thrice their number of Bolsheviks.

"How long have you been talking with Khuseff?" asked Smith.

"Almost two months." Despite his confidence, Broster's reply reflected the effort behind his work.

"Do you think you'll be successful?"

"In a way..." Broster resumed his seat on the sofa. "We won't get cash compensation, but both we and the Bolsheviks want British commerce involved in the Russian economy again, they even more than we, though they won't admit to it. It's in that degree of their desire that we'll be able to force some advantages that will be as good as money."

As Broster's maid entered to announce that dinner was ready, Smith decided that though his host's sympathy may have been with the Russians, he would probably not let that prevent him from striking a hard bargain. He emptied his glass and walked with Broster into the next room.

Smith felt that reading the products of the Russian press proved a relatively simple accomplishment these days. The newspapers of the new Soviet republic were no more than organs of the Bolshevik Party, and were filled with the same sorts of stories day after day. Internationalism and the proletariat, world revolution and world capitalism, exploitation by the bourgeoisie and sabotage by their lackeys, and the ceaseless efforts by the heroic workers to combat them, were all that one could find in Red journalism. The words of one article differed almost not at all from those of the next. Smith estimated that the knowledge of but a handful of nouns and verbs, and even fewer adjectives, was all that was required to understand any printed story in the Russia of 1922.

He folded his newspaper and set it on the empty chair beside him. The restaurant of the Europa Hotel was nearly deserted, though, after his initial perusal of the menu, Smith did not wonder. The champagne on the wine list, as mediocre as it was, could not have been had for less than the equivalent of £2 10s. He chose instead a Moselle at half the other's price, and it turned out to be second-rate at best.

The Europa had been a good hotel under the old régime; that, and the fact that it was one of the few still operating, had determined Smith's choice of accommodation. Broster had protested that he was welcome to stay at his house indefinitely. As sincere as the offer was, Smith knew that his decision to seek out other shelter came as a relief to the diplomatist. There was no guarantee that Misolov's invitation was not a trap, and if things went awry this Tuesday, it would be bad enough that Geoffrey Scovell and Basil Broster were countrymen, let alone residing under the same roof. Besides, Smith had no notion how long he would be required to remain in Russia.

In deference to Britain's official agent, the Soviet authorities had made available a couple of once beautiful rooms on the Europa's first floor at a cost of a mere eighteen million roubles. This was not as cheap as it sounded.

A waiter made his way around the other tables, most of them empty, and approached the Englishman. The servant's white jacket, rather dated but clean and pressed, like the cloth draped smoothly over the table-tops, was a relic of the hotel's glorious past. The waiter was so practised and polite that Smith suspected that he too was a survival from the old days.

"May I bring you anything else, sir?" The tone implied that the customer was more than welcome to stay as long as he desired. "No? Very good, sir. This was delivered to the front desk for you, sir." The waiter presented his small, silver, circular tray, upon which was a sealed envelope. Smith took it, noting that his name and address, the temporary ones, had been roughly scrawled on the face. "It was known that you were here at dinner, so I was requested to bring it."

Smith thanked the waiter, who retreated with a small smile, as if pleased to receive some civility. Judging from the few other diners' behaviour, Smith thought respect for the staff may have been at a premium. One man, not far away, was sitting with an attractive young woman, and was dressed like a peasant. His typical rural Russian's blouse was belted, but not tucked into his trousers, and he wore top-boots that smelled, even at a distance, strongly of polish. He had kept his peaked cap on throughout the meal. His comrades, in pairs at a couple more tables, were conventionally dressed but had become louder as they ate — and drank — their way through dinner. Each had lit a cigarette before his food had arrived, smoking it and several others, while they consumed their successive courses.

Smith's observations were interrupted as the small chamber orchestra, on its shallow stage at the far end of the room, finished playing. They had already been performing when Smith had sat down, and, when not ignored by the others present, were the subjects of snide comments made in voluble whispers. Smith applauded, quietly, as he had at the end of each piece, and the group's leader half-rose in a bow of appreciation. Russia was full of excellent musicians, many of whom would have distinguished themselves were it not for the revolution. Now, they considered themselves fortunate to be playing in hotel restaurants before indifferent audiences.

Done with his meal, Smith set aside its dishes and utensils, lighting a cigarette as the orchestra began a Mozart string quartet. He opened the envelope, not knowing what to make of the delivery, and was surprised to pull out an invitation.

Smith was accustomed to being asked to functions wherever he went. As an Englishman with a respectable military title — most of his aliases were similarly characterised — he was considered a safe risk, even by hostesses unacquainted with him, or who did not remember him from previous associations. But a request for his presence at a Bolshevik government banquet was not something he had anticipated. And he had not thought to bring evening dress.

He checked the date printed on the card he held; the event was this coming Thursday. He inhaled a breath full of smoke and wondered if three days were enough time to find a tail-coat and white waistcoat in revolutionary Russia.

It would have surprised no one to have learned that winter came early in Moscow. That Russia could be cold and snow-bound by early November was probably one of the more widely-professed, and accurate, beliefs that foreigners held about the country. The Moskva River, and its small tributary, the Yauza, had frozen completely the week of Smith's arrival, and the slight warmth of his first day in the capital had not altered the water's solid status.

For ten million roubles, Smith secured the services of a taxi to carry him to the Zamoskvoryechie, the principal district of the old merchant families in the latter days of the tsars. It was as well that the gloomy afternoon skies, smeared with unfriendly grey clouds from one horizon to the other, had not added to the snow on the ground, since that which had already fallen gave the taxi a rough time as it was. The motor-car was, Smith was informed, an 'international' — made from diverse kinds of vehicles from several countries — and the driver, his teeth rattling painfully with every bump and bang, assured his passenger that they would reach their destination in spite of the obstacles. For his part, Smith was not persuaded that the bouncing, jarring and tossing were due entirely to the condition of the streets.

The Misolov family townhouse was known to the cabbie. The clan had been rich, and respected in Moscow. Their home was typical of those in the Zamoskvoryechie, and had once been the centre of what was in effect a little suburban estate. But the few short years since the revolution had changed its character, if the sad, breathless oath from the driver was any indication.

The house still stood, almost defiant in its grounds, but the gates were missing from where they had sometimes barred the main entrance in the surrounding walls. Shoddy out-houses had been erected about the residence, and existing dependencies adapted, so that each was now a separate abode. The curious, makeshift chimneys that poked their way through roofs and glassless windows reminded Smith of drainpipes.

"They *are* drainpipes, comrade," responded the taxi-driver, chuckling grimly. "They are torn off buildings, and come the spring, roofs throughout the city will leak like waterfalls because of it."

The interior of the house presented a more discouraging sight than the outside. It had not been cleaned in years, dirt and grime clinging to the walls like another coat of paint, with moisture trickling down several well-watered paths. A kind of rude booth of pieces of scrap wood, had been raised in a corner of the hall. A concierge sat nonchalantly within, barely noticing Smith as he passed. Certainly the Englishman felt no tension in the air, and though he did not abandon his guard, he began to think that he was not walking into a trap.

The Misolov house had never been a nobleman's home, but it had belonged to a merchant family whose ambitions had been fulfilled, and this happy state had been reflected in the construction of the building. Not ostentatious, the broad staircase of stone and wood was nonetheless impressive. Under its top-light, now cracked and leaking in a number of places, it suggested something both homely and lofty.

"Comrade Nasonov, how good of you to come."

Anatole Misolov had been awaiting Smith's arrival, and had seen the Briton look into one of the grand chambers on the first floor after another. The Russian quickly stepped forward, his hands held out in greeting. The interior of the house was chilly, but its relative warmth in comparison to that of the two men's previous meetings had not improved Misolov's appearance. His eyes peered from deep sockets in his square face and his nostrils dilated and contracted with his nervous breathing.

"Come and meet my wife and son."

Smith was led into what he guessed had once been a parlour or principal bedroom. It was now partitioned into cubicles by blankets of various hues and fabrics hung over cords above the height of a man's head. Low voices and slow movements emanated from behind these screens, though one or two had been pulled back, probably for air, revealing the spaces behind. From one, with no other furnishing than an old cot, the floor covered with dirty clothes, a pair of rheumy, malevolent eyes followed Smith's progress.

"What's this, comrade? Another repentant ex-bourgeoisie?"

The voice was loud and belligerent, the words slurring into one another. The speaker was squatting on a pile of rags, his back to the wall. He had just finished re-charging the chipped glass tumbler that he held in one hand with vodka from the bottle he grasped in the other. His next bellow was so full of obscenities that Smith made a motion toward the inebriate, literally forgetting his place.

"It's this way, comrade..."

Misolov pulled at the Englishman's sleeve, and the two passed beyond the view of the drunkard. The Russian tugged back the coarse grey cloth that hung farthest from the door and invited his guest into his home; the irony in his tone was nearly palpable.

The Misolovs' portion of the room was in a corner, and had the distinction of a window, though on a cold day such as this, the advantage was dubious. The remains of the family fortune was arranged in neat and orderly stacks: clothes, a few books, a photographic album and a tiny store of food. Each had its own place. The smell of damp garments hovered about a string of washing suspended across the rear of the space, as far as possible from the small form lying under several blankets by the nearest partition. The boy, asleep, had an unhealthy colour.

"Comrade Nasonov, my wife, Elizavetta."

Mrs Misolova rose from one of the two rickety chairs she and her husband possessed. She was thin, the naturally high cheekbones adding to the gauntness of her face, which had once been pretty. The skin of the hand she extended to Smith was almost translucent. She wore a dated but clean dress, and around her shoulders was a man's sweater.

"A pleasure, sir..." she said, her whisper as slender as her frame. She knelt by the lad, pride and pain in her pinched visage. "Our son, Pavel..."

There was no source of heat in the Misolovs' space, but from the other side of the screen next to which the boy lie came the warmth of a small stove. Even with this advantage, Pavel, not more than four or five, shivered periodically, involuntarily. Misolov, gazing down at his son, began to blink his eyes. His wife gently recalled him to his duties as a host.

"Yes, of course," he said, chuckling distractedly. "There is some water boiling across the corridor. Tea, comrade?"

"Oh, that reminds me..." Smith reached into his long, fleece-lined coat. "A poor guest I would be if I didn't bring a gift or two." The small, carefully wrapped packages that he produced contained tea, butter, sugar, salt and fresh white bread. The last item, a little but plump orange, caused Elizavetta's eyes to widen.

"For the boy, perhaps," Smith commented quietly.

Misolov had intended to make new, stronger tea with the supply his visitor had brought, but Smith had dissuaded him. He was not about to have any more food or drink wasted on him than his hosts had already prepared. Elizavetta insisted, however, on serving out the rolls he had brought, and spreading them with a decent amount of butter.

After Misolov had returned from the communal stove with a steaming samovar, the conversation was easy and innocuous. At first, Smith assumed that the conscientious parents feared waking their son. Though this may have been a factor, what the couple wished to avoid was the attention of their drunken neighbour.

Smith could hear him, a big man, moving clumsily about and muttering, several spaces away. Now and then, he would raise his voice in a shout, damning all the enemies of the proletariat. These seemed to be without number, so his rambling tirades were long and ended in incomprehensibility. Eventually, the sounds of anger grew faint and, at last, ceased.

"He's passed out," said Misolov, with a sigh. His wife's relief, written patently across her wan face, was greater. Smith could only have imagined her apprehension when left alone with her son, her husband working, and the champion of the world's workers intoxicated with vodka and rage. "He'll wake suddenly in a couple of hours and rush out."

Smith had been given a cushioned chair in which to sit, despite his protest that Elizavetta should have continued to use it. The woman politely but resolutely refused the offer, even refusing her husband's hard-seated chair. The men therefore reclined in relative comfort, while the woman sat on the floor and spent most of Smith's visit gently caressing her sleeping child's brown hair.

"I have thought over what we spoke of last Friday, Mr Nasonov," Misolov stated. His voice was conversational yet low, flat. The sound of it would not carry more than a couple of feet. He glanced at his spouse, then drank from his metal-handled glass cup. "Elizavetta and I have agreed that I should help you all I can..."

Smith nodded and sipped from his own tea. It was so weak that it was little better than boiled water. When he spoke, his words were as likely as Misolov's to be heard by those who should not.

"I don't suppose I need to stress that this may prove a dangerous activity."

Misolov smiled, cynical lines pulling the loose skin of his square face.

"Grek has a deputy who doesn't simply report to the GPU, but is one of its officers. Since the commissariat deals constantly with foreigners, the secret police feel that the opportunity for spying against the workers' republic is great." He shook his head. "No, you needn't tell us about the dangers. What sort of information would you want?"

Smith swallowed the mouthful of bread that he had been chewing, and replied, "Anything that you hear from your chief, or from anyone else. News regarding trade talks, the economic situation, personal intelligence, government gossip..." He paused. "How difficult would it be to deposit your reports at arranged locations?"

Misolov shook his head.

"Not difficult," he answered. His response was almost cheerful. "Grek sends me on errands all the time. Though I wouldn't have the time I do now, I'd find it easy enough to slip away to a park or a building — at least in the central part of the city."

"Good." Smith drank some more tasteless water. He was almost done; he had not wished to offend his hosts but drinking the barely flavoured fluid had been a chore. "I'll prepare a plan for regular contact." He looked first at Misolov, then at Elizavetta, and back again. "I want you both to realise that if, at any time, you feel yourselves to be in peril, you may end your involvement. I'll set up a separate means of communicating problems, simply and rapidly. Now, as for remuneration..."

Misolov emptied his glass, his sunken eyes peering over the rim. He indicated their surroundings.

"Mr Nasonov, this...what you see here...is all we have left. A fortune it took generations to collect is gone, taken without warning. We live in a corner, literally, of what used to be our house, while pigs wallow in the rest of it. I am humiliated daily by a semi-literate criminal for whom I must work, while my wife is afraid to leave our son even to wash her hands. Our boy is sick — again..." He stopped talking for a moment. "And our daughter...murdered because some chairman of a revolutionary committee took a fancy to her..." His wife turned to peer at him, almost in astonishment; perhaps surprised, thought Smith, that he had divulged this information. "I will do these things for you, Mr Nasonov," the Russian added. "I will do them for nothing..."

Procuring a suit of evening clothes was an easier deed than Smith had imagined. Even before the limited capitalism of Lenin's New Economic Policy, individuals had been permitted to sell goods in the streets of the cities. Throughout Moscow, but principally in the central districts, by the Kremlin and the government offices, where high-ranking bureaucrats worked and where the rare foreigner may have been seen, thousands of hawkers displayed all manner

The Art Lover

of goods in baskets and bags, on wheelbarrows and carts. These peddlers stood in the frigid open all day, trying to sell what they could of what property remained to them.

From their manners and speech, indeed, from the very way in which they stood, it was obvious that many of these petty merchants were men and women of good breeding, and of education. What they offered posed no competition for the mendicants who also haunted the pavements, as one group sold while the other begged. Nonetheless, public space for bargaining was limited, and former aristocrats and bourgeoisie were sometimes forced to move on by the more veteran denizens of the streets.

"Here it is, sir, as I promised."

The speaker presented to Smith a bundle neatly wrapped in uncoloured paper and tied with string. His voice may have been stuttering with the cold but still held pride that his actions had been as good as his word, and his long, lean face, unshaven and peeling from extensive exposure to the cold, was not that of a defeated man.

"My friend couldn't believe his ears when I told him that I knew somebody who wanted evening dress, and in his size." The hawker looked as though he wanted to put his hands, free once more, in his pockets for warmth, but would not be so impolite in front of another person.

The former retail thoroughfare of Tverskaya had suffered the fate of Kuznetsky Most, the majority of its shops closed and empty, a few replaced with businesses purveying loot. Most of those in the street now had come to sell where they had once come to buy.

"This is more than the amount to which we had agreed, sir," the Russian protested gently when Smith gave him an envelope full of rouble notes.

"I thought you may want to treat that friend of yours to something, as he's done me a great favour," Smith responded, though he hoped that the seller would instead purchase a good, warm hat. The silk scarf tied around his bald head barely covered his ears. "Besides, I consider it worth extra just to hear someone in this country say 'sir' again, like a gentleman, rather than 'comrade'."

The other man laughed, the brittle air forcing the sound out like a series of small coughs.

"It does grate after a while, doesn't it, sir?..."

The coat, trousers and waistcoat were a bit large for Smith, though years of travel in peace-time and campaigning in war had provided many hints on how to deal with such problems. The solutions would be temporary but satisfactory.

An hour later, Smith appraised himself in the cracked surface of his hotel

Inductions Dangerous

room's cheval glass. The adjustments to the clothes had been timely made, for Basil Broster was due in minutes. There had been no success in finding a hat for the suit, so Smith would have to go without. Though he would feel rather naked without one, it was one of the least necessary appurtenances of formal wear.

He turned away from the mirror and picked up his long overcoat. The room he had rented had indeed been one of the best available in Moscow a decade before. The rich upholstery and carpeting, the workmanship of the furniture, even the art on the walls, bespoke of a consideration to the guests in which hotels such as the Europa had once taken such pride.

For Smith, the evidence of the current régime's attitude toward foreigners — at best it may have been described as naïve — was not the curtainless windows, or the torn and stained fabric on the sofas and chairs, or the bullet holes in the painting opposite the bed. It was not even the dark patch of the carpet in one corner that reeked of stale urine. It was the fact that there had been no effort to improve the room's condition; not even a simple cleaning.

"Well, yes, I can understand your opinion, Mr Scovell, but you must concede that the Bolsheviks have more pressing matters than tidy hotel rooms."

Basil Broster and Linus Smith sat in the back of the Fiat that served as the British Mission's principal item of transportation. The driver, Olson, was, when he was less mobile, the envoy's chief clerk.

"I disagree, Mr Broster. I feel that a society that routinely allows human waste to remain unexpunged in a room's carpet, and rents that room so stained to guests, has its priorities mis-scheduled." Smith may have been mistaken, since he could see only the back of Olson's head, but he thought the chauffeur found the assertion amusing. Smith used an analogy. "If you offer to take in lodgers to your house, and find that one of the previous boarders has been sick in the hall, would you clean it up, or merely ask the new tenants to step over it?"

"Really, Mr Scovell..." Despite his scolding, the diplomatist could not help smiling. He was, Smith observed with a little envy, the better dressed. Though he bore more weight, and his girth was somewhat wider than Smith's, his evening wear was perfectly tailored. And he had a top hat that somehow managed to reduce the size of his ears.

Sokolniki was rated as a suburb of Moscow, though it was in fact a distance from the city. By its forest, more than four square miles in extent, a number of summer residences had been erected, primarily for the wealthy merchant class; Broster commented that the Misolovs had had a big villa in the district. Some manufactories had been built in the vicinity, but Sokolniki retained its charm, so Broster believed, though most Muscovites reportedly found it a dull place.

"Even the people who lived there?" Smith asked.

"*Especially* the people who lived there, so I gathered," replied the other.

The Art Lover

The sun had long since set before the Englishmen approached their destination. It was tricky going over bad roads most of the way, but Olson seemed equal to the task, conquering the lanes down which they had to progress, riven as they were by small, frozen chasms.

The house to which the Britons were heading was obvious. It blazed with lights, beacons which aided Olson's navigation from some miles away. But so many motor-cars, not one pair alike, had been parked so inexpertly — or inconsiderately — that despite Olson's efforts, Smith and Broster had to trudge through deep snow for the last few hundred yards.

The house itself may have been taken for a shooting box on any backwoods estate in England. In the shape of an L, it looked to be made of stone and clapboard, and but for the window frames' embellishments, the lodge could very well have been set in Northumberland, rather than Sokolniki.

In each of the automobiles sitting idle before the house, a driver was seated, trying to stay warm. Smith could not determine if Misolov was present. The Britons passed on to the house, where they were glared at by several GPU sentries, in mufti but obvious just the same, lounging about smoking cigarettes on the veranda. A final obstacle was the more polite security officer, just within the front door, who examined each guest's invitation.

After this, Smith and Broster were ushered into a big hall, lofty and wide, furnished as a living room. It was filled with so many people that the closeness and heat of the atmosphere was breath-taking, especially after emerging from the cold.

From out of the milling throng, over which hung a pulsating roar of conversation, almost as oppressive as the sharp smoke of hundreds of burning cigarettes, a huge human form descended upon the newcomers. Tall and broad, it was surprising that such a figure was not in the midst of his seasonal hibernation. His dark hair was thick and unkempt, as was the curling moustache that hid the mouth under the big nose. The man's flat face was florid, but at least it smiled.

"Broster! Glad you come!" the man shouted over the verbal din as he seized the diplomatist's shoulders. In spite of the room's high temperature, the Russian, for such he was, wore a leather jacket over his tightly-buttoned blouse, and felt-lined galoshes on his feet. It was little wonder that the man's skin shone with sweat.

"Mr Scovell," Smith's countryman said, "I'd like you to meet Ivan Khuseff; Mr Khuseff, Geoffrey Scovell."

The president of the Council of Labour and Defence started, a slight tremor shooting through his large body. He had not noticed Smith standing beside Broster.

Inductions Dangerous

"Ah, yes, from Treasury, no? To price everything the British Mission has..." Khuseff had obviously been informed of Smith's stated reason for visiting Russia. The Bolshevik extended a massive hand, the back of which was almost covered with coarse black hair. Smith considered that the man would have been a gift to the illustrators of *Punch*, if they had known of him. "Welcome, then. Come!"

The mixture of types at what was termed the Commissariat of Foreign Trade's 'night of food and entertainment' was great; Smith had not seen such a mixture of costume outside fancy dress. A number of the men were attired like Khuseff, in the clothes one worker out of two would have worn every day. Others were garbed in a sort of pre-War evening suit. Between the extremes was every degree of difference. Smith observed several men in smoking jackets, one a velvet affair with quilted satin lapels, as if he had hastened here directly from a relaxing hour before bed. There were a couple of well-dressed gentlemen, but Smith was told that one was a German, and the other a Czech.

The women presented less of a diversity than a polarity, for between one sort and the other there were few grades. The younger half seemed to have come straight from the floor of an industrial plant, pausing only to apply a tremendous amount of make-up. They contrasted with ladies in dated but attractive gowns and a modicum of cosmetics. The only things that they had in common were the smouldering cigarettes in one hand and the glasses of vodka or champagne — or a cocktail thereof — in the other.

During the next hour, as he filtered through the mob, which did irreparable damage to his reach-me-down suit, Smith met and conversed with a great many of the powerful in the new Russia, and their hangers-on. The president of the State Bank was present, coughing over an immense cigar; the director of the Chief Economic Administration was arguing loudly with two women, one his wife and the other, it was rumoured, his mistress; the little chairman of the government export conglomerate, sweaty and smelly, was attempting to win a drinking contest with the more reserved head of the Central Statistical Department.

Two individuals who interested Smith more than did any of the others included one pointed out to him as Nikolai Krasny, deputy chief of the GPU's Counterespionage Section (his identity and position were evidently not state secrets; their public knowledge was, rather, desirable for the Bolsheviks). He resembled a mere boy, tall, pale, impassive, apathetic. The second person was Commissar Dmitri Grek, everyone's host.

"Don't eat too much, comrade; supper will be served later."

Grek was of average height, the top of his bald head shining over the remaining fringe of red hair at the back and sides. His face was ordinary but his

The Art Lover

eyes always moving. He grinned a great deal, and shrugged, as though he were aware of something that would lead to trouble, but not for him. It was clear that the commissar was tipsy.

"But have some of this salt herring," he urged Smith, grabbing an unfortunate waiter as he passed, and causing the servant to spill the contents of his tray. Grek swore at him, then, the fish forgotten, turned back to Smith, throwing an arm over the Briton's shoulder as the waiter made his escape. "I call you 'comrade' because I feel that we are working toward the same goal..." Smith's confusion over how the Russian may have arrived at this astonishing conclusion was distracted by Grek nearly dumping his tumbler of vodka on him. "Are you having fun, comrade?"

"Oh, yes, quite." Grek had spoken Russian, either not realising that he was doing so in the company of a foreigner, or not caring. Smith consequently replied in the same language.

"Good! The entertainment is about to start!"

Smith did not bother to look at his watch. He knew that it was past midnight, and thus still somewhat early for the main activity of any Russian party, but indeed, there was a commotion among the tightly-packed guests, as the staff tried to make space for tables, chairs and, least likely, a kind of stage.

"For this cabaret, I brought people from the state theatres," explained Grek. He directed a couple of over-worked servants to place the table they were carrying before him, and to bring a pair of chairs. Smith had been hoping to sit by a window. Though all of these were shut fast in the native style, osmosis may have provided some relieving cold. "I will describe them as they perform."

To Smith's dismay, Grek was as good as his boast. After more tables and chairs were produced — many guests were nonetheless left standing — the lights were dimmed over most of the hall (by the simple expedient of unscrewing the electric bulbs) and the entertainers brought out. Most of the government institutions from which they had been borrowed had taken them in turn from those favoured by the former imperial family and aristocracy. They were very good, and Smith was glad to see that their new audiences were, for the most, appreciative of their talents, unlike the few diners at the Hotel Europa's restaurant.

Unfortunately, Grek, seated next to Smith, provided a commentary for each act.

"That cellist, he played for the tsar. He became quite well off because of it. Somebody with a patron like that can demand high fees. We deprived him of more than twenty thousand roubles — twenty thousand eight hundred and thirteen — and that was before inflation. That was in 1920, April fifth. I remember because his brother had been conscripted into the Red Army to fight the Poles, and had been reported killed that same day. Bad time for him, huh?" Even as he grinned, Grek's eyes continued to move.

"These comedians now, they're from the Alexandroffsky. They all live together, I'm told: three actors, their wives, children — four boys, four girls — parents-in-law, all in one room, fifteen feet by fifteen feet... And they hate each other! Now that's comedy!

"The conjurer used to work with Chinizelli. When he was brought into state service, he was found hiding in a cellar in Petrograd, under a house in the Boulevard of 25th October — Nevsky Prospect. If you'll look closely, you'll notice he has only a...a... What is it called? Vestige! Vestige of an index finger on his left hand, three sixteenths of an inch long... Yet he's very good, isn't he?

"I believe in making these bourgeoisie work. Yes, even circus clowns. All my menial staff were once rich. A cleaning lady in my townhouse was a countess. She had a place in the Fontanka, an estate next to Tsarskoe Selo, another estate in the country that was fifty and three fifths square versts. My chauffeur had a fortune worth four million four hundred and twenty-one thousand five hundred and eight roubles — on the day we confiscated it! Where is he now? In part of a room with his wife and sick son, while a daughter washes walls in the party headquarters in Orel. My cook used to work in a grand duke's kitchen. He once prepared a banquet for five hundred and twenty-seven people. Now, he cooks for me. Oh, watch this ballerina. She weighs just seventy-nine and four fifths funts!"

Grek's impressive memory for details was no compensation for the constant and grating distractions they entailed. The rest of the audience, between shovelling caviar and hot potatoes into their mouths, forced down by glass-fulls of vodka, applauded and shouted. Grek talked.

"Of course they clap loudly," said the Foreign Trade Commissar derisively. Ash fell from his burning cigarette into the alcohol by his hand. He chuckled. "Most of them are peasants, and couldn't even read before the revolution. Some of them had to be tutored by university professors before they could sign their names...

"Krasny's an exception... Personal secretary to the chairman of the Cheka at eighteen, you know. He's a cold one, though. He even keeps track of how many death warrants he's signed. Twenty-two hundred and sixty during a single year as head of the Frontier Department. We were at war then, I think...

"And Khuseff, forty-nine years old, six foot five inches tall, two hundred and fifty-six funts... A factory foreman in the old days... Good at economics, I'll give him that... The woman? Oh, she's beautiful, yes... his wife, I suppose..."

"Have some more semgi, Scovell..."

The Art Lover

The narration continued for the rest of the night, even into and through the supper. Smith considered it his duty to listen, as he was in truth learning a great deal about the Soviet leadership, even if much of it was trivial. The tuition was trying, however, and after three hours — three hours, twelve minutes and sixteen seconds, Grek would have said — Smith was more than ready to leave. But it was early yet by Russian standards, and after supper, there would be dancing...

Smith awoke the next afternoon to find it gloomy and cloud-bound. The sky had refrained from snowing, but the day was cold again and, as there was no heat in his hotel room — the flue in his fireplace was blocked and none of the staff inclined to clear it — it was almost as cold inside as out. It served a purpose, though, as he had drunk far too much the night, and morning, previous, and he was paying for it now. With the air chilled, the price did not feel as high.

Even in the days of the old régime, water provision had not kept pace with the growth of Moscow's population. Many of the city's residents drew water from the rivers, or, in the winter, from snow and ice, all dubious sources. Little less suspect were the unprotected wells to which the poor of the outlying districts resorted. The pressure in the pipes was not enough to force their contents to the upper storeys of those buildings which had optimistically laid on water, and in the Hotel Europa, Smith had to bribe a page to bring a pail of it for the purposes of washing and shaving.

"Yes sir, the water isn't what I'd call safe, not in the cities in this country. Since most of the people don't have the money to pay yardmen to take away the rubbish from their buildings, those that live by the rivers throw it into the water."

Walter Olson had temporarily shed his guise of chauffeur, reverting to that of clerk, a position in which Broster found him just as capable. He was full of local knowledge, some useful, most entertaining. His means of imparting it was certainly more interesting than that employed by Commissar Grek. More importantly, he waited until he was asked before providing the intelligence.

"Do you know Angelskaya?"

Smith was relaxing in the comfortable sitting room at the rear of the mission's ground floor, where the lower ranks of the British delegation gathered for quick meals or slower snacks between duties. Ordinarily, he would not have dreamed of violating such a preserve, where, like a servants' hall in a country house, staff members could be assured of escaping, if only momentarily, their superiors. But Olson had taken pity on Smith when the latter, entering the building, pulled off his hat and gloves and inquired hopefully after a cup of tea. A kettle was just whistling in the pantry, Olson explained, as he had felt like a cup himself.

"Angelskaya, sir?"

Olson raised his eyebrows and grinned amiably. His was a friendly face, openly proclaiming his willingness to help any who asked for it. He was the sort of man businesses would have wanted for their advertisements, a professional ready to please but without a trace of sycophancy.

"Yes sir, I can tell you where that is. Know some wealthy comrades, do you, sir?" Olson sat back with his tea on a bulging sofa, quite at ease.

"Is that who lives there?"

"Mm." Olson licked his lips after a drink from his cup. Smith had to look twice upon his first meeting with the clerk; the man had a moustache, quite full, but its blond hue made it almost transparent. "I don't know if the people in that street these days are rich in terms of money, sir, but I suppose if everyone and everything is at your beck and call, you might as well be rich, coin or no."

"Very true," agreed Smith.

"You might've noticed, sir, a lot of streets that were full of gentry in the old days are empty now." Olson gestured with his cup, as though he were indicating the courtyard just outside the frosted windows. "A pal of mine with the official agent in Petrograd tells me it's the same there. The main boulevard — Nevsky, I think it's called — is mostly deserted, except for a few squatters. Right after the revolution, a crowd of factory hands moved in, I suppose just because they could. But with fuel so dear, they couldn't heat all those big rooms. You know what they did, sir?" Olson's mouth hung open in anticipation of his own story. "They tried to burn the houses down, or tear them apart! My pal, he heard it straight from some of these rock-headed idiots — pardon my language, sir. But they bragged about the state they left those buildings in." The clerk shook his head in incomprehension. "That's the sort who have a say in Russia now, sir."

"But people have moved back into Angelskaya?" Smith set aside his empty cup. It had been perfectly brewed.

"Yes sir." Olson laughed lightly, but not with real humour. "It's the big Bolshies who *can* afford the high prices of coal and wood, so they don't worry too much about buying them. The new leaders of the country are starting to take over the property of the old."

"Well, as a matter of fact, Olson, what you mentioned earlier may happen: I may indeed meet some wealthy comrades in Angelskaya, though, if so, it will be incidental." Smith smiled. "I want to visit the art auctions that are held there."

"Mm." Again, the clerk interrupted his swallow of tea. "That's right; I'd forgotten them. I hear the prices are sometimes a tenth of what they were before the revolution. It's too bad all the money goes into Bolshie pockets."

The Art Lover

"They have to afford living in Angelskaya somehow," Smith pointed out dryly.

The Fomin brothers had been fixtures in the pre-revolutionary Muscovite art world, and their gallery in Angelskaya had been famous for the works exhibited and sold there, and for the people who visited it. Now, the items displayed in the big rooms were more eclectic, less expertly arranged and even ignorantly advertised, but were nonetheless fine and valuable.

Smith discovered that, contrary to his initial beliefs, it was not just paintings and sculptures that were being offered by the so-called State Art Repository. The revolution had resulted in the abolition of private property. Consequently, a vast number of pictures, tapestries, marble, porcelain and furniture had been seized by the government, which needed real currency more than it did manifest culture.

The main exhibition hall at the gallery was wide and high, with the objects to be auctioned placed haphazardly on a small dais at the far end. The attendant crowd was not big, and Smith, unobtrusive by the near wall behind a screen of columns, suspected that the majority had come either out of curiosity, or from discomfort, seeking to warm themselves in the heated building. Most present were Russian, and therefore too poor to afford even the notional prices demanded. Others who had come were foreign, and could reasonably be expected to participate in the auction.

Indeed, it was this element that was responsible for all the purchases this Tuesday. A few, Germans, Scandinavians, Italians, appeared discerning, while others, blind to the cultural value of what they bought, hoped to have their choices validated when they re-sold the items outside of Russia. A third group comprised agents acting for others, and they knew precisely for what they had come to bid. There was little rivalry over any of the articles, though two men competed shortly for a suite of furniture, which reminded Smith of that which he had seen in Broster's office and home.

The brief day was ending when Smith emerged from the auction a few hours later. He had not seen the item he had come to find, but then, he had not really believed that he would. The air was freezing outside the former Fomin Gallery, which darkened behind him as those in authority turned off the lights and themselves departed. The sudden transition to the cold caused Smith to shiver a little, even under the layers of garments he wore. But he had time to waste outside, according to his watch, and pulled his coat's collar more tightly around his neck.

A week later, the temperature was no higher; the winter would be a long one.

Inductions Dangerous

As Smith loitered near the door of an abandoned house in Angelskaya, he could barely see the snow that swirled heavily through the dark air. He was dressed more like a native than he had been while attending the auction, and was almost invisible to the casual observer.

At last, a figure emerged from one of the buildings opposite, a house, much like the one by which Smith stood, but inhabited, its windows glowing. Even in the unpleasant weather, the form moved jauntily, and whistled. Smith's sharp eyes followed the man — for such the figure was — as he walked the quarter-mile to the whilom art gallery. Behind its papered windows, another auction was in progress, and despite the seedy appearance, the former Fomin headquarters looked warm and inviting. Nonetheless, the man stood on the pavements outside, waiting. Smith crossed the broad street.

"Good afternoon, Commissar," he greeted in Russian. Despite Grek's watchfulness, he had failed to see Smith approach.

"Oh...yes...good afternoon..." Grek squinted against the drifting snow, his eyes pausing in their frenetic movements. He could not identify the speaker.

"Or is it evening? By the time, it would be day, by the darkness, night..."

"Yes, yes, I suppose it would. It's thirty-two and a half minutes after four, so... Do I know you, comrade?" Recovering from his surprise, Grek became annoyed. He was not a member of the Soviet republic's government so that he could be bothered by any citizen on the pavements.

"You weren't at the auction today," Smith said, "nor were you at last week's." He stood beside Grek, facing the empty street. "I was told that you visited the gallery every Tuesday, but that isn't true, is it?"

"Who are you? What business—? How dare you!" Grek turned to confront the stranger, his eyes darting about, as if searching for the man's hidden accomplices.

"You've been visiting the home of Ivan Khuseff, just down Angelskaya, haven't you?" The Englishman cut off the Bolshevik's protests, without looking at him. "But he wasn't home; his wife, however, was."

The simple statement caused a minor but audible inhalation on Grek's part. He then began to question the point of Smith's remarks, but the damage was done: the Russian's eyes had stopped, abruptly, as though frozen in the cold air, and then continued moving. Any words he uttered after this were meaningless.

"You claimed to have been visiting the auctions when in truth you've been having a weekly assignation with Maria Khuseffa, while her husband was regularly occupied with the British envoy." Smith nodded over his shoulder. "It was convenient that the Fomin Gallery was situated in the same street as the Khuseff home."

Angelskaya was empty but for the two men talking on the pavements, half-lit

The Art Lover

by dim street lamps, half-obscured by the darkness and the swirling snow. But soon, the auction would end and the buyers and spectators would be disbursed from its exhibition hall. Grek was quiet, in welcome contrast to his loquaciousness at the banquet he had given. But his eyes sought a means of escape, settling once or twice on Smith beside him.

The Briton had hunted animals on three continents. He could read their intentions in most cases; it was one of the reasons he had survived so long. Grek was no leopard or buffalo, merely an opportunist, a mild bully, who used, or abused, the trappings of his office. So it was only a second or two after the Russian considered physical force against his accuser that he abandoned the idea. Smith nodded, and placed a gloved hand on Grek's shoulder. The Bolshevik jumped.

"A wise decision, Commissar," said Smith.

"What do you want?" The question was hoarse, low. Behind the two men, a rush of voices gathered behind the doors of the former Fomin building. The auction was over.

"Tell me about your chauffeur."

"What about him?" Grek asked blandly.

Smith's grip on the other man's shoulder tightened a little.

"Very well," hissed Grek, almost cringing. "He spoke to me, two weeks ago last Friday, at twelve minutes past one. He told me a foreigner wished for him to spy on me."

The doors to the gallery opened and through them the people who had attended this week's sale debouched. They resembled the crowd who had been present seven days before. Smith took Grek's arm and led him a few yards away.

"He was in a difficult situation, no doubt," Smith commented, sympathetically. "Someone had obviously decided that Misolov was in the perfect position to give false information to these foreigners. Who was it?"

"Krasny." Grek nervously regarded the art buyers, but they, scattering in every direction, were more concerned with getting home, or otherwise out of the flurried snow and painful cold. "He has used disinformation before."

Disinformation, Smith repeated mentally; it sounded a typically Bolshevik word.

"As far as the GPU is concerned, the...disinformation...will be given to the foreigners," insisted Smith, "but you will add to it genuine intelligence, from your commissariat, from the Council of Labour and Defence... We'll let you know exactly what—"

"I can't," protested Grek, though with more passion than conviction. "My deputy is a GPU officer. His room is a mere forty-five feet from mine, down the corridor to the left. Krasny trusts nobody."

"He won't discover a thing. Misolov will be the conduit for the disinformation reaching the foreigners and, as he is your driver, you will have no difficulty in finding opportunities to give him the real intelligence to pass on."

"I won't."

Smith found Grek's defiance tiresome.

"Would you prefer Khuseff to learn that you've been visiting his beautiful wife every week?"

"He wouldn't believe you," the Russian remarked. He and Smith were alone again in Angelskaya. Far up the street, a motor-car, heralded by its shining headlamps, advanced fitfully upon the pair.

"Not immediately, perhaps, but he'd investigate. What man wouldn't?" Smith gestured. "Here is your ride, Commissar." The automobile, crunching over the frozen snow of weeks before, and through the more recent, softer, precipitation, drew up beside them. Smith added, "And have your chauffeur moved to a decent home, a room or two for just himself and his family, something heated. He deserves it. After all, he's working for important people."

The walk back to the Hotel Europa was not a long one, for which Smith was grateful: the going was rough and tricky, and the snow was stinging, driven by a wind that was increasing in strength.

Smith was by himself on most of the streets down which he trudged, though the odd pedestrian was glimpsed from time to time. He reflected that, after all, he was grateful to Grek's loquacity and, even more so, to his obsession with detail. The fate that the commissar had described for Misolov's daughter was so different than that given by her father during the Englishman's visit that both versions could not have been correct. Grek had had no reason to falsify the girl's status. Even if he had, he possessed still less excuse to put it in such detail. Her parent had at least one purpose for lying: such a falsehood about the girl would have led Smith to wonder why he had been told such a tale, and perhaps to conclude that Misolov was not acting under his own will. The chauffeur's clues as to Grek's illicit behaviour had been merely fortuitous, and, in the end, quite fortunate.

So far as the GPU would know, Misolov could still be trusted to lead astray those foreigners who wanted him as their agent. Smith hoped that those foreigners could now trust Misolov to lead astray the GPU.

At last, the weak lights of the Europa could be seen through the increasing descent of snow. Smith sighed. He hoped the storm would not delay his departure the next day from the comforts of Moscow's best hotel.

The Sundering Seas

"Sit down, my boys, sit down."

With a typically fatherly phrase, C invited his two subordinates to take chairs at the big, oblong table that filled half of his room on the first floor of Number 1, Melbury Road, in Kensington. The chief of Britain's Secret Service was already comfortably seated in his usual spot, under the life-size portrait of his late son, and was leaning forward, his arms on the glass-like table top, his hands folded. His red, weather-lined face beamed as his officers took their places.

Major Linus Smith, Royal Fusiliers, had re-joined the Service just two and a half months before, at the end of September. He had received no extraordinary training for the Secret Service when he had become one of its handful of members before the War, and was not really surprised at the brevity of the fortnight's training he was given upon returning. It had been a busy, concentrated course, dealing principally with codes, ciphers, communications, procedures and finances. More detailed preparations for his new role as field operator was, Smith knew, unnecessary: he had been recruited precisely because his knowledge and experience fitted him for the part.

"The two of you've already met, what?" C's full, white eyebrows rose like signals on a ship's yards as he glanced from Smith to his colleague.

Indeed, the soldier had been introduced to Commander Thomas Brand a few days before. Though Brand and C were both officers of the Senior Service, their personalities differed like contrasting types of vessels. Whereas C was broad of beam and powerful, open and blustery, built to engage the enemy at close quarters — an old sailing ship-of-the-line — Brand was plain and reticent, prepared to identify a foe and fire from distances — an iron-clad steamship — his logical mind its turbines, his constantly smoking pipe its funnel.

"We received an interesting message last night from Evan Loder, our head of station in Paris." C screwed a monocle into his right eye and regarded his audience. Smith's nonchalance rendered him, as usual, almost invisible, while Brand's contemplative puffing indicated engines stoked and ready. "He reported that the embassy's naval attaché has been offered intelligence concerning France's maritime defences."

Inductions Dangerous

"Was the type of intelligence specified, sir?" Brand wanted to know. "What is the source of the offer?"

" 'No' to the first question and 'unknown' to the second," replied C.

"Such information about the French forces could prove useful," observed Smith. Though it was but four years since Britain and France co-operated to defeat Germany in the Great War, peace had brought a divergence of interests, and history had demonstrated repeatedly that yesterday's friend might become tomorrow's foe. Even if the two countries extended their war-time entente, it would have been useful to know the secretive French's capabilities. Nonetheless, Smith added, "But would it be worth the furore if England were discovered spying on its one-time ally?"

"Which is why you'll need to be very careful, my boy." C smiled and turned to Brand. "And you'll have to evaluate this kind offer. I want the pair of you to catch the next boat train to Dover. Smith you'll require false colours, so see Herriott, in Docs." C dropped his eye-glass into an open palm. "Use your imagination."

It was well enough for C to urge some flamboyance in Smith's alias. After he had first been appointed head of the Secret Service, C had periodically enjoyed adventures as he personally gathered information on the Continent. In the carefree days prior to the Great War, a Briton could travel anywhere in Europe but Russia and Turkey without a passport or any other documentation. If C had chosen to spy on the shipyards at Kiel disguised as an eccentric entomologist armed with a butterfly net and notepad, the German authorities would have been at a loss to prove him otherwise.

In 1922, the game of fake identities had become a bit more of a science. The chief of the Secret Service's Documents Department was, fortunately, the right man for the position. Michael Herriott soon outfitted Smith with papers to persuade anybody that he was Captain Charles Sutter, late of the Middlesex Regiment. Thus, he entered France.

"It's just as well I'm not a field operator, Sutter," said Brand, after examining Smith's new passport. "I like things more straight-forward."

The two gentlemen were alone in their railway compartment as the train rumbled suddenly into the compact urban environs of Paris. Smith had not found the six and a half hours to the French capital dull. He could, if the occasion demanded, provide enough vapid small-talk to challenge even the most feared club bore (a good talent for a spy to possess) but preferred to listen while others spoke (an even better talent for a spy to possess). He came to know something of Brand during the journey.

An exact contemporary of Smith's, Brand appeared older than forty, with steel-grey hair swept back from a high forehead, an angular visage like metal plates riveted together, rather unsympathetic in repose, and a tight-lipped mouth, usually pegged shut by a pipe.

As the head of Section III, the unit of the Secret Service responsible for receiving, collating and distributing intelligence relating to naval affairs, Brand's duties were basically bureaucratic. Whether behind his desk at Melbury Road or on the deck of a cruiser, Brand liked matters to be clear and uncomplicated. He was, however, a professional, no matter what the assignment: apprised of Smith's new, albeit temporary, identity, the commander referred to his companion as Sutter, whether they were alone or otherwise.

"Are you familiar with the Paris head of station?" Smith stubbed out the cigarette he had been smoking as he peered out the window at the flashing buildings. He had yet to meet any of the station officers who represented the post-War Secret Service abroad.

"Loder?" Brand's eyebrows winched upward. "I've met him. His father was an Austrian, dead before the War broke out; his mother is Welsh. He speaks German like a native and performed, so I inferred, valuable work for C in Vienna while the fighting was on."

It had not taken the train long to clatter into the heart of Paris, still largely confined within the circular line of fortifications erected in the middle of the previous century. The two Englishmen gathered their bags from the racks over their seats as the carriages neared the Gare du Nord.

"It's surprising that Loder wasn't posted to Austria or Germany instead of France," stated Smith. "He'd be useful there."

"I gather he is just as much at home here," Brand replied.

Smith understood that comment when he met the head of station. Evan Loder did not look Austrian, or Welsh, for that matter. He could have passed as a countryman of any of the affluent French gentlemen Smith had observed on the boulevards as he and Brand rode in a taxi to the embassy on the Rue du Faubourg Saint-Honoré. Loder was a slender man with oiled hair parted down the middle. He wore a moustache so thin that it appeared little more than a shadow of the Gallic nose above it. His suit was excellently cut but of obvious French tailoring. When he spoke English, however, his heritage may have been no more than Eton and Oxford.

He greeted his visitors with firm handshakes, a few words of welcome to Smith and an enquiry as to the health of Brand's family.

"I figured that C would be quick to respond to the offer we've had."

Loder squeezed himself into the seat behind his desk and gestured to the pair of shallow armchairs, like jaws of a vice, in front of him. The office was in an attic, tucked under the roof. Smith's impression was that Loder had been given an undesirable garret at the top of the embassy building because the ambassador or, more likely, the head of chancery, wanted him nowhere else. Secret Service and diplomatic staffs around the world were still unaccustomed to each other. Despite the altitude of the room, Smith could hear street sounds through the open window, motor-cars driving and pedestrians shopping in the cold December air.

"The anonymous letter arrived only yesterday morning and you're here by tea-time today. Speaking of which..."

Loder's secretary, a pretty thing still in her first quarter century, entered with a tray. Smith noted the shingled hair and make-up, and sighed inwardly. The girl smiled at the visitors and left the tray, covered with refreshments, on the tiny round table near the one window. Loder urged his guests to help themselves; to struggle out from behind his desk for the purpose was obviously not worth the effort. He did, however, lean forward to offer his guests the contents of his deep wooden cigarette box.

"The letter is rather like an invitation," he said. From a drawer of his desk, Loder had removed the letter Smith and Brand had come about. He handed it to the army officer. "Time and place, and vague idea of the occasion."

The stationery was plain and common. The words typed upon it were in French, and had been placed there by an unremarkable machine. Posted within Paris, the envelope had been addressed to 'Captain Kelly, British Embassy'.

"The fact that the letter's author knows that Hubert Kelly is the naval attaché means only that he has access to a recent *Whitaker's Almanac*," Loder pointed out. "And he might or might not realise that a service attaché doesn't engage in clandestine intelligence gathering, since he could have been relying upon Kelly forwarding it to those who do."

Smith gave the letter and its envelope to Brand, saying, "As you observed, Loder, the only definite references are to a time and place for meeting." He drank some tea.

"Yes, Wednesday...tomorrow." Brand read the missive through a cloud of tobacco smoke, then tapped the paper with his pipe's stem. "At a café called L'Ourson, in the Rue Jacob. Where is that?"

"Just below the Place Saint-Germaine," answered the station head.

"He wants someone to sit near the stairs to the loo, with a coffee-stained copy of *Le Figaro* on his table." Brand's wide brow creased like the churned water of a ship's wake, but the expression on his disapproving face was dry. "Melodramatic, don't you think?"

"Out of a Le Queux novel," agreed Loder, trying to lean back in his chair and encountering the dull green wall behind him. A line of chipped paint demonstrated that previous attempts to recline had been no more successful. "But in spite of the trappings, I think it might be wise to follow the plot and see what happens in the next chapter."

The next day, Paris was being streaked by a cold, leaden rain that left the cityscape resembling a painted canvas that had been smeared by a dissatisfied artist. Smith rather liked it.

The Héron was a family-run hotel in a formerly elegant eighteenth century townhouse, hidden in a side street between the Rue de Rivoli and the Pont-Neuf. Since Smith was visiting Paris under a name he had not used before, he had chosen to stay at an inn he had not used before. The recommendation of a club acquaintance had been a good one.

The hotel was rather typical of the Marais, the district that largely accounted for the city's Fourth Arrondisement. Once the urban home of an aristocrat, the Héron had, physically, seen better days, many of them, and was now serving a purpose not entirely different than that which its builders had intended. Run by a solidly middle class proprietress, who managed the front desk herself, the hotel boasted small, comfortable rooms, a cage-like lift, an antique porter whom Smith was afraid for health reasons to let carry his bags, and a little breakfast chamber that had never seen a meal more substantial than a croissant.

Smith's appointment at L'Ourson was for one o'clock. He arrived at the restaurant, therefore, at eleven, and ordered luncheon. L'Ourson was a quiet place, ordinary; an adequate situation, to Smith's mind. The district of Saint-Germaine was similar. Now that Montparnasse, to the south, had displaced Montmartre as Paris's artistic quarter, and was filling with writers and painters — and would-be writers and would-be painters — and their assorted myrmidons, Saint-Germaine was beginning to collect its overflow. But few had found the Rue Jacob, or L'Ourson, yet.

The café's interior was simple, its walls beige, formerly white; framed pictures and sketches had been hung at one time and then forgotten, at least by the char ladies.

Smith had brought a book to while away the hours and to provide a diversion if his palate found disfavour with the menu. L'Ourson, as it turned out, served fare from the east of France, and the usual midday meal was veal with a salad of goat's cheese. This was accompanied by an unpleasant onion-coloured wine. To kill that fluid's awful taste, Smith swallowed several cups of equally awful coffee.

L'Ourson began filling with Frenchmen before noon. They appeared to be, for the most part, bourgeois shop assistants and office clerks. Then, as one o'clock approached, Smith saw through the front plate glass windows — he had made certain that such a view was possible from his table — a tall man approach the café through the rain from across the street. Carrying no umbrella but wearing a felt hat and a belted Burberry, he rather resembled a police detective of the continental variety. Upon entering the building, he removed his hat, revealing yellow hair.

Ignored by the patrons already present — the restaurant was crowded now and one more customer was hardly noteworthy — the blonde man made his way around most of the tables to the one in the corner by the tightly-wound circular staircase.

That table's occupant had been concentrating on the copy of *Le Figaro* he had been given, despite its brown discoloration and crumpled texture, and did not hear anyone approach. He was startled, and nearly dropped his wine glass when the stranger spoke.

"I'm sorry, sir. I think you have me confused with somebody else," the diner said.

"With me, most likely," Smith stated, in excellent French. He had come up to the two men noiselessly and now turned to the blonde newcomer. "I believe your appointment is with me." The Englishman withdrew from his coat pocket the envelope Captain Kelly had received Monday, and showed it to the blonde.

The latter said, "Very sensible of you to take precautions, sir. I assume you met this gentleman," he indicated the bewildered patron with the damp newspaper, "no earlier than when you paid him to sit here and pretend to be you. Good. Now, let us adjourn to your table and talk."

Smith did not hurry back to the embassy after his meeting. This had nothing to do with reluctance, or with a desire to explore Saint-Germaine, which he considered a very unremarkable part of the French capital. It was, rather, a matter of professional curiosity and caution.

Not until tea-time did Smith return to the embassy and climb the several flights of stairs to Loder's attic office. The station head's secretary ushered him in with a bright smile (as well she might; the anteroom in which she worked was bigger than her boss's tiny burrow).

"There you are, Sutter," Loder said, peering past Brand, who was seated before him. The naval officer turned in his chair, or as much as space allowed. "We were wondering if you'd met with an accident instead of our mysterious correspondent."

"Did the fellow show?" Brand wanted to know.

"Oh, yes." Smith handed back to Loder the envelope he had borrowed. "And I think you might find this interesting, Brand."

Smith pulled a bulky brown package from within his damp overcoat. The

The Sundering Seas

commander clamped his teeth down on his pipe and took the offering with both hands.

"Our mystery man gave it to me," explained Smith, divesting himself of his hat and coat.

"Do you know what's in this?" queried Brand, untying the string that bound the paper wrapping of the package.

"No. I was told simply that it was a 'promise of bigger things'." Smith forced himself into a chair between the little table and the room's humble fireplace. Loder signalled that he should help himself to the tea set before him.

"Why don't you use Kelly's office downstairs?" Loder had chuckled as he had watched Brand, his hands full of documents taken from the parcel, cast about for an unused bit of horizontal surface on which to spread his find. "He's gone to Cherbourg today, and won't mind."

Brand nodded seriously, and left the room, billowing smoke.

"Aside from what I've just given the commander, we're being offered quite a bit," Smith said, as Loder turned to him and lit a cigarette. "This man informed me that he can supply the latest intelligence on every French naval installation, from Dunkirk to Saigon, every base, dockyard and harbour. And he'll continue to do it for as long as we pay him, thus keeping us current with events."

"Ah, yes, pay..." Loder, Smith noted, even held his cigarette like a Frenchman.

"He made no pretence concerning his motive." Smith attempted to find more space for his legs under the table. "He wants £1,000 for everything that he can provide right now, and five hundred every year as a kind of retaining fee, for which he will give the latest information as it becomes available to him."

Loder knocked some ash into an open desk drawer. Smith hoped that there was a satisfactory receptacle under the debris, and not sensitive documents or secret papers.

"Those are rather large amounts," the head of station commented, his thin eyebrows knitting together, "but not unreasonable considering... Did he tell you anything about himself?"

"Not wittingly," replied Smith, swallowing some hot tea. "He's about thirty-five, six feet tall, with yellow hair and blue eyes. He speaks French distinctly, a Picard accent, perhaps, and carries himself as would an officer. He doesn't live far from L'Ourson, in the Rue de l'Université—"

"You followed him?" Loder interrupted a pull on his cigarette to raise the surprised question. "Is that what took you so long?"

"It gave me the opportunity to ensure that I myself was not being followed. I wasn't. Oh, and he carried his right arm stiffly, never using it."

At this revelation, Loder dropped his unfinished cigarette into the open drawer and, asking Smith to wait, struggled out from behind the furniture and left the room. The major was helping himself to another cup of tea when his host reappeared, bearing a slim folder of the sort that the Secret Service Registry used to hold files on foreigners of interest.

"This is from Kelly's records," Loder said. Instead of trying to resume his place behind his desk, he simply stood beside the little table and Smith's chair. "Thanks to Brand and his pipe, the naval attaché's office resembles London in the midst of a November pea-souper." The head of station coughed and smiled.

"Jules Monory." Smith read the name from the cover of the folder and nodded. "That was the name on the directory in the lobby of the building he entered in the Rue de l'Université."

"You knew his name?" Loder paused as he lit another cigarette.

"I wanted to see if you could confirm his identity without such a clue."

"Your description was good enough for that."

Smith opened the file and read from the first page. Monory was a capitaine de corvette, the French Navy's equivalent of a lieutenant commander, and worked, according to the latest information, in what Smith and his compatriots would have termed the Admiralty's Plans Division.

The folder's contents were actually few. They included newspaper clippings from an official gazette and from periodicals' society pages; a photograph of a seated couple from the first decade of the century labelled simply 'parents'; another picture displaying a light-haired blur standing next to a dark-haired blur; a biography written in point-form by several hands; and a note, with the words 'Denny, Vine Street, 1913' jotted upon it. There were also several signed letters, dated 1920, from Monory to Captain Kelly's predecessor. Loder explained that Monory worked on the staff of the Ministry of Marine at that time, as well, but had much to do with ceremonial functions. Indeed, the letters were invitations to official events.

"Well, this sounds like our would-be benefactor," Smith said, perusing Monory's biography. "Born in 1888 — making him 34 — six foot with blond hair and blue eyes."

"And his arm..."

"Yes." Further on in the précis of his life, Monory is described as having been badly injured in an accident. "An explosion on board the cruiser *Senegal* in Marseilles harbour in 1917. He was decorated for saving the lives of sailors, but his right arm was damaged."

"Permanently, to judge by your description," Loder stated, exhaling smoke. Glancing at the file, he added, "Hmm, it was after a stay in hospital that he was posted back to the ministry, and, a year later, to Plans."

"But before the War..." Smith tapped the page at the appropriate entry. "

'Assistant Naval Attaché, London, 1910-3'. His eyes moved to the notation regarding 'Denny'. "There's a police station in Vine Street."

The office door opened suddenly, hitting the back of Smith's chair with violence, and forcing Loder to jump to avoid being struck. Brand peered around the edge of the door.

"Sorry." The commander's apology was strained through the clenched teeth that held his pipe. He climbed around his colleagues and set down on the seat of an unoccupied chair the documents that he had been examining.

"Your chap's gift *is* interesting, Sutter. There isn't much that wouldn't be obvious to a student of naval intelligence; the information isn't intrinsically valuable. But it is definitely of a sensitive, perhaps secret, nature."

"He stole an apple from the orchard not to eat it," Loder reasoned, "but to prove that he could steal it."

"Mm." Brand nodded as he chewed his pipe stem.

"Monory doesn't expect an answer to his proposition immediately," Smith said. "If we do agree to it, we are to place an advertisement, relating to a Mr François from Bordeaux, in the personal column of *Le Petit Parisien*."

"Monory?" Brand removed the pipe from his mouth to repeat the name. Loder enlightened him regarding the Frenchman. "Naval attaché? I've an acquaintance who may, possibly, have met this fellow. My friend's ship and mine were in the same squadron in '15, but prior to that, he worked at the Admiralty. I recall him talking about one of his duties there being as periodic bear-leader to a lot of foreigners. The last time I spoke to him, he was marooned on half-pay."

Smith nodded.

"If you'll write me an introduction, I will speak to him — and Mr Denny — when I return to England."

Smith's reappearance across the Channel was not long delayed. By Thursday night, he was in London.

He had been lodging at the Metropolitan Club pending the acquisition of a more permanent home. He had found something at last in a block of flats in Cayleb's Yard, a quiet backwater in Mayfair, and its furnishing and decoration was currently under the supervision of Odways, Smith's valet and general factotum — the reason the servant had not accompanied his employer to France. Though the rooms were full of wooden crates, packing paper, straw and miscellaneous disorder, Smith's bed was ready for him.

The next morning, after an unhurried breakfast, Smith walked to New Scotland Yard. He had telephoned Vine Street police station the night before and had been informed that an officer named Denny had indeed worked there —

had been the head of the division's CID, in fact — but had since been posted. At Scotland Yard, Smith found that Bertram Denny was now one of the several detective chief inspectors assigned to the Criminal Investigation Department's Central Office. As such, Denny had his own room. It was small but still larger than Loder's.

"Good morning, Captain..." the police officer glanced surreptitiously at the card he had been given "...Sutter. Please, sit down."

Denny was a diminutive man who, even when standing, would not have been able to peer over Smith's shoulder. He was almost completely bald and had the face for a moustache, and though none was present, his habit of stroking his upper lip suggested that its absence was new.

"I'm sorry you had difficulty finding me," Denny said, resuming his task of feeding a caged canary, interrupted by Smith's arrival. "I was at C Division until 1918, when I was promoted."

Indeed, there seemed to be about four years' accumulation of paper-work in Denny's cluttered room. But for the bird, in its wicker cage on a stand, the room resembled every police detective's office that Smith had seen, regardless of nationality. The proliferation of what the army called 'bumf' seemed a common constabulary characteristic.

"When I received your note earlier this morning," Denny said, watching his little yellow pet peck at its food, "I contacted the War Office. I was asked to help you if I could." The inspector stood by the open window, his thumbs in his belt. "You want to know about the Monory case..."

"Yes, anything that you might feel would be informative." As Denny returned to his desk, Smith glanced at the bird cage. Its door had been left open.

"I had this brought up from Criminal Records." The detective sat and produced from a desk drawer a cardboard folder, as slim as the one from Captain Kelly's files in Paris. "Don't worry, Captain, nothing in it is — what did you army blokes call it during the War? Classified?" He laughed, his eyes disappearing into the folds of his face.

The canary, perhaps curious as to what lie beyond the confines of his home, hopped over to the cage's open door. Smith tried to direct his host's attention to the bird, but Denny was browsing through the folder's sparse contents.

"Lieutenant Dee Vay-see-aw..." The detective rubbed his upper lip and shook his head cheerfully. "French is not a language I ever learned, Captain. The way I behaved in school, it's surprising I can speak English."

Smith suspected that the inspector's attempted pronunciation was meant to convey 'lieutenant de vaisseau', the French naval rank immediately below Monory's current grade. Meanwhile, Denny's pet, after cautiously surveying the landscape, fluttered from her threshold over to the sill of the window. The chilly

The Sundering Seas

air of early December ruffled her tiny feathers.

"Inspector..."

"Anyway, Lieutenant Monory was the assistant naval attaché at the French embassy in 1913," Denny said, recalling events. "He was caught writing several bad cheques. The amounts were not stupendous: £5 here, £2 there. Nonetheless, he did not have the funds to cover them, and wrote more, even after his bank warned him of his empty account."

"Inspector..." Smith tried again. With a courageous leap, the little canary flew out the window and was, a moment later, past the Embankment and over the Thames. Smith sighed and turned back to Denny. "And this was when you became involved?"

"Respectable merchants complained and most were in the West End. I thought a discreet approach might work."

"Did it?"

"Oh yes," Denny again traced the imaginary lines of a moustache. "Monory's superior, a Captain Colbert, I think, was very polite, but I could tell that he was none too pleased with the lieutenant. He promised that the bad cheques would be honoured if no charges were laid." The police officer chuckled. "Anything an English court could have handed Monory would have paled next to what Colbert looked ready to dole out, so I talked to my bosses and the matter was dropped."

"And the aftermath?" To Smith's surprise, Denny's bird reappeared on the window's sill, looking cold but pleased.

"Oh, the cheques *were* honoured — with interest, I might add — and when I enquired a week later, Monory had already been sent back to France."

The canary flew energetically to the inspector's shoulder. Denny walked back to the animal's cage, while Smith glanced through the items in Monory's file, open on the desktop. Included was a brief report on the affair, with Denny's name at the bottom. Several retail establishments' written complaints were in the folder, as was a letter, in French, apologising for the trouble. The signature on that page was identical to those on Monory's letters that Smith had seen in Loder's office.

"Hardly the case of the century," said Denny, grinning. His pet, back on its perch, was singing merrily. The detective scanned the sheets — notes, memoranda, official circulars — pinned to the wall behind his desk and chose what appeared to be the oldest (or at least, the most faded). This he pulled with a jerk from its ancient place and inserted onto the floor of the canary's cage. "If it hadn't involved a foreigner from an embassy, one of my men would have handled it."

"Did you ever meet Monory?" Smith wanted to know, passing the closed folder across the inspector's desktop. When Denny nodded, the soldier asked him to describe the Frenchman.

"In his early twenties, I'd wager..." The policeman stroked his face in thought. "Good-looking chap, blond hair, blue eyes, tall and straight-forward..." He smiled widely and shut the door to the little bamboo bird cage. "...Or so it seemed..."

Captain Reginald Powers, RN, lived in semi-retirement on the coast of Essex. His name was on the Special Duties List, that catalogue kept by the services (both the armed and the secret) of men (and a few women) whose extraordinary abilities or talents may some day prove useful to their country.

Powers's life of leisure was not a voluntary one. Like many officers of the army, navy and air force, he had been placed on half-pay, the result of post-War reductions in manpower and budgets, which left no place for him. For a surprisingly large number, this meant a kind of poverty, half-pay rarely being enough for anybody but the most frugal bachelor to live upon. Fortunately, Powers had independent means; the opportunities he was missing were professional, not financial.

An hour and a half by train took Smith from London to Colchester, and ten minutes more brought him to the village of Penby. Enquiry at Powers's house sent the army officer along a path through tall grass, lined by skeletal trees. The smell of the sea was ubiquitous and shortly Smith emerged from the brown wilderness, almost stepping into the salt water itself.

"Careful..."

Smith saw a man rise from the cabin of a boat, moored alongside a rickety wooden quay. The vessel's mast, lofty and straight, would have been a beacon to follow but it was disguised by the bare trees along the shore as one of their own, and the boat's hull had been obscured by the reedy grass that surrounded this natural little harbour.

"It's rather soggy ground here," the man said. "Not really ground at all, sometimes. May I help you?"

"Are you Powers?"

"That's right."

The captain was not the stereotyped image of an ocean-going naval officer. He was too youthful, with a face almost plump in its babyishness, eyes too wide for squinting into a stiff sea-wind, hair too thick. Nevertheless, Smith discerned that Powers belonged on the water, and that his rubber-booted feet were at ease on a rolling deck.

"I should help you but not ask why." The captain handed Smith back the letter of introduction Brand had written for him. "The likes of you and I have lived our lives by those orders, Major. Come aboard."

Smith stepped over the gunwale of the *Iolanthe*, a seven-ton, thirty-foot cutter, wishing that he had dressed more warmly. Powers wore a big woollen jumper, but the visitor's suit, hat and overcoat were too thin. The morning, which Smith had spent in London with Chief Inspector Denny, had been cool and clear, the sky a pale blue. During his passage to Essex, the temperature had tumbled and the wind freshened, bringing dark, laden clouds with it. Here on the coast, it was winter.

"I've just returned from a sail. Do you know this part of the country?" Powers indicated Stone Water, several square miles of tidal creeks, marshes, islands and mud flats, the topography of which was highly changeable, confusing the transient sailor but delighting the local.

"My knowledge is more earthbound," replied Smith.

Powers's mouth grew perfectly horizontal, which Smith guessed was his version of a smile. The captain led the way below. Smith was, as usual, surprised at the roominess of watercraft. It was true that landsmen often found boats to be cramped, the smaller ones matchboxes in size, the larger ones Chinese puzzles. But Smith was of the opposite mind, the vessels' low situations and squat cabins preparing him for less space than the average badger burrow, but expanding under the deck. The *Iolanthe*'s high-ceilinged cabin provided four berths, a table, plenty of cupboards and a little stove, on which a pot was trembling with heat.

"You knew Monory, then?" asked Smith, sitting on one of the berths.

"It was my duty at the time to be acquainted with the foreign naval attachés, in a way. I've been lucky enough to spend most of my career at sea, travelling to different, far-away places. The only shore duty I've had was just before the War, in the Admiralty's Intelligence Division."

Powers poured some hot chocolate and passed a mug of it to his appreciative guest.

"You were in the section that liaised with foreign representatives." Smith's surmise was not a guess. The War Office had a similar branch.

"That was only one aspect of the work, mind you, but one I enjoyed." Powers drank some of the thick brown chocolate from his own cup. "If I couldn't go to distant lands, their people came to me."

"What was Monory like?"

"Gregarious, lively, slightly disdainful of the mundane..." Powers nodded. "In other words, a Frenchman. An excellent swordsman, too. He and I met periodically for fencing matches. Nothing serious, since I was below his level of skill, but they were healthy, and instructive."

"Do you recall his having difficulty with money?"

"Not that I know of," Powers answered. Outside the cabin, the wind gusted, shaking the boat a bit. "He always spent generously, rather than extravagantly. I assumed that he had a private income, since he surely couldn't have lived the way he did on his naval pay. He was sent home, I understand, after I left to join the *Westmorland*. Something to do with bad cheques...?"

So it would appear, Smith said to himself, that Jules Monory had a history of living beyond his means; the incident with the cheques was, however, nine years previously.

"I won't enquire as to why an army major is interested in the past of a French naval officer," stated Powers, knowingly. "I wouldn't mind encountering Monory again, sword-to-sword. Does he still fence, I wonder."

Smith asked which of Monory's hands used to hold his weapon.

"His right," answered Powers.

"Then his fencing days are probably over." Smith emptied his mug of chocolate.

Smith enjoyed Paris in the rain, the autumn rain, to be exact. He had visited the city before, but never during a wet December. That he liked the French capital under grey skies, its streets slick and reflecting the lights along the pavements, shops and theatres, was not surprising: it was one of the ways in which he liked many cities. He was uncertain if this was because, or in spite, of the dry regions in which he had spent much of his early life.

The Englishman had whiled away most of Monday evening in an Alsatian brasserie in the Rue de l'Université. It was a dismal little place that served unimaginative pork dishes at high prices. Its primary, indeed only, appeal to Smith was its view of the attractive First Empire-style building Jules Monory called home. Enquiring as if to rent one of the block's flats allowed Smith to infer that the Frenchman was again (or still) living beyond his means.

Not long after Smith had finished his meal (sauerkraut and sausages; but the beer was good), he spied his quarry emerge from his building's deeply recessed doorway, across the street. Even with a hat obscuring his yellow hair and a beige Burberry to ward off the rain, Smith recognised the man. He followed him discreetly down the pavements to a taxi stand. There, Monory stepped into one of the waiting motor-cars, and Smith signalled for his own.

"Yes sir?" The cabby, a middle-aged man who spoke French with a decidedly Russian accent, he did not turn to view his customer.

"Don't lose sight of your colleague ahead."

Smith indicated Monory's taxi, now pulling out into the light traffic of the Rue de l'Université. The driver knew what to do. A former captain in the tsar's Chevalier Guards, he was one of the dozens of useful, low-level agents employed by the Paris Station. His vehicle had been parked in an alley, awaiting Smith's instructions.

Monory's journey took him to the Seine's Right Bank, via the Pont Alexandre-III, and further, to the Grands Boulevards. This thoroughfare, known officially by several names throughout its length, had been where fashionable Paris had come to see and be seen, though its famous cafés were now less popular than they had once been. Monory's taxi halted not far from the Opéra Garnier.

"A girl, sir," said the Russian, watching through the rain-brushed windscreen as Monory brought a laughing young woman out of a narrow apartment building. The two piled into the rear seat of their taxi and they were off again a moment later.

It was outside a subterranean night club that Monory paid his cabby and dismissed him. The naval officer, in dinner jacket, topper and silk scarf, then gave his left arm to the befeathered girl, and they rushed inside, out of the rain.

"Would you like me to wait, sir?" the Russian asked, not uncooperatively.

"For a quarter of an hour," replied Smith.

The Champs-Elysée, leading to the Arc de Triomphe, was lined at this point with dignified mansions. But the twentieth century was beginning to deal roughly with these aristocratic buildings. Night clubs, along the lines of those in London and New York, were opening here; a few were garish, with electric lights and gaudy signs. From where he stood on the broad pavements, the Briton could see as well the blinking, beckoning beacons of a cinema, a harbinger of things to come. He sighed.

He was out of place in the Chat Nouveau, as he would have been at Ciro's or The 44, in London, or any other night club. Despite this, he managed to blend in quite naturally; he did everywhere. After descending a flight of stairs and passing the inspection of a nominal doorman, a provocatively clad waitress showed him through the smoky gloom to a small table, where he was automatically furnished with a glass of bad champagne.

The Chat Nouveau was trying hard to appear modern. Its tables, dance floor and stage (for singers and a band, occupied currently by only the latter) were all of a blue, metallic look, as if constructed of aluminium scraps left over from the War. Lights blazed and winked for little reason other than to cause headaches, and even the musicians sounded as if they were a tinny gramophone recording.

The dress of the women added colour to the scene, and the men were, Smith was satisfied to see, attired well: principally in dinner jackets, though a few, like the Englishman, preferred the tails of an evening coat.

Monory and his girlfriend were seated at a table across the room. For two hours or so, they behaved like any other couple present, conversing, drinking, dancing (Monory did quite well, with one arm stiff and immobile).

Smith had been following Monory for three days. C wished to know more about this prospective agent before paying for any information. Smith was certain that this constant presence had not been detected by the Frenchman, and the latter's behaviour had been normal for a young, handsome gentleman about town, though he had spent some of Sunday in church.

Smith was just wondering how long he would have to remain at the Chat Nouveau when the fighting broke out.

"Who hit you?"

Evan Loder had been asleep when Smith called at his home, situated in a cobbled street near the Passy Cemetery. Pulling a robe over his pyjamas, the head of station had opened the double doors of his flat to see Smith in damp, rumpled evening dress, his face starting to swell under his left eye.

"I didn't have time to learn his name, but I think he was one of the staff."

Smith accepted a thin towel filled with ice and applied it to his cheek. He was sitting on a rather severe chesterfield in Loder's drawing room, which resembled a public exhibit of the latest French décor. More comfortable was the glass of sherry his host provided.

"The cause seemed to be a woman," said Smith, after a sip.

"It often is." Loder grinned and relaxed, as much as he could, in an austere, straight-backed chair. He smoothed out his hair, indisciplined by sleep.

"A blow was struck, knocking a man into a table, whose occupants took umbrage with this interruption, and a moment later, the room resembled a Johannesburg gold-miners' pub in the '90s. But I didn't lose sight of Monory until the police arrived."

"The police?" Loder leaned forward.

"Monory stayed aloof from the fracas, as I attempted to do," Smith stated. "Though, considering his right arm, he couldn't have done much else."

"What about the police?" Loder could not rid himself of the unpleasant image of being recalled to London to explain why his operation had resulted in the arrest of a Secret Service officer.

"They arrived very quickly." Smith nodded, as he drank some more wine. It was excellent. "They gathered in everyone and took them away in motor-vans."

"Everyone?" Loder stood and walked to the impressive array of decanters on the sideboard by the curtained window. He poured whisky into two glasses.

"Everyone," replied Smith, "but me."

The head of station paused, but decided that the drink would do him good anyway, and gulped from his glass.

"I was able to escape through the kitchen in the rear. Then it was over a wall

The Sundering Seas

and down the Rue L'Attique, where I caught a taxi back to the night club."

"*Back* to the night club?" Loder recharged his glass, and brought the other to his unexpected guest.

"I wanted to see what was being done. The police had halted traffic on that part of the Champs-Elysée, and were arresting everybody who had been in the Chat Nouveau, even the waiters."

"That seems a bit excessive," Loder decided.

"It does, rather," Smith responded blandly. He emptied his glass and, standing, handed the ice-filled towel back to his host. "I think we can tell Monory that we're ready to buy his wares, and arrange a meeting with him."

Loder's high brow wrinkled.

"Are you certain?"

"I am," answered Smith.

Paris from the river looked like a painting, especially in the evening. As the sun set early behind dark December clouds, the lines that defined the individual buildings, trees and statues began to blur. Even the great structures, Notre Dame Cathedral, the Louvre, the Eiffel Tower, lost their distinctions as the gloom fell and the city's lights rose. They melded with the less grand, the modest houses, and became simply Paris at night.

Smith stood in the darkness created by a corner of the French Institute. He pulled his battered hat low and tugged at his ragged coat (badly-cut, ill-fitting and, he suspected, originally ready-to-wear) around him. This was for warmth against the chilly night, and not just for disguise. Police had already moved him on from two locations, confirming that he did indeed resemble a beggar, and that the authorities in the vicinity of the Pont des Arts were particularly vigilant this evening.

As Jules Monory walked along the Quai Malaquais, to stop by the steps leading from the end of the bridge to the embankment below, Smith was not the only one who noted the naval officer's awkward attempt to make his stroll seem nonchalant. When Monory leaned on the balustrade lining the quai's edge, a package in his left hand, he was watched by a dozen pairs of eyes.

Policemen, observed Smith.

"You've no idea, Smith, how anxious I've been during the last week."

Evan Loder exhaled cigarette smoke as he and Smith paused at a book stall on the Quai d'Orsay, near the French Foreign Ministry. The head of station did indeed look tired, a little drawn, as if recently sleep had been coming to him infrequently. But his speech and movements were those of a man suddenly at ease.

"Jules Monory — the real one — returned from his holidays in Provence yesterday. Do we know who the 'Monory' was who met you?"

Smith ran his fingers along the spines of volumes the bouquiniste was offering for sale, laid out in shallow boxes just inside the shelter of the stall. A gust of cold air off the river fluttered the black-and-white and tinted prints pegged to the inside walls.

"He was the bait." Smith flipped through the pages of one of the books he had picked up. "I don't think he was working for the French. If the SR had been behind this, they needn't have used a false Monory; the real one would have done his duty willingly enough."

"That's a good point," agreed Loder. "The Germans, perhaps?"

"They would certainly benefit from a rift — a greater rift — in Anglo-French relations." The major selected a faded guide-book to Paris, published in the decade following the Commune, and handed several coins to the merchant who stood patiently behind his wares. He was a middle-aged man, whose empty left sleeve and good turn-out, even in frayed and worn clothes, spoke of honourable military service. "But a French police officer was probably involved."

Loder nodded and tossed away the stub of his cigarette.

"Yes, the fake Monory and his masters couldn't very well have gone to the authorities with news of a British spy ready to be caught accepting secret papers, without raising questions they themselves didn't want to answer."

As the two English continued their walk down the pavements, a crocodile of little schoolgirls clattered past in their wooden-soled boots. Their footwear, chatter and giggles temporarily drowned all other noises.

"Yet they required someone to set the police trap for you on the Pont des Arts last week. It's good that you smelled something rotten by then." Loder peered sidelong at his colleague. "Which brings me to the question..."

"What put me on the line of the false Monory?..." Smith, having slipped his new book into an overcoat pocket, was diverted by a couple standing near-by and arguing. Their words were flung at each other almost too fast for anyone to comprehend, but the meaning of their gestures was clear. "It was his — or rather, the real Monory's — signatures."

"Where did you see them?" Loder reflexively glanced up at the Eiffel Tower, looming over them and the surrounding buildings.

"On the letters you showed me in Captain Kelly's files; they had been written in 1920. And again on a note in the police file Chief Inspector Denny let me examine; it was dated 1913. The signatures were identical."

"Of course they would—" Loder jabbed the air with a finger and smiled, a bright, toothy expression. "The accident that hurt Monory's right hand occurred in '17. If the signatures before and after that were identical, then his arm hadn't been permanently damaged after all."

"Correct," Smith said. "So why did the Monory I met have a nearly useless right hand? The Germans, or whoever was responsible for this hoax, thought as we had: that the genuine Monory was incapacitated in that manner."

"Why would they use a fake Monory if he was so identifiable?"

The French couple whom Smith had watched arguing vehemently a minute previously were now kissing — and in public, the Englishman noted. They laughed and, with their arms around each other's waist, entered a small bistro.

"The Germans no doubt couldn't procure a doppelgänger for the relevant French officer, so they chose to impersonate one with a characteristic that we would readily accept. Tall, blond, living in the Rue de l'Université — the real occupant on his holidays — he wouldn't require further confirmation. We accepted the impostor as Monory largely because of his disability."

"Clever." Loder indicated the bistro the couple had just entered. He sat at one of the empty tables arranged on the pavements. Disregarding the cold temperature, Loder reclined in the wood and metal chair. "And the arrests at the Chat Nouveau? Did they have a connection with all this?"

"I think so." Smith enjoyed strolling through chilly or wet or even snowy weather; sitting outside for a meal was, however, something for warmer days. He sighed and pulled out a chair at Loder's table. "I have no proof of this, but I believe that the fake Monory's masters were prepared for him to be followed. They may not have been able to identify his watcher, so a fight was staged — or started — and the police, under orders of the suborned officer, were ready to collect everyone present. That officer could then sift through those detained at his leisure, and confirm who was following his associate."

A waiter, seemingly reluctant to leave the comfort of the crowded bistro, hastened out in his shirtsleeves, wiping his big hands on his apron. Loder requested some black coffee.

"And the plans we were initially given?" the head of station asked, after the waiter had departed.

"Jules Monory may be a loyal citizen of France but someone with similar privileges is not. Whoever prepared this trap has a real spy in the navy of the French Republic."

"Though we're not formally organised for such, I'm responsible for counter-espionage, among other things."

Ernst Bauer was a fifty year old former colonel in the German Army. The manner in which he sat behind his desk on the third floor of the Reichswehr Ministry building was the same in which his large head rested on his narrow shoulders — uncomfortably. His face was stern and pale. Captain Joss von Grim, newly posted from the 13th Brigade, would not have minded a more welcoming expression.

"You'll be working under me," Bauer said, continuing to shift the papers on his desk from one of the many piles there to another, "but be prepared to lend a hand wherever you can. We're a small unit: four serving officers, including you, seven ex-officers, like myself, and a few clerks. We old-timers are lucky to be salaried." Bauer located several pieces of paper which, to judge from his grunts, he had believed lost.

"The Intelligence Division of the Army Troops' Office, to which we're attached, would like us to concentrate on domestic politics. *We'd* like to deal in foreign espionage, but lack money, personnel and equipment. And what resources we have are often squandered by other departments."

"Sir?"

"Here." Bauer handed Grim the pages he had just found. "This is a report on an action conducted by the navy's secret service. It was intended to cause trouble between England and France. They called it Operation 'Sundering Sea'. Get it? Nothing came of it except possibly to expose one of *our* agents, a commissaire in the Paris Police. We've been blackmailing him, but his involvement with us may have been inferred by now."

The retired colonel pointed to a bare desk by a window overlooking the Tirpitz-Ufer.

"Skim through the report. As an old sergeant-major I knew used to say, the best way to learn is from mistakes — *others'* mistakes." Bauer stood, held out his hand to Grim and smiled, in a way. "Welcome to the Abwehr."

Thirteenth Night

"It was up less than a fortnight. Why does the room look so bare without the Christmas tree?"

At his friend's question, Linus Smith cast about the drawing room. Indeed, it did seem to him rather empty; this despite the furniture that filled much of the space, the rugs that covered the floors and the pictures that leaned in from where they hung on the papered walls. And though a fire blazed in the grate, the chamber had lost some of the cosiness Smith had found when he had first arrived at Blaney Lodge the previous week. Still, he thought, from the depths of a snug armchair, a glass of good port at his elbow, the room nonetheless had much to recommend it.

"One must take the tree down on the Twelfth Day of Christmas," he reminded his host; "bad luck otherwise." But Smith did concede that, as a consequence, the action made the thirteenth night almost forlorn.

"We should leave the tree up all year!"

Thus, into the quiet reflection that had settled over the drawing room, burst energy that could have come only from a child. Nikki Hopkins, clad in her nightgown and robe, bounded across the room and launched herself on to one of the big, cushioned arms of Smith's chair. The girl did not have the consideration even to be out of breath, he mused.

"What in the world are you doing awake?" he demanded, with an outrage that was neither real nor convincing. "It's after ten."

Nikki giggled, her smile dimpling her cheeks, and it was up to her mother to answer the question.

"She wanted to say 'good night' to her Uncle Linus," Trudy Hopkins explained, in her Norwegian-tinged tones, as she quietly followed her daughter. She shook her head, as though she were admonishing herself for finding the girl's behaviour so adorable.

"And not to me?" asked Rupert Hopkins, seated on a sofa across the hearth from Smith. He did his best to adopt an expression of hurt feelings.

"I see you *much* more often than I do Uncle Linus, Daddy," Nikki informed him, matter-of-factly.

"So now I'm old hat. Thank you very much." Hopkins peered imploringly at his wife, who stooped and kissed him, as if to compensate him for any insult. It seemed to work.

"You're not really my uncle," Nikki told Smith, her blue eyes regarding him almost critically. She was leaning on his chair's arm now, using it as a fulcrum, and nearly lost her balance twice. She was thirteen, and all arms and legs, entering into that stage of adolescence when the body rejected any sense of proportion and grace in exchange for speedy growth. In a few years' time, Smith realised, he would not even recognise his goddaughter.

"That's hardly a shocking discovery," he said. "You've been aware of that for quite a while."

"Yes, but if you're not really related to me, we can get married when I grow up."

Smith nodded, as if seriously considering the proposal, and responded, "I see. I'll tell you what, Nikki: if you feel the same way in ten years, I'll talk to the vicar about it."

Nikki frowned and glanced at her parents, whose amusement disappeared from their faces too swiftly for the girl to observe it. But her father's brow beetled, and he implied that Smith's offer was a good one.

"Ten years is an awfully long time," Nikki stated, slowly.

Smith pointed out to her, with a private sigh, that the older she became, the more rapidly the years passed. Nikki found this truth exceedingly funny, and giggled again.

"And speaking of time, young miss, you should be in bed by now." Trudy's tone was warm, but left no room for negotiations.

"All right, Mummy." Nikki pushed away some of her brown hair, now cut into a short bob, in imitation of more mature styles. She looked at Smith once more. "You're going to be here a few days longer?" she asked, as she had in the morning, and in the afternoon. When Smith replied in the affirmative, the child decided that she had to be satisfied with that situation, then threw her arms around her godfather's neck and squeezed.

"She's off to Switzerland in a couple of weeks," said Rupert Hopkins, after he had watched his wife and daughter leave the room. He stood and strolled to the wide, many-paned window. The landscape beyond the glass was invisible in the darkness. "I hope she won't be too lonely."

"And you hope that *you* won't be too lonely," Smith responded. He too rose, and joined his friend. "After missing so much of her childhood, you've grown accustomed to her being just sixty minutes' away by rail at her prep school."

Hopkins grinned, and said, "You always know what I'm thinking, Nemo."

Rupert Hopkins was one of the two friends whom Smith had managed to make in his life. Hopkins was a handsome man, tall and strong, with the sort of good looks typical of those that were beginning to grace the large silver screens of motion picture houses. A month younger than Smith, Hopkins had always caused female hearts to flutter. With sandy-blond hair, eyes the same hue as his daughter's, and a face that may have been shaped by a Renaissance sculptor, he could very well have played the ladies' man into old age. But that had not interested him, and he had married young the only woman who would ever capture his attention. Smith envied his friend's fifteen years of matrimony.

"Don't forget that Will won't be ready for school for a few more years," he added.

"Master Willoughby will be four in the spring, as he never ceases to explain. He's worn out as many nurses, and seems only to be gaining steam."

Trudy Hopkins re-entered the drawing room, having tucked her daughter in bed. As Smith turned from his reflection in the glass, he considered again that Trudy was one of the very few women who could wear to advantage the usually unflattering post-War fashions. Smith concluded that this had little to do with her figure (as shapely as it was), as attractive forms were usually obscured in the modern tubular dresses, anyway. Rather, it was her poise and natural charm that appealed.

She did not resemble her daughter much at all. True, the blue of their eyes was identical, but no one could have guessed that they were related. Perhaps, Smith mused, it was the purely adult appearance of the woman. There was nothing girlish or childish about Trudy, and though not strictly beautiful, she was undeniably attractive.

"And while we're on the topic..." Trudy accepted a glass of sherry from her husband and thanked him with a glance that was both quick and deep "...when might we expect some minors from you, Major?" She turned a steady gaze upon Smith.

"Oh, well..." Smith was slightly nonplussed at the inquiry, and deflected it. "I think it might be best to be married first. It'll obviate all those awkward questions."

"Linus..." Trudy's laugh caught her by surprise as she was about to sip from her glass. "Rupert, who do we know who is unattached?"

Hopkins' eyes met his friend's for an instant, and he answered, "Well, my darling, your mother has been widowed these seven years now..."

Smith relaxed again in his chair. He was glad that he had accepted Hopkins's invitation. Blaney Lodge was almost a home to him. It was of course more than that to the Hopkins family, though less than an ancestral hall, having been acquired a scant century before. A military clan, the Hopkinses had lived in army cantonments and stations around the globe since the Restoration. Though this house in the Lincolnshire countryside usually passed in ownership among the senior branch, it was a haven for any stray Hopkins. By extension, it welcomed the family's friends, as well.

Smith had not been able to arrive for Christmas Day, but had come for the second half of the season, and had enjoyed the fun of Twelfth Night, twenty-four hours before. He loved the Yuletide and its traditions, though it often found him, a soldier like Hopkins, in odd corners of the planet, sometimes in the company of strangers. He had spent just one Christmas in England since before the War and, with his new employment by the Secret Service, he wondered if that pattern would change.

The ringing of the telephone in the hall was shrill and jarring. Trudy glanced at her husband and, as people frequently did when receiving an unexpected call, wondered aloud who it might be.

"We should speculate upon the question more before Hap answers it," remarked Smith smugly.

"Shush," ordered Trudy, with a poisonous look that was belied by her laugh. "Who calls at a quarter past ten at night?"

Blaney Lodge was solidly constructed, the brick core and wood of the walls soaking up sound as cotton absorbed water. Trudy, whose curiosity was as great as that assigned by stereotype to womanhood, frowned in frustration. She could hear her spouse's voice only as a dull murmur through the door left ajar. Even Smith's acute ears picked up only some of the words spoken; enough, however, not to be surprised by Hopkins's offer when the latter came back to the drawing room.

"I say, Nemo, care to go for a drive in my new Hillman?"

Trudy greeted the sentence with incredulity, and hoped that her husband was joking.

"That was Fowler, the village constable," Hopkins explained. "He's having a bit of trouble at The Firs."

"Captain Doyle's house?" This surprised Trudy more than had the telephone call. "What sort of trouble?"

"Doyle is dead, I'm afraid," replied Hopkins, resignation in his voice, as if the decedent had been in his care and had finally succumbed to an anticipated illness. Trudy felt genuine disappointment and regret.

"Oh, no. He was such a dear man. What happened?"

"Fowler didn't say," her husband said. "But he's by himself in a snowbound night, and his superiors can't get to Kingsby to help. Even his sergeant is stranded in Pagthorpe until the roads are cleared. So he was instructed to get in touch with a responsible local individual and ask for assistance."

"Having failed in that, he called you," Smith surmised, draining his glass and standing.

Thirteenth Night

The night was not very cold. The temperature was just below freezing and so, though perhaps uncomfortable to hazard without adequately warm clothing, the chill in the air was not dangerous to life and limb. But the incapacity of Constable Fowler's colleagues to render him help was explicable as soon as Smith and Hopkins left Blaney Lodge.

The flat countryside was covered by deep, wet snow. It had been falling, gently but steadily, for days and, where undisturbed, was over a man's knees. It was heavy when it clung to boots and trouser legs, and scattered only with difficulty when brushed from coat sleeves and hat crowns. The night was dark, except half a mile to the east, where some lights from Kingsby pierced the gloom, but in the illumination provided by the Hillman's headlamps, big weighty flakes could be seen adding to the amount already landed.

The route to The Firs ran along a sunken lane, the steep sides of which had sheltered its surface from much of the snowfall. Consequently, the light motor-car that Hopkins drove would, his passenger figured, reach their destination. But the going was slow and troublesome, and just a couple more hours of precipitation would probably preclude any return trips in the same vehicle.

"I assume that Captain Doyle did not die in bed, of natural causes, or was not found at the bottom of a flight of stairs, the victim of an obviously innocent accident."

"Why do you say that, Nemo?" asked Hopkins, his words slightly bumped by the vibration of the car in the rutted lane.

"The average village constable doesn't require help in registering someone's demise from simple misadventure," Smith pointed out. He tried to peer through the windscreen, as it rapidly became obscured with snow. "Despite the rural policeman's popular reputation for stolidity over ingenuity, most are fully capable of handling such circumstances by themselves."

"Being in the Secret Service has made you suspicious." Hopkins wore what could have been described as a smirk.

"How do you know I'm in the Secret Service?" Smith narrowed his eyes at his friend.

"Until August, I worked in the War Office's Intelligence Directorate, remember." Hopkins raised his chin and sniffed ostentatiously.

"You were in charge of MI4, the topographical section; you handed out maps, you ass."

"Besides," Hopkins chuckled, "you told me about your new appointment."

"Well, yes, there is that," Smith conceded.

"Won't you get in trouble for doing that, contravening the first half of *Secret Service*?"

"They are very sensible about it," answered Smith, after the vehicle slewed about and recovered. "One may tell the people the Service considers trustworthy."

"I say, Nemo, that's quite a compliment." Hopkins beamed.

"I said that the *Service* thinks you're trustworthy. Is that Doyle's place?"

On clear nights, lights burning at The Firs were plainly seen from Blaney Lodge, half a mile away, even through the former's screen of eponymous trees. Now, the captain's house was almost invisible until one was upon it.

The Firs was a tall, Victorian villa, with several gables under its steep roof, and a tower rising an extra storey over the entrance, and ending in an even steeper roof. The current reaction against all things Victorian, especially in art and fashion, was not shared by Smith. Many would have disparaged The Firs's appearance as busy, even overwrought, but Smith viewed it as particularly attractive with the thick cap of snow making it seem small, and cosy. It reminded him of the candy-constructed witch's house in the tale of Hansel and Gretel, and it came complete with icing on top.

"The lights are on," Hopkins observed needlessly, as he piloted his motor-car to a stop by the front door, between two heavily burdened evergreen trees. A moment later, after the two men had stepped from the automobile, he added, just as necessarily, "But no one is answering the bell." He pulled again on the chain that hung by the door. Snow stuck even to this, and clumps of it came away with his action.

"We were almost an hour getting here after Fowler's telephone call," Smith said. "Perhaps he had to leave for some reason." He glanced behind him, but the only footprints to be seen were his own and Hopkins's, the only tire tracks, those of the Hillman; all of these signs were already vanishing under relentless precipitation.

The door was unlocked, and the newcomers entered the house. Electric light bulbs glowed in the hall, and in several of the rooms beyond. The colour scheme of The Firs's interior was neutral, and the house smelled of polish.

"Oh, Colonel Hopkins... I'm glad you've come."

Constable Fowler emerged from a door to one side. He was a youngish man, stocky, his weight filling out his uniform. His face did not move with much expression ('stolid', thought Smith) but he seemed capable. Hopkins introduced Smith, who greeted the policeman with a friendly nod.

"When the door opened, I thought you might be Doctor Stoller," said Fowler. "I called him even before I called you, Colonel."

Just in the short time Smith and Hopkins had spent outside, between the car and the house, snow had gathered thickly on their outer garments. These they brushed off and hung on pegs that jutted from the wall. Seeing near by a small table with a telephone, Hopkins was reminded to call Trudy, to let her know that he and Smith had arrived in safety. In the meantime, his friend was led into the small room from which Fowler had just emerged.

At first glance, it seemed little different from any other billiard room. Dominated by a ponderous table, the remaining space was occupied by chairs, and racks for cues. A dying fire glowed fitfully in the grate, to one side of which another door was slightly ajar. It opened into a small w.c. The only items that lifted the chamber from the ordinary were the policeman's helmet on the mantelpiece and the corpse behind the table's massive, buttress-like legs.

"This is Captain Doyle?" Smith asked as he knelt beside the body. It lay crumpled, like a stocking stripped off and dropped. Fowler's affirmative response was confirmed a moment later by Hopkins.

The dead man had been about sixty years of age, bald, but with the usual fringe of hair about the back and sides, grey in this case. Clean-shaven, his face was neither handsome nor ugly, and was double-chinned. He was dressed, like Hopkins, in the standard evening wear of white, starch-fronted shirt and waistcoat, black dinner jacket and slacks, all of which curved around Doyle's girth. Smith fingered the lapel of his own tailed dinner *coat*; sometimes he imagined that he was the only one who still favoured the older fashion.

Doyle had been struck forcefully on the head by a heavy, pointed object that had created a horrible wound. Blood had flowed from the injury onto the imitation Persian carpet on which the body lie. Next to the corpse was a loving cup, a trophy of championship at golf of a local variety, with a weighty, cubic base, one corner of which was smeared red.

"You can see, sirs, why I thought I should call someone," Fowler said, in a voice that was deep, thick and rheumy, like the Fens from which it had come. "I first telephoned my sergeant at Pagthorpe, of course, and then the division headquarters at Louth. Both times, I was told it would be tomorrow before anyone arrived to help. The superintendent at Louth ordered me to call someone nearer."

"Why not a justice of the peace?" Smith queried, standing again.

"This is the j.p., Major." Fowler's gaze indicated Doyle. The men paused, almost out of respect for the man at their feet, then, as one, moved away from the still form, over to the fireplace. Once there, the constable added, "I never touched anything, except to make sure he wasn't alive."

"Dead about three and a half hours, I'd say," Smith deduced, "possibly four."

"Around eight o'clock, then," estimated Hopkins, after glancing at his watch. "Who found him like this, Fowler?"

"Mrs Wills, sir — sirs," the policeman replied. He appeared quite comfortable now, with superior officers on the scene. "She's a sort of 'cook-general', the only permanent help the captain has — had — and the only one here today, aside from the captain. After I arrived, I sent her to Mrs Brimmel's."

"When did she discover Doyle dead?"

"About nine o'clock. The police house just had a telephone put in a few months ago. It hasn't rung much, since few others in Kingsby have telephones." The logic of this reasoning was unassailable, but the constable admitted that the instrument had come into its own this evening. "Mrs Wills told me the captain had been murdered but, between you and me, sirs," Fowler lowered his voice still further, as if there were others about who might wish to eavesdrop, "I thought she was exaggerating."

"You believed that you would find Doyle at the bottom of a staircase, the victim of an obviously innocent accident, did you?" Smith leaned against the chimneypiece.

"Exactly, sir," Fowler said, matter-of-factly. "But when I got here, well... It looked to me like no accident."

"How long did it take you to get here?" Hopkins asked.

"Just over an hour, Colonel."

"From Kingsby?" Hopkins was surprised. "Major Smith and I travelled half that distance by automobile in only a little less time."

"But I came by horse, sir," replied the policeman, the slight hint of a smile forming at the corners of his hitherto flat mouth, "and an animal like that can do better in weather like this than a motor-car. I borrowed Mr Underhill's horse."

"The butcher's?"

"Yes sir. That's why I'll need to get him back for Mr Underhill's deliveries tomorrow. He's out behind the house, in a sheltered spot."

Smith assumed that Fowler was referring not to Underhill, but to his steed.

"An imaginative approach, Constable," Hopkins commented. "Well done."

The sound of a door opening near the rear of the hall was followed by that of heavy footfalls. Fowler looked perplexed, and the three men stepped from the billiard room.

"Mrs Wills, what are you doing back?" the policeman asked politely. A large, middle-aged woman returned his gaze, shifted it to Smith and Hopkins, then settled it back on Fowler.

"May wants me to spend the night at Lane End Cottage," Mrs Wills replied, exasperation tinged with warmth. "She thinks whoever killed poor Captain Doyle will come back and finish with me. But she's a dear. And it'll probably be better for you men if I'm out of the way. I came back to get some things..." The woman's heavily-lidded eyes moved again to consider the others.

"Mrs Wills, this is Colonel Hopkins, who you might know, and Major, er, Major...Smith. They're helping with inquiries," Fowler explained. "You don't mind talking with them, do you, Mrs Wills?"

"Of course not," replied the woman, almost scoffing at what she thought was the constable's implication that she might have been too unnerved by events to be interviewed.

"Thank you, madam," said Smith. "Constable, will you take Mrs Wills into the drawing room?"

The servant of the house preceded Fowler, who was stopped before he had left the hall.

"You mentioned a Doctor Stoller, Constable," Smith stated. "Is he the local police surgeon?"

"That's right, sir," answered Fowler; "he's worked with B Division for twenty years or more. He and Captain Doyle are friends. Terrible to have to perform his duty in these conditions." His face turned to the front door, at the far end of the hall. "I thought he'd be here by now. He owns a motor. You don't think anything happened to him, do you, sirs?"

"From what I know of Geoffrey Stoller, he can handle his Ford better than most. And if my Hillman can get here, so can Stoller's vehicle." Hopkins was confident of the surgeon's imminent appearance, and Fowler accepted the verdict. As the constable continued into the drawing room, the two army officers returned to the entrance to the billiard room. From where they stood, the unfortunate victim of the night's crime could not be seen behind the huge table.

"Fowler seems as capable as you predicted he would be, Nemo," Hopkins told his friend in a low voice.

"I wasn't worried about it." Smith's face bore a puzzled expression. "What in the world is a 'cook-general'?"

Hopkins chuckled, his grin wide, in spite of the situation.

"That's right, you've been out of the country for some time, until just recently. The explanation will appeal to the social historian in you. It's because of the economy being the way it is now: small households can't afford the staff they could before the War. Some have to make do with a single servant. Her principal duties are usually in the kitchen, but extend elsewhere, so people started using the term 'cook-general'."

Smith agreed silently that the facts did interest that scholarly part of him, but a condition caused by a worsening financial environment, left him sad, more than anything else.

"I say, Nemo, should we...?" Hopkins gestured into the billiard room. "Should we cover up the poor fellow?"

"I'd like to, Hap, but I think the police surgeon should examine the body the way it was found, even if the CID won't arrive until tomorrow."

"Yes, of course..."

"Were you acquainted with Doyle at all?" Smith asked his friend.

"We'd met a few times socially," replied Hopkins, inclining his head, "at a bridge party, a couple of dinners. But Trudy and I are up to Blaney only for Saturday-to-Mondays, and not every one, so I didn't get to know Doyle closely. He seemed a little dull, I think I can say, though he could appreciate a joke. No family that I'm aware of."

"What about enemies?"

"No obvious ones," Hopkins continued, his smooth brow now rippled in thought, "though he was, as you've heard, a justice of the peace, and he was a former chief constable of the county police."

"Well, that provides a fertile field for motive," Smith considered. "Doyle may have made his share of opponents, and most of them from a class of men not averse to breaking the law."

"True," concurred Hopkins, nodding, "but it may have been something as simple as robbery."

Smith admitted that this was certainly a possibility. However, he had examined the hall and the billiard room with a critical eye. Neither seemed to be missing anything, and what they contained was not worth stealing, in his opinion, or worth the risk of stealing. Even the rug upon which the captain had expired, though well-made of wool and with a floral pattern resembling that found in similar products of western Persia, was probably purchased in England for a few pounds. The average burglar would not have been so discerning; nor, however, would the average burglar have committed murder.

"Let's not keep Mrs Wills waiting, Nemo," Hopkins said at length. "She may not be afraid to stay at The Firs, but it's inconsiderate not to let her leave."

The drawing room in which the late Stephen Doyle's cook-general sat waiting was as unremarkable as the billiard room. The usual compliment of sofas, chairs and tables occupied much of the space, while uninspired paintings added some colour to the beige walls. Again, Smith was given the impression that The Firs contained nothing valuable. Here too electricity provided the illumination; the grate was cold and empty.

"We're sorry to keep you waiting, Mrs Wills—" Smith's apology was terminated by a loud click from the woman's tongue and the flap of a flabby hand.

"Don't think on it, Major," she said in a loud voice. "Whatever you can do to find whoever killed poor Captain Doyle... You do it and never mind me."

Mrs Olivia Wills was a large woman, her body an oval from whichever vantage point one cared to view it. Her head was small and squarish, as if taken from atop a completely different torso, and supported a mass of mouse-coloured hair bundled neatly in a small globe; no modern bob for this woman.

"It's a horrible thing, sirs, horrible," she said, her small eyes expanding with speech, as if her words surprised her. "Who would want to hurt Captain Doyle? Such a decent man. That's him, atop the mantel."

Smith glanced at Hopkins before turning his eyes in the direction Mrs Wills had indicated. Hopkins too had expected, for just an instant, to see the woman's late employer laid out along the smooth wooden chimneypiece. But Mrs Wills had been referring to photographs.

"That's him in his uniform. Very handsome, don't you think?" Smith observed a slightly portly gunner officer, a young version of Doyle, with the ribbons of half a dozen minor campaigns on his chest. "And with his friends, probably from his army days." Another picture showed two dozen gentlemen in the mess dress of the Royal Artillery, in some dining hall. "And with Doctor Stoller. That's them at last year's village fête." A man as spindly as Doyle was stocky stood with the dead man in front of a large striped tent. "And that's him with his old dog, Tiger. He passed away just last year — the dog, I mean." Tiger appeared to be of no particular breed, and definitely of no resemblance to a jungle cat, striped or otherwise, despite his name.

"Oh, yes, a decent man," Mrs Wills stated, finally, and without expectation of contradiction.

"Can you tell us about tonight, madam?" Smith asked after a moment. He was about to sit on the sofa opposite Mrs Wills, but moved to another cushion farther down, just in time.

"Yes. Oh, you saw that, did you, Major?" Mrs Wills nodded her cubic head toward the spot of Smith's first choice. "Someone has been in here with snow on his clothes — and boots. Disgraceful." Hopkins glanced at his shoes, out of reflex, but Mrs Wills added, in a motherly tone. "Oh, not you, Colonel, or you, Major. Gentlemen know better. It was probably whoever killed Captain Doyle."

"Why do you say that, madam?" Smith wanted to know.

"The captain would *have* to be dead not to do something about a visitor who did that." Mrs Wills's eyes were large, and her head nodded sagaciously.

An interesting observation, Smith thought. Aloud, he asked:

"Did the captain today receive any visitors of whom you know, madam?"

"None while I was here, Major, but I think he was expecting one." Again the woman's small head bobbed, portentously this time. "I have no idea who it might have been, but yesterday Captain Doyle told me to take this evening off. My usual day is Saturday."

To Smith, as to Mrs Wills, the inference drawn from the re-arranged schedule was clear: Doyle had planned something that required privacy. An expected guest was a possibility.

"The captain wouldn't normally send you out of the house when he had visitors, would he?" Smith said, with some incredulity plain in his tone.

"Indeed not, Major." The woman leaned forward for emphasis, the effort causing her oblong body to balance precariously on the edge of her seat. "All other times I was kept here when the captain entertained. He sometimes had me stay up quite late, though when that happened, I was usually given the next morning off. He was very considerate, was Captain Doyle."

"He does seem a most fair employer," Hopkins observed, sitting on a mediocre replica of a Sheraton chair. Constable Fowler remained standing, a pencil scribbling in his open notebook. "You decided to spend your free evening with a friend?"

"That's right: May Brimmel, at Lane End Cottage." Mrs Wills pointed at the room's far wall, decorated with a couple of painted landscapes. "I went over before seven of the clock."

"You didn't walk, did you?" Hopkins said, with some apprehension.

"Why, Colonel, it's just through the hedge. You can see Lane End Cottage from the kitchen." Mrs Wills's face adopted a mildly reproving look, tinged with genuine delight that she was the object of the gentleman's concern.

"No one likes the idea of a lady going out in such weather, madam," explained Smith, with a smile.

" 'Lady'?" repeated Mrs Wills. Her small eyes grew soft, as if a secret admirer had left a bouquet of flowers on her cutting board. "Bless you, sirs, I've been out in snow twice as deep and air thrice as cold. You needn't worry about me." A slight rosiness in her cheeks was a while dissipating.

"How long did you stay at Lane End Cottage, Mrs Wills?"

"It must have been two hours, Major." The cook seemed quite definite in her answer. "I know because May was just putting her second set to bed." She did not think that her statement required elaboration. Hopkins dissented.

"Second set?"

"Oh, yes, Colonel, May Brimmel is famous for her children. She's been married thrice and has a set of three boys from each time. Her first set is almost grown now: Albert's the last still at home. A big strong lad of seventeen; fancies the sexton's daughter." Mrs Wills's practical countenance became coy, and for the briefest moment she appeared seventeen herself. "The middle set go to bed at nine o'clock."

"What happened when you returned here?" Smith wanted to know.

"I went to see if Captain Doyle needed anything," she replied, becoming quite serious again. "Though he gave me the night off, I thought I'd just see if he might want something."

Smith wondered if the cook-general had also been motivated by a not unnatural curiosity about her employer's possible visitor. He refrained from posing such a question, however.

"At night, the captain usually likes a fire in the billiard room, where he plays after dinner, and in his study, where he writes letters before bed," the woman continued. "He wasn't anywhere, so I thought. It didn't seem right, somehow. So I started looking again. I went back to the billiard room and I found him..." She shook her block-like head, her little eyes gazing at the floor, as if re-living her discovery. "Horrible, just horrible..."

After a few seconds' silence, Smith said, "That's when you telephoned Constable Fowler?" The servant responded in the affirmative, and the policeman nodded in confirmation over his notes.

"You weren't afraid that the killer might still have been in the house?" Hopkins was a little alarmed at such lack of caution on the woman's part.

Mrs Wills paused before answering, as if considering the possibilities for the first time, but then said, "I never thought of it, sir..."

Smith was not surprised by this admission. Mrs Wills struck him as very capable, but lacking in imagination; similar, he thought, to Constable Fowler. He inquired aloud if she had noticed anything out of the ordinary in the house (not an easy sentence to phrase, considering that a corpse in a billiard room was hardly a regular feature of country villas.) Upon a negative response, he told the woman that she need not be kept further. But as he stood, Smith did ask how long she had worked at The Firs.

"I started in the summer of 1919, Major — two and a half years ago," Mrs Wills replied, in a voice full of reminiscence. "I came here after I left the Ampervilles."

"The Ampervilles?" reiterated Hopkins. "The Ampervilles of Betton Grange?"

Smith too had heard of that gentry family. The qualification in his friend's question was redundant, however, as there had been but a single branch of that family since the beginning of the nineteenth century. Now that too was extinct.

"That's right, Colonel," the servant said, pleased at the recognition of her former employers. "Very sad: four brothers, all but the youngest killed in the War, and him dead of the influenza soon after. If that wasn't bad enough, they left the world in the order they came in, so each inherited the estate and had to pay taxes on it each time. When young Master Davy passed away of the 'flu, his sister had to sell what was left to pay the death duties. Very sad."

"And then you came here?" Hopkins said to Mrs Wills.

"That's right. And now this house is a sad one." The woman glanced from one gentleman to the other. "I can't think of who would want to hurt Captain Doyle. Horrible, just horrible..."

"Hello! I'm Carey, Herbert Carey, doctor of medicine."

The newcomer had stepped through the front door of The Firs not more than a minute after Mrs Wills had left through the back, returning to Lane End Cottage, with Constable Fowler as her escort. Carey set down his black leather bag and shed his hat and overcoat in the hall. The garments had as much snow on them as had Smith's and Hopkins's when they had arrived.

Hopkins grinned and advanced on Carey, his right hand extended.

"I've heard your name before, Doctor," he said. "You're taking over Stoller's practice, is that right?"

"Eventually," agreed Carey, his reaction curiously guarded.

Smith did not think that Carey could have been a physician for long, as he was not far removed from his mid-twenties. Such was the eagerness that he radiated, though, that the major, who shook his hand a moment later, would not have been surprised if the young man had passed through the prescribed course of study at his medical college in half the allotted time. Divested of his heavy coat and boots, his natural posture was seen to be a forward lean, as if at the start of a race. His red hair, a contrast to the pallor of his skin, was brushed straight back, as if blown thus by his running at great speed.

"Did Stoller send you?" Smith asked.

"Ah, no...no, he did not. In fact, I kept him from coming," announced Carey, not for effect but as though he were learning this for the first time himself. "It's why I didn't want to say too much about inheriting his practice. You see, he's had a heart attack."

"Good Lord," breathed Hopkins.

"Nothing devastating," Carey was quick to point out. "I think he had a bit of a shock when he heard the news of Captain Doyle's death. I gather they were friends. But then he dug his motor-car out of the snow, intending to drive here. His heart couldn't stand the strain."

"Wielding a shovel in this weather would tax a fit man," commented Smith truthfully.

"And Doctor Stoller is not fit. Oh, he's still capable — a better physician than I'll be for years, if ever. But there was a reason I was brought in as a partner." Carey stooped to retrieve his bag. "Tonight, he knew he'd had an attack, so he telephoned me. That's why I'm late getting here. I visited him first."

"Will he be all right?" Smith wanted to know.

"As long as he rests, stays off his feet and avoids any work. Now he'll have to take that holiday everyone has been urging on him. No stress or disturbance of any kind." Carey turned his head at an angle. "It could have been far worse," he added. Then he clapped a hand against one side of his bag. "I'm ready, gentlemen."

Smith and Hopkins led the youthful doctor into the billiard room, Carey almost bursting to get there ahead of them. But he paused when he saw the crumpled body and, if he had some with which to start, might have lost some colour.

"One more thing, Doctor, and then we'll let you work in peace." Smith glanced at Carey with a slightly puckered brow. "How did you get to The Firs?"

"I drove Doctor Stoller's motor-car," Carey replied, just before kneeling beside the corpse. "He had finished clearing away much of the snow before his heart attack, and though more had fallen by the time I was ready to come here, the Ford is strong enough to plough through it. Is that your Hillman out front? You chaps may be coming back to Kingsby with me."

Stephen Doyle's study was a small chamber, tucked unexpectedly behind the billiard room, near the back stairs. The few books in his fewer shelves, the bland prints on the walls and the odd memento of the former owner's past were none of them striking, and could have come from any gentleman's own room.

"Doyle may have been expecting to come here after his visitor of the night had left."

Rupert Hopkins indicated the fire, lit by Mrs Wills before her first departure of the evening. Untended, it was slowly burning itself out, though it warmed the study adequately as it did so. Smith sat behind Doyle's desk and opened on the blotter before him a small notebook, taken from a drawer.

"They may have started conversing here and ended in the billiard room," he remarked, almost absently. He glanced up. "Do you know anyone in Kingsby named Turpin?"

"No," answered his friend. "Why? Are you trying to blame the murder on a long-dead highwayman?"

"Of course not," Smith countered indignantly; "on his descendant."

"There was a Dick Turpin in the pantomime that we took Nikki and Will to on Boxing Day."

"I suspect that wasn't the actor's real name," said Smith.

"Nikki wanted *you* to take her to the panto," Hopkins stated, standing before the fire and warming his backside. "I'm jealous. She wants you to take her everywhere."

Smith rather enjoyed his role of godfather, and always looked forward with anticipation to playing it whenever he could.

"So far, all I've managed these holidays has been the village production of *Twelfth Night* yesterday," he told Hopkins.

"And she really understood it?" Hopkins's grin was a genuine display of parental pride.

"Just because such literature surpasses *your* understanding, doesn't mean that your daughter is as handicapped," Smith pointed out.

Hopkins's retort was forestalled by a rap on the jamb of the open door. Herbert Carey peered almost excitedly into the study, still drying his hands with a towel after having washed them.

"Have you reached any conclusions about Doyle's death, Doctor?" asked Smith, folding his hands on the desk's top. Simultaneously, he heard Constable Fowler step through the door from the kitchen, stamping his feet to free them from snow. The policeman appeared behind the physician a moment later, his smooth cheeks rosy from the chilly air outside.

"Yes, some, yes..." Carey set the towel aside and clapped his hands together. "Dead since about eight o'clock, perhaps a little after, though there's always room on either side of an estimate like that, due to varying temperatures, individual body characteristics and such, but yes...about eight o'clock."

"What about the cause?" Hopkins queried. "The trophy on the floor?"

"More like trophy on the head," replied Carey, turning serious before anyone could disapprove of his joke. "I don't doubt the trophy was what killed him. Again, there are other possibilities. Doyle may have been poisoned, then struck to mask the real weapon, but... That sort of thing occurs more in fiction than in real life."

"Anything else remarkable?" added Smith.

Carey breathed in, placed his arms akimbo and thrust his face forward.

"No, no, I couldn't see anything else. I think a post-mortem examination is in order, of course, but I don't have anything further right now."

Smith nodded, then moved his eyes to Fowler, his face returning to room temperature.

"Is Mrs Wills safely back at Lane End Cottage, Constable? Tell me, do you know anyone in the parish named Turpin? No? Do you, Doctor?"

Hopkins reacted as if he had just been reminded of something forgotten and said, "How did you come up with the name, anyway?"

"I found it in Doyle's appointment book," his friend replied, tapping the little volume before him. "The calendar was hardly heavy with activities but the captain did print, quite clearly, the name 'Turpin' in the space provided on the sixth of January. If that indicated an arranged meeting, then it may very well have taken place between seven and nine o'clock tonight. Certainly, Mrs Wills knew of no other."

"Shall I call the Fox and Hounds, sir, to see if they have a guest staying there under that name?" Fowler suggested.

"I assume that's the name of the inn in Kingsby? Yes, Constable, do that."

Thirteenth Night

Privately, Smith thought it would be most obliging of a murder suspect not only to stay overnight near the scene of the crime, but to register at a local hostelry under the name by which he was known to the victim.

Fowler was absent for a minute. Carey filled the time by explaining, almost as a reminder to himself, what he necessarily had to do while deputising for the divisional police surgeon. Though he listened to the doctor, Smith was able nevertheless to eavesdrop on the constable's part of his conversation with the landlord of the Fox and Hounds. He was therefore not taken aback by what Fowler had to say when he returned to the study from the telephone in the hall.

"There is a William Turpin at the inn right now." Fowler was surprised and even showed it to some extent on his smooth face. "Mr Aitchison — the landlord — says Turpin left the Fox and Hounds about seven o'clock, came back about two and a half hours later covered in snow. Turpin's in his room now..."

Doctor Carey's assessment of his motor-car was correct. The Ford proved powerful, though its triumph over the snow-deepened road between The Firs and Kingsby could not be faithfully duplicated on the return journey. Precipitation had continued to fall while Carey was at Doyle's house, and several times proved a match for the automobile. Smith and Hopkins had wisely abandoned the latter's Hillman, which would not have made its way out of The Firs's drive, and the two gentlemen joined the physician and the constable in the heavier American car. The new passengers were useful in pushing the vehicle whenever it stalled.

Fowler, for his part, had wished to ride Underhill's horse back into the village but, as Smith observed, any interview of William Turpin must include a regularly appointed agent of the law; the policeman had to accompany the others. Fortunately, a solution was found in Albert Brimmel. One of his mother's 'first set', the strong, broad lad was concerned that the sexton's daughter would be afraid on such a stormy night. Despite his mother's insistence, probably quite correct, that the damsel in question was fully able to care for herself, her son made the most of the fact that the butcher's horse had to be back with its owner for the next morning's deliveries. When taxed with his proposed method of return to Lane End Cottage, Albert mentioned something about staying the night with a friend in the village.

It was no longer the thirteenth day of Christmas when the four passengers alighted from the Ford, now stopped in front of the Fox and Hounds. The hours passed seemed to have made little difference, however, from the time at which Smith had arrived at The Firs. The temperature was the same, as were the volume and rate of snowfall. Smith stretched his legs and glanced up at the building before him. A couple of windows in the upper storeys glowed with lamplight, as did the hall behind the front door.

"Aitchison hasn't alerted Turpin that we wish to speak to him?" Smith asked, adjusting his coat's collar against the descending snow.

"No sir. He's a sensible fellow." Fowler raised his fist to knock on the inn's door, then hesitated. "Are you sure you want to question Turpin now, Major?"

"Quite sure." Smith knew from a lifetime's experience that intelligence was always best gathered from unwilling informers in the early morning, when they were at their weakest, both mentally and physically.

Henry Aitchison was a startled-looking man, with a moustache so full and wide that it seemed to want to be a beard. With no apron and his shirt-sleeves rolled down, he might have been one of his own patrons. He greeted Fowler conspiratorially, peering pigeon-eyed at the gentlemen who followed the constable into the Fox and Hounds.

"That's right, he's upstairs. Not what I'd call sociable, but decent enough. What's he done? Sorry, Doctor? The telephone? Oh, yes, of course, through that door, into the parlour."

While Carey excused himself to call the police superintendent at Louth, Aitchison led Fowler up the solid but age-warped stairs to Turpin's room on the first floor. Smith and Hopkins, meanwhile, were directed into the saloon bar, off the hall and deserted at this time of night.

"I've been dying for one of these," Hopkins said, as he lit a cigarette. "I didn't want to smoke in Doyle's house, it being a crime scene...and someone else's home."

Smith too chose a cigarette from Hopkins's silver case when it was offered, but longed more for a cup of tea. He pulled a chair up to the young fire, which the landlord had considerately ignited in the hearth before the visitors' arrival. The shadows of the two men, bounding about with the dancing flames, created a weird atmosphere. Smith's thoughts of Yuletide ghost stories were terminated by Carey's entry from the neighbouring parlour.

"The snow must have brought down some of the telephone wires," said the doctor, declining a cigarette. "I can't get through to Louth." This problem was set aside as the tramp of several feet was heard on the stairs.

When the door to the saloon bar was opened and a young man stepped in from the hall, he seemed momentarily to share something of Smith's fancy regarding the eeriness of the room, for he paused briefly, more shades bouncing off the low, open-beamed ceiling as the three gentlemen at the fireside turned.

"Looks more like an inquisition than an interview." The comment, almost snide, and no doubt in response to a remark Fowler had made earlier, showed that William Turpin had quickly recovered his aplomb.

Thirteenth Night

The policeman announced the newcomer's identity, and Smith took in the young man's appearance. Under thick, almost longish, wiry, brown hair Turpin's complexion was florid and freckled. Green eyes viewed all before them with a certain amount of cynicism, while a mocking expression on the face made ready to scorn everything. Smith thought the fellow's years — under twenty-five in number — rather few to have such a permanent attitude.

"We were in luck, sir: Mr Turpin hadn't gone to bed yet," Fowler declared, in that matter-of-fact tone that policemen throughout the world had perfected. And indeed, the younger man was dressed casually, in a brown suit, worn and cheaply-made, with a soft-collared shirt, open at the throat, as if he had been interrupted reading or relaxing.

"Mr Turpin, I am Major Smith. This is Colonel Hopkins and Doctor Carey. We'd like to ask you a few questions, if we may."

Turpin glanced at Smith, as if he had not seen him until he spoke.

"Major? Colonel? Those don't sound like police ranks to me."

Smith could tell that interviewing Turpin would be a struggle. Nevertheless, he smiled in a friendly way.

"You're quite right, of course. We are not members of the county constabulary, or any other police force, for that matter. But we are assisting the local authorities, with the sanction of Constable Fowler's superiors." To these statements, Turpin responding merely by shrugging his narrow shoulders, as if the explanation did not concern him. Smith produced a flat case from within his jacket. "Cigarette?"

"Sure. I have a feeling I'm going to be a while." Turpin grabbed a cigarette with one hand while fishing a box of matches from a pocket of his trousers with his other. He was soon expelling smoke from his lungs, and sitting on one of the old but hardy wooden chairs the room offered.

"You don't seem surprised to receive a late night visit from the police, Mr Turpin." Smith sat opposite the younger man, across a table. The bar was growing warm, thanks to the fire, which was also providing the only illumination. The room was also slowly becoming more welcoming, especially when Aitchison, in a white apron and with his shirt's sleeves rolled up to the elbow, entered a minute later with a tray full of cups, saucers and tea pots.

"Why should I?" demanded Turpin, a knowing smile twisting his thick lips. "I'm never surprised when the establishment closes ranks."

"Sorry?" Hopkins, having taken a seat near by, thought that he had misunderstood.

"This is about Doyle, isn't it?" Turpin's complaisance was smug, which seemed misplaced to Smith.

"Yes, it is..." replied the major, slowly. Fowler, standing behind Turpin, with his note book poised, frowned at the man, while Doctor Carey had placed himself on the edge of a table, and was leaning forward eagerly.

"I thought as much," said Turpin, nodding. "A former chief constable still has influence, I see; still has friends in high places. I ask him for justice and he calls his lackeys to give me the third degree."

Smith tapped his cigarette's end into the glass ashtray that Aitchison had brought over from another table.

"No one is going to torture you, Mr Turpin, physically or otherwise," he asserted. "And as for the justice that you wanted from Captain Doyle... What form was that to take?"

"He didn't tell you?" Though he had begun his cigarette after the others had started theirs, Turpin had burned through his rapidly. "You don't have an idea why you're here?" He chuckled. "Ask Doyle."

Smith paused in his drink of tea and gazed over the rim of the cup at Hopkins. The latter was confused, and Carey, perched with some balance on the edge of his table, also looked bewildered.

"We would indeed like to speak with Captain Doyle about this matter," Smith responded honestly, "but we can't, as you may very well know." He set down his cup in its saucer with a small ceramic clink. "Stephen Doyle is dead, murdered just a few hours ago."

Turpin appeared to think, momentarily, that he was the victim of a joke, or perhaps a ruse, crude and obvious, and the start of a smile flickered across his ruddy countenance. Then he may have reasoned that if Smith's statement were a falsehood, it would achieve nothing for anyone. Finally, he must have drawn the conclusion that Doyle was actually dead, and that the men assembled to interview him in the saloon bar of the Fox and Hounds public house believed he had something to do with the captain's demise.

"I didn't kill him," he stated simply. "He was alive when I left him."

"When was that?" Smith's eye noticed Fowler's pencil moving across a page of his note book.

"It must have been eight o'clock, a little later, maybe..." Turpin's narrow green eyes moved rapidly. They were not seeking a means of escape, but rather to recall his memory. "I wasn't there long."

"Where? At The Firs?" Hopkins stubbed out his cigarette.

"That's Doyle's house, right? Yes, I meant there..." Turpin was uncomfortable now. He repeated, "He was alive when I left."

No one spoke after Turpin made his claim. Smith finished his tea and set aside his cup.

"Very well, Mr Turpin, let's hear your story. We may as well start at the beginning. Why did you visit Captain Doyle's home?"

Turpin squinted at Smith, his expression full of suspicion, but he saw nothing in the bland face that hinted at what the brain behind it was thinking. As if to perplex the young man further, Smith poured hot tea from a pot into a cup, hitherto unused, and pushed it toward Turpin. The latter kept his gaze upon Smith, and moved slowly, like prey watching predator in a dusk truce at a jungle water-hole.

"My father is John Turpin. The name will mean nothing to you now, but it made the papers ten years ago. He was convicted of killing a woman, Alice Biggars. He didn't do it." The suspect glanced about him defiantly, but was disappointed if he had expected to see disdain or incredulity on the faces of his audience. Smith's visage was dull, unresponsive, and Hopkins was nodding, as though to prompt greater exposition. Carey was leaning forward earnestly, and Fowler was too busy writing to react.

"The evidence was against my father," resumed Turpin, a bit more deliberately. "Alice Biggars was found strangled in her cottage. My father didn't have a witness to support his story of being elsewhere at the time of her death. He admitted to being in love with her — my mother had passed away a few years before — and had asked her to marry him. Most men who knew her were infatuated with her. But dad was turned down. And it was known he had a foul temper."

Smith held out his cigarette case to Turpin once more, surprising the younger man, who thanked Smith this time.

"There must have been more evidence against your father than that," insisted the major. "The most unsophisticated jury would not have returned a 'guilty' verdict in such a case."

Turpin shrugged, as though the legal arguments bore little significance in the matter.

"There was more," he said, almost apathetically. "Medical evidence mostly, physical evidence... Enough to convict dad of manslaughter. The belief was he went crazy when Alice rejected him, and he strangled her in a fit of rage." He sighed. "Life imprisonment... Dad would've preferred hanging."

Aitchison entered again, this time from the direction of the kitchen and, coming as he did in the silence after Turpin's last statement, became the focus of everyone's attention. The landlord swallowed, and held up the heavy tray he had borne in.

"I thought you gentlemen might like some sandwiches..." he said, cheerfully, hopefully. "And some more tea..."

Hopkins smiled gratefully, and waved the hotelier closer.

"An excellent idea, Mr Aitchison," he commented. "It's been a while since I've eaten, and I dare say the others are in the same boat."

Smith agreed with his friend, and mentally reminded himself to compensate the landlord later. After Aitchison had retired once more, the major said:

"The matter of justice you raised with Captain Doyle, Mr Turpin... I assume that it was a demand for an inquiry into your father's case. Why Doyle? He had been, it is true, the chief constable of Lincolnshire's police ten years ago, but why not talk to his current successor?"

"Or someone at the Home Office?" suggested Hopkins.

"The lord lieutenant?" put in Carey, helpfully.

The jerk of Turpin's mouth was half sneer and half genuine smile. He inhaled more from his second cigarette, then drank from the cup before him.

"I tried all of society's legal avenues. I don't have the money or the friends to be heard. Doyle was involved in the investigation a decade ago. I thought I would try the personal approach."

Smith picked up a triangular sandwich from the platter on his table and bit into it. The bread was fresh and the cheese sharp. Turpin, once he had selected a couple of sandwiches, ate the first quickly, and the second just as fast.

"I thought he might be willing to listen to me, at least. My father never confessed to killing the girl, and has told me often enough he didn't even see Alice Biggars the day she died. I wrote Doyle a letter from Manchester the day before last, explaining what I wanted, and that I'd be in Kingsby today." Among bites of food, drinks of tea and puffs on his cigarette, Turpin made it seem as if he had not tasted the delights of civilisation for some time. "When I registered here, the landlord let me use his 'phone to call Doyle."

"He agreed to talk to you?" Hopkins asked. Smith noted the slight disbelief in his friend's tone, though no one else did.

"Yes, he told me he would see me at seven." Turpin's own voice betrayed a little incredulity of its own. "I left here about six-thirty, a little later. I had to walk, and I must've underestimated the amount of snow in the road. It took more than an hour to get to Doyle's house."

"What happened then?" Smith's second cup of tea perfectly complimented the sandwiches.

"I rang the bell at the front door but no one answered. I figured somebody was home because lights were on in the house. I knocked and knocked..." Turpin regarded the last half-inch of his cigarette and, after a final draw, extinguished it. "I came all that way, and I wasn't going to go back without at least seeing Doyle. I went in." The statement was rather defensive, but no one challenged his unbidden entry into The Firs. "He was in the billiard room. I think I must've startled him, but I did try to be polite. I asked if he was Captain Doyle, and told him who I was. He seemed irritated, and snapped that I should have wrung the doorbell, then ordered me to wait in the drawing room."

Thirteenth Night

"How long did you wait there?" Smith sipped some more tea.

Turpin must have thought the question irrelevant, for he replied scoffingly: "Five minutes, maybe six or seven..."

That would have been long enough for snow brought in on boots and a coat to melt, Smith thought. He asked the younger man if he had heard or seen anyone else in the house during his visit.

"No, there was no one; just Doyle and me. But I didn't go anywhere else in the house." Turpin was impatient with anything that he did not consider directly related to the topic. But his manner changed somewhat and he ran a hand through his coarse hair. "I was...nervous... I couldn't sit still... I wandered about the room, looked at some photographs..."

"The ones on the mantelpiece?" Hopkins queried. He and Carey had swiftly finished their sandwiches and tea. Even Constable Fowler had been hungry.

"Yes, yes," Turpin answered, annoyed again. "One of a group of soldiers, one of Doyle and another man outside a big tent — Does it matter?" He drained his cup and set it on its saucer with some violence. He relented, and gently pushed the items away.

After a few seconds, Smith said, "The interview with Doyle did not go well, I take it."

"No," replied Turpin, still testy. He sighed and rubbed his face, rendering it a little more red than had nature. "No," he repeated. "Despite the impression you may get here and now," he glanced at his audience in the fire-lighted room, "I can be tactful, if I try. And this was for my father, so I didn't want to ruin my chance. But Doyle seemed ready for a fight from the first. He described Alice Biggars's death as the worst crime he'd ever known, and told me my father should've hung for killing her. I tried to reason with him, tried to stay calm, tried to—" The rising volume of Turpin's voice was climaxed by his hand slamming down upon the table, jarring everything on it. Constable Fowler eyed the suspect warily, but Turpin calmed himself.

"How long were you at The Firs all together?" Smith asked, acting as if the outburst had not occurred.

"It couldn't have been more than a quarter-hour. Probably half of that I was alone in the drawing room. Eventually Doyle just shouted at me to leave, which I did. He was by himself when I walked out the front door — by himself and alive."

"And then?" Hopkins wanted to know the sequel.

"And then...I walked back here and sulked by the fire in my room, until the local guardian of law and order fetched me to your little inquiry."

The only sound that could be heard in the next minute was the odd crack of coal burning in the grate. Smith reclined in his chair.

"You can understand, Mr Turpin, that it would be in the interests of justice for you to remain a while in Kingsby," he said.

Turpin chuckled and reiterated, contemptuously, "Justice..."

Smith sighed. He found the young man's attitude to be growing tiresome. He amended his statement.

"In *your* interests, then."

"And who will pay for my room? I wasn't planning to stay for more than one or two nights."

"If you prefer, Constable Fowler will arrange alternate accommodation, at the county's expense." At Smith's words, the policeman flexed his hand, cramped after several pages' worth of small writing, and stepped forward. The implication of the offer was not lost on Turpin. His sarcasm was checked, to a degree.

"Am I under arrest, then?" he said, in a low tone.

"That probably won't be necessary, as long as you don't leave the village."

"It doesn't look like I have a choice, does it?"

"One always has a choice, Mr Turpin," countered Smith, rising to his feet amid the noise of chair legs scraping across an ancient wooden floor. "Sometimes, however, it's simply a bad one."

The snow ceased falling at some point during the dark hours of the early morning. Soon after the last flake had descended, the thick overcast started to break up, and when dawn came, the sun would be seen. But the temperature would not climb much higher, and what snow had landed over the past few days would remain for a few more.

Smith and Hopkins had arrived back at Blaney Lodge a little after two o'clock, and neither man retired to his bed for another hour after that. Trudy had waited for them (or, rather, had fallen asleep on a drawing room sofa and then complained that she had waited) and demanded that she be told the whole story, which she was certain would be exciting. She was both disappointed and annoyed to be given a verbal précis of the whole affair in just a few sentences. It was, she claimed, one of the disadvantages of knowing military officers experienced in composing succinct reports.

To Smith, though, it was clear that Trudy's principal motive for remaining awake (metaphorically, at least) was to set her mind at rest about her husband returning safely. It was yet another facet of married life that Smith envied.

It was before the sun had made its appearance over the horizon that Smith was awake, even earlier than usual, roused by young Willoughby Hopkins, who wanted him to come and see the pretty colours in the eastern sky. For his part, tired as he was, Smith did not believe that watching a winter sunrise with an

Thirteenth Night

awe-struck little boy was something to be missed.

"That was Detective Inspector Wragg, of the Lincolnshire Constabulary CID," said Hopkins, walking into the dining room an hour later. "He called to let us know he's sending us a motor-car in twenty minutes."

"That's quite generous of him," Smith responded, as he spread strawberry jam on a slice of toast. "We can use it on alternate days."

The remark caused Nikki Hopkins to giggle, which made her little brother do the same. Trudy could not resist laughing at the contagion, and her husband sighed (though without conviction) and inquired if his friend remembered breakfasts in their regimental mess.

"A silent meal," said Smith. "I recall entering the dining room for my first breakfast with the Royal Fusiliers. I had only experienced the messes of irregular regiments until then. I wished everyone present a good morning. The colonel threw down the newspaper he had been reading and demanded how he could possibly digest his food with all the bl—" He glanced at the children, sitting on one side of the table and listening closely "—horrible racket going on."

"Well, don't look for a quiet breakfast after you have a family, Nemo," Hopkins warned, taking his place at the head of the table.

"Are you going to be away *all* day, Uncle Linus?" Nikki demanded, lifting her hands so that the maid could remove her empty dishes. "I was hoping we could build a snowman."

"Snowman," echoed Willoughby.

"I don't think we'll be gone long, Nikki," Smith answered the girl.

"We'll probably be back before the three of you return from church," added her father.

The roads of Lincolnshire had not been cleared of snow, but traffic had begun to move on them nonetheless. The sunken lane to The Firs had been travelled by a number of police vehicles. As a result, the snow on its surface had been rutted and tamped down enough, in Smith's opinion, for his friend to be able to drive his Hillman home.

When the motor-car sent for them reached The Firs, the two army officers observed several other automobiles parked near Hopkins's in front of the house. Activity inside the house was betrayed by the comings and goings outside of men in police uniform and civilian attire.

"Colonel Smith? Major Hopkins?"

As the constable who had driven them to The Firs ushered the soldiers into the house, they were immediately noticed by a sharply-dressed man at the far end of the hall. He dismissed the police sergeant to whom he had been talking, and walked toward the newcomers.

"Major Smith and Colonel Hopkins, actually," corrected the former. He explained who was whom.

"I'm Detective Inspector Wragg."

The police officer's appearance made Smith think of those individuals now being termed 'lounge lizards', reptilian habitués of night clubs whose appreciation of anything beyond themselves and their prospects was rare, and superficial when it existed at all. Nonetheless, Wragg's handshake was firm and something in his dark eyes gave the impression that his character was strong and solid. The oiled hair and the exceedingly thin moustache were, however, unfortunate adornments.

"Constable Fowler's report made it clear that you two gentlemen were essential to last night's investigation. I'm grateful." Wragg smiled, displaying too many teeth, the front upper two separated by a notable gap. "Naturally, I wanted to confer with you myself."

"Fowler did well," Hopkins reciprocated; "very professional."

"I'll be sure to include that in my own report," said the inspector. "At the moment, he's with Turpin at the Fox and Hounds."

"Have you questioned the young man?" Smith asked.

"I have. And placed him under arrest for suspicion of murder. He'll be taken to the divisional station in Louth. You're done?" The query was directed toward a photographer, emerging from the billiard room and laden with the equipment of his trade. The Firs was indeed a busy place this morning, though it seemed to Smith that he and Hopkins had arrived just as immediate police interest in the house was concluding.

"You're convinced that he murdered Captain Doyle?" Hopkins said.

Wragg, instead of answering the question right away, indicated the open door of the drawing room. There was an air of peace within that chamber, a contrast to the pace without, and the inspector obviously felt that the three could converse without interruption there.

"Turpin? I'm not a hundred per cent certain of his guilt," he stated, pulling a packet of cigarettes from out of his tan suit's jacket. "However, he is a radical, generally hostile to society, with a genuine grievance against the victim, and the means and opportunity to kill him. All of this suggests to me he's the criminal. Even if he's not, he might decide to make himself unavailable for an interview at a later date." After offering a cigarette to each of the others, Wragg chose one for himself and put it to his lips. "Better safe than sorry, I say."

Smith admitted the wisdom of the precaution.

"Are you familiar with Turpin's grievance, Inspector?" he wanted to know. "The death of Alice Biggars, ten years ago?"

"Indeed I am, Major." Wragg lowered himself onto the cushions of the same sofa on which Smith had sat hours before. "It was the first case I was involved in as a detective sergeant. I was working out of B Division CID, then as now." The police officer leisurely blew smoke from his nostrils. "The murder took place at Ermsby, not far from here. She was a pretty girl, Alice was, the sort of pretty, flighty female who starts a lot of fights, without meaning to."

"Captain Doyle took personal charge of the investigation?" Smith sat opposite Wragg, where Mrs Wills had been seated the previous night, while Hopkins leaned against the mantelpiece, with its array of photographs.

"He oversaw it," Wragg clarified. He smiled, a smug expression that was almost certainly not the implication intended. The inspector was probably a long-time victim of his disreputable looks. "He supervised rather more than my boss at the time, Inspector Fitzroy, would've liked. But there aren't many murders in Lincolnshire, thank God, and people like to see as high-ranking an officer as possible in charge."

"But I think you'll agree that there is plenty of scope in this current affair for someone other than Turpin to have committed the crime," ventured Smith.

"Turpin left The Firs at about a quarter to eight," Hopkins pointed out. "If he is telling the truth, there was roughly seventy-five minutes between then and Mrs Wills's return at nine, during which Doyle may have received another visitor."

"I'm not ignoring that possibility, Colonel," Wragg said, genially, leaning to one side to deposit some burned tobacco from his cigarette into an ashtray. "It's true that someone may have come here after Turpin."

"Or before..." added Smith, thoughtfully.

"And remained in the house throughout Turpin's time here?" The inspector's eyes narrowed, making him appear distinctly untrustworthy.

"Perhaps even next door to the billiard room. There's a w.c. to one side of the fireplace, and would provide a convenient spot in which to wait." Smith spread his hands. "Turpin did tell us that Doyle was several minutes in joining him here in the drawing room."

"And Doyle was startled by Turpin's sudden appearance," said Hopkins, "startled and annoyed. Perhaps someone else was responsible for his bad temper."

Wragg nodded, and did not dispute the theory.

"However, Turpin is the likeliest suspect I have at the moment, I'm sure you'll agree, gentlemen."

A uniformed constable knocked on the jamb of the half-closed door and, leaning into the room, announced to his superior that all was ready. Wragg put out his cigarette and rose.

"I think the way back to Kingsby should be travelled enough by now for you to get your motor away, Colonel."

The Firs was almost empty now. The last of the policemen had left, except for a sergeant, noisily searching through a bunch of keys, preparatory to locking the house. As Smith stepped across the threshold of the front door, following Wragg and Hopkins outside, he almost bumped against a man standing on the steps, staring at the chain of the bell.

"I'm sorry," Smith apologised automatically; "my fault."

"Oh, no sir, mine," retorted the man, haltingly, whisking off his cloth cap and almost bowing in deference, "mine, mine." He was middle-aged, dressed in old and dirty garments of tough fabric, his coat open to the cold. He wore no waistcoat, and the shirt thus revealed was rumpled, the tie unevenly knotted. His slightly bleary eyes returned after a moment to the bell's chain.

"Is something wrong?" Smith asked, peering up.

Again, the man's cap came off, and his eyes lowered.

"Yes, yes sir, it's broken, yes, yes. Captain Doyle wants me to repair it, he told me to repair it yesterday. I'll do it, I says, right away. No, tomorrow will be fine, Gid, he says, fix it tomorrow."

"That's you, is it? Gid?" Smith smiled.

"Yes, yes sir, that's me, Gid." This confession was accompanied by more bowing. "Gid Perfoy."

"I don't think there is any rush to repairing the bell today, Perfoy."

"Because the captain's dead? Yes, yes sir, I know." Perfoy's voice sank in tone and speed. "But I promised to fix it today. You can't break a promise, right, sir?"

"No, you can't," agreed Smith, patting Perfoy on the shoulder.

"He is *not* lop-sided!"

Nikki Hopkins, her dimpled cheeks pink from exertion in the cold, gazed defiantly out Blaney Lodge's dining room windows. This chamber gave the best view of the back lawn that stretched from the house to the hedge, exedra-like behind a dense line of bare trees. Dominating the scene was the big snowman Smith and his goddaughter had raised.

"Yes, a clear lean to the left, my dear," said the girl's father, the teasing note in his voice not missed by any present.

"I beg your pardon?" Smith stepped forward. His face was not as rosy as Nikki's, but nonetheless showed definite signs of prolonged play outside. He had just divested himself of his hat, coat, scarf and gloves, and stood next to his friend, drinking from a mug of hot cocoa. "I think you've been acquainted with me long enough to know, Hap, that I tend not to lean to the left."

"I'm not so sure, Nemo," Hopkins retorted, grinning, and regarding Smith sidelong. "Your defence of young Turpin smacks of comrades closing ranks."

"He's also a veteran: two years in the Royal Engineers Signal Service, and as many wounds."

"Uncle Linus didn't want to put a scarf on the snowman," said Nikki, from the other side of her father. A drink of her own cocoa left her upper lip brown and foamy.

"Why not?" Hopkins queried.

"Because he thinks snowmen shouldn't want to stay warm." Nikki started to giggle. "And if the scarf heats up his neck, it'll melt, and his head will topple off." The last words were spoken with difficulty through laughter.

"That makes sense," Hopkins conceded, "in a distorted way..."

Smith sipped his beverage and examined through the window the large effigy he and Nikki had created. He was happy that he had been able to spend time with her today. He would play with little Willoughby this evening, he decided. The boy had been feeling a bit neglected since not being taken to see *Twelfth Night*. He would have fallen asleep during the performance, anyway; he took after his father as regards to Shakespeare.

Smith turned to Hopkins.

"I believe there *was* a second visitor to The Firs last night," he said.

Hopkins, chatting with his child, looked at his friend and asked, "Before or after Turpin came to call?"

"During," responded Smith.

"I say, Nemo, you really must get a family of your own," Hopkins said. "It's most disconcerting to see them more upset with your departure than with mine."

Smith turned from his scrutiny of the white countryside, almost painfully bright under the morning sun. The road from Kingsby to Louth was not sufficiently cleared to permit traffic in light automobiles. The railway was, however, available, and Monday, just after breakfast, the two gentlemen were bound for the town in a compartment of a first-class carriage.

"I won't be leaving for London until tomorrow," Smith reminded Hopkins. The train was decelerating preparatory to stopping at Louth's station.

"That's hardly the point," the other remarked dryly. "Is Wragg expecting us?"

"Yes, he'll be at the divisional headquarters."

The detective inspector, greeting the two army officers in the charge room of the police station, sounded genuinely glad to see them, but his smooth smile, with a cigarette dangling from one upturned corner, made it appear as though he were about to press a used motor-car upon them.

"I wasn't really surprised when you 'phoned me last night and told me you had an idea about the Doyle case," he said. "What's got me curious is you explained it involved not new evidence but old." He gestured beyond the charge desk, with its attentive station sergeant, and indicated a gloomy corridor that led farther into the building.

"Turpin hasn't wavered in the least in maintaining his innocence," Wragg continued. "Just like his father did, ten years ago."

"And still does," Hopkins added.

After a turn down a subsidiary passage, the inspector halted before a closed door, and opened it. At a table under a high, small window, and guarded by a police constable standing just over the threshold, William Turpin sat impatiently. He looked very much the same as he had early the previous morning, and was dressed in the same suit and shirt. He regarded the gentlemen who now entered the interview room and, his thick lips curling derisively, spoke.

"Well, Colonel Hopkins...and Major...whatever your name is... My benefactors from the other night. I must've given you the answers you wanted to your questions, because the inspector there didn't waste any time in arresting me soon after." He shook his red head and turned away. "The police have always been tools of the gentry."

"I'll have to remind the constable that the next time one endorses my licence for speeding," murmured Hopkins to Smith as they stood on the other side of the table from Turpin.

"As a matter of fact, you did provide the responses necessary for solving the mystery of Captain Doyle's death," Smith said to the prisoner. "I simply didn't put them in the right order until yesterday."

Turpin's eyes narrowed, as if suspecting a trap.

"You have enough evidence to hang me, do you, Major?" he asked, more as a legitimate question than a taunt.

"Not you, Turpin."

Smith reached into his jacket and removed a rectangular photograph. Turpin recognised it as something familiar. When it was laid before him, flat on the rough table, he confirmed that he had seen it, framed, on the mantelpiece of the drawing room at The Firs. Inspector Wragg, standing near by, leaned over the table to examine the picture. It showed the late Stephen Doyle next to his friend, Doctor Geoffrey Stoller, in front of a large, striped, canvas tent.

"For the official history, Turpin," said Smith, "please identify Captain Doyle."

The younger man's brow wrinkled in incomprehension, and he snorted contemptuously.

Thirteenth Night

"Is this some sort of trick?" he demanded. "All right, I'll play along. That's him, right there. That's Doyle." And he jabbed his index finger on the likeness of tall, lanky Geoffrey Stoller.

"I don't understand."

Detective Inspector Wragg had barely closed the door to his office before he gave vent to his frustration. Hopkins sat, as invited, in one of the chairs in the room, its overstuffed cushion squeaking with escaping air. Smith sat on a sofa next to a precarious pile of reports detailing local criminal statistics from before the War.

"It was *Twelfth Night*, wasn't it?" Hopkins leaned over the wooden back of his chair and grinned at his friend.

"Yes, it was," Smith replied. To the police officer, standing with his back to the office door, as if ready to confine his visitors until they divulged what they knew, he said, "Do you know the play, Inspector?"

"Is that the one with the dragon?" Wragg pulled a comb from his waistcoat and ran it through his oiled hair. It was difficult to believe that he had thought it in disarray.

"No, not a dragon," answered Smith. "*Twelfth Night* is full of mistaken and false identities, similar to the situation surrounding Doyle's death." He paused, then added, "When Turpin arrived at The Firs for his chat with the captain, the front doorbell did not function. He eventually entered the house without an invitation, as Colonel Hopkins and I did later that night. Earlier in the day, however, Doyle had suggested to a local man, Gid Perfoy, that the bell be repaired. Yet, when Turpin met him in the billiard room, Doyle upbraided him for not ringing first."

"Doyle forgot the bell wasn't working," suggested Wragg. He held out a package of cigarettes to his guests and, upon their refusals, took one of the contents for himself.

"The man Turpin saw in the billiard room didn't know," Smith countered. "If Turpin were telling the truth, and hadn't murdered anyone, then the inescapable conclusion is that he was not Doyle's only visitor that night. This mystery man may have come afterward or before and, perhaps, was still at The Firs when Turpin arrived."

"You mean he was hiding..." said Wragg, nodding.

"In plain sight."

"In plain sight..." The inspector's head tilted to one side, as if avoiding the exhaled tobacco smoke around it. Then he straightened. "Do you mean to say...?"

"Yes, it was Doctor Geoffrey Stoller whom Turpin came upon in the billiard room." Smith reclined on the sofa, nearly unbalancing the stack of reports beside him. "And he was not only startled, but frightened — naturally so, since he had probably just murdered Doyle a minute or two previously. The body was behind the billiard table, and if Turpin had walked even a foot or two into the room he would no doubt have seen it. As it was, he was instructed — by Doyle, so far as he knew — to wait in the drawing room. That gave Stoller a chance to collect himself before joining the young man."

"Good God," Wragg breathed, unconscious of the smoke blowing from his nostrils.

"Stoller must be very quick-witted." Smith frowned, yet smiled simultaneously. "Not only did he realise, immediately upon seeing Turpin, that the visitor had never met Doyle and, in fact, could not identify him—"

"How did he know that?" the inspector posed his question seconds before Hopkins asked a similar one.

"The first thing Turpin wanted to know of Stoller was whether or not he was Captain Doyle..."

Hopkins and Wragg exchanged glances, and seemed in slight embarrassment, as if they had been bested at a simple game.

"Stoller also thought that he stood a stronger chance of survival if someone else could be blamed for his crime," continued Smith. "Again thinking swiftly, 'Doyle' became combative, forcing Turpin into an argument."

"Of course." The police officer nodded once more. "It might provide further evidence against the young man. The crime was obviously one of passion, committed in the heat of the moment, as during a fierce quarrel."

"But how could Stoller hope to maintain his charade?" asked Hopkins. "Turpin was bound to see him some time, in court perhaps, or..." His voice trailed, then halted. He grinned and wagged a finger at his friend. Meanwhile, for Wragg, the pieces of the puzzle were coming together.

"Stoller faked his heart attack," he said. "What was it Carey reported? It was nothing serious, but enough to keep Stoller from working. No stress of any kind..."

"Correct, including his duties as police surgeon. Certainly, Stoller didn't suffer heart trouble from removing snow from his motor-car just before Carey arrived at his house. The Ford had been dug out for his previous trip to The Firs, during which he had killed Doyle, and the falling snow covered all recent tire marks."

Wragg's sly eyes regarded Smith as though the latter were the potential purchaser of several drinks at a bar, perhaps of a whole meal.

"What about the motive, Major? That still eludes me, unless..."

"It couldn't be a coincidence that Doyle was killed the day Turpin appeared to talk to him about the Alice Biggars murder," Hopkins commented, thinking aloud.

"Yes," Wragg agreed, "yes."

"It had to do with Turpin's father," concluded Hopkins.

"I think it might profit the Lincolnshire Constabulary to re-examine that old investigation, Inspector," Smith remarked, "and Doctor Stoller's involvement. You may find that the physician murdered the girl — perhaps from the same motive popularly ascribed to John Turpin's alleged actions: unrequited love — and then persuaded his good friend, Captain Doyle, to assist in disguising the facts. The evidence against Turpin Senior would have been strong indeed if the county's chief constable and the local police surgeon had colluded in making it so."

"Lord..." Wragg at last sat, on a wobbly stool that tipped dangerously. No doubt in consideration of what he was being told, the detective ignored such piddling matters as balance. He glanced at Smith. "But Doyle had agreed to see young Turpin on the sixth."

"Conscience had most likely got the better of him," theorised Smith, who added dryly, "at last. I suspect that he contacted Stoller and informed him of what he was going to do."

"Stoller drove out to The Firs to dissuade his old accomplice, probably walking right in without recourse to the doorbell. His efforts to turn Doyle from his intentions failed," Hopkins said, "so Stoller killed Doyle to keep him silent." He nodded.

Inspector Wragg put the remains of his cigarette on the saucer of a forgotten tea cup. Anger was distorting his face, turning it from that of an effete wastrel into that of a righteous but merciless avenger. "Ten years John Turpin's been in prison — ten years! I can't wait to see Stoller's expression when I drag him down here to be identified."

"That's all it should take to make the villain crumble," agreed Smith. "After all, his plan relied on not being seen by Turpin after the thirteenth night of Christmas."

A Lesson in Politics

And Major E. Smith.

Major L. Smith sighed. One would not have thought, he mused, that there would have been much to confuse about his name. But whenever it appeared in public print, it was wrong: it was, in this case, not his name at all. It was the custom of the *Morning Post* each day to list those who had attended Society functions the night before; in this instance, a Saturday-to-Monday at Lady Coverham's house in Surrey. Smith had long since resigned himself, however, to receiving the world's disregard, but it unreasonably irked him when it was in print.

He set the newspaper aside as his valet entered the dining room of his new flat bearing a heavy tea pot, a cup and saucer, and other paraphernalia of refreshment. The morning papers, to several of which Smith subscribed, told him this day little of interest. He kept himself apprised of events, domestic and international, but this third week of 1923 seemed to be seeing the world at last catching its breath after the Great War and the lesser but still significant upheavals that had followed.

Deserving of greater attention were the letters that had come in the post, though several were the inevitable bills. (One, from his tailor, he had been dreading in a minor way: his secondment to the Secret Service four months previously had necessitated an entirely new wardrobe, since he had rarely worn anything but military uniforms for years before it).

"Were you mentioned in the *Post*, sir?" Odways inquired, as he handed his employer a filled cup.

"A relative of mine was," replied Smith, dryly.

"Never mind, sir. Your acquaintances know who you are."

Smith smiled as his servant left the room again. Then his expression fell as he wondered how accurate Odways's statement was.

It was true that among the letters just delivered were two more invitations to country house parties. (It was, of course, winter, so nobody remained in London unless they had to.) But Smith did not fool himself. He was a convenient bachelor, a gentleman and officer of the King's army who would 'make up' a hostess's young men, provide a respectable twelfth at dinner or, even if, upon inspection, he should prove not suitable for an unmarried daughter, he might know someone more appropriate.

"Who was that officer Lady So-and-so had at her fancy dress ball last Christmas? He seemed quite nice. Yes, put him down." And so he would again be the last mentioned in the *Morning Post*'s list the next day, an incorrectly spelled name after 'and'.

Smith shook his head. He was becoming self-pitying in his middle-age, he observed.

He was surprised a moment later when the door-bell rang. The clock on the fireplace mantel showed that it was not yet nine.

The dining room door opened, and Odways announced, "Captain Crawford, sir."

The chief of the Secret Service, colloquially known among his colleagues and subordinates as C, stepped into the room with his habitual rolling bounce. Despite two decades of shore duty, the old naval officer still walked as if he were on board a ship. He grinned and extended a lined, red hand.

"Good morning, my boy, good morning. I hope I'm not disturbing you, calling so early. Damned rude of me, I know, but I was near by..."

Smith doubted that C's presence in Mayfair was as casual as he implied. He lived in an apartment at Secret Service Headquarters in Kensington, and his wont, as many of his subordinates knew, was to rise early, breakfast, then go downstairs to his first floor office to begin his day's work. A close behind Little Mount Street was out of his way.

"Another cup, Odways. Please, sir, sit..."

"Oh, these old spars are creaking more and more, my boy," C said, easing his legs — one of them wooden — with a sigh as he settled into a chair at the dining table. His attention was caught by Smith's newspapers, discarded and pushed to one side of the shiny surface. He screwed in a rimless eyeglass and peered at the journals. "*The Times...Pall Mall Gazette...The Post...*" C glanced up, his monocle dropping from a bright blue eye into an open palm. "*The Daily Herald?*..."

"A Labour paper will, if not gauge the mood of the working class, at least reflect the opinions of sympathetic editors," Smith explained. "Besides, it's socialist, not communist."

C nodded, but then raised one white eyebrow as he tapped another newspaper.

"*Pravda?* That definitely *is* Bolo..."

"It's good to know what the other side is thinking," Smith said, "at least officially."

For a moment, C's weather-battered face remained as wooden as a sailing ship's figurehead, the nutcracker shape of his nose and chin aimed directly at his underling. Then he laughed.

"Quite right, my boy. I get the blasted rag sent to Headquarters myself. I used to get *Izvestia*, too, but it just parroted what *Pravda* wrote, so we saved our money."

Odways had poured tea for the guest, who drank the hot beverage gratefully. Despite his dark blue woollen suit, reminiscent of his uniform, C had been chilled by the low temperature outside.

"I'll wager you're surprised I'm here, what?" he said at last. "The fact is, I need you to go to Ireland; to Rambard's Castle, to be precise."

"It can't be a coincidence that I'm acquainted with the house's owner, can it?" retorted Smith.

"Few things are fortuitous in our line," acknowledged his chief, pausing for another gulp of tea. "Kilkelty is having some people to visit next week. One of them will be a chap named McGarry, Joseph McGarry. Heard of him?"

"I think so, yes." Smith's brow lined as he tried to recall what he had read of the man. "A physician; moderate in all things. Worried himself into a heart attack trying to negotiate an end to the Troubles; refuses to condemn either side in the current civil war, despite pressure to do so. He's seen as an honest broker, comparatively non-partisan. He's about sixty; had one son killed by the Black and Tans, another by the IRA. His daughter is the apple of his eye." Smith shrugged his shoulders. "Other than the fact that he has just accepted an appointment to the Irish Free State's Senate, I know little about him."

C was regarding his host through an eyeglass.

"Have you ever considered writing for *Who's Who*?" The old sailor chuckled and, nodding, added, "Yes, that's the chap. Some think his Senate seat means the abandonment of his disinterest. He's expected to make his maiden speech in the Dublin parliament in about a fortnight, just after his visit to Rambard's Castle. His Majesty's Government want to know what course he will take; in particular, whether he will speak against the new emergency powers the Free State has just enacted or support them, however reluctantly."

"It seems a straightforward assignment," Smith said thoughtfully.

"It should be. But then sudden squalls and hidden shoals aren't restricted to the sea, as I've found in my time." C's boyish expression implied that he had not always considered danger and fun mutually exclusive. "Don't try to influence the fellow. Just get to know him and keep a weather-eye open. Now, let's not put the stern before the bow: can you get yourself invited to Rambard's Castle in the first place?"

"It shouldn't be difficult," answered Smith, glancing at the invitations he had received that morning, lying in their opened envelopes near the newspapers. "I spent a couple of months at Rambard's Castle before the War. When I again met

A Lesson in Politics

Lord Kilkelty some years afterward, he seemed to have remembered me, after a fashion. Where is he now?"

"Here in London. He's had some business with his solicitor and is staying at his club."

" 'The Regiments'? Then it's quite possible our paths will cross..."

"Excellent!" C brought his thick hand down on the table and made the cups rattle in their saucers. He had fortunately emptied his own half a minute before. "I'll leave the rest to you, then. You'll be travelling as yourself, of course, so you needn't worry about false papers and the like." He rose and held out his right hand once more. "Good luck, my boy, and send me a signal if you run aground."

It turned out relatively simple for Smith to get himself invited to Rambard's Castle. The first step (or rather, steps) involved a walk to the United Regiments Club, in Berrow Street.

Though the Metropolitan was the principal seat of his affection in Clubland, he had joined 'The Regiments' first, in 1904, primarily as a means of widening his contacts within his own profession. Smith had become fond of this, his initial club. It possessed a slightly anonymous character, over-shadowed by larger, older and better known clubs.

An 'accidental' encounter between Smith and Lord Kilkelty just before luncheon was followed by the inevitable discussion of what each man had been doing since they had last met. Among Smith's talents, two were especially useful in his new field: a great capacity for small-talk, and the almost subconscious encouragement he gave to the speech of others.

It was over the soup that Kilkelty explained that he was having some friends to his home, and it was over the fish that he learned Smith had no plans for the coming week. Having already described the amenities that he would be offering to his guests, it would have been ungenerous of the nobleman not to have asked Smith, over the cutlets, if he would like to come.

"You like shooting, don't you?" Kilkelty did not recall much about Smith, but a fondness for gun-sport was a safe bet.

"Why, yes, I do." This was true, but Smith would have answered similarly no matter what his predilections.

"Good, then; it's settled. You remember how to get to the old place, don't you?"

Smith had spent his last full leave before the War at Rambard's Castle (that of 1914 had been interrupted) and had had to travel across the breadth of Ireland to reach it. The countryside at the beginning of the journey was much like

England's, but even greener, though it became more bleak, more barren with each mile traversed.

"Well, Odways?"

Smith and his valet were alone in the compartment and may have been, by now, alone on the train. Its population had diminished with each stop.

"It's a wonder any farmer can make a living here, sir," Odways said, disapprovingly, as he viewed the landscape through the window.

Indeed, the more prosperous parts of the island were behind them by this time. Brown blanket bog, its roiling undulations like moss-hidden rubble, covered most of what could be seen, with grey rock irregularly breaking to the surface here and there, growing to become blue and purple mountains in the distance. Patches of cultivated soil were tucked between stretches of turf and miniature massifs of stone, as if a squatter had scattered seeds and hoped his surroundings would not notice. Cows and donkeys blinked at the passing carriages from behind crumbling drystone walls, exhibits in a nature preserve that no one visited.

"For the most part, they just manage," responded Smith. "I imagine that if they want more than mere subsistence, they emigrate."

Odways shook his head. The servant, usually a generous and sympathetic man, had a hard-headed, and hard-hearted, view of the Irish. Smith, on the other hand, thought their character perfectly suited for survival in their contrary land.

"Is there anybody there for here?"

As the train slowed beside the platform of the Tobinstown station, the stationmaster ambled beside the carriages, calling out the strange but appropriate question. In answer, Smith and Odways stepped from their compartment. As they did, a stout man in a battered bowler and a checked tweed suit, both too small for him, rose expectantly from a bench under the eaves of the station's roof. Odways mistook him for a vagrant, but the major rightly guessed this to be one of Lord Kilkelty's retainers.

"Is it to Rambard's Castle that you'll be going, your honour?" The Irishman asked the question as if the destination were a royal palace.

"It is," Smith responded with fitting dignity.

"Then it's Hurley who'll get you there." With this statement, the Irishman removed his hat and, with a flourish, bowed from the waist. "This way, your honour."

Two horse-drawn vehicles awaited the newcomers on the far side of the building. Hurley was a bit surprised when Odways followed his master into the first, instead of riding with the bags that were loaded into the second. To cover his confusion, Hurley barked a few sharp words at the driver of the luggage van, a slow-looking lad who had been nodding over the reins, then took his own

A Lesson in Politics

place, behind the horses on the seat of the passenger cart.

"Aren't there some rugs just there for the comfort of your honour," he said, over his shoulder; "and for your honour's footman."

The weather in County Mayo was no more clement than it had been in London a few days before. There was no snow on the barren ground but Smith could smell it in the air. The clouds that coloured the mid-morning sky a pearly white became grey to the west, where their rolling texture reflected the waves of the ocean that began there.

Rambard's Castle was about three miles from Tobinstown over rutted roads, the mud of which seemed to have frozen during the night into sharp-edged crevices, and would not thaw this day. But Smith had ridden worse courses (so he assured himself, as his molars were nearly dislodged by a particularly deep canyon). Even Odways wore a disgusted expression, simply because these bad lanes were Irish.

Between walls of stone that made the land resemble a provincial touring company's version of Yorkshire, the carts creaked and banged past numerous white-washed cottages, smoke curling from the chimneys protruding through the thatched roofs. Here and there were small pastures, grubby green in hue, and smaller arable fields. Everywhere else was bog, which provided the peat that Smith could scent being burned by the cotters.

"There she is, your honour. Isn't she a sight?"

Hurley spoke the words with blatant pride, a smile in his voice. He might have been the owner of the house now in view, rather than a member of its staff.

Beyond a dip in the road that widened to become a dell were some of the first trees that Smith had witnessed since entering the county. They were bare, asleep in the winter's chill, but welcome to his eyes nonetheless. They gathered more thickly as the little valley progressed, the lattice-work of their branches providing a grey hide for the house, its hipped roof and attic windows visible above.

"Rambard's Castle, your honour." Hurley paused the wagon respectfully, as if introducing a princess.

It had in fact been several centuries since the ancestral home of the Tobins had been fortified. The tall, rather narrow-sided structure raised in Napoleonic times (after its predecessor had been razed in revolutionary times) had not been built for defence, though it was difficult to conceive of it existing entirely for comfort. It was ascetic, rather than aesthetic, the only ornamentation being stone urns placed along the edge of the roof, in lieu of a balustrade, and a half-hearted Venetian window in the middle of the first floor, above the entrance.

But, with chimneys puffing smoke, a few lights showing behind glass panes, and Smith's host standing on the front steps awaiting his latest guest,

Rambard's Castle did, after all, possess more than a little homeliness.

"Good morning, Smith," the Earl of Kilkelty said, smiling, as the Englishman dropped to the gravel of the drive. Both wagons, with Odways still in the first, continued around the back. "You're the penultimate. One more party is yet to arrive."

As Smith was ushered through the front doors, he asked whom he had preceded.

"Doctor McGarry and his daughter. They're due later today."

"That's enough, Aunt Mercea," Lady Violet Harris said to the currently-speaking Tobin relative, "and the rest of you, too. I promised to show Major Smith around the house after luncheon. At this rate, you'll use up the whole afternoon."

The rebuke was a kind one, and the aunts, all seven or eight of them, were no doubt used to such chaffing, and twittered with laughter. Violet rose and took Smith's arm to lead him from the dining room.

"You needn't have done that, Lady Violet," Smith told her, once they were in the hall.

"Oh, yes, I did," the woman responded with a smile. "They really would have talked your ears off all day. Besides, even though we didn't have a tour planned, no one has shown the convent such patient selflessness in a long time, and I thought it needed rewarding."

"The convent? A family name for the unmarried Tobin females, I assume?"

"And there are a few more about, too shy to take their meals with strangers."

Lady Violet Harris had changed little in the decade since Smith had last seen her. Married to Malcolm Harris, Ireland's 'Champion of the Slums', she apparently eschewed politics and, though her husband necessarily spent most of his time in Dublin, Violet preferred County Mayo and Rambard's Castle. She was not conventionally attractive, having strong features and a look men called striking, meaning it as a compliment. Her eyes were green and her hair red, the latter kept thick if not long. Though wearing the new cylindrical fashions, she bore them with grace and femininity. Smith believed that few women achieved those qualities these days.

"But as long as I have an audience," Violet said with an arch of one of her light-hued eyebrows, "and one who hasn't seen Rambard's Castle before, I may as well show you around."

Smith sighed mentally. The woman did not recall his initial visit to the house in 1913, though she had been present at the time. He was, however, for good or ill, accustomed to being forgotten. Aloud, he said:

"That would be delightful, Lady Violet."

A Lesson in Politics

Rambard's Castle was as ordinary on the inside as on the out. Not one exciting decorative feature met the eye as Smith was led through one bland room after another. The architect and interior designer might well have worked from factory-replicated books of patterns. The workmanship was not bad, but it was hardly of a standard one would have expected in a house of this size and local importance. Floors sagged and walls bowed almost imperceptibly — almost. The house had been built to last, but not built well.

But as they walked, Smith observed that his hostess could find no fault in the house. Where he saw an uneven dado, she saw the spot at which, as a child, her growth had been measured; where he noticed an unimaginative balustrade, she remembered sneaking girlhood glances at adult dancers long after she should have been abed. Her familiarity with the large staff (Irish households, even now in the leaner days following the Great War, kept an almost feudal number of servants; as in India, the rich considered it a duty to employ as many of the poor as they could) demonstrated that the love she felt for her home included a strong human element.

"And here we are on the ground floor again," Violet announced, as she and Smith descended the staircase, slightly too narrow and a little too steep. "We'll go through the music room into the library, and I'll show you where the patriots set the fire when they burned down the old place in 1798."

"Oh, Vi, you're not dragging Smith about the draughty wreck, are you?"

Lord Kilkelty was in the hall, taking his hat from a footman; he was dressed for the chilly outdoors. He bore a masculine version of his sister's features, and they were more successful on him. Tall, handsome and strong, he was characteristic of the Anglo-Irish Ascendancy: loyal to the old ways, yet careless in their application; devoted to field sports; generous to his friends; uncomprehending of his enemies; vaguely bored much of the time. In fashion, he was slightly anachronistic compared to his fellow aristocrats in England: with his paper collar, his full and broad moustache, his hair oiled and parted down the middle, he resembled an Edwardian beau rather than a gentleman of the 1920s.

"I'll thank you not to speak of our ancestral home in that manner," Violet said. Though Smith surmised that similar exchanges were a regular feature of the siblings' dialogue, he nonetheless could hear a sharpness in the woman's response.

"Besides, he's seen it before." The earl positioned his hat just so on his head before accepting the stick proffered by his servant.

"You have?" Violet looked at Smith in surprise.

"It was long ago," the Englishman replied. "I don't think you were here."

Kilkelty smiled and supported his guest's lie: "Yes, you were away, Vi. And speaking of 'away', I must be, as well. One of the tenants — er, farmers — is making a fuss about tomorrow's sport. I'm going to sort it out. Oh, and you'll find Pat and Mike in the music room." The earl grinned, inclined his head toward a near-by door and took his leave.

Violet sighed and said, quietly, "Oh, those two."

As she and Smith entered the music room, they interrupted Hunter O'Brien and General Egan in an earnest debate of recent Irish history, just as the announcement of luncheon had done two hours before.

"Just a friendly discussion, Vi, that's all."

It had been explained to Smith that O'Brien had been a fighter in the Irish Republican Army. He had held from it a colonel's commission, which seemed to have implied a sometime command of fifteen or twenty men. O'Brien was honest enough not to use the title in his retirement. Whatever his rank, he had apparently seen some military action against British forces. Nevertheless, Smith found it easy to take a liking to the small man, whose Leinster accent sounded more gentle in the ears than the local speech. O'Brien did not become heated when the subject under discussion was the past. Rather, his eyes sank farther back into their deep sockets, his ruddy cheeks distended in a wry expression, and his crooked mouth was always ready to smile.

"That's right, Lady Violet."

Charles Egan had been using his height (extensive when compared to O'Brien's) to advantage, towering over his verbal opponent. He came by his rank from having commanded a brigade in France in 1915, and though his bony frame, over which his pale skin stretched like a tanned hide, was healthy for its age, he had realised that the rigours of modern battle had surpassed him. He had retired to his house in Cavan, which, due to his outspoken support of unionism, was burned in '20. But he had stayed on, simply moving to one of the estate's cottages, and damning his foes from there. Those enemies — who appreciated a brave man when they attacked one, and admired an obstinate man even more — had left him unmolested thereafter.

"You see, Major," said Violet, turning to Smith, a smile playing on her thin lips, "Ireland can inflict much on itself, but as long as we keep our sense of humour, we'll get through."

"This fossil has no sense of humour, Vi," declared O'Brien, jerking his thumb at the general. "He's just so archaic that people have to laugh at him."

"I'd rather be considered ridiculous," Egan retorted, drawing himself up and jutting out his wide chin, "than be humoured out of pity." His thick, neat eyebrows and carefully trimmed moustache bristled meaningfully.

O'Brien opened his mouth in feigned shock and muttered something about pity being extended to the one old enough to be knocking on death's door.

A Lesson in Politics

"Do the historical debates here always attain such a level of brilliance?" Smith's aside made Violet laugh.

"If someone who actually cared about British prestige had been prime minister during the Troubles, rather than that blackguard Lloyd George, your IRA would have been thrashed within six months," said Egan. "They can't even put up a decent fight in this district."

The implication surprised Smith. He asked if there was an IRA unit near Tobinstown.

"Both kinds," replied O'Brien, with a pop-eyed grin.

"He means the Irregulars and the National Army," Violet clarified.

"The Irregulars in these parts are just local boys, from what I hear," O'Brien said breezily, dropping onto a couch. "They don't even take orders from Dev." He shrugged. "Units in remote regions have always been like that."

"Undisciplined brigands," opined Egan fiercely, "who don't even follow their own chief's commands."

"How long have you lived in Ireland, General?" O'Brien's question was filled with mischievous incredulity and innocence. He lit a cigarette and offered one to the other debater. "We Irish take orders from nobody. We merely consider suggestions."

"Are the Irregulars active?" Smith wanted to know.

"They robbed the pub last week," said Violet, who seemed almost embarrassed at such criminal activities by those claiming to be freedom-fighters.

"As I stated: brigands." Egan puffed on his cigarette triumphantly.

"That must be why the National Army is here, then," Smith theorised: "to show the flag."

"Exactly so, Major," concurred O'Brien. He propped his stubby legs up on a wobbly table and, turning to Egan, added, "It's rather a change to meet an Englishman with sense."

Before the general could rebut the inference of this statement, Violet hurriedly said, "I hope neither party will do anything to ruin your shooting tomorrow, gentlemen."

"Indeed," answered Egan.

"Glory!" O'Brien exclaimed. "I think we agree on something, General."

"Then there can't be a better note on which to exit," Violet said with a quick smile and exaggerated relief in her voice. Taking Smith's arm, she pulled him out of the music room and into the thankfully deserted library beyond.

But for the clothes worn by its participants, dinner that evening at Rambard's Castle might have been taking place a century earlier. Outside the plainly trimmed windows, the temperature of the dark January night stood at several degrees of frost. Within, the poor lighting thrown by a crooked chandelier cast an orange glow over the dining room. The crowd of servants, moving from kitchen to sideboard to table, were little more than eerie shadows, while from the walls, dark portraits of nearly invisible Tobins gone by stared at the assembly eating below. Smith believed that he was now on the main course, but, as he could barely see the food, he had to judge from smell and taste.

Listening to the general conversation, he could not but be relieved that the custom had evolved at Rambard's Castle that the Tobin aunts dined earlier, in the breakfast room, thus leaving the space and time now for others' words.

"It's a shame that your daughter could not have come with you, Doctor," said Lady Violet Harris. She was seated on Smith's right, and though the skin of her oval face shone in the candlelight, it was the warmth of her body and the ease of her movements which most alerted the major's senses. "I saw her in Dublin last year, already well on her way to becoming a beautiful young lady."

Across the table sat Joseph McGarry, physician, and the newest member of the Irish Free State's Senate. Smith had met him upon his arrival, just before dinner. He looked an ordinary man, bald, with a monk's fringe of grey hair around the sides of his head. His appearance was that of a fifty year old, though he was sixty; his face, however, was showing definite signs of recent strain.

McGarry smiled, almost unwillingly, and replied, "She'll be eighteen next year. A most disconcerting age for a father, I can tell you."

"Is she in school, then? Is that why she couldn't come? Shouldn't she be still on holidays?" Lady Duggan leaned over her plate of beef as if she were making an accusation. Famous more for the vehemence of her speech than for her logic or interest, she made simple conversation sound combative. O'Brien once quipped that she could fight the civil war by herself.

Sir Horace Duggan, eating quietly, was equally well-known for the inevitable reaction he made to almost everything his wife uttered. This was to roll his little eyes upward and to repeat his lady's words verbatim, but in a low, nearly unintelligible mumble. How — or why — the two had maintained a marriage for three decades was a national mystery.

"Er, yes, she is still on holiday, Lady Duggan," responded McGarry, who was inured to the provocative behaviour the woman habitually used. "She's with her mother in Antibes."

"Foreign parts are not the places to spend the hunting and shooting seasons, McGarry," said Egan, after a satisfying drink of claret, "though I do remember once in '05—"

"Nobody wants to hear your boring reminiscences," O'Brien assured him. "You should write your memoirs, so that people the world over can ignore your bilious stories."

"Of course *you* would ignore them," remarked the general; "you'd have to learn how to read first."

O'Brien once more registered shock, quite unrealistically.

"I fear," interjected Lord Kilkelty, from the head of the table, "that Mrs McGarry is not in the south of France by choice...?"

McGarry smiled, wanly, and confirmed his host's suspicion.

"My wife has been feeling poorly of late, and our daughter's presence always comforts her."

There was a murmur of general good wishes from the other diners, and Alan Pollock, farther down the table from Smith and Violet, added, "If Mrs McGarry is not in the best of health, Doctor, you may be assured that the French Riviera will affect a wondrous change in her, though she may have preferred Menton."

Pollock was a rather timid man, whose eyes and ears made Smith think of a deer on the run from staghounds. The major would hardly have been surprised if, when leaving the table, Pollock leaped from his chair, right over dishes, candles and his fellow guests. His gasping delivery and high voice augmented the illusion by sounding perpetually startled.

"Why, during the War, Mrs Pollock was in such a state that her physician recommended a prolonged stay in Menton, and she has returned much better, much better. Haven't you, dear?"

This addendum to his recommendation was perhaps a mistake, for Dervla Pollock was present. She was quite sickly in appearance, pale, sad, with hair that looked as if it had been recently slept on. Smith did not need his powerful olfactory sense to notice the strong, medicine-like aroma she exuded.

"Oh, indeed, dear Doctor McGarry," she confirmed, "I was much worse."

In the uncomfortable silence which followed this declaration, Smith lifted his glass of wine in a miniature salute to the woman, who smiled almost prettily. Then a telephone rang.

"You're connected to the lines out here, my lord?" Lady Duggan turned her sharp gaze on Kilkelty, who raised his eyebrows.

"We are," he answered, "though, to be honest, I'm surprised at it."

"Care to explain that remark, Kilkelty?" chuckled O'Brien. Even General Egan seemed curious about it.

"The lines here have been cut before," said Violet, "by the Irregulars."

"Oh yes, I've heard that it's something they do habitually," Pollock informed the table, as if expecting an attack momentarily.

"...The lines have been repaired as often as they have been cut," Kilkelty finished. "It appears now that the IRA are falling behind in their destructive duties."

"Maybe the blasted National Army is doing some good after all," muttered Egan, as he set down his knife and fork. "I'd be impressed if they merely bestirred themselves out of the old RIC barracks they've occupied in the village."

Before O'Brien could compose a retort to this jibe, a broad-shouldered servant, who was in fact Mains, the butler, strode into the dining room, his jinking shadow twice as tall and thrice as wide as anyone else's.

"The telephone is for Doctor McGarry," he said. "It's from Dublin."

Smith was not alone in wondering if Mains's statement was a comment on the instrument's point of manufacture. He sensed Lady Violet suppress a laugh.

"The government have cancelled your appointment, Doctor," barked Lady Duggan aggressively. "You've been tossed out of the Senate!" It had been meant as a joke, but the woman's confrontational tone had rendered her words humourless. She never failed to miss the true effects of her sentences, and laughed heartily.

"It's good that we can reach Dublin," Violet said quickly, as McGarry left the room.

"Yes, indeed," said her brother, his smirk hidden by the napkin he applied to his moustache. "When the telephone was installed, the only connection we could make locally was with Colonel Ivers, at Mount Myrtle, the nearest house to us. Then it was burnt out during the Troubles, he left, and we lost contact even with him. At least now, we can call the police station, if no one else in the district."

"You seem rather to be on the edge of the world out here, Lord Kilkelty," said Pollock, looking as if he took the phrase literally, and was afraid that Rambard's Castle might slip over the rim and into an abyss.

"My husband is merely being facetious," cautioned Mrs Pollock, thinking perhaps that there were doubts. "We believe that the Earth is round."

Pollock smiled warmly at his wife. His opinion was, evidently, that she had just saved him from being embarrassingly misunderstood. The other guests smiled as well, though whether out of relief at their discovery of the Pollocks' geographical orthodoxy or for another reason, it was difficult, in the dim room, to judge.

"What do you think of the place, Odways?"

Smith was in his pyjamas and robe, peering at the patterns the frost was making on the panes of his bedroom window. There was little to be seen beyond the crystalline shapes, even had the room not been glowing with the light of numerous candles. It was a dark night, not moonless, but cloudy and cold.

"It's rather primitive, sir. It must have been like this in England in the

A Lesson in Politics

eighteenth century," the valet said, as he carefully poked among the coals glowing in the fireplace. "But at least we haven't been given dirt to burn."

Smith grinned and, turning from the glass, said, "To be precise, what you are thinking of is called peat. And we've been in more backward settings than this."

"True, sir," the servant admitted, as he straightened and set the poker amid its fellow tools by the hearth, "but never in so confusing a land. Why is there still fighting, sir? Who is this National Army, and are they different than the IRA?"

"Even some of the natives find the whole thing trying," Smith remarked, nodding. "The chaps who form the Irish Free State's government are those of the old Irish Republican Army who negotiated a peace with London, in order to end the Troubles. Some of their colleagues weren't satisfied with the terms they brought home, and started battling against those who accepted them. The new Irish government formed its own force, the National Army, to deal with the new rebels — most of whom are old rebels."

Odways, his hands held before him as if they were weighing two disparate objects, "And these rebels...they're the IRA, sir?"

"We call them that for convenience," replied Smith, "but since the government is formed from former IRA leaders, it's understandable that the Irish named the current rebels 'Irregulars'."

"Are these Irregulars likely to cause some bother, sir?" Odways's impassive face turned again to the poker, a possible weapon.

"They may," admitted his employer. "The local unit doesn't seem too keen on taking commands, either from De Valera, the Irregulars' leader, or from anyone else."

Odways shook his head. He was a true gentleman's gentleman, and preferred order in all things, even an insurrection.

"What of the staff here in the house?" Smith ran his fingers over the books he had borrowed from the small library on the ground floor, trying to decide which would be a good friend to sleep.

"They constitute an army in themselves, sir, at least in terms of numbers," observed Odways, pausing as he wound a clock. "His lordship of course knows his needs best, but there are enough staff, inside and out, to furnish several English earls' households, I'm sure, sir." He frowned. "And they are almost all unintelligible. Except for the higher servants, I can scarcely understand any of them. Mind you, Mr Mains does keep order well enough."

"And Doctor McGarry's man?" This was the real question, and Smith's attention was not wholly concentrated on the well-bound family history of the Tobins that he held.

"Grace is his name, sir," Odways stated, almost dubiously. "I believe it is his surname. He seems conscientious, sir; and ill at ease."

"Interesting." Smith sat on his bed. "His master might be described the same way. The cause?"

"None that I could see, sir." Odways set a tumbler, half-full of water, on the night-stand beside the wide, heavily-quilted bed. "If I should guess, sir, I'd say that Grace was waiting for events to happen."

Shooting at Rambard's Castle was not entirely like similarly-termed sport on an English estate, or even on a property in a less isolated portion of Ireland. Smith, having been a guest of Lord Kilkelty before, knew something of what to expect. He wondered if the other visitors did.

It was not a good sign that Pollock, rubbing his eyes and yawning in the cold gloom of the hall the next morning, expressed surprise that there was no breakfast laid on in the dining room. O'Brien and Egan, again breaking tradition by agreeing, expressed a hope that Pollock at least had handled a shotgun before.

There were no beaters, no drive, no butts. A handful of gentlemen, cursing at various obstacles rarely seen but eventually encountered in the leaden dawn, spread out over an expanse of bog and marshland after jumping down from wagons. Some headed for a small, rush-bordered lake on the property, aiming for duck or teal; others navigated toward the tiny arable fields, where partridges lurked amid the stubble. Smith, with Odways behind him as loader, remained in the bog, where the heathery bits sheltered grouse, and the marsh, snipe. The valet was displeased by the fact that they were accompanied by Hurley, in the rôle of keeper, and a mongrel that vaguely resembled a setter.

"At least he wasn't entrusted with a gun," was Odways's last comment on the subject, muttered under his breath.

Though largely raised in the open country, and further accustomed to it by his varied military duties, Smith was not a man who loved discomfort, as many sportsmen seemed to be. He enjoyed shooting and hunting, but also liked the warmth of a good bed, so that it took him a little time to enter into the day's spirit.

But the early morning, especially in the autumn or winter, with its late dawn, grey and bleak, made him feel alive and strong, as no other hour of the day could, not even the dusk twilight that he preferred. And when the first brace of startled grouse flew up before his approach, he brought them down within half a second of each other.

"Be gob, that's quick shooting, your honour," enthused Hurley. He loosed the dog, to whom he spoke in whirling Gaelic, to retrieve the dead birds. "And you hit them, too!"

A Lesson in Politics

As if his action had broken a spell of silence, Smith heard other shots crack across the tumbled landscape. Somewhere, Egan bellowed an oath, and the major guessed from its angry, rather than disappointed tone, that the general had merely been *nearly* hit.

The light grew stronger, spilling from the east behind a thick and seamless overcast. Game birds were not plentiful in this part of the country, which was why organised shoots were dispensed with, but Smith nevertheless bagged a goodly number. It was as he neared the soggier patches of the estate's bog, feeling the brittle, frozen water within the turf crunch under his feet, that he met with another member of the party.

"Hullo, Doctor. Any luck?"

McGarry stepped across some bulging peat, seeming to watch his step. But Smith noticed that the physician's attention was unfocussed, or perhaps elsewhere. McGarry stumbled over a tussock, as if fatigued. His breathing, however, was steady and strong, as it might have been with someone deep in thought.

"Not a blessed thing, Major," said the new Irish senator, though his tone implied apathy rather than disappointment. "I think the birds hear me coming."

"Well, this district doesn't really provide much in the way of targets," Smith replied, "though I believe I heard General Egan almost become one."

"It's true. Kilkelty's retention of the sporting rights upon the sale of his estate was academic." McGarry opined. "Er, what time do you have, Smith?"

"Just after nine o'clock."

McGarry turned behind him. One of the two men who had been following him at a respectful distance wore a grey tail-coat of homespun, the likes of which had been used by Irish peasants for two centuries. By his stockinged legs trotted a contented dog. The other man, dressed well but not really for a day in the bogs, was tall and handsome, carrying himself with dignity.

"Grace?"

"That's right, sir," the doctor's valet responded, after pulling out his own watch.

McGarry nodded and, turning back to the Englishman, perhaps fearing that he had insulted Smith, explained, "I'm expecting a telephone call — from Dublin."

"I understand that maiden speeches can sometimes be worrisome." Smith thought the new politician's nervousness comprehensible.

"Mm? Oh, yes, yes, quite right." When Smith suggested that, as he seemed to be enjoying the better luck, the doctor might wish to walk with him, McGarry did not answer. Then, brushing a fleshy hand across his mouth, the Irishman seemed to recall that his fellow sportsman was speaking. "Yes... Why not?"

Inductions Dangerous

Despite the agreement, McGarry's fortune did not improve. Smith observed that the doctor moved heavily (something that had little to do with weight), his footfalls warning birds into flight far in advance of the men's approach. Even at long range, Smith hit every fowl at which he aimed, but McGarry's reactions were too slow. When Smith delayed his own firing in order to give his companion opportunities, the only result was another day of life for all his targets.

The morning progressed but grew no warmer. It was not far now, either in distance or time, until the party would reassemble at the head keeper's lodge by the River Hobe. Already, that sluggish but deep stream was in sight, winding its twisting way through porous bog, its water the same unattractive hue as the sky. Clumps of thorn now became common, and from them upon disturbance flew magpies, most Irishmen hoping to see a pair, for their traditional luck.

"It's difficult to believe, on a day like this, in a place like this, that this country can be undergoing civil strife," said Smith conversationally. A rabbit bolted from underfoot, and both Hurley's and the other keeper's dog ran after it. There followed much shouting, both in Gaelic and some form of English. Smith did not mind pausing until the animals had rejoined the six men.

"Mm, yes, that's true, Smith." McGarry handed his gun to Grace. A small flock of curlews wheeled overhead, one bird after another giving its shrill cry. "Who would think that people could do things — such as we Irish are doing — to their own race?"

Smith glanced at the doctor. This was the line of talk that he hoped to encourage.

"The Troubles, involving the English, were bad enough — no offence," said McGarry.

"None taken," responded Smith.

"There is something very sad about a civil war." The physician's low voice sounded sad, troubled. "My father, bless him, strove for amity between British and Irish, between Protestant and Catholic. And now, the hatred is between Irish Catholic and Irish Catholic." He shook his bald head. "I sometimes think—"

From a dense spinney emerged Sir Horace Duggan, his lofty head covered by a tweed hat pulled so far down that it hid much of his pink face. Smith had heard someone trampling through the brush and thorns but had hoped that his chat with McGarry would have proceeded uninterrupted.

"Hello, Duggan," greeted the doctor. His smile seemed pretended, though the newcomer did not notice. "Did you hit anything?"

"Two couples of snipe and a plover," answered Duggan.

It was the first time Smith had heard the man utter words that were not a repetition of his wife's. He glanced behind Duggan but as he had heard, so he

A Lesson in Politics

saw. The newcomer was alone.

"Where is your loader, Sir Horace? And the keeper?"

"Hit them, too." Duggan's attitude, as he stomped past the others on his way to breakfast at the lodge, was one of indignation. No doubt the servants had ruined a pair of perfectly good shots with their blundering.

As it transpired, neither Duggan's loader nor the keeper, two of Lord Kilkelty's many employees, had been seriously injured. Each had received a 12-gauge pellet or two in the arm. In the time-honoured tradition, the guest was punished for the accident monetarily, and the servants correspondingly compensated.

The rest of the shooting party had enjoyed themselves. No one but Smith had brought down many of anything, though all except McGarry had encountered some success. Even Pollock could brag to his wife of his first official bag, a large partridge that more than made up for the nest of swallows he had inadvertently blown out of a tree at Lord Willerton's, the previous November.

Smith, for his part, was frustrated in his attempts to speak to the doctor about politics again. For reasons of amicability, this topic was forsworn among the party. Talk at the keeper's lodge over breakfast was of the morning's shoot, game in general, Rambard's Castle and other innocuous subjects. While there, Hurley somewhat mollified Odways's feelings toward Irish servants by praising Smith's skill with a shotgun.

"Sure, I've seen only one other gentleman so quick and deadly, another Saxon here just before the War."

Odways's annoyance returned: Hurley did not realise that he was referring to Smith's previous visit to Lord Kilkelty's home.

The rest of the day was spent closer to the house, where it was the earl's habit to retire to the library after luncheon, not to read, but to escape his aunts, whose domain the drawing room became soon after the meal. The male guests tended to join him there, while the ladies were generally trapped with the maiden Tobins.

Sunday brought no shooting but, rather, church, for those who wished to attend. Most of Kilkelty's guests did so, walking behind carriages loaded with aunts to the Protestant church outside the park gates. Only Hunter O'Brien accompanied the staff to the Catholic church in the village.

"You're extraordinarily kind to spend so much time with my aunts."

Monday's luncheon was over. The morning's shoot had been similar to Saturday's, though Duggan's targets this time had excluded humans. Pollock had again brought down half a brace, a teal this time, and Smith's bag was once more the biggest. The major was growing concerned, however, as McGarry's first appearance in the Senate was now only a week away, and the doctor's intentions once there remained a secret.

Smith was crossing the hall to the library when he observed the earl's sister descending the principal stairs from the first floor. Violet Harris was dressed in the long, full skirts and tight jacket of a riding habit, with a plain bowler and a short whip in her hands. Smith could not help noticing how attractively the contrasting black clothes and plaited red hair set off her pale face.

"Not at all," Smith answered. "They're delightful."

"Liar." Violet's lips smiled. "Are you busy?"

"I was just going to the library..."

"That's where my brother is, and most of the others — though I think Doctor McGarry has gone for a walk. Do you like to ride, Major?"

"I do, yes."

"I'll have another horse brought around to the front, if you wish."

After Smith had changed and emerged from the main door of Rambard's Castle, ten minutes later, he saw Violet mounted on a handsome white mare she called Bianca. Beside her was a restless black stallion, a groom holding its reins. The woman was surprised when Smith spent some time walking around his horse, and amused when he spent more murmuring to the animal. Then he swung himself effortlessly into the saddle.

"Strange..." the woman said. "Actor doesn't usually tolerate strangers on him."

Smith ignored the obvious opportunity to ask why such a horse had been chosen for an English visitor.

Monday was as chilly as Saturday had been, despite an unobscured sun. Under the dull blue sky, the ride warmed Smith and Violet quickly. She led the way, over bulging ground covered in bracken and broken by boulders. For every rabbit hole seen, two were not, so they remained on the paths trodden across the land.

Harder riding was reserved for the pale green water meadows by the river, grass and dirt flying freely as the horses joyfully galloped without urging. Smith watched his companion, marvelling, not for the first time, at how a woman maintained herself in a side-saddle. Legs were of little use to a lady in such a position; it was all a matter of balance.

"The people here are wonderful." Violet was just a little out of breath as the two riders slowed their mounts to a gentle walk. They were approaching Tobinstown, its white- and colour-washed cottages, with thatched roofs resembling straw hats pulled low over the eyes, clustered close together. "They

A Lesson in Politics

deserve better than they have had." The feelings Violet had for the locals seemed reciprocated, as men raised their hats, smiling as they tugged at their forelocks; some men bowed and women curtseyed as she rode by.

Smith glanced at his companion as their horses ambled down Tobinstown's one street. Violet brushed strands of red hair from her face, which glowed slightly with moisture. Her graceful reactions to the friendly and respectful salutes of the villagers made her seem very much the lady of this manor. But she was not. Even before Smith's first visit to Rambard's Castle, the 20,000 acres that had been gathered under the ownership of her family for three and a half centuries had been dispersed.

It had been a voluntarily decision, taken a few years before. The British Government, determined to achieve land reform in Ireland, hit upon the plan of buying whole estates from the gentry. Many of the latter, offered very good terms, especially considering prices in Edwardian Ireland, accepted the deal, pleased that, as incentive, they were to retain sporting rights. The Government then re-sold the land to the tenantry who farmed it, loaning them the money to buy, if necessary, at even better rates than those given the previous owners. The third Earl of Kilkelty was one who had sold his patrimony, leaving only the house, garden and park (the 'demesne') to his heir, the present earl.

"Do you regret that all of this land is no longer Kilkelty property?" queried Smith.

"Sometimes..." Violet turned to him with a disarmingly wistful expression, which rapidly changed. "But the Irish who worked it now own it. It is as it should be."

"But aren't you and your brother Irish?"

Violet stopped her mare at the low wall that kept the lawn before the church, dedicated to Saint Brendan, from the rutted dirt street. She looked as though she were contemplating that modest building, standing in the centre of the village, with its little cemetery beside it, full of old, leaning stones. Smith noticed that opposite the church was the public house.

"John is thinking of moving to England, buying an estate there."

A village mongrel took offence to Actor trespassing on its territory. The horse stomped menacingly in the dog's direction, but a few words from Smith soothed the beast.

"He's a Protestant in a Catholic country. You must've seen on Sunday how empty Saint George's was... He was sent to school in England, first Hawtrey's, then Harrow. Up to Sandhurst, from which he was commissioned into an English regiment. Until father died, John thought of Rambard's Castle as little more than a holiday home, a shooting box... Other than a bit of sport now and then, he's dreadfully bored here. There's precious little society, except the vicar whom John thinks dull... He'd be a good landlord, but there's no estate anymore. He's English, Major; he just resides in Ireland..."

The two cantered up the road, the village ending as suddenly as it began, the horses scattering some chickens that had been pecking the clotted dirt outside the last little cottage.

"And what of the house?" Smith asked. "What will happen to Rambard's Castle if your brother moves?"

By way of response, Violet glanced at him, then put the whip to Bianca's flank. Smith was hard-pressed to catch her as she fairly flew down the lane, past the old Royal Irish Constabulary barracks, above which an orange, white and green flag flapped listlessly.

"McGarry is a bothersome fellow."

This judgement, delivered the next evening by Lord Kilkelty from the comfort of a deep library armchair, was in jest. The earl and Smith were the only ones remaining on the ground floor of Rambard's Castle, all others having retired to their beds. Hunter O'Brien was the last to leave them, a little wobbly, thanks to his host's whiskey.

"He does play his political cards close to his chest," agreed Smith, who preferred Kilkelty's port. Whatever else about the house may have been mediocre, its cellar's quality was high.

"Exactly: a very conscientious chap. He realises that whatever he says before next week *about* next week might be used the wrong way, so he remains silent regarding the special powers legislation. Still..." the nobleman stood and helped himself to some whiskey from a table under one of the rectangular windows "...with his daily telephone conversations with Dublin, you'd think he would let something slip." Though Kilkelty had been resorting to the decanter since soon after dinner, he always added liberal amounts to his glass from a siphon. English or Irish, the aristocrat was a gentleman; if he became drunk, he was not going to let anyone see it.

"What is your opinion?" Smith queried of his host. He heard the mismatched footfalls of the night watchman shuffling through the corridor beyond the library; the practically enfeebled old man's only recourse if he had discovered intruders would have been, indeed, to watch.

"I believe that McGarry will come down against the special powers," Kilkelty answered. He brushed aside several strands of reddish blonde hair from his brow, and nodded as he returned to his seat by the fire. "He'll support the government but not its emergency legislation. I think he sees it as too divisive."

Kilkelty's father had been a good friend of McGarry's, and the present earl had known the doctor since the former's infancy, so his opinion was valuable.

A Lesson in Politics

Smith could not but agree, however, that the new senator's reticence was frustrating.

For several minutes, the two acquaintances drank in silence. Outside, a cold January night was accentuated by the brittle shine of a silver half-moon, suspended above the bare trees of the Castle's park. Inside, the library, lit and warmed only by the fire in the grate, was a snug retreat.

Violet was right, Smith thought: her brother was bored. He spent most evenings, it seemed, in the library, while his aunts gossiped or played whist in the drawing room. With his guests about him, the earl was bright enough, but without friends near by, he had little to do. Perhaps an estate in England, purchased with the proceeds of the sale of the Kilkelty lands — unspent and accruing interest since 1905 — would be just the tonic he needed.

"Hullo, who's calling this late?"

Kilkelty sat up in his chair. The dull thud of the heavy brass knocker against the thick front door had summoned the decrepit watchman, whose clip-clop footsteps made him sound like a two-legged draught horse. Smith listened to the low mumble of conversation as his host quietly rose and set his glass on the mantelpiece. Kilkelty pulled back a panel in the wall by a bookcase. The servant's distinctive approach was echoed by the tread of a younger man who had had, Smith discerned, military discipline.

The earl had just enough time to remove from the small hidden chamber a brace of revolvers and hand one of them — heavy with a full cylinder — to his guest before the library door opened. While Smith quickly put his hands behind his back, Kilkelty hid his own weapon by standing behind his chair.

"Captain Neal, milord," croaked the watchman, a wizened ancient, one of the Tobin family retainers, who would always be retained, working or not. The introduction, more exhaled than spoken, brought a uniformed man into the aura of the firelight.

Kilkelty relaxed, and placed his revolver on a small table. Smith was more wary.

"Lord Kilkelty..." Neal stepped forward and took the aristocrat's proffered hand. He was about twenty-seven, his face alert and intelligent. He moved with economy and intention.

"Major Smith, Royal Fusiliers," Kilkelty indicated the Englishman.

A twinkle shone in Neal's eye as he shook Smith's hand.

"Royal *Irish* Fusiliers," the captain said, referring to his own erstwhile regiment.

Smith nodded. The khaki uniform of the Irish Free State's National Army resembled that of the British, excepting the low-slung holster strapped to the thigh; its wearer looked like a former British Army officer. Then, Neal was

Inductions Dangerous

business-like, at Rambard's Castle on professional matters.

"I'm very sorry to trouble you at this hour, gentlemen," he stated, without a trace of brogue, "but I thought you would want to know that we've received word of a unit of Irregulars moving into the district."

"Something to drink, Captain?" Kilkelty said, indicating the decanter half-full of whiskey. When Neal declined, the earl placed his hand on the stopper of another crystal vessel. "Some brandy then, to keep off the chill..." The captain hesitated a second before politely refusing.

"We'd heard that there were IRA already in the area," Smith said.

"I suspect there are, sir, but in no organised unit," replied Neal. "The locals are irregulars in more than one sense of the term." He might have added that such rebels would have been doubly difficult to find, being men from and familiar with the vicinity. "The unit I'm referring to now is of Galway men, just arrived and, as 'foreigners', if you will, easier to identify. They may have moved into the area over the week-end."

"Why are they here?" Kilkelty wanted to know.

"It's only conjecture, but we believe that the Irregulars' high command think the Mayo men are too independent." Neal seemed pleased with his own force's intelligence. "If that's the case, the Galway unit will be here to impose a little discipline."

"And no doubt to give a practical demonstration of who's in control," said Smith. "Thus, your warning."

"Yes sir."

"Thank you, Captain," Kilkelty said. "I'll let my guests and staff know to take extra precautions."

Once the watchman, who went by the name of Old Nolan (his son, Young Nolan, and grandson, Younger Nolan, both worked at Rambard's Castle, no doubt to be followed one day by the great-grandson, Youngest Nolan), had escorted the captain to the front door, the earl turned to his guest.

"You came to Ireland armed, I take it?" Kilkelty's expression showed that he already surmised Smith's answer. "And your man?"

"Odways can handle himself in an emergency."

"Good. Old Nolan, however, cannot make such a boast," the nobleman stated with a grin, pocketing the firearm he had set aside earlier. "I'm just going to help him in his rounds."

"Sir?"

"I hear it, Odways."

The valet had knocked quietly on his master's door and, hearing no instructions to wait, had entered. The chamber, rather low for one on the first floor of a large house, was dark. The only illumination came from the half-moon, shining into the room at a sharp angle. Smith was in his pyjamas and robe, his Webley service revolver in his right hand, and was kneeling on the cushion of the small settle under one of the windows. The room was cold, air wafting in from under the raised sashes.

"What do you think it is, sir?" Odways too was dressed for bed and had, indeed, been in it. Roused, he had thrown on his coat, taken his own weapon from its drawer and hastened down the stairs from his attic room to check on his employer.

"It sounds as if young Captain Neal may have found his 'foreign' IRA unit," Smith replied.

Odways closed the door slowly and moved to the window. The discharge of firearms — Lee Enfield rifles, to judge by the noises — punctuated the delicate stillness of the night, each shot echoing and lonely, as if there had been none before it. Smith's eyes were closed.

"About five miles away, to the northwest..."

"Not in the village, then, sir?" Odways had been envisioning, with dread, the uselessness of the average mud cottage's walls as protection against modern bullets, and of families huddled for their lives on beaten dirt floors.

"No, Tobinstown is to the northeast," Smith replied. "I'd say, twenty, possibly twenty-five men are involved." For a moment, the firing escalated to a panicky zenith, then eased. "What time is it?"

"Sixteen minutes past three o'clock, sir." The valet slipped his watch back into a wide pocket of his black coat.

"Neal found his quarry very quickly... I hope he is all right. He was in the Irish Fusiliers; he should know his business." Smith opened his eyes. The reports were infrequent now, widely scattered in both time and distance. "Odways, go to the hall and check the telephone, would you?"

Two minutes later, the servant, moving quietly enough to earn mental praise from his master, returned.

"The instrument is not operational, sir."

Smith nodded and said, "That may cause some anxiety later this morning..."

Actor kicked and jumped like a colt. It was not an effort to remove Smith, who was seated securely in the saddle, but simple exuberance. If the dark, shiny-coated stallion had been his own, the major would have tempered his enthusiasm somewhat. But the horse was happy to have a sympathetic rider and, after testing the Englishman cautiously on Monday, played with him on Wednesday.

Lady Violet Harris watched from her white horse, Bianca. She and the major had raced each other over the uneven fields of the Castle's park, and when Violet had had to rein in Bianca at the crumbling boundary wall, Smith usurped the lead by whispering permission to Actor to leap, if he could. The beast cleared the obstacle easily, and now frisked in celebration.

"I've never seen him behave like that before," Violet said, in wonder.

"He's glad," Smith said simply. "Shall we meet you round by the gate?"

The pair cantered for some distance, eventually through hard, brown fields that were sleepily awaiting a spring planting. Beyond the house's northwest corner, the land was a bit more productive, with arable acreage taking the place of bog. At a pleasant pace, Smith and Violet passed the miles to the railway station, located an inconvenient space from Tobinstown.

" 'Morning, your ladyship...sir...'"

The stationmaster, Shaughnessy by name, the collar of his coat turned up against the low temperature, was standing just outside his front door facing the early sun, as though attempting to catch what warmth it could provide. He had been speaking to a member of the Free State's new Civic Guard — the term 'police', it had been decided in Dublin, having negative historical connotations. That man too touched the brim of his peaked cap out of respect to the riders, while his other hand was putting a small black notebook into a pocket of his blue tunic.

"Good morning, Constable," Smith greeted.

"Guard, sir," the policeman corrected conversationally.

"My apologies, Guard. Are you busy this morning?"

"Guard Bailey was just interviewing me about the fuss last night," stated the stationmaster, polishing his spectacles with studied nonchalance.

"The shooting, you mean? Oh, Lord, yes," said Violet, her green eyes widening a little. "I must admit, it terrified me."

"The telephone lines have been cut again," Bailey pointed out. "Is yours working at the Castle, my lady?"

"No, it's not, and it's causing some bother."

Indeed, thought Smith, Violet was speaking of the worry he had foreseen hours before. Doctor McGarry, when informed that communication with the rest of Ireland had been severed, was visibly perturbed. Though he blamed no one — he was too fair a man to require a scapegoat — his concern and even anger over the telephone line's disrepair was manifest.

"The station's telephone is dead, as well," said Bailey, significantly.

"There isn't a telephone in the station, Guard," said Shaughnessy, glancing at the small stone building behind them, "as you know."

"Was I meaning *that* station?" demanded the other. "I was not. I was meaning the Civic Guard station." With a triumphant inhalation of cold air,

A Lesson in Politics

Bailey once more put his gloved hand to his cap, bid good day to the riders and departed, walking away, as did complacent policemen the world over.

After availing himself of a disdainful stare at Bailey's retreating back, and a pregnant shake of the head, Shaughnessy took a step toward Violet.

"Begging your pardon, my lady, but would anyone at the Castle be missing luggage?"

The question surprised the earl's sister, who had been patting Bianca's thick neck. The animal, like Actor under Smith, was impatient to be off.

"Luggage?" Violet glanced at the major with a humorous expression.

"Yes, my lady, probably belonging to a woman of the female kind, to judge from all the hat boxes. They were on the train last Friday, with 'Tobinstown' marked on them, but no one's claimed them."

Smith watched his companion's face grow a little more pale. Seconds before, Violet's cheeks had not yet recovered from the flush that had come from her ride.

"Is there no name at all on them, Mr Shaughnessy?"

"There is not, sir," the stationmaster responded to Smith's query. "There is not one label on them."

"I'm afraid we can't help you," Violet said. "No one at Rambard's Castle has complained of lost bags. Have they, Major?"

"True," confirmed Smith, thinking to himself that while Mrs Pollock might have remained silent in such a situation, Lady Duggan would certainly have informed all and sundry about any missing personal item.

"Oh, well, perhaps they were marked for the wrong stop, and someone at Rathcreel or Duncogan is wondering where their clothes are," said the railway official. He smiled wryly and added, "A mystery for our Guard Bailey to solve."

Violet rode hard after that, giving Bianca her head. The horses and their riders ranged over the meadows bordering the River Hobe, then charged down paths between bogs that resembled mounds of debris carpeted in dingy brown and dull green. As they rounded several piles of boulders, like rubble from a giant's construction site, Smith coaxed Actor to a halt.

"Is that Colonel Ivers's late residence?"

Violet reined in her beast and, pulling the veil of her hat upwards, looked in the direction Smith was pointing. Half a mile away, behind a wicker-work of sleeping trees, some felled and cut up for fuel by former tenants, was what had once been a handsome stone-built mansion. Aside from the entrance facade of steps, pediment and tall, fluted columns, that hinted at a Baroque origin, and smooth bows that suggested the Regency, little remained. Fire, which had discoloured much of what was left, had burned out the house's interior, and the roof had collapsed. One wing, small and forlorn, appeared as if it might still prove habitable, but the rest was mere ruin.

"How did you know?" Violet's strong face was bright and pink again, heated by a good ride.

"Your brother mentioned that it was the nearest house to Rambard's Castle, and that it had been destroyed," answered Smith.

The woman turned in her saddle to gaze more fully at the wreck of Mount Myrtle, the wild state of its park contrasting all the more sharply with the surrounding bog.

"Yes. It was quite lovely. Two hundred years and with many a treasure in its rooms. Colonel Ivers was a Protestant, and often absent, so it was fired. It's one of the reasons Johnny likes me to live at the Castle: I'm someone in residence." Her eyes softened. When in its prime, Mount Myrtle would have been a familiar sight on many of her childhood and adolescent rides. "We are destroying our heritage." She sighed.

A minute later, Violet turned again to speak to Smith, but Actor's saddle was empty. The major was about twenty yards away, on the cushioned earth of the bog. He knelt and picked up several spent cartridge casings from where they had lain, scattered about.

"I knew that we were near the scene of last night's fighting," he said, almost to himself. He glanced up at Violet, who had dismounted by him. Smith rose and indicated a number of spots that looked unremarkable to the woman.

"A man was lying here, shooting. Another there, and there... Perhaps twelve, in a line." Smith stepped carefully, examining the ground. "Here, one was struck in the head by a bullet. Here..." he spread a hand to encompass an area near a boulder "...another fighter was shot, in the abdomen, perhaps the liver." He chanced to see Violet's expression and part of him was gratified to observe that it was one of interest. Nevertheless, he felt that he must apologise.

"I'm sorry, Lady Violet. This is hardly a fit subject for such company." Before the woman could dispute Smith's words, he added, "No doubt Captain Neal would concur."

The National Army officer was approaching across the turf. Smith's keen ears had detected the slow walk of a horse, and he had seen the captain drop from his mount.

"I was rather hoping that his lordship had given publicity to my warning," said Neal, after introductions had been made.

"Oh, he had," responded Violet. "My brother can be personally reckless but is a good host and a considerate sibling. Nonetheless, I insisted upon continuing as if there were no danger. And I have Major Smith's protection."

"I hope none of your men was among those injured, Captain," the

Englishman said.

"Two were killed."

Neal's voice reminded Smith of a thousand other conscientious officers he had known, each of whom had sensed the stab of remorse whenever he had lost a man under his command. It was a feeling that made one certain that if one had performed a duty better, or more quickly, things would have ended differently.

"They were on sentry duty, and must have been kidnapped some time in the night, probably for intelligence purposes. We were alerted when the shooting began. I figure that they escaped and then put up this struggle. Their bodies were discovered just beyond that rise."

Smith's brow wrinkled and he queried, "Do you think that's what happened, Captain? There appears to have been at least two groups of men, roughly equal in numbers: one here and another back along the path."

"It's possible that the Irregulars changed their position during the battle, isn't it, sir?"

Smith nodded, agreeing with the younger officer, but he was not convinced. However, it was not within his assignment to reconstruct skirmishes to which he had not been party.

"I'm sorry about your two men, in any case, Captain." Smith wiped his hands with a handkerchief. "May I ask where in the body they were shot?"

"In the head," answered Neal darkly.

"Both in the head?" The major's face was thoughtful, as he and Violet returned to the saddle. "That's a very unfortunate pair of chances, wouldn't you say? Well, good day, Captain, and good luck."

The rain that started to fall, spattering in sludgy grey drops against the windows of Rambard's Castle shortly after dusk, seemed to match the mood of the guests within the house. The Tobin aunts were uninfluenced by the gloom, and talked in excited tones and present tenses about a society that had long-since vanished. This was followed, as it was every evening, by innumerable games of whist (or 'whisht', as they called it) at tables set up in the drawing room, accompanied by endless cups of tea.

Smith spoke with the maiden aunts for perhaps a couple of hours, as he had each night after dinner. When the cards were dealt, he, pleading that bridge was his game, wandered into the library.

"Sir Horace seemed unusually quiet this evening."

Smith's comment, made four hours later, after Duggan had stormed off to bed, surprised the others in the room. Talk at dinner had been subdued but nonetheless had occurred. Sir Horace Duggan had, as was his wont, restricted his contribution to sarcastic echoes of his wife's words. Hunter O'Brien was the first to laugh at the major's remark.

"Lord, Smith, you're a cool one. To meet you, nobody'd suspect you of having a sense of humour."

"Not that O'Brien knows one to hear it," said Egan, as he rose from his chair and cast a cigarette end into the dying embers of the fireplace. "Good night to you all."

After the general had shut the door behind him, Alan Pollock, who had been warming the same glass of port in his hands all evening, said, "Why do the two of you dislike each other so, Mr O'Brien?" His face, with its startled appearance, looked innocent and unused.

"Dislike, Pollock? Bless you, the man loves me like a brother." O'Brien grinned, the expression pushing his eyes more deeply into their sockets. Then his face sagged, and the humour left it. "But I'll tell you this: that fellow feels what's happening in this country more than Dev and Michael Collins, rest his soul, put together ever could. That blasted beggar Egan loves Ireland, and when his kind dies out, we'll be all the poorer for it."

Kilkelty, reclining in his usual easy chair by the hearth, slowly smiled. O'Brien frowned and peered at the empty glass in his hand.

"This whiskey of yours is potent stuff, Kilkelty. It's time for me to sleep it off before I start becoming sentimental about Cromwell." He stood, pretending to struggle more than he needed to stay upright.

"Yes, I as well." Pollock downed his port in one gulp and reacted as Smith had done, the first time he had tasted home-brewed alcohol as an adolescent. Once his eyes managed to focus again, Pollock said, "Oh, my. Mrs Pollock will have something to tell me about my state."

"Come on, then," declared O'Brien from the door. "We'll help each other up the stairs..."

"At least you were able to communicate with Dublin tonight, Doctor."

Kilkelty spoke to fill the silence left by O'Brien and Pollock's departure. McGarry, as he had been much of the evening — indeed, for most of his visit — was far into his own reverie. He started mildly and blinked his clear blue eyes.

"Yes, yes, I'm very glad that the telephone line was repaired. I must admit that I found it distressing not to be able to talk to my advisers."

"Never mind, Doctor," said the earl sympathetically, after a sip from his glass. "This time next week, your maiden speech will be over and you'll be able to relax."

"Yes," agreed McGarry. "I pray for that."

Smith, watching the sparking end of his cigarette in the library's gloom, thought that the conclusion of an appearance in the Irish legislature to be a poor thing for which to request divine help. But then, politicians had called upon the Deity for less.

The door to Smith's bedroom swung inward slowly, quietly. Of it, he was aware instantly. When he slept, he did so soundly. But the same process which allowed him when conscious to concentrate fully upon two or more subjects kept part of his sleeping mind alert for the smallest change in his surroundings. His revolver, kept in his night-stand's drawer, was in his hand a second later.

"Major?"

Against the dull black of the night, the darker silhouette of Lady Violet Harris evinced her presence as much as did her anxious voice. Smith set his weapon aside and lit a candle.

"What's wrong?"

Violet's hair was loose, hanging in a red, thick carpet down her back. It was tousled, as if by hands run through it, and her green eyes were uncertain, nervous. She wore a thin, silk robe, unadorned, the colour of her name, and cinched at the waist with a matching cord. She shut the door.

"Is something the matter?" Smith reached for his own robe, which lay across the bottom of his heavily-covered bed.

"Yes..." Violet sat on a chair facing the man. "Do you recall the baggage Stationmaster Shaughnessy mentioned to us today?"

Smith tried to make his own hair, mussed by sleep, more presentable.

"Yes: ladies' luggage, unclaimed."

"It's mine."

"Yours?" Smith sat on the edge of the mattress. "I don't understand."

"It's from Dublin," answered the woman, staring at the cold, stone-flagged floor. "My husband and I...are separated. Johnny knows. I've had to have all my belongings sent here. I...I don't want anyone else to find out. It's embarrassing...shameful..."

Smith leaned forward to pat Violet's arm comfortingly. To his surprise, she tightly clasped his hand. Her touch was very warm.

"I have to tell you because you might tell someone about the bags at the station. Then the other guests would have asked questions." Her pale face looked into Smith's.

"You needn't have worried, Lady Violet," he said with a smile. "I wouldn't have brought it up."

Violet nodded and closed her eyes, obviously relieved. She slipped down onto the floor, still holding one of Smith's hands, while one of her own rested on his knee.

"Thank you, Major. I'll have all the bags and boxes brought to the Castle after everyone is gone. This is such a weight off my mind." A catch in her voice made her pause. "You've no idea how lonely it's been. I dread having to tell the children about their father and me..."

She moved forward, her left hand slipped under Smith's robe and up the thigh of his pyjamas, while she brought her face to his and kissed him. Their lips parted while she waited for his reaction. A second later, he kissed her in return.

The early morning was the traditional time for arrests to be made by secret police, and for attacks to be launched by enemy troops. In truth, these actions were moveable from one hour to another, according to many factors. The essence of their timing, however, was always the same: to take advantage of the torpor that fatigue or a sudden waking produced. Thus, three o'clock found Smith dressed for travel.

Odways, seeing his employer's bedroom door ajar, entered. He observed, in the aura of a burning candle stub, Lady Violet Harris asleep under blankets and quilts. Smith, pulling on the cloth cap that he habitually wore for shooting, motioned his servant out into the corridor.

"Complications, sir?" Odways whispered, once the door had been gently closed.

"No, though Lady Violet thought there might be," Smith replied cryptically. "Are the horses ready?"

"Yes sir. Grace is seeing to them."

Outside, in the cold, deep blue night, a diminishing moon had broken through the clouds and was throwing a narrow light onto the landscape, still wet with the late rain. McGarry's valet, shivering in the shadow of the house, held the reins of two horses, saddled and ready for riding. Smith was pleased to see that one, blacker than the air, was Actor.

The lines of Mount Myrtle were imprecise in the vague light of the truncated moon. The irregular, crooked walls cast grotesque half-shades that vanished and grew, depending on the scattering clouds that scudded across the sky. Lights flickered in two of the east wing's glassless windows, and thin smoke ascended from a chimney. By a tangle of severed branches, the relics of a vanished tree, the riders stopped and dismounted. Giving Actor's reins to Odways and imploring the horse to behave, Smith set off to cross the remaining two hundred yards to the ruined house.

Entry to Mount Myrtle's remaining rooms was simple. Though habitable within, the weakened walls of the pavilion exhibited at least one crack large enough to accommodate an intruder. Inside, voices reached Smith's ears as a low buzz, like the noise one might have heard from a badly-tuned wireless. A quick reconnaissance through several chambers determined the major's tactics.

Thus it was that, five minutes later, the door to what had once been Colonel Ivers's study burst open, and three members of the Irish Republican Army beheld a plain looking man with a pair of revolvers aimed at them.

" 'Morning to you, boys," the newcomer greeted, sounding like a Mayo native. "I've come for the girl."

"I didn't hear any shooting, sir. All went well?"

"Yes. None of the kidnappers favoured death to unconsciousness."

Once behind the trees where Odways and the horses had waited, Smith gently lowered his burden to the damp grass. Isobel McGarry was dishevelled, hungry, thirsty and unwashed after days of captivity. Her eyes were big with fear as she glanced from Smith to his valet and back again, and her legs were wobbly beneath her. A quick flick of the major's knife freed her wrists from the rope that had bound them since Friday.

Smith smiled and said, "Don't worry, Miss McGarry. We're going to take you to your father." Under the dull moon, he saw silver tears well in her eyes.

Something else luminous caught Smith's attention just then: a white, riderless horse, wandering in the remains of Mount Myrtle's park. A low groan, like that of someone uncomfortable in her sleep, caused the major to peer over a thick and unkempt hedge of yew. Lady Violet Harris, hastily dressed, lie on her back on the grass; beside her body was a large heavy bough, taken from the pile of arboreal debris.

"I hope her ladyship is all right, sir," said Odways with real concern, as he joined his master to look down upon the earl's sister. "She came riding very fast indeed toward Mount Myrtle. I was afraid she'd give the game away to her friends inside."

Smith stooped and checked Violet's pulse.

"She'll be fine, I expect, other than a broken rib or two. No worse than a fall out hunting." Smith returned to Isobel McGarry and smiled once more at the confused girl. "Back home for you, young lady." He rapidly but carefully deposited her on Actor's back, the animal standing still and co-operatively.

A moment later, Violet Harris awoke with a pained chest, a great headache and nausea. She was alone on a damp sward, except for her horse, Bianca, grazing a little distance away.

" 'McGarry makes impassioned plea for an end to the special powers'."

C read the leader from his copy of the *Irish Independent* before folding it and setting it aside. In return for a previous invitation to his chief's club, Smith had asked him to dine at his own. The Metropolitan's Strangers' Dining Room was not full this dim January evening. There was less noise from conversation than from tinkling utensils and clinking dishes. Even the waiters could be heard moving.

"How in the Seven Seas did you fathom that he'd come out against the Free State's emergency powers even after the IRA kidnapped his daughter?" C's voice, surprisingly silky, despite years of shouting into strong ocean winds and over crashing waves, was low, and indiscernible beyond the table he shared with Smith.

"It was the nature of the man, sir. Even a crime such as his child's abduction wouldn't move him from an action he thought to be in his country's best interests." Smith used a fork to split the mulberry tart on the plate before him. The dessert was a speciality of the Metropolitan Club. "At least, that's what I guessed he would do."

"It's too bad His Majesty's Government hadn't faith in your judgement — or McGarry's honour," C said, shaking his big head. "In spite of our report, they chose to base their actions on the opposite opinion. Still, they won't forget that we got it right, my boy." C dipped into his ice cream with boyish delight. "So, the daily telephone calls McGarry received from 'Dublin' were actually calls from the kidnappers, assuring him of his daughter's safety."

"Yes sir," confirmed Smith, swallowing a mouthful of crust. "They called every day since she was taken from the train just before Tobinstown. It was meant to appear as if she hadn't accompanied her father. Her bags couldn't be taken off the train with her but the labels with her name on them were removed."

"And when the telephone lines were cut, by the Galway IRA men, the doctor became fretful."

"Right. The local rebels had their own plans. They hoped to force McGarry to denounce the government — not realising that he intended anyway to do so, however politely. These Mayo rebels, taking unkindly to interference from their 'foreign' IRA comrades, drove them off after a battle, later repairing the telephone wires. They also captured and murdered two National Army soldiers — to provide a more or less plausible reason for all the shooting."

C enjoyed the taste of his dessert in silence for a moment. Then he jutted out his chin; the nose came with it, giving him the appearance of a living nutcracker.

"Two things, my boy: how did you know that the kidnappers would be at the ruined house...?"

"Mount Myrtle was the only location in the vicinity to which Rambard's Castle was still connected by telephone. One wing looked to be still habitable."

"...And the woman. Was she involved from the start?"

A Lesson in Politics

"I believe so, sir," replied Smith, gathering the last of the crumbs and filling from his plate onto his fork. "Lady Violet identifies herself completely with Ireland, which she no doubt equates with the Republican cause. I recall her remarking upon Mount Myrtle, stating that 'we' were destroying 'our' heritage. I thought at the time that she meant the Irish in general. But she was probably referring to the IRA, who had burned the house."

"And she claimed to own the unclaimed luggage from the railway station to divert you from thinking that it was Isobel McGarry's..."

"Yes sir." Smith had not mentioned in his report the other diversion Violet Harris had attempted. It was, alas, an irrelevant episode anyway, he mused wistfully. He glanced up to find C regarding him through a rimless eyeglass.

"Hmm..." The Secret Service chief let the monocle fall into his open hand. "And Miss McGarry... How is she?"

"Physically unhurt, but terribly shaken. She really has gone with her mother to the south of France now. Her father plans to join them in a couple of days."

"Best thing for her!" C set aside his empty dish and produced another newspaper, that day's *Morning Post*. "And as for you, I see you've wasted no time in accepting more invitations. You're listed among those at Lord and Lady Ragby's dinner party last night. At least, I assume it was you..." With an expression of mixed humour and sympathy on his red and lined face, C pushed the newspaper, open at the appropriate page, across the shining surface of the table. Smith tilted his head to read the column.

"Yes sir," he confessed with a sigh, "that's me: *Major L. Smeeth*..."

Misericord at Dawn

Count Julius Polnicki stood on the trampled slush and swung the blade of his sword back and forth in the air as if he were bored, which he very well might have been. He was in his shirtsleeves, but had not even deigned to unbutton (or remove, since they were of paper) his cuffs or collar. He had not expected the duel to last long. Of the four men present, he was the most calm, to judge by the breath they were visibly exhaling into the chilly morning air.

Behind Polnicki, his second, Baron Norwis, was pulling on the thumb of his gloved hand with his teeth. He was not a man easily frightened, and he had never disgraced the military uniform he wore. He was, however, prone to anxiety, especially over social matters and etiquette. Someone was dying this March morning, and he was certain that the whole affair would be condemned as bad form.

In the background, even more upset than Norwis, but for a more relevant reason, stood the doctor, his black bag at the ready. Competent and dedicated, he hated what he was witnessing, but when a Polnicki requested one's services, one did not refuse. The count regarded the doctor, a Jew, as 'good enough for whomever I kill today'.

Jan Leszinski was a young man, a Polish pacifist, which meant that he fought only when his passions were inflamed. As a Polish aristocrat, his passions were inflamed constantly. He stood, doubled over, his hands gripping his knees, blood dripping as long, red spittle from his mouth. He too was without a coat, but he no longer felt the cold. He was thrice wounded. His sword, lying in a patch of dirty, half-melted snow by his feet, had not even touched his opponent. He slowly stooped further to retrieve it.

The sky was translucent, a milky grey, and the sun was somewhere behind it, just above the eastern horizon. The countryside was awakening.

With a final burst of energy, Leszinski lunged at the count, who had a surprisingly difficult time avoiding his opponent's thrusts. But the imbalance was temporary and half a minute later, Polnicki's blade was through Leszinski's throat, and withdrawn again.

Such was the victor's disdain for the vanquished that he walked from the field even as Leszinski lie on the wet earth bleeding to death, despite the doctor's fervent efforts.

Misericord at Dawn

"Just time for some breakfast, I think," Polnicki said, as he took his coat from Norwis's arm, "before good taste dictates that we leave my opponent's house."

Nine days later, Major Linus Smith, Royal Fusiliers, ostensibly a half-pay officer on the Active List and employed by the Foreign Office, in its Historical Section (in reality, a field operator of the Secret Service), was in Warsaw, walking south on the pavements of Nowy Swiat Street. The sun, in its pale blue sky, both still dulled by the last effects of winter, did little to warm the early afternoon. But Smith's fellow pedestrians did not seem bothered. They were gentlemen who may have been sauntering down the Strand and ladies walking down the Champs Elysee, and they were peasants from the countryside, whose appearances had not changed for centuries. The vehicular traffic, almost entirely horsed, was heavy, directed, when it wanted to be, by policemen. One and all, people, animals, buildings, bore a slightly shabby look, the clothes running to thread-bare, the horses thin, the city dingy. Little else could have been expected after the country had suffered through six years as a battlefield. But, being Polish, the men and women wore friendly, optimistic expressions, and may have been dressed in the robes of kings for all their concern. Even the horses in their traces appeared game.

Passing the British Embassy beyond its gate, Smith continued until Nowy Swiat, a rather short passage, became Ujazdow Avenue. These attractive thoroughfares were Warsaw's principal concourse, and were lined with the town residences of the wealthy. One of the most impressive was the palace of the Leszinskis, behind its high and grimy stone wall.

The Englishman was expected. When a liveried footman allowed him past the lofty neo-classical façade, Smith was a bit disappointed to find himself in a low-ceilinged entrance hall that for some reason put him in mind of the egress to a public bath.

But, relieved of his hat and coat, he was led through a screen of pillars into the great hall. It was a cavern of immense size that soared to a sky-lit dome, ringed half-way up by columned galleries and holding a staircase reminiscent of that in Stafford House. All was marble and bronze, rich hangings and deep carpets. There was nothing small in this vastness except Smith and his guide. A thousand could, and at times no doubt had, entered the room and not filled it.

"Major Selby, welcome."

Prince Tadeusz Leszinski had been awaiting his visitor in one of the drawing rooms. It, like most of the mansion, was decorated in the style of Louis XV, opulent in white and gold, with little colour outside the crimson of the furniture and the paintings on the walls. It gave the newcomer the feeling of having just been woken from a long sleep.

Smith shook hands with the nobleman and was offered his choice of seats. The room was densely furnished, as an English chamber would have been toward the end of the Victorian era. The Briton settled onto a plushly upholstered divan by a thickly curtained window, while his host sat near by.

Leszinski was a handsome man in his late fifties, with grey hair, rather long for modern fashion, and side whiskers, a broad brown moustache and a tiny 'thumb-piece' beard just under the lower lip. The Pole must have been devastating to the ladies in his youth, thought Smith, and, with his sharp blue eyes, perhaps still was. With a cloak and a wide-brimmed hat cocked to one side, he would have been the model of a dashing Bohemian figure. Like many continental gentlemen, he was wearing scent.

"I received a letter of introduction for you from Colonel Sanction," said the prince. "You know him?"

"We've met," answered Smith.

"He and I became acquainted in 1920, when he was in command of the British Military Mission here in Poland. He recommended you to me, stating that you are much interested in shooting."

Smith considered Leszinski's English to be nearly perfect, betraying only the hint of an accent.

"Indeed I am, sir," replied the guest.

"When Sanction mentioned another acquaintance, a Commander Creighton, I realised that you were coming in response to my plea."

A door opened and several servants entered in line, each bearing a tray of refreshments. Smith took the opportunity to study Leszinski more fully and saw no trace of grief in his well-defined features. The Briton might very well have come to Poland for no other reason than sport on the prince's lands, as was the pretext for his — or rather, Major Selby's — visit. His attention was directed to the array of treats laid out for his enjoyment. He selected a small cake with pink icing, and a cup of tea. All the servants but one retreated the way they had come. Smith looked askance at the remaining staff member, standing immobile to one side.

"It's quite all right, Selby," Leszinski said. "This is Kisiel, my valet. He is aware of my association with the British Secret Service. You need hide nothing from him."

"Yes sir." Smith did not share his host's complaisance, but had to trust his judgement. He stirred some cream and sugar into his tea. "I assume that this Commander Creighton was your contact during the War?"

"Correct. His name was no doubt fictional; it was nevertheless to, or through, him that I passed my information." Leszinski smiled. Here was the first hint of a father's sorrow: it was meant to be an amused expression, but it struck Smith as empty. "As I stated, Creighton may have been no more than a postal box, but when Sanction mentioned him in his letter, I guessed the connotation."

Smith had taken a bite from his cake. It was moist and tasty, and filled with smooth strawberry jam. Kisiel was immediate in handing the Englishman a napkin.

"I'm afraid I must touch upon the painful reason for my visit," said Smith. "If at any time—"

Leszinski waved a hand and smiled again, saying, "We Poles have a reputation for being emotional, I know, Major. But during our conversation, I intend to imitate the phlegm of your race."

"Yes sir. Your son was killed in a duel with a Count Polnicki, on the tenth. It was fought at your country estate of Styrzyn. Is that right?"

"It is. My eldest son, Jan is — was — very headstrong, very passionate. He had never fought a duel before, but certainly would not have shrunk from one."

"Polnicki challenged him," Smith assumed.

"No, he didn't."

"Your son, then, challenged him."

"No, Major..."

Smith swallowed some more tea, set down his cup and glanced from the stony expression on Kisiel's face to his host.

"A friend of my son's, a captain in the army named Zulkos, had been the one challenged by Polnicki," revealed the prince, whose features were not as steady as they had been. "Jan volunteered to be his second. I was aware of this arrangement but was not overly concerned by it. Young Zulkos is an excellent swordsman and not one to neglect responsibility. In such a situation, choosing a second should have been a mere formality."

"But it wasn't," Smith commented.

"On the morning of the tenth, Jan and Zulkos set off on horseback for their appointment. Zulkos's mount trod on some ice and threw him. His arm was broken. He sent Jan on with a message that the combat would have to be postponed." Leszinski's eyes had fallen to the rich, piled Turkey carpet beneath his chair. Kisiel was at his elbow a moment later with a glass of vodka.

"Polnicki did not accept the postponement?"

"According to witnesses, the question of re-scheduling was not posed." The prince gained some strength from the alcohol and went on. "Jan informed Polnicki that Zulkos was injured and that, fulfilling the role of the second, *he* would take the principal's place."

"I see." Smith's cup was replenished without request by the servant. "The count accepted this?"

"Polnicki is not the sort to object to killing a man simply because he has no quarrel with him." Leszinski's voice was hard.

"You know him?"

"I do. He had been staying at Styrzyn for a month before the duel. Polish aristocratic households, Major, are something like their English counterparts were two centuries ago. Many are invited for long periods." Leszinski's tone recovered its equilibrium as he discussed a slightly different topic. "Some who are asked are friends, some are acquaintances, while others...are a matter of expediency."

"A matter of politics?" Smith queried over the rim of his cup.

"Exactly." The prince smiled again.

"You stated that Polnicki did not need a quarrel to fight a man," said Smith. "He has duelled much, then?"

"Much," confirmed Leszinski. "His people come from Poznania, that part of my country that was occupied by the Prussians since the partitions of Poland in the eighteenth century. He is most definitely a Pole but has taken on what German characteristics amuse him. He has been duelling since his youth."

Smith was quiet for a moment, during which he noted that the drawing room not only looked huge, but sounded huge. Even silences echoed. He inquired as to witnesses to the deadly encounter.

"Baron Norwis was Polnicki's second," Leszinski answered. "Despite their friendship, he is honest. A doctor was present as well. Peretz. He is a Jew but his word may be trusted nonetheless."

Smith had heard of the average Pole's prejudice against the Hebrew race. He hoped that such unattractive feelings had no place in this affair.

"Well, sir," he said slowly, "to be frank, I don't know what I can do—"

"Major," Leszinski leaned forward in his chair, his face set, "for three years during the War, I provided British intelligence with information from my position as a staff officer in the Austrian Army. I did so at considerable risk to my life and my family's position. I asked for nothing in return; I did it for a free Poland. Though I have had no contact with your country's secret service since 1918, I think I may have earned a little credit, if not for the results of my efforts, then for the efforts themselves. I felt that I could turn to nobody in my own land for this assistance in regard to the killing of my eldest son, so I believed—"

"Prince Leszinski..." Smith could understand the nobleman's anger, and that it required a direction, even if it was not the right one. But he was not about to let his organisation be maligned, even by implication. His words were polite, his tone strong. "You want to know if something was amiss in the duel. I am here to find out. What I meant to say was that it does not appear as if anything was untoward. But appearances are easy to manipulate. My assignment has not yet started."

Another silence hummed in the big room. Leszinski smiled once more, this time with genuine feeling.

"Forgive me, Selby," he said finally. "I am a Pole, after all."

"It's quite all right, sir. I can only imagine the pain you are enduring."

"You must allow me to extend the hospitality of my country house to you. You are, ostensibly, in Poland for the shooting. And Captain Zulkos is still at Styrzyn."

"Thank you, sir," replied Smith. "I do wish to speak to him. But first," the Englishman set aside his cup and saucer before the vigilant Kisiel could re-fill the former, "I have some matters to attend to at my hotel. And then..."

"Yes?" The prince raised his thin eyebrows.

"I want to be introduced to Count Polnicki."

The Klub Mysliwiski was a gathering spot for the élite of Polish society. Prince Leszinski was of course a member, indeed, a leading member, as was Count Polnicki, though he did not visit the institution as frequently. The prince knew that Polnicki and a coterie of admirers resorted to the club periodically for dinner, and agreed to arrange an encounter for Smith that evening.

The Briton sensed an apprehension among those present as soon as they observed Leszinski walk into the building. Smith was certain that he himself was not the cause of this unease, for nobody ever noticed him, so he assumed that a clash between Leszinski and his son's killer was feared. Smith and Leszinski in fact met the count at the doorway to the dining room, as he was leaving with some friends.

"Leszinski." Polnicki was surprised to run into his fellow aristocrat but was hardly unnerved at the meeting. "You haven't been to dinner here since you returned to Warsaw. It is a pleasure to see you." He spoke French excellently

"Selby, may I present to you Julius, Count Polnicki. Count, this is Major James Selby."

"British Army?" surmised Polnicki, switching to English.

"Yes. Northumberland Fusiliers, retired."

"An honour, sir."

Julius Polnicki was a tall, svelte man, immaculate in the uniform of a lancer regiment. The top of his head was bald, but ringed on the sides and back with short black hair. He was striking, rather than handsome, with sable eyes, a long nose, and a luxuriant moustache which ended in waxed points. He exuded strength and confidence, and Smith doubted that the man ever regretted any action he had taken or word he had uttered.

"You are visiting Leszinski here in the capital, Major?"

"And at his country estate. I've been invited to do some shooting." Smith noticed that other gentlemen were avoiding Leszinski and Polnicki, though keeping wary eyes on them.

"A sportsman? I enjoy the company of sportsmen." The count glanced over his shoulder at the four or five men, friends, who were gathered behind him. They too were attired in military uniform, and smiled and nodded at his words. "There is no higher activity for a man than the hunt."

"I can think of one or two, sir," Smith said diffidently.

"Do you mean war, sir? Or the seduction of women? All one with hunting, I assure you." Polnicki's cronies laughed and the count himself grinned. Smith thought it rather a cynical expression. "But, Major, if it is sport you crave, you must come to Koszow, my house in Poznania, after you have finished shooting Leszinski's birds. Have you ever hunted wolf?"

"I've killed wolves," responded Smith, "but the hunting was on their part."

Polnicki laughed, and his friends followed suit.

"Then you will turn the tables! My invitation is open. Send me a note when you wish to visit and you will be welcome!"

Smith shook the count's hand in parting and Polnicki, with his myrmidons trailing behind, walked past. The Englishman glanced at Leszinski but the prince betrayed no emotion.

"That was easy." Smith generally distrusted events that ran smoothly.

"He intended it to be so," Leszinski answered. "He has made a practice to entertain people after they have been my guests. The Polnickis have always been a competitive family." The Pole sighed and shook his grey head. But a moment later, he smiled. "While you are here, Selby, and Polnicki is not, let us have dinner. The club offers an excellent menu."

"What do you think of Styrzyn, Perry?"

Smith's valet, Odways — whose name, for the duration of their Polish sojourn, would be Perry — entered the major's bedroom from the dressing room next door, where he had just finished laying out his master's clothes for the next morning. Everything was illuminated by the soft glow of fire: from the grate, where a big log blaze was now burning itself out, and from dozens of candles set about the room. Smith was in a long chair, enjoying a cup of tea and a book before retiring for the night.

"Quite fine, sir, if I may venture such an opinion," said Odways. "Larger than I expected."

Indeed, Styrzyn was a palace, the centre of its own kingdom. Much of the journey from Warsaw had been by train, passing villages of wooden cottages with thatched roofs. From the town of Dobricgrod, the Britons travelled by

Misericord at Dawn

carriage, an old but well-made machine drawn by four identical horses. The roads were, in places, barely recognisable as such, but were nonetheless crowded. In some spots, despite the earliness of the year, gangs of menders, men and women, were already at work. Peasant carts met on the route made way, and labourers in the fields uncovered and bobbed their heads, out of respect for the Leszinski arms on the carriage doors.

Smith had been given an apartment at Styrzyn twice as spacious as his flat in London and furnished considerably more richly. From his second floor windows, he could look down upon the parterres and paths of the extensive formal gardens, just now recovering their vitality after winter. Beyond these were the three thousand acres of park, created two centuries before from the forests of the Carpathian foothills. Farther away, could be seen some of the four hundred square miles of wood and meadow, farm and village that his host owned.

"Many of the Polish aristocracy still live in a semi-feudal manner," commented Smith, thinking of dinner earlier in the evening, served in one of Styrzyn's five eating halls. The procession of guests to their meal (the number of temporary residents at the prince's house always allowed for a procession or two) had been flanked all the way by servants in breeches and powdered hair.

"I spoke to one footman, sir, whose father had worked for the prince, as *his* father had, and *his* father, and *his* father, too." Odways was ensuring that the maid assigned to Smith's room had properly prepared the sheets on the wide, canopied bed.

"On the subject of the staff," Smith said, closing his book: "I was hoping that you might ingratiate yourself with Kisiel or one of the other upper servants while we are here. I'd like to know what they thought of Leszinski junior, and of Polnicki's visit."

"Actually, sir, Kisiel has already invited me to his rooms for a nip of something Thursday evening. That's his night off." If Odways was proud of this achievement, he did not show it. "He worked for years in America, so he speaks a debased sort of English. If you can spare me, sir."

"Don't be too conscientious, Perry," warned Smith, good-naturedly. "I can't afford for you to become more valuable to the Service than I."

"Very good, sir."

Smith had experienced dawn in many lands, under many conditions. Friday's first light had been proceeded, as every morning's was, by nature waking itself. The cranes had started the day before anyone else, calling shrilly to each other. Then the snipe had begun their throaty drumming and the woodcock their cries, like children snoring. As the sun rose, all the other birds of the countryside commenced their songs. They reminded Smith of an army that was shaking off the sleep of a night that had been far too short.

The Englishman was standing in tall reeds by the edge of a pond on Prince Leszinski's property. His knees were cramped from squatting in a hide for hours on end, his legs ached from straining and bending, and his shoulder was sore from the recoil of his gun. It seemed to him that these minor pains had been much more minor just a few years before. Nonetheless, after the perspiration he had sweated finally evaporated, he was growing tolerably warm in the spring sunshine, and he felt good.

He heard a man, young from the sounds of his exertions, approaching through the marshy grass that covered much of the area, and smelled the cigarette he was smoking and the eau de cologne he was wearing.

"The keepers tell me that you have exceeded everyone else's bag, Major," Andrei Zulkos said in French, as he neared Smith.

The Englishman glanced across the soggy ground to where the staff were collecting the ducks from the dogs, who had retrieved almost every bird that had fallen into the cold water. The other guns, most of whom had been staying at Styrzyn for weeks, if not months, were happily congratulating each other on their morning's sport.

"They say they have never seen anyone shoot so fast yet so accurately."

Zulkos was twenty-five, only a couple of years older than his late friend, Jan Leszinski. His face was an oval, with its small features gathered near its centre. When in repose, the little green eyes, thimble-like nose and carefully groomed moustache could have belonged to the editor of a moderately popular gardening magazine. When excited, the animated visage could have had no other owner but an infantry officer.

"It was a good morning for shooting," Smith remarked simply.

"A glorious morning," agreed Zulkos, gesturing toward the lightening sky with his left hand. The other hand's fingers, emerging from a cast carried by a sling of linen, were immobile. "Jan would have loved it today."

"He was good with a gun?" asked Smith, absently watching one of the dogs bounding through drowned plants, a dead drake in its mouth.

"Not really, no." Zulkos chuckled. "He simply enjoyed the sport of it. Rising at two a.m. — not an easy thing for a Pole of the better classes to accomplish, I must impress upon you — trudging out to the ponds through these boggy marshes, waiting in the hides, the first blasts from the guns..." Zulkos paused, as if in thought, then harshly threw his cigarette, only half-consumed, into the water.

"I still can't believe he's dead," the younger man said. "I'd arrived only the day before...the duel. We hadn't seen each other for months, and now it's as if he's merely...elsewhere. Do you understand what I mean?"

Smith could empathise. He had lost many acquaintances during the War — wars, in fact. When one met a fellow only intermittently, it sometimes took a while to realise that one would never meet him again.

"His poor father... He is the best of Poland, you see." Zulkos turned his eyes to where the towers of Styrzyn could be seen through clumps of trees, its grey walls seeming, in the early sun's rays, to be a bastion of the Carpathian Mountains beyond. "He is a nobleman, a prince of the House of Leszinski. He cried at the funeral and, I suspect, will never do so again, at least not in public." Zulkos grinned sadly. "We Poles are proverbially demonstrative, but the prince must have had an English ancestor, for he has a stiff upper lip."

"I'm still confused over what happened," said Smith, a statement only partially true. "What caused the duel in the first place?"

Zulkos peered at the dozen or so men who comprised the other guns of the shoot.

"It was my fault." The Pole began to walk, aimlessly, stepping first one way, then another. "Do you know much about etiquette in Poland, Major?"

"Not a great deal."

"It can be complicated, even for a native. I had arrived at Styrzyn on the ninth. That evening, a big dinner, with a dance to follow, was given by the prince. Those already at Styrzyn were of course invited, which explains my presence at the events, but many of the prince's political associates came, too. It was a grand affair.

"At dinner, I discovered that I was to be seated next to Countess Polnicki. I think in England it is the duty of a gentleman to engage the lady next to him in conversation, is it not?"

"It's considered a privilege, rather than a duty, but yes, the expectation is the same." The major neglected to add that modern times were unfortunately eroding even the most polite customs.

"So it is here," commented Zulkos. "What if the gentleman does not know the lady?"

Smith nodded his head, indicating that this was a practical problem on occasion.

"It's to be hoped that a good host or hostess would not let that happen," he replied. "But if it did, there would be no great impropriety in the gentleman introducing himself."

"It is a grave error here, Major." Zulkos frowned heavily, though the expression had nothing to do with the bright sunlight now strengthening across the landscape. "I think it may be a punctilio derived from the days of the old Austrian Empire, for I've not encountered it save here in Galicia. But, perhaps, that may be because I've not known the circumstances to arise anywhere else."

"I assume that you were not introduced to the countess," Smith said.

"And I could not very well ignore her throughout dinner," stated Zulkos. He raised his left arm in resignation. "I tried to find Polnicki to present me, but he must have been absent for a few minutes. At last, I realised that there was nothing for it and took my place." The young man struggled to withdraw his cigarette case from inside his coat, his sling and unfamiliar left-handedness making it all but impossible. Smith offered his own.

"Thank you, Major." The Pole paused in his narrative to inhale some smoke. "I couldn't have asked for a more agreeable neighbour during the meal. But her sensibilities were fickle, and she reported my breach of etiquette to her husband."

"And he challenged you to a duel."

The other guns called over to Smith and Zulkos, telling them that breakfast was laid on at the head gamekeeper's lodge. The Briton signalled that they would join the group later.

"I was in the ballroom, standing with Jan and admiring the ladies as they danced by. Polnicki strode across the floor toward us." Zulkos shook his head, the features on his face growing even smaller as he expressed exasperation. "The fellow amiably mentioned that I had been conversing with his wife. Then he dashed a tumbler of vodka in my face."

" 'You will give me satisfaction for the insult, will you not?' " Zulkos imitated the deeper voice of the count. "All the while, most charming, even disarming in his manner."

Smith thought 'disarming' an ironic description in the circumstances.

"Jan volunteered then and there to be my second." Zulkos frowned, his abbreviated eyebrows knitting together, and he kicked at a tussock of sodden grass. "I saw no harm in it, damn it... I am a capable swordsman, and I guessed that Polnicki would choose that weapon."

Smith was aware that, unlike the English custom, on the Continent it was the challenger who selected the means by which an affair of honour was to be settled.

"And the next morning?" More birds flew overhead.

"The next morning was cold, after a slight thaw." Zulkos's topical non sequiter was, in fact, to the point. "Jan and I were riding to the field, a spot several miles from here. We left very early, for though most at Styrzyn knew of the duel, we purposely put it about that it was to take place several days later, and we didn't wish to be seen that morning."

"To avoid interference."

"Yes." The Pole drew deeply on his diminishing cigarette. "We set off before dawn and conversed as we rode. I wasn't paying attention and my horse lost his footing on some ice. I am considered a fine rider, but some things are beyond one's control. The animal fell; I landed awkwardly."

"Your arm was broken," said the Englishman, "and you despatched Leszinski to arrange a postponement of the duel."

"Correct, Major." Zulkos's little eyes followed the arc of his second cigarette as he tossed it into the pond. "I was specific in the instructions I gave Jan. As my second, he should have carried them out. But he took my place."

"Were you surprised?" The sun was now pleasant on Smith's face. The day would be warm and fair.

"I was, yes, though perhaps I should not have been." Zulkos kept his gaze downcast. "I made my way back to Styrzyn, feeling very sorry for myself. It wasn't until I reached the house that I remembered a foolish remark I had made the previous night."

Smith sensed bad news creeping relentlessly up the back of his neck.

"I had been at Styrzyn for a month or so and commented to Maria — Jan's sister — that Polnicki would be visiting. She seemed disturbed by the news, so much so that I selected another subject for our discussion." The Pole sighed. "The count's reputation as a womaniser is wide-spread. I deduced, perhaps correctly, perhaps not, what the cause of Maria's distress might have been."

"And you communicated this to your friend?" Smith did not try to keep admonition from his voice.

"I merely remarked that I would be fighting Polnicki for both of us." Zulkos shook his head once more. "Jan is — was — as capable of deduction as I."

The two men were alone in the landscape. The prince's other guests, the game keepers, loaders and dogs, had all disappeared, having tramped through the marshy ground to a lodge a mile or so away to slake their appetites. The light of the sun had turned the pond's surface into a glaring sheet. Smith and Zulkos were not enough of a presence to frighten away wildlife, and the returning ducks broke the harsh reflection as they landed in the water.

"As soon as I can move the fingers of my right hand," Zulkos said, patting his cast, "I will cross swords with Count Polnicki, for my friend."

"He's very good, I understand," Smith countered.

"I will be better," stated the Pole, with determination.

The size and shape of Poland kept changing throughout history. When it first coalesced as a political entity, it was even then larger than England. Union in the fourteenth century with Lithuania, at the time a powerful grand duchy, expanded it to vast proportions, while subsequent weak periods brought successive dismemberment by stronger neighbours. Napoleon erected a French client state but for a hundred years before the Great War, Poland's only existence was a vague one, governed as little more than a Russian province, with millions of Poles living as minorities in Germany and Austria.

The new, independent Republic of Poland, founded in 1918, was extensive, the sixth largest state in Europe, in both area and population.

"So Prince Leszinski lives in what used to be part of the Austrian Empire, sir?"

From the window of their train compartment, Smith and Odways could see the plains that formed central Poland, with their intermittent forests. Villages appeared to be rare, and farmsteads not much more common. Cottages were of wood, sometimes of whole logs, with thatched roofs, the walls often painted with primitive designs. The fields were returning to life, and labourers worked the brown land.

"Yes," answered Smith, turning from the window, "the southern portion of this country used to be the Austrian crownland of Galicia."

"And this Count Polnicki lives in the western part, that belonged to Germany before the War."

"That's why Prince Leszinski was in the Austrian Army for much of his life, and Polnicki in the German." Before Odways could ask, Smith said, "Captain Zulkos was raised in the Russian zone of Poland, and was in the tsar's army."

"It must make running the new country hard," Odways stated, peering out the window again.

"It does; each part has its own history, customs, administration, school system." Smith almost smiled. "Not only that, but thanks to the settlements after the War, a third of the country's populace isn't even Polish. German minorities in Poznania, Bylorussians in Polesie — most of the prince's tenants are Ukrainians. Every country created or enlarged by the peace treaties has sizeable ethnic minorities: bitter resentful groups who refuse to assimilate and are hated by their new masters."

"Won't this lead to trouble later, sir?"

"Indeed, Perry," assured Smith. "Politicians love their countries' soldiers, to make such provision for their future employment."

"Yes sir." Odways's face did not reflect any emotion he may have been feeling. Smith decided to distract himself — if not his valet — from such thoughts.

"Tell me again about your conversation with the prince's manservant."

"Kisiel? Yes sir." Odways settled back into the cushioned upholstery of the compartment's seat.

As was the case when British country houses were visited, the servant of a guest was considered a guest of the host's staff, and dined with them. Odways had eaten a fine meal Thursday night (a meal prepared by the second-cook, a French-trained Swiss whose skills would have surpassed those of the best chefs in many first-rate restaurants) with the upper servants in the steward's room. Several of his fellow diners could speak English, after a fashion, and everyone was kept entertained by Odways's attempts at the native tongue.

Afterward, he retired with Kisiel to the latter's apartment, which consisted of a bedroom and two parlours. Kisiel was a well-mannered person, as might have been expected of a nobleman's valet, who had spent his youth working in the townhouse of a wealthy Lublin solicitor, and his early manhood working as an employee in an elegant New York City hotel, whither he had emigrated. The Great War had brought him back to Poland and, despite his American-accented English, he was in some ways quite cosmopolitan.

"Vodka does make him talk, though, sir," Odways explained, as their train trundled jerkily through the city of Lodz, "and he falls under its influence quickly. After two glasses, he started telling me more than he ought to have."

"And he spoke of everyone," said Smith.

"Nearly everyone in the country, sir," Odways answered, possibly impressed in spite of himself. "I know who on the prince's staff has a liking for who else; why the previous housekeeper had to resign; why the groom of the chambers puts so much sugar in his tea..."

"Did Kisiel mention guests, visitors to Styrzyn?" Smith's eyes were on the rolling landscape outside the compartment window. The train was in the ethnic heart of Polish territory, known as the Kresy (from the German word 'kreis', wondered the major, meaning circuit or district?) but would soon be in former Prussian lands, if the wheezing engine, betraying signs of great fatigue, held out.

"Oh, yes sir. Members of their parliament, generals of their army, officers of the French military mission, aristocrats... All their stories came tumbling out. Few of their names were pronounceable, though, sir." By way of explanation, the valet added, "They're all foreigners..."

"Would a spy or blackmailer find Kisiel useful, do you think?" Smith judged the Polish manservant to be too indiscreet for his position.

"I don't know about that, sir," replied Odways, giving the question some consideration. "A funny thing about the man is, he told me much, but got his facts mixed up. He'd be describing Lady So-and-so as very fussy and then," the valet imitated the intoxicated gesticulations of his continental counterpart: " 'No, wait... That's Lady So-and-so's daughter... Or is it Countess What's-it? And Colonel Such-and-such is having an affair with his brother's wife... No, I'm thinking of General Whoever...' " The waving of the arms and the slapping of the forehead ceased and, clearing his throat, Odways resumed his own persona. "Mr Kisiel was very entertaining, but I can't say that his stories made complete sense, sir."

"I see." Smith regarded his employee with disguised good humour. "If his facts cannot be trusted, what of his opinions? Did he have anything to say of Count Polnicki?"

"Nothing good, sir," revealed Odways. "Kisiel thought him a villain, improper in his manner toward any and all female staff pretty enough to attract him, and the same with the female guests. Though Kisiel did seem to get along famously with the count's own valet." Odways noted. "The fellow doesn't hold his liquor as well as Kisiel himself, I was told..."

The Englishmen arrived at Polnicki's house, Koszow, in the early evening. The countryside in the former German province of Poznania was flatter than Galicia and, since its geography included many small lakes, marshes and fens, Smith guessed that the opportunity for duck and snipe shooting would be even greater than on Leszinski's property.

Spring was more advanced here than in the foothills of the Carpathian Mountains, so the Englishmen's journey from the tiny village railway station, where they left the train, was by country cart. As the primitive vehicle, with the even more primitive driver, bumped uncomfortably along back roads with the speed of erosion, Smith decided that he would have been unsurprised if they had had to have ridden on top of a pile of mangolds or potatoes, or whatever crops were grown here.

Fortunately, Koszow was only a mile away from the station. When the Britons arrived, Smith was taken directly to his host. Koszow was, apparently, a two-storey mansion in the baroque style, a small version of that favoured by German princes of the early eighteenth century. Despite the imposing portico, with its columns supporting the heavy attic-level pediment, the visitor surmised that this was a former farmhouse, overgrown and, eventually, given a fashionable façade. It had no doubt originally been the home of yeomen, whose place in society had improved with their finances.

Smith, tired and dusty from his journey, was led to a rather spacious room on the first floor, that had been converted into a kind of gymnasium. Ropes hung from the ceiling, which had been raised; mats, weights and a wooden horse all testified to the chamber's purpose. Two servants stood by the door, while Julius Polnicki fenced with another man in the centre of the room.

The count moved fluidly, his body supple and seemingly untroubled by the limits of physics. He parried the thrusts of his opponent as if the latter were an old man, yet both swordsmen were skilled, it was plain to see. Dressed in white, with quilted beige padding as armour, Polnicki could have been wearing tennis flannels and been in no danger of injury. After he noted Smith's arrival, he ended the exercise with an easy victory.

The two duellists bowed to one another and Polnicki strode over to his visitor. The aristocrat was hardly perspiring, the disarranged hair on either side of his otherwise bald head the only sign that his fencing practice had constituted an effort.

"Welcome to Koszow, Selby." Polnicki shook the Briton's hand. The count's servants quickly divested him of his protection, leaving him stripped to the waist. He was handed a towel. "I won't ask if you had a pleasant journey, since I suspect that you did not. The railways in this country haven't recovered from the War yet, and most of the carriages we're using are Russian and so they stink." He wiped his face and chest with the towel and left it on the unpolished wooden floor for one of his footmen to retrieve. "Do you speak German? Yes? Let us use that, then, for though my English and French pronunciation are adequate, my vocabulary is less so."

The count's English, Smith thought, was very good, and his French probably of the same quality. But his German could not have been bettered by a Berliner.

"I always do something very physically demanding just before dinner," said Polnicki, "whether it is fencing, riding..." He eyed one of his maids, a strong, big-boned girl with a blank expression hauling two large pails of steaming water down the corridor outside the gym. "...Or something else. It stimulates the appetite. One of my servants will show you to your room."

Smith quickly discovered that Polnicki was an unpleasant man. He also possessed much charm so that, for short periods of acquaintance, his ruthless and unsympathetic nature was masked by a rough but companionable exterior.

While at Styrzyn, Smith had been fed a rich and imaginative menu, prepared by a French chef who could have learned his craft at the court of the Sun King, and served in fabulous dining rooms that may have been modelled upon a wing of Versailles. The fare at Koszow was simple: the main dish (here preceded by fewer courses) being something that his host had shot and then had had roasted by his plain cook. Instead of the array of wines at Styrzyn, vodka and beer were the staple beverages.

During dinner, at which Smith and Polnicki were the only ones present, the count related anecdotes of his services with the German Army. Those years seemed to comprise nothing but violent, bawdy and careless stories. The Pole had fought throughout the Great War on the Eastern Front, and treated even the sacking of hapless villages as if they were grand jokes.

"When am I to have the honour of meeting your wife?"

The dinner had at last ended and Smith was led into a long, narrow sitting room with ceilings low enough to touch. The decor here, as everywhere in the house, was masculine, from the mediocre family portraits on the walls of men in uniform to the thick fur rugs strewn across the cold, stone-flagged floor. There was no indication that Countess Polnicka had ever resided at Koszow.

"Not during this visit, I'm afraid, Selby," replied the Pole.

While the Briton sat in a large armchair before a blazing wood fire, his host reclined in a duplicate. His long legs, stretched out before him, the soles of his boots nearly singed by the flames in the grate, accentuated his tall, slender form: a supple body, agile and dangerous in combat. He let his hand fall next to his chair, where he scratched the head of a dozing greyhound, elongated beside him.

"She lives for the most part in Warsaw. We still see each other for special occasions — our visit to Styrzyn last month, for example."

A maid, quiet and pretty, but with a spiritless look on her freckled face, entered with drinks for the men. Smith had been relieved to be provided Madeira; wine was available, it seemed, after dinner. Polnicki's choice was another large glass of vodka. He almost spilled it as he seized the servant and pulled her across his lap.

"But for some reason, my darling wife has long disapproved of the way I live here."

"I can't imagine why," responded Smith, with mock incredulity.

"Ha!" bellowed Polnicki. The girl's expression was a study in acceptance in the face of a lack of options. The count threw her to her feet and slapped her rear end. She left without haste but, it seemed to Smith, had enough emotion remaining to be relieved. "By the way, Selby, if you want one for the night, just take her."

Smith shook his head, saying, "I prefer a bit more sport in my sport." Despite his disgust, he was trying to maintain a comradely spirit.

"Suit yourself." Polnicki took a great swallow of alcohol, then stood and took a box from the mantelpiece. "Speaking of sport, did you enjoy what you had in Galicia?"

"Yes, very much."

"Did Prince Leszinski join you for any shooting?" Polnicki's black eyes watched Smith's nondescript face. He offered the Englishman a cigarette from the teak casket he was holding. Smith accepted one.

"No, he was not in the mood, so it appeared to me."

"Ha! I wouldn't have thought so." The count sniffed in disdain. Then he laughed as Smith, inhaling cigarette smoke coughed suddenly and forcefully. "That's my own special blend. I grew to like it after I relieved a Russian officer of his tobacco in '15. It's of Uzbek origin, from Turkistan. Take some, if you

Misericord at Dawn

wish."

Smith thought the cigarettes a most foul concoction, but he put half a dozen in his pocket, to be polite.

"What do you think of my duel with Leszinski's son?" Polnicki was sitting again, his head back against the stained top of his chair, but he regarded the Briton carefully down the length of his curved nose.

"It was a matter entered into freely by both parties," declared Smith, almost without interest in his voice. In fact, he believed duels to be wasteful, and invariably unfair to one or the other combatant. He would never, however, have refused a challenge himself.

"Exactly!" The Pole slapped the palm of his hand onto the small battered table between the chairs, rattling his glass and making the dog at his feet glance up. Polnicki yelled for more vodka. The maid hurried into the room with a pitcher.

"It is the kind of sport I enjoy: one against one. Do you see these wolves' skins here, Selby?" Polnicki indicated several of the rugs upon the floor. The silvery-grey fur could not have come from any other animal. "I killed each of them. Do you know how these magnificent beasts were done to death on the estate in my father's time?"

Smith admitted his ignorance. He could see that, in spite of his tolerance for alcohol in large quantities, Polnicki was drunk. His speech was slowing, while his actions were becoming exaggerated.

"The foresters here used to track the wolves in the snow, a feat involving no great skill. Once located, the area was cordoned off with rope, which was hung about with coloured rags. The wolves wouldn't approach this barrier. But one side was left free and open, and there the guns waited, to shoot the animals when they were driven."

This method was similar to tiger shoots in India, mused Smith, though one tiger loose in a jungle was a different proposition than a pack of wolves. Still, he preferred stalking to any other means.

"The peasants like that way of doing it," Polnicki said, scratching the chest of his hound as it obligingly rolled over. "The wolves destroy their livestock."

"This isn't how it's done now?" guessed Smith.

"No! I wait until spring, when the snow melts, as it has now. The wolves become difficult to track, yet they retain their winter coats."

"That can't result in the same numbers being killed."

"Then there will be more for me to hunt!" said Polnicki happily, waving a hand. "There is no more roping of enclosures and wholesale slaughter. The peasants will simply have to live with fewer cattle and sheep." He laughed again, though now it was a sloppy sound. "What is a cow compared to a wolf?

What is a peasant compared to a wolf, for that matter?" He leaned over the little table toward his guest, as if to speak confidentially. "Shall we stalk the wolf tomorrow, Selby?"

At this point, the Briton was undecided as to whether he would have preferred to shoot the wolf or his host.

"How does Koszow compare with Styrzyn, Perry?"

It was some time after midnight, and the full moon, visible over the trees that crowded close to Polnicki's ancestral home, was bright, shining sharp and white through the windows of Smith's bedroom. The major was enjoying a final cigarette (one of his own) before retiring, hoping to rid his mouth of the taste of the count's noxious tobacco and indifferent Madeira. His valet, who had insisted in this strange setting on staying up until his employer went to bed, had just finished laying out Smith's clothes for the morning.

"I don't mind the house, sir. It is simple and plain; a bit of a rest-cure after Styrzyn." Odways's reticent face clouded just a little. "It's the air in the place, sir. Poisonous, you might say."

"Yes," agreed Smith. "It's the count. His influence in these parts is, I suspect, both strong and malevolent. Did you get an impression of life below stairs yet?"

Odways turned from his task, saying, "The closest I can come to explaining it, sir, is to say it's a bit like trench-life in the War."

"How so?" Smith was intrigued by the simile. He sat down in a creaky chair.

"Everyone seems to be tense, anxious. They go about their duties normally enough. But they're waiting for something unpleasant to happen; nothing tremendous, but routine, routinely unpleasant. The feeling is everywhere, sir, all the time; so they make the best of it..." Odways's explanation petered out, and he finished setting out his master's garments. "Of course, I may be mistaken, sir," he added, self-effacingly.

"On the contrary, I think—"

A tentative knock on the bedroom door suspended Smith's words. He stood as his valet opened the door and revealed the late night caller to be the maid who had waited upon the major and Polnicki after dinner. Smith made certain that his robe was tied about him to present a decent appearance as the girl, her eyes lowered, handed a note to Odways. As he passed the folded paper on to Smith, the maid, unusually, followed him into the room.

"Thank you," the valet said to her, nodding and smiling, hoping to make her understand that her duty was done. "You can go now. This wasn't a telegram, my girl; you don't have to hang about for a reply."

"She didn't bring the note," Smith said quietly. "The note brought her."

"Sir?" Odways turned and was surprised to be given the piece of paper. On it was written, in a scrawling, drunken script, Smith's alias. Beneath were the English words,

Enjoy. With my compliments. P

"The count sent her as a gift?" Odways glanced up, startled.
Smith set down his cigarette and, smiling warmly, took the young girl's hands. In spite of the resignation she habitually displayed on her pale face, she jumped, and swallowed hard. The major shook his head and gently led her to the door. There, he uttered three of the words he had learned of Polish.
"Sleep well, child."
Smith closed the door behind the astonished offering and put his back to it.
"Count Polnicki is no gentleman, sir," Odways said. He saved such insults for the truly deserving.
"Very true," his employer concurred. His eyes moved to regard nothing in particular and he added, "But it gives me an idea. You may put those away." He indicated his shooting clothes. He was now ready for the wolf hunt on the morrow.

"You look as though you are ready for travelling, Selby, not for stalking dangerous game."
Before the sun had risen, Count Polnicki, prepared for the morning's proposed activities, had found Smith sitting in a stiff wooden chair in the hall. The Briton had been awaiting his host for some time, having foregone breakfast in the hope of catching the Pole unawares. He had succeeded.
"I am leaving Koszow immediately," said Smith peremptorily, standing, holding his hat and gloves. He wore upon his face an expression of exaggerated indignation.
"But why, my friend? What is wrong?"
Polnicki, dressed nattily in various shades of green, with high, polished leather boots over well-worn corduroy breeches, was unsure if his guest was serious. His black eyes, though questioning, were not the unfocussed eyes of the previous night, and the hair that fringed the dome of his head was not unkempt but carefully combed.
"The present you sent to my room last night."
"Did she not give enough pleasure?" The count shook his head. "I will remedy that tonight. Another girl—"
"Did you think that I couldn't get my own?" demanded Smith with ire. "I consider myself to have been grossly insulted."

"But Selby—"

"Your seconds may call upon me at the Hotel Splendide, in Warsaw," the Englishman declared. "It is continental tradition that the challenger chooses the weapons to be used?"

"Yes, but—"

"Good. When your people visit me, I'll have made my selection. And now, Count," Smith drew on each of his gloves with a swift motion, "may I have the dubious convenience of one of your carts?"

"Of course..."

Polnicki watched, incredulous, as his erstwhile guest donned his hat and strode from the hall into the grey hues of the dawn. The nobleman had recovered from his surprise, if not from his incomprehension, and smiled. The expression told of better game in the offing than even a forest wolf!

"But you must have a second, my dear fellow."

Prince Tadeusz Leszinski stood worried and careless of showing it by the fireplace in Smith's sitting room at the Hotel Splendide, four days later. He had received word of Smith's upcoming duel with Polnicki and had come to visit the Englishman, full of concern.

"*At least* one second, Selby, preferably two."

Andrei Zulkos sat on a couch near by, his plastered limb resting immobile on the furnishing's arm. With his other hand, he was attempting once more to free his cigarette case from within his jacket. Smith offered one of the contents of his own case, though he had yet to replenish its stock and only those cigarettes made from Polnicki's poisonous blend remained. Zulkos was too distracted by the subject under discussion to care.

"I volunteer," said the young captain, smoothly exhaling smoke; "I volunteer in the strongest terms to be one of your seconds."

"And I the other," said Leszinski.

Smith had been quietly reading when his visitors had arrived, having travelled north from Galicia together. The Briton observed that the older Pole's somewhat romantic features were constricted, and realised that the prince was feeling greatly that the impending duel was his fault. It was true that Smith was fighting Polnicki because of the earlier combat involving Leszinski's son, but he would have been equally pleased to fight his opponent for any reason.

"Whatever excuse you used, Selby, cannot be the genuine reason for your challenge," Leszinski said, putting a hand to his broad brow. "Why are you doing this?"

"Polnicki offended my sensibilities," answered Smith, truthfully enough.

With his usual excellent timing, Odways entered the room and handed the major his Webley revolver.

"Revolvers?" Zulkos leaned forward, breathing in tobacco fumes. "You've chosen revolvers?"

"Yes." Smith broke open the weapon to examine its chambers. "I'm no match for Polnicki's fencing skills, and I've always considered the rules governing pistol-duelling to be too artificial. I therefore selected something that would appeal to the count, and place us on an equal footing." He slipped the Webley into the drawer of the room's desk and locked it in.

"How so?" Leszinski was still worried.

"On the train to Warsaw, I noticed a wood, some miles to the west of the city." Smith accepted a glass of sherry from his valet. "It suggested to me that Polnicki and I could meet in a similar setting, entering a wood from opposite sides and then stalking each other. We'll need a wood that is not so large that we would never find each other, nor too small as to make the episode ridiculous."

"Good Lord..." Zulkos considered the possibilities, a smile playing over his small, almost feminine mouth. He was brought back to the present by Odways's offer of wine.

"How good are you?" Leszinski wanted to know.

"Excuse me, sir, but the dining room will have your table ready in twenty minutes," Smith's servant said to his master.

"Excellent. The hotel does itself rather well with wine, don't you think, gentlemen?" Smith's change of subject was not intended to be subtle, merely friendly.

Smith arrived at the chosen wood early Sunday morning, about an hour after dawn. The weather promised to be unsettled later, but at the moment the ragged, grey clouds, like dirty, discarded fleece, gave no trouble. The setting belonged to a member of the Klub Mysliwiski, who had been more than willing to lend it to the duellists, and to see that they were undisturbed.

Smith had come by motor-car, journeying from Warsaw with Leszinski and Zulkos in one of the nobleman's Daimlers. A surgeon, an acquaintance of the prince's, had followed in his own automobile, and had parked it behind the Daimler at the roadside. Leszinski's chauffeur waited with the vehicles while the other four walked to the wood, the doctor strolling leisurely, humming a tune and swinging his black bag in the cool air.

Polnicki and his party were not yet present, so some self-conscious small-talk passed the time. Zulkos mentioned the rubble left by the road-mending gangs that they had encountered a few miles back, and wondered if the count might have been held up by a similar obstacle. Leszinski stated that Polnicki was probably late on purpose. Smith wished that he had brought a book.

Then he smiled inwardly as he recalled Odways's reaction to learning that he would not be accompanying his employer to the duel. The valet thought it most unfair; he understood that this was a gentleman's matter but, as he unassailably argued, when the major was asked to a country house party, accommodation was always provided for the inevitable servant, though none was invited. Odways had to settle for ensuring that his master dressed warmly. Thinking perhaps of King Charles I, he explained that he did not want the major trembling due to the chilly morning, and his enemy mistaking it for fear.

"The King was on his way to his execution," Smith had reminded his valet.

"All accounted for, are we?"

Polnicki rode up to the three on a great black cavalry charger; a fine animal, Smith observed, and obviously as wilful as its rider. The count was seconded by two of the gentlemen Smith had seen with him at the Klub Mysliwiski when they had first met. They were also mounted, though garbed in their army uniforms, whereas Polnicki was dressed for a day in the country.

"Leszinski, I thought I might find you here." The count, tossing away the Uzbeki cigarette he had been smoking, spoke German. Smith attributed the idiosyncrasy to Polnicki's desire to annoy. "And Zulkos: always a bride's maid, never a bride."

"Once I can grip with my right hand again, you and I will go through the ceremony together, Polnicki," predicted Zulkos, his features gathering together in anger.

"Oh, so you assume that I will be the survivor of today's activities, do you? Very kind of you, I'm sure."

The count, laughing, dropped to the ground from his horse and tossed the reins to one of his seconds. He asked the other for his revolver. This, taken from a saddlebag, was exchanged with Smith's, for inspection.

"A Reichs," observed Smith, a little surprised: "model 1883. A German Army weapon, but surely not the one you took into the War."

Polnicki raised his thin eyebrows and said, "You're right, Selby. That was my father's and, since it is in perfect condition and fits the requirements of today's arbitrament, I thought that it should see battle once more."

"Its single-action may put you at a disadvantage." The duellists returned each other's firearm.

"I have the feeling that neither of us will afford each other the opportunity for rapid shooting. That's why I never mentioned the subject of ammunition. I suspect neither of us will require extra." The count stood back, his arms akimbo. "This is a shame, Selby. The more I speak to you, the more I dislike the idea of having to kill you. We are similar."

Misericord at Dawn

"Come then, gentlemen," said Leszinski. "If neither of you desires to fight, call this off."

Polnicki turned his black eyes on to the prince, smiling unkindly.

"You would want to see me unharmed, Leszinski?"

"If I must save your life to save Selby's so be it," the prince answered darkly.

"Neither of your seconds seems to have confidence in you, Selby," Polnicki said, chuckling. Then he threw up his hands. "Alas, Leszinski, Selby and I are sportsmen, and the field for today's hunt is settled." He glanced at the Englishman without a hint of reluctance in his strong face. "Is that not so?"

"I propose that we enter the wood there, and there," The Briton indicated two points opposite each other across the wood's width, "at half-past eight. That gives us, by my watch, exactly five minutes to reach our places."

"And if one spots the other after that, the latter is fair game."

Polnicki grinned, and Smith could tell that the count was enjoying himself. The Pole put his hand out and the Englishman shook it. Five minutes later, the two men were intent on killing each other.

The wood was mixed, of coniferous — pine for the most part — and birch. The undergrowth was moderate but the tangle of vegetation that did exist indicated no management by a forester or gamekeeper. The deciduous trees were budding but still largely skeletal; distance was obscured by the thick branches of the evergreens. Smith found their scent strong in the morning air, and he could hear nothing of his opponent.

He moved slowly, caring about every footfall, and he was silent, as if stalking a lion in the Rhodesian bush. Certainly Polnicki was as dangerous as any four-footed predator. He had not its speed or strength, but with his hunting experience, and a loaded revolver, he did not need them.

Time barely moved. Each second required a minute to become the next. Smith stepped so deliberately that the sparrows overhead were undisturbed on their branches. But then, somewhere up ahead, a capercailzie, frightened, burst from where it had been hiding. Smith tried to fix the spot with his eyes, failed, and so closed them.

Old, long-dead leaves mouldering on the damp earth rustled against each other. A breath of breeze brought an odour to the Englishman's nostrils: Polnicki's repellent tobacco; the aroma clung to the count long after his last cigarette had been smoked. Smith could not see his adversary but nonetheless knew his location, to within a yard or two.

Smith levelled his revolver and fired off two rounds in the Pole's general direction, immediately dropping to a squat. The Pole responded with one, then another shot. They showed Smith precisely where the count stood. Even as the second of Polnicki's bullets flew above the major's head, through the air where his chest had been an instant previously — he's good, judged the Briton — Smith fired once more. He was gratified to hear a grunt, and the sound of a falling body hitting the ground. He would have feared a trap, but caught the noise of a heavy metal object striking the detritus out of Polnicki's reach.

The situation in which the count found himself did not prevent him from attempting to seize his weapon before Smith closed the distance between them. But Polnicki's legs would not move, and the pain from his abdominal wound practically immobilised the rest of his body.

"Congratulations, Major Selby," he said, as the Briton stooped to retrieve the Reichs revolver. "I genuinely thought that I would have the better of you."

Smith admired the nobleman's ability to keep a level tone of voice. Supporting himself on an arm, Polnicki might have been relaxing at a country picnic. But perspiration beaded heavily on his bald pate, and his thin lips were set like the jaws of a vice.

"Perhaps you would do a dying man a favour, and tell me the real reason for this duel." The count gazed up at the victor, his eyes as carefree as they ever were. "I assume it had nothing to do with the maid servant I sent you at Koszow last week."

"It was the murder of Jan Leszinski," stated Smith. "And though you killed him in a duel, you may as well have arranged to have him run down by a van in a city street. He was no match for you, but you made the challenge irresistible."

"He required execution. He was a spy, a traitor to his country." Polnicki blinked away the sweat that was now dribbling in rivulets onto his face, and he struggled among half-decayed leaves to find a less agonising position.

"So you learned from your valet, who in turn gleaned it from Kisiel, Prince Leszinski's man, during your last visit to Styrzyn."

The count almost forgot his pain as he regarded Smith strangely. He had no idea how the Englishman came to be aware of these things; but he supposed that it did not matter now. He smiled charmingly.

"Kisiel is a loquacious fool when in his cups," he said.

"He is also an unreliable informant," observed Smith. "He attributes the characteristics of one to another, then to a third or a fourth. *Jan* Leszinski was never a spy."

Starlings flitted on to the bare branch of a birch above, wondering if the humans below were done making their frightening noises.

"The prince then? Yes, I see...Well, the loss of a son is strong punishment, isn't it?" Polnicki now seemed bored with the subject and indicated his revolver in Smith's left hand. "I have no son for an heir, only an effete cousin with a

Misericord at Dawn

pigeon-brained wife. I give that weapon to you. Mount it on your wall as a trophy in lieu of my head." His features squeezed together as he barely controlled his reaction to a flame of pain firing through his torso. "Now... We both know that my wound is mortal, with or without medical attention. Will you be a gentleman and administer the misericord?"

Smith did not hesitate. The bullet between Polnicki's eyes killed him instantly.

That evening, Prince Leszinski played host to Smith at the Klub Mysliwiski. A private dining room was secured and a dozen or so of the nobleman's friends were invited to meet the Englishman. He realised that he was someone easily forgotten, and Smith considered it unusual to be the centre of attention, if only for a while.

Andrei Zulkos termed the dinner a celebration, though neither Smith nor his host agreed. The Briton never found jubilation in the killing of men, no matter who or why, and Leszinski, however satisfied he may have been to have his son's death avenged, would have preferred there to have been no reason for vengeance.

The meal was excellent notwithstanding, prepared by the club's finest chef, and the wine was from the prince's own cellar. Afterward, the gentlemen smoked. Zulkos, his right arm still encased in plaster, its fingers useless, had his usual trouble in igniting his cigarette.

"I'll be happy when I can at least move my hand," complained the young army captain, sitting to Smith's side. He accepted a light from the Briton.

For a few minutes, everyone around the table in the dark, panelled room enjoyed smoking in silence. Smith watched Zulkos.

It had been too much to expect, he mused, that Jan Leszinski would offer himself up as Polnicki's victim just when the count had required him to do so. It had been Zulkos, the younger Leszinski's friend, who had, as he no doubt saw it, sacrificed Jan for his country's honour. Persuaded by Polnicki that Jan was a traitor to Poland, Zulkos knew that his impetuous crony would volunteer to be his second in any duel against the count. If he had not stepped forward of his own volition, he would have been asked to do so; he would never have refused. The head-strong Leszinski would not have begged to have the duel postponed, if, per chance, a debilitating accident had rendered Zulkos *hors de combat*; a remark or two concerning Polnicki and Jan's sister would see to that.

It had been a plot, engineered by Polnicki, for genuine, if twisted, reasons of patriotism; but it had required a second conspirator, who could only have been Zulkos. The latter claimed not to have been acquainted with the count, but Zulkos had grown accustomed to smoking Polnicki's cigarettes at some time.

Otherwise, he could not have smoked one so smoothly in Smith's hotel room the previous day.

"Tell us, Selby," said Zulkos, his little mouth exhaling a grey cloud, "what are you going to do with Polnicki's revolver?"

All the men at the table turned with amused interest to watch Smith. They appeared honourable men, ready to right an injustice in the old-fashioned way. Really, Zulkos would not have a hope.

"This?" Smith removed the Reichs pistol from his evening coat and languidly spun its cylinder. "I thought I'd give it to you."

As he spoke, the Englishman tossed the weapon sharply to Zulkos, who reacted reflexively, catching and grasping it tightly with the fingers of his plastered right hand. An automatic movement, the Pole had instantaneously forgotten to pretend that his arm was broken, its grip useless.

Every man present peered at Zulkos, at first with incredulity, then with confusion, and finally, with understanding and anger.

"I think you'll know what to do with it," ventured Smith, as he stubbed out his cigarette, and stood to leave.

One Soft to Petrograd

"One soft to Petrograd."

The very phrase had an outlandish sound to it. But the small man in the ticket office had appeared uncomfortable even before Linus Smith had made his request, and it was not simply because he had already spent several hours on a hard stool in an unheated room. He had seen Smith approach and, though he barely noticed the man, he had quickly appraised the worn but serviceable black leather coat and peaked cap that he wore. No one in the new Russia of the Soviets wished to displease a member of the Extraordinary Commission.

"All the softs are taken, comrade," the station agent said, uneasily.

"Find one anyway," said Smith, as if this solution should have occurred to the ticket-seller. "I don't intend to travel hard."

"Yes, comrade." The railway official complied, after a slight hesitation, and issued another ticket for a soft compartment.

As Smith turned away from the barred window, other travellers, waiting in line to purchase their tickets, or milling about on the platform after having acquired them, made way for him. The personnel of the Cheka did not wear uniforms as such, yet everyone in the country had rapidly come to recognise their appearance, and even Smith caused something of a reaction when he was so garbed. This, the fact that there were still classes to rail journeys in Russia, and that the secret police were implicitly entitled to the better grade, should have demonstrated to all who cared to look that things were not as they were claimed in the proletarian paradise.

A 'soft' compartment was what Russians might have considered first class, but no Englishman would have thought so. Russia's industry had not recovered after years of war and revolution, so few carriages had been built in the last decade. Consequently, what was now 'soft' varied in degree: some instances bore the last traces of luxury, while others were little better than freight cars with compartments.

Undoubtedly, more people would be shoved into the compartment Smith chose, as the train had yet to leave the village station, and no one could depend on the time of the next. But at the moment, his compartment was the least densely populated in the soft carriages. He settled himself into the farthest corner of the seat. The stuffing was almost absent from the cushions underneath him, the carpet had been ripped from the floor at one time or another and not replaced, and the window, its pane cracked, was tightly shut against the cold spring night, and allowed for no passage of air. This characteristic was typical of Russian windows, in trains or buildings, and had been, probably since Russian windows had first boasted of glass, Smith believed, and so could not be blamed on the Bolsheviks. But any attempt to force it open, he knew from experience, would have been bootless and, what was more, would have suggested that he was no native.

The situation was not so bad, he mused. Petrograd was only seventy-five miles away: how long, after all, would he have to endure the stuffy, smelly, crowded, uncomfortable ride?

Just a few days previously, Smith had been in Talinn, wearing proper clothes and drinking tea on the thickly-padded cushions of a chintz-covered couch. From the office in which he sat, he could see little of the city's grey buildings with their red-tiled roofs, but felt the salty breeze wafting off the sea. The warmth of the sunshine made it easy to believe that the shores of Estonia had been a playground of aristocracy not long before, when the newly-independent republic had been but a province of the Russian Empire.

"What did they tell you at Headquarters about Gridissov?"

Smith turned from the view and declined a second cigarette from his host. Andrew Beckwith was the passport officer attached to His Majesty's legation, and head of the Secret Service station, in Talinn.

"Not a great deal," replied Smith, after a drink of tea. "Only that he's one of the agents run out of this station, and that he may be in trouble."

"That's about it, too."

Beckwith did not resemble the stereotype of either a bureaucrat or a spy. Tall, thin, elegant, with a relaxed, almost lazy manner, he looked, rather, like a vapid man about town, or a black sheep, sent to the colonies to await his quarterly remittance. A pointed nose accentuated the slopes of both his forehead and his chin, creating a supercilious, jutting impression. When he had been a junior officer in a lancer regiment, he had worn, in accordance with regulations, a moustache, which gave him an air of responsibility. When the Secret Service posted him to Estonia, he shaved his upper lip. Viewing him for the first (or even fiftieth) time, few would have associated him with intelligence — in any form. This disguise, with the invitations he received to almost every social function in the country, made him a prolific source of information on this side of the Baltic Sea.

"Yuri Gridissov is a clerk on the staff of the Petrograd Soviet," he explained, igniting another cigarette for himself. "It doesn't sound like much, I know, but as a clerk, he is shifted from one committee to another, and records most of what goes on in each of them."

Smith set his cup and saucer on the table before him, in a beam of April sunshine as if to keep the tea heated, and accepted the folder Beckwith gave him.

"The quality of his intelligence varies." The head of station leaned back against his desk, his long legs crossed in front of him at the ankles. "But that has to do with where he's put to work. Sometimes, His Majesty's Government finds what Gridissov has to report extremely interesting." He might have been speaking of a horse's capabilities in the hunting field.

"Is he your best agent in Russia?" Smith glanced up from one of the pages he had been perusing.

"I'd say so, yes," confirmed Beckwith, blowing smoke. "We have others, but none as highly placed. Comes of not having a station in the country, I suppose."

"But now, Gridissov needs help."

"So it would appear, old boy. Two days ago, we received word from Petrograd, from one of those agents who aren't as significant as Gridissov. This chap's principal duty is to walk about the city checking for messages from others. The day before, he'd found one: a slip of paper stuffed into a crack in an old brick wall. Written on it was nothing more than a list of groceries and their prices."

"A cipher?" Smith reached for his tea.

"In a way." Beckwith languidly scratched his ear. "Sometimes this second agent will find scraps of newspaper, other times, a child's scribble. Each comes from a different agent, and each means a different thing, something simple. Complicated messages are sent by courier; the grocery list and its like are intended as no more than notifications. If Gridissov had left a torn piece of a ten-kopeck note, it would have signified that he was being re-assigned; if a burned match, he had an unscheduled report for us to pick up."

"And the grocery list indicates danger," Smith said. "I assume that, since Gridissov normally despatches his reports to someone other than the insignificant finder of messages, the trouble he is in must be immediate, and he hasn't time to go through usual channels."

"Exactly, old boy." Beckwith tossed his cigarette out the open window. "One of the problems is, of course, that the chap's distress signal is already three days old." His expression, almost of apology, made it seem as if he were sorry to have spilled a drink on a host's rug at a party.

"Do you think he's been uncovered by the Cheka?" asked Smith.

"I do. The other implication of his cry for help, however, is that, having had time to send it at all, he might have had time to go to ground before an arrest was made."

"Where would he go?"

"To a little bolt-hole we'd prepared for such emergencies," answered Beckwith, as he lit another cigarette. He seemed barely to notice it once he started smoking. "It's not intended to keep a fellow hidden for long, though." Despite his appearance, the head of station's mind was working, and he took a guess at what his visitor was thinking. "All very improvised, isn't it?" His mouth spread in a silly smile. "True, I'm afraid. But until we can get a station in Russia, we'll be at this disadvantage. We've done pretty well, so far. The sad thing is that if Gridissov is in danger, then he, our best man in the country, may very well have to come out."

"You think that's what it will come to?" Smith too believed that to be the case.

"With a gang like the Cheka, there's no half-way measure. If you are suspected, you will be found guilty. And..." Beckwith shrugged with resignation. "We gave the chap our word, you see, to bring him and his wife to safety, wherever that may be, if things went wrong for him."

It was clear to Smith that his host disliked breaking a promise as much as he did himself.

"Then if that's what the situation demands, we'll do just that," Smith said simply. "Now...if Gridissov sent his signal three days ago, then the chances are good that he's been on the run from the Cheka for as long as four, perhaps five. If he's been captured, he won't have been with them for long." He patted the folder beside him. "Condense this for me, Beckwith. Tell me all you know of the man."

"Goin' to Roosha, are you, sir? Bin there once; that was enough."

Henry Chivers was the junior of the two clerks who supported Beckwith in his station work. Not being officers of the Service, the clerks would not normally have been called upon to perform duties in the field, and Smith was curious as to when and how Chivers had crossed the border.

"You didn't like the workers' paradise, then?" he asked.

Chivers peered sidelong at Smith, as if the two were sharing a joke, and repeated, "'Paradise'... If some people who thought that place was a paradise was to go there, without no commissar as escort... Well, you can't persuade some people, eh, Major?"

The clerk was about the same age as Beckwith but was prematurely balding. His pale pate and the sagging skin of his face made him appear older than his years. His expression seemed almost permanently cynical, yet he was cheerful, in the knowing way of the Cockney, and looked as if he might have ended every complaint, however justified, with a resigned shrug of the shoulders.

The two men were seated at a table in a small room next to the clerks' office. The little chamber had the atmosphere of a treasury, its only door opened with a key, its single window overlooking a shear drop of fifty feet to the pavements below. The space within was almost filled with cabinets, bulging with records and documents.

"Now, Major, what sort of name would you like to 'ave?"

Chivers had removed a box from one of the innumerable drawers surrounding him, and had carefully chosen several sheets of stationery from within. He returned the box to its depository and replaced it on the table with a typewriter.

"I once knew a man named Isakov, a book-seller," said Smith, after a moment.

"Right. 'Ow about Alexander Alexandrovich Isakov? Position?"

"Why not reach for the top?" Smith suggested. "Put me in the Cheka."

A wide smile curved across Chivers's droopy visage.

"Now, your talkin', Major. The All-Russian Extraordinary Commission for Combating Counterrevolution, Speculation, Sabotage and Misconduct in Office. No wonder they shortened it to Cheka." Between the carriage rollers of the typewriter, the clerk inserted one of the pages he had previously selected. "No one'll question you with these documents."

Smith watched as Chivers's fingers slowly created a certificate testifying that Alexander Isakov was in the service of the Extraordinary Commission. The clerk apologised for his low speed among the keys, as he had never become accustomed to the Cyrillic alphabet. When he had finished, Chivers placed the paper flat upon the tabletop, pulled a fountain pen from his waistcoat and, hesitating a couple of seconds, scribbled a signature above the words 'Commissar, Extraordinary Commission, Petrograd Council of Workers' and Soldiers' Deputies'. With a grin of anticipation, he then withdrew a folder from another drawer, this one immediately behind his chair. From it, he took a letter and laid it next to the forgery. The signatures at the bottom of the two items were very similar.

"Not bad, not bad," Chivers decided, obviously pleased. "That's Ivan Stigga. 'E's easy. I never could master the bloke what come before him." The clerk put back the letter, which he assured Smith was the station's only example — and a hard-won example at that — of the signature of the current chief of Petrograd's secret police. "Now, for good measure, we'll give you a personal identification, too. You was told a photograph was needed, right? Right. Then we'll do likewise for the mister and missus what's coming out of Russia with you." Chivers grinned. "By the time I add the latest seals and stamps, Major, you'll be able to walk up and shake hands with Lenin 'imself." The clerk glanced at the soldier a little sheepishly. "Well, not quite..."

Beckwith accompanied Smith from Talinn to the Russian frontier east of Narva. The railway crossed the boundary there, and it was the principal port of entry into the Soviet republic from its tiny Baltic neighbour. Smith would be leaving Estonia at a point farther south.

"We have our own gateway into the Bolshevik domain," Beckwith said, as he urged the steering wheel of the station's Model A Ford to keep a straight course on the highway. "Our relations with the Estonian Defence Police are excellent; consequently, we may rely on their assistance whenever we need to go in or come out."

The roads in this part of the world were not horrendous, but were close to it. Beckwith, however, a cigarette between his fingers, behaved as if he were at the tiller of a small sailboat on a summer sea, with no particular course to maintain. The short spring day was ending already, and the vehicle's headlamps were the only illumination, other than a weak blue smear, diminishing by the moment, on the western horizon.

"The Defence Police arrange matters with their colleagues in the Border Guard?" Smith guessed. Bouncing in his lap with every swerve from one hole in the road to the next was a plain Gladstone bag, rather worn and supple, which contained the garb he would wear in Russia. The station maintained a small wardrobe for such occasions.

"Exactly, old boy, but more than that..." Beckwith paused as he peered through the windscreen, searching for a sign in the densely forested landscape. In spite of the hastening gloom, he evidently found it, for he made a turn onto an even less-travelled road. "More than that, the frontier troops just opposite in Russia have been paid handsomely — at least from their point of view — to cooperate. Chivers gets most of his stationery and paraphernalia through them."

"How far up the hierarchy can you bribe?" Smith wanted to know.

"It depends." Dragging on his cigarette, Beckwith was too distracted to avoid a particularly deep trough in the path, and the automobile bounced with a loud bang. The head of station seemed not to notice. "In the case of this specific border post, all the troops there are in my pay, except for their commander; a sergeant, he'd be in our army; over there, he's a commissar." He grinned. "Anyone in charge of anything in Russia these days is a commissar, whether it's a regiment or a cow shed."

"And the rest of the frontier?"

"Much the same, but without the bribes. There are no fences or walls — not yet, anyway. A growing number of troops, all ready to shoot quickly enough, but some open to temptation. Here we are."

The Estonian border post turned out to be a little clapboard-sided cottage; in the night, it might have been any dark colour. Those inside must have heard the approaching vehicle, for the door opened and two men emerged, silhouetted on the porch by the brightness within.

"Hello," greeted one, "we were told that you were coming." He spoke a heavily-accented Russian, as many Estonians did.

Beckwith knew both men, calling them by their names and shaking each by his hand. The ritual was repeated with the pair who had remained in the cottage. The head of station introduced Smith merely as a colleague.

"You choose a good night to cross," said one of the Estonians, the corporal in charge of the post. He was referring to the new moon, but had not an inkling of course that Smith had had no choice in the matter, having to infiltrate Russia as soon as possible. The corporal warmed his hands by the huge stove that took up much of the cottage's interior and, in fact seemed to prop up the roof of the dilapidated building. He still wore his greatcoat and the snow on his boots indicated a very recent excursion outside. "Our friends across the brook have been warned not to look too closely at any passing shadow tonight. But if their commander bids them shoot, they will."

"I understand," said Smith. He hefted his bag. "Is there somewhere I may change?"

The corporal nodded toward an ill-fitting door. It led to a tiny bedroom, almost filled by its beds, stacked one above the other, as in a train compartment. As Smith dressed in the darkness, Beckwith sat at the table in the next room, conversing with the Estonians in their own tongue by the flickering light of a single oil lamp. He produced from his coat a package, filled with bars of chocolate, and Smith heard cries of "Cadbury, Cadbury!"

"We don't bribe the Estonians," the head of station had explained to Smith earlier. "They help because they are ordered and because they know we share relevant information with their government. But a small gift now and then demonstrates a more personal appreciation."

When Smith stepped from the bedroom, handing his everyday clothes to Beckwith, one of the Border Guards, a young private, muttered something in his native language.

"He says you look like a chekist," the corporal translated, his nod indicating agreement, "but that you 'have no face'... Nobody will remember you."

Smith sighed mentally. That was always the case, he thought.

Beckwith glanced at his watch.

"Right on time, colleague. Are you ready?"

Inductions Dangerous

Smith could see the stars from where he sat in the train compartment, next to the dirty window. No illumination cast an internal reflection upon the cracked glass. Neither was there heat, and the temperature was barely above freezing. Remarkably, even the bodies of his fellow passengers, seven tightly packed peasants, failed to produce much warmth. Smith could have been travelling through some sort of bleak underworld, his carriage reeking of black bread and borscht.

There had been no moon this night, as the Estonian corporal had implied, but the stars could throw a surprising amount of light on their own. However, Smith had invaded Russia without attracting attention as he noiselessly jumped the narrow stream marking the country's limits, vanishing quickly into the fir woods that covered the region regardless of politically-drawn boundaries. He had not disturbed the occupants of the Russian border post, a primitive log cabin half a mile away, and his illegal entry was accomplished unchallenged.

Petrograd, though seventy-five miles away by railway timetables, was actually four and a half hours distant as the train squealed and rumbled to a stop at every village and rural halt, to be emptied and filled repeatedly. The only indication that time was indeed moving was the growing greyness that haunted the eastern horizon.

Smith mused that he would probably not have an opportunity to rest once he reached Russia's second city. Gridissov was somewhere there, hopefully hiding in the bolt-hole, the address of which Beckwith had given Smith before the latter's departure. The agent could, unfortunately, just as likely be in detention at Number Two, Goróhovaya, the Cheka's Petrograd headquarters. And as for Gridissov's wife, Smith could only guess where she might be: arrested, free, a fugitive running from capture with her husband, alone. She was aware of Gridissov's work for the British; this was both an advantage and otherwise. Having her know of, and sympathise with, her spouse's clandestine activities, would make the exfiltration easier, Smith realised, once she was found. If, on the other hand, she had been arrested, then the Cheka would be the ones to benefit from the information she possessed.

The hour before dawn might have meant a deserted platform when the train arrived at its destination, yet it did not. Even at Okhta, a small station at Petrograd's edge, crowds waited as the carriages were at last pulled next to the rambling wooden buildings. The prospective passengers were a communist's true proletariat, peasants and factory workers, and they knew well that they outnumbered the spaces available on the train. They began their surging and shoving even before the vehicles stopped. Smith had to be even more forceful in order to fight the tide and escape his compartment.

One Soft to Petrograd

A tram, acting and sounding rather like the railway carriage from which he had just issued, thumped and cracked its way from Okhta toward the centre of the city. Before it reached its terminal at Mihailovsky Square, the horde of travellers it had picked up at the station had evaporated by ones and twos, and only a handful remained to disembark with Smith.

The sky above Petrograd was growing lighter as the sun breached the horizon behind the low overcast. The nights were shortening, slowly but certainly. Smith glanced about him. He had been in this city before and had, in fact, seen the revolution erupt and become the upheaval that toppled the Romanov Dynasty and changed the world. He could only guess what sort of nation Russia might have become if it had been ruled all this time by the democratically-minded liberals who had come to power then, rather than by the Bolsheviks, who seized power in a coup d'état months later.

People were beginning to move about the streets in the dawn's cold bleakness. The snow here was dirty, as it always seemed to be in large cities, crusty brown where it remained untrammelled, otherwise crushed into slush, sluggish, lumpy water running slowly in gutters. But it was clear that none of the snow had been cleared, not even from the main thoroughfares. The last fall looked to have been a week or more previous, yet the only paths cut through it had been made by pedestrians on the pavements, or vehicles, primarily horse-drawn, on the streets, as they forced their way through. At points, even the trams became stuck, their lines still clogged.

Nonetheless, Smith was eventually able to ride out to The Islands, that district of Petrograd raised on what had been the delta of the Neva River, and to Kamenovstrovsky Prospect, where the Gridissovs lived. Their flat was in one of the big houses near the end of the avenue, not far from a large hospital. The house seemed almost a keystone in a terrace of similar buildings, disadvantageously placed for unprepared surveillance. Smith could spend little time on preliminaries anyway, since it was now four days since Gridissov's distress signal had been fired off.

Smith stood opposite his objective, in the shelter of a doorway, for the amount of time it took to smoke a cigarette. It was too cold for the clothes he wore, and the tobacco he consumed was a Russian blend that tasted unpleasant. But at least none of the men and women, stolidly passing him in increasing numbers, noticed anything foreign about him.

"Yes, comrade?"

The building's concierge (if, Smith thought, such a bourgeois term might be used for a representative of the newly-powerful proletariat) was in the hall as Smith entered the Gridissovs' house. He was a thin, nervous man, timid in his approach. Quickly taking in Smith's attire, without bothering to glance at his face, the Russian's manner instantly became deferential.

"Yuri Gridissov." Smith's tone was dismissive.

"Oh... He hasn't returned..." The concierge stepped back, as if hoping to camouflage himself against the dingy tiled walls. "I will inform the Cheka if he does, as ordered..."

"I know he hasn't returned," responded Smith, sounding annoyed. In fact, what the man revealed was news to the Briton — good news, as it implied that the secret police were unaware of Gridissov's location. "It's routine to make certain. And to make certain that you are doing your duty, comrade."

"But of course..."

The old man's rheumy eyes blinked and he paused, as if searching for more subservient words. Smith told him to go about his business, whereupon the concierge gratefully disappeared into his tiny, ground floor room, closing the door behind him.

Flat number eleven was on the third floor of the once elegant building. The whole edifice had, before the revolution, been the home of a single family, and their attendant servants. The owners had been wealthy and their status had been reflected in the house. The steps that curved upward from the entrance hall were of marble, though they and the balustrade were damaged, great chips knocked out, caused perhaps when the heavy furniture had been looted. Indeed, nothing that had been moveable remained from the old days. And above, the plasterwork of the stairwell ceiling had been deliberately vandalised, the glass of the circular skylight at its centre largely replaced by small planks of wood.

The door to flat eleven, the number painted crudely on one of the panels, was unsealed, and ajar. Smith paused on the landing, and felt for the Mauser pistol hidden under his coat. The noises he heard from the other apartments were routine, domestic sounds of the day's commencement. Smith cocked his ear to the door before him and heard nothing beyond it. The flat smelled empty.

The room just within had been ransacked. What furniture there had been was broken up, wood gouged, upholstery slashed; paintings, worthless landscapes and still-lifes, had been torn off the walls; books were scattered, their bindings ripped. In the little bedroom behind the parlour, the scene was repeated, with the linen of a small cot cut up and splinters from a smashed mirror strewn about. Smith shook his head. The Cheka could not have been searching for anything with these methods. It had been wrought through sheer malice.

Smith did not think that anyone had been in the flat for several days. The secret police had seized what they wanted, wrecked the place, and departed. He had refrained from asking the concierge whether Mrs Gridissova had been removed by the Cheka. As a member of the Extraordinary Commission, he surely would have known such a detail.

One Soft to Petrograd

He bent and retrieved a broken picture frame from the debris on the floor of the sitting room. The photograph had been taken, as had all the others that might have been in the flat. There was certainly no likeness of Gridissov, whom Smith knew to recognise, or of anyone else. The pictures could very well have been confiscated for identification purposes, especially useful if a wanted man were still at large.

Before he left the room, he peered from its windows, two overlooking Kamenovstrovsky Prospect, another a drop of ten feet onto a neighbouring roof. He confirmed his earlier observation: the Gridissovs' home was not being watched.

Back in the city, the temperature had risen in the past few hours. The ice that had frozen the river over the winter had broken up and water was running, if not freely at least steadily. If there had been precipitation from the grey clouds above, it might very well have been rain — a cold rain, but not snow. The day remained dry, however, and the only moisture was trampled under foot or running off roofs.

The sad start of spring in Petrograd was mirrored in the faces and attitudes of the people who moved about on their business. Though people were returning to the principal streets, the Nevsky and Leitny Prospects, the Fontanka and the squares, they moved seemingly automatically, their actions as grey as the day, and their clothes as shabby as the grimy buildings they passed.

There were places of vitality, though, such as the Siennaya Market. To recover from world war, civil war, famine, administrative ineptitude, the Bolsheviks had created the New Economic Policy, a temporary 'retreat from communism', which allowed capitalism to flourish on a small scale. Siennaya Square, by the Ekaterina Canal, was filled with tables, booths and sheds, all displaying merchandise for sale. Smith wondered if it struck anyone as telling that in order to revive the country it had been necessary to resort to mass 'speculation', regarded by Bolsheviks as an economy's worst evil.

Probably not, he sighed; at least not so they spoke it aloud.

He wove his way through the stalls and among the buyers and sellers of the market. Here, at least, there was energy. People haggled over prices, almost pointless due to the outrageous inflation, men debated the merits of the various items, women argued over who had seen what bargain first, and children stared, astonished at things they had not seen before. Smith was generally ignored by the throng though, when his garb was noticed, customers and vendors lowered their voices, as if what they were doing were still illegal.

South of Siennaya Square, Smith slipped into a tangle of little streets, some no more than alleys, though the principal doors of the houses opened into them.

His progress was slow, as he made unnecessary turns, doubling back on his route; he eventually assured himself that he was not being followed. His destination was a rubbish-filled court beyond an arch in a crumbling brick wall. Several tenements, on different levels, had their entrances ranged around the yard, each distinguished by a number scrawled in chalk upon its door.

The court stank of decay, and the external staircase which Smith climbed was littered with refuse that even the old, dirty snow of Petrograd had not effectively covered. Flat number eight, on the second floor of one of the buildings, was situated around a corner, with a window on either side of the angle. Smith paused by the window perpendicular to the entrance. Its panes were cracked so badly that they resembled spiders' webs, and the remaining glass so dingy as to be almost opaque. But Smith could see that the room beyond held no occupant.

He rapped on the flimsy door and an instant later, was beyond the corner, peering through the window at the response, his hand near the butt of his secreted firearm.

A man appeared in the sitting room of the flat, having moved, afraid, from what was probably a bedroom. Smith identified him immediately as Yuri Gridissov, though he was altered somewhat from the man in the photograph Beckwith possessed. The Russian was motionless now, but for the trembling that shook his body. He was alone. Smith returned to the door and knocked again.

"Good morning," he said, as Gridissov pulled back the door just enough to reveal a bloodshot eye. "I'm seeking a friend of mine, Mikhail Passov..." The eye blinked. "Mikhail Ivanovich Passov... I was told that he lived here... Mikhail Ivanovich Passov..."

It was almost half a minute before a sharp but almost inaudible "Oh" escaped from behind the door.

"I'm sorry... He's in...Pskov..." Gridissov's voice was high and halting.

"Then I have something to leave for him," Smith said. "May I come in?"

The door opened further, to admit the visitor. Then it was quickly shut again, and bolted.

"Forgive me," said the Russian, gulping. "I nearly forgot what I was supposed to say. I've been waiting for days."

Smith removed his cap and smiled.

"We responded as rapidly as possible. I'm sorry it was not sooner."

Gridissov was a short man, bald but for a monk's fringe about the sides and back of his head, and that a dusty grey hue. His hair must have vanished relatively recently, to judge from his timorous habit of running his hand over where it had once been. His face, long and frightened, like a trapped deer's, looked as prematurely aged as the rest of his head, though how much of the appearance was permanent, and how much due to exhaustion, physical and emotional, was open to conjecture. That he had not shaved for the better part of a week was certain, as was the fact that he appeared unwashed.

"Of course, of course," Gridissov acknowledged, pushing his fingers over his pate. "Thank you for coming..." The pitiful statement of gratitude sounded like a lonely man whose many invitations, long ignored, had finally brought guests, and it affected Smith more than anything else about the agent.

The Englishman searched the flat, confirming his belief that the two men were alone. The bolt-hole was furnished sparingly, cheaply and rudimentarily. Nothing decorated the walls. But it had served its purpose, and had provided a refuge when one was required.

"It's cold in here," Smith said. Unwarmed even to the temperature outside, the rooms were almost uncomfortable enough to see the men's exhalation. "There is wood for the stove... Why didn't you use any?"

Gridissov shrugged, embarrassed, and replied, "I didn't want anybody to know I was here. Perhaps someone would smell the wood burning, or see the fire's glow in the window..."

Smith noticed that the man was still shaking. He smiled again and patted the man good-naturedly on the shoulder.

"Never mind, Mr Gridissov. Sit down." As the pair sat on unadorned wooden chairs facing each others, Smith asked, gently, "Where is your wife?"

Gridissov had absently pulled a pipe from under his frayed jacket. He put it to his mouth and drew on it, trying to suck smoke through the stem. But its bowl was empty.

"Would you like some tobacco for that?" Smith reached into his own coat, intending to break up some of his cigarettes for the man. Gridissov removed his pipe and stared at it. He smiled, thinly, sadly, and shook his head.

"No, thank you. I have tobacco... It's just that...my wife always has my pipe ready for me. When I wish to smoke, I merely pick it up, put it to my lips and light it. She's always done that for me..." Gridissov was silent. "My wife..." He said at last, as though just now recalling the original question. "I don't know where my wife is..." He regarded Smith, blinking.

"Tell me what happened."

"It was Monday, I think..." Gridissov paused again, squinting. "What day is it?"

"Thursday."

"Is it?... Monday, then, yes, very early in the morning, almost still Sunday..." The Russian set aside his pipe and pushed at his scalp again. He was no longer shaking. "I should have been in bed, but I couldn't sleep. Often, when I have a bout of insomnia like that, the only thing that seems to help is a stroll in the night air."

Smith had stood and moved to one of the windows, gently parting the grey curtains. Gridissov looked up to see if the Briton was listening.

"I was gone for about half an hour. It couldn't have been more. When I returned, I saw members of the Cheka coming out of my building. The man in flat six is a well-known anti-Bolshevik. The woman in fifteen assists in illegal abortions. The Cheka may have been there for either of them, or for anyone else, but... Well, I suppose I have a bit of a guilty conscience. I was certain that they were there for me. My wife was in the flat when I left..." He sighed. "Perhaps I should have..." His voice faltered.

"There was nothing useful that you could have done," Smith asserted, returning to his seat. "Was she arrested?"

The Russian glanced at his small hands, lined like his face.

"I don't know," he admitted. "I didn't see her brought out, and there were no black ravens in the street..." Smith assumed that the term referred to police vehicles used to transport prisoners. "But if she was arrested, she may have been taken away before I was there to see... I hid around a corner until the Cheka left, and even after. The windows of my flat were dark. I don't know how long I waited..."

"Did you go up eventually?" asked Smith.

"Yes, and there was no sign of Sonia, no clue as to where she was." Gridissov rubbed his red eyes, as if they had grown even more tired from trying to peer back in time. "Our home was wrecked, torn apart by the Cheka. I didn't know what to do. I couldn't go to work that morning, of course... I left the distress signal where it would be found, and then came here."

"You've been here since?"

Gridissov nodded. It was not difficult for Smith to believe him. He thought now that some of the man's wretched appearance may have been due to hunger. He inquired as to when the agent had last eaten.

"Not since I came here," the agent responded. "For water, I've taken snow from outside, at night..."

That, in Smith's opinion, was an excellent indication of how terrified Gridissov was. The Englishman had had to drink some unpleasant versions of water in his time, but he would have gone without for a very long period before matching his health against the crusty, discoloured snow in the courtyard.

"What about my wife?" the Russian asked, plaintively.

"First things first," Smith said objectively, but with a kind smile. "I'm going to move you from here."

"Where?" Gridissov cast about the dilapidated flat, as if it were the last word in security.

"A safer place. But I'll want to make certain of it first, so you'll have to remain here a bit longer. But there should be no problem, and soon you'll be fed, washed and asleep in a clean bed."

"And my wife...?"

"I'll do my best to reunite the two of you, I promise."

The safe-house was in a lane at one end of Kazanskaya, near the cathedral. Smith had to be sure that it was indeed safe before bringing fugitive there, and so visited it alone. The building's hall porter (looking nothing like the individual who made the term one of responsibility and respect at the Metropolitan Club) expressed no surprise at being asked by a stranger about the flat at the top of the house, and answered dismissively that it was occupied, even intimating a fervent wish for Smith to go away. He remembered that the lodging was in fact empty when Smith explained that he had been directed to the address by an acquaintance named Irene Yonanova. The Russian did not seem less desirous of Smith's departure, however.

The porter, Makiev by name, led the way up the stairs, limping heavily on his right leg. Once the house's attic, the flat tucked under the roof may have been adequate storage, a space for crates of books, or boxes of clothes long out of fashion. But as a habitation for humans, it was cramped and low.

"My cousin will be coming to reside for a few days," Smith informed Makiev, after he had looked over the wide single room. "Has there been trouble with the, er, housing councils?"

"No, none at all," the porter said, in a dry, hoarse voice. "The building's committee has lost interest in putting a tenant in here since your other cousin's visit." One of Beckwith's agents had been providing money for the porter to disburse to anyone in the house who might have inquired too deeply into why the space was not filled. Makiev kicked at the unwaxed wooden floor with his good leg. "Your new cousin... Is he the sort who might pass for a bourgeoisie?"

"He is."

"Good. The city is full of bourgeois squatters. If the Cheka come, I'll simply tell them that I thought he was squatter." Makiev seemed to want it clear to Smith that he was paid to maintain the safe-house, not to defend it. Smith thought this fair.

"My cousin will need food and drink, and soap and hot water with which to wash," said Smith, searching in his coat for a wallet. He glanced at the tiny square window that provided the room's only illumination. "Candles, as well. And clothes. Whatever size you wear will be serviceable."

Makiev accepted the cash Smith handed to him. After he had counted it, the

Russian nodded. The amount given was rather more than that required to buy the listed items, and both men knew it.

"And a woman may be joining my cousin a little later," Smith stated, pausing as he was about to leave the room.

"Another relative of yours?" the porter questioned, almost with humour. "You come from a large family, obviously. Never mind." He shoved the money under his blouse. "We'll manage."

Gridissov was installed in the safe-house before mid-afternoon. After a wash, a shave and a decent meal, he was more relaxed; once he had changed, he was considerably more presentable, even in the used garments Makiev had provided. Smith had never stopped marvelling at how physical well-being could affect its emotional counterpart, and vice versa.

Smith drew from Gridissov information about his wife, the names and addresses of friends or kin to whom she may have had recourse if fleeing from the Cheka. The Briton refrained from mentioning the likeliest possibility, that the woman had been arrested, and was sitting in a cell under the secret police headquarters.

"I'm sorry I don't have a photograph of Sonia to give you," Gridissov apologised, drinking tea from a tall glass. "I didn't have one with me when I went for my walk Monday morning, and all the others were taken by the Cheka."

"That's quite all right," responded Smith, though in fact he felt that the description he had been given of Mrs Gridissova, in lieu of a picture, would be less than useful under the circumstances. Smith was dubious that Sonia would be as radiantly beautiful as the mental image her husband had glowingly painted.

"It's a good sign, isn't it?" asked Gridissov. "It's a good sign that the Cheka took the pictures from our apartment? Doesn't it mean they need them in a search? That would mean she's still free." He pushed a hand over his head.

"Yes," Smith answered, "it's a good sign."

Outside, the short April day had ended, and the subsequent darkness had brought an emptiness to the streets of Petrograd once more. There was no curfew in place, however, and now and then, a wraith-like individual would shuffle down the pavements, head bent, booted feet moving quickly, urged on by the temperature, now freezing again. More startling were the sudden bursts of voices, as pairs or groups broke the quiet with their talk, on their way home from a rare evening out. Even laughter could be heard, floating disembodied through the air, then ending abruptly. Petrograd, Smith found, could be an eerie city.

One Soft to Petrograd

Though his papers would have persuaded any member of the people's militia that Smith belonged to the more powerful Cheka, and indeed would most likely have deceived even an official of the Extraordinary Commission itself — at least until the documents were verified — Smith did not wish to put them unnecessarily to the test. He therefore kept to the side streets, blending his form into the deep shadows cast against buildings by the intermittent light of lamps overhead. In that fashion, he passed from one quarter of the city to another.

The first address he visited gave him cause to think that he may have been on his way to becoming a pessimist. Sonia Gridissova's parents had owned a large and popular restaurant in Sadovaya Street before the revolution. Though the establishment had become 'Communal Eating House Number 22' (with, Smith suspected, a corresponding drop in the quality of both food and service), the old couple still lived in a room above their former business.

Outside the building, overlooking both the front and rear entrances were pairs of militiamen. As Smith observed them from a distance, he wondered if Gridissov could have been correct, and have reason to hope that his wife was still uncaptured. The militiamen, the revolution's replacement for the *ancien régime's* police, did not seem too concerned with trapping a fugitive as she sought refuge with her mother and father. They conversed in normal tones, stamped their heavy feet to induce warmth and smoked cigarettes, the burning tips of which would have indicated the men's locations to all but the truly blind. Wrapped in their greatcoats, their bayonet-tipped rifles leaning against the nearest wall, they did not present Smith with a threatening image. But then, he thought, he was not a woman on the run from the authorities of her own country.

Mrs Gridissova had an uncle who inhabited a part of a basement under his whilom home on the Nevsky Prospect, the house above coming to be inhabited once more, this time by many proletarian families. It too was guarded, in a similarly leisurely fashion, by two pairs of militiamen. A friend's flat near the Fontanka rated six policemen, ranged in couples; but then, there were more doors to guard.

Smith paused behind a wall and ruminated, watched by a curious cat. After the animal had grown bored and moved on, the human asked himself where Sonia Gridissova might have gone had she been confronted with what he had seen. It occurred to him that, since his arrival in Petrograd, he had found only one location associated with the Gridissovs that had not been guarded or under surveillance. The only reason Sonia might have to return to her own home was the best one: she could have had nowhere else to go. Smith lit a cigarette and caught an empty tram, bound for The Islands.

The building on the Kamenovstrovsky was indeed unwatched by the police, secret or otherwise. Smith explored the area carefully, more so than he had done the previous morning. This time, he had greater reason to fear a trap. But except for routine activity near the hospital at the far end of the street, no one was to be seen. He slipped into the house unnoticed. The concierge was absent, no doubt asleep, and Smith was on the third floor in seconds.

It was odd, he told himself, how one could sometimes feel another's presence. Smith's senses had been tuned in the Rhodesian veldt, honed during hunts and skirmishes, and during wonderfully calm nights, when there was nothing else to do but listen and smell. He knew that someone was in the Gridissovs' flat, probably a woman.

Nothing had been touched in the sitting room, it seemed; the floor was still covered with debris from the Cheka's visit. There was almost no illumination from the street lamps outside the windows, and Smith could see only by letting his eyes adjust to the gloom. Beyond, in the tiny bedroom, even his stealth could not prevent his detection by someone awake and alert.

"Who is it?" A woman sat up from where she had been lying, sleepless on the remains of the cot. "Who's there?" The frame of the simple bed squeaked as she put her feet on the floor.

"Mrs Gridissova?"

Smith struck a match. He had been right about the woman's description: it had indeed been somewhat idealised. Yet she did resemble the general image Gridissov had conveyed. The face was more oval, the nose larger, the eyes farther apart and the hair coarser than Smith had been told. But the basic elements were there. Besides which, he admitted that any opinion formed now might not be entirely valid. The woman's face was partially disfigured — temporarily, it was to be hoped — by the extensive bruising that was colouring and swelling some of her countenance.

"Who are you?" she demanded, with some fear, but just as much aggression, as if making ready to fight her way out of a bad situation. She moved her head, painfully, it seemed to Smith, trying to see his face in the fading light of the dying match. He lit another. "Who are you?"

"My name is unimportant," the Briton informed her, "but I've come to take you to your husband."

"You're a chekist," Mrs Gridissova declared, jutting her squarish chin at Smith's garb. When he denied the charge, she challenged him to prove the claim.

Smith said, "You'll simply have to trust me." Certainly he had nothing to show the veracity of his words. Everything he possessed about his person at that moment was meant to indicate just the opposite. "But if I were with the Cheka, you would be under arrest and would have to accompany me anyway." Sonia

Gridissova nodded, her head's movement matching the flickering of the failing match's flame. "Do you have a coat?"

The woman's clothes were dishevelled and of an odd assortment, as if she had attired herself with the remnants of a jumble sale. From the debris that had once been the contents of a wardrobe, she managed to find not only a coat but a hat. With many quick, nervous glances at Smith, she followed him down the stairs to the hall, and to the front door of the building.

"Where is my husband?" she asked on the way. "Is it far? How will we get there?" The questions were not those of a frightened person, but someone careful and reasoned.

"We'll take the tram," answered Smith, in a low tone.

"Openly?" Sonia's small eyes registered incredulity. "I am wanted by the Extraordinary Commission..."

Smith paused after opening the door, and peered out to the street, then turned and said, "As long as you are with me, it will be believed by anyone who thinks about it that that is who you are with. If you are challenged, don't speak; leave it to me."

"All right." Sonia sounded wary.

Smith did not have a hard time crediting the notion that such a woman might have avoided capture by the Cheka. Sonia was tall, only an inch or two shorter than he was himself, bigger than Gridissov, and correspondingly strong. Despite the bruising that mottled much of one side of her face, Sonia's eyes clearly suggested intelligence.

"Am I presentable?"

Smith was uncertain if the concern addressed the woman's attempt to appear unconnected with a Cheka manhunt, or mere feminine vanity. He glanced at her and nodded.

"Quite presentable. Let's go."

Few people rode the trams this early in the morning, fewer still rode them to or from The Islands. Smith and Sonia sought the relative privacy of the car's rear seats, as far as possible from the driver, who could not see them in the lightless interior.

"How did you evade the Cheka when they came to your flat Monday morning?" Smith asked eventually. Sonia's visage was a silhouette against the intermittent passing streetlamp. "Did they hurt you?"

The woman shrugged, replying in an almost nonchalant manner: "When they came, they knocked on the door and announced themselves. They always do, I'm told. I saw that my husband was not in bed — probably on one of his nocturnal walks — so I knew that he was safer at the moment than I was. Before the Cheka broke through the door, I'd pulled on a sweater and stepped through the window."

"There isn't much of a ledge to cling to," Smith recalled of her house.

"Not the windows facing the street," said Sonia, almost with exasperation. "There is another overlooking a neighbouring roof. In my haste, I fell. That is how I injured my face."

"Is it painful?" asked Smith sympathetically. The query met with another shrug, this one implying stoicism.

"It didn't occur to the Cheka that I might have simply slipped outside, through a window, so they didn't look. I heard them tearing up the flat..." She paused, until the tram's bell concentrated her thoughts again. "Once they left, I climbed back in, nearly frozen but still free."

"We'll get off up here," Smith interjected. "What did you do then?"

"I put on some clothes and tried to find a place of refuge, until I could think of what to do next. I knew my husband had instructions on how to act in such a situation, but I had no idea where he was. Wherever I tried to go was guarded by militiamen: my parents' rooms, my uncle's... So I returned home..." The hesitation at the end of the sentence reflected the limbo Sonia Gridissova felt herself to be in at the time.

"That was impressive presence of mind, stepping through the window as you did when the Cheka arrived," remarked Smith. Sonia peered at him sidelong.

"I am fully aware of what Yuri has been doing," she said dryly. "Acting quickly has been at the back of my mind since he started living his double life...since *we* started living it. In that situation, one acts quickly or doesn't get the chance to act again. Here?"

The two disembarked. As they passed the Kazan Cathedral, dark and empty, the eastern sky behind the horizon of buildings was starting to lighten. Other people were on the streets now, intent on their business, and unconcerned with Smith and Sonia's. The Englishman kept an eye on passers-by but saw nothing suspicious, and within minutes had brought his charge to the attic room where Gridissov waited.

Smith opened the door and saw the man sitting on the narrow iron-framed bed within, his face thin and lined in the aura of a low candle. Sonia stepped past the Briton, out of the shadows of the landing and into the room, where what light there was caught her. Gridissov's eyes widened and he opened his mouth to speak.

"Yes, Yuri, it is I, your wife..." the woman said, walking slowly, almost shyly, forward. Her words were almost breathless. "Your wife is alive and unhurt..."

The last sentence was not strictly true, thought Smith, but relative to what her condition might have been, Sonia's injuries were not significant. She smiled — almost fetching in her nervousness, Smith considered — and held out her arms. Gridissov reacted slowly, as if bewildered by her bruises, but at last stood and embraced her.

Smoking a cigarette on the landing half a minute later, Smith was relieved. He had not been entirely certain of the woman's identity until Gridissov hugged her. But he had had little means of confirming who she was other than by simply presenting her to the waiting man.

The hall-porter limped up the stairs and accepted one of Smith's cigarettes. His pale face grew whiter as he inhaled the smoke, and he coughed.

"Everything is all right?" he asked after he had recovered. "Your cousins are happy?"

Smith nodded, saying, "I thought I'd give them some privacy."

Makiev regarded the closed door of the attic flat.

"You will be leaving soon?"

"Tonight, most likely." Smith listened as a woman's laughter floated from within the room. "We'll need some food to travel with."

"That should be no problem," the Russian said, taking the money Smith offered him. "But I will need to wait. It's very early yet." Finishing his cigarette in a burst of choking, Makiev slowly retreated down the stairs again, almost dragging his damaged limb after him.

Smith knocked gently on the floor of the flat before entering. Sonia was sitting close to Gridissov on the edge of the cot. She was smiling, while his expression was, paradoxically, one of anxiety mixed with relief.

"Yuri was afraid that I would be angry with him," the woman told Smith, as she took Gridissov's hands and squeezed them. "He thought I would feel he'd abandoned me when the Cheka came to our home." She glanced at the man next to her and her smile grew. "He knows now that is nonsense."

"I've explained...to Sonia...that you will get us out of Russia," Gridissov said, freeing his hands and filling his pipe with tobacco, "even though I don't know how you will accomplish it."

Smith offered the Russian his small box of matches.

Sonia was studying the Briton's nondescript face, as if seeking a clue to their escape but, finding none, stated, "The border is guarded, with constant patrols; everyone knows it."

"There are ways through," Smith assured her in a confident voice. "But we won't leave until nightfall. We'll eat, and the two of you will get some rest." He tossed the stub of his cigarette into the flat's small stove, which was producing barely enough heat to be considered warm.

Sonia still seemed doubtful of Smith's ability, and looked to Gridissov again.

Inductions Dangerous

He, puffing on his pipe, told her not to worry.

It was dark again. Despite the lessening hours of night, Smith had not seen the sun the whole time he had been in Russia. Such pervasive gloom and cold made it difficult for him to recall that he had travelled through this land when it had broiled under a blazing summer sun. Russia was a nation of contrasts, in almost every respect.

As if to make that observation personal, Smith no longer wore a leather coat, with a peaked cap to match. He knew that he was an anonymous man, but if anything were to draw attention to him, it was the garb of a Cheka official. As helpful as that might have been to him on the inward journey, he did not wish his party noticed on its way out. Now, his coat was cloth and shabby, and the astrakhan on his head was of dirty wool. He retained his false identification as a member of the Extraordinary Commission, however, as it might have proved useful yet.

A train whistle, strained and thin, signalled the approach of the long-awaited transportation. The would-be passengers, most of whom had been sitting or squatting on the suburban station's wooden platform for hours, stood slowly and gathered their belongings which, though relatively meagre, would make the cramped journey tighter still. The Gridissovs rose as well, Yuri nervous, indecisive, while Sonia pulled her scarf closer about her head, both to keep her face warm and to hide its bruises.

There would be no 'soft' ride this time, Smith realised with a sigh; no separate compartment, not even an over-crowded one. He and his charges would be travelling as ordinary citizens of the new proletarian republic, and would have to fight for what they wanted. But whatever the case, he warned his companions, they must have places on this train.

Smith kept telling himself that he had been in more uncomfortable situations. He always tried to mitigate wretched circumstances in this manner, and, for the most part, such statements were true. But they rarely made him feel better.

The narrow space of a 'hard' railway carriage was nearly filled with rows of planks, like berths, but fixed lengthways along the inside of the walls, three high, with an aisle down the vehicle's middle. Officially, one passenger was allotted to each plank, which would serve as both his bed and his seat for the journey. The paucity of rolling stock in the new Russia meant that the windowless carriage was filled beyond capacity, and even the aisle between the rows of triple berths was congested with passengers and their baggage.

The Gridissovs shared a plank, and neither of them looked to be enjoying the experience. Opposite them, Smith sweated within the layers of his clothes,

One Soft to Petrograd

trapped between a snoring soldier on one side and a mother with her wailing infant on the other. His endurance was tested by the six hours he spent in that position.

Like the tram ride to The Islands in Petrograd, the farther the train journeyed from the centre of population, the more passengers disembarked than got on at each station. The sound of the train as it rumbled through the dense woods of northwest Russia changed as it neared Lake Peipus, on the Estonian border. Fewer trees between the rails and the water altered the noise Smith heard, until the lake was left behind, and the old, more solid sound returned. Smith knew that he would soon be breathing fresh air again.

He dropped to the floor of the carriage the next time the train began decelerating. Gridissov did the same, and Sonia, waking from a restless half-slumber, followed. Once the train stopped, no one accompanied them through the sliding door of the vehicle, into the night outside, numbingly and suddenly cold after the airless fug within.

There was not even a station to signify this stop. The engine pulled away with a squealing, clanking noise, dragging its cars with it, leaving Smith and his companions standing on a platform of badly-hewn boards, amidst an oval clearing in the forest. At the far end of the platform, a rudimentary hut had been erected, and from a little tin pipe in its roof, a curl of smoke drifted into the now clear sky. From the shack's tiny window, came the only addition to the natural illumination provided by the stars.

"Where are we?" Sonia whispered. She peered about her forlornly, and grasped her little string-tied bundle, containing a few extra garments and some food.

The door of the hut opened joltingly, and a yellowish light streamed into the night. A member of the Russian Border Guard stepped out, his unlaced boots crunching on the old snow. He approached the newcomers, drawing on a greatcoat. A couple more soldiers, curious rather than dutiful, appeared behind him.

"Good evening, comrades," the first sentry greeted, in an urban accent. His tone carried a suggestion that he did not wish to be bothered more than was necessary. Smith thought of him as a corporal, though in the new Russia, he held no rank. "We don't get many stopping here, this close to the frontier."

Smith ignored the Gridissovs' furtive glances and casually asked, "How far away is it?"

The corporal regarded Smith with suspicion but, as he buttoned his coat, asked simply, "Who are you, comrade?"

"Isakov," replied Smith, producing his documents, "of the Extraordinary Commission."

Inductions Dangerous

The corporal paused almost imperceptibly as he adjusted his wide wool hat, and his attitude became slightly more respectful. One of his colleagues had brought a lantern, and the three of them examined Smith's papers.

"Nobody told us you'd be visiting our little wayside halt," said the corporal, returning the forgeries.

Smith smiled, as one might at an unfortunate but hardly unexpected situation.

"Does anyone ever inform you fellows of anything?"

The frontier guards chuckled.

"How may we help you?" the corporal queried, a little more good-humouredly.

"I need to keep the border near without crossing it. Can you tell me where it is?"

"Not far at all," responded the senior sentry, explaining that Russia ended not half a mile distant, due west. "If not for the forest, you'd see a long, low hill, with a kind of natural ditch beyond it. On the other side of that, is Estonia."

"Excellent." Smith replaced his documents inside his coat. When he withdrew his hand again, it held a flask of vodka. He shook it. "There isn't much left, but why don't you boys have what there is?"

Two of the guards grinned, but the corporal frowned.

"You won't need it, comrade?" he wanted to know.

"I'll have my fill where I'm going," Smith said mysteriously, making the sentries wonder about the chekist's secret — and no doubt enviable — mission. "But I'll want the flask back when I return this way tomorrow." He tapped the silver vessel, with a coat of arms of noble provenance engraved upon the surface. "It's a souvenir, you see."

"Good luck to you, then." The corporal glanced at the Gridissovs, as if unsure where to place their participation in the chekist's assignment. "Good luck to you."

As soon as Smith and the Gridissovs disappeared into the forest, they headed west. The snow here was as old as that in Petrograd, but it was clean and white; between its reflective smoothness, even under the heavily laden branches of the evergreen trees, and the sky full of stars, Smith had no difficulty keeping his bearings. Gridissov expressed some doubt as to the trustworthiness of the border guards, but Smith had had a rough idea of their location, and the corporal had merely confirmed it.

The Englishman's companions were not in a condition for a long journey by foot. Physically and emotionally drained by the past week's adventures, they were further tested by having to trudge through the deep snow of untracked wilderness. Where the density of the trees had lessened the fall of snow on the ground, there were boughs and bracken to negotiate. The temperature had not risen but Smith, having grown used to it, felt the cold less; the Gridissovs did not and trembled as they walked. Not more than an hour after the train had deposited them in the woods, they were nearing the limit of their endurance.

"Keep going," Smith urged them sympathetically. Through breaks in the trees, he showed them the low ridge the corporal had mentioned, a smear of purple across the dark blue of the night's horizon. "It's not far now."

The Russians were slowing, moving with ever less willing, automatic steps. Smith decreased his speed as well, and no one noticed when he dropped behind and blended with their indistinct surroundings.

Sonia felt the first bullet's impact before she heard its report. The little bundle to which she pointlessly clung flew apart, ragged clothes spreading out before her as the shot passed within inches of her body. A sharp crack followed immediately. Both she and Gridissov turned to see Smith sprinting toward them from the blackness of the trees.

"Run!" he ordered, gesturing with his drawn Mauser pistol. "Run!"

Gridissov started ploughing through the hard snow, causing white explosions with every lift of his feet. Sonia hurried after him, calling out for him to wait. Smith was surprised at the speed with which Gridissov moved, fuelled by the genuine fear of being caught, so close to freedom. Sonia, on the other hand, no more tired than he, was being left behind.

"Don't stop!" Smith yelled needlessly. He caught up to the woman and turned again, firing two rounds from his weapon. Startled, Sonia was spurred on, rushing inelegantly in her clumsy attire, but at least narrowing the gap to Gridissov.

The three climbed up the obtuse incline of the ridge, then slid down the other side, repeating the process, in reverse, in the ditch beyond. A brief struggle with the bushes growing in the bottom of the gully was followed by the more difficult fight upward. Neither Gridissov's determination to escape nor Sonia's fear of being shot were enough to propel them through the crumbling snow, and Smith had to haul first one, then the other to level ground again.

"They won't follow us here," he declared, breathing hard despite his fitness. Gridissov suffered a coughing fit, bent double and spat. Sonia, surrounded by clouds of exhalation, was shaking with the exertion of the past two minutes. She gestured insensibly, and could not make herself understood until she was able to speak.

"You...almost...got us...killed..." she cried loudly, incredulously. Her small eyes narrowed with fury. "You promised...to help us... That was how...you get your...friends out...of Russia...?"

Inductions Dangerous

"No, of course not," replied Smith. He had replaced his pistol and was mopping his brow with a gloved hand. He seemed to be looking for something amid the scattered pines among which they stood. "I chose that spot at random, spontaneously, picking one of the halts where the train paused. I wasn't about to let a Cheka operator learn how and where we cross the Russian border." He breathed deeply, recovering now from his efforts, and brushed crystal snow from his coat. "That is why you were sent to accompany us, isn't it?"

Smith disliked sweating profusely in cold air. It not only chilled him but made his clothes uncomfortable to wear, rather like walking in soaked shoes. His brow, armpits and more sensitive areas began to tickle now, as the perspiration evaporated, and would soon start to chafe.

He turned to Gridissov, whose aching limbs and pounding head appeared to have been forgotten with Smith's words. The expression on the Russian's face, already drawn with fatigue, was not only one of fear, but also of hope, as well.

"You can admit it now," Smith told him. "We're in Estonia."

"Yuri," the woman said softly, "your wife loves you. She—"

"My wife is in the Cheka headquarters in Petrograd," Gridissov interrupted wretchedly. "This person is a stranger to me. I never saw her before this time yesterday."

"You fool!" The woman spat the exclamation remorselessly, her strong features growing hard. "You will never lay eyes on your wife again."

Gridissov turned from the remark, his countenance stricken. Perhaps more to divert his thoughts than from a real desire to know, he asked Smith how he had guessed the truth.

"Let's walk while we talk," the Briton suggested. Part of his attention was still diverted, and he indicated a direction.

"I will go nowhere with you!" the false Sonia stated.

"You're a woman," responded Smith, "so I can't strike you even in this situation. But you are also my prisoner, and I feel within my rights to bind and gag you, and drag you after me, if needs must. Or..." He glanced at Gridissov, standing distraught near by "...I'll simply let your husband shoot you."

After a few minutes of tramping through the dark woods, the chekist stumbling in front and the two men walking abreast behind her, Smith explained that it had been Gridissov's pipe that had given the game away.

"My pipe?" the Russian repeated, instinctively reaching for the item, tucked away under several garments.

"You told me that your wife always tended to its preparation, and that you never gave it a thought until you actually smoked it. Yet..." Smith inclined his head, as if listening for something just within earshot. He straightened again.

"Yet when you were re-united with your 'spouse' in the safe-house, not only did she not fill your pipe, but you did, without comment. You clearly did not expect her to do what your wife usually did."

Despite the situation, Gridissov smiled.

"Very clever," he said. "But that couldn't have been everything."

For a moment, no one spoke, only the clock-like trudging of six feet making a dent in the silence

"No," admitted Smith, talking again at last, "but because of it, other things that had seemed odd made sense. The first thing that struck me was the fact that your flat had not been sealed after the Cheka had searched it; they wanted me to go inside and see that no one was there. They had removed all photographs of you and your wife, so that I could not identify the latter. Then there were the words the impostor uttered when she met you at the safe-house. 'Your wife is alive and unhurt'. She knew that you would be shocked by her impersonation of Sonia. What she was telling you, before you could react, was that your wife was well, but implying that she would remain so only if you co-operated."

"Yes, yes, exactly so," confirmed Gridissov. "She informed me of this explicitly when you left us alone after we met. But...but what is this all about, this charade?"

Smith stopped.

"I'm afraid further elucidation must wait," he responded. He raised his hands over his head. "Do this. It will keep them from shooting you. I hope."

A second or two later, the three travellers were surrounded by members of the Estonian Border Guard, all armed with rifles pointed in their direction.

"So what *was* it all about? The exfiltration routes?"

Andrew Beckwith lit Smith's cigarette with a match, then lit his own. Smith breathed in contentedly. It was the first British-prepared tobacco he had enjoyed in a week, and after smoking Russian blends in the interval, it was rather like sleeping in a bed after nights of camping rough.

The greyness of the hour before dawn had metamorphosed into a translucence, followed by the appearance of the orb of the sun itself. Smith had spent the short period since his arrest by the Estonians in the stuffy warmth of one of their frontier posts, larger than the one from which he had entered Russia, but more primitive, largely of sod, like the cabin of a settler newly arrived on the Canadian prairies, though strengthened with timber. The hospitality was advanced, however, and Smith was partly restored by the refreshments of salted black bread and strong, hot tea with sugar. His claim to be British, despite the papers he still carried, had provoked caution among his captors. The young subaltern in charge of the sector had summoned his captain

Inductions Dangerous

from company headquarters, ten miles away. That officer realised that whatever was afoot required more authority than he possessed. This vacuum was eventually filled by the arrival of the commandant of the Border Guard, the director of the Defence Police and Beckwith, all coming from Talinn.

"Yes..." Smith answered his countryman's question. Still dressed as a fugitive Russian, he pulled his shabby coat more closely around him. The dawn, the orange of the sun still fresh on the land, felt colder than had the dark night. "I suspect that your 'doors' into Russia have been causing a draught in the committee rooms of the Cheka. The latter had no idea where your entry points were, so they devised a plan. They would force one of your agents to flee, then watch how we spirited him to safety."

The door to the hut near by opened and the director of the Defence Police, a harmless-seeming man named Torop, stepped out to ask Beckwith if he was ready to return to Talinn. The head of station begged a few more minutes. When the door shut again, the Britons resumed their conversation.

"How long do you think the Cheka knew Gridissov was working for us?" Beckwith tucked his coloured scarf more tightly about his throat, giving the jutting look of his face more force, as if it were being squeezed off. He drew on his cigarette. "His intelligence has been verified as genuine as late as last month."

"He's probably been compromised only a little while. The Cheka needed to give us very little time in their scheme, to make us take their bait out of Russia as quickly as possible, by the shortest route. As well, they required someone above suspicion in your mind, so that there would be no thought of it being a trap. Therefore, they couldn't afford to use anyone to whom they had been giving false information; on the other hand, they couldn't afford to allow a genuine spy to continue siphoning off good intelligence. I think they implemented the plan as soon as they uncovered what Gridissov was up to." Smith watched ash from his cigarette darken the white snow at his feet.

"They most likely planned to capture both Gridissovs," he continued, "keep the wife as a hostage and replace her with an impostor. As actually happened, it was planned to have the 'wife' tell whoever was sent to help them that she had eluded the Cheka, and hid where I was likely to find her."

"Why replace the wife?" Beckwith stamped his feet to reclaim some feeling in his extremities.

"Even with Sonia as their prisoner, the secret police couldn't be sure Gridissov wouldn't lie when he was forced to describe the route and precautions used on his eventual escape. So he became nothing more than the bait, Sonia the insurance that he would not tell me the truth, and the impersonator the informer who would report to the Cheka about the exfiltration."

One Soft to Petrograd

"But it turned out that Gridissov accidentally avoided arrest."

"Yes, which necessitated the impostor being rather quick-witted when she at last met him." Smith shook his head as he tossed away the stub of his cigarette. "It was damned clever. Finding a woman who somewhat resembled Sonia Gridissova; removing the real woman's photographs, so I would have to rely upon a verbal description of her; even disguising the false Sonia with bruises..."

"That took dedication," said Beckwith.

"And audacity," Smith responded. "But the same can be said for the whole plan. It had its risks, such as putting the impostor in the Gridissovs' flat. The Cheka had to narrow down the number of places I could find her, and hope I'd go back to the couple's home when I'd found all the other possible refuges guarded."

Beckwith too discarded the remnants of his cigarette, only to light up another, as the two walked back to the guards' hut.

"I think the biggest gamble, though, was yours," the head of station remarked. "How could you be certain of crossing the frontier at a spot sufficiently discouraging to persuade 'Sonia' that it wasn't the usual exfiltration point? After all, you couldn't depend on the Russian border troops firing at you."

"I didn't depend on them," Smith stated. "Those lazy fellows were nowhere to be seen. *I* had to play their role..."

At the far end of the little stretch of road was a throng of men, some attired in leather coats, others in plain, unadorned grey uniforms. With them, under a red banner, furling and unfurling in the ambivalent breeze, were two women and several more men, seeming to press both fearfully and impatiently against the pole, striped scarlet and black, barring their way.

At the near end, by a similar turnpike, was another knot of men, some in civilian garb, the rest in a variety of uniforms. A lone woman stood here, waiting under another restless flag, this one coloured white, black and blue.

Anton Torop, director of Estonia's Defence Police, wearing uniform for the occasion, looked up from his watch and nodded. Two members of his country's Border Guard pulled back the barrier and Linus Smith, definitely not in uniform but, rather, wearing one of his better suits, hidden by a long overcoat, stepped forward. Between him and the police chief was the woman who had masqueraded as Sonia Gridissova two weeks before. The swelling under the bruises on her face had vanished and the discoloration itself was much reduced. Her strong features had become more attractive, in an ordinary way, thought Smith.

"You did very well," he told her, gazing straight ahead. Simultaneous to their progress, a group started walking toward them from the Russian barrier. "Your superiors must agree. You're valuable enough to exchange not only for the real Sonia Gridissova, but her parents, uncle, and some Estonians, too."

"That means nothing," replied the female chekist, almost scornfully. "I am experienced and trained, with knowledge of intelligence operations. That is why my comrades want me back."

"I think you're underestimating yourself," pressed Smith. "It isn't your fault that the plan failed. I can explain that to your bosses, if you wish." He did not bother to see what expression the woman wore in response to his offer.

Smith and his companions halted. The Russian group stopped two yards away. Smith considered the real Sonia Gridissova, her identity eagerly confirmed by her husband as he had peered through binoculars a few minutes before. The impostor did not resemble her much at all.

"Welcome back, comrade," said one of Sonia's escorts, as the impostor traded places with those being exchanged for her.

Smith glanced at the speaker. Torop had recognised him as Nikolai Krasny, deputy chief of the Cheka's Counterintelligence Department; his presence suggested his authorship of the recent scheme.

With the newly released prisoners preceding them into Estonia, Smith and Torop turned and deliberately retraced their steps. But their pace was too slow for Sonia Gridissova who, smiling, broke into a run and threw herself into her husband's waiting arms.

Smith sighed. That was the sort of proof he should have expected in Petrograd, he told himself.

The Old Ally

"I should mention that for some time it has been the consensus of the Service that you would one day end up here."

"In Lisbon?"

"In gaol."

The lonely sound, from somewhere in the gloomy, subterranean cell, of consecutive drops of water striking with pathetic regularity the damp stone floor was the only break in the heavy silence that followed this exchange. Edward Lightfoot stared across the scratched top of the wooden table at his visitor. Then he burst out laughing.

"It's jolly to know that my colleagues have such a ripping opinion of my character," he said. A broad smile brightened his handsome face, otherwise dirtied with the unusual addition of several days' growth of beard. Even the stubble did not make him appear overly mature.

"It was confidence in your actions, rather than a lack of confidence in your personality, that led to such a judgement, I think," Linus Smith responded. He held out to the young Royal Air Force officer his open cigarette case. Lightfoot accepted one of the contents and reciprocated the pleasantry by hospitably pouring water from a grimy pitcher into a marginally clean though chipped glass, and placing it before Smith. The latter raised an eyebrow at the swirling grey clouds within the fluid.

'Well, yes, that's fair," Lightfoot conceded good-naturedly, thinking of Smith's words. He leaned back in his chair — with its twin, in which Smith sat, and the table, the only furniture in the dark room. "And I *have* met some dashed interesting chaps here." He exhaled smoke and gestured to what lie beyond the chamber's peeling walls. "All quite innocent of the charges for which they've been incarcerated."

"As are you?" asked Smith.

"It goes without saying," Lightfoot replied.

"Which accounts for you not saying it."

"Still," Lightfoot's boyish grin was replaced, briefly, by an expression of annoyance, "it is rather an inconvenience that I've had to spend much of the week-end here."

"Why is that?" Smith queried.

"I was invited to enjoy it with a delightful little thing who works in one of the antique shops up beyond the Carmo. She had promised to tell me all about Portugal's great national poet, Louise D. Cameo."

"Luis de Camoens?"

"That's the johnnie," said Lightfoot, jabbing the air with his cigarette, the end of which glowed red in the twilight of the cell. "Marvellous eyes, she has, by Farnborough! I don't mean Louise—"

"No?"

"No, this girl. Joan. Portuguese, I believe."

"In Lisbon? Surprising."

Lightfoot chuckled and dropped spent ash into the jug of water on the table, causing Smith to regard his glass even more suspiciously. He found it hard to believe that this was his countryman's fourth day in prison, his whiskers notwithstanding. But for his unshaven face, he may have been spending a week at a friend's house, from the way he was behaving. Yet Smith knew that this was not an act on Lightfoot's part.

Smith had met the young war hero at a couple of social functions in England. This was to have been expected. Smith, anonymous, forgettable, but able to provide and withstand hours of small-talk, and Lightfoot, handsome, famous and vibrant, were invited everywhere, and frequently. Otherwise, they had little in common: Lightfoot was, after all, little older than the century, and the other's junior by a couple of decades. Their employment by the Secret Service was, the senior man believed, the only other uniting factor.

"I say, would you care to hear how I arrived at this sorry end?" the flyer asked, as if encouraging a friend to go with him to the newest most popular night club in the West End. He drew on his cigarette. "It's not exciting, as stories go, but I do seem to have the time..." He glanced past Smith at the solid oaken door, bound by iron, like a remnant from a medieval fortress — which it may well have been — barely visible in the darkness. "What shall we do about being overheard?"

Smith too cast about the room. The pair of Englishmen were the only occupants. Far up one wall, squat, barred windows permitted some light to enter, though it was periodically eclipsed by the feet of pedestrians; the windows were, in fact, at ground level. Beyond the chamber's only door was an anteroom, probably empty, the warder who had let the visitor in having no doubt retreated down the corridor to the sagging cane chair in which Smith had found him, peacefully slumbering.

"Just to be on the safe side, I'll speak Latin, shall I?" Lightfoot suggested. With a facial flourish, he began. "About three half pennies ago, I arrived from under Spain to push out the flying sea. Most likely, it's not the intoxication that

The Old Ally

created the prince of the happy flamingos."

"I don't think this is going to work," Smith responded in English.

"Er, no...?" Lightfoot peered warily at the other man.

"I don't know the language." Smith's lack of formal schooling had resulted in Latin being one of the few tongues which he could not comprehend.

"Really?" Lightfoot seemed to brighten. "And I was tops in my class... How about Greek, then?" He cleared his throat. "Green apples, according to trammelled exhaust, when I can't fountain the moon with a quandary at quarter-past mouse."

Smith's upbringing had taught him the more practical languages of the Rhodesian veldt while schoolboys his age in Britain were learning Classics. Even so, he was almost certain that he was not hearing ancient Greek the way Socrates or Plato had spoken it.

"I've heard that you're familiar with Russian," he said at last.

Lightfoot's visage, slightly clouded with perplexity, like a child doing sums he was not sure were correct, was cleared by a big smile.

"First-rate idea, old boyar."

The young pilot launched into his exposition. His Russian was perfectly adequate and, though his accent made him sound like a goat-herd from Tyrol attempting to sing a Slavic dirge, he was at least comprehensible.

The task to which C, the chief of the Secret Service, had set Edward Lightfoot was to have been simple and congenial. Economic exigencies had forced the closure of C's station in Lisbon, so when Britain's principal agent in Portugal reported that he would have some important information for London, Lightfoot, having just completed an assignment in neighbouring Spain, had been directed to collect it on his way home.

"Do you know about the ruffians in Morocco?" Lightfoot asked his visitor. He was nearing the end of his cigarette.

"I imagine that there are any number of ruffians in Morocco," Smith opined. "Do you mean the Riffians? Natives of the Rif region?"

"The very chaps! You *are* good at geometry, aren't you? Apparently, these blighters have become dissatisfied with Spanish rule in their little corner of the world, and have been trying to give them the old heave ho for some time. Spain has a — What are those bally things like colonies but not?"

"Protectorates?" Smith ventured.

"And politics, too! By Upavon, you are a cosmopolitan fellow! I heard someone describe another with that word; I think it's a compliment. Protectorate, yes! Sounds rather homely, doesn't it?" The air force officer tossed himself back in his chair. His cigarette he left on the table's surface, to burn itself out. "Spain has one of those things over the north coast of Morocco and inland to some mountains, or valleys; I can't remember which. Living under the Spaniards must have grated on the nerves a bit for these Riffians — naturally enough — and was interfering with the ancient traditions of the people to slaughter each other on a daily basis. These people...they're all barbers, you know."

"Berbers." Smith could not determine if his countryman genuinely believed that a generous portion of north-western Africa's populace was composed of hair dressers, or if he had simply mispronounced the ethnic group's name.

"Oh." Lightfoot sounded disappointed. As with most negative emotions, however, it was quickly gone from his voice and face. "Well, whatever their trade, things had apparently changed since their last big set-to, and they found that bows and arrows just don't put the fear of Ali Baba into the Latin heart as they once did."

"Not since the advent of the magazine rifle and howitzer."

"Exactly." Lightfoot laced his fingers behind his head. "So the entire clipper-and-comb brigade put themselves to work getting some of the twentieth century's marvels of destruction."

"There is a flourishing trade in illegal firearms to the Rif," said Smith, nodding. "Most of them, it's suspected, are smuggled by the Rüdiger brothers, out of their warehouses in Barcelona and into Tangier."

Smith was hoping to move the narrative along a bit; he was fully aware of the situation in northern Morocco, as both a professional intelligence officer and an amateur historian.

"I say, it's no fair flipping to the end of the book," protested Lightfoot, regarding the older man with a critical sky-blue eye. "Let's leap ahead to the interesting parts, then. I gather C's been keeping a shell-like ear cupped in this direction, to learn what he can about the toing and froing of guns, in case it gets out of hand and involves the old Sceptred Isle. Having just finished a tale of derring-do in Spain, I was the chap in the right place when C needed someone to visit the splendidly named Count of Caprica. I suppose C told you all about him? The old count seemed to know everything worth knowing in Portugal, and then some. What's more, he passes on what he discovers to us."

"When did you arrive in Lisbon?"

Lightfoot rolled his eyes toward the ceiling, in the centre of which burned, barely, a moribund electric bulb.

"Tuesday morning." He lowered his eyes again. "I sent word to the good count immediately. He replied that, like the feast given for the prodigal son, a fatted calf, or some such creature, would be duly slaughtered, skinned, seasoned and the pieces trundled into his kitchen in my honour. Even so, that gave me plenty of time to look for a gift for my mother and father's wedding

The Old Ally

anniversary. In the hunt for said token of filial devotion, I met Joan, and arranged for the aforementioned poetry lessons. Then I had tea with Sophie, a wonderful girl from the embassy, and then prepared for dinner at the Quinta de Caprica. It was quite a banquet, though between you and me..." Lightfoot glanced about, first to the right, then to the left, adding emphasis to his warning of confidentiality, "I don't think the old boy is well off."

"That's likely," agreed Smith. "There isn't a great deal of money circulating in Portugal, even among the aristocracy. Who was in attendance at the dinner?"

"Let's see..." The air force officer enumerated the guests on his fingertips. "There was a duke, a second count, the director of the national police, a general of the army, a member of parliament — theirs, not ours — and a bishop. Everyone brought his wife or girlfriend — except the bishop. The general brought both; I suppose to make up for the bishop." He grinned. "We all had a smashing time."

"Until the violent death of your host," reminded Smith.

Lightfoot sighed sadly, concurring.

"Yes, until then. But Caprica, being the gentleman that he was, had the good manners to wait until everyone had departed before doing so himself. The meal started late — nine or ten is the usual hour for strapping on the feed bag, I gather — so it ended late, or early, depending on one's point of view. By three o'clock, all but your narrator, dear reader, had left."

"When did Caprica give you the information he had?"

"He never did," answered Lightfoot simply. "He explained that he had someone he wanted me to meet, someone just waiting to blurt out all sorts of state secrets about arms smuggling to the Rif. This mystery man was supposed to have popped up that very night, but didn't."

Smith frowned and asked if Caprica had found his agent's absence strange.

"Not a bit," the pilot replied, shaking his head. "The old boy told me that this chap had to be careful due to his position, and that he'd probably be by the next evening and shed the cloak and dagger long enough for a stiff drink and a good chat."

"The count definitely stated that his agent would be available the next day?"

"He said either that or 'I'm a little teapot short and stout'."

Smith nodded and commented that both phrases were pregnant with portent.

"Did he reveal the identity of this man? Or the intelligence he was providing?" Smith could guess the answer to his query.

"Not even in the game of charades, which, by the bye, the bishop won hands down." Lightfoot's mouth twisted in a wry expression. "I don't think Caprica was willing to trust the fellow's name to a stranger, even one from C. And as for giving over the information expected, well, I imagine the old boy didn't think there was a need for it. He no doubt expected to be still hopping, skipping *and* jumping the next day."

"As do we all," Smith remarked, at which Lightfoot smiled widely. "When did you leave Caprica's house?"

"About an hour after everyone else. Aside from being a spy, the chap was a very entertaining fellow. He rather reminded me of a master I knew at school; we called him the Pelican, because of the armfuls of funny stories he always had ready."

Smith had the urge to ask how the teacher's sobriquet could possibly have related to his nature as a raconteur, but decided against it.

"The staff had long since been sent away, except for Fatso—"

"Vasco?" suggested Smith.

"By Trenchard! That was it! Dead on! How did you know?"

"Vasco is a Portuguese name, and Fatso...isn't..."

"And this johnnie is thin, too," Lightfoot pointed out. "Anyway, Caprica was proud of this servant because he actually rose early, in order to wake the rest of the household, or feed chickens, or make table legs... I forget what his duties exactly were. Vasco was probably awake by the time I left, though I didn't see him." He shrugged. "Before I went, the count showed me his digs."

"Nice?" Smith asked out of curiosity.

"Not much furniture for the size of the place," answered the younger man; "a few paintings, a fountain in the courtyard — and a pistol collection! You may be right about the coin being few and far between in *this* realm, but what Caprica had, he seems to have spent on his hobby. He brought out most of them for me to see."

"And touch?"

"The fingerprints of the alleged murderer, what? Yes, and touch." Lightfoot leaned forward again, his elbows on the surface of the table making it wobble. "We talked, he sang some 'fado', which I think is a Portuguese ditty. In return, I taught him the first twenty stanzas from my old school's song — he has a rather horrid voice, I'm afraid — and I left about four o'clock. Caprica asked me if I wanted to stay the night — he was quite pleased that one of his guest rooms was habitable — but I had a date with a tour guide from the Estrella and didn't want to over-sleep. Then he was all for going to find Vasco, and have him take me back to my hotel in a dog cart, but I didn't need him to do that. It wasn't far and the night at that hour is heaven to walk through. Besides, a farmer came along in a wagon, going to market. He had quite a fetching daughter, so when he offered me a ride..."

"And later?" Smith prompted.

"Later — not later enough, though — a couple of policemen woke me. They walked right into my room and shook me." Lightfoot mimicked the action which he had found so abrupt and unpleasant.

"The nerve."

"Well, they were foreigners." Lightfoot was an understanding sort. "They told me — I think, for they don't seem to know English too well here; or I don't know it too well myself at that hour — that I had to accompany them. It sounded official. I suggested to them — in the kindest of terms, mind you — that they should buzz off and that I'd tootle along when I was ready. They didn't care for my attitude, but I did get another hour's sleep. They retreated, but came back, this time with an officer named Barbosa, small and oily but, I strongly suspect, competent. I thought I'd come along this time and the result you see before you." Lightfoot spread his arms, then folded them with finality. "End of chapter one."

After a moment, Smith inquired if there was anything he could bring the prisoner.

"A decent meal, old angel of mercy, would not go unappreciated," said Lightfoot, adopting a thoughtful pose. "A bottle of champers, some clean clothes, including the unmentionable bits and...oh, yes..." He rubbed the lower half of his face. "A good razor. I tried the knife one of my fellow inmates had smuggled in, but he seems to have dulled it on the ribs of the previous chap he had given it to."

"Did you want me to pass a message on to anyone?"

"You could let my parents know that I may not be visiting them next week as planned," the pilot replied. "But by Netheravon, don't tell them I've been gaoled for murder! They'll find it in appalling bad taste. Tell them that I got roaring drunk at a diplomatic ball and tried to invade a convent. It'll liven up the drawing room conversation."

Smith had not before been in Portugal. As someone with an interest in history, he of course knew that the country was England's oldest ally, with a treaty of friendship dating back to the fourteenth century, and co-operation in military affairs as recent as the last year of the Great War. He had read much about the land — he had read much about everything — but was personally unacquainted with it. Thus his interest had been piqued by more than just his mission when he and his valet had come ashore that afternoon, crossing a tossing harbour from the P & O liner anchored in Lisbon roads.

Smith's first experience of Portugal's personality — described as lazy and inefficient by its detractors and easygoing and carefree by its champions — had come before landfall, in the form of a four-hour wait to disembark. This delay was occasioned by the arrival on the ship of various port officials — customs examiners, document inspectors, harbour doctor — who fancied luncheon in the first-class dining saloon while there. They tarried at the meal, conversing at length with the captain and his officers, who, though displeased with the slow course of events, were apparently accustomed and, certainly, resigned to it.

But for the absence of minarets, Lisbon reminded Smith of Constantinople. Neither city was situated on the open sea, despite impressions caused by small-scale maps: the Portuguese capital was located on a wide estuary of the swift River Tagus, a full twenty miles from where it debouched into the ocean. The ships, straining at their chains some distance from the shore, the stone jetty with its customs shed, the busy traffic of ferries, tenders and lateen-sailed boats surging up and down on the rolling water, all could have been borrowed from the Turkish metropolis. Even the weather, turning to rain as Smith and Odways clambered into a decrepit motor-taxi, so ancient it may have been powered by steam, was reminiscent of Constantinople.

"Settled in?"

Smith handed the valet his rain-shined umbrella as he entered the sitting room of his hotel suite. He had set out for the municipal gaol as soon as their rooms had been secured, leaving his servant to sort out the domestic arrangements. From Odways's expression, Smith could determine that Portuguese hospitality may have become a source of dissatisfaction for his employee.

"The hotel, sir, though in need of considerable restoration, will serve your requirements," Odways said, flatly.

"It's conveniently placed, don't you think?"

The open window through which Smith peered was on the third floor of the Hotel Avenida Palace. Below was the Praça Dom Pedro IV, called by all the locals the Rocio. Though spacious enough for two large fountains and their basins — just now topped up by the recent rain — and a monument to the eponymous monarch higher than the surrounding buildings, it was nonetheless crowded. This may have been partly illusory: across the square was bustle and movement, and coffee houses and billiard rooms filled to capacity. From their viewpoint, the windows of Smith's suite were part of a calmer façade. But certainly the relentless clanging of the tram-cars' bells made it sound as if all of Lisbon were passing through the neighbourhood.

"Sir."

Odways indicated the dampness on the cuffs of Smith's grey trousers and jacket. It would have dried in a few minutes without damaging the fabric, but Smith knew that that was not the point of his servant's observation. He nodded and retired without comment to the bedroom, where a dark blue suit had already been laid out for him.

The Old Ally

"It is conveniently placed, sir, no doubt," the valet agreed belatedly; "the central railway station is just next door."

To many, railway hotels conveyed the image of the middle class, provincial, small-town families come to the metropolis to gape. It would do little, Smith realised, to argue that Portugal was different than England, and that the Avenida Palace, despite its situation, was not a railway hotel as such, but rather the best hostelry in the city. The two Britons had spent nights in flea-ridden caravanserais; had hidden for days in malarial swamps; been served dog dressed up as horse in evil-smelling inns; but to Odways, a railway hotel seemed, really, the limit. Smith returned to the sitting room, dry-clad, and accepted a cup of coffee from a tray a page had delivered moments before.

"None of the staff seems to be able to speak or understand English, sir," continued Odways, "and though the hall porter can manage a kind of French, it doesn't sound the sort that is readily tolerated by a Frenchman."

Smith tasted his beverage and acknowledged his valet's point. Smith himself was fluent in so many modern languages that he was almost at a loss when he travelled in a land where communication with the natives was not automatic. The fact that he did not know Portuguese was the reason for his temporary abode at the Avenida Palace. Smith preferred, when abroad, to stay at an inn more unique to the country. Even when on professional business, he disliked sleeping in a hotel that was little different from the one he would have just left.

"One expects more from a city's best offering, sir," Odways remarked, encapsulating his principle, as he walked to the bedroom to gather his master's discarded clothes.

Smith smiled. His valet was not unreasonable. If a guest at a house without electricity, he would not have bemoaned the necessity of candles; but if all the modern conveniences were installed, one had a right to expect them to work. To be fair, though, the Avenida Palace did not make boasts it could not sustain. And its kitchens did brew excellent coffee.

Smith's introduction to Portugal, being ferried to the shores of its capital under wet, grey skies, the tender crewed by tremendously filthy but skilled sailors, had not been auspicious. But the waterfront of most towns were usually their least attractive prospect. Coming from the opposite direction, descending the gentle incline from the Rocio, down the Rua Aura — the fact that the 'street of gold' was lined with the headquarters of many banks was probably merely a coincidence, mused Smith — to the Praça do Commerçio, offered much the better approach.

At first glance, from a relative distance, the plaza, nicknamed 'Black Horse Square', was rather appealing. The eighteenth century buildings, along three sides of the square and united by a continuous arcade, were graceful and symmetrical in the best neo-classical manner. The fourth side was open to the broad Tagus, an almost splendid view, full of movement, from the vessels on the water to the gulls that wheeled about the equestrian statue in the square's centre.

The headquarters of the city's Public Security Police were in a tall building on the plaza's north side, facing the harbour. The structure's exterior was peeling away; gentle decay was having its slow way with both paint and stone. The lobby just beyond the main doors seemed not to have been cleaned in the one hundred and seventy years since it was put together, following the devastating earthquake of 1755. The corners and surfaces of corridors and rooms had collected grime like unused books stacked too long in one place. The policemen who were standing sentry were of a similar condition.

The civil service of Portugal did not operate until after luncheon. Government departments were open, in theory, during the forenoon, bureaucrats of the national, district and municipal administrations worked, in theory, and the machinery that allowed the country to function rumbled and moved, in theory. Smith had been warned of the worth of theory in Portugal and had, indeed, found the caution justified.

Wandering about police headquarters, both unescorted and unquestioned, Smith was viewed with indifference by everyone he passed and when he paused to query a clerk or constable, was greeted with puzzlement. The one policeman who could speak a form of English left the visitor rather more confused than he had been before.

"Commissario Barbosa? Sí, senhor, three floor."

Since the statement was accompanied by the gesture of a finger pointing straight at the ceiling, Smith was left wondering if he were being directed up three storeys from where he stood or to the third floor.

The term 'commissar', Smith mused in his sojourn, could be found in its varied forms in most countries of Europe and even (as commissary) in England. The German word 'kommissar' was a police rank equivalent to a British inspector, while the French 'commissaire' was of a slightly loftier station. Grudgingly, Smith conceded that the Bolsheviks used the term in its purest sense: Russian commissars led government ministries, little road-mending gangs, and every sort of organisation in between. In Latin — Smith knew individual words, if not the whole language — 'commissarius' meant simply a person to whom something is committed, the one in charge.

Commissario Joao Barbosa was in charge of Lightfoot's criminal case.

Smith's first glimpse of this senior police officer was through a half-open door. Even sitting behind his desk, the man appeared short and round. His eyes were watery, as if he had just been weeping over a tragedy, and his full lips kept pressing against each other, as though trying to suppress a strong emotion. He appeared to be still at lunch, a stained napkin tucked into the open collar of his uniform's shirt, and a cup of chocolate on the desktop in front of him.

He spied Smith eyeing him, and signalled enthusiastically for the Briton to enter. Simultaneously, he launched into a torrent of Portuguese, which, even if it had been English, would have been ejected far too rapidly for comprehension.

"I'm sorry, Commissario," Smith said, putting up his hands as he stopped before the officer's desk. "I'm afraid that I don't speak your language."

This caused Barbosa to pause, his thick, dark eyebrows raised almost to the forelock of the black hair plastered by oil to his scalp.

"You are not, uh, from Ministry of Interior?" he asked, in clear, almost lyrical English.

"No. My name is Sinclair," lied Smith. "I'm from the Foreign Office — the British Foreign Office. I've come to see you about Squadron Leader Lightfoot. I do have an appointment."

Barbosa threw back his head and roared with laughter. He swallowed the remains of his chocolate — while still laughing heartily, a rather dangerous accomplishment — tugged away the napkin at his throat, scattering the crumbs that it had no doubt been meant to capture, and used it to wipe his eyes.

"Very droll, senhor, very droll!" he exclaimed, as if Smith had planned and executed a particularly hilarious joke. He stood and forced his bulky way around his desk to grasp his visitor by the hand. "I am Barbosa, and yes, you had, uh, an appointment. My clerk — where is he, that fool?" He indicated the little, windowless cell through which anyone coming to see the police officer had to pass.

"Never mind, senhor!" Barbosa waved away all concern. "Sit down, sit! Would you, uh, like something? Some chocolate? Have you eaten? Some coffee, then? When my, uh, useless clerk returns... He is lazy! Sleeping, no doubt!" And he laughed at his subordinate's irresponsibility, as if it were a comedic turn on a music hall stage.

Smith's estimate of his host's height and girth had been correct, for the man stood barely five feet tall. This made his width, which was substantial, appear even greater. When the small size of the room was added to these factors, Barbosa seemed to fill the space, to dominate it, as a parent would his child's nursery, where the furniture would be a relative half-size. He at last pushed his way back into the tight fit of his chair, a pliable wicker affair, and, leaning forward, offered his guest a cigar, taken from a full box in one of the drawers. Using the discarded napkin once more, he wiped his swarthy face, dabbed at the corners of his eyes, and slapped the grease-spotted wooden surface before him.

"Yes, yes, Chef de Esquadra Lightfoot," he said: "a character!"

"I suppose he can be, Commissario," Smith agreed, "but hardly a murderer." He set the cigar he had been given in a tall ashtray by his chair. The tobacco tasted as if it had been blended with dirty rags.

"Aaah, but Senhor Sinclair, we have *evidence!*" The zest with which Barbosa made this declaration led Smith to infer that having proof of someone's guilt was an extraordinary thing in this part of the world.

The police officer wrenched open a drawer of his desk and rifled through its contents. Behind him, through an open window, came sounds of the city and the harbour, the river sparkling blue and silver in Monday's sunshine and wind, dotted with the red triangular sails of small boats. On the farther shore could be seen the bright white buildings of the new naval college, with low hills rolling into the distance beyond.

"Yes, yes, evidence!" cried Barbosa again, raising aloft an aged cardboard folder, creased so often and in so many places that it resembled thin, blue leather. He dropped it dramatically on to the desktop, then reached for the cigar Smith had abandoned. "No? You mind?" He picked it up and popped one end into his mouth, where it bobbed up and down with his words.

"Your friend's, uh, fingerprints were found on the, uh, murder weapon, yes? Do you know how the Count of Caprica was, uh, killed?" Frenetically, Barbosa imitated the action of seizing something as if it were a hammer and striking it against another object. "Whap! Whap! Whap! The count was hit to death with one of his own, uh, pistols. He was a collector..."

"He showed Lightfoot the weapons," countered Smith, "and Lightfoot handled them. You no doubt found his prints on several of the count's guns."

"Aaah, may be, senhor, but they were, uh, very much on the one that killed Caprica." The commissario removed one of the folder's pages and held it inches from his dark eyes, so close that Smith feared that it would be ignited by the lit end of Barbosa's cigar. "It was a Bergmann-Bayard automatic pistol."

"Danish," elaborated Smith, matter-of-factly.

"Aaah, a collector yourself, senhor?"

"No, but I read a great deal."

Barbosa considered this statement uproariously funny and laughed loudly. As he calmed down, he wiped his nose and eyes with the napkin.

"More evidence, senhor," he continued, adjusting himself in his chair. "There were no signs of someone forcing themselves into Quintas de Caprica. Doors were not broken, locks were not, uh, disabled. The count let his killer in!"

"But Caprica must have had many acquaintances," responded Smith. "There were a dozen other guests at the dinner party Lightfoot attended Tuesday night."

"It is true, yes, the count was, uh, popular, good at, uh, conversation, always

The Old Ally

wanting to know things." Barbosa paused, removing the cigar from his mouth to exhale a thin plume of smoke. "But do you think a bishop murdered him? Or the wife of one of our, uh, legislators? Lightfoot was the last to see him alive." A chubby finger went up. "Evidence, senhor: the count's old servant..." he rubbed his eyes and consulted another piece of paper "...Vasco Correia was just, uh, woken to begin the day when he heard his master and the chef de esquadra shouting. Arguing, no?"

"That was probably Lightfoot's old school song," Smith said dryly.

"And Correia saw someone leaving, not at, uh, four o'clock as Lightfoot claimed but, uh half an hour later," the police officer stated.

"Was this Vasco in a position to see Lightfoot depart at four?" asked Smith. "It's possible that the squadron leader left when he claimed he did, and that the individual seen going at four-thirty was someone else. When is it believed that Caprica died?"

"Aaah..." Barbosa shrugged his shoulders. "Between three o'clock and five?" he said, as if he were asking the question. "The Duke of Segora, his duchess and General Macedo and his wife and, uh, friend, all left about three, so unless all are, uh, liars, Caprica was living still, and alone with Lightfoot at that time."

"You must admit, Commissario, that this is all quite circumstantial," Smith said, sceptically.

The police officer hesitated. His grasp of English was very good but not comprehensive. Then he laughed strongly.

"Yes, yes, true," he conceded good-naturedly. Then he added, "Uh, circumstantial or not, it is proof." He spread his hands in a sign of helplessness.

"May I visit the crime scene, Commissario?" inquired Smith. "I assume your people have finished with Caprica's house by now."

"Finished...?" Barbosa's olive face grew puzzled, but then he smiled. "Aaah, the evidence, uh, physical. Yes, yes, all done, you may visit. The staff was, uh, ordered not to touch anything in the library. That is where the count was, uh, found. But yes, we are finished there."

"Then I will take my leave. Thank you for your time, Commissario." Smith stood, and Barbosa struggled to free himself from his chair, and rise also. "Would you object to my provision of some amenities to Squadron Leader Lightfoot, during his incarceration?"

After another pause for understanding, Barbosa grinned happily and shook his head.

"No, no, Lightfoot is the gentleman. He should be in comfort." He tossed aside his cigar and shook his visitor's hand. As Smith reached the office door — the anteroom still missing its clerk — Barbosa spoke again.

"Aaah, Senhor Sinclair, you did arrive most rapidly to assist your, uh, countryman. What section of your Foreign Office do you, uh, represent?"

"The Treaty Department," replied Smith, turning. "It was thought fitting, considering the old alliance between our two nations."

Barbosa laughed until his eyes were running with tears.

"Wonderful, yes! Excellent! Thank you, senhor..."

The Quinta de Caprica was a large, squarish house in Lumiar, a village that served as a suburb of Lisbon. The building was in a beautiful state of decay, not like the squalid crumbling of the government structures in the Black Horse Square, but rather like a roué who, after a lifetime of good-humoured debauchery, is content to look upon other people's fun from an idle retirement. The building's pink stucco was falling away from the walls, the tiles were slipping from the roof and the windows had been cleared of their dirt only when and where someone had wanted to see out.

The grounds were on several levels, smoothed by terraces and connected by short, unexpected staircases. The lawns were fuzzy with grass unchecked by mowing, and moss crept up every stone surface. Masses of bougainvillaea, purple and vibrant, vied for attention with giant nasturtiums where the paths, growing indistinct through a lack of maintenance, separated the beds of hydrangeas and sweet marjoram, guarded by jacaranda trees, asleep on duty.

Smith entered the house through a side door. It was unlocked, and every window in sight was open to the gentle breezes and flowery fragrances on this warm, cloudless day. An intruder, whether friend or stranger, would have had no need to force his way into the late count's home.

The rooms were, as Lightfoot had described, sparsely furnished. They reminded Smith of a catalogue he had once read, an inventory from the Elizabethan era, listing the items in an old house: ninety pieces of furniture in fifty rooms. The fashion in English country house décor of three and a half centuries before may have encouraged bare chambers, but Smith doubted that style had motivated the interior design of the Quinta de Caprica. The few chairs and tables that the count had owned included, Smith was certain, some genuine Chippendale pieces; that woodworker had been employed at the Portuguese royal court for a few years. There was no way of telling how many examples of his artistry Caprica had sacrificed to economic necessity.

The library was a long room, perhaps once a picture gallery, facing the cobbled courtyard, cool in partial shadow. If the library's tiled walls had held shelves, it would have been able to accommodate several thousands of books, but Smith theorised that the room's name had always been a mere courtesy. Instead, it was a kind of museum, fitted with large wooden cases, glass-topped,

The Old Ally

in which were neatly stored a variety of handguns. They were of all shapes and sizes, and from the newest to what certainly appeared to be very old items. Smith thought that the displays, weapons of violence, were rather jarring in a room in which the only sound heard was the tranquil plashing of water from the fountain in the court.

Two of the cases were unlocked and open, and a number of firearms were lying on the lengthy table in the middle of the room. Smith recognised a 'Baby' Nambu, a Japanese pistol that resembled the more popular German Parabellum; next to it was another semi-automatic, the Austrian Mannlicher M1901, a unique weapon Smith had first examined in Vienna before the War. His eyes were caught, however, by a more ordinary article, a Colt Army Special. He picked it up and, reflexively, swung out the cylinder. It was loaded. Smith set it down again.

The display cases were no more than deep trays with legs and glazed covers. Between a pair of them, however, was a short cabinet, fitted with several drawers, one not quite shut. He opened it further and discovered a box of ammunition, .38 calibre, like the Colt revolver; six rounds were missing.

The sound of distant footsteps, quiet but nonetheless audible to Smith's ears, preceded the brief glimpse of a shadow passing across a wall. The Englishman turned to see a man, tall and slender, peering worriedly through the glass of the French doors. Smith gestured for him to enter.

The man was probably a servant, Smith thought, and, for his part, may have believed the Briton was a police officer, for he approached deferentially, his old straw hat hastily removed and clutched anxiously in two bony hands. He began to speak, but in Portuguese, which the visitor halted with an upraised hand.

"Do you speak English?" he asked.

"Oh...yes, senhor... A little..." The man indicated, metaphorically, how much of the language he knew by placing the thumb and forefinger of one hand an inch apart.

"My name is Sinclair," Smith lied. "Commissario Barbosa sent me." Though not quite the falsehood his first sentence had been, the second statement stretched the truth somewhat. "Who are you?"

"Vasco...Vasco Correia..."

The appearance of the Count of Caprica's servant would not have found approval with Smith's own valet. Correia's long, gaunt face was unshaven, and he was dressed in trousers, a shirt and jacket that did not fit properly, and the whiteness of which had been dimmed to a dingy beige. His feet were partially shod in sandals, which had not prevented his toes from turning grubby. Perhaps, Smith thought, giving the Portuguese the benefit of the doubt, this was his off-duty attire, or his outside livery, for work in the garden. Whatever the case, something about Correia's attitude struck Smith as sincere, and his manner was that of a person lost, bereft of a guide. As unprepossessing as he looked, Vasco Correia had most likely made the count an excellent servant. Smith had learned as a boy not to judge by appearances.

"I'm sorry about your master, Correia," he said, slowly and gently. "I've heard excellent things about him." He punctuated the compliment by offering the other man a cigarette. After a hesitation, Correia accepted the gift.

"Yes, senhor. The count...good, good man... Everybody his friend." Correia's face became even more emaciated as he drew in the cigarette's smoke, and did not become much more full as he exhaled again. "Police...they arrest..."

"Edward Lightfoot," supplied Smith.

"Yes..." Correia sounded unconvinced.

"I don't think he killed your master."

"No?" The servant seemed pleased to hear this opinion. A small smile, almost imperceptible, moved the cigarette in his mouth. "British man, the count liked... Everybody liked..." He shook his head. "I don't think...killer..." Correia was distracted by the length of tobacco that had already burned to ash at the end of his cigarette. There was an ashtray conveniently placed on the library's long table, and still containing crushed cigarettes from, Smith guessed, the night of the murder. But Correia did not use it; that had been the count's prerogative. Instead, the servant knocked his cigarette against the outside of the door, ash falling to the stones that paved the courtyard.

"The count had many friends, did he?" asked Smith.

"Oh, many, many..." The response brightened Correia's visage briefly, and he moved his hat back and forth in front of him. "They come, they go, all time, all time... Music, food, laugh... All time, many friends..."

"Any..." Smith considered how best to phrase his question "...any secret friends? Quiet, alone?"

Correia paused before answering, perhaps wondering if he had the right to divulge confidential information to this stranger. The argument was decided in Smith's favour. The Portuguese nodded.

"Someone...not...secret, but... Oh, quiet..." Correia put a finger to his colourless lips. "The count tell...do not say, not to anybody..." He looked dubious, and guilty about disobeying his master's command.

"If Lightfoot did not murder your master, Correia, then the man who did is still free," Smith pointed out.

"Yes, yes," the other responded, almost impatiently, knowing that to help justice he had to break a confidence. His brow was lined. "One, he come...two times..." He held up a couple of fingers.

"An enemy?"

The Old Ally

"Oh, no." The answer was emphatic. "The count tell...brave man...good man... Come at night...come alone..." After a moment of confusion, Correia tossed the tiny remnant of his cigarette into the courtyard and donned his disintegrating straw hat, pulling it low over his dull eyes, then flipped the collar of his discoloured jacket up, hunching his slender shoulders.

"Oh, yes, I see," said Smith, nodding. Correia relaxed and removed his hat, restoring himself to what he probably considered to be his dignity.

"He Spanish," he stated, unexpectedly.

This claim raised Smith's eyebrows, and he inquired as to how the servant had discovered the nationality of his master's most secret guest.

"Secret, yes...not to me. The count, he trust me... I hear..."

"You heard them speak together?" This was a stroke of luck, Smith thought. "What did they say?"

Correia grinned, a just a little, in embarrassment, perhaps, and shrugged his shoulders. He held up a hand, with his thumb and forefinger once more an inch apart.

"...English..." he said. Then, adjusting the distance almost negligibly, added, "Spanish... But I know when I hear..."

"I see." Now it was Smith who smiled. "You recognised the language but didn't understand it. Did you ever see this Spaniard?"

Correia gave the visitor a contrite expression, and shook his head.

"Little here...little there... Anyone...anyone..."

Caprica's brave and good visitor was anonymous, and Correia was confessing that he could not have identified him. Smith nodded, and reached for his own hat.

"Tell me, did the count have enemies?"

"Enemies...?" The servant seemed not to understand the word, but then shook his head vigorously. "No, no...no enemies... Friends, only friends..."

"And women... Any difficulties with women? Ladies?" Smith smiled when posing the question, to diffuse any offence it may give.

"Ladies?" Correia straightened, growing tall and cool, giving an indication of how impressive he may have appeared with proper hygiene and fashion. "Come, please."

Smith followed the Portuguese from the library, not into the courtyard but through a pair of interior double doors, the paint on which had turned brittle and was falling away. Beyond was what may have been the drawing room, barely furnished. Dominating the chamber was its single picture, a portrait of full-length but almost twice life's size.

The subject was a lady, not beautiful, rather plain, in fact, but whose entrancing eyes and somewhat off-centred mouth suggested a great depth of

222

sensitivity, intelligence and passion. Those qualities, and the trace of a smile on the lips, perhaps demonstrating how the woman had not taken everything too seriously, would surely have retained any heart that they captured.

"Countess..." remarked Correia, gazing adoringly at the image. "Dead ten years... No one else for count, not ever..."

The servant bowed deeply toward the painting, and Smith surmised that it had not been only Caprica who had loved no other these past ten years.

"You're looking better."

Smith appraised Lightfoot as the latter was escorted into the interview room of the municipal gaol once more. The air force officer was joking with the warder who accompanied him, though neither understood the other's language. After a loud, shared chuckle, the warder, whose advanced age looked to keep him from adequately guarding a baby in its pram, shook the prisoner's hand, uttered what sounded like a completely facetious caution, and left the room, closing the medieval door behind him.

"Yes, it's astounding what a shave will do," said Lightfoot, stroking the rounded angles that comprised his face. He sat easily in a chair opposite Smith's, across the table which, this time, supported a clean ashtray as well as a couple of undamaged glasses and a jug of fresh, sweet water. The visitor noted, in addition to Lightfoot's smooth visage, the neatly brushed blond hair, and the new collar under the well-knotted tie.

"I didn't think the authorities permitted inmates to wear neck-ties," Smith commented.

"Hm? Why not?" Lightfoot withdrew a cigarette case from within his neat jacket and offered it to Smith.

"Well, I suppose it's believed that an attempt at suicide would be made."

"Suicide?" Lightfoot laughed as he lit first his guest's cigarette and then his own. "By Bleriot, what a dismal thought. Besides, they allowed me a razor. I imagine they figure that if I were to kill myself, it would be with that. Can you conceive how long it would take to cut one's throat with a silk tie?" He breathed out smoke. "Mind you, my friend Miguel — the warder you just saw — did ask me not to share the razor with my left-hand neighbour, Sebastian — the 'Vivisectionist of Bucellas', as the yellow press dubbed him."

Smith spoke Russian when he asked, "Do you know any of Caprica's acquaintances who may have been intelligence agents for him, specifically, a Spaniard?"

"I know only the friends the poor chap invited to the party I attended Tuesday night," replied Lightfoot, "any one of whom may have been giving the old boy bits of news. But there was no Spaniard. I gather Caprica knew

The Old Ally

everyone who knew anything worth knowing in Portugal, native or foreign. Always on the go, dinners, parties, country house weekends... He must have had a wonderful life."

"Until its violent end," Smith put in.

"I say, you can be a bit gloomy," said Lightfoot. "Must you continually bring that up?"

"Besides, his life sounds much like yours."

"Except for its violent end," Lightfoot added.

"There's plenty of time for that." Smith made use of the ashtray that had been provided. "I really came to tell you that I will be off to Madrid tomorrow, and didn't want you to think that you'd been abandoned to filth and squalor."

Lightfoot nodded gravely as he drank some water.

"Dashed decent of you," he said. "And thanks for the champagne you sent. It was very useful. The chap across the corridor from my cell is a polygamist, and he becomes quite thirsty relating the stories of his misses...missuses...missi..."

"He would," reasoned Smith.

"You don't think they'll close me down, do you?"

Frederic Tremarne was a youngish man, not yet thirty-five years old, with a nervous way of talking, and walking, of sitting and smoking, eating, breathing and, Smith had no doubt, of sleeping. He paced his office with the energy of a regimental band and sucked tobacco through the carved amber of his cigarette holder as if he were a dying man imbibing the elixir of immortality.

"They did abolish Lisbon, didn't they?"

"Not the entire city."

Tremarne peered worriedly at Smith, who was seated in the depths of a print-covered armchair, and continued pacing.

"I'm next, geographically speaking," the younger man said. "Besides, it would save money. That's all government think about now: economy."

"That's all they've ever thought of. Anyway, I'm certain that Headquarters will want to retain Madrid Station." Smith drank from his tea cup, surely an antique, the hand-painted Chinese landscape on its side still bright and colourful. "Your proximity to Lisbon should bring you security, not anxiety. After shutting down the service's permanent representation in Portugal, Headquarters wouldn't want to lose its only other station in the Iberian Peninsula."

Tremarne hesitated in his aimless perambulations, as a tramp might when he had come to the end of a path, and stared again at Smith from under a fringe of brown locks. He pushed the hair back and drew on his cigarette once more.

"Yes...true... You're quite right..." He nodded, as if hammering a nail into wood with his chin. "Yes, that makes sense."

Smith thought that his colleague may now find something else to worry about, but Tremarne returned to his own chair behind the ornately carved walnut desk. His long fingers removed what was left unsmoked of the cigarette in its holder and inserted a fresh one, which he lit almost calmly.

Darkness had just fallen over the Spanish capital, and a bright white moon could have illuminated the city by itself, even though only half visible. Voices, their words indistinct, but their tone cheerful, drifted in through the open windows of the room, originating from a café, or two, and were the loudest sounds at this time of night. Smith had long held the impression of Madrid as a continuously festive place, full of gaiety, dance and song emanating from every street corner. He had been somewhat surprised to find that this unrealistic fancy was not far from the truth, as noise competed with noise, all loud and none malevolent, throughout most of the day and much of the night. But even in this city such a cacophony had to end eventually, temporarily, and along the Calle Fernando del Santo, over which the British Embassy looked, the quiet was now comparable to that in a provincial English town after midnight.

"Has C mentioned me at all, Major Smith?" Tremarne's thin hands trembled slightly, a condition that followed an attack of nerves, or preceded one. "I understand that he is unlikely to discuss any one officer with another..." The head of station's intense green eyes blinked, suddenly startled. "Unless of course he *has* discussed me... But then, you wouldn't tell me if he had, would you? No, certainly; that would be unprofessional..." Tremarne chuckled like a boy hurrying through a cemetery at night. "But you are not here to talk about my problems, are you, Major?" He exhaled smoke and reached for his cup on its saucer.

Though C had not spoken of his principal man in Spain, others had. The staff of the Secret Service's Headquarters were generally amused that someone who performed such consistently good work could be so frightened of being sacked for doing the opposite. Frederic Tremarne was one of the few officers of the Service who had not served in the army or navy, having been rejected, repeatedly, by various medical boards during the War, no doubt for neurasthenia. Even the French Foreign Legion had declined his desperate application. C, whose sailor's eyes saw opportunity in the bleakest of situations, had decided that their loss would be his organisation's gain.

"You've no doubt heard of the death of the Count of Caprica," said Smith. He set aside his own cup, placing it on the lacy cloth that covered the small round table next his chair. While the furniture of the room may have come from the study of an eighteenth century dilettante, the décor reminded Smith of every grandmother's parlour he had ever entered.

The Old Ally

"Oh, of course, yes," replied Tremarne, nodding in his staccato manner. "I met him, twice. I was made his controller after the Lisbon Station closed. Have you had any luck finding his killer?"

Smith smiled to himself. No one who knew Edward Lightfoot, even if only by reputation could have placed him in the role of murderer; the assumption of his innocence was automatic.

"No, but you may be able to assist me in that matter. Do you know anything regarding the count's agents? In particular, a Spaniard?"

Tremarne chewed at the end of a thumb, the nail of which was the exception to an otherwise superbly manicured hand.

"I'm afraid I don't have any information about Caprica's people," he said, shaking his head like a child faced with strong medicine. "He was given a great deal of latitude when it came to his agents; he was that trusted. I doubt that even Leeson, who ran the Lisbon Station — when there was one..." a distressed expression once more crowded onto Tremarne's pale face "...was aware of everyone who supplied the count with intelligence. It's hardly surprising though that he would have Spanish agents. This country is usually in more turmoil than is Portugal, especially with the current trouble in Morocco. I know he was gathering information on the arms smuggled to the Rif." Tremarne adjusted the collar of his shirt. "I of course was doing something similar here."

Setting his cigarette aside, the head of station left his chair again and moved to a tall wooden filing cabinet with a porcelain gewgaw of indeterminate shape on top.

"Try talking to this man, Major," he said, removing a file folder from a drawer. From its pages, he pulled a photograph, the sort a gentleman might have taken for a special event, such as a promotion in rank. "Colonel Ricardo Ortega Rodriguez, Spain's military attaché in Lisbon. As much as the Spanish have an intelligence presence in Portugal, he's it."

"Thank you." Smith glanced at the picture, that of a dark, almost feeble looking man in the dress uniform of a cavalry officer. The head of station blinked nervously.

"And you'll let me know if you hear anything?" Tremarne asked guardedly.

"Once the person responsible for Caprica's death is—"

"No, no, I mean..." Tremarne leaned forward conspiratorially "...about my situation here."

"Oh...yes," Smith promised, nodding, "of course."

The journey from the Spanish capital to the Portuguese — and vice versa, for that matter — was along the railway that followed the valley of the Tagus River. In spite of the large and full stream's propinquity, the land was turning brown. The last of the early summer rains was past, and the fields appeared unattractive to an Englishman, whose eyes were accustomed to lush, green grass and trees. The towns and villages that Smith's train passed gave him little to look at, as the permanent way, and consequently the stations, were rarely close to the communities they served. Old mansions and abandoned castles, their stone walls dull even in the strong sunshine, were always glimpsed at a distance. Adding to the unappealing countryside was the inconvenience of Smith's inability to communicate to any great extent with his fellow travellers. All combined to make him glad that he never sojourned far without a book.

If the frontal approach to Lisbon, that by sea, gave an initial impression of a semi-oriental, ocean-side metropolis, exotic and unknown, coming in through the tradesmen's entrance, at the rear, thrust the visitor rather more abruptly into the capital, as he emerged into its upper reaches after progressing through a tunnel.

As Smith had observed to Odways, the Avenida Palace Hotel was nothing if not strategically placed. After leaving the city's central station, he merely walked next door. Even so, the late afternoon crowds of the Rocio gave him something formidable to penetrate. Shiners of shoes, peddlers of lottery tickets and small-time photographers were all insistent on custom from the passers-by. The disadvantage of not being able to speak Portuguese, even badly, marked Smith as a foreigner, and made him more of a target for the costers and the hawkers than was any native. The policemen at the corners of the square were uninterested in the problems of a besieged guest in their country, having to concentrate on directing the constant flow of traffic, both motored and horsed.

"A pleasant trip, sir?"

Smith glanced at Odways as the valet relieved him of his hat and overnight bag. His employee was being amusing, Smith knew.

"Was there an answer to my telegram?"

"Yes sir."

Smith accepted the envelope he was given. It had been delivered to the hotel by hand.

"Good. Colonel Ortega will be able to see me at seven o'clock." Smith pulled his watch from a pocket. "I've plenty of time."

He had to raise his voice somewhat, as his servant was already in the bathroom, running water into the tub. Odways's judgement regarding domestic matters was invariably sound, and he realised that an overnight journey across the dusty plains of the Iberian Peninsula rarely left one feeling fresh and clean. But a cloud of steam was already floating through the open door from which the valet emerged a minute later.

"The colonel suggests that we meet at a place called the Beresford-Bar,"

The Old Ally

Smith said as he passed Odways on his way to the bathroom. "Find out where that is while I'm scrubbing, would you?"

"Very good, sir."

The Beresford-Bar was a small restaurant in the Rua Garrett, which, like many addresses in Lisbon, had another, more informal name: in this case, it was the Chiado. It lie on the sudden slope of the city's western ridge which, in spite of Lisbon's claim to be built, like Rome, on seven hills, was one of only two natural eminences that most observers could discern. Though some distance from the Rocio, Black Horse Square, and other points in the valley below, the Chiado could be reached in just a few minutes. Smith simply boarded the public lift in the tall and ugly lattice-work steel tower that disfigured the skyline, paid a few pennies and ascended two hundred feet.

"Ah, Mr Sinclair? It is a pleasure to meet you. I am Ricardo Ortega Rodriguez, colonel, of the army of His Most Catholic Majesty the King of Spain." Smith and his new acquaintance shook hands, the latter smiling. "Forgive me, sir. It is such a grand formula, I never tire of using it."

The Spaniard looked to be the sort of man that cartoonists of *Punch* and other humorous periodicals draw when they require an effete caricature to do or say something asinine. The man's thinning black hair was combed carefully back on a round pate, discreet side-whiskers framing a brown face. Two little eyes squeezed the sides of a convex nose, which in turn sprouted from its nostrils a travesty of a moustache. The whole visage funnelled into a chin that almost disappeared in a neatly folded collar. His grip was strong.

"I had just walked through the doors of the legation when your telegram was given to me by the porter," he said, as the two gentlemen took seats at one of the Beresford-Bar's outside tables. These spilled across the establishment's front terrace without regard for the traffic, vehicular or pedestrian, which was increasing in the thoroughfare with the ending of the day. "I had the sad duty of escorting back to Madrid the body of one of my clerks. He contracted cholera Tuesday night and was dead Wednesday morning."

Smith had been about to comment on Portuguese hygiene, but recalled that cholera in Britain had disappeared only a couple of generations previously, and so limited his response to a condolence.

"I've had some experience of losing colleagues to that illness," he said. "Its speed is perhaps the most frightening thing about it."

"Indeed," Ortega concurred.

"But we may as well have met in Spain, Colonel," Smith added, "for I returned from Madrid just hours ago."

"Oh?" Ortega smiled, pushing his thin moustache upwards, further into his nostrils, it seemed. "A coincidence." A waiter approached, wiping his damp hands on his apron. Smith recognised the word 'porto' in the colonel's order, and was not surprised when the Spaniard turned to him and asked, "Will you join me in a bottle of this country's most famous export?"

It would have been rude of Smith to point out that, as an Englishman, he preferred port *after* dinner, and sherry, from Ortega's homeland, before. Instead, he acquiesced in the suggestion.

"Port wine is excellent here, as one would expect." The colonel reclined in his chair, relaxing, as if he had already sampled a glass or two. His English was very good, accented but fluent. He had spoken it automatically to Smith, perhaps out of politeness, but perhaps as well thinking that a Briton would be ignorant of Spanish. The fact that this assumption would have been correct in this case made Smith decide that it was time he expanded his stock of languages. When the beverage arrived, Ortega held up his glass to the orange light of the evening sun, its orb already having vanished.

"Now, Mr Sinclair, how may I help you?" he asked, after a taste.

"I wondered, Colonel, if you had known the Count of Caprica well." The wine in Smith's own glass was good, but no better than in England for being drunk in its land of origin.

"Yes, indeed, I did. I would believe that most ladies and gentlemen resident in Lisbon have met the good count, and have even been invited to his table. I myself had many congenial discussions with him during the two years I have been posted here." Ortega shook his head sadly, his shirt collar turning with each movement. "I returned from the aftermath of my clerk's death only to be told of another. How did Caprica die, do you know, Mr Sinclair?"

"He was murdered," answered Smith, "in his own house, with one of his own firearms."

"Good Lord..." Ortega sipped again from his glass, afterward dabbing gently at his upper lip with a handkerchief. His small eyes displayed sorrow, but also a certain fecklessness, as if he would have been powerless to prevent harm coming to anyone. He glanced at his companion. "Forgive me, Mr Sinclair, but how do you figure in this affair?"

"A legitimate question, Colonel," Smith conceded. "I represent the British Foreign Office, and I am looking into the matter of Squadron Leader Edward Lightfoot's arrest for the Count of Caprica's murder."

The Spaniard's eyes expanded and, reflected the illumination now coming from the café's interior.

"Edward Lightfoot, a murderer? Impossible!" Such was the colonel's apparent indignation that his chin, almost non-existent, jutted forward. He made a sweeping gesture with one hand, as if clearing a table of something offensive.

The Old Ally

"You know Lightfoot?" Smith should not have been surprised; everyone was acquainted with the young Royal Air Force officer. It was claimed — not by Lightfoot himself — that he possessed more friends than anyone else in the world.

"Ah yes, I met him last year at a dinner party hosted by the military attaché of my country's embassy in London." Ortega's chin retreated back into his throat as he smiled. "A most energetic young man, Lightfoot; a most humorous man. The very idea that he would break an old man's head is absurd." As if to emphasise that his position would stand no argument, Ortega tossed back the remains of his wine.

"You are not the only one to believe so, Colonel," commented Smith, smiling, "but I think the police are determined to hold him until a more promising suspect is found."

Ortega's head moved from side to side, scornfully this time.

"How can I help?"

"Caprica appeared to know a great deal about gun-running to the Riffians," Smith said. "I know this is a subject that interests your government, Colonel. I've no doubt that the count's interest was one of curiosity, but do you think it's possible that his knowledge in this respect may have led to his death?"

Ortega raised his eyebrows, very thin lines, like his moustache.

"I wouldn't have thought so," he stated, after half a minute's rumination. "My own conversations with Caprica were those of friends, of course, certainly nothing official. We did touch on events in Morocco, of course, as we talked also of the occupation of the Rhineland, the Teapot Dome scandal and modern art. From what I recall of the pertinent discussions, I can say that he believed the Rüdiger brothers were responsible for most of the arms smuggled to the rebels. That's a common theory, really. I am not convinced holding that opinion would have got Caprica killed. The Rüdigers care nothing for what the public think."

"Unless the count had discovered proof of their involvement," suggested Smith.

Ortega nodded, concurring in theory.

"I suppose that would be a motive," he stated, still not persuaded.

The sun was nothing but a reddish glow in the west, silhouetting the near by statue of Luis de Camoens, the poet about whom Lightfoot had been so looking forward to learning. The day was dim now, and street lamps and lights from restaurants and late-night shops were providing the illumination. The Chiado was a fashionable street, somewhat out of place on these heights of Lisbon. With its milliners, jewellers and dress-makers, it would have fit better in the sloping valley below, along the Avenida do Liberdade. The street was growing crowded as clerks, shop assistants, mannequins and customers left behind the business of the day, and gathered at the tables of restaurants. The Beresford-Bar filled and became noisy, inside and out, on the terrace under its string of lanterns. For a moment, the gentlemen's dialogue lagged, and they observed in admiring silence the movements of pretty women as they walked by.

"Shall we continue our conversation over dinner, Mr Sinclair?" the Spaniard asked. "Which would you prefer, English fare or Portuguese?"

Smith was unconcerned with the sort of food that he ate. Though he favoured Portuguese food when he was in Portugal, he had learned something useful in the last quarter-hour: port should be drunk on a full stomach.

Rain seemed to come in gusts in Lisbon, blowing up the slope of the city from the wide roadstead of the Tagus, propelled by the southerly wind. These were showers rather than storms, light and cool, but nothing that would return the green to the late spring grass in the countryside surrounding the city. And after the rain had ceased, the sun shone more strongly, drying the buildings and pavements quickly.

Along the waterfront, west of Black Horse Square, was the Portuguese capital's biggest market, broad but cluttered nonetheless with small, open-fronted huts, most roofed with corrugated iron, rusted and dirty. It reminded Smith of a shanty town and, but for its building material, had probably changed little in several centuries. The scene was livelier than any slum, however, with hundreds, perhaps thousands of women, wearing colourful kerchiefs or round, flat hats, bringing food to the market in baskets perched upon their heads. As many customers, principally housewives or their servants, made up the other half of the dynamic crowd, all talking, arguing, bargaining.

Smith had smelled fish almost from his hotel, and could have found the market blindfolded. At one point, he followed the fishwives, delivering their produce to the Praça da Figueira straight from their husbands' boats, their bare feet slapping a beat as they padded along the market's damp floors.

As he passed by the various stalls, Smith observed that the bounty of the sea was merely the most olfactorily pressing of all the items for sale. The shabby, drab sheds incongruously offered vibrantly-coloured vegetables and fresh meat, and millions of blossoms of brilliant hues. The din may have seemed riotous, and the crowds appeared to surge aimlessly, but everything had a purpose, and by the end of the day that was just beginning, most who would have visited the market would be satisfied. Smith hoped that he would be able to say the same after his errand.

Beyond the ugly stalls and the populous aisles that separated them was the Caës de Sodré. From this railway station departed the trains that serviced the

The Old Ally

resorts of Estoril, twenty-five minutes away. About the station were gathered public houses familiar to sea-going traders, cafés where stories could be told and deals sealed. Above the Tamariz, a bar with dark windows and a quiet clientele of sailors, was the Lisbon office of Rüdiger Brothers, Importers and Exporters.

Neither the street entrance nor the first floor door at the top of the narrow staircase was marked with a name or number. The attractive middle-aged woman who sat at a desk in the outer office was surprised, almost startled, when Smith walked in. She had to struggle to recall what was probably the stock answer to visitors requesting to see Adolf Tappen.

"Mr Tappen sees nobody without an appointment." Her accent was heavily accented with German.

Smith removed a card from his waistcoat pocket and, with a short, sharp pencil, wrote several words on its plain back. He presented it with a smile to the receptionist.

"Perhaps he will make an exception in my case," Smith told the woman, in his friendliest manner.

With a mixture of anxiety over not announcing a possibly important individual, and of curiosity at seeing her superior's reaction, the receptionist stood and took the card uncertainly through the anteroom's second door, anonymous like the first, its ground glass revealing nothing. Smith stood to wait; the single chair ostensibly provided for visitors looked filthy. The room's only décor was a set of dilapidated filing cabinets and an ancient photograph on the wall of Hamburg harbour. The woman emerged a moment later and informed Smith that he could pass into the inner office.

The chamber into Smith walked was hardly larger than the preceding one, but had two bigger windows, through which the sounds and smells of the waterfront and its market drifted. Though the window gave an illusion of space, what there was of it was occupied by a desk, a couple of chairs, more cabinets, in better shape than their brothers in the outer office, and a small table, around which there was no opportunity to place even the smallest of stools. Evidently, company was something Adolf Tappen wished to discourage.

"Well, Herr Sinclair..." Tappen said slowly, not bothering to stand in greeting. "Your card tells...you make talk...Graf von Caprica..."

The German regarded Smith provocatively, as if challenging him to an argument. He was of average height and medium build, and thus should have had difficulty making himself comfortable in the small space he had allotted to himself. But Tappen seemed almost fluid, even when still. Or perhaps, Smith amended his observation, the proper analogy was to gas, which filled whatever container into which it was put. The German's face looked hard and unforgiving, yet yielding at the same time.

Obviously, conversation in English would not only take considerable time, but probably be confusing, so Smith responded to Tappen's remark in the trader's own language.

"That's right, Mr Tappen," he said. "As you may or may not know, a countryman of mine, a Royal Air Force officer named Lightfoot, has been arrested in connection with the Count of Caprica's murder. I've been despatched by His Majesty's Government to make inquiries."

The German considered the card Smith had given him, but it contained no information other than the visitor's name and address, both false. Tappen gestured for Smith to sit in one of the rickety chairs before his desk. They were, fortunately, cleaner than those in the outer office. After some further rumination, the trader told Smith that he could smoke if he so desired, though no cigarette was offered.

"Yes, I am aware of the count's death," Tappen said, in a curiously neutral version of German. He lit a cigarette for himself. "I didn't know him well, but I met him once, at a garden party hosted by the minister of trade." He waved a hand, its motion seeming almost to defy the bones within it. "I can't pretend that I am sorry over what happened to the man, though it is nothing personal."

"Professional, then?" guessed Smith.

"I discovered that Caprica had been asking questions about arms smuggling to the Riffians in Morocco," Tappen replied, blowing out smoke.

"And that concerns you, professionally?"

Provoked, Tappen's eyes narrowed, the lids lowering as if weighted.

"It is commonly believed, here and in Spain, that Rüdiger Brothers is involved in gun-running to the Rif. This is a malicious lie. The Rüdiger brothers do not commit crimes."

Smith allowed Tappen praise for credibility. His indignation sounded genuinely righteous. This was the more remarkable in that not only were his employers the leading exporters, through various contacts and middle-men, of weapons and ammunition to the Moroccan rebels, but they were also surrogates for the reborn German military intelligence organisation. The Abwehr, as it was called, was tiny, constrained by budget and manpower limits, as well as foreign vigilance. Its representation abroad was, in terms of its own personnel, non-existent, and it relied upon unofficial assets. Adolf Tappen was, in effect, the Abwehr's head of station in Lisbon.

"And the count was spreading this...inaccuracy?" Smith managed to sound as if speaking ill of the murdered Portuguese were shameful. Tappen, surprisingly, was a little embarrassed.

"Well, no..." He ran a hand over his greying hair, which rebounded from the

The Old Ally

slight pressure in waves like a rolling sea. Smith thought it possible that the man was honest enough when his duties permitted. "But he was causing talk about the Rif. He spoke very casually about it, all just a matter of curiosity. But it gave people ideas."

Smith almost smiled. Many Germans in authority did not like people thinking too much.

"The interests of the Rüdigers, then, would not have been impaired if Caprica were silenced..." Smith put the notion as a theory.

Tappen's eyes squinted effortlessly again, but he considered his answer this time, the singing of the fishwives from the market plainly heard in the pause.

"They would be neither improved nor hindered, Mr Sinclair," the German stated, drawing on his cigarette once more. "And if you are interested in freeing Lightfoot, you might look in other directions. After all, I hear that Caprica liked to collect information on everything, like every rumourmonger."

"It *is* claimed that he had his finger on Portugal's pulse," said Smith.

"Well, he certainly listened to it," Tappen agreed, in a way. "There is much to learn about this country, if you care to, Mr Sinclair. Government inefficiency, police corruption, intrigues for and against Spain, monarchist plots, communist agitation... Caprica would have made many enemies."

"True, but it's probable that only one killed him," observed Smith.

"But not me," Tappen asserted, as he squashed his cigarette in an ashtray, "not me."

"I say, welcome back, old bean! How goes the quest for my freedom?"

Edward Lightfoot glanced up from a chair at the familiar table in the dungeon-like interview room of Lisbon's central gaol. He wore a newly-pressed suit, with flecks of grey in its medium brown fabric, and his blond hair seemed to have been trimmed since Smith's previous visit. He set aside the newspaper he had been perusing and picked up the pot of a china tea service.

"Care for some refreshment?"

"Thanks." Smith sat in the chair opposite Lightfoot's. The latter's was no longer identical to his visitor's, but looked as if it had come out of a pleasant café, its wood varnished and its seat softened with a thick cushion. "Are you certain you want to be freed?"

Lightfoot laughed and answered, "Quite certain, old comic. Oh, Miguel, may we have some of those biscuits the governor brought for me? The tin is in my cell."

Peering over Smith's shoulder, the air force officer performed a brief mime, imitating the selection and consumption of a light snack. The old warder, who had paused at the chamber's door like a waiter expecting to take an order, smiled and nodded, then withdrew and closed the door behind him. Smith did not hear it lock.

"Can you read that?" he asked, indicating the journal Lightfoot had set aside. The *Diaris Noticia* was Portugal's leading newspaper, and was printed, naturally, in the native language.

"Oh, no, of course not," said Lightfoot, handing his guest a filled cup. "But I find the foreign words amusing. And I think I discovered a story about me. Look here."

Indeed, the article to which the pilot pointed did mention his name, three times, though what it may have claimed about him was lost in non-translation. As the two Englishmen examined the story, Miguel returned and deposited a tin half full of biscuits on the table, with some cheerful, incomprehensible words.

"Now, you were referring to my incarceration in this hellish pit," Lightfoot said, as he added cream and sugar to the tea already in his own cup. "Was that an implication that my time behind bars is almost over?"

"It's possible," Smith replied blandly. His beverage tasted very good and the biscuits were rich and tasty. "If all goes well, I may have you out tomorrow."

"I say, that is good news. It means that I may just make it."

"Make what?"

"I have a date with a delightful angel at the Embassy next Tuesday."

"The girl you had tea with last week?" asked Smith. "You'll be able to meet with her several times by next Tuesday, I should think."

Lightfoot grinned, explaining, "Not His Majesty's embassy; the Embassy night club, in Mayfair. An entirely different girl. By Cranwell, you do lag behind the times."

Smith's last day in Portugal was, like those preceding it, sunny. The blue sky was fathomless and bright, and the temperature was high. The warmth was mitigated, however, by a breeze that drifted gently up the ridge that supported the eastern third of Lisbon.

There was built the older part of the city, its streets much narrower than those below, more serpentine than those on the western eminence opposite, where the Chiado and the Carmo cut straight lines through the architecture. The trams that etched their routes down the various thoroughfares and up the little alleys did not penetrate as far as the old cathedral and unlike the other ridge, the eastern was not served by public lifts. Smith walked a portion of the way to the grand church.

Though damaged in the great earthquake of 1755 which destroyed much of the city, the cathedral survived in such a condition as still to be considered a twelfth century building. As Smith approached it, in company with worshippers

The Old Ally

and tourists, it put him in mind of a kind of fortress. It never would have withstood a siege, and would have succumbed even to a half-hearted assault, yet with its square towers and grim appearance, it resembled in some ways a stronghold. It reminded the historian in Smith that much of what was now Portugal had been under Saracen domination, and the Church had been very much the Church Militant.

The interior had been simple and spare, but centuries of popular devotions had added to it, rather like a plain room would have become busy under the influence of an inveterate collector of figurines. Slowly though, the authorities were restoring the original beauty of the cathedral.

"Quite lovely, wouldn't you agree, Mr Sinclair?"

Among those kneeling in prayer or gazing at the decorations, Colonel Ortega Rodriguez stood, having entered a few minutes before Smith. He likely would not have observed the nondescript Briton, had the latter not made himself known.

"Indeed," concurred Smith, though he added, regarding those milling about near them, "but let's see if we can't find a bit of privacy."

It looked as though the cathedral's cloisters had suffered the worst of the damage from the tremors. The arcades that surrounded this deserted garden were not all standing, and many that were seemed ready to topple. Smith thought the spot a sad one; here were tombs, ancient and forgotten, great bits of the church disused and deposited, like bits remaining after an inexpert assembly of a machine. But, perhaps for this reason, the enclosure, unattended, unrepaired for more than a century and a half, was left to Smith and Ortega, and no one else.

"Well, Mr Sinclair, like your telegram from Madrid, last night's note, asking me to meet this morning, was a surprise." Ortega raised his face to the sky. Its blue depth, uninterrupted by clouds, was all that could be seen from within the cloisters. The Spaniard smiled and lowered his eyes to Smith. As he did so, he momentarily had a chin, but it quickly disappeared into the smooth line of his throat. "How may I help you today?"

"I'd like you to write a letter, addressed to Commissario Barbosa, of the Lisbon Public Security Police, stating that you have proof that Squadron Leader Edward Lightfoot is innocent of killing the Count of Caprica."

Ortega seemed genuinely taken aback, and he opened his mouth, the flat lips almost attempting to form letters.

"An extraordinary request," he said, after a moment. "How could I know that Lightfoot did not commit the murder?"

Smith sat on a fallen stone column.

"Because you did," he said.

Ortega again appeared to be at a loss. He searched his jacket's pockets for his cigarette case, and was relaxed once more before he found it. Smith did not wait for his acquaintance's response.

"You killed Caprica soon after Lightfoot left his house that Wednesday morning," he explained. "The count knew you, and probably admitted you himself; there was no forced entry."

"I have been to Quintas de Caprica, of course," the Spaniard stated, inhaling the first fumes from his cigarette. "But anybody could have slipped into that building: no doors or windows were ever locked or barred."

"As well, when we last spoke," said Smith, "you claimed that the count believed Rüdiger Brothers to be involved in gun-smuggling to the Rif. But even that company's own representative in Lisbon, who has no reason to protect Caprica's reputation, told me that Caprica thought no such thing."

"Really?" The colonel shrugged his slender shoulders and leaned against a cracked column that nonetheless managed to support one section of the arcade around the cloisters. "Everybody has an opinion."

"You also informed me that you had 'other ideas'," Smith went on. "In fact, it was the count who had those ideas. The Rüdigers may be selling arms to the Riffians, but they have help. A Spanish intelligence officer would be a great asset to the brothers."

Ortega looked hurt, and shook his head.

"You are quite wrong, Sinclair."

"Last Wednesday morning, you were probably waiting for the last of Caprica's dinner guests to depart. Most of the staff were still in bed, and the one who had already arisen was employed elsewhere." Smith, for Vasco Correia's protection, forebore to mention that the servant had indeed seen Ortega leave the count's home, mistaking him for Lightfoot.

"Caprica let you into his house, little suspecting that you had come to kill him," Smith theorised, "yet, at some point, he became frightened. He loaded a weapon from his collection, a mundane revolver, one with the most convenient ammunition. But you struck first. You seized one of the other pistols and bludgeoned the old man with it."

The colonel took his time answering the charge, drawing in more smoke from his cigarette and leisurely exhaling it again, as if time and effort were of no concern to him.

"A fanciful tale, Sinclair," he said, half-wearily and half-warily. "How on Earth did you arrive at your incredible conclusion?"

Smith himself now paused, as a pair of tourists stepped into the cloisters: an American couple, from that country's mid-west, to judge from their accents. They were apparently bored with the sights they were seeing, and withdrew

The Old Ally

after a comment about 'more darned ruins'.

"Do you recall when we met at the Beresford-Bar, Colonel? You made it clear that you knew nothing about Caprica's death, other than that it had occurred. I mentioned that he had been killed with one of his own firearms. When you then heard that Lightfoot had been arrested for the crime, you observed that it was most unlikely that he would have 'broken an old man's head'." Smith watched Ortega's limp face, but it reflected nothing. "A much more credible assumption — by anyone ignorant of the truth — would have been that Caprica had been shot, not clubbed, by one of his pistols or revolvers."

The Spaniard's eyes fluttered to a close, and the ends of his moustache disappeared as he pressed his lips together. He put his cigarette to those lips one last time.

"If Caprica had his suspicions of me," he asked, "why not tell somebody of them?"

"Despite what a few may have thought, the count was not a rumourmonger," replied Smith, respect in his voice for the late British agent: "he gathered information. He was probably unsure of his theories, and was awaiting an individual who would confirm them. He was expecting that man to visit him last Tuesday evening. At first, I thought that it may have been you. But this man arrived once or twice in disguise. You were an acquaintance, had been a dinner guest, so you needn't have had any recourse to subterfuge just to supply news to Caprica. I think the count's informant had been your clerk, Colonel. He didn't arrive as planned that Tuesday night, for he was already dying of... What was it? Cholera?"

Several ravens flew cautiously over the open enclosure, their wings beating deliberately. No other sound disturbed the two men. Ortega dropped his cigarette stub into the grass and ground it underfoot.

"A clever story, Sinclair," he admitted. "But the only proof you have, if I may dignify it with the word, is my remark about how the count was killed. I will simply deny that I uttered it, if it comes to that. Or perhaps... Yes, I think, after all, I must have overheard people discussing the murder at the Beresford-Bar while I was waiting for you." He smiled with a sickly confidence, and pushed himself away from the column against which he had been leaning.

"Could your background withstand scrutiny, Colonel?" Smith pondered aloud. "A senior officer in the army of His Most Catholic Majesty the King of Spain would not, I expect, sell his services cheaply; would your finances reflect only your legitimate income? And your clerk's death: would that bear investigation?"

Ortega had halted at the other man's words, but now resumed walking from the enclosure. As he vanished under the arcade, Smith sighed quietly, stretched his legs before him and pulled out his cigarette case.

Smith watched as Edward Lightfoot shook hands with the governor of Lisbon's central gaol, thanking him for his kindness and regard. The Royal Air Force officer, with a wistful expression on his boyish visage, then bade farewell to the prison's warders, who were drawn up as if for review by a general, in the next room; Smith wondered who was minding the inmates. It was the privilege of Miguel, the elderly guard under whose amiable watch Lightfoot had been incarcerated, to escort the former prisoner out of the building.

"Commissario Barbosa!" Lightfoot exclaimed happily. The policeman was waiting by a Public Security Department motor-car in the cobbled lane outside the gaol's main gate. "How nice of you to come and see me off! As kind as mutton that's turned itself into lamb, what, Sinclair?"

"My very words," Smith agreed.

The morning was another bright and cheerful one, with nothing in the sky but birds. Barbosa's expression matched the sunny day and as he stepped forward to shake the Englishmen's hands, he laughed uproariously.

"I have come, uh, to wish you well, senhor!" he said in his melodious accent. "And to apologise for, uh, arresting a man so obviously innocent." Barbosa whisked off his uniform's cap, reducing himself to the height of Smith's shoulders and nearly overwhelming the Britons with the sudden scent of his abundant hair oil.

"Well, I'm as glad as a crushed peanut shell that Colonel Ortega remembered seeing me at that theatre in the Park Mayer," said Lightfoot, his countenance showing an exaggerated sense of relief. "I'm sorry I left that bit out of my statement to you last week, Commissario. It must have slipped my mind in the excitement."

The Portuguese wiped at his rheumy eyes with a large, square handkerchief, and dismissed any worries.

"For myself," he said, "I was not aware that there were, uh, performances at that early hour, but..." Barbosa shrugged his shoulders which were, like the rest of his body, round and large. Then he turned with a flourish to the motor-car, its driver keeping the engine idling. "I have come also to, uh, offer you gentlemen a ride to wherever you need to go."

Smith and Lightfoot glanced at the small, almost delicate vehicle, then at the width of the police officer, and finally at each other.

"Thank you very much, Commissario," said Smith, convincingly.

"I say, dashed kind of you," added Lightfoot. He waved a last good-bye to

The Old Ally

Miguel, who was still standing, stooped and frail, in the open gateway of the stone-walled prison, and walked to the automobile with his companions. "Sinclair and I were about to nourish the inner chap, Commissario; would you care to join us?"

Barbosa laughed, genuinely pleased and able to show it best this way, but he declined with profuse apologies.

"I am very busy today. I must go to meet a good friend of mine, who is in some, uh, authority in Madrid. Colonel Ortega's poor clerk, you see... The only case of cholera in Lisbon last week..."

"Very tragic," remarked Smith, following Lightfoot into the rear seat of the motor-car.

"Yes, yes, most unusual..." said Barbosa, forcing his bulk into the empty passenger's seat, next the driver. "Yes, I must see my, uh, friend in Madrid..." And he laughed some more.

The Heart of Betrayal

Linus Smith considered it one of the pleasures of his native land that each month was different than the one which preceded it or followed it; each had its own characteristics that made it unique in the calendar. Thus it was that May, less wet than April but not as warm as June, represented spring in its fullness, bringing to England the lushness of its fields and the vividness of its gardens.

So Smith thought as he climbed the oak staircase of Number 1, Melbury Road, and was, after pausing for permission in the secretaries' ante-room, shown into his chief's conference room, next to his office. The room was almost deserted. Fresh air stirred the curtains of the open windows and two sparrows, standing on a sill to which they had resorted from the burgeoning garden below, regarded the newcomer as an interloper.

C was seated at the big round table to one side, his chair under the huge portrait of his son. The chief of the Secret Service was dressed in a dark blue suit, reminding Smith of the older man's career in the Royal Navy, and was reclining with his eyes closed. Smith noted with some concern that C's face, normally red from all the years he had spent in the elements on the open oceans, seemed pale and tired. Smith cleared his throat.

Instantly, C's eyes were wide, and alert as ever.

"Damn it, my boy, you are the only person I can never hear approach." The old sailor smiled. The expression, combined with the downward-cutting nose and upward-thrusting chin, made him resemble a most benevolent Punch. "Sit yourself down."

C, quite his old self, offered his guest refreshment but, as Smith had just come from having luncheon at his club, the invitation was declined.

"A cigarette, then."

C held out an open box, taken from the mantelpiece. After he had resumed his seat, he glanced across the table at the army officer.

"Do you know who Sir Nicholas Boisragon is?"

"Yes sir. He is His Majesty's minister to Rumania," Smith replied. "Though I'm sure he would not remember me, I met him while he was on the high commission in Constantinople in 1920."

"That's the chap, my boy. Last night, we received a cable from Ward, our man in Bucharest. It seems that Boisragon's wife has left him."

The Heart of Betrayal

Smith made a noncommittal remark and C smiled. Whenever he did so, he seemed less like the head of the country's intelligence organisation and more like a kindly uncle, who, in this case, felt he might have been humoured.

"Yes, I realise that you must be wondering what concern a diplomatist's domestic arrangements — or disarrangements — are to us." C inhaled smoke from his own cigarette. "Lady Boisragon's a Russian, a White refugee from the late civil war. She's young and beautiful, and captured Boisragon's middle-aged heart in a few days three years ago."

"It's thought that she might be a GPU agent?" Smith referred to the Soviet secret police force.

"And that is why this matter concerns us. It's not inconceivable that she was sent to wreck Boisragon's career. The fellow is a terrific anti-Bolshevik and has a very bright future in his field. Or had, I should say, if this affair becomes a scandal."

"If she is a GPU agent, she would have been very well placed to obtain information through her husband." Smith dropped burned tobacco into an ashtray. "Though that would necessitate her remaining with him."

"It will be your task to go to Bucharest and investigate the matter. Boisragon cabled a frank report to the Foreign Office, so I had Anstruther collect a copy of it this morning; you'll be able to get Ward's report from him as well."

"You don't want to use Ward in this case, sir?"

"No," replied C. "Everyone in Bucharest knows him as the chap in charge of the legation's passport office. They would all think it odd if he busied himself making inquiries about the minister's private life. He'll provide you with whatever support you require, however." C extinguished his cigarette. "How soon can you get there?"

Smith thought for a moment, then answered that the next boat train left for Dover at ten after three, giving him a couple of hours to catch it. After the Channel crossing and the trip to Paris, the new Simplon-Orient Express took seventy-eight hours to travel to the Rumanian capital.

C chuckled: "You're better than a *Bradshaw's*, my boy."

Two hours did not, in fact, give Smith much time, considering what he had to do. Fortunately, Anstruther, in charge of the Secret Service's Section I, which collated, analysed and disseminated political intelligence gained through covert means, was prepared. He had copies of the reports forwarded by both Ward and Boisragon ready for Smith and, in addition, was able to provide information on the minister that Smith lacked.

Even more efficient was Odways, Smith's valet, who, having served as his batman throughout the Great War, was more than a match for his employer's peripatetic lifestyle. He ensured that they were waiting at Victoria Station when the train commenced boarding at three o'clock. This allowed Smith enough time to despatch a short letter to his acquaintance, Prince Kostromov, before departure.

The journey to the most northerly of the Balkan states was uneventful, though delays were incurred by customs inspections and the odd detour, both dictated by conditions imposed by the end of the War, just four and a half years previously. The train route, and its service, at least, was being improved all the time, as Europe, and especially its new nations, adjusted to the post-war era. A postponed departure from Paris's Gare de Lyon meant that the Englishmen reached Bucharest early Tuesday afternoon. This was fine with Smith.

"It'll probably be different from the last time we were here," he said, closing the book he had been reading for most of the day. He handed it to his valet. Odways put it in one of his employer's bags, then gathered together the suitcases — Smith's two and his own one — as the train steamed through Bucharest's outskirts toward the city centre.

"I'm sure you are right, sir."

Indeed, the only prior visit the two had made to Rumania's capital had been in December of 1916. The country's mis-timed declaration of war against Germany and Austria had led to the spectacularly rapid collapse of its army. Smith's primary recollection had been of a cold, panicky city, rather like an overgrown market town, being deserted by all those capable of flight.

May, however, was just as pleasant a month in Bucharest as it was in London, though much sunnier and warmer. Flower sellers thronged the streets and with their baskets of blooms — roses being especially numerous — turned the exterior of the railway station, where Smith hailed a motor-taxi, into a garden.

"Strada Jules Michelet 24, please."

Smith tried English on the driver first, as he and Odways settled into the back of the automobile. It and French were the first foreign tongues most Rumanians learned, though how far below the aristocracy its knowledge seeped, the major was uncertain. French was close to the native language (one of the few he did not know), so he thought that he might be understood in that, if need be.

"British legation?" the driver said, after some hesitation. The accent was unmistakably Russian, and upper class.

"That's right," replied Smith, in the man's language. "I'll get out there and my man will go on to the Wallachia Hotel."

"Very good, sir."

The Heart of Betrayal

The driver, almost cheerful at hearing this hint of his homeland, put his vehicle in gear and pulled out into the boulevard.

Smith was not surprised at meeting a Russian behind the wheel of a Bucharest taxi. Many White Russians, exiled because of their opposition to the Bolsheviks, had taken up similar work in the French capital. It made sense that those who had found it impossible to travel so far might have settled in Rumania, migrating to its chief city, often hailed as the 'Paris of the Balkans'.

At the legation, Smith left his card and signed his own name in the guest-book; this was not a mission which required an alias. He asked the porter, a jovial but authoritative man with the air of an ex-soldier, if he might pass another of his cards to Colonel Ward. A minute later, the porter returned and requested Smith to follow him.

"Come in, man, come in."

Joseph Ward, late of the King's Dragoon Guards, strode across his first floor office and grasped Smith by the hand. Accustomed as the major was to firm grips, Ward's was like a knot of silk, gentle but powerful all the same. He was tall and wide and thick, all bone and muscle, with a little space grudgingly left for internal organs. Even in a heavy cavalry regiment, it must have been a challenge to find the horse that could have supported him.

"Headquarters let me know someone was coming. I don't think we've ever met."

"We did, briefly," Smith corrected, flexing his hand surreptitiously, hoping the blood would start circulating in it again. "It was in November of '16. I was with the 'Corn and Oil Stores' Mission."

"Oh yes..." Ward smiled. His mouth, usually set in a deceptive-looking pout, was rather low on his face, which was principally covered by a big nose and canine brown eyes. The mission of which Smith had been part had been sent to Rumania primarily to destroy its namesake commodities before they fell under German control. Ward had been sent at the same time directly to Bucharest by C to provide much needed intelligence. "Dashed sorry I can't remember you."

"The situation was hectic," observed Smith, though in fact people forgot meeting him even under the most favourable circumstances.

"Can I get something for you? Tea? Cigarette? No? Do you mind, then?" Ward held up his pipe and packed its bowl with tobacco. The head of the Secret Service station then closed his office door. "Sit down and tell me how I can help."

"I know some things about Boisragon," said Smith, taking a hard, straight-backed chair. "He comes from a very distinguished family which accounts for a number of pages in *Burke's*. Educated at Eton and Oxford, he entered the Foreign Service in 1894. He's served in several posts, always doing sterling work. Some opinions hold that he could have progressed faster than he has but refused some promotions because of the good he believed that he was doing in his then-current appointments."

"True, true," Ward responded. He was sitting precariously on the corner of his desk, and Smith feared that the man's bulk would snap it off, sending Ward crashing down on top of him. "I was already here when he was posted to the legation in 1920... July, I think, perhaps August. He's the only minister I've known who doesn't act as if the local Secret Service station is in the pay of a hostile country. He doesn't get involved in our duties, mind you," Ward pointed with the stem of his pipe; "he's very correct in such matters."

Though, as was the way with small groups, most diplomatic staff in missions abroad became informally aware of who represented the Secret Service, a minister was often required definitely to know this for the smooth working of the station. At best, most diplomatists simply preferred to pretend that the resident intelligence personnel did not exist.

"And now he's wealthy. The Earl of Dantry died early this year."

"Right. Boisragon isn't a close relative, but all of Lord Dantry's nearer kin are dead, the last killed in the War. So he left Boisragon his estates, worth £22,000 a year, I hear."

"And Lady Boisragon?"

"Much younger, I'm sure you know." Ward held his pipe in his mouth, where it resembled a slender twig growing from a massive tree trunk. "She can't be more than twenty-three. Beautiful, vital, friendly, warm. One of those women who have a natural and universal sex appeal, if you can understand my meaning."

Ward's tone was neither lewd nor insinuous but rather surprised, as if he had met too many women hiding behind façades, and had been pleasantly taken aback by Irina Boisragon.

"They were happy?" asked Smith.

"One couldn't help noticing how happy a couple they were..." The station head contemplatively puffed smoke from the corner of his wide mouth. "And it didn't seem an act. But then, one never really knows."

"Tell me about last week."

"It was Wednesday," Ward said, nodding. "Boisragon went out in the morning, having received, I think, a private letter or note by the early post. He returned to the legation in the afternoon, missing his usual time for luncheon. I didn't see him so I know he seemed disturbed only from other witnesses. Lady Boisragon, who'd been out as well, came back later. It was clear something had happened. The next day, early, Lady Boisragon left with her maid and three or four suitcases for the station, bound for England." The colonel shrugged, the shoulders of his grey suit moving like plates of armour. "I don't spy on the staff here, but I keep my ears open."

"That's sensible," agreed Smith.

"I sent a report to Headquarters, since this seemed the sort of thing the other side might exploit."

"The minister forwarded his own account a little later. It matched yours in essentials."

"That's like him," said the head of station. "He wouldn't hide anything unpleasant, especially if it might concern matters of state."

"Well, that should be all for now, I think." His visitor stood. "Thank you for your help, Ward. I hope," Smith added slowly, "my coming doesn't put you out in any way."

"Not a bit, man; I'm glad you're here. It's always awkward inquiring into someone you work with. C knew what he was doing by dispatching an operator from outside the station to investigate." The two shook hands again, Smith wincing mentally with the effect.

The Hotel Wallachia was an ageing but still genteel establishment opposite the Old Princely Court in the Lipscani district, the original heart of Bucharest. The hotel had never been of the same class as the elegant and popular Athenée Palace, inspired by the Ritz in Paris, nor the aristocratic Ambassador, but then, it had never attempted to match them. Smith liked the Wallachia's quiet atmosphere, the shady courtyard around which it had been built, and its respectable, unostentatious reputation.

"Adequate, Odways?"

Smith selected a book from the several he had brought with him. His valet had quickly unpacked his clothes upon arrival at the suite Smith had rented, and had placed his employer's evening wear neatly on the bed.

"Yes sir," Odways replied, coming into the sitting room. "More than adequate for a continental hotel."

Odways's opinions of life abroad were insular. Electricity, central heating and indoor plumbing were all well and good, but if a British inn were stocked only with lamps, a coal-burning fireplace and a chamber pot, he would have rated it superior. Though the Wallachia had, in fact, electric lighting, no further concessions had been made to modernity. This hardly bothered Smith and, indeed, Odways found other aspects of the hotel more important.

"Quite clean for these parts, sir, and the staff are reasonably efficient and respectful. I noticed that the page-boy's fingernails were not at all dirty."

"I'm glad to hear it."

Smith had chosen a slightly shabby armchair in the sitting room and found that it conformed well to the shape of his body, due no doubt to a half-century of other patrons' posteriors moulding it for him. Through the open doors of the balcony, he could see the orange light of the setting sun colouring the faded walls across the courtyard. A rap on the door announced an arrival.

"A letter for you, sir," said Odways, after dismissing the hotel messenger.

"It's an invitation." The paper was thick, of excellent quality and all the words written by hand, though the penmanship was so perfect that they might have been machine-printed. "From a Countess Arionescu, for Thursday evening."

"Rapid work among the hostesses, sir. Will you be attending?"

"Oh, yes. One can learn much from these society parties, even if it's only unreliable gossip gleaned from rumour. And I expect that the Boisragons have generated much of that."

"And tonight, sir?"

"Colonel Ward is taking me to a place called the Traian. I fear it may be an imitation Moulin Rouge sort of affair; hardly an informative venue. Though, I suppose..." Smith amended, opening his book "...it depends upon what one wishes to learn."

The invitation for which Smith had actually been hoping arrived the next day. He had returned very late from his excursion with Ward, walking into the Wallachia's lobby with the first rays of dawn. The Traian had been as bad as he had anticipated, a night club near the National Theatre that had adopted a classical theme. The décor was, allegedly, second century Roman, the chorus girls clad in diaphanous 'nymphs' garb'. The women were so beautiful and their dancing so terrible that Smith was torn for most of the night between looking and not.

During a late breakfast of sausages, eggs, toast and tea (the Wallachia had catered to English patrons before), an invitation from Nicholas Boisragon's secretary arrived, asking Smith to dinner that evening at the legation.

Smith had never flattered himself that such invitations were due to his wit, charm, ebullience or the like, for he averred that he had none. His presence was requested at functions because he was a convenient bachelor, a neutral party, a respectable-sounding name. Countess Arionescu had sent him a summons so quickly because he was new in a city whose Society was small. The invitation from the legation was due to the custom of diplomatic and consular officers showing fellow Britons hospitality when they travelled. Smith could have been almost anyone of the same nationality and class, and the result would have been identical.

Odways had performed a minor miracle in repairing a rent in the leg of his

The Heart of Betrayal

employer's dress trousers, caused by a Rumanian cavalry officer's spurs. A brawl had developed over one of the Traian's dancers and, as she had appealed for protection to Smith and Ward, the two Englishmen felt honour-bound to intervene. Fortunately, the others involved were mostly beneficent toward Great Britain and the tear in the trousers was merely incidental to the general bedlam. The fracas, like Smith's garment, was soon healed, and in both cases everything returned to normal.

As the major discovered when he arrived at the legation that evening, the dinner was an all-male affair. Smith surmised that including ladies might have accentuated Lady Boisragon's absence. That the dinner was held at all was of course necessary: a diplomatist did not represent his country by remaining hidden from his host-nation's Society.

Among Boisragon's other guests were a general and a colonel of the Rumanian Army; the French minister; several aristocrats; a government prefect and a minor oil magnate. The conversation was largely interesting (from Smith's professional point of view) and the major made several successful but intentionally banal additions to the talk. The evening broke up about midnight, keeping a debate between two of the Rumanians about currency administration from becoming an argument.

As the others were departing, Smith asked Boisragon if they might speak in private. The minister agreed and led the other to his study in the residential wing.

"Colonel Ward mentioned that you might wish to talk to me," he said, after the door closed behind them. "I alone among the staff here know of his true role at the legation, though to be honest others might have guessed by now."

"I didn't want you to think that I was here under false colours, sir," said Smith. "I've been sent by the Foreign Office to make certain inquiries."

Sir Nicholas Boisragon was a man of average appearance; not so average that, like Smith, he was in danger of being camouflaged by the very background. But he nonetheless had few outstanding superficial features. Though in his early fifties, he seemed younger, and as smart as he was in evening apparel, the insignia of a CMG on the breast of his coat over several foreign orders, he could easily have been mistaken for a second secretary or another middle level functionary, rather than the head of a mission.

"I was rather expecting someone to show up regarding my...debacle." Boisragon was a little embarrassed, and hid it behind hospitality. "Would like something to drink, Smith? Port? Something else, perhaps?"

"Port would be fine, sir. Thank you."

The study was a personal room, not an office. The photographs on the fireplace's mantel were of smiling people and happy groups in informal settings. The paintings on the walls were not of great artistic merit but no doubt of emotional attachment. The books in the shelves had well-worn bindings and the chair behind the desk was probably accustomed to generations of Boisragons. The minister poured wine into a pair of glasses at a sideboard.

"The legation, I'm told, had an excellent stock of port, as well as claret, before the War. It disappeared during the occupation by the Central Powers."

Smith accepted his glass and tasted its contents.

"Please don't interpret my presence here as an indication of any conclusion drawn by the Foreign Office, sir."

"I suspect that you must be rather like a police detective looking into a suicide, to make certain that it wasn't a murder," responded Boisragon. The two sat in wing chairs near the grate.

"You've had a successful career, sir. Our country's enemies would benefit if that were shortened."

"You would like to know about my wife."

"If it's not too painful."

"Everything is painful now, Major." The minister sipped his port and leaned his head back. "I was on the staff of the high commission at Constantinople in 1920. The city was full of White Russians, homeless, stateless, friendless for the most part, and more on the way. The Bolsheviks were sweeping them out of their country, and many of them came to Constantinople, at least temporarily. You can't imagine the scenes we saw then."

Smith could indeed imagine the scenes, for he had seen them from both ends. He had witnessed the dreadful evacuations from Novorossisk that March and, soon after, served with the British Army's headquarters in Constantinople.

"Irina Globova — as she was then — was attached to a committee attempting to succour the refugees. She was educated, multi-lingual and beautiful. She was also alone. As a member of the British high commission, I had dealings with this committee, and as soon as I saw her..."

Though his head was back and facing upward, Boisragon's eyes were not, for the moment, seeing the plaster patterns on the ceiling. What he saw was hundreds of miles and three years away.

"The intoxication I felt was complete," he continued, half a minute later. "Irina and I were married less than two months later. Many told me that I might regret such a precipitous action. Some actually suggested that I simply keep her as my mistress." A dark frown of anger lowered over Boisragon's brow and he emptied his glass. Smith thought the port too good to drink so quickly.

"But your career prospered," he said.

"Yes." Boisragon seemed reluctant to come back to the present. "Sir Horace — Sir Horace Brunte, then high commissioner, now ambassador to Turkey —

used his influence in my favour and fortune smiled on me, at least for the time. I was appointed to this legation."

"Had there been any sign of trouble in your marriage before last week?"

"None to which I was party. We'd been perfectly happy." The minister's face took on an expression of confusion. "A fortnight ago, we had our first disagreement, the first in three years. The way Irina behaved... It wasn't like her. Or perhaps it was, and I simply didn't know the real woman." He tipped his glass to his mouth, forgetting that he had finished his wine. He set it on a small table near by.

"What was the disagreement about, sir?"

"My career," Boisragon said with incredulity, as if the subject had been time-travel or something equally outlandish. "I recently inherited some property and we were arguing over whether we should retire to it."

"And last Wednesday..."

Boisragon did not speak immediately. Two clocks ticked somewhere in the room.

"I received a letter by the morning post. It was addressed to me personally and marked 'confidential'. Inside was a single sheet of note paper on which was typed 'Your wife will be at the Phanar Hotel, room 18, at noon today, with her lover'." The sentence had apparently been chiselled into the diplomatist's memory.

"Are you married, Major? If you are not, you can only pretend to know what I felt at that moment. I tried to dismiss it as a cruel prank, a ridiculous joke. But I *had* to know, of course. The Phanar is a little hotel, as it turns out, in the Strada Bazarul, not quite respectable but not quite not...if you understand me."

"You arrived at noon?"

"A bit before, rather." Boisragon rubbed his eyes, as though he had been staring at something too long without blinking. "I knocked on the door of room 18 and it was opened by...someone I recognised..."

"Sir." Smith had no desire to press but the identity of Lady Boisragon's paramour might have been important.

"It was Prince Stefan Movilesco." Boisragon stared unseeingly ahead. "If it had been anyone else..." He glanced over at his guest. "You're probably unfamiliar with the bounder, but Movilesco is well-known in Rumanian Society, Major. His appetite for seduction is unparalleled even among that company, which can rival Louis XIV's Versailles for romantic intrigue."

"What was his reaction?" Smith wanted to know.

"He laughed. He was just leaving anyway, and as he put on his hat, he tipped it to me and called me by my name." Boisragon's face, reflecting horror, surprise and astonishment, might have been that which he had worn the previous Wednesday. "I was speechless. He walked past me and I simply stood on the threshold. Eventually, I entered the room. Irina was still..."

Smith finished his wine while waiting for the minister to collect himself.

"I will not repeat what my wife and I said to each other, Major. I will never repeat it, just as I will never forget it. Suffice it to say that I never would have believed her to be capable of such heartlessness. If she'd shown the least remorse, I would have forgiven her, but..."

Again, the two clocks ticked mechanically, a fraction of a second out of synchronicity.

"I told her that she would have to leave the legation, to which she agreed." The diplomatist sighed, a sad, puzzled exhalation. "She informed me that she would go to England, and imply that it was for reasons of health. She would give me time to think of what I wanted to do. I returned to the legation, as she did later, acting as if nothing untoward had taken place. I was not so nonchalant. I spent the night on the settee in my dressing room, and early the next morning Irina departed with her maid."

After a respectful moment, Smith said, "I appreciate the candour you have shown, sir. I imagine that this interview has been most painful. I assure you that nothing you have stated will be repeated, even to my superiors, unless absolutely necessary."

The minister was surprised.

"Won't they require a report?" he asked.

"They will be satisfied with knowing the results of my inquiry, not its stages."

"Thank you, Major." Boisragon rose, as did his guest, and the two shook hands. "If I can do anything for you during your stay, you have only to mention it."

Smith was struck by how still the legation was when he left the study a moment later. In the large lobby, the night porter was in his chair, reading a week-old English newspaper, but the rest of the staff were abed. Smith wondered if his mind, so full of questions, would admit of sleep this evening.

A waiter removed Smith's dishes and the Briton relaxed in the shade offered by a large chestnut tree. He had just finished his luncheon: pork stew and a kind of corn mush. It was hardly the sort of mid-day meal to which he was accustomed, but he always favoured sampling the local cuisine when he travelled. He decided that he preferred the venue to the food.

The Café Gradina was a pleasant, clean restaurant, with more tables outside on its stone-flagged terrace than inside, and located near Cismigiu Park, thus giving the establishment its name. The number of cafés with facilities for

The Heart of Betrayal

streetside-dining was one of the aspects which led some to compare this capital to that of France. In some ways, Bucharest did resemble Paris.

Or rather, Smith amended as he took a drink of his beer, the physical features of Bucharest resembled those of Paris. Several wide, tree-lined boulevards ran through the city, some, traversing north to south, tracing the pre-historic trade routes from the Carpathian Mountains to the Danube River. Between these principal avenues were narrower passages, flanked with slender buildings. The pastel-hued plaster on even the newer structures was already peeling and falling away.

The more prominent structures were big and heavy. Any characteristic of which a Parisian architect would use some, his Bucharest counterpart would use more. Ornate became ostentatious, baroque became grotesque. The city made Smith think that modern Rumania had sprung from the minds of men who had heard of Paris but not seen it. Bucharest became a sort of stage-Paris, the chief village of a medieval principality which had been made a kingdom, and needed a metropolis.

But it contained an array of sights not to be copied in France. From his table, Smith observed smart army officers walking past peasants in their local costumes; melon-sellers with their panniers; a Gypsy woman peddling paprika. The streets were busy with every kind of conveyance, from ox-carts to motor-buses — and a greater number of automobiles than anywhere else in eastern Europe.

Smith barely contained a rude belch and frowned at the glass before him on the wooden table. Rumanian beer at least was as gassy as its Gallic counterpart.

"Will you require anything else, sir?" The waiters seemed anxious to please. Smith's had several phrases that he could deliver in English. Everything else was comprehended with signs and gestures.

"Just the bill."

Smith removed from his jacket's inner pocket the letter he had received in the early post. Prince Kostromov had been able to provide him with information regarding Irina Boisragon, née Globova.

Her family had been wealthy, the result of a century in trade, primarily in tea. Their main home had been a palace on the Nevski Prospect, in Saint Petersburg, next door to the equally princely house of a grand duke. They owned a smaller mansion in Moscow and several estates in the country, as well as a seaside villa in the Crimea. Irina was the youngest of four children. Kostromov listed her siblings' names and their fates, none of the latter of which were pleasant, since they had come under the hands of the Bolsheviks. Her parents, though, simply vanished in the maelstrom of the Russian Civil War. Smith was apprised of the young woman's hobbies (music and interior decoration), favourite wine (Tokay) and driving skills (poor). She possessed no close friends of whom anyone knew.

Smith noted the date at the top of the letter and nodded. Kostromov had despatched his missive only a couple of days after the major had visited him the past Friday. By now, the prince would have learned, through his usual channels, of the woman's indiscretion. What interested Smith was that, according to his informant, Irina had committed none before.

Countess Arionescu lived in a large house of a vaguely Mediterranean style, set in spacious walled and flowered grounds beyond the Soseaua Kiseleff, Bucharest's Rotten Row. Smith arrived promptly at eight o'clock, his invitation's appointed time. As his taxi drove through the tall iron gates, his nose caught hints of cows and pigs, probably kept within further walls behind the house. He also smelled the more pleasing traces of wet laundry hung out to dry — hopefully some distance from the livestock.

The servants who ushered Smith into the cavernous drawing room were liveried in the manner of the early nineteenth century, and even had powdered hair. But Smith's attention was diverted by the assault of his hostess.

"My dear, sweet, Major! How kind of you to attend! You are the first Englishman I have had to one of my parties, excluding Sir Nicholas Boisragon, two previous ministers, their staffs and a few travellers."

"I'm honoured," Smith responded.

The countess was a thin, almost frail-looking woman of the major's age. Dark-haired but pale-skinned, she accentuated this contrast by an exuberant use of black make-up about the eyes which, to Smith's old-fashioned tastes, made her appear very sleepless (or beaten) but which many these days found becoming. He did not really consider her pretty, but her movement and speech were both vibrant and attractive. It was clear that her sickly-slender frame had nothing to do with ill health.

The drawing room, as large as a ballroom, was decorated as a French salon of the Belle Époque, gold and black being the predominant colours. No other guest was present and Smith wondered if he had read his invitation inaccurately.

"Not at all, Major!" the countess laughed, a light and appealing sound, genuine. "You are merely early."

Smith, frowning as if at a puzzle, looked at his watch, then at the room's several clocks, all of which showed a minute or two had passed since eight o'clock. The lady laughed again.

"You *must* be English, Major. Nobody in Rumania ever arrives on time. Come, sit with me. We will have an apéritif while we wait for the others."

Smith was seated on a chaise-lounge of the sort that accommodated Madame

The Heart of Betrayal

Récamier in David's famous portrait. When pressed with a number of possible libations, he chose his usual pre-prandial beverage. His hostess wafted her wispy form onto the patterned upholstery beside him, her thigh, clad in the filmy fabric that every woman who followed Parisian fashion now wore, touching his own.

"Your English is flawless, Countess," Smith commented. Ironically, it was his ability to initiate and sustain small-talk that helped to keep him unremembered the morning after any party. One who faltered or failed in this essential social activity would be considered a bore, one who rose above it would become a centre of attention; as neither, Smith was invisible. "Did you learn it in Britain?"

The woman smiled coyly and replied, "No, Major. I have alas never been farther west than Paris. But many Rumanian families employ English governesses, and mine was no exception. A French nurse, an English nanny and an Austrian lover during the occupation and voila! I am multi-lingual, and please, call me Sissy."

Smith did not delve into the woman's method of mastering German, but sipped the sherry he had been given by an elegantly-attired footman.

"But now, Major," Sissy said, in a conspiratorial tone, "before the others arrive, tell me about your very proper minister and his very improper wife."

"Sorry?"

"Come, come, Major..." Sissy slipped her hand onto Smith's leg. The soldier had, on numerous occasions during the War, tossed away German grenades with nearly spent fuses, so he was able to maintain his composure in this situation, too. "I invited you because a new face is always welcome in Bucharest, especially at this time of year, and especially an officer — our own, you understand, can create ecstasy with their words, but with little else. But now, this scandal breaks about the British Legation. You must tell me more."

"I'm afraid I'll disappoint you, Sissy," Smith confessed, "for you probably know more about the matter than I. For instance, I'm not even aware with whom Lady Boisragon is supposed to have committed her folly."

"Why, it was Prince Stefan Movilesco, of course," said Sissy, playfully slapping her guest's leg and taking a drink from her glass. Her refreshment seemed to be a discoloured cocktail. "He is a positive wolf in Society. He is rumoured to have been the queen's first lover."

"Quite successful with the ladies, then?" Smith asked innocently.

"Among the very young, and the less discriminating, yes." Sissy's eyebrows, which, if they had been thinner, would not have existed, arched. "In spite of his title, he is rather common. I invite him to this house when I wish to annoy my husband. Those new to Society or to Bucharest might be swayed by his manners."

The countess's opinion of Irina Boisragon's paramour seemed genuine. Smith found himself watching Sissy's violet eyes and decided that she may have known something after all, in applying the heavy black cosmetics. Though she rather resembled a scheming adventuress in a moving-picture show, the effect of her make-up had grown on her visitor.

"That is why I did not think that Movilesco would ever win Lady Boisragon's body," the countess stated, leaning close to the Englishman. "In spite of her youth, she seemed mature, and the faintest whiff of scandal had never come from the British mission."

"You didn't think 'he would ever'... Had he been trying to seduce Lady Boisragon for long?"

"As long as she and her husband have been in the kingdom, my dear. I suppose that is why the prince has remained in Bucharest." Sissy peered at her guest's unremarkable face, which Smith made deliberately questioning. "Oh, yes, you might not be aware... Our Season begins in November, with the return of parliament. Society leaves for the country come spring."

"But Movilesco stayed?"

"He sometimes does, if he is in pursuit of some poor girl. He usually takes them back to his villa, one of those houses with the railings on the chausée. Most nights he has some body there."

Smith drank the last of his sherry and wondered aloud, "How did the minister discover the affair?"

"Oh, Major, a man like Movilesco has many enemies," Sissy remarked. When Smith suggested that the informer might have been a previously cuckolded husband, the countess laughed. "Heavens, no, my dear: a no-longer-cuckolding wife. Passions rule the aristocracy in Rumania, completely unhindered by anything resembling self-control." As if to illustrate the point, she emptied her glass, leaned across Smith to place it on a small table beyond their seat and said, "Now, Major, my second guest will, I guarantee, not appear for at least half an hour and I, as hostess, need not show myself for another half-hour after that. So, why don't I offer you a more...intimate...hospitality upstairs?"

"Well, uh, your husband—"

"My husband is at our country house in the mountains and does not mind me entertaining. You see, Major," the smile on Sissy's face was almost girlish, "infidelity is hardly a sin in Rumanian Society but, oh, missed opportunities are condemned as the darkest of vices."

"Good morning, sir."

The Heart of Betrayal

The sun had long since passed its dawn and was strong, uninhibited by clouds over a city already about its business. Around the Wallachia Hotel, the tradesmen of the Lipscani had opened for the day, the big black iron doors of their shops wide. The tables of the coffee shops were being cleared of the stained cups and crumb-littered dishes of their breakfast customers. Traffic, horse-drawn and motorised, was steady on the boulevards.

"Was the countess's party a success, sir?"

Linus Smith had returned to his hotel suite a minute before. He handed his tall, silk hat to Odways, who was waiting in the hall.

"It's rather difficult to know how to answer that," Smith replied. "Suffice it to state that there were no fatalities."

"And no casualties among the garments, sir?"

"Not among mine."

The major stood on his balcony, leaning on the railings and inhaling the fresh morning air. His eyes were sore from peering through ten or eleven hours' worth of tobacco smoke (the Rumanian gentlemen at Countess Arionescu's table had not waited until the ladies had taken their leave before indulging; indeed, some of the ladies had joined them). His head ached from the constantly high noise level that Sissy contended was the norm at her gatherings; his stomach rumbled and twisted in response to an indifferently prepared Black Sea fish dish.

"Were you able to obtain information from the countess, sir?"

"She provided all that I could have wanted," said Smith, turning away from the serene and cool courtyard below. "What of your errand?"

"Pease will be able to meet you tonight at nine o'clock, sir." After Smith had made an appropriately approbationate response, Odways excused himself. "I'll prepare your bath, sir, and ready your bed."

Smith nodded. He was not an habitué of the night-life; the more raucous the event, the rarer his attendance upon it. But when he had been a young officer, guest night in the mess could be a long, arduous but enjoyable ordeal, though he did not recall feeling so 'pushed and pulled' (as his father may have put it) after one of those occasions. He was getting old, he told himself, with nothing to show for the years past but less time remaining.

The Butoiul de Aur was a little restaurant off the Soseaua Kiseleff, near Bucharest's triumphal arch. This monument, still of temporary wooden construction, had been raised to commemorate Rumania's part in the Allied victory just four and a half years before. Smith shook his head as he viewed it. Considering the effect Rumania had on the War, the arch came very close to being a celebration of Germany's victory.

Inductions Dangerous

The Butoiul de Aur itself was a bit of a disappointment. The name, which, thanks to Rumanian's affinity to other Romance languages, Smith knew to mean 'The Golden Cask', resembled an A.B.C. tea shop in Paddington more than a fine dining house. This was why, perhaps, Robert Pease routinely stopped here whenever he had a free evening.

Pease was a porter at the British Legation and was, in fact, the diplomatic servant whom Smith met when he first visited the mission. Pease was about fifty years of age, round of belly and of face, with jowls serving as a foundation for an impressive pair of Victorian side-whiskers. Despite his girth, he sat as straight as a rifle barrel in his chair.

Beside him at his table was a woman of about forty. She seemed nervous as Smith approached, and she bit her lower lip, which was painted very tentatively with a red cosmetic. Smith thought that it was as well that she had not used more make-up for, in spite of her fidgety manner and the unappealing hat she wore, she was rather attractive. More lipstick and rouge would have ruined the effect.

Smith greeted Pease and was invited to sit down in the table's third chair.

"Major, this is Mary Anne Conroy. She works at the legation as one of the maids." The woman was slightly flustered, but pleased, when Smith rose from his chair and lightly took her hand.

"You look like an old soldier, Pease," Smith remarked.

The porter gave a small grin, displaying several gaps in his teeth, and said, "That's right, sir. I did my twenty-one years in the Loyals."

"A South Africa man?"

"Yes sir. I would have been in the last war but I suppose they thought me past my prime, so they kept me at the legation here."

"You were in Bucharest when the Germans invaded? Then I suspect you were of more value to the minister and his staff than you would have been as one of the millions in France."

"Just what I always tells him, sir," said Conroy, her support of Pease overcoming her shyness of Smith. She put her small hand on the bulk of the porter's arm and he smiled. A waiter, evidently one of only two working this evening, made his way through the crowded, humming room to the Britons' isolated table.

"The beer here is pretty good, sir," urged Pease. "It ain't like a pint at the local back home, but it ain't like the usual around Bucharest neither."

Smith acquiesced and Pease pointed to the half-empty glasses, holding up three fingers. The waiter nodded and left.

"I have to assure you, Pease, and you, Conroy, that I do not wish to damage any reputations," stated Smith. "As Odways informed you, I was sent by the

The Heart of Betrayal

Government to examine this unfortunate matter concerning the Boisragons. Nothing you tell me will end up in a newspaper tomorrow. I want the truth, not rumour."

"Fair enough, sir." Both legation servants were relieved at Smith's declaration. "But in a city like this one, anybody wanting the truth will be outnumbered by scandal-mongers."

"As far as you know, when did trouble begin between the minister and his wife?"

The waiter returned with a trio of filled glasses on a tray, and Smith paid him before Pease could. The major sampled his beverage and found it just as watery as that served at the Café Gradina. Perhaps the porter had been absent from England for too long. Smith nevertheless made gratifying noises as he drank.

"Myself, sir, I always thought they were happy," Pease replied: "a model couple, you might say."

"But I heard from Lewis — Lady Boisragon's own maid — that she — Lady Boisragon — was crying in her room one night about two weeks ago." As she spoke, Conroy dabbed at her mouth with a delicate but aged handkerchief, the Butoiul de Aur apparently not counting napkins among its stock. "I know it's second-hand news, sir, but Lewis is reliable."

"What might have caused this behaviour on Lady Boisragon's part? I assume that it was behaviour that was uncharacteristic."

"It *was* unchar...racter...istic, sir..." Conroy said.

"Lewis told us," Pease continued, reaching for his second glass, "that Sir Nicholas and Lady Boisragon had argued over staying in the Diplomatic Service."

Smith drank some more beer, realising that he would regret it later, and asked, "When was this argument?"

His informants had to think for a moment. They turned to each other and concluded that it had occurred on a Tuesday.

"Did Lady Boisragon have a routine that she followed most days? Tea with friends one afternoon; charity work another morning?" Smith's guess was rewarded with affirmative answers. "And she broke with her habit that Tuesday."

Pease raised his thick eyebrows and Conroy nodded energetically.

"Yes sir," she said. "Mrs Basarascu generally came over to Lady Boisragon's drawing room on Tuesdays. She's the wife of the prime minister...or someone..." Smith recognised the name as that of Bucharest's mayor. "But that day, Lady Boisragon cancelled the appointment and went out in the afternoon."

"And the argument with her husband followed in the evening."

"Yes sir."

Things were falling into place for Smith. Amid the low babble of the café, he was beginning to understand the situation. Even as he spoke to the two legation servants and listened to their stories, he was thinking of how to form his theory. His ability to concentrate simultaneously upon two disparate mental subjects always served him well.

"Thank you, Pease, Conroy," he said at last. The porter nodded, his jowls bouncing somewhat. He may have been surprised at the sudden end of the interview, but as a veteran soldier, he did not question a superior's behaviour. Conroy, however, opened her hazel eyes wide. "I cannot tell you much," Smith added, "but I want you to remember that things are not always what they seem."

"Do you mean about Lady Boisragon, sir?" the maid asked breathlessly.

"Now, Mary Anne," said Pease, "the major can't talk about it anymore. If we've helped, that's good enough for us."

"And you have helped, Pease," Smith confirmed, "greatly."

Allard's Hotel, in Hythe Street, was about seventy years old, having been founded by its namesake in 1850. It had long been popular with gentlefolk visiting or passing through London, and while those at the top of Society might have preferred the Savoy or the Northumberland, many still enjoyed the quiet luxury of Allard's. In this, it had been rather like the Wallachia in Bucharest. Alas, the recent owners had not maintained their predecessors' standards and, during the War, Allard's had become little more than a lodging house for young officers on leave and, it must be admitted, a convenient rendezvous for their transitory *affairs de couer*.

Things were changing though, since, even as Linus Smith entered the small lobby and walked to the front desk, the hotel was for sale, with several potential buyers already interested.

Smith was escorted in the lift up to the third floor by a smart young page, who showed him to the door of one of the Allard's suites. A maid took charge there, asking the visitor to wait in the drawing room. Left alone, Smith's senses absorbed the atmosphere of fading splendour: the heavy curtains roped back in the doorways, the worn chintz on the chairs, the heavily-trodden Persian rugs on the floors. He liked his surroundings, and felt sad that they were past their best.

"I meet few Englishmen who can write in Russian, Major." Irina Boisragon emerged from a room behind double sliding doors. "I am curious as to how you attained this skill."

The diplomatist's wife was indeed young, no older than the century itself. Her hair was so black that it seemed to consist not of strands but of a mass, cut and turned inward at the ends, in the latest bob. She wore sable-hued eye make-up as well; not as much as Sissy Arionescu, but enough to remind the soldier of portraits of ancient Egyptian queens. Thus, the stark blue irises were all the more startling. Her face was a very pale pink and beautiful, everything in perfect proportion. She pursed her red lips as she glanced from the card that she held to Smith himself, and waited for her curiosity to be sated.

"And the contents of the words, madam?" the major ventured after his hostess had introduced herself.

Lady Boisragon dismissed her maid and brought Smith into a drawing room, where she offered to provide him with refreshments herself. Upon his refusal, she urged him to sit and removed a long cigarette from a wooden box on a simply carved table.

"I hope you don't object to women smoking, Major. I acquired the habit when I was fourteen and never quit."

Though Smith indeed disapproved of ladies using tobacco, he was unsurprised by Lady Boisragon's affinity for it. Dressed in a daring, satiny pair of dark trousers and matching blouse, she appeared ready more for bed than for receiving guests. She seemed very much a modern woman.

" 'I know the truth about Bucharest'." After quoting from the back of the card Smith had initially sent up, the lady slipped it into a pocket of her blouse. "Do you intend blackmail?" Despite her words, or perhaps because of them, she sounded composed as she took a seat on a long settee. Smith sat opposite.

"I was sent to Rumania to inquire into the matter concerning you and your husband," Smith responded blandly. "There were several aspects over which anxiety was felt."

The woman nodded, as if this fact had already been discussed, and said, "What did you learn?"

"That three weeks ago now you were contacted by someone, most likely an agent of the Russian GPU. You cancelled your appointments for that day and met with him. I believe that he gave you with proof that the Bolsheviks were holding members of your family prisoner, probably your parents, and demanded that in return for their continued health, you spy on your husband for Russia."

For a full minute, neither spoke. Lady Boisragon pulled a tiny bit of tobacco from the end of her cigarette, moved to ignite her lighter, remembered that her cigarette was still lit, and waved her hand.

"How do you know this?" she queried quietly.

"The evidence points to it: your altered schedule, parents missing but not dead, an argument with your husband... He wished to leave the Diplomatic Service and take up the inheritance he'd received from Lord Dantry; you urged him to remain, so that you could do the GPU's bidding."

Lady Boisragon's beautiful, pale face had been growing sorrowful during

Smith's explanation, for which she was showing unmistakable respect. Upon the mention of the fight with her husband, however, her expression became rather superior.

"You know it all," she said. "Am I under arrest?"

"I think I do know it all, madam," Smith agreed, "but I require confirmation."

"Why? I am separated from my husband; he is unlikely to take me back. I can do him and England no more harm."

"It was your affair with Prince Movilesco which puzzled me." Smith glanced at the woman, who had hardly touched her cigarette. It lay smouldering in a heavy, black, glass ashtray by her seat. "I was informed that he had been pursuing you since your arrival in Bucharest, the inference being that you succumbed to his efforts only lately."

Lady Boisragon was watching her guest warily. Her jaw was set firmly, as if prepared for a physical fight.

"You are an intelligent, worldly woman, madam, despite your age. Not the sort, I would have thought, to fall for the blandishments of a professional lothario. Yet you did, recently and suddenly. Your tryst was at a hotel, though Movilesco prefers his own house on the Soseaua Kiseleff for such occasions. Why?"

"Why not, Major? We Russian women are impulsive. Since you know our language, you probably have some familiarity with our moods, our passions." She took up her cigarette, found that it had gone out and set it aside again.

"No, your reasons were more definite. You did it because you love your parents, and you love your husband." The woman stared at Smith as he continued. "You agreed to an affair with the most common sort of womaniser, in a place at which your husband could discover the two of you, then you informed him of your encounter, anonymously, of course."

"Why in the world would I do that?" Lady Boisragon laughed, but it was a nervous and unconvincing sound. Logical planning was her forté, not bluff.

"Because you needed to make yourself useless to the GPU."

The woman almost gasped. She stood, the folds of her voluminous outfit flowing about her slender form. She began to speak, stilled her voice and started to pace the room instead.

"If you had refused their extortionate demands, your parents' lives would have been forfeit," explained Smith, after rising himself. "If you'd consented, you would have been abusing your husband, his career and his country, but...if he were no longer your husband, what would the Bolsheviks do? They would keep your parents in relative safety, in case you and your husband reconciled, and they required them again. The GPU would not bother you to spy for them, since you would have nothing worthwhile upon which to spy."

A pause followed Smith's words, but at last Lady Boisragon spoke.

"After that horrid man from the GPU talked to me, it took me a day to see what needed to be done — and six days to work up the nerve to do it. It killed the best part of me to do such a monstrous thing to Nicky." Her voice was small now, a child's voice, and the voice of a stricken old lady, too. She was facing an open window, through which a sunny afternoon was brilliantly visible. "When he walked in on me and that odious dog Movilesco, it took every ounce of my strength not to fall at his feet and beg his forgiveness."

"He told me that he would gladly have taken you back but for your callousness at that moment," Smith said.

"And that I couldn't have had, Major. I had to end my marriage. I had to be simply another Russian refugee with relatives in the old country, not the wife of a British minister."

Smith was silent for a moment and stood to leave. But he paused and asked his hostess why she had not explained her cruel dilemma to her spouse.

"He would have retired, gladly. He would have been just as useless to the GPU as you've made yourself."

"No, not at all, Major, as I think you are aware." Lady Boisragon turned to face her guest. "The secrets he holds, the people he knows... He would have been a source of information to the Bolsheviks until the day he died — and after. I would have been their informant, copying his personal papers, eavesdropping on conversations with old friends..." But there was more in her heart.

"My husband is a great man, Major. He could be prime minister one day, or at the least, at the very least, an ambassador whose wisdom could prevent wars. He is the best man I will ever meet, and I will *not* have him throw away his career, his destiny, because of me. He would do just that to live quietly with me in the country. The GPU would win, even then. The waste of a career like Nicky's would be a celebration to them, and they would still use me against him, in retirement. That was why I urged him not to give up diplomacy for his new estates. My way was the only way to defeat the GPU."

Irina Boisragon was close to tears. Her eyes were wet and filled but not a drop spilled down her silky cheeks.

"I'll see myself out, madam," Smith said. "Thank you for your time."

The woman extended her hand, unexpectedly, and Smith shook it once. As he left, he hoped one day to meet a woman who would love him as much as this Russian girl loved her husband. And then he hoped *never* to meet a woman like that.

Fallen to Earth

The *Times* had recorded the death as that of Sir James Crawford, Captain, RN (Ret.), KCMG, CB. Little information was provided concerning the decedent, other than a short list of the clubs to which he belonged, and the name of his wife, who survived him. No mention was made of his fondness for stories and games; nothing written of the son he had lost during the War; certainly it was not published that the subject of the obituary had been the founder and first head of the latest incarnation of the Secret Service.

Those who had known C — as Crawford had been called in his clandestine profession — would not have needed to be told any of these facts. And those who had not been acquainted with his unique personality would not have benefited from any post-mortem revelations.

From the tiny glade in the woods, the sea, reached by the tidal creek just down an overgrown slope, was invisible. But a slight waft of air brought the smell of salt, and gulls whirled overhead, as though wondering at the curious gathering of people below. The spot at which C had chosen to be laid to rest was just a stone's roll away from the ocean, hidden by a ferny oak wood.

"Always start a voyage on a warm, sunny, summer morning, if you can, my boy. It presages a fair passage."

Linus Smith could almost hear his late chief's words, uttered in his cheerful voice, not so long before. The funeral service was over and the crowd of mourners — C had always been a gregarious and amiable man — began to move, individually or in pairs, from the open grave, and Smith found himself standing on a small tongue of lawn just the other side of the trees. The sun was bright, and the day, full of cloud-flecked blue skies, was a pleasant one. Smith could see sails meandering back and forth on the waves, far beyond the sandy beach, below the crumbling edges of his vantage point. C could not have followed his own advice better if he had chosen the day himself.

"Excuse me, sir."

Smith turned to see his valet, having emerged from the woods a few seconds before, and hesitant to interrupt his employer's reverie.

"Yes, Odways?"

"There is a message for you, sir. A Foreign Office man brought it. He's awaiting a reply."

Curious, Smith tossed away the cigarette he had been smoking and took the unopened envelope. Reading the contents, he glanced up.

"We must go," he said, thrusting the message into a pocket of his dark grey suit's jacket. "Tell the Foreign Office chap that I'm on my way."

"Very good, sir. Lady Crawford is still at the graveside."

Smith nodded. He would have preferred to have gone back to the house with the other mourners, to talk with the widow or simply reminisce about the gentleman just laid to rest. As it turned out, Lady Crawford understood perfectly; never privy to the details of her husband's work, she nonetheless appreciated its demands.

"It would have been almost disappointing if one of you gentlemen hadn't had to rush off without a moment to lose," she said, with a smile on her lips and a twinkle in her eye.

"London, sir?" Odways ventured, as he accompanied his master to the motor-car that would take them to the station.

"Just long enough to pack for Hungary," replied Smith, adjusting his hat. He was glad that he had decided against wearing uniform to the funeral. It had not been, after all, a military affair, and the only ones so garbed had been a couple of C's brother officers from the navy, in their sombre blue. As if reminded, Smith added, "And C has suggested I bring some clothes suited to a stiff hike in the woods."

"Yes sir." To his professional credit, the valet did not even pause before they reached the car. "C, sir?"

"The new C, as it were, Odways, the new C."

The new C indeed. Other departments of state could have afforded an interregnum between one chief and the next; it was doubtful if many Britons would have been alarmed even if the country had gone without a prime minister for some time. But in the Secret Service, it was a matter of 'the king is dead, long live the king'. Its late director would have been the first to approve of such a policy. He had done just that, in fact, proposing to his superiors his own successor, during a spell of ill health in the spring.

Smith had time to contemplate the effect a change of regime might have on his department. Even the fastest air service on the continent required a day and a half to travel from Paris to Budapest. Smith's orders had been explicit in urging speed, but until regular service was achieved between nations, even a journey by air would not have got him to his destination more quickly than rail. That he need not have flown was, in any case, a relief to him. The Switzerland-Arlberg-Vienna Express, little sister to the Orient Express, had been inaugurated four years previously to avoid the bad tracks, lack of fuel and obstructive government of post-War Germany, but it ran only three days a week. He chose instead the route from Ostend through Munich. It was rarely punctual but certainly comfortable enough.

Smith had been to Budapest once before, a lamentably short visit in the performance of his duties, fourteen years before, in 1909. In that brief time, he had gained the impression of a great European capital, yet one almost not European. He missed the approaches on this present occasion, as his train pulled into Keleti Station at 11.30, Thursday night, and the Hungarian metropolis, at a distance, had been little more than brilliantly lit masonry. This, as he recalled, was no great deficit to tourism. The railway, when entering Budapest, passed through the usual grimy, industrial outskirts that railways always seemed to do when arriving at a major city; the advance upon Hungary's capital, however, appeared to stretch the process over a much greater length.

"It looks a very modern hotel, sir."

Odways watched the porters as they gathered the Englishmen's small amount of luggage from the motor-taxi that had delivered them to the Hotel Kastelly, in Szent Gellert Square, on the hill of Budapest's citadel. Seeing that the bags were being handled with satisfactory care, the valet spared a glance for the edifice before him. He knew his employer's taste for the traditional, a place with the flavour of location.

"It's been here for a few decades, but yes, it's quite up-to-date," Smith responded, adding somewhat dubiously, "It's noted for its 'radioactive waters'." As they entered the lobby, he wondered why the movement toward modernity often involved the loss of distinction. "But C is staying here, and it was simple for rooms to be reserved for us in the same hotel."

And it saved time. Smith washed, changed his shirt and called on his new chief a quarter of an hour later.

"You don't look like the description in your file," were C's first words to his subordinate. "But then, I was told that you frequently don't."

Smith was unsure what the last phrase meant, though he suspected that it had something to do with his innate ability to go unnoticed. It was a rather desirable trait in a secret service operator, but left its owner with mixed feelings, socially.

"Sit down."

The new C was certainly not going to blend into any crowd. Tall and handsome, only a little older than Smith's forty-one years, C cut a striking figure. Under a head of full, thick, brown hair, was a face of strong features made fierce by a bristling moustache, and by the black patch covering the socket where his right eye had once been. The left sleeve of his brown suit was empty, and pinned to his lapel. He was the holder of the Victoria Cross, and the DSO and Bar, but he had paid heavily for the awards.

Being offered a chair seemed the extent of C's hospitality: no refreshments were forthcoming, and the collection of decanters on the sideboard remained unopened. At least the room was cool; Hungary's summer nights were warmer than England's, and the doors to the balcony admitted a breeze that swept up the Castle Hill from the river.

"How was the funeral?"

The question caught Smith by surprise, but he answered, "Very satisfactory. Just as C — Captain Crawford — would have wanted."

"I would have preferred to be there, of course." C frowned as he sat opposite Smith. It was clear that he was unaccustomed to being put in a defensive position, even if he were the only person who considered it so. "The secretary of the Committee of Imperial Defence notified me as soon as he heard of Crawford's death. It was to have been a smoother transition, but the next day, Headquarters received a request from Colonel Sághy. Do you know the name?"

"Yes sir." Smith nodded. "Istvan Sághy, an Hungarian Army officer, a baron, of a moderately important aristocratic family. He was a member of the Kundschaftsstelle," he said, referring to the old Austro-Hungarian military intelligence organisation, "both before and during the War, and now he's in Hungary's National Defence Service."

C regarded his subordinate starkly, as might a schoolmaster who, seeking to test a pupil, had elicited too much information to confirm.

"Anything else?" he asked tonelessly.

"He owns several thousand acres of rich farmland, has been married twice, once widowed, with a son and a daughter from each union; had a brother who was murdered during the short-lived Communist government in 1919, and is, unsurprisingly, a reactionary in politics," replied Smith, as if reading from a list.

"He was also, as an officer of the Kundschaftsstelle, in charge of Austro-Hungarian intelligence in occupied Rumania, in 1918," said C, seemingly pleased to know something that Smith did not.

"Yes sir," confirmed the other. "He went to Bucharest in February of '17, and remained until the War's end."

C was silent for a moment, then breathed in deeply.

"Right... That fact touches upon why you are here. We'll be calling on Sághy first thing tomorrow morning, and he'll explain matters to you. I know what he wants, but I'd like to see your reaction to it. If you have any concerns at that time, don't hesitate to explain them."

"Yes sir." Smith was somewhat mystified by this preface to the next day's meeting, but intrigued. In the meantime, he had a query to pose in the present. "Why was I sent for, sir? My orders were for speed, and there must have been operators closer to Budapest than I was."

C's expression changed slightly, becoming more confident, as might a traveller's who had just found his bearings again after being momentarily lost. He placed his right hand on his abdomen, and the fingers made an odd motion as though interlocking with the long-gone digits of his missing left hand. Smith wondered how ingrained such a habit had to have been to continue a decade after it was no longer practicable.

"When I was alerted to my eventual succession to Captain Crawford, I was shown the Service's personnel files." C inclined his head toward his visitor. "Yours proved of some interest. Raised in Southern Rhodesia; fought in the rebellions there when you must have been but, what, fourteen? In the Rhodesia Regiment to start the South African War, then intelligence work in Hopkins's column... I understand the Boers found that one so dangerous they made a special target of it. Where was that, now?"

"Zandbosch, sir," Smith responded.

"After that, your work with this very department in its early days, and what you did in Russia and Transcaspia during the War, indicate someone who is resourceful and self-sufficient, and good at bushcraft." Smith remained silent, and C stated, "And *that's* why you're here. We'll be meeting Sághy at nine o'clock tomorrow morning." He glanced at his wrist watch. "Nine o'clock later this morning."

Smith nodded and stood, but then, pausing, asked, "Was there anything else interesting in my file, sir?"

"A few items, here and there. The most arresting was the fact that across your name, Crawford had written 'Any job at all'. What do you make of that?"

"I believe that Captain Crawford realised that I would never have declined an assignment because it was too easy."

It was a response the old C might have considered worth a laugh. His successor merely dismissed Smith with a reminder of the hour at which they would be meeting the Hungarian.

Once the door had closed behind his guest and C was alone, the intelligence chief sat again, grunted and said, " 'Would never decline an assignment because it was too easy'... Good answer."

Budapest had not suffered from battle in the Great War, but it had been the second city of the Austro-Hungarian Empire, and a vibrant capital in its own right. The empire's dissolution, and the loss of vast tracts of Hungary's territory in the peace settlements had disrupted the lives of almost everyone in Budapest, ruining many. It had been a financial centre, now in the middle of a nation impoverished by defeat; its great enterprises were separated from former customers by new borders; refugees, driven from their homes in the lost provinces, had swelled the population of the unemployed and unhoused.

But as Smith and C were taken by motor-taxi farther up Castle Hill, the former thought that he detected few signs of surrender. There was not the sullen resentfulness or fabulous hedonism of Berlin, nor the reckless resignation of Vienna. Having grown tremendously in the previous century, Budapest was now too large for its truncated hinterland, but the tone Smith detected about him was one of definite optimism.

Or perhaps, he thought, it was simply the beautiful summer morning.

Uri Street ran near the very top of Citadel Hill, and was overlooked by the now-vacant royal residence. As might have been inferred by its lofty position and the name the Austrians had given it — Die Herren Gasse — Uri Street had always been the home of aristocracy. Gothic townhouses, rather grandly and misleadingly termed 'palaces', after the French style, lined the wiggling lane, one of the oldest in the city, and, in some cases, were built on Turkish vaults and basements.

The taxi's loud engine seemed to violate the cloister-like atmosphere of the street, and Smith was glad when it drove off, leaving him and his chief before one of the larger houses.

"A private residence?" questioned Smith.

C replied, "Yes. Sághy prefers the informality." He pulled the chain, suspended at the entrance.

The house loomed over the street, its upper windows seeming to push out to see who might be calling. Over the recessed door was carved a coat of arms. Smith held no doubt that they were those of the Barons Sághy, placed there in pride and duty when the edifice was raised.

The Englishmen were led by an elderly footman from the high, vaulted hall to a wide morning room. Despite the open windows, the big chamber smelled of wax and tobacco, the must of centuries. In the centre of an expansive, rectangular carpet, worn almost through, stood their host.

"Welcome again, General," said Istvan Sághy, shaking C's hand. "Is this the gentleman whose arrival from London we have been awaiting?"

Smith wondered if he had not detected a hint of reproach in the query.

"This is Peter Shaw," C said, indicating his subordinate.

Even as they took their seats — Smith in a chair so ancient and pliable that his action made no sound at all — the colonel's manservant was entering the room again, this time pushing a trolley of refreshments. Considering the frailty with which the footman seemed to move, Smith would gladly have foregone food and drink; he was afraid the poor fellow would topple over in the midst of his work. But Sághy dismissed the servant curtly; through impatience, Smith considered, rather than rudeness. The colonel was anxious to begin the meeting, in private, and his man was very slow.

"I have explained to General Sanction why I need his service's help, Mr Shaw, but he suggested that I reiterate it to you. I must stress, however, that time is of some significance in this matter."

Sághy prepared cups of coffee and dishes of cake as he spoke, his English practically flawless, though his accent made the words sound as if they were tumbling over smooth boulders in a stream's bed. He looked to be about sixty years of age, though his thick hair had remained very black. His face was blunt, and though creased in every direction, most of the lines were short and shallow. It was a handsome countenance, with an almost ingrained expression of hauteur.

"I myself prefer the bare essentials of an affair, Baron," said Smith, a statement which was quite false, but which pleased the Hungarian.

"Excellent."

Sághy sat back in his chair. As he had leaned forward to offer Smith his coffee, the latter had noted a hint of scent about his host, nothing unusual among continental gentlemen.

"It was at the very end of the War, the first week of November, 1918, in fact," Sághy commenced his story. "An aeroplane of the Austro-Hungarian air service crashed in that range of the Carpathian Mountains that formed the frontier of Transylvania. The pilot had been given information to take to Vienna, information regarding the identities of Austro-Hungarian military intelligence officers stationed in Rumania, which, as you probably are aware, Mr Shaw, was under a joint occupation with Germany at the time."

Smith chewed his cake, an orange-flavoured confection, and nodded. Rumania had the dubious distinction of being the only Allied nation to be invaded by forces from all four Central Powers.

"It has—" Sághy stopped speaking and, rising, walked to the wide door of the morning room. He opened it, glanced into the hall beyond, then shut it once more. As he returned to his seat, he continued his narrative without apology. "It has come to our attention that the Rumanian Army has taken official notice of the aeroplane's wreckage. Its whereabouts have been, I should mention, known for a while," he added, as if divulging an open secret. "The local authorities were informed of the crash as soon as it occurred, but with conditions prevailing then — armies in retreat, governments in disarray — nothing was done about it."

"So the crash's existence has been *re*-discovered," Smith commented.

"Just so, Mr Shaw. The appropriate department in Bucharest has found the relevant file with the original report of the crash, and will be despatching a team soon to recover the pilot's body — and any papers he may have been carrying."

How Sághy knew of proceedings within a Rumanian government ministry did not puzzle Smith. It had no doubt been an Hungarian agent who had alerted the National Defence Service to this development.

"I am certain the Rumanians are unaware of the information the pilot had with him when he went down," Sághy asserted. "To them, it is simply a routine operation to pick up another long-dead war casualty. The fact that they attach no urgency to this duty has undoubtedly bought us time. My department needs to get that information first." He glanced at C, who had remained quiet, eating his own piece of cake. "I have requested General Sanction's help in this matter."

Smith, over the rim of his porcelain coffee cup, very briefly caught his chief's eye. He realised why C had wanted him to hear the Hungarian's plea for himself. It was hardly the usual favour asked by one secret service of another. C's silence gave Smith permission to delve more deeply.

"Excuse me, Baron," as a nominal civilian, Smith felt it better to use Sághy's aristocratic rank rather than the military, "but could your own people not complete this task?"

"A natural question, Mr Shaw," Sághy replied beneficently. "The truth is that..." He helped himself to more coffee from the big urn on the trolley his servant had provided. "Well, I take great pride in my country, and in the organisation I lead. But the truth is that we have no capacity for such an operation — not at this time."

"And time is vital." Smith too re-charged his cup with his host's excellent beverage. Then he continued, with an impression of reluctance. "Still, it's usually a simple thing to determine the regular staff of any military department, isn't it? Even an intelligence branch? Given the appropriate government directories and army lists, a person, someone perhaps no more than a civilian such as myself, could probably reconstruct any part of Hungary's general staff after a few days' research. Most competent military intelligence officers could identity each other's personnel — barring secret operators and agents."

The many little lines of Sághy's face disappeared into an impassivity that revealed no emotion. C, to one side of the conversation, regarded his subordinate with mild approval.

"What's more," continued Smith, after a swallow of coffee, "considering the inflated size of any army's administration in a major conflict, it must be that few of those named in the documents you want retrieved are still affiliated with the Hungarian military. A large portion of the regular officers would have retired, and some may even have died by now." He was tactful enough to refrain from stating explicitly that his host country's armed forces had been ruthlessly reduced by the peace treaties after the War. "Why do these papers need to be retrieved so urgently?"

There was little noise in the high-ceiled chamber after Smith had finished speaking. C set his cup and saucer on the surface of the small circular table between his chair and his subordinate's, the porcelain making a brief but sharp rattle. At the windows, the curtains stirred, brushing over the tops of several framed photographs displayed on a desk there.

"You're quite right, Mr Shaw," said Sághy at last, a slight smile creasing the lower half of his visage. He appeared as one might who had just witnessed a clever move by an opponent in a chess match. "The truth is that these records contain not only names of Austro-Hungarian intelligence staff who had been stationed in Rumania..." He stood and walked to the intricately carved marble chimneypiece over the hearth, and returned with a lacquered wood box, bound by brass. He offered the cigarettes within to the Britons. "Also included are the identities of agents and potential agents — Rumanians — whose lives would be endangered if their own government found the documents first."

"Then I can understand your concern, Baron." Smith breathed in his cigarette's smoke. It was strong, almost harsh. "Though I find myself wondering why these records were being transported anywhere at all."

"I'm afraid I don't know what you mean." Sághy sat once more.

C glanced at Smith through pale blue smoke. The secret service chief had, until now, held worries parallel to those Smith had voiced. But he had not been anxious over this new question.

"Surely the War Ministry in Vienna had copies of such records as those kept in Bucharest," Smith elaborated. "It's a sound and common policy for intelligence departments to keep duplicate files on their agents at headquarters, for control, accounting, security and convenience. I can't imagine Agent X, employed by Austria-Hungary in Bucharest, being a complete mystery to his superiors in Vienna. That being the case, it would have been far safer, and simpler, to destroy the files kept in Bucharest, rather than attempt to fly them anywhere."

The silence that covered the morning room this time was no longer than the first, but to Smith it felt deeper. Peripherally, he observed C nonchalantly tipping the end of his cigarette into an ashtray on the round table. Smith had surprised him with this latest point, but the junior officer saw no disapprobation.

"This fellow is sharp, General," declared Sághy suddenly, speaking to C but indicating Smith with a flick of his finger. The baron's countenance may have reflected respect or annoyance; it was impossible to tell. "Do you know much of the Austrian Empire's history, Mr Shaw? Forgive me," Sághy held up a long, slender hand to forestall indignation which, in the event, was not shown, "but I've found foreigners' knowledge on that subject...confused."

"Especially British, I've no doubt," responded Smith good-naturedly. "I know that from 1867, the country was, in effect, two: Austria and Hungary. It was a union bound by the person of the monarch, who was emperor of one and king of the other. In foreign affairs, finance and defence, the administration and policies were shared."

"Excellent, Mr Shaw," Sághy replied, smiling. "I have compatriots who couldn't describe the constitution as succinctly. At the end of the War, my country's transition to complete independence was achieved quite simply. Acting for Hungary's good was not disloyalty, and our oaths to the king remained unbroken."

C was growing slightly restive with the history lesson, but his attention focused again with Smith's next words.

"The records lost in the aeroplane crash... You were transferring them for independent Hungary's use, because you might not have been able to get at the ones in Vienna."

"Yes," Sághy confirmed, waving away smoke. "Though in spirit, our fidelity to the king was intact, sending the files to Budapest was done without the permission which, if sought, might have been withheld. I think you can appreciate the reasons for my actions."

Smith nodded, saying, "Rumanian agents would be of much more value to the new Hungary, than to the new Austria."

He was not alone in thinking that the treaties which had ended the Great War were far from the diplomatic master-strokes needed to maintain peace and security in Europe after 1918. Revisionist sentiment in Hungary was strong, and directed in large part toward Transylvania and other territories lost to Rumania. If Hungary became involved in another war in the near future, it would, Smith predicted, be with its neighbour to the southeast. Intelligence from Rumania would be required in abundance.

"The pilot chosen to fly the aeroplane was cognisant of the plot?" Smith asked. "And trustworthy?"

Sághy, having been forced to reveal so much to the Englishman, was now on more certain ground, and smiled confidently.

"Yes, to both questions, Mr Shaw. Like all of us Hungarians, he had been loyal to the Dual Monarchy, but when the bonds were cut, he was eager to do his part for his homeland." The baron extinguished his cigarette. "But the aeroplane went down in the first bad storm of the season, while it was crossing the Transylvanian Alps."

Now it was Smith's turn to pause.

"And you trust us to recover your records for you, assuming that they are to be found?"

"I have considered the possibility that you might use for your own purposes the identities of the agents listed in the files, once you collect them," the Hungarian admitted. "But I think your chief knows that helping me would be of greater worth to his organisation than would possessing the names of several middle-level Rumanian civil servants: to us, they would be valuable assets, but not so to the British Secret Service. My department's gratitude, however, would provide far more opportunities for you, and on a greater scale."

C stirred himself and, leaning forward in his chair, gestured with his cigarette, saying, "I assume, Colonel, that you have available detailed maps of the district under discussion..."

Odways was uneasy that he would not be accompanying his employer into Rumania. This was hardly a matter of competence or capacity, as the valet, younger than and nearly as fit as Smith, would have been able to match the latter stride for stride. But Smith would be travelling as Mr Peter Shaw, of Oak Leys Cottage, Staffordshire, an aspiring novelist. A writer researching the setting of his book — to be described to anyone who asked as a sort of middle European *Kidnapped* — was not likely to bring a servant with him on a trek through the Transylvanian mountains. Odways, a reasonable man, reluctantly accepted this argument, and contented himself with preparing a restful reception in the relative civilisation of Bucharest.

Smith had begun his journey as soon as the briefing by Sághy had ended. The remainder of the morning passed in a train, traversing the Alföld, the plain that covered western Hungary, and he reached the Rumanian border as noon approached. He was the only passenger to cross the frontier at Curtici, but even so, the Rumanian customs official barely acknowledged the passport that he stamped. Neither Smith's belongings, packed carefully in a small ruck sack, a rolled greatcoat tied atop, nor his clothes, tough but comfortable tweed, with soft leather boots, excited comment. When he boarded the train at Decebal, he was just another ticket-holder.

From the notices in his compartment, embossed on metal plaques and affixed to the walls, Smith determined that his carriage had been looted by the Rumanian Army during its short-lived invasion of Hungary just after the War. Vehicles, machinery, art and personal property had all been carried back when the occupiers left Budapest. And, beyond the window, were what all Hungarians considered the greatest plunder: rectangles of grain, alternating with brown fallow fields, relieved periodically by groves of trees, surprisingly dense; dropped among the crops, marked first by the towers of their churches, were villages. These told Smith that he was entering the land not only of three languages but of three denominations, once a province of Hungary, now of Rumania.

Fallen to Earth

People came and went at each little station, with many more at the town of Arad. Some were middle class, as clearly such as their counterparts in England. Others were peasants, piling into the carriages farther back, wearing attire that varied from valley to valley.

Those who briefly shared Smith's compartment were more curious about his garb than had been the bureaucrats at the frontier. Some of these travellers understood German, others French; only one of Smith's passing acquaintances was conversant in English.

"So... You go to Trapburg?"

The man seated across from the Briton had Nordic blond hair and strong features, and his heavy accent reminded Smith of the German spoken along the Rhine River, where it met the Moselle. Yet Jacob Engelhardt had been born and raised in Transylvania, and had probably spent most, if not all, of his fifty-odd years there.

"A wonderful place to begin a walking tour," he said cheerfully. "I teach in Eisendorf, and sometimes in Szelinczag, not ten miles farther on." He shrugged, which, given his Teutonic economy of movement, was most expressive. "It is a Szekler village, but the people are decent."

Smith felt gravity gently urge him back into the thin cushioning of his seat. The train was climbing slowly, but continually, and soon the hills, at one glimpse so distant, would become surrounding mountains.

"Szeklers... They are Hungarians?" Smith was aware of the group, but everyone who knew of them had their own ideas.

"Well, they themselves claim to be descendants of Atilla's tribe, true *Hun*garians," Engelhardt answered, the pun almost lost in the thickness of his accent. "Others believe that they are Magyarised Turks. I, on the other hand," he leaned forward, as if to impart slightly confidential information, "think that they are no different than any other Hungarian, simply a detached band who settled in these parts while the others carried on to the Danube."

Smith liked the theory. He had found, in studying history, that uncomplicated explanations usually provided the most accurate solutions to mysteries.

"They speak Magyar, then?" he asked.

"A dialect of it, yes, but not so distinct that they couldn't understand a Budapest shopkeeper. But they are expanding their linguistic knowledge, at least in Szelinczag." Engelhardt grinned and put a hand on his chest. "That is why I work there, from time to time: I teach Rumanian. The new masters of Transylvania offered to send an instructor, but the Szecklers are more comfortable with a neighbour, even a Saxon such as myself."

"That is what German-speakers are called here?"

Inductions Dangerous

"Nothing is so simple here, my friend." Engelhardt shook his head, as if at a child falling after taking his first steps. "Just as there are two kinds of Hungarians in Transylvania — Szeklers and the later Magyars — so there are two kinds of Germans. We Saxons were brought in centuries ago, so that our industry and sense would re-vitalise the land. 'Swabians' arrived later, mainly merchants. Naturally, they are probably no more from Swabia than we were from Saxony," he added, almost carelessly, "though they are Catholic."

Smith had met Engelhardt on the platform of the station at Zam, where the Briton had chosen to spend the train's halt reading on a bench under the acacia trees. Engelhardt, a student as well as a teacher of languages, started a conversation when he had observed the English title of Smith's book.

"Is there a good inn at Trapburg?" Smith inquired of his new acquaintance.

The day was gathering to a close. There was still light, even if it was only the reflections off the steep hills which rose next to either bank of the Mures River. Smith planned to wake very early the next morning, and he wished to be well-rested for the next stage of his journey.

"You are in luck, Herr Shaw." Engelhardt reached into the jacket of his suit, locally made but decently tailored. "My brother-in-law is the landlord of the Weissehunde, a very satisfactory guest-house. Not a Ritz or a Bristol, but..." From a pocket, the teacher had taken a note book, in which he wrote, in neat German Gothic script, a short letter of introduction. "Heinz is rather a peasant but a good man, honest and hard-working. Don't tell him I told you so. His rooms are clean."

The train, tired and no doubt relieved to gain some respite, steamed breathlessly into Trapburg as darkness settled onto the hills, now high enough to be mountains. Engelhardt had disembarked at the previous halt, his home of Eisendorf, wishing the Englishman a pleasant journey. Now, Smith slung his pack on to his back, placed his hat firmly on his head, grasped the staff that would serve as a walking stick, and stepped out into the evening in what might have been Hesse or Westphalia.

Here, amid their crops of corn, maize and tobacco, beside rivers and almost hidden by forest trees, were tidy, picturesque villages. Trapburg was full of tall, gabled houses with casement windows, the walls plastered with pastel-hued rendering and half-timbering, reminiscent of Bavaria — or Cheshire, for that matter. In the half-gloom of twilight, Smith read German names above shop doors, and the conversations he overheard were easily interpreted by a man who had learned German from a Hanoverian.

The Weissehunde was indeed clean. It was a neat establishment situated at the far end of the village's principal street. Its doors were open to the warm summer evening, and the glow of lamps and candles from within, as if carried on waves of low voices and laughter, was welcoming. Those already at tables or on benches in the equivalent of the public bar barely noticed Smith's entry, and he soon had a room placed at his disposal by the hospitable Heinz.

Smith held the burning wick of a lamp to the end of his cigarette, then sat back in the one chair with which his room had been furnished. Its wooden components, like those of the square table on which he had opened his map, were worn with decades, perhaps centuries, of use. Dating items made in the vernacular was difficult: peasant styles changed slowly, when at all.

The charts with which he had been provided by Baron Sághy were common government productions from before the War. According to their creased images, the Austro-Hungarian Empire still ruled Trapburg, and the city of Sibiu, a dozen miles to the east, was still called Hermannstadt. But Sághy had known his business: topography would not have changed in the interval, however much the names had, and nobody would question an English traveller guided only by old, outdated maps.

The object of Smith's search had fallen to Earth just this side of the pre-War Rumanian boundary, not far at all from Trapburg. Smith planned to approach the wreckage of the aeroplane in a straight line, though he was fully aware that the rugged terrain would throw a dozen detours into his path. He was prepared to sleep rough, if it was required: the price he might have to pay for not being able to hire a local guide. His initial 'discovery' of the downed machine could not be seen as intentional.

In mountains, even summer mornings rarely began warmly, and Smith wore his gruel-coloured Norfolk jacket as he left the Weissehunde at sunrise. After shaking hands with the smiling landlord at the door of his inn, Smith was followed to the edge of town by a crowd of small children, respectful but whispering amongst themselves. He was struck by the large number in Trapburg of boys and girls four to seven years of age. Perhaps the villagers had been concerned with the high loss of life during the War, and had decided that they would do what they could about it. Smith reasoned, however, that the disproportionately young population may have had more to do with the German Army pioneer battalion stationed there until the conflict's end, than with the demographic worries of the town elders.

The path Smith took had been trod for a millennium, a narrow canyon, carved by feet, not always peaceable, not always human, through the increasingly lofty Transylvanian Alps. The temperature of the day increased before Trapburg's squarish church steeple, or even the roofs of its houses, were lost to sight in the deep green of the enveloping trees. Smith was about to remove his jacket and add it to the roll of his coat on his back. But then, just past a flat, smooth meadow, twice the length and breadth of a cricket pitch, he stepped into the woods.

A deep stillness fell upon him as much as did the cool dimness. His sensitive eyes and ears quickly adjusted, and his nose too caught the signs of a new world. Orioles flitted among the oaks and alders, and somewhere, in an arboreal pasture, a cowbell clanked. The people who had settled these woods knew how to live there. Fields enclosed by huge trees and filled with ripe grain alternated with tracts of forest so dense that they were impassable; cottages were tucked into the undergrowth like fairy-tale dwellings, while pigs dug for roots and distant peasant voices sang as their owners worked. Had it been so in his own country's remote past? Smith wondered. And when the press of a land-hungry rural population grew, would the wild trees be felled and the survivors tamed, in Transylvania, as in England?

The day passed quickly. Smith ate sausages by the banks of a little brook that was fighting its way among scattered rocks. Hours later, famished again, he stopped for dinner. Since he had left Trapburg, he had covered ten miles by his reckoning, but never more than a hundred yards in a straight line. Nonetheless, following strict compass readings, he knew that he was on course. From his vantage point, the sun had set some time before, but it was not late, and sleep, though well-earned, would not come yet. He had to urge himself to further ascents after he had stopped for a cigarette in a tiny glade. Pigeons nesting in the column-like beeches high above had a most soporific effect. Smith pushed his hat back on his head, crushed his tobacco under foot and set off again.

It was about an hour later, as the fragrance of pine first began to make itself noticed among the still-predominantly deciduous trees, that Smith heard long, ethereal notes, coming from a pipe. Low for the most part, drawn out, they resolved themselves into a tune only eventually, with the aid of rather rare higher trills. He followed the sound, as though led, and soon the dolorous music was accompanied by the plaintive bleating of sheep.

A few yards more brought a scene to Smith's eyes that another traveller might have beheld four or five centuries before. In the greying light, a flock of sheep grazed the fresh, level grass of a field, small and smooth, tucked away amid ancient hornbeams. A shepherd, his crook in the bend of his arm, stood with his back to a tree's smooth trunk, and produced the otherworldly melody on a flageolet, his fingers moving deliberately up and down the wooden pipe. It was his dog, jealous of his woolly charges, who alerted his master to the interloper.

Smith was reluctant to speak. He had stepped into a painting by Lorrain, a depiction of deepest Arcadia, and was loathe to break the spell of bucolic serenity. But he felt that he had to justify his intrusion.

"Good evening," he said. "Please forgive the interruption, but I was walking this way, and heard the music..."

The shepherd pushed up the brim of his hat, shaped like a flattened bell, and smiled genially.

"Say, that's okay, mister. I ain't no expert on this here flute, anyway!"

Ion Joja had not had the chance to practice his English since he had returned from the United States two years previously. Smith accurately guessed the location of his tuition as somewhere near Chicago. The shepherd was pleasantly surprised at meeting an English-speaker in this part of the world, and immediately invited his new acquaintance to share the dinner that he knew was being readied.

"Besides," he added, with another ready grin, "Mom and Dad'd kill me if I let on I met a stranger and didn't extended the family's hospitality."

He effortlessly guided the sheep to a path at the far end of the field, abetted by his dog. This animal was suspicious of Smith, perhaps thinking that the newcomer might be an unknown species of predator. But the dog went about its duties, deciding that if its master tolerated the stranger's presence, then he was probably acceptable.

The Jojas — the name made it clear that they were ethnic Rumanians, like most rural Transylvanians — lived half a mile away in another natural clearing, with wide vistas. Their whitewashed cottage, roofed with wooden shingles, was surrounded by a waist-high paling, which encompassed several out-buildings and a sheepfold. Though overlooked by the tall trees climbing a steep slope behind, the flock would be safe within their little stockade. But even here, not far from the edge of a precipitous cliff, where the eye could take in hundreds of miles of ridged and furrowed countryside, the sun had departed for the day. Wolves howled not far away.

"Just in time," Ion commented, chuckling, as he shut the gate behind the tardiest of his livestock.

Introductions to the rest of the Joja family were made through Ion, who alone of his kin could speak English. Smith met the father of the clan as the latter was carrying a load of chopped wood to the house. He set down his burden after a brief hesitation and shook Smith's hand, after wiping his own on the front of his blouse. He was much like his son, spare, fit and tanned by a life spent out of doors. Age had worked its way on his face which, dissimilar to Ion's, was deeply graven with lines, and had the dignity of a wide, greying moustache, something not yet attempted by his offspring. Carol, the younger brother, was next, and he continued the resemblance that ran through the males of the family, though he was much more shy than his sibling, carefully polite but very reserved.

All three men were dressed alike, in white homespun. The collars of the tunics worn by the boys were open, while the elder Joja kept his buttoned, the sleeves widening until the cuffs flared like those of a Chinese mandarin's gown. Tied at the waist by a belt, the baggy shirt spread below it like a skirt, hiding the tops of their trousers. Such clothes had not changed for generations.

There was no discussion as to whether Smith would be staying for dinner. As the men entered the cottage, Joja Senior made a matter-of-fact remark to a similarly-aged woman tending a boiling pot on the hearth. Mrs Joja — it seemed to Smith as incongruous to refer to her thus as it did to call her madam — greeted the Briton as though he were a farm labourer who habitually joined the family for meals, and then went on with her work. Her daughter was even more shy than Carol, and continued her own chores with difficulty.

Night came quickly thereafter, but with candles on the rough, well-used table and a fire in the primitive grate, the plainness of the Joja household became cosy. Smith won a smile from Mrs Joja when his compliment about the rabbit stew, which he thought quite tasty, was translated. Despite the odd remark from the woman — non-sequiturs thrust into the conversation haphazardly — she and her daughter were almost part of the background. Their dresses, aprons and leather bodices, tied at the sides, were dark, and seemed unconsciously to emphasise this status.

If Ion had forgotten any English since his return home, it came back to him rapidly enough. He was both a principal in, and a conduit for, the discussions that accompanied and followed the meal. Carol, some years junior to his brother, smiled as easily, but more uncertainly; he was curious about everything beyond his mountains. His father, at first listening more than talking, became almost loquacious when he discovered that his guest was also a sportsman. (Peter Shaw's walking tour in aid of his book had left the old man unimpressed.)

"You fought in the War, did you?"

The women had cleared the dishes from the table, and the aroma of the stew and maize porridge was being replaced by that of Virginia tobacco. Cigarettes, and a flask of brandy, were the only reciprocation Smith could offer, but the gifts were accepted with gratitude.

"Yes," Ion said, in answer to the Englishman's question. "By 1917, I'd already spent two years in the States, and it would've been plain mean not to pay back some of the good fortune I got there."

Smith glanced at Carol, whose youthful face was smiling at his first taste of brandy, and said, "I hope your brother was too young to fight."

Ion too peered at the youngest of the family, who returned the gaze quizzically.

"Yeah, he was, thank God, though..." Ion looked back at Smith and gestured with his cigarette "...the War came pretty darn close to home once." Now it was Smith's turn to appear puzzled, and his host elucidated. "A 'plane crashed a couple miles from here, near the end of the War; October, I think..." He spoke to his brother, who replied after a short dialogue with their father. "November," Ion corrected with certainty, "the first week."

"Really?" Smith raised his eyebrows. He tapped ash from his cigarette and let it fall onto the hardened dirt floor. Most reluctant to do this initially, his reticence had been brushed aside by Mr Joja, who disposed of his own burned tobacco in that fashion. "Did the airman survive?"

"No," Ion said, shaking his head. "When I got back home, they told me all about it. It was in the first storm of the fall, and the wind and snow were strong. Carol reached the crash almost right away; he always could move through the forest like a fox. He found the pilot, and came back for dad. Together they brought the pilot here. He was awake but hurt awful bad. Dad knew he probably wouldn't make it." As he was speaking to Smith, Ion was translating for his family, and relayed their comments to their guest. "Carol ran for Doctor Kovacs in Szelinczag. No one here could make out what the poor pilot was saying, so they sent for Herr Waldheim, too. But by the time he arrived from Trapburg, the guy was dead."

The silence that followed was contemplative, each person thinking his own thoughts. Then, Mr Joja asked, through his son, if Smith had served in the War.

"Yes," the Briton answered truthfully, then lied about the details. "I was in the air force, as a matter of fact. I didn't fly but was on the staff. Many of the men I knew didn't survive." That last statement was, unfortunately, too genuine.

After these words were interpreted, Mr Joja spoke further.

"Dad's wondering if you want to see where the 'plane went down," said Ion. Then he added, as if by explanation, "Many of our neighbours never returned to their farms and villages, either."

Smith nodded slowly, as if the notion of visiting the aeroplane's wreckage had not occurred to him before now. In fact, he had hoped that by placing himself in the RAF during the War, a connection with the dead pilot might have been made in the Jojas' minds.

"Yes," he responded simply, "I'd like that."

Ion smiled sympathetically and stated, "I can take you there tomorrow morning. It's a bit of a tramp through the woods — nothing's ever in a straight line 'round these parts — but," he gestured to Smith's garb, "I guess you're dressed for it."

Inductions Dangerous

Several deer started at the approach of the two men and bounded off through the densely packed trees, leaping over the rotting corpses of long-dead oaks and pines, and quickly vanishing to the accompaniment of cracks and snaps. Smith had observed the animals standing still and, had he been alone, would have tried to come closer to them. But Ion Joja moved with the stolid steps of a countryman, confident but uncaring who heard him, and the leather boots he wore did not muffle his arrival.

Smith had spent the night out of doors, wrapped in his warm greatcoat, supplemented by a blanket Mrs Joja had loaned him, and lulled by the sounds of nature in the dark. There had been no room for him in the Jojas' little cottage, and Smith had not given the family the chance to be embarrassed at the cramped quarters. He had risen stiff this morning, but the subsequent walk through the forest had limbered his body with little delay.

Rock, bare and raw, forced its way through the vegetation here and there, and the aspect of the wooded landscape grew harder, wilder. Except for the occasional need of a farm, the trees here died natural deaths, collapsing with old age and, now and then, laid low by slips of earth, eroded by weather and pulled by gravity. Bracken often acted like barbed wire against Smith's booted feet, and branches grabbed at his sleeves and hat.

"Here..."

Ion Joja, slightly breathless, despite his healthier age, stopped and pointed. Even Smith, whose eyes, attuned to discerning patterns against nature's backcloth, was momentarily mystified. Then he saw it. The large trunk, fallen across his path, was too squarish, and the lichen hanging from the surrounding tree limbs was cloth-like. These were the remains of an aeroplane, torn asunder upon impact, and left to decay for four and a half years.

Smith observed from the tops of pines, sheared off at increasing heights the farther the trees were behind the machine, that the aeroplane had descended at an acute angle. The wings had been pulled off before it struck the ground, their wooden skeletons and linen skin drooping from branches still. The machine had finally hit the unmoving body of an oak, inertia propelling the tail still further. Fifty feet away, an engine lie among saplings, rusting.

Smith was unsure of the aeroplane's type; it was possibly an LVG. Though of German manufacture, many products from that nation had been supplied to its war-time ally. Weather and vegetation had combined to provide the remains with almost perfect camouflage, though the straight-armed black crosses that both Germany and Austria used to mark their flying property at the end of the War could be identified.

"This was a two-seater," remarked Smith. He paused by the fuselage, a hand on the rim of each empty nacelle.

"Yeah, but there was only one guy in it. Dad and Carol made sure."

Ion moved with high, slow steps, as if making his way through mud. Plants grew thickly over and among the splintered wood and broken metal, like vines upon a lattice. Smith waited a moment before following his guide, and surreptitiously removed a compass from a jacket pocket. The wreckage was in a direct line to Trapburg, its smashed nose pointing straight toward that village miles away. Smith almost smiled, pleased that, even if unaided by the Jojas, he would have found the object of his search.

"He was still strapped into this..." Ion was saying as Smith caught him up. The Rumanian was kneeling among thistles, and next to the battered seat from an aeroplane cockpit. Its cushions were ripped and decayed, pulled from their frames and chewed by animals. "I always think about how much force it needed to throw this thing from the 'plane it was bolted into..."

Both men were silent. Smith had never gloried in the deaths of enemies, and felt them almost as keenly as those of his countrymen. How many men had died alone, he mused, suffering in desperation, without even the unfamiliar comfort of strangers at the end?

"A two-seater was probably used for the extra fuel it could carry, and the extra power, to get it over the mountains," he theorised. Before him was the fan of a small landslide, largely covered now by thistles and dwarf pines, and strewn with bits of the aeroplane. He prodded with his foot a large piece of the air screw, now held fast by dirt and roots.

"Yeah, that makes sense," agreed Ion, standing and absently slapping his brown hands together to dislodge soil. "Carol told me aeroplanes used to fly over the house once in a while, really low, like they were just skimming the mountain-tops. But all of them were big, like this one, and slow."

Smith uncorked his water bottle and offered it to his companion.

"You want a bite to eat before we head back?" the latter suggested. "We can see what Mom put in my pack, and I know there's a field of wild strawberries over this ridge, if..." he grinned spontaneously "...if Carol didn't get to it first."

"Mom really hated it that we couldn't send the pilot home to be buried. I think partly it was 'cause he was my age, so they tell me, and reminded her that I might end up like that: another dead body, unknown and God knows how far from home."

Ion chewed as if testing the taste of the biltong Smith had given him. It was not made of buffalo meat, as had been the real biltong Smith had eaten throughout his youth in Rhodesia. But he had come across a butcher in London who was from the Cape, and Smith kept a standing order for the product, to take with him on his travels. Though beef provided the principal ingredient, it was prepared the same way. The Rumanian took a liking to the 'jerky', as he called it.

"There was no identity disk around the pilot's neck?" Smith queried. Between the dried meat, bread, cheese and strawberries, the two men were not wanting for refreshment. Water came from a tiny rivulet finding its new course through the recently tossed boulders of a landslide. The morning was past its mid-point, the sun high enough to cause the hikers to picnic under the shade of trees.

Ion shook his head and answered, "The force of the crash must've been terrific. It threw one of his boots a hundred yards into the branches; never did find the other one. The guy's dog tags are likely buried in the grass somewhere... Mom insisted that they put him next to Grandma and Grandpa, even though they figured it would only be a temporary arrangement."

"A very Christian thing to do," Smith said, after a drink from his bottle.

"Heck, that's Mom and Dad all over," replied Ion with a chuckle. It was a light-hearted sound, but it had pride in it.

"I don't suppose the pilot had any personal papers with him, either..." ventured Smith. British air crew, he knew, never flew carrying anything that might, if they were brought down, give their enemies more information than their names, ranks and regimental numbers. He was certain that other air forces differed little in policy. But then, it was not the dead man's identity that he was probing.

"No, nothing like that," the shepherd said, biting off more bread. "He did have a briefcase; it was under his seat, I think. It was, you know, the soft leather kind. Attaché case, I think they call them. Losing it was the only thing that brought some life out of him. In the crash, it flew off into the woods, and most of the pages were scattered. But Carol found it, and gathered the papers. The pilot held on to it like it was gold or something."

Smith popped a final strawberry into his mouth. It was small, as were most wild fruits, but tasted full and sweet.

"Doctor Kovacs reported the crash and the death of the pilot afterward, not only to the police in Trapburg, but to the district government in Sibiu." He lie on his back, with his hat, like the top of a large mushroom, pulled over his eyes. "That's a big town, headquarters for a Hungarian division and an army corps in the War; you'd think somebody'd have come to look into it."

"Well, it was at the end of the War," Smith pointed out, "a war Austria-Hungary was losing. They probably had tens of thousands of such reports, and were more likely concerned with getting the living home."

"Yeah, I'll bet you're right there."

"If you — and your parents — would like, I could pass word on to the authorities when I reach Bucharest," offered Smith. "This is Rumanian territory now, so it's their responsibility. I can take the pilot's attaché case with me as proof."

Ion raised the brim of his hat to consider his companion.

"Say, that's a great idea. Maybe a reminder is what they need." He propped himself up on his elbows. "I guess red tape can tie up any government. But now that peace is here... I think the poor guy's mom and dad'd appreciate knowing what happened to their boy." He stood up, shook the goat-skin bag that carried his drinking water and sighed. "We should be getting back, I guess."

Smith was as reluctant to leave the warm, peaceful clearing as was his acquaintance. Out of sight of the aeroplane's grisly remains and its implication of war and death, this spot was idyllic. But Ion was right: they had lingered too long among the lotos.

It was perhaps unfair that the next big city Smith visited was Bucharest. He was not one to rail against the towns of the world. He was indeed a countryman at heart, but he had many happy memories of London and Paris, Vienna and Constantinople, and would, he hoped, have more.

But returning to paved streets and congested traffic, loud crowds and big stone buildings after the Arcadia through which he had passed was discouraging. And since he had always thought Bucharest a 'set-piece city', the change was doubly disheartening when he reached the Rumanian capital a few days later.

"Aaaah, yes, Mr Shaw... I did receive your letter from Craiova. It was kind of you to come in person."

Mihai Dragu was a chubby man, a little under medium height, whose undress uniform, that of a captain of dragoons — it was unlikely that he had ever sat a horse for long — strained somewhat against his wide torso. His expressions were just as expansive as his body, his gestures grand, and he wore make-up. Smith knew that this was a habit once common among Rumanian gentlemen, and far from extinct now. It cast no implication upon their characters, and yet, as an Englishman, Smith could not regard it favourably.

"I was coming through Bucharest anyway," he said, wiping his forehead with a handkerchief. The temperature was over a hundred degrees Fahrenheit, admittedly hot for this time of summer, even in the Wallachian Plain, but it was not rare.

"It is a coincidence, really," remarked Dragu. His French being much better than his English, the conversation, begun in the latter tongue, was continued in the former. It made his gestures more natural, somehow. "My department had just come across a report on that same body, a pilot, whose aeroplane crashed in the Carpathians, in late 1918. The file was in a batch of paper-work sent down from Sibiu." The captain used his people's name for Hermannstadt. "We are so far behind the documentation from the War, Mr Shaw, we can only pray that Europe stays at peace until we catch up."

Dragu laughed heartily, and, with a flourish, unfurled a large square of scented linen to mop up the resultant perspiration. His office was well-appointed, more like a parlour than a staff captain's room at the War Ministry. Nonetheless, it was small, and the air within was stale, the atmosphere stifling; the single window being open did little to alleviate the discomfort.

"But knowing that the — Joja, you say? — Joja family are expecting us will facilitate matters. It was very kind of them to care for the remains of the unfortunate pilot, don't you think? Typical of peasants, simple, not a thought amongst them, but very kind." Dragu peered at the torn and dirty attaché case he had had Smith deposit upon a plain, unupholstered chair, after covering its seat with a sheet of newsprint.

"And no identification, but this?..." The captain used a long pencil to push back the flap of the case and regarded the mouldy, rodent-chewed pieces of paper disintegrating within. Smith had examined the case's contents carefully during the night he had spent in Craiova, and had removed the few documents remaining that named any but obvious military personnel. "Very sad. Still, when our people have had a look at the aeroplane, and have compared records of officers and units, the fellow will soon have his identity back."

"That's excellent news, Captain," said Smith, rising to his feet. The fabric of his trousers wanted to stay stuck to the sweaty chair. "Perhaps, in a few weeks' time, there will be one less family wondering what happened to their son."

"Undoubtedly, Mr Shaw," Dragu concurred, standing as well. "I'm sure it will all be sorted out soon."

C's office had changed. The previous occupant had had few professional reminders of his days at sea, though the interior decoration had been quite personal, typified by the large portrait of his late son that covered much of one wall.

The new chief of the Secret Service had created a new effect. This C had already spent a quarter-century in the army before his current secondment. But a visitor would not have known it by his office. It had been as empty of his military past as the first C's had been of his naval history. But the similarity ended there.

Other than portraits of the King and Queen, the walls were devoted to maps, coloured and framed, of the world, of Europe and the Far East, in particular. Several bookcases contained reference works: encyclopaedia, government directories, almanacs and various versions of *Who's Who*. The original C's casual décor had given way to his successor's utilitarianism.

Smith was, however, pleased to see, and more pleased to feel, that comfort had not been altogether abandoned. He sat deep in one of the armchairs before C's desk a week after his visit to Captain Dragu in Bucharest. The doors to the balcony, overlooking the back garden, were ajar, and the fresh scent from the sunny summer day without indicated that the garden was in full bloom.

"I received a wire from Colonel Sághy yesterday," C said as he regarded his subordinate. "He was quite satisfied with the results of your mission. He also approved of your decision to give the Rumanians the least harmful portions of the records retrieved."

"It might have proven suspicious if the attaché case had arrived in Bucharest empty, after the Jojas told the Rumanian investigators that it had left their care with papers inside." Smith's hands rested on the arms of his chair. He had been offered no refreshments.

"Indeed." C scanned the page facing him in the open folder on his desk as if he were searching for an obscure location in the index of an atlas. "Yes, the Jojas... The farmers near the crash site..." He glanced up. "Sághy will be most grateful for the assistance we've provided, and having the Hungarian Secret Service on our side will be useful."

"Perhaps more useful than it will first appear, sir," Smith responded. C's one eye questioned him. "I believe that Colonel Sághy was a German agent during the War, and may be still."

C was silent for an inordinately long time, as if trying to determine the credibility of the last statement, or perhaps of its speaker. Then he closed the folder before him and, reaching inside the jacket of his grey suit, brought out his cigarette case. He held it open for his visitor. Smith had noticed that there was no box of cigarettes on the desk, as there had been in the old C's time. It was a new desk, too.

"Would you care to explain that theory?" The chief's tone was neither sarcastic nor sympathetic.

"It occurred to me as soon as he had made it, that Sághy's request for our help was strange." Smith suspected that C had shared his concern, but the latter said nothing now. "Ion Joja told me that the pilot fatally injured in the crash had spoken to his rescuers, but that they 'couldn't make out' what he was saying. I thought at first that this implied incoherence. Then I realised the significance of their summons of a Mr Waldheim, from Trapburg, a 'Saxon' village."

" 'Saxon'?"

Smith briefly pieced together for his chief the fragmented ethnology of Transylvania: the German-speaking 'Saxons' and the later 'Swabians'; the

Hungarian-speaking 'Magyars' and the longer-established 'Szeklers'; and of course the Rumanians.

"You believe the pilot was talking German," C said, following the elucidation.

"Yes sir. If he had been muttering in Hungarian, then the Szekler physician, already sent for, could have translated; a German-speaker, who was not a doctor, would not have been needed." C nodded, and Smith continued. "I'm certain the Jojas would have recognised Hungarian and German, even if they wouldn't have comprehended the words. The three groups have lived beside each other for centuries; they'd know the sound of each others' tongues, I'm sure."

C grunted. It was a kind of acknowledgement of Smith's notion, not concurrence with it.

"Then there was the position of the aeroplane when it went down," Smith tipped ash from his cigarette. "The machine had been flying in a direct line toward Trapburg, where a German Army battalion was stationed at the time, even though an Hungarian division was headquartered a dozen miles away in Hermannstadt. There was even a level field near Trapburg large enough for 'plane to land safely."

"You think the pilot had been ordered to take the shortest route to the nearest German unit in undisputed territory." C's mind mulled over this possibility.

"With the War almost over, formations in occupied Rumania, an Allied country, might have been interned. Once over the Transylvanian Alps, in Hungary — Hungary extending that far then — German forces would be more secure, and also more likely simply to be commanded to return home intact, rather than surrender to the Allies. If I'm right, and Sághy had been told by his German masters to give them his intelligence records, the Germans in Trapburg would be the ideal destination. The German High Command had every reason to believe they would be allowed to go home unmolested, and the files of Austro-Hungarian agents in Rumania could be used by Berlin after the War."

C grunted again.

Smith added, "It would explain why Sághy wanted us to retrieve the records for him. Even if kept most secret, an operation conducted by his own people would have required pay, expense accounting, false documents... It would have been known soon enough within the National Defence Service. And if Sághy had worked secretly for another country, he wouldn't have wanted even one of his colleagues asking questions; they would have expected the records after they were retrieved, if only for bureaucratic reasons. And what if he is still a German agent?" Smith put the remains of his cigarette in the small, round ashtray by his chair.

C nodded slowly, and said, "Even in their reduced capacity, the Germans wouldn't want to relinquish such a valuable asset: having the director of the Hungarian Secret Service in their pay puts his whole organisation in Berlin's pocket. On the other hand, our knowledge of his true colours puts us in a position to demand more than just gratitude from Sághy, if we wanted." C reclined in his chair, a more austere furnishing than the one that it had replaced. He glanced again at his subordinate, and then pushed a button on the wall by his desk. "Tea, Smith?"

The Rhine Maidens

"How was the shooting?"

Linus Smith hesitated before answering C's question. The chief of the Secret Service had posed it in a voice more gruff than usual, and in a tone that carried an under-current of sarcasm. The trouble was that just the day before, Smith had been at the Duke of Beynhurst's lodge in Yorkshire, to which he had been invited for a week's sport. The occasion had been the opening of the grouse season on the twelfth of August, in which almost every British gentleman aspired to participate.

Unfortunately, not all of those aspirations were fulfilled. It was certainly not envy of Smith's opportunity to shoot over His Grace's moors that prompted C's resentment. After all, he himself had been asked by numerous friends and acquaintances to visit them for The Glorious Twelfth. It was the inability to accept such hospitality this year that rankled.

However, Smith did not always feel the need to indulge his superior's moods.

"It was excellent, sir," he answered; "most enjoyable."

The weather in the North Riding had been perfect for shooting: a slight overcast screened the glare of a bright blue sky; warm, with cooling breezes. Those tied to London by their duties had to suffer days of rain, which were continuing even as Smith and C entered the main doors of the War Office, facing Whitehall.

"I suppose you've heard of Christopher Grey?" C brushed the moisture off his hat and coat before handing them to the porter in the lobby. The frown that indented the space between C's left eye and the leather patch that obscured the empty socket of his right suggested to Smith that his boss was not prepared for humour to be made of the subject.

"Yes sir, I have."

"Of course..." muttered C. He did not wait for Smith to dispose of his own coat and hat before ascending the principal staircase that rose before them.

"Royal Engineers, commissioned in 1890, I think, and seconded to the Egyptian Army after Omdurman." Smith caught up to his chief as the latter reached the first floor landing. "He's had much operational experience in the Sudan and the Near East, was promoted major general in 1918, attained the rank

The Rhine Maidens

of ferik in the Egyptian service a couple of years later. He was recently knighted and, I believe, is currently on long leave here in England."

Though both men were out of uniform, they may as well have been wearing ammunition boots as they strode down the stone corridors, for the noise their footfalls couldn't help making. The building was certainly different from the old War Office in Pall Mall; Smith visited that venerable building twice, and remembered its honeycomb of rooms of all shapes and sizes, each one, it seemed, on a different level to the one next to it. Moving military administration into the new headquarters in 1906 was almost symbolic of the army's reorganisation, undertaken at the same time. But Smith had found something endearing in the ramshackle array of past days. Some things could be too orderly.

"What you may not know," C said, as if Smith had neglected the most important fact, "is that Grey has just been appointed sirdar of the Egyptian Army."

"Oh?" Smith was not aware of this development, but he saw no reason to let his superior know it. "That was confirmed, was it?"

C did not respond, but turned and pushed open an unmarked door to an isolated suite of rooms. One was a small office with a large desk, piled with papers, both bound and loose. All of the three gentlemen within were standing, as though waiting, and despite the open windows, the atmosphere was close and uncomfortable.

"Sanction?" The oldest of the three men was surprised to find C striding through the door. "No wonder you disappeared from the Active List. I was told that I'd be meeting someone from the Secret Service, but I'd no idea it would be you."

"You still have no idea," stated C, in a surprisingly friendly tone. The two shook hands.

"Of course."

Smith did not require the introductions which followed to be told that this was Sir Christopher Grey. Dressed as a major general, his tunic's left breast decorated with four rows of medal ribbons, Grey looked very much the military commander. Tall, broad-chested, with a full moustache and dark hair parted down the middle of his scalp, he resembled the late Lord Kitchener, but with bright green eyes, instead of blue. He seemed relieved that C was the man with whom he would be dealing, and equally buoyed to see that he was not in a mind for small-talk. The atmosphere in the room relaxed marginally.

C gestured to the man on Grey's left and said, "Smith, this is my opposite number at the Home Office."

The reference was to the director-general of MI5, the Security Service, responsible for protecting Britain and the Empire from foreign intelligence organisations. K, as he was usually called, was about fifty, on the small side, with a face that seemed perpetually screwed up, as if he were forever trying to observe something that was just out of sight. Oddly, the most prominent individual feature of that countenance was the little toothbrush moustache which, due to the man's habitual expression, seemed always to be in the very centre of his face.

"And this is my aide-de-camp, Lieutenant Boyd-Foster," the general said, turning to his right. The subaltern, in the uniform of the Rifle Brigade, had an honest and eager visage, and could not have been long out of Sandhurst.

"Smith knows nothing of the situation, gentlemen," C stated, after K, playing host, had suggested that they sit. Chairs were pulled into as spacious a circle as the room's dimensions allowed. "I myself was told only the bare facts, so why don't we start at the beginning?"

Grey nodded and, after inhaling forcefully, slowly emptied his lungs again.

"Yesterday, I received a letter," he revealed, speaking to no one in particular. "It claimed that one of my daughters had been abducted."

K had brought a polished leather attaché case to his lap from where it had reposed out of sight behind the unused desk. He now removed from it a manila folder and handed it to C. Within the folder was a large envelope and what it had contained: a creased sheet of foolscap, upon which had been pasted letters, cut from a newspaper or magazine and arranged to form words.

"Is it safe to touch this?" C queried, passing it to his subordinate.

"Yes," replied K. "We've had it examined for fingerprints: nothing identifiable, I'm afraid."

Smith spread the letter before him. Its surface was bumpy and uneven, the result of the paste.

" 'Do not go to Egypt. Resign your appointment. We have your daughter. Do as we say and she will not be harmed. Do not call police'." As the letter's text was read, K presented the Secret Service men with a photograph on stiff paper. It depicted a girl of mid-adolescence, well on her way to being very pretty, with curled, dark hair, light-hued eyes and an intelligent and energetic expression. The resemblance to the general was clear.

"I didn't know what to do," Grey continued. "Then I remembered that when I worked in the Intelligence Department in Cairo, we had dealings with a branch of the home government to do with security. The chap I'd met back then turned out to be heading MI5 now." He indicated K.

Smith had been examining the envelope and held it up, face forward.

"And we were called because of this?" He tapped the cancelled German stamps.

"Exactly." K seemed please that Smith had noticed the clue. "It was mailed from outside the country. Not my bailiwick."

Smith observed that the envelope had been sent to Grey's house in Belgravia. That address was hardly a secret; it was listed in his *Who's Who* entry. His eyes followed the circular postmark.

"It left a place called Eberkirch, on the tenth." Smith glanced up. "Do you know Eberkirch, General?"

"Yes, I do. I've been there. It's the location of my father-in-law's estate...and my daughters went there for their holidays at the start of the month." Grey patted his chest, feeling unsuccessfully for his cigarette case. Boyd-Foster quickly produced his, and the general was smoking several seconds later.

"The letter mentions only 'daughter'," commented C.

"It's Sophie," responded Grey, in a low voice. "They have Sophie."

Despite his outward appearance of calm, the general's anxiety was almost palpable. He drew strongly on his cigarette, and quickly consumed half of it. Boyd-Foster had taken an ashtray from the top of an empty filing cabinet and placed it at his superior's elbow.

"Why don't you tell us about your family, sir?" Smith suggested, returning the items he had been given. Grey regarded Smith suddenly, then blinked.

"Yes...my family..." The general cleared his throat. "My wife, who died ten years ago, a month before the War, was German, the only daughter of Albrecht, Count von Reitfels. Even though my opinion of Germans suffered because of the War, I didn't want my children growing up in ignorance of their grandfather, or their continental heritage. Therefore, I arranged that my girls, Sophie and Frances, should spend a couple of months' holiday with him." Grey was speaking easily now, as if concentrating on a narrative distracted him somewhat.

"And your father-in-law, sir," prompted Smith, as if he were interviewing a subject for a magazine article, "what sort of man is he?"

"Decent, considering that he's a Hun," answered Grey, inhaling from his cigarette. He then put it down and shook his head. "No, he's decent, full-stop. Proud of his family's history, mindful of his dignity, almost to the point of arrogance, but not quite. He comes from a large family, with relatives everywhere, yet he has time for all of them, if they need it." He set his jaw firmly, but his green eyes softened, as he said, "It will be a tremendous blow when he learns what has happened. He'll see it as a personal failure on his part to keep Sophie safe."

Both Smith and C noticed the statement, but only the latter put the observation into words.

" 'When he learns...' Surely, he knows his granddaughter is missing."

"As a matter of fact, it appears he doesn't." K was the one to respond, pursing his lips and forcing his facial features together once more. "When General Grey received the letter, he needed to confirm its claim."

Smith had been wondering if this had been done.

"There was little sense in creating a furore if the letter was meant simply to frighten me," explained Grey. "So I telephoned Schloss Reitfels. Not wanting to alarm anyone, I pretended that I was intending to surprise my girls with the call. The castle has just had its telephone lines installed, you see."

"You found Sophie absent but accounted for," guessed Smith. The others turned to him questioningly. "The only way Count von Reitfels could not have realised that his granddaughter had been abducted, if she had been, was for there to be a legitimate reason for her to be elsewhere."

"Yes...yes, precisely, Major." Grey seemed to regard Smith for the first time as a person in his own right, and not simply one of C's underlings. "Frankie — my daughter, Frances — was at the castle. Sophie had apparently gone to visit their great-aunt, Wilhelmina, Baroness von Bockmann, who lives about a hundred miles away."

"You made certain that Sophie was not there, either," Smith assumed.

"Precisely. I made a second telephone call, again using a pretext. I informed the baroness that I thought my girls would enjoy a visit with her, and acted as if I were arranging a surprise for them. That way, if Sophie had genuinely gone there, it could have been seen as a simple case of her forestalling the surprise."

"But she wasn't there." C's statement was unnecessary.

"No, and it was clear that the baroness, though she liked the idea of a visit, was not expecting either of them." Grey reached for his cigarette, to discover that he had finished it. His a.d.c. produced another.

A stillness enveloped the room again, and though the humid air and the rain made the atmosphere close, it was less charged than it had been. The general looked tired, drained from re-living the experience of discovering his daughter missing.

Smith listened for a moment to the precipitation, falling beyond the windows. Then he said:

"Tell me about your children, General." His tone was conversational. Grey remained quiet for half a minute, smoking.

"Sophie...is fifteen, and resembles me, so I'm informed. I rather hope that isn't entirely true..." The thick moustache moved a little, as if hiding a small smile. "She's very intelligent, very clever; too much so, for her age, I sometimes think. She's too trusting, and lives for her books, which she's always reading. She is in a hurry to grow up and get out into the world, to experience the things she reads about. She wants to attend university." The final sentence was added as if the speaker were unsure what to make of the fact.

The Rhine Maidens

"And the other?"

"Frankie, as she's always been called; she's twelve." Grey smiled more plainly this time. "She looks like her mother. Smart, and *very* curious about everything, less scientific, I suppose you could say, than Sophie; her mind moves all over." He sighed.

"I'm afraid I've been rather jealous of their affection, not wanting to share them with anyone. For their part, they've always been concerned about my welfare. Not having a mother has made them over-protective of the parent they have, I suppose. They haven't been pleased about my going to Egypt at all, because of the threats and outrages against Englishmen there. I explained to them that it's not dangerous in the least, compared to some places I've been." The general's face took on a wry look. "I'm afraid that only started them worrying about the things I've already done."

The room was quiet again. Grey lowered his eyes and concentrated on his cigarette, perhaps slightly embarrassed at how much he had told the others.

"I assume MI5 are looking into possible clues here at home?" C asked his counterpart in the Security Service.

"Yes, and the Egyptian Secret Police are investigating matters at their end," asserted K.

"And in the meantime, Smith will go to Germany," said C.

"I don't want the regular police involved, British or German," Grey said, with finality. "There is no way to know if the people who have Sophie are watching events on the continent — or here, for all that. I don't want to take the chance that their threats are not bluffs." He glanced at Smith, then looked at C. "How will your man look into things in Germany?"

C was unprepared for the question, and was himself unsure of the course his subordinate would take. Smith, however, was already thinking.

"General, you mentioned that Count von Reitfels's family has ramifications everywhere. Tell me, do you think that there might be a second cousin twice removed, or some such creature, with whom he could have lost contact?"

It was curious, thought Smith, what sort of topography symbolised a country, especially to a foreigner. When he was a child, still living in his native Northumberland, Africa was the Dark Continent, all of it covered in impenetrable jungle — except those bits in the north that were barren desert. When he was sent to the Cape, and lived in Rhodesia, a different landscape confronted him, and the open veldt, with its tumbled boulders of granite, became his home. But that was Rhodesia; 'Africa' was still jungle.

Never mind that Smith had been to different lands and had seen that they comprised a variety of terrain and vegetation; youthful impressions remained.

Inductions Dangerous

So it was that Italy brought to mind rural lanes lined with tall, slender Lombardy poplars; Russia, vast forests of never-ending trees; the United States, great plains, empty of all but waving, pale grass. And Germany meant castles on the Rhine.

Smith travelled to Cologne using his own identity, a British Army major, his uniform facilitating the passage. Beyond it, however, he journeyed as someone else, wearing civilian attire, purchased before his arrival by a colleague. Dressed in used, and abused, but still presentable second- or third-hand garments, he made his way south on a river steamer. And there were castles on the Rhine.

The neat and clean towns and villages that had grown on either shore seemed devoid of the industry that dominated the landscape farther north, and the closest approximation to great factories that Smith saw were Victorian and Edwardian hotels and villas, a little seedy now, but as tidy as German efficiency could make them. Between these communities, and above them, chunks of stone loomed over the water from ever-increasing heights. These became mountains, hardly the giants of the Alps or the Tatras, though they nonetheless rose dramatically, in some instances from the river's very edge. They added to the effect of the fortresses that topped them; or perhaps it was that the castles added to the mountains, for one strengthened the other.

The morning sun came and went, now hidden by a deteriorating tower, long-since abandoned by its knights, now shining over the walls of a prince's ornate palace. Some of these magnificent buildings had been raised for defence, and had been so forbidding to both owner and visitor that they were deserted when more secure times at last arrived. Others were residences to this day, the newest generations of occupants playing on the terraces, and waving to the passing vessels from the balustrades.

Smith had seen these castles and mansions before, though he never ceased to marvel at the fairy-tale turrets and story-book settings. More prosaic was his wonder when he stepped ashore at Coblenz, the slanted city at the confluence of the Rhine and its tributary, the Moselle. Cutting sharply into the water, on its little promontory, was the huge statue of William I, German Emperor, astride his horse.

The Briton was not astounded by the likeness itself, but rather by its continued existence. Above the fortifications of Ehrenbreitstein floated an enormous flag of blue, white and red; the Gallic tricolour flapping over the headquarters of the French army of occupation. The French had tried almost everything to lower the spirits of their vanquished enemies; perhaps throwing down the imperial bronze giant would have been too much, even for them.

Smith had to be careful, though, for little else seemed to be beyond the

The Rhine Maidens

ungracious victors. He had been provided with false identification papers before leaving London, but these documents had not been intended to withstand close scrutiny; as good as the Secret Service was in that regard, there had not been time available for convincing work. Fortunately, Smith himself rarely invited close scrutiny and, as long as he was prompt, as a temporary German, in removing his hat to any passing Frenchman, he was ignored. Soldierly habits were nearly his undoing, though, as he was unaccustomed to saluting other ranks, as well as senior officers.

Eberkirch was a little village not far up the left bank of the river from Coblenz. Smith covered the distance by train. He might very well have imagined himself travelling up the Rhône, rather than the Rhine, as the crew, staff and most of the passengers were French. France's seizure of the Ruhr district in January had prompted a policy of passive resistance among the Germans. Among other boycotts, native personnel refused to service trains running through French-occupied territory, so Paris had ordered in its own corps of railwaymen. Germans still rode the Rhineland trains, as a matter of necessity, but as he sat unobtrusively in a carriage grown shabby after years of war and defeat, Smith was fully conscious of being its only non-Gallic inhabitant.

"The Count of Reitfels? Of course! Everybody knows him."

So declared a stocky baker who, to judge by his clothes, had once been stockier. The tradesman was loading baskets of fresh bread, grey and gritty, into the rear of an ancient van, while a horse, a contemporary of the conveyance to which he had been harnessed, and looking much thinner than its owner, waited patiently in the traces.

"I'm making a delivery to the castle right now," the baker said, his last loaf settled. He glanced at the suitcase Smith had put down at his feet. "I can give you a ride there, if you like."

Eberkirch's founders had taken advantage of a wide, flat tract of land that spilled out between the river and two rocky crags behind. A modest pair of jetties made riparian trade convenient but not prevalent, and the lack of an hotel indicated that the tourist trade had passed the village by. The community wore a down-at-the-heels appearance, like the home of a former genteel family who possessed the culture and manners of their class, but not the money. What with the usual discomforts that accompanied a major war, the Royal Navy's highly effective blockade, Germany's eventual defeat and rampant inflation that made printed currency more valuable in a water closet than in a bank, Smith was surprised at the almost buoyant attitude he observed among the people.

Along Eberkirch's principal street, around the more southerly of its neighbouring massifs and up a country road that had probably never seen motored vehicles, the baker maintained a staccato dialogue with Smith, seated next to him behind the bony horse. Speaking of the warm weather, the paucity of good flour, the French soldiery, the paucity of good flour, his wife's relatives, and the paucity of good flour, the German tossed his comments into a rustic quiet otherwise broken only by the plodding of the poorly shod animal and the creaking of the van's axles.

"I'll tell you, after the rationing during the War, the inflation, the embargo... I can't remember the last time I took pride in a loaf I made," he said, shaking his head regretfully.

"Come now, with what you had to work with during the War, I'm sure you created wonders," responded Smith, sympathetically.

The baker grinned a little, then let the expression subside.

"Well, *I* thought so," he agreed, reservedly, "but everybody else just complained. Did they criticise the British navy for keeping food out of our bellies? Did they whine about the socialist politicians who sabotaged the war effort? They didn't even blame the Jews. You know things are bad when the Jews aren't being blamed."

As a gauge of morale, Smith considered the baker's remark valid; as a gauge of morality, it was something else.

The river, even under a bright blue summer sky, the sun now past its mid-point, did not sparkle here, but ran deep and dark. This was the Rhine of legend. Along its shores, Germany first experienced civilisation, and its history began.

"There it is, sir," the tradesman said abruptly and, to Smith's surprise, without a reference to wheat, flour or bread. "That's Castle Reitfels."

Like the English word 'castle', 'schloss' had originally denoted a fortress. And like castle, schloss could now have been applied as much to a baroque palace of indefensible situation and elevation, as to an impregnable keep. Though from a distance, the home of the Counts of Reitfels might have appeared to belong to the latter category, it was most definitely of the former.

Placed solidly on the end of a ridge which soared over the river but sloped downward to the hinterland, Schloss Reitfels was a tall, long, seemingly rambling affair. It resembled something, to Smith's mind, that might have been raised in England during the Regency by a wealthy aristocrat casting his eye back to his medieval ancestors. It rose out of a small forest that climbed its ridge, and made the house look as though it had always been there.

"The count is at home?" Smith asked.

"Oh, yes, there are several guests this week. That means extra loaves and pastries." The baker glanced over his shoulder at his wares in the van and added, almost inevitably, "But I can't say they'll be getting the best I've ever made..."

The German halted long enough to drop off his passenger at the main gate,

The Rhine Maidens

before progressing around to the tradesmen's entrance at the rear. Smith hefted his suitcase and walked the long avenue of lime trees that pointed the way to the castle's primary entrance. The castle was a grand sight approached from this direction, as its architect had intended. Smith wondered if he would find here the answers General Grey anxiously sought.

"Good afternoon, sir. I am told that you are Hans von Reitfels, a cousin of mine, from Africa..."

The statement might as well have ended on a higher inflection than that with which it began, since the speaker was certainly regarding Smith questioningly. The Englishman had been deposited in a morning room — or the German equivalent thereof — after stepping into the front hall. The young footman who had answered the deep summons of the door bell had been rather at a loss, probably because no Hans von Reitfels had been expected. Perhaps the servant had been suspicious. After all, Germany was not what it had been; transients, sharpers, profiteers and strangers who committed all sorts of senseless crimes, were the subject of leaders in even respectable newspapers. So in the morning room Smith had waited, pausing before a mirror to brush at his clothes.

"From Africa, yes..." Smith said to his host.

Albrecht, Count von Reitfels, did not resemble a stereotypical German. His face was long and white, its lower half hidden behind a similarly-hued beard and moustache, both of which grew luxuriantly but neatly. The pate was bald, and minute lines wrinkled the skin about the pale, watery eyes. Though the rest of the visage was remarkably smooth, Smith guessed the aristocrat's age to be about eighty years. Yet Reitfels held himself erect and strong, his voice and his hands steady.

"I realise that my materialisation is most irregular," continued Smith, glancing over the count's shoulder to the door; it had been kept slightly ajar. "I have no invitation, and did not write beforehand, but..." He retrieved an envelope from within his jacket. "...I think this will explain matters."

The nobleman accepted the letter slowly, and was cautious as he withdrew the folded piece of paper from the envelope. After a moment's reading, he glanced up. His expression had hardly changed, yet he seemed almost stunned. He had difficulty speaking.

"Come to my study, please..." Reitfels turned and saw the open door. "I have some of my favourite plum schnapps, and we will celebrate this visit from a long-lost branch of the family..."

The count's own room was opposite the morning room, across the vast hall that soared three storeys to a distant circular skylight. The study was obviously the gentleman's private domain, decorated with books and hunting trophies, almost in equal proportions. Reitfels ushered Smith inside, then closed the door.

Inductions Dangerous

After a moment's hesitation, the aristocrat removed a key from his watch-chain and turned it in the lock.

"This letter..." The older man cleared his throat. "This letter... Do you know what it says, sir?"

"Yes, Count." Indeed, it had been at Smith's direction that General Grey had written it.

"My son-in-law informs me that my granddaughter has been abducted..." Reitfels held up the paper he had read, as if challenging Smith to deny its existence.

"Yes, I know."

Again, the nobleman seemed to have difficulty in finding his voice. He gestured vaguely to an armchair under a particularly fine stag's head mounted on the wall. Smith sat, thanking his host, though the latter remained standing, still gripping Grey's letter. Reitfels again cleared his throat and, as though the sound signalled a return to control, said calmly:

"My son-in-law further states that he received a message demanding that he resign his latest appointments. If not, Sophie..." The count's struggle for mastery over his emotions fluctuated again and he lowered his eyes. "She is supposed to be at my sister's house..."

"Perhaps you should confirm that, Count," suggested Smith.

"No." Reitfels face came up, and he stood tall. He placed Grey's letter upon the desk before him and put his hands behind his back. "Christopher has explained how he determined that Sophie is not there. To call my sister and ask... Well, she is not an idiot and would know that something was amiss. And she is no longer physically strong enough to stand such a shock. I thought that was why she consented to only one of the girls visiting her at a time."

"I'm sorry, Count, but do you mean that the baroness put forward an idea that one of your granddaughters go to see her?" Smith found this incongruous. Grey had stated explicitly that Baroness von Bockmann had not been expecting any relatives to come calling.

"No, I am sorry, but I mislead you unintentionally." Reitfels shook his head. Retaining the control he had now won, he stepped behind his desk and sat in the chair there, having first offered Smith a cigarette from a mahogany box kept on the study's mantelpiece. "Sophie and Frankie received a letter last week. There wasn't a reason to think it hadn't come from my sister. The girls had no suspicion that the handwriting was not hers, and I barely glanced at the letter myself."

"It was an invitation to the baroness's house?"

"Albenburg, yes, about a hundred and ten miles east of here. Sophie left on the tenth. Frankie and I drove with her to the station in the village to see her off.

The Rhine Maidens

She was nervous but very happy."

"Nervous?" repeated Smith.

"She had not met her Great-aunt Wilhelmina before," explained Reitfels. He made the comment as if it were incidental. Smith noticed that the German seemed to have recovered completely from the shock of the news. But Smith had long before learned what appearances might hide, and he was sure that it was a fight for the nobleman to remain so calm.

"The demands the kidnappers have made of my son-in-law, that he resign his appointments..."

"Yes, General Grey has just been made sirdar of the Egyptian Army." Smith observed an uncertain expression on Reitfels's face, the tiny lines about his eyes bunching together somewhat. "Sirdar is the title held by the commander-in-chief. Since the 1880s, the post has been held by a British general officer seconded to the Egyptian service. Its holder is also governor-general of the Sudan."

"A responsible position, then," said Reitfels, nodding.

"Indeed. Inquiries have been started in both England and Egypt." Smith refrained from giving details of the investigations under way. As K had informed him two days before, the likeliest culprits were Egyptians harbouring anti-British sentiments; MI5 and the Egyptian Secret Police were working to determine the validity of the theory. But Smith admitted to Reitfels that this event was unprecedented. "The usual anti-foreign crimes are straightforward assaults on the principal; if the main target's family is injured, it is usually unintended, or at least unconsidered. And kidnapping has been alien to Egyptian nationalists, so far."

"It seems personal..." the count stated. He examined Grey's letter once more. "It seems directed against Christopher himself, not the English as a whole."

"I agree. That aspect is not being ignored in the inquiry. Nothing is being overlooked, Count," Smith set aside his cigarette, "which is why I am here."

"Yes..." Reitfels nodded slowly. "Christopher writes that I may entirely trust the bearer of this communication in the matter of my granddaughter. But he doesn't identify you." The nobleman was not quite suspicious of his visitor, yet he was plainly uneasy with any charade, as would be any gentleman. Smith knew that a pretence could not be helped.

"For the time being, I am Hans von Reitfels, with your permission; second cousin twice removed, from Africa. I believe you have such a kinsman?"

"I do; a farmer, in what is now called Tanganyika, the last I heard." The aristocrat looked at Smith carefully. "How is he, now?"

"I think you'll be pleased to know that the real Hans served with distinction as an officer of General von Lettow-Vorbeck's *schutztruppen* during the War.

He was wounded, however, and captured in 1917. He lost his farm, but is a reasonably prosperous trader just inside the border of Portuguese East Africa. General Grey recalled that you had a relative in that part of the world, and this was confirmed just before I left London."

"How recent is your intelligence?"

"Three months old."

The count nodded again, this time with confidence, and said, "Then he is a good choice for impersonation. I've several guests staying already at the castle, and Hans's anonymity will prove useful." Smith was not unaccustomed to anonymity. Reitfels's brow furrowed, several lines, deeper than those about his eyes, creasing his forehead. "Your German is excellent for an Englishman — I'm assuming that that is your nationality. You have a Hanoverian accent that will be noticed in this district."

"If Hans von Reitfels's immediate family is as unknown as he, perhaps we might postulate a mother from northwestern Germany," suggested Smith lightly, "to account for my speech."

This was acceptable to the count.

"You will of course be my guest here at the castle for as long as is necessary. Any resource, material, monetary or moral, that I can provide, will be at your disposal." Reitfels leaned to one side and tugged on an old-fashioned bell-pull that hung from the ceiling. He then inquired about his visitor's baggage.

"I left it outside," responded Smith. "I didn't want it to appear as if I were certain of accommodation."

"Of course." Reitfels's expression implied that he approved of such a detail, however small. He rose and, walking to the door, unlocked it, leaving it ajar. A moment later, a footman, the one who had ushered Smith into the house, stepped into the study. "Have one of the bedrooms prepared for my cousin," he was told by his employer. "You will find his bag just outside the front door."

After the servant had departed, shutting the door again, Smith asked about the castle's staff.

"Sixteen indoors and as many outside," replied the count, returning to the chair behind his desk. He glanced at his guest and deducing his thought, added, "A large number for these times, I know, but with the economy in ruins, I have found it difficult to turn anyone away when they come seeking work, and I refuse to let anyone go on economic grounds."

"Do you trust them all?"

"An interesting question." The German's long face seemed to grow longer as he pulled absently at his neat beard. "I trust them all to perform the duties for which they were hired... But you are thinking of another kind of trust, aren't you? Gunther," he indicated the servant Smith had already met, "is one of

The Rhine Maidens

several new employees. Not all have the best, or most recent, references, and some have been unemployed since the War."

"Is there one upon whom you would stake your life?"

"You mean my granddaughter's life, don't you?" Reitfels's tone demonstrated that he thought the question a fair one; well-asked, in fact. "My personal manservant, Heinrich."

"Then it would be as well to acquaint him with the situation, including my part in it."

Reitfels again pulled the length of embroidered silk to summon one of the staff. Then he sat back in his chair. He was quiet for half a minute.

"Will you be able to find Sophie?" he asked. He raised his eyes to Smith's. "I have lost one of my sons to the War, a daughter to an accident, a wife to disease. I am a German, practical, almost as stoic as the English. But I am as well a Rhinelander: the steel in my character softens as it nears my heart. What of my granddaughter?"

"Right now, Count, I have high hopes of finding her alive and well," his visitor said.

"And if the time comes when your opinion changes?" The aristocrat's eyes did not shift.

"I will tell you so," promised Smith.

"Thank you." Reitfels said as a knock heralded a servant's arrival. "Thank you."

Smith sat on the deep softness of the feather mattress of his temporary bed. The chamber that Count von Reitfels allotted him was spacious and simply furnished: a typical bachelor's bedroom in a country house. Its windows overlooked one of the castle's courtyards, grassed and shady, and the crenellated walls that enclosed it. Beyond were the tops of the trees that covered the slope upon which the house had been built. For the next indefinite while, this was to be his home, in more ways than one, for, until his mission ended, he would be a German.

Smith was ambivalent about his new position. He had fought Germans during the War, had killed many of them — not without remorse, but almost always without hesitation. They had been soldiers; the thought of waging war upon civilians was repulsive to him. How then had the Germans themselves done it so readily? The murder of six hundred Belgians, the youngest not a month old, at Dinant; unrestricted submarine warfare; the bombardment of undefended Yarmouth; the shooting of hostages on the eastern front... In the early days of the War, Smith had watched as red and orange lights had flared up on the horizon in Belgium, like beacons signalling danger: they were villages, fired by the Germans troops passing through them, one after the other. What had Count von Reitfels thought of such barbarism? Had Smith's cultured and compassionate host approved of this savagery? Two centuries before, learned Englishmen had made fortunes from buying and selling slaves. Was it simply a matter of time? Had the Germans merely to catch up?

"May I bring you any refreshments, Mr von Reitfels?"

Gunther, the new footman, had been detailed by Smith's host as his valet for the duration of the Briton's stay at the castle. He had just put away Smith's clothes — all rather used, obtained in Cologne — and waited expectantly. He was young, eager to please yet seemingly competent.

"No, thank you," replied Smith. He turned toward the servant. "Tell me, Gunther, who are my fellow guests?"

"Important people, sir," replied the footman with a kind of enthusiasm. "Prince and Princess von Esbeck are here, with their children. The prince is well-known and respected in the Rhineland, sir, so notable that the French have occupied his house as officers' quarters. Baron and Baroness von Keller are visiting from Düsseldorf with their little son. The baron is a great industrialist, sir, who owns iron works in the Ruhr," he continued, stabbing his palm with a forefinger, as if progressing down a list. "Mr Weidner, the provincial governor, is to stay a week longer, and then there is Baron von Bockmann..."

Smith had been pushing at the full, downy pillows at the head of his bed, testing their firmness, when he asked, "Bockmann... A relative, isn't he?" He almost appended 'of the count's'. That would have been an odd thing for him to say. As long as he was Hans von Reitfels, any kin of the count was his, as well.

"Yes sir, the count's nephew, I think."

"Thank you, Gunther. I believe it's only polite to know with whom one is sitting down to dinner. Oh..." Smith held up a hand, as if imploring for silence in which to remember an almost forgotten fact. "There are two English girls staying at the castle, aren't there?"

Dinner that evening seemed to Smith to have been stretched, not in time but rather in content. It reminded him of occasions on which individuals had had to make a little material go a long way. The problem for Count von Reitfels, indeed for all Germans at this time, was not insufficient funds, but a surfeit. The mark was worthless: thousands of millions were required to buy a dozen eggs, twice that amount for a link of sausages. The most unskilled labourer could, in theory, become a millionaire after an hour's work. Yet he not only remained poor in practice, but actually became poorer, as the value of the mark would have dropped between accepting the wage and being paid it.

But the count was an excellent host, and what he had to offer was good and

The Rhine Maidens

hearty, if rather provincial. Nothing uncomplimentary, however, could have been said about the wine, from the castle's own vineyards.

"So you fought with Lettow-Vorbeck, did you, cousin?"

The dishes had been cleared. The ladies had retreated to the Drawing Room, while their children had, Smith assumed, eaten in an entirely different room. Smith sat with five Germans at a flawlessly made table, longer than any off of which he had previously dined, but still almost lost in the cavernous chamber. The chandeliers, suspended from the high ceiling, held hundreds of candles, though only a fraction of these had been lighted. Consequently, little of the vast room could be seen, and the portraits on the walls, no doubt of past Reitfels, were no more than vague and ghostly images almost out of sight.

"It's strange indeed that Vorbeck's darkies proved more loyal than many Germans here at home."

Lothar, Baron von Bockmann nodded as he spoke, the fat cigar, gripped in his teeth, moving up and down as if by its own dying inertia. Though a little older than Smith, Bockmann had a youthful face, resembling his uncle's somewhat, though smoother and plumper, and his features were slightly irregular. His eyes had the half-closed look, and his mouth the set smugness, of someone whose egotism would not have allowed him to think that others' opinions differed from his own.

"Quite right, Bockmann, though those who stabbed us in the back and sold the country to the French and English can hardly be considered Germans." Baron von Keller, the industrialist, was short and round, bald like Reitfels, but with his pate skimmed by the brown strands left to it. His eyes were magnified by a pair of very strong spectacles, making him appear almost comic, and a kind of parody of his own type. He poked the table with a thick forefinger. "Jews are a race apart, thank God, and socialists have abdicated their rights in the Fatherland."

"True," Bockmann agreed smoothly, "true."

The 'stab in the back' was a theme Smith had been hearing more often from Germans. The belief that their armies had not been vanquished on the battlefield but had been betrayed by politicians and profiteers, comforted many Germans, and salved their pride. Smith had no sympathy for such a view for, not only was it inaccurate historically, but it was a theory that required scapegoats. His empathetic nature, however, understood how many could credit such a story. Berlin had kept all news of defeat and desperation at the front from its people, and when they were suddenly presented with a virtual surrender to their foes, it was not to be wondered that they were stunned by this occurrence, happening as if over night.

But those sitting with him at the table should have been positioned to know better. Perhaps one did. Prince von Esbeck spoke up.

"Still, one has to admit that our opponents fought better than we had thought possible." The prince had hardly touched the glass of brandy before him; he had eaten just enough of his meal to be polite. Tall and tired-looking, he wore the gauntness of one debilitated by disease. But his voice was hollow, and Smith could tell that illness had not injured him, but rather, poison gas had burned out his lungs. His words, however, were delivered with authority. "I remember how we had laughed at the English before we met them in battle at Ypres. Yet half my battalion couldn't laugh ever again after our first encounter."

"The English fought like gentlemen, that's true," said Bockmann, permitting himself to be generous, perhaps for the sake of his host, whose daughter had married a Briton, "and I understand that the administration of their zone of occupation is quite fair, compared to the French. But," he waved his cigar dismissively, "they are weak at heart, and their politicians are fools."

Reitfels, sitting silently at the head of his table, near to which all the other men had gathered, glanced at Smith.

"Perhaps these old animosities will heal some day," ventured Smith. The Germans looked at him and, excepting the count and Esbeck, wore expressions that were almost unfriendly.

"It may have been different in the colonies, but here in Europe, we do not forget, and we do not forgive," growled the man sitting next to Smith. Otto Weidner was the *oberpräsident*, or governor, of the Rhineland Province. He looked a very ordinary man, who might have passed as a middle-level bureaucrat in any country, were it not for the scars, diagonally gouged into his cheeks. They had been gained, it was easy to see, not in battle, but in ritualistic duelling, relics no doubt of his university days, about thirty years before. He spoke with the accent of a Berliner, and the harshness of a Prussian.

"It is conceivable that we might one day come to an accommodation with the English, if they return the colonies that they took in the War," he explained, his voice a low, gravelly rumble, "but the French? Never!" Weidner's fist came down hard on the table's surface. It caused no reverberation, the furnishing's length, weight and workmanship ensuring that it was much more solid than anything a man's hand could damage. Consequently, Weidner's gesture had the futility of anti-climax about it. He quickly filled the self-conscious moment that followed with anger. "Not only did they behave as filthy dogs during the War and now treat us as slaves, but they dare to attempt to separate the Rhineland from the rest of Germany! The damned frogs and their schemes... The time will come when we will give them what they deserve..." The governor's face coloured with passion, though his scars stood out white against it.

Smith marvelled that a civil servant could become so worked up that the footmen, re-charging glasses around the table, were reluctant to approach Weidner.

"Come, Weidner, I didn't invite you to frighten my staff." Reitfels spoke lightly, his paternal face smiling under its beard and moustache, yet under that Smith sensed displeasure. The governor's rage would probably not have stopped on its own, and even Bockmann and Keller seemed a little embarrassed. "Some more brandy..." He signalled to the servants, one of whom was Gunther, temporarily returned to his regular duties. "And let's not speak of the French, or the English," the count peered benignly at Smith, "for the rest of the evening."

Weidner adjusted his collar and straightened his white tie, but did not apologise for his outburst.

"Grandfather?"

The men turned in their chairs. A small girl, indescribably tiny in the vastness of the Dining Hall, despite being almost tall for her age, stood in the half-open, distant doorway.

"When are you coming to join us? Why do the men always stay behind?"

A warm smile, as of one who was reminded of comfort and warmth after a day amid cold and pain, grew on Reitfels's face.

"So we can prepare our answers for all the questions you ask, child," said the count. The girl laughed and, upon being motioned in, walked slowly forward, glancing apprehensively at the men's faces. "Frankie, you haven't met another of your cousins. This is Hans, from Africa."

Frances Grey looked at Smith, not fearfully or shyly, but carefully, as if examining a curiosity. Her brown hair was wavy and arranged in a simple manner, while her pretty face was soft and round, without any angles. Her limbs were just beginning to leave proportion behind and were about to embark on the spindly stage that made adolescence such an awkward time for children. Smith stood to greet her, recalling to click his heels, like a polite German.

"You're from Africa?" Frankie said, in her grandfather's language. "Why aren't you black?"

The comment raised a chuckle from Reitfels, but Bockmann's eyes widened, perhaps in shock at the thought of a non-white German.

"Not all Africans are black," Smith replied, with a smile. "Many are brown, others are yellow, and there are quite a few white ones, too."

Still not satisfied, the girl tilted her head on one side and asked, "Where's your tan?"

The count opened his mouth as if to intercede, but clearly did not know what to say. The other men at the table, who obviously had not thought of this question themselves, turned to Smith, who said:

"I stopped off to visit a friend in Silesia on my way here. I was there for a couple of months, and probably left my tan near Gleiwitz."

Frankie giggled and Reitfels relaxed.

"We'll be in presently, my dear," he told his granddaughter.

Smith slept well that night, though he did not sleep much. After he drifted off, he woke unwontedly late and, subsequent to washing, shaving and dressing, was knotting his tie before one of the open windows. Besides the courtyard immediately below, the prospect included some of the castle's out-buildings, and he could just see a corner of the stables. He leaned out over the sill, his eyes, still fondly recalling their interrupted slumber, squinting in the high summer's sunshine.

His host was standing by one of the stables' exterior walls, accompanied by a pair of servants, grooms, to judge by their garb, and a couple of his guests. Smith could not hear the discussion underway, but no one's attitude conveyed pleasure. He drew on his jacket and walked downstairs to join them.

"Yes, Count, it can be cleaned off," one of Reitfels's employees was saying as Smith approached, out of the nearest of the grassed courtyards that comprised much of the castle's intricate topography. "I'll see to it immediately." The servant, elderly but like the aristocrat, standing erect and with some dignity, spoke lowly to his underling, little more than a boy, who hurried away.

"Ah, cousin," said Baron von Bockmann, turning to Smith, "I hope you slept well."

The self-satisfied expression on the speaker's face implied that not only had he risen early but had done something useful with his time.

"I did, thank you," answered Smith, ignoring the look. "But I see someone was awake in the night."

On the stone wall of the stables, blank and grey, had been painted '*Rheinland Freiheit*', in large, capital letters. The white words stood out clearly.

"Rhineland freedom." Smith glanced at the others. "Why on this wall?"

Prince von Esbeck shrugged his thin shoulders, and looked as if the effort were about to give him a coughing fit.

"That's a good question," he said. "The count is well-known as a political moderate, against the separation of the Rhineland, but ready to talk to anyone of either side of the argument."

"Disgusting that this should happen to such a patriot," said Bockmann, his round face becoming grim and angry.

"Have the police been called?" asked Smith.

"Oh, yes," his host answered, with a sidelong consideration of the Englishman. "That was the natural thing to do, don't you think?"

"Here comes the gendarme now, Count," the senior groom, still standing by,

The Rhine Maidens

observed.

Having been re-directed from the house, a constable of the *Landjagerei*, or state gendarmerie, was almost upon the men at the wall. He looked very much like a private soldier of the army, something most uniformed bureaucrats of Germany, and there were many of them, resembled. His shako and shoes, and the colour of his neat tunic — green, rather than field-grey — made the distinction, though even the tall, flat-topped hat had been the sort worn by the infantry in the mid-nineteenth century.

"Count." The gendarme saluted the nobleman, and greeted the other gentlemen respectfully. The groom was ignored. "I was told what happened. Is this the only instance of vandalism?" The policeman indicated with distaste the graffiti on the wall.

"Isn't this enough?" demanded Bockmann haughtily.

"Well, yes sir, of course—"

"You still haven't recovered the cuff links that went missing from my room last week, and you want more crimes to bumble over?" The baron obviously had scant regard for the local agent of law enforcement. "And Mr Weidner, another guest at the castle, is missing a watch chain. Did you know that?"

"Perhaps I could take the details of the matter after—"

"Who would do such a thing, Constable?" Smith had decided to help the wretched-looking policeman. "Malcontents? French spies?" As if having a sudden thought, he added, "Are there any strangers in the village?"

"Yes sir, there are," replied the gendarme, his stout chin doubling as he nodded. In this matter, he seemed to have confidence, and was not a little grateful to be able to display it. "But they are known to me. The inn at Eberkirch reports to my office, of course, as do the lodging houses. I have informants in town who warn me of newcomers and transients. I assure you, sir, the old ways of law and order are not forgotten in my parish."

Smith made his bland face register approval. In Imperial Germany, the police had complete oversight over every district, keeping records of foreign visitors, new residents, people moving house, guests at hotels, businesses opening and closing, clubs and their memberships, associations, meetings and even concerts. Officially discouraged by the post-war democracy, the policy was a habit with the country's authorities.

"Did your spies tell you of Mr von Reitfels's arrival, Constable?" Esbeck asked with a twitch of humour about his drawn face.

"Well... Yes sir," responded the gendarme, with a mixture of pride and embarrassment, "though there was no need for any further information, when I learned that he was a guest, indeed a kinsman, of the count's."

If the policeman had discovered his appearance in Eberkirch before his call upon Count von Reitfels, Smith would have been surprised. Yet, he sometimes felt that he relied too much upon his anonymity, and the German police system *was* efficient...

"I should hope so," said Bockmann, staring at the gendarme as if he were a beggar. "We don't need protecting from the gentry."

Ignoring the baron, Smith said to the policeman, "You will of course be able to provide Count von Reitfels with a list of names and descriptions, so that he can determine if any are familiar as personal enemies, people with a grievance or some other sort of trouble-maker."

"Oh...yes...of course..." The gendarme was uncertain about this, but the double chin eventually formed several times more as his head nodded in compliance. "And as for the losses of property—"

"Theft!" corrected Bockmann, none too gently.

"Er, yes..."

"I understand that inquiries such as these take time, Constable," said Reitfels. "But my guests are leaving at the end of the week, with the exception of my cousin here. This matter," he gestured to the words painted on the stables' wall, "can wait until you see to the missing items. My staff is at your service for questions, and I'm sure my visitors will provide any help they can."

Smith admired the manner in which the count's eyes, the wrinkles about them moving ever so slightly as he glanced at Bockmann, told the baron that the latter would give the constable assistance. Bockmann caught the look and was silent in acquiescence. The old nobleman was a moral force in these parts, it was obvious.

Leaving the policeman and the groom to ponder the wall before them, Smith and the others walked back toward the house, even as the junior servant returned, hastening up with a bucket of soapy water in each hand. The gentlemen crossed an open, paved courtyard, and the strong smell of hay and horses brought a dozen wistful memories to the surface of the Briton's mind.

"That was rather clever," Reitfels said quietly, his moustache interfering with the words. Esbeck and Bockmann were some distance ahead, Smith having kept pace with the count, who had slowed. "The letter my son-in-law received warned against police involvement in this affair, so you contrived to bring them in, connected with a completely different crime. I assume your late sleep this morning is the result of your nocturnal artistry..."

"I used to be able to deface private property far into the night and not feel it at all the next day," Smith declared in a hoarse whisper. "The most efficient means of discovering any stranger in the district belong to the police." The two followed the other pair through a door out of the cobbled court and into a grassed one. The sun was already high enough to shine over the jumble of walls and roofs around them. "It's improbable that the kidnappers would observe any contact we might have had with the police, but still..."

"Yes, still... The vandalism was an excellent pretext on which to speak to the gendarme."

Smith and Reitfels continued into the castle, through one of the many subsidiary entrances, of which a genuine medieval fortress would have had a very limited number. This more modern version was a warren of rooms and passages, less spontaneous and arbitrary in construction than the old War Office of which Smith had been thinking the day he had left London, but still a challenge to any frontiersman's bushcraft. Eventually, however, they emerged into the lofty, three-storeyed entrance hall, with its massive, double, curved staircase.

"Is there anybody else to whom you wish to speak?" Reitfels asked, pausing by the door of his study.

"As a matter of fact, yes: your granddaughter, Frankie."

As if she were an actress cued by a stage prompter, the girl materialised just then, trotting so lightly down the monumental left-hand flight of stone stairs that her footfalls made no sound at all. She bounced off the final step with the energy and carelessness of the child that she was.

"Grandfather!" she cried, running up to the old man. "Hello, Cousin Hans," she added to Smith, brushing at the fringe of brown hair that was too long for her forehead. "Grandfather, may I go to the village this morning?"

"With whom, my dear?"

"Why, by myself, of course!"

The count's face fell, and he shook his head, stating, "No, my dear, not today."

"Why not?" The girl's face was a study in disappointment, and her forthright question probably would not have demanded an answer so starkly had she not been taken by surprise. She had clearly believed that permission would have been granted and that asking constituted a mere formality. "You let me walk back to the castle last week, when we took Sophie to the station. You came back in the carriage and I walked back."

"That was before—" Reitfels caught himself. He again shook his head, the lines near his eyes seeming to stretch across his face at having to refuse the girl something. "I'm sure someone will be going to Eberkirch tomorrow. Some of the Esbeck children will go with you."

"But Grandfather, I want to go today!"

Frankie did not seem to Smith to be a spoiled child, in spite of the obvious devotion with which her parent and grandparent doted upon her. He knew from his own childhood memories, however, that an adult's inconstant and, seemingly, unreasonable behaviour could be most provoking to young minds.

"Uncle, I saw the village so briefly on my way here yesterday," said Smith suddenly, turning to Reitfels, "that I made up my mind to visit it when I had more time at my disposal. Perhaps Frankie could accompany me. It would also provide a perfect occasion to learn more about the English branch of the family."

Frankie jumped for joy, literally, as her grandfather was won over by the other's argument.

"Well, yes, I suppose that would be all right," he responded, still rather hesitant.

"Excellent." Smith smiled at the happy girl. "Go and get your hat, Frankie, and we'll have something for lunch while sitting by the river."

General Grey's description of his younger daughter as 'very curious' had been a gross understatement, Smith felt a couple of hours later. Her questions were interminable, and covered every subject with which Smith, as Hans von Reitfels, might have been acquainted, and many with which he was not. Frankie's ability to elicit information would have been the envy of any secret service.

Schloss Reitfels was more than a mile from Eberkirch, and a hundred and fifty feet above it. Even with gravity on one's side, the distance constituted a healthy walk. Smith, as fit as he was, was not looking forward with joy to the return journey. Frankie had hopped, skipped and run all the way down; only the desire earnestly to hear the answers to her questions had kept her within earshot of her escort. The latter was now hoping that a heavy meal before going back to the castle would weigh the girl down somewhat.

But for all the effort, Smith found the child a delightful companion, and made him wonder, as he had many times in his life, how good a father he would have been.

"How do you like Germany, Frankie?"

Smith considered himself lucky to have fit in a query of his own. He and the girl had switched to their native language, Frankie rather surprised at how well her cousin spoke it. She peered at him rather suspiciously over the remains of her pastry, a large confection that left some of its cream filling on her chin and cheeks.

"You needn't worry about hurting my feelings." Smith smiled. "I tend to think of myself as more African than German." This was certainly true.

Frankie grinned and wiped ineffectually at her mouth with a napkin. Her appetite had already consumed as much sauerkraut soup and chicken salad as the restaurant had provided and, as her reactions slowed in response, she had turned her talk from the subject of Smith himself to that of their surroundings. From their table under a big linden tree on a riverside terrace, they could see across the wide, dark Rhine to the wooded hills on the far side. Sailboats glided, and engined craft, silent at this distance, puffed about under a sky too blue to stare at for long.

"It is very beautiful," replied Frankie at last, having finished a last mouthful. "I wish we had mountains and forests like these in England. And I like the food..." She blushed a little, and regarded the empty plate before her. At twelve, the sensibilities of womanhood were just beginning to affect her, and she had a twinge of guilt concerning her over-indulgence. But then, it was clear, as she swallowed a whole glass of lemonade at one gulp, that these feelings had much to develop.

"And the people are nice," Frankie added, when she could breathe again. Her face took on a quizzical look, that made her appear even younger than her age. "But I think many of them are angry. But most don't show it."

Smith would never have thought to characterise the German national mood in such terms, yet the words fit.

"You and Grandfather aren't like that. And Prince von Esbeck isn't angry; he seems tired out..."

"And what about your sister?" Smith asked, watching a waiter re-charge Frankie's tumbler from a big ceramic pitcher. The restaurant staff had waved away the idea of Smith paying for anything he and the girl ordered, implying that, as guests of Count von Reitfels, their money was no good. In Germany this day, the phrase had a literal meaning. "She's visiting your great aunt, isn't she?"

"Mmm... Yes..." Frankie seemed distracted or simply uninterested.

"You didn't want to go?"

"Great-aunt Wilhelmina is frail, Grandfather told us." She turned to regard a gentleman, in a suit with frayed cuffs, seated at a near by table reading a newspaper. "We explained to him her invitation, and he said that was why Great-aunt wanted only one of us to visit at a time." She twisted her head at an angle, her thick brown hair falling over her chubby cheeks, as she tried to read the words on the newspaper's first page. The French army of occupation controlled the Rhineland press, and so the *Koblenzer Zeitung* had little of significance to report.

"Would you like me to buy you a newspaper?" Smith inquired, smiling.

"Oh, no, thank you." Frankie sat upright and faced Smith again, apologising for her rudeness. "Sophie reads newspapers at home all the time, but she's just showing off." She paused, wondering if the statement had constituted telling a tale. "She couldn't read the German ones, though; she can't understand the spiky printing." She giggled, enjoying an implied superiority over her sister.

Inductions Dangerous

"Why do Germans use spiky letters?"

Smith set down his coffee cup; he wondered if it was entirely real coffee, anyway. Two or three newspapers were for sale in Eberkirch, along with several periodicals. All were thin, of reduced dimensions, the inflation and the collapse of the national economy having driven most journals out of business altogether. The survivors were forced to take measures they had avoided even in war.

"It's called 'black-letter' or 'Gothic'," Smith explained. The thick, pointed typestyle reminded many Englishmen of medieval printing, and was generally difficult for foreigners to read. Certainly, it was easily distinguished from the type used by British newspapers.

"There are some French papers for sale, too," observed Frankie. "Oh, very many! Why are there so many French papers here, Cousin Hans?"

"The French soldiers in the Rhineland like them," responded Smith, "and I suppose there are so many because the Germans *don't* like them and don't buy them." His mind, while talking to the girl, was also recalling the letter sent to her father, informing him of Sophie's abduction. It had been posted from Eberkirch, but had been composed of English words — neither French nor in German type — and cut from an English journal or magazine.

Sophie's kidnappers must have brought the letter to Eberkirch already prepared, and posted it once the girl had been taken. Had they been so certain of their success? pondered Smith.

"Did you shoot any lions or elephants in Africa, Cousin Hans?" The high voice brought Smith back to his surroundings, and Frankie was regarding him with large, excited eyes. "What about cannibals? What did you do in the War? Is it true that water drains the opposite way south of the Equator? Did you fall in love with a beautiful native princess? Do they really kiss by rubbing noses? Or is that Eskimos? May I have another cream bun, please?"

"Do you recognise any of the names?"

As he asked the question, Smith glanced up from the sheet of paper Count von Reitfels had handed him. Twenty names had been neatly printed on the page by a typewriter with a nearly expired ink-ribbon. The list was the result of the village gendarme's vigilance. They were strangers, transients and newcomers to Eberkirch and, as such, suspicious in the eyes of the German police. Before the War, the identities of appropriate individuals would have been recorded in the National Registry of Inhabitants, a detailed survey of every man, woman and child who had moved, travelled through, visited, departed from, arrived or simply existed in, every district of the country.

"No, nobody." The elderly aristocrat shook his head.

The sun was still some distance from the hills that crowded the Rhine to the

The Rhine Maidens

west, even though it was after nine o'clock on a warm, high summer evening. Smith was chafing in an uncomfortable dinner coat which was not only someone else's but of a foreign cut; nonetheless, he was thankful to the count for having provided it. He had retired to a wide, circular terrace that gave off of the Drawing and Music Rooms, on the second floor of the castle's main block. The space, flagged with flat stones, was called the Battery, and though it was defended with genuine, Napoleonic-era cannon, it had probably witnessed no scene more bellicose than the odd family argument.

"Still, it's your son-in-law who is the focus of the kidnappers' attentions, and he might know a name or two. May I keep this?" Smith asked his host, who nodded. Smith folded the paper and slipped it into an inner pocket. "I'll be speaking to a colleague of mine in Cologne tomorrow. I can give him the list as well. I'll then be able to learn of any news from England and Egypt."

Reitfels looked at Smith and smiled, thinly. The expression was heartfelt but nevertheless small and tired. The tiny lines about the nobleman's eyes had grown and multiplied. He offered his visitor a cigarette, and the two smoked without words. A melody from a piano well-played indicated that the evening's entertainments continued inside.

"The princess has a light touch," Reitfels commented at last, his bald head to one side. "She is suited to Chopin."

"Baron von Bockmann, on the other hand, evidently feels an affinity for Wagner," Smith said, referring to the earlier selections which had driven him to the Battery. "Though I wouldn't have thought arias from the *Niebelungen* to be readily adapted for the piano."

Again, Reitfels smiled, smoke escaping from under his moustache. Then he sighed.

"It's the 18th tomorrow," he remarked, peering out over the Rhine. The river was in shade now, waterborne traffic cutting luminous wakes on the surface. "More than a week since Sophie...since she vanished. Is there any chance of bringing her safely home?"

The aristocrat stared steadily out over the crenellated stone wall that curved around the terrace. Smith could not see his face.

"Yes, every chance. It is, after all, in the interests of those who abducted her to keep her alive and healthy." Smith dashed some ash from his cigarette by brushing it against the barrel of a cannon. "If she were hurt or ill, she would require treatment, a doctor or nurse, perhaps; if treated privately, medicine would be needed. In any case, someone would be alerted. The villains we are seeking would not want that, so they will be treating Sophie well. The worst for their purpose that they could do is to kill her. It would be discovered sooner or later, and then, not only would they lose their advantage in gaining what they want, but every man's hand would be against them." Smith exhaled calmly. "No, Count, your granddaughter is alive and well."

Reitfels turned again to Smith, who responded with his most bland countenance.

"I can't determine if you credit your own words or not," the German said slowly. "Either way, you are convincing. But I suppose that I am dismayed at the criminals' silence, the lack of any further demands..."

"I'm not," Smith stated. "General Grey hardly needs a reminder that his child is missing. The kidnappers profit from his fear and uncertainty. Reticence on their part is not necessarily ominous." So he spoke. Yet he too was far from easy.

"Grandfather! Cousin Hans!"

The little figure of Frankie Grey emerged from the glass doors of the Blue Parlour, behind the Music Room, where she and the other children had been enjoying themselves. She ran to her elders, her arms and legs looking rather spindly in their action, but stopped before them and smoothed the skirt of her frock before addressing them breathlessly.

"Come and play hide-and-go-seek!" she urged eagerly, seizing a hand from each of the gentlemen.

"I'm sure your cousin will oblige, Frankie, but I am too old and dignified," pleaded the count.

Smith glanced at his host, as if to inquire silently why he was not excused with his dignity, but was forestalled when the child laughed that Baron von Bockmann would be playing.

"Well, I can't miss that," Smith asserted. "I'll be there in a moment. You and the others hide, and I'll seek." The girl needed no further encouragement and ran inside.

"I'm surprised that you have the energy to play, after spending much of the day with her," observed the nobleman, a benign expression on his face.

"She *is* vibrant," Smith admitted, with a bit of an understatement, "but rather a tonic to middle-age. And I admire the way her mind is like blotting paper." He crushed his cigarette against a huge block of smooth stone. "She wants to know everything. She insisted on purchasing stamps at the post office this afternoon by herself, to send her letters home. I had to wait outside." Smith held up his hands and reassured Reitfels when he saw the latter start. "Don't worry, Count. She wasn't out of my sight at any time."

The older man relaxed, and Smith moved to follow Frankie into the castle. Then he stopped.

"I should mention that I found it impossible to pay anyone in Eberkirch today," he said. "The money I had—"

The Rhine Maidens

"Dropped in value, minute by minute..." Reitfels nodded, his bearded, bald head making the motion implicit of wisdom. "These times make barter, in one form or another, more realistic than currency. I will honour my debts, and those of my guests."

Smith was about to speak further but, knowing that anything else on the subject would merely offend the aristocrat, he simply smiled and walked toward the house, having given the children plenty of time in which to hide.

The spires of Cologne's cathedral — the Dom — were landmarks before any more of the city came into view. Paradoxically, they were seen less and less the closer one approached, until they were hidden altogether by intervening buildings. Smith had to cross the square on which the great edifice was situated just to view it again.

It was another warm and sunny day in the Rhineland, its promise evident even when Smith had caught the early train heading north out of Eberkirch. It took twice as long to reach his destination as it had before the War. One of the reasons involved having to switch trains when the line left the French zone of occupation and entered the British, and German railway workers took over operations.

The Secret Service's little Rhineland station was headquartered in the Dom Hotel, and was responsible for gathering clandestine intelligence within the bounds of Allied-controlled territory. It was independent of the station in Berlin, a sensible arrangement considering the restricted communications between the Rhineland and the rest of the nation.

"Yes, we did meet: eleven months ago, when you were assistant provost-marshal here."

Terence Osborne regarded Smith more closely after the latter uttered this remark, but still could not place his visitor. Nonetheless, the head of station shook Smith's hand genially, offered him the chair in front of his desk, a cigarette and tea, and only then took his own seat.

"It wasn't during that smuggling case, was it?" he asked, leaning forward and folding his hands on his ancient desk's top. "The black market in foodstuffs, down in Komödiengasse? The white slavery ring we broke up? The one working out of the little tavern in Am Bollwerk? What about the French soldiers who caused the riot down by the quays?"

Smith sipped some of the tea Osborne had prepared himself. The fellow had evidently been very busy when he had headed law enforcement in Cologne.

"No, it was the Warner murder. I was the chap the Foreign Office sent over."

"That was you?" Osborne pointed, shocked that he had not recognised Smith; in fact, he still did not. "Dreadfully sorry, old man."

Inductions Dangerous

Smith was used to being forgotten, and waved the apology away as unnecessary. To make his host feel better, he lied and claimed that he had changed over the past year. Osborne certainly had not, though the exchange of his captain's uniform for civilian garb had made him appear thinner, something Smith would not have believed possible. The heaviest attributes Osborne possessed were his sandy-hued hair and moustache.

"I suspect now though that you weren't from the Foreign Office at all, not directly," said the head of station, relaxing in his chair once that he knew that his bad memory was not to be used against him.

"No, C had sent me. How did he bring you aboard?"

"My time in the army ended in February," Osborne explained, testing his tea for temperature. "I had no prospects, but C liked my experience. I changed my suit, walked over from my office at the Excelsior and started here the next week." He shook his head. "It's a damn' shame that C went west so early. The Service could have used him for a while yet."

Smith could not have agreed more, though he was willing to give the first C's hand-picked successor a chance.

"It's a tiny station here," said Osborne, glancing about, as if one could see the whole operation from where the two men sat, "just me and one other. But the German economy right now allows for the recruitment of a great many agents, some of them even reliable, and we work closely with Military Intelligence upstairs, so it's rather a nice billet to start with."

"And you were apprised of my current interests?"

"I was, yes." Osborne nodded, his attitude becoming more business-like. "Bloody awful affair, kidnapping a child. But I'm afraid that I have no good news, old man." He stood and crossed to a tall cabinet by an open window, and withdrew from one of its drawers a slender folder. "Headquarters forwarded the first files, Berlin the ones underneath." He handed Smith the contents of the folder, just a few pieces of paper, covered in typescript.

"Not a hint of a threat against us from any organised group in Europe, either indigenous or from other continents," Smith summarised after reading the pages. "Other than some rather ineffectual students, no Egyptians are known to be in Germany."

"There is a handful in Mainz, but they are here to learn about jurisprudence, or some such thing." Osborne sat behind his desk once more, and at last decided that his tea was cool enough to drink. He pointed. "You'll notice that the Secret Police in Cairo found no indication that revolutionaries are currently plotting against British officials, whether inside Egypt or out."

Smith set the pages on the desk before him and frowned.

"Has General Grey any enemies of a more personal nature, I wonder..."

The Rhine Maidens

Osborne shrugged, rising a little in his chair, as if the action had almost provided the inertia required for flight.

"Most men who attain general officer rank have enemies of one sort or another," he answered, "even if no one consciously thinks of them that way. There are more than a few Germans who feel personally aggrieved about the War. But then, Grey didn't serve in Europe."

"Yet the threat from the kidnappers does seem directed against him specifically." Smith finished his tea. "If he did relinquish his appointment as sirdar, it would just be taken up by another Briton." He produced from an inner pocket the list of strangers whom the gendarme in Eberkirch had found suspicious, and handed it to Osborne with a few words of explanation.

"I'll pass this one to both London and Berlin," the head of station promised, reading the names to himself. He glanced up. "Do you have another line you can follow in the meantime?"

"One," replied Smith, sighing, "but I'm reluctant to suggest it."

"Absolutely not."

Count von Reitfels sat upright behind the heavy desk in his study, his hands flat on the unsoiled blotter, and a strong frown forcing the features on his face downward. Outside the room's windows, birds called to each other in the late afternoon warmth, but Smith felt a distinct drain of temperature within.

"We must tell Frankie about her sister, Count," he insisted. "She knows Sophie better than anyone and might provide real clues to her disappearance."

"And upset herself tremendously in the doing," countered the aristocrat sternly. "You've seen how happy she is, how carefree. She needs to be protected."

"She needs to help, any way that she can." Smith paused, then added, "We have no other option, Count."

Reitfels was silent for half a minute. The absurd notion occurred to Smith that the deer heads, mounted on the walls above the men, were bending their ears to catch the nobleman's next words.

"*I* will tell her," he declared. Less starkly, he consented to Smith accompanying him.

Frankie and Sophie had been given a large room half-way up the castle's square, northeast tower. The younger girl had pleaded for lodging in the tall structure even before the carriage drawing them to their grandfather's house had stopped in front of the main doors. Frankie claimed that she would feel like Rapunzel, despite her hair falling no further than her shoulders; her sister, citing Frankie's alleged laziness, suggested Sleeping Beauty. Perhaps realising the dishonesty of the comparison, Sophie acquiesced in Frankie's wish.

"Hello, Grandfather!" Frankie greeted excitedly, as the two men were admitted to her chamber, minutes after their discussion in the study. "Cousin Hans! You're back from Cologne! Is the cathedral as beautiful as in the pictures? However did they build it so long ago? When was it built? Do the bells really chime every quarter-hour? Do you like this hat?"

She had only just returned to her room, having been outside in the garden with the Esbeck and Keller girls, and was retrieving a hat that she had brought with her from England. With a high crown and a narrow brim, it aped adult fashion, but its like had not yet appeared in Germany.

"Sit down, my darling," said Reitfels, gravely, as Smith closed the door behind then. "Sit down."

Though the room had been occupied for less than a fortnight — by Sophie for even less time — the Grey girls had made it their own. There was no mistaking that it was home, albeit temporarily, to two females. Men, Smith mused, were usually reluctant to stake a claim to any space that they would soon be vacating.

Clothes hung in the half-open wardrobes, more lie upon one of the wide, soft beds. Some of the garments were clearly too old for Frankie to wear; too old for Sophie, in fact, Smith considered. But he recalled the girls' father telling of his elder daughter's desire to mature quickly. Some jars of cosmetic powder and paste sat, partially used, on a bureau before an expansive mirror, accoutrements Smith would have allowed no child of his to use until she was of age — if then. Shoes were scattered about the rug-strewn floor, in some cases, on or covered by copies of periodicals such as *Girls' Own Paper* and *Modern Little Miss*. Books of more substance were stacked on the night-stand beside the bed Smith assumed Sophie had used.

"What is it, Grandfather?" asked Frankie. She lowered her voice in mock solemnity. "You sound very serious."

"What we have to tell you *is* very serious, my dear," the count replied. He put the child on the edge of the bed, and sat next to her. Smith remained standing. "It's about Sophie..."

"Yes?" Frankie removed her hat, seeing that this was not a moment for frivolity.

"She...she is not at your great-aunt's... She is...missing..."

Frankie blinked her big eyes several times, as if not understanding.

"Why isn't she at Great-aunt Wilhelmina's? She got on the train to go there..." She was watching her grandparent's face intently, trying to interpret each line on its surface.

"She never arrived... Your father received..." Reitfels paused. When he did not continue, Smith stepped forward.

The Rhine Maidens

"Your father received a letter a week ago, Frankie, telling him that Sophie had been abducted," he explained. "We think the letter is genuine." The girl lowered her eyes and slowly started revolving the hat by its brim, like the driver of a motor-car twisting its steering wheel in perpetual circles. Smith added, "The kidnappers have demanded that your father do something in return for your sister's release." Frankie remained silent, but bit her lower lip with the front teeth that were becoming prominent with adolescence.

"The reason we are telling you this, my dear," the count resumed, speaking gently, "is that we are hoping that you may have seen or heard something that will help us find Sophie. When we went with her to the village station, to see her off on the train, did you notice anybody, anywhere, who was acting strangely?"

It seemed to Smith as though the girl was about to speak, but then decided to hold her tongue.

"What about afterward?" her grandfather pressed. "I came home in the carriage, while you walked back on your own. Did anybody follow you, or talk to you?"

"I saw people," Frankie volunteered helpfully, "but they weren't dangerous. Just ordinary people." Abruptly, she pushed herself off the bed, leaving her hat behind, and walked nervously to the tall, dark cherrywood wardrobe in which her coat, among other things, was stored. From one of the garment's pockets, she removed a folded piece of paper.

"This came the day after Sophie left," she stated apprehensively, handing the page to the count.

Reitfels quickly read what was written on the sheet, then, giving it to Smith, looked at Frankie. He took her into his arms and held her tightly.

The stationery of this new letter, Smith's fingers informed him, was of the same stock as that posted to Christopher Grey. The creamy colour was identical but, instead of bits of magazine pasted to its surface, this letter was covered in neat, curving, girlish script.

"This is your sister's hand?" he asked Frankie.

She still stood very near the count, but faced Smith. Tears welled in her eyes and shook loose as she nodded. In the letter's text, Sophie explained that she had been abducted but was unhurt, and would remain so. But for her safety's sake, Frankie had to pretend that her sibling was indeed visiting their Great-aunt Wilhelmina.

"That's why I didn't say anything," said Frankie fretfully. "I knew but I had to act as if she was at Albenburg."

"My dear, we completely understand," Reitfels said, squeezing the child's hand tenderly. "Don't we?" The aristocrat peered up at Smith, who was still examining the letter.

"Of course." He smiled at Frankie, who appeared to him frightened and confused for the first time in their acquaintance. "You did just fine."

Smith's mind was not in the mood for bridge that night. But with his ability to concentrate on more than one subject at a time, he and his partner, Baroness von Keller, had little difficulty triumphing over Baron von Bockmann and Princess von Esbeck. The baron was, however, a graceless loser, and though he never explicitly blamed the princess for their defeats, the intimation was unmistakable.

"Eleven o'clock," noted Smith, after a glance at the clock, of unique craftsmanship, marking time on the lintel of one of the long Drawing Room's doors. "Why don't we pause? My legs are craving exercise, however mild."

"An excellent idea, Mr von Reitfels," concurred his partner, who had also witnessed the rising temperature among their foursome. Indeed, it had escaped no one's attention, and the prince, playing a round at a second table, silently indicated his appreciation to Smith, and suggested a similar intermission to his group.

The exterior doors of the room were open to the garden that grew on a narrow terrace between the castle's walls and the wooded slopes that fell precipitously to the river below. A cooling breeze gently turned the chandeliers as they hung from the plastered ceiling, and made the flame of Smith's match wobble as he lit his cigarette. Across the deep darkness that represented the descent to the Rhine, only the pinpoint illumination of another mansion could be seen.

"You must forgive Bockmann, Prince," urged Otto Weidner, as he relaxed in his chair, one arm over its back, the other's hand holding a long cigar. "He exerts himself in cards as he does in politics: with passion, and a full heart."

"It's merely a game, Mr Weidner," Smith reminded the provincial governor.

"Only a game?" Weidner repeated, a little taken aback. Colour seeped dangerously into his cheeks, except for the scars carved there, which remained pale. "Why, Reitfels, I think you've been too long among the savages. Nothing in life is merely a game. Bockmann realises this." The civil servant's voice began, slowly, to rise. "Bockmann realises, as I do, and I think Keller too, that we Germans must forget the old ways of thinking. We were too merciful, too piteous in days gone by; that attitude cost us the War. We must be hard, Reitfels, hard in everything we do!" Weidner slammed a fist down hard on the table. This one was of lighter make than that in the Dining Hall, and it reverberated with the action, cards scattering as if in a wind.

Smith thought that the fellow must be great fun at committee meetings.

The Rhine Maidens

"Yet if we treat everything that we do with the same seriousness, we risk losing perspective," observed Esbeck, standing quietly just outside the drift of Weidner's tobacco smoke. "I agree with you, Reitfels," he said, nodding to Smith. "Bridge is just a game."

"And speaking of which," Baron von Keller commented, "you seem to be down on your game tonight, Count." A couple of footmen, including the ubiquitous Gunther, entered the room bearing trays and urns. Keller held out his cup automatically and had it re-filled with coffee as he sat on a wide sofa, his round torso straining at its waistcoat. He turned to his wife as she and Princess von Esbeck joined him. "I was just telling the count, my dear, that he is not playing to his usual standard."

"I'm afraid I'm a little tired tonight," their host confessed, with a small smile. Indeed, he appeared drawn, his eyes sunk into a welter of lines, and ringed in grey.

"Are you concerned about the vandalism at the stables, Count?" Princess von Esbeck asked, standing close to her husband, and almost reflexively taking his hand.

"Yes, yes, I suppose I am." Reitfels glanced very briefly at Smith, who understood that the nobleman was grateful for the camouflage for his worry. The count was not about to tell his guests about the heartache he felt over his granddaughters.

"It's the French," Keller said, matter-of-factly, as if one were blaming the cold air of winter for dry skin. "They and their lackeys are behind every evil in the Rhineland these days."

"Quite right, Baron," Weidner inevitably agreed. His voice was low and raspy, as though he had a Frenchman before him at that very minute, and was about to pounce upon him. "Have I told you what I and my fellow administrators plan to do about it next week? We—"

"Clumsy oaf!"

A bellow from Bockmann, still standing petulantly aloof from Reitfels and the other guests, startled everyone in the long room. Smith turned to see Gunther, an astonished and terrified expression on his youthful face, holding a silver urn, steam rising from its top and boiling coffee dripping from its spout. Bockmann was shaking his hand, which was reddening, while his plump face was draining of colour.

"My dear Baron!" exclaimed Keller uselessly, as he realised that his friend had just been scalded. The cup and saucer that Gunther's aim had missed lie in pieces on the rug at his feet.

Smith had seized from a tray a large pitcher of cold water and, as Bockmann advanced menacingly toward the cringing servant, took the baron's injured hand

and plunged it into the soothing fluid.

"I'll kill the ignorant peasant," growled Bockmann, the veins standing out in his neck, as if fuelling his rage. Keller and Weidner belatedly gathered about him.

"Not until you can grip a weapon again," Smith responded. The German, thinking he was being made fun of, glared at his benefactor. But, as Smith had placed one of Bockmann's hands in water and the other on the pitcher's handle to hold it, there was little else he could do.

"How could you employ such an incompetent, Count?" demanded Weidner, staring angrily at the now thoroughly frightened footman. "Is this what service has come to in the great households of Germany?"

"I employ whom I wish, Weidner." The calm, hard, coldness of Reitfels's reply was more shocking than Bockmann's shriek of pain and fury. "If you are dissatisfied with the hospitality offered under my roof, you are free to leave — now — and seek your entertainment elsewhere."

Weidner paled, as though he too had been burned, and he waved his cigar tentatively as he sought to mitigate his offensive words. Keller as well tried to soothe feelings, and even Bockmann had the instinct to remain quiet under the steely gaze of his host. It was a moment when all the men in the room remembered that Count von Reitfels was one of the most influential and powerful men in the province.

Smith slipped out of the knot of guests who were now orbiting Bockmann and moved unnoticed to where Gunther stood, not yet dismissed, in the shadows, his hand still grasping the metal urn, with its steaming contents.

"Why don't you return to the kitchens for a moment?" suggested Smith. The footman was surprised by the gentleman's sudden appearance beside him. "Ask the steward to arrange other duties for you for the remainder of the evening. Count von Reitfels would approve, I'm sure."

"Yes sir, thank you..." Gunther swallowed dryly and looked past the Englishman to Bockmann, who had consented to being led to a couch, and tended there. "Do you think I'll be sacked, sir?"

"I think the count is a fair man," answered Smith. In a whispery voice of warning, he added, "But if I were you, I would pay more attention to my duties than to others' conversations."

Gunther's eyes, still wide with fear, returned to Smith's bland face, as though he were unsure of the words he had just heard. But Smith turned, and walked back to his fellow guests, and the servant then followed his advice without further delay.

Count von Reitfels soon regretted the comments he had made to Weidner, though he did not retract them. They had had a dampening effect on the rest of the evening, though this had its advantages, too. Bockmann eventually accepted his injury manfully, and his reverses at cards more maturely. Bridge was continued for a couple of hours, but Smith could see that Reitfels considered that he had behaved badly as a host, and the night's entertainment ended without gladness.

The mystery of the kidnapped girl was nearing its solution, Smith believed. He had a theory concerning the affair, and he hoped fervently that it was correct, otherwise Sophie would be in grave danger. He sat on the sill of one of his bedroom's windows far into the early morning, enjoying a cigarette in the darkness and silence, and blowing the smoke out the open casement. The lights were off in his room, but sufficient light shone from the half-moon for him to read. He had spent an hour or so with his latest book, and now, his coat off, he let his mind wander.

But his eyes forced it to concentrate once more.

From his vantage point, the white, shadow-tossed illumination showed him a figure moving away from the castle and toward the woods that covered the slope to the west. The form was that of a man, Smith could tell, a young man, walking quickly and furtively, obviously hoping not to be seen.

An exterior route to intercept the mysterious person was quicker than negotiating the dozen corridors, staircases and doors inside the castle, so Smith, tossing his cigarette before him, swung his legs over the sill of the window and dropped to the balcony immediately below, Another, less convenient jump brought him to the verge of the lawn. He rolled as he landed: a concession to middle-aged bones that would no longer tolerate a less cushioned descent.

Nonetheless, Smith easily kept pace with his quarry who, despite his youth, seemed to be in slightly worse physical condition. That, incidentally, made Smith feel a bit better about his bones. He ran through the gate of the courtyard, across the grass beyond and into the woods, following a path well-trodden and very clear in the moonlight. Despite the illumination, the man leading Smith stumbled every dozen yards, over roots, stones and the irregularity of the path. His footfalls, dinting the dirt surface with the clumsy marks of indoor shoes, could have been tracked by the most inexperienced of Boy Scouts.

Then Smith stopped. The traces of shoes on the ground before him met with another set, heading in the opposite direction, toward Schloss Reitfels. Then, they disappeared together from the path, and continued in the dense undergrowth of oak and alder forest that pressed close by.

This sign alerted Smith, and he had a second or two to prepare his defence before a huge, heavy form sprang at him from the darkness of the trees. Smith was ready, and avoided the swung fist which gripped a kind of cudgel. The prospective victim used his assailant's inertia to throw him over his shoulder. The attacker flashed as he was caught by the silver of the moon and landed with a crash amid the shrubbery and bracken on the far side of the path.

The determined but hasty adversary was soon on his feet again. Smith had stepped back into the shadows from which his opponent had so suddenly emerged, and was thus virtually invisible. The stranger swung his right fist with tremendous force, striking only night air, while Smith delivered an open-palmed blow that caused a startled grunt when it hit the attacker's arm at the elbow, putting it at an unnatural angle. The pain was incapacitating but short-lived. Before it subsided, however, Smith's left connected with the bridge of the other man's nose. The assailant collapsed and lie still.

Smith stood without moving. Between him and the house, someone was charging about, frantically running for the safety of the castle. It was Smith's original quarry, panicked by the brawl he had overheard. But otherwise, the night was quiet, animals normally about and noisy patiently awaiting the conclusion of the human disturbances.

The man unconscious on the ground was big, taller than Smith, and broader. The thin moustache that he wore, like a single line of ink from a pen, was certainly not a German fashion, and his suit, now soiled and torn at the seam of a shoulder, was not tailored locally. Smith knelt and searched the stranger.

He was armed, with a revolver tucked snugly into a holster under his jacket. The weapon was a Lebel; hardly surprising, as Smith had already correctly guessed that his former opponent was a French soldier. The papers he carried identified him as Albert Corosi, a captain, and *Kreis* officer of Coblenz.

Smith smiled. What would the representative of the French occupation forces in the Circle of Coblenz be doing in the woods around Schloss Reitfels, trying to club an honest German at three o'clock in the morning? Smith felt the weight of the small, rubber-encased lead block that Corosi had been wielding.

The Frenchman stirred. He would be angry when he awoke, with a dislocated arm, a couple of black eyes from concussion, and a general sense of nausea. It did not matter, Smith concluded, as he replaced Corosi's property. He already had his answers.

Sophie Grey hugged her legs and pressed her cheeks against her knees. She had spent most of the past few days sitting on the narrow bed of her room, listening to the sounds about her. The cacophony of the Zoo Station never ceased, trains coming and going, vendors shouting, passengers talking and laughing. She wished that she could have shut the room's only window, but the August sun heated the air to the point of stifling her. Motor-cars and lorries, and horsed vehicles, thronged the few streets between her building and the railway station, and their roar and rattle was continuous, merely diminishing a little at night. Worse were the sounds in the hotel, in the neighbouring rooms and in the corridor. She told herself repeatedly that each noise was innocent: men and women from the provinces, excitedly discussing the sights of Berlin; commercial travellers tired from their rounds; maids delivering sheets and making beds.

But at every closing door, every creaking floorboard, it was almost more than she could do to keep from bursting into tears.

Sophie was hungry. She was tired of sneaking out to the Aschauer's, across the street, buying the little sausages and bowls of pea soup that were sold there at ever-increasing prices. She detested German food, anyway. She had money, but its value had plummeted daily, and nothing more had come in the post. If she did not pay her rent this afternoon, the manager would evict her.

And she was frightened. She had arrived in Berlin more than a week before, rouge and lipstick on her face, her prized silk stockings on her legs and wearing her most adult dress. It had been almost fun, despite the reason for the charade. But now, she trembled at every sound, and cried at the loneliness. When she did venture out, she no longer felt twenty-one, as she had been pretending to be, and her flesh crawled at some of the glances she received.

Sophie bent her head and wept some more. She was but fifteen, after all.

Tentative rapping upon the door of her room put a stop to her sniffling. She was silent and still, like a rabbit fearing that a prowling fox had caught her scent. Then she heard the unexpected and joyous sound of her sister's voice.

"Sophie! It's me! Are you in there?"

Sophie jumped from her neatly made bed, nearly falling in her haste. She struggled frustratingly with the lock until the key turned and the door was wrenched open. The siblings leaped into each other's arms, Frankie almost smothered by her taller sister. Only after prolonged hugging did Sophie draw back, wipe at her wet eyes and ask, in a small voice, what Frankie was doing in Berlin.

"He brought me."

Frankie, her own cheeks damp, sheepishly indicated the man standing next to her in the corridor. Sophie almost screamed, not having noticed Linus Smith.

"It's all right," her sister asserted, with a shaking mixture of relief and anxiety. "He knows everything."

"It's almost unbelievable that the whole abduction was concocted by the two girls themselves."

Terence Osborne led the way into one of the several cafés scattered about Cologne's central railway station. Smith was glad no longer to be a counterfeit

German, and to wear his own clothes, comfortable and English, once again.

"They had heard of the threats made against British officials serving in Egypt, and were very concerned about their father's welfare if he went there," Smith responded.

The coffee house was nearly deserted, Germans not keeping four o'clock as a meal-time. At one of the round tables, covered with aged but clean cloths, two elderly men, resembling retired schoolmasters, played a desultory game of chess, while at a second, a younger gentleman smoked a pipe while reading a newspaper. Ignored by these patrons, the Englishmen chose a third table equidistant from the others.

"Well, that accounts for the naiveté of the scheme. The girls believed that they simply had to force their father to resign his appointments, and he'd be safe." Osborne sighed. They ordered from the waiter, a large, tired man, who looked as if he enjoyed this leisurely time of the day. "But how did you arrive at the truth?" The conversation paused as coffee arrived in old porcelain cups.

"There were a number of clues, really," answered Smith, drinking. He much preferred tea, whether at tea-time or any other moment of the day, but when in foreign lands, he drank foreign beverages. "For instance, the note sent to General Grey comprised words, English words, cut from a journal or magazine. It had been posted from Eberkirch, yet the only newspapers and periodicals sold there were German — easily identified by the black-letter Gothic type that they use — and French. This hardly reduced the possible range of suspects, but it proved the writer had access to English publications, like the kind I saw in Frankie and Sophie's room, at Schloss Reitfels."

Smith seemed distracted for a moment by the domestic scene of a young family strolling by the windows of the café, all hand in hand. But he continued to speak as he watched their happy walk.

"Minor jewellery had vanished from the castle on two occasions. The first instance occurred just prior to Sophie's disappearance; I felt it unlikely to have been a coincidence. The next time it happened was just before Frankie and I visited Eberkirch, where she begged me to let her mail her own letters at the village post office."

Osborne smiled. He had not touched his coffee, allowing it still to cool.

"She was taking the opportunity to post something to Sophie, something to pay for her room and board in Berlin."

"Yes," confirmed Smith. "She also had to have had a chance to post the previously prepared letter to her father. After she and Count von Reitfels had seen Sophie off at the station, Frankie walked back to the castle, stopping surreptitiously at the village post-box, while her grandfather rode in the carriage that had brought them." He drank some more coffee, then continued.

The Rhine Maidens

"There were clothes in the girls' room that seemed much too old for either to wear, and one of them had also been using cosmetics. At first, I thought that these items had solely to do with Sophie's desire to grow up, to become an adult, but I doubt that even the most indulgent parent would allow a fifteen year old to wear make-up."

"I certainly wouldn't," Osborne stated with certainty, as indignant as if he were a parent already.

"Nor I. Nor General Grey, I believe. But the garments and cosmetics were, of course, elements of Sophie's disguise."

The waiter sauntered over to the Britons' table again, and re-filled Smith's diminished supply of coffee. He peered askance at Osborne's cup, still untouched, and seemed almost aggrieved as he retreated again.

"But there was one thing above all that made me think that Frankie, at least, knew more about her sister's situation than she let on," said Smith. "Her father had described her as very curious, about everything. My own experience in her company fully proved that." He smiled as he remembered the child's endless questions. "Yet when the count revealed to her that Sophie had been abducted and demands for her release made of her father, Frankie not only didn't ask what those demands were, but didn't want to know whether he would accede to them."

Osborne nodded, and his mouth spread in a grin.

"The two things she should have been *most* curious about."

"Her behaviour was wrong," Smith pointed out. "The principal reasons a person doesn't ask 'why', about anything, are because she doesn't care or because she already knows the answer. I couldn't believe that Frankie was apathetic about her sister's fate. So, taking the other possibility, I re-examined all the other clues I had noticed. They suddenly made perfect sense."

Osborne's beverage was finally cool enough to drink. He hefted the cup, which may very well have out-weighed him, to his lips, and sipped an amount which made the waiting hardly worthwhile. After he had swallowed, he wondered aloud what would happen to the girls.

"Oh..." Smith inhaled and raised his eyebrows, recognising that he was entering the realm of the hypothetical. "They'll have to replace what they stole, but they are sensitive and sensible children. They realise the anxiety they caused, and I doubt that any of it will sit easily on their consciences. Besides," his expression indicated a certain inside knowledge, "General Grey and Count von Reitfels are not the kind to let such behaviour, however well-intentioned, go completely unpunished."

"Well, the important thing is that Sophie is safe and sound. I was frightened to death that something terrible would happen to her." The head of station paused with his cup half-way to his mouth again. "But not everyone emerged from this adventure unhurt. I hear Captain Corosi's arm is in a sling."

"Hm, yes..." Smith's reluctance to comment was almost apologetic. "That series of events was unconnected with the Grey family. A footman in Count von Reitfels's employ, Gunther Schilling by name, was also in the pay of the French *Kreis* control officer. He was to report on any anti-Gallic sentiment or activity he might come across at the castle."

"Considering the count's guests, he must have been kept busy," observed Osborne.

"In many ways, yes. But Schilling was severely unnerved by the fact that Corosi felt anyone following his agent needed to be frightened — or beaten — off, and he has left Reitfels's staff." Smith nonchalantly leaned back in his chair. "I've put him up at the Berner Hof Hotel. I thought you might find a useful billet for him; somewhere quiet, where he doesn't have to pour any hot drinks..."

Secret House

"Pearson here is just out of a six-weeks' conclave with his clerks, Smith, and he's found your next assignment."

Linus Smith, Royal Fusiliers, had barely had time to settle into one of the deep leather chairs before his chief's desk, when this statement intimated that he had better not become too comfortable.

He took no exception to the situation, however. When he had re-joined the Secret Service the previous year, he had been informed that irregularity in his new work would be the norm. September, for instance, had been uneventful, and he had been left to his own devices the entire month. October, on the other hand, had produced four short missions, one after the other, his suitcase rarely unpacked, and had ended with him sailing off to South America. He had returned from the New World only the day before and, when turning in the report he had written during the voyage home, had been told to call back the next morning for a meeting with C.

When he had entered his chief's office at 9.30, he had discovered C already in conference with someone. Arthur Pearson was not a stranger to Smith. He was in charge of the Secret Service's Financial Section, having been recruited by the first C after spending a quarter-century at the Exchequer. It was through his counting room that all the money allotted by the Government passed, most of it in the form of figures in ledgers.

"I don't think we've met..." Pearson stated, staring at Smith through thick-lensed, round-rimmed spectacles and half-closed eyes.

"We have, yes," responded Smith. "When I first joined you were the one who explained to me the Service's system of pay." He was used to people not remembering him, and thought that anyone with Pearson's obviously limited vision should be excused the oversight.

"Did I?" Pearson leaned back in his chair, identical to Smith's and next to it, and tapped his fingers on the top of the stack of hard-bound volumes resting on his lap. He raised his spectacles and squinted. Then his long, bony face brightened, and he smiled, his mouth full of crooked but white teeth. "You were in Germany in August, weren't you? And Rumania before that? Yes, yes, a very economical officer," he explained to C, turning to his superior but pointing a lengthy digit at Smith. "The lowest expenses of any field operator. I await the receipts from your latest mission with anticipation."

Smith marvelled that anyone would look forward to such things gladly. But then, everyone had his fads.

Outside, the weather had become chilly, hardly surprising for the first week in December. A fog had started to creep over and about London, isolating each house, each gate, making the closing of a door behind one's entry a welcome into a refuge. But, Smith thought as C sighed with impatience, some refuges were more welcoming than others.

"Shall we proceed?" C asked, as if he were the chairman of a parish council meeting, rather than the head of the Secret Service. His black patch, its strings disappearing into brown hair brushed straight back, made his remaining eye sharper, more piercing, than it otherwise would have been. He gestured with his remaining hand. "Pearson and most of his staff have been in isolation recently, to go over the books." He indicated that his subordinate should explain.

"Indeed, yes," confirmed the financial officer, his fingers interlaced upon the pile of what may very well have been the actual 'books'. "We perform an audit on the accounts every year. I regret to say that we are still behind somewhat in that regard, due to the War, the great expansion of the Service and, consequently, its budget. Alas..." he removed his glasses and peered almost sightlessly at Smith, sighing as if over a lost dream "...Treasury retrenchment is greater now than one would have expected following the conclusion of a great conflict." He replaced his spectacles. "Still, it has allowed us to delve into some areas that, regrettably but necessarily, have been neglected. It's part of the reason why this year's audit was greater than others, and why it took the form of a retreat."

"Secret house," said Smith, words that sounded irrelevant to C but which intrigued Pearson.

"I'm sorry?" He cocked his head and squinted at Smith. "Er, secret house?"

"Yes, it was a custom in the later middle ages, at least among the more powerful aristocracy," replied Smith. "The lord of the manor, his chamberlain and a few especially trusted retainers would take themselves to a lodge or other small house on the estate and go over the annual accounts. Due to the subject under consideration, the smaller household kept for the period and the private setting, the process came to be called 'secret house'."

No one spoke for a moment after Smith had finished speaking. C's expression was undoubtedly similar to what he would have worn when listening to a particularly dry lecture while a cadet at Sandhurst. Pearson, however, slowly grinned and wagged a finger at Smith.

"What a marvellous phrase," he declared: "secret house; I like it very much."

C leaned forward and said, with audible exasperation, "Yes, it's a magical pair of words, Pearson. You can use it as the title of your autobiography when you retire: *Secret House - My Life as Treasurer of the Secret Service.*"

"Oh, by Jove, sir." Pearson's grin expanded, the misaligned teeth filling half of his head now. When he began rummaging in his jacket for paper and pencil, C recalled him none too gently to the matter at hand. "Er, yes, yes, Major, uh, Smith..." Pearson cleared his throat but seemed reluctant to return to more mundane matters. "The result of our...secret house..." his eyes shot quickly toward C, then squeezed themselves almost shut as they considered Smith "...is the discovery that some £15,000 is unaccounted for."

"The Service has lost £15,000?" Smith rarely displayed surprise, but could not help himself this time. "You don't know where it went?"

"We do know where it went." C placed his hand on his trim midriff as he reclined in his chair. "It was paid to a Lieutenant Colonel Hugh Coutts-Grogan — or Major Coutts-Grogan, as he was then — over a period of five years."

"Rather more than that was disbursed to him," Pearson amended, desirous of accuracy in matters fiscal, "but £15,000 represents the amount that is...missing."

Smith suspected that this was the start of a fuller explanation. He settled more deeply in his armchair, its leather creaking satisfactorily, and wished that C's hospitality extended to tea.

"Grogan retired from the Leinster Regiment in 1913," C stated. "He wasn't fit enough for an active regimental posting, and he and his wife moved to Tangier for the climate. My predecessor needed a man there, and so brought him into the Service." He regarded his subordinate from under his prominent eyebrows with a mixture of wariness and tedium, adding, "I assume you know the recent history of Morocco, Smith?"

"Yes sir." Smith was well aware that his chief would have preferred a simple affirmative or negative response to his question. This was why he decided to give a more comprehensive exposition, or at least attempt one. "It was the focal point for two international crises in the decade before the War, and became something of a symbol to—"

"Right." C's raised hand slowly lowered, as if he were afraid Smith would erupt in narrative again. "Grogan was sent to be the one-man station there."

"No doubt a very useful situation to the Service, sir," Smith observed. "Tangier wasn't really under anyone's control, a haven for large-scale gamblers, gun-runners, mercenaries and spies. During the War, the city increased in importance—"

"Yes," agreed C sternly, "yes...and so did our station."

"As you may surmise, Major," Pearson interjected, "as the Service grew in the War years, so did its expenses; the Tangier station was a good example, if not entirely typical. Sums that were enormous compared to previous amounts were spent on a daily basis. In what was, in effect, an on-going emergency, accountability was, er, relaxed..." Pearson's large bald head drooped, as if in shame.

"Coutts-Grogan's office expanded, I assume," Smith guessed.

"Just so, Major, just so." Pearson nodded vigorously. "Of course, it wasn't a case of the funds supplied simply being thrown away."

"Grogan provided excellent intelligence during his tenure in Morocco," C revealed. "He had quite a few agents, most of marginal importance, of course, who were paid correspondingly small amounts. But several of his people were very well placed — and expensive. His information, however, turned out always to be accurate and timely, so no one complained."

"I recall being troubled about the cost," Pearson smiled, as one might have done over a hopeless situation, "but not because I feared it was being wasted. I simply thought it was extravagant."

"But the War Office, Admiralty, Foreign Office, all thought the cost worth the result," C said, glancing briefly at the financial officer. "The amount of money spent wasn't — and isn't — the issue."

"But I suppose that, in the event, Grogan's intelligence was a better bargain than anyone thought," said Smith, "because, I take it, not all the money sent him for the pay of his agents went that way."

"Exactly, Major, exactly." Pearson nodded some more, as if a difficult riddle had been solved. "Since the end of the War, we've been able to examine many matters from new aspects, using, in some cases, records to which we hadn't access before." He raised his eyebrows, no doubt to demonstrate significance but, as the action widened his eyes, the effect was to blind him. He squinted once more. "We were able thus to fill gaps in our knowledge."

"How do we know that it's Coutts-Grogan who should be under suspicion?" Smith asked of C. "Since Tangier station expanded during the War, there were other members with access to the funds."

"True," confirmed C. "There were, in fact, several officers and numerous clerks, all working under Grogan at various times."

"But, according to our researches, Major," Pearson added, "the money in question disappeared more or less constantly during most of the colonel's administration, before and after all the others who had worked with him had come and gone."

"Besides which, as head of station, only Grogan had final approval for the spending of any funds sent to his office." C's tone implied that Smith should have known this fact, as indeed he had. But the chief of the Secret Service realised that Smith was being thorough.

"How long was he head of station? Throughout the War?" Smith wanted to know.

"No," C replied. "In early 1918, Coutts-Grogan started reporting his suspicions that he was being watched by what he believed to be agents of Germany. He was certainly not an imaginative man," the words conveyed the impression that the less imagination someone possessed the better "and when his suspicions became stronger, my predecessor took notice. Eventually, there was what was generally thought to have been an attempt on Coutts-Grogan's life, disguised as a robbery. It couldn't be chanced that the Huns were trying to get rid of him, so we did it first: we posted him from Tangier to somewhere safer."

"Where was he sent?"

"To an infantry company in France."

Smith raised an eyebrow.

"To the world at large," C concluded, "Grogan was just a member of the Reserve of Officers being mobilised. His health had improved in Morocco and he did good service in Europe, eventually being promoted to command a New Army battalion of his old regiment."

A few seconds of silence ensued, C waiting for further questions, Pearson peering near-sightedly at the major, and Smith himself thinking. At last, he spoke.

"But no one is sure that Coutts-Grogan has the missing money."

"That's why you are here," said C, with an indication that the expositional phase of the interview was at an end. "You won't need any false names or documents for this mission, though Production is finding you a house near where the Coutts-Grogans live, as we speak."

"Is there urgency in the matter, sir?" Smith wanted to know.

C shook his head, almost casually, saying, "The money has been missing for years, so I don't think it needs to be recovered before Christmas. But remember, the longer you take, the more expenses poor Pearson here will have to pay out."

And from the stricken face the financial officer adopted, it seemed as if the Secret Service's funds might have come directly from his own pockets.

"Very homely, Odways."

Smith relaxed in an armchair, having just inspected the cottage from which he would be conducting his new assignment. He had arrived on the afternoon train from London twenty minutes before, to be met at the village station by his valet, who had preceded him. Now, in his temporary home's parlour, a fire glowed in the grate, and a pot of tea steamed on a trolley, surrounded by its usual accoutrements.

"Thank you, sir," said the servant, pouring the hot beverage into a cup. "I must confess, however, that the cottage was in a satisfactory condition when I came, so the preparation required was minimal."

It had taken almost a week for the Secret Service's Production Department to find an adequate house in the little Herefordshire village of Marlton. The research conducted had paid dividends, though: Ruscote, as the cottage was named, was not only clean and comfortable, and the sort of place a gentleman might rent for a fortnight's holiday, but it was within sight of the thatched roof under which Colonel and Mrs Coutts-Grogan lived, at the end of a well-trodden path through thin woods.

"Are there any special instructions for the next few days, sir?" Odways asked, handing a filled cup on its saucer to his employer.

"The first thing is to establish contact with Coutts-Grogan. I'll watch his movements for a while. His file stated that he enjoys walking, having taken it up for his health's sake in Morocco, so an early morning constitutional might be a habit of his. To confirm this, I will need to rise even earlier than he does each day."

"Very good, sir. Five o'clock, then?"

Smith sipped his tea, prepared with the perfect complement of cream and sugar, warmed his feet near the fire, and gazed through the many-paned casement window, and at the unfriendly greyness beyond it. He sighed.

"Five-thirty will suffice, I think..."

Marlton was an attractive village, but Smith thought that its black and white half-timbered houses and few brick shops, its yew hedges and numerous oak trees would have appeared to much greater advantage in the high summer. Then, trees that were now bare, bony and leafless, would have been fresh and alive; the little gardens lying next to cottages would have been blooming with colour, and the narrow river winding through the heart of the community would have reflected the depth of the blue sky.

As the first day of winter approached, Marlton nonetheless looked appealing beneath a chilly overcast. The woods that spotted the countryside, and the many individual trees within the bounds of the village, were relics of the expansive forest which once covered the region, so close to the Welsh border. This day, a desultory rain fell across the stripped boughs of the trees, and the low temperature drew one's breath out in clouds of vapour. Smith rather enjoyed such gloomy autumnal weather, but at seven o'clock in the morning, he envied those who could view the day while still snug behind the lamp-yellowed windows of Marlton's homes.

His watchfulness had been successful. He had discovered, that Coutts-Grogan, recognised from his photograph in the Secret Service records, always took a stroll through the village just as its other inhabitants were beginning their daily work. Smith noted the man's route from his house, and the most convenient spot at which to make his acquaintance. It was not difficult to arrange.

"I'm dreadfully sorry."

"Not at all, my fault."

The foot-bridge over the stream that coursed through Marlton was wide enough for two, even three men to cross abreast. But as sometimes happened when individuals met walking toward each other, Smith and Coutts-Grogan moved the same way to let the other pass. The action on Smith's part even looked accidental.

"Excuse me, but I'm new to the district, and my local knowledge is limited. Do you by chance happen to know the name of that cottage?" Smith pointed with a gloved finger, through a gap in the near by screen of trees, to Coutts-Grogan's own residence.

"I do," said the colonel, just a little impatient to be on his way and out of the rain, "for I live there. It's called Fellings," then, as if admitting something to himself, added, "though I don't know why." He frowned and tapped the ferrule of his stick on the boards of the arched bridge. "I've tried to find a past owner of the house or land whose name might have been Felling, but so far I've not met with success."

"Perhaps it derives from a description," suggested Smith. "The Middle English word for 'clearings', perhaps, or Anglo-Saxon for 'newly cultivated land'." He regarded Coutts-Grogan.

"Good Lord..." that gentleman muttered. "That may very well be it. As a matter of fact," he indicated the distinctive roof of his house with his stick, the inconvenience of the precipitation apparently forgotten, "do you see how the trees gather close to the place? I have discovered that it was only in the fourteenth century that the site was cleared for a small-holding. The current building is of course only as old as the seventeenth century, but its earliest predecessor shared its name, and it would have been natural to call such a farm Fellings." He swung his stick in the air, as if at a vanquished foe, and turned to Smith with a grin. "Good Lord, sir, that's wonderful! How did you arrive at such an idea?"

"Languages are rather a fad of mine," said Smith, quite truthfully, having mastered a dozen of them. "Learning them has led me to dabble in their origins, especially that of our own."

"Really? That's similar to an interest of mine; you can probably guess what it is," said Coutts-Grogan cheerfully. "I research place-names — just for fun, you know."

"Intriguing," remarked Smith. His evident surprise at Grogan's hobby was exaggerated. He was at times astounded at the useful bits of information that may be recorded in a man's personal file. Coutts-Grogan extended his hand.

"Coutts-Grogan, Leinster Regiment, retired."

"I'm Smith, Royal Fusiliers, half-pay," replied the other.

Philip Coutts-Grogan was a few years older than Smith. His face had a naturally aloof expression, even one of superiority, though his newest acquaintance suspected that these traits were not reflected in his personality. Grogan's narrow, almost disdainful eyes widened when he spoke, and his small mouth, the upper lip of which was hidden by a generous moustache, was not reluctant to smile. His tweed suit, fit for a walk in the autumnal countryside, was less fitted for his figure, and Smith guessed that he had not purchased a new suit since he had been thinner.

"It isn't that often I meet someone with an interest similar to mine. My wife, I'm afraid, sees no enjoyment in it."

"I'd be glad to discuss the topic with you at length," responded Smith.

"Why don't you come for dinner, then?" invited Coutts-Grogan, almost enthusiastically. "What about tomorrow evening? My wife has to go into Hereford, but she should be back by seven... What about eight o'clock?"

"I will be there," Smith promised happily.

"The only public house in the village, sir, is the Ullington Arms, in the High Street."

Odways drew the curtains against the dreary day outside the cottage, as the afternoon ended. In the sitting room, oil lamps added illumination to the dying coal fire. Ruscote had no electricity, and glowed with the intimate burning of cloth wicks.

"I am afraid I had to imply a certain restlessness in your employ, sir," the valet said, turning to his master, "to stimulate a conversation."

"There's no truth to it, Odways?"

Smith drew on a cigarette, the ignited end glowing stark and clear before fading to ash. He was dressed for dinner, his black suit supple after years of use, his shoes shining with distorted reflections. He would have liked a drink of something — tea, to be honest — but he would be knocking on the Coutts-Grogans' door within minutes, and they would undoubtedly be offering him something else.

"Not at all, sir," Odways declared, with no particular emphasis. Though possessed of an adequate sense of humour, the valet did not believe that the servant-master relationship was an appropriate subject on which to use it. "It seemed the most expedient means of determining the staff arrangements at

Fellings." He placed an ashtray at Smith's elbow, the heavy, opaque glass sounding thick on the wood of the side-table. "I am most satisfied with my current situation, sir," he felt compelled to add.

"I'm glad to hear it," commented Smith, with feigned severity. He stretched himself out in the chair, and had to guard against becoming too satisfied in *his* situation. "What did you learn?"

"Colonel Coutts-Grogan employs two servants, sir," answered Odways, standing to one side. "A cook and a housemaid. I did not gather that either considers herself overpaid."

"You spoke with both?"

"I did, sir, in the Ullington Arms. They are both moderate in their habits," — by this, Odways meant that the women did not drink excessively — "and appear honest. The maid in particular hopes to better her situation, if not her station."

"Will she succeed, do you think?" Smith asked with curiosity.

"Probably not, sir."

Smith disliked dreams being dashed.

"A cook and a housemaid," he mused. "Hardly the establishment one might have with £15,000 to play with."

"Colonel Coutts-Grogan may no longer have the money, sir," Odways pointed out.

"True. He may never have had it." Smith threw his cigarette among the coals afire. He pulled a watch from his waistcoat. "Time?"

"Time, sir." The servant had noiselessly retrieved his master's hat and coat. Smith stood.

"Who knows?" he postulated. "Perhaps the missing money will be found invested in a wall covered with Rembrandts, or shelves of priceless porcelain." He slipped his arms into the wide, warm sleeves of his coat. "It wouldn't be the first instance of impressions being false."

But Smith observed no Dutch masters hanging in Fellings's hall or drawing room, and the only pottery he saw had to have been of sentimental value, as its monetary worth was undoubtedly low.

Nonetheless, Coutts-Grogan's house was a pleasant one of black and white wooden construction, like most in Marlton, though its thatched roof had the unusual distinction of possessing dormer windows, three of them, poking through the wheat-reed, facing the visitor as he arrived. Under that roof, the rooms were spacious, though the ceilings were low, as would have been common in the seventeenth century, when the house was raised.

"Yes, it is rather a nice old place," the colonel said, peering about his drawing room warmly. He had provided Smith with a glass of sherry. "We've lived here four years now, coming to the village in...November? Yes, November, of '19. My wife's people come from Herefordshire." Coutts-Grogan glanced at a large, elaborate clock on the mantelpiece. "Dreadfully sorry about this," he apologised, with a hint of annoyance. "She really ought to have been back by now."

Smith assured his host that he was not offended, and the two continued their easy conversation about place-names. Small-talk was a simple thing for Smith. Indeed, two of his greatest assets as a field operator of the Secret Service were his anonymity — he had once been called 'the most unrecognised man in the Empire' — and his ability to keep up a constant flow of idle chat about almost any topic. His contributions to a discussion were uniformly polite and forgettable; they could also be leading, intensive, inquisitive, all without his listeners realising it. Information he gleaned from them, however, was often valuable.

It was as he and Grogan were debating the name of the village (not, as it might have seemed, from 'marl', a type of soil, found nowhere near, but rather from a term signifying 'boundary manor') that they heard the front door open and someone step lightly into the small hall. Mrs Coutts-Grogan had returned.

The colonel excused himself and slipped out of the room, shutting the door behind him. Smith disliked eavesdropping, though it was sometimes necessary in his line of work. To the relief of his conscience, the discussion which followed was inaudible, even to his sensitive ears, coming through the thick walls of the old house only as a series of murmurs. He did, however, clearly hear the distinctive sound of British silver being dropped into an open palm. It seemed unlikely that Coutts-Grogan was the one giving, and not receiving.

A carefully-run household, Smith ruminated. His host would indeed have been a miser to demand his spouse's small change after he had embezzled £15,000. Smith sipped his sherry and wondered if the transaction could have been performed for his benefit, or for the servants'. He shook his head. He was getting ahead of himself, and the facts.

"It's my wife," Coutts-Grogan confirmed as he returned to the drawing room, his hand just leaving a trouser pocket in which coins were jingling. "She apparently missed the afternoon train and had to wait for the later. She will join us in a moment." He paused. "Where were we...?" His eyes widened happily with the resumption of his favourite subject. "Oh, yes... Marlton *was* in fact a manor very near the Welsh frontier in pre-Conquest days, so it makes perfect sense for its name to be derived from its location..."

"You must think me horribly rude, Major. I'm sure my husband has explained my tardiness, but I must apologise for myself. I do *not* make it a habit to neglect my duties as hostess."

Diana Coutts-Grogan entered the drawing room twenty minutes after she had arrived home. Smith could not have considered her a pretty woman, for her face was too long and her cheeks too thin for his tastes, but she was nonetheless attractive. She wore her brown hair long, which was rare these days, and in a long plait down her back, which was rarer. Her brown eyes looked lively and observant, but at the same time sad, while her skin, smooth and unblemished, youthfully reflected the glow from the fire.

"That's quite all right, Mrs Coutts-Grogan," Smith addressed her concerns chivalrously. "I myself have missed the odd train while poring over the shelves of book shops. I know such distractions."

"It does, my dear, mean that you will have to forego your pre-prandial cocktail," said the woman's husband, as the maid opened the door from the dining room, "for I believe that our meal is ready."

The dinner was prepared well and served promptly. The Coutts-Grogans' maid and cook, however they considered their wages, performed adequately for them. The conversation was good as well, even though it tended to leave out the lady of the house, despite Smith's efforts.

"Tangier?" Smith said, as if hearing the name for the first time. He drank some of the claret that had been served with the roast beef. Just as Fellings contained no artistic masterpieces, so no fortune had been spent on its cellar. "That's an interesting choice for a home." Though he directed his words to Mrs Coutts-Grogan, sitting along one side of the dining table, the response came from her husband, opposite Smith at its head.

"Unexpected, you mean." The colonel laughed. He was a genial host, cheerful and friendly, without the emotions seeming forced. "I was half-way to being an invalid when I left the army. Someone at the club suggested Tangier, for my health. As luck would have it, an old school chum, who worked there for an import-export firm was being promoted. He'd heard I was moving to Morocco, and suggested I apply for the agency in his place." Grogan skewered a piece of meat from his plate and gestured with his fork. "Soon everything was settled."

"And you accompanied your husband, Mrs Coutts-Grogan?" the guest asked.

"Of course," the woman answered with a smile.

"Completely different world, I can tell you," remarked the colonel, as if unconcerned as to whether his wife had come to Morocco with him. "Yet parts of it familiar..."

"Were you there throughout the War?" Smith inquired of his host.

"I thought I would be," Coutts-Grogan replied. "But after repeated requests, the War Office eventually decided that even a broken old soldier could serve some purpose."

"You were hardly broken down, Philip," his wife interjected, and turning to Smith, added, "though the climate in Tangier seemed to do him every bit of good."

"I wasn't in prime condition, but, as an officer yourself, Smith, you know that what might be unsuited for employment in peace-time can be perfectly acceptable in an emergency."

"Of course," Smith concurred. "The army tends to dismiss its members a little too easily. Most of those can serve in any number of capacities. I know a gentleman who lost an eye *and* an arm, yet commanded not only a battalion but a brigade in the War."

"Nowadays, he'd not be given a platoon." Coutts-Grogan nodded. He laid his knife and fork across his empty plate. Smith too had finished the meat course. "I was sent to a New Army battalion of my old regiment, but it was only six months or so until I was knocked out of the War for good," the colonel mentioned, with a wry grin.

Smith glanced at Diana, quietly eating the last of her beef. She was across the table from the fire, and her skin was radiant.

"I suspect that you considered your husband's posting to the infantry as something less than lucky, Mrs Coutts-Grogan."

Before his wife could answer, the colonel shook his head and said, "Women don't always appreciate the feelings of a soldier forced to live out a war in safety while his comrades fight."

"I suppose that's true," Diana concurred. She at last set down her utensils, though a slice of meat still lie on her plate untouched. "Does your wife have a similar difficulty, Major?"

"I'm a bachelor, Mrs Coutts-Grogan," answered Smith, "though if I were married, I strongly believe that my spouse would prefer to have me safe and guilty."

"Rather selfish, I'd say," stated Coutts-Grogan, frowning.

"But also, much to a woman's credit," Smith postulated.

Coutts-Grogan's face had been growing less animated as the conversation had progressed, until it displayed a distant, uninterested expression. He shrugged noncommittally. As the maid entered the dining room, carrying a heavily-laden tray, the colonel's smile returned.

"But enough about my past. Smith, tell me..." Grogan's eyes widened with pleasure as the servant set dishes of the sweet course before those at the table. "How did you become involved in languages, and the words they use?"

Hours later, Odways removed his employer's dinner coat and set it aside;

though spotless, it would be carefully brushed before it was ready to be worn again. Though more than a decade old, Smith saw no need to modernise that part of his wardrobe. He was secretly proud of the fact that the suit fit as well this day as it had when he was thirty. For his part, Odways thought the garment to be in excellent repair.

"Colonel Coutts-Grogan's house is not, after all, a treasure trove, sir?"

"You may indeed conclude that, Odways, without the slightest fear of being wrong." Smith pulled apart his white tie, unbuttoned his paper collar and removed a cigarette from his silver case. "He and his wife are living the existence of a retired British Army lieutenant colonel. There were not even four courses to dinner."

"That might merely be contemporary hospitality, sir, rather than economy." If there was a man in Britain more old-fashioned than Smith, it was his valet.

"True," conceded Smith. He blinked several times as the smoke he exhaled swirled about his head. "Just because there is no evidence of high spending doesn't mean that Coutts-Grogan didn't embezzle the Service's money. He may have put it into something as unexciting as an annuity, or an insurance policy... But then, one doesn't usually steal a great amount of money for something so gradual."

"To have taken the funds years ago and to wait — to continue to wait — all this time would involve much patience and discipline," remarked Odways, as he set aside more of Smith's clothes, ready for the morning.

"Very true. Patience and a great desire for whatever it was that one was waiting for," said Smith.

Outside the cottage, the night was dark. The moon, half-way from new to full, was obscured by a uniform sheet of low clouds. The air drifting in through the window's open casement was cold, and the fire in the grate was a small one, not being meant to last through the night. An extra blanket or two would be required for a comfortable sleep.

"I remember a chap in the regiment, Fourth Battalion," Smith stated, smoking leisurely as Odways turned down his bed, "in Z Company. Do you recall a Captain Seaton?"

"Yes, sir," the valet replied, pausing in his duties, "I think so: tall gentleman, with red hair?"

"That's the fellow." Smith picked a piece of tobacco from his mouth. "He had a badly concealed affection for a brother officer's wife. He never ventured to do anything about it, and there was no question of the lady's fidelity. The point is that Seaton was content to wait. The lady's husband was reckless in action and had been wounded twice or thrice already. Seaton kept his eye on events and deduced that we would be in battle before long. The husband would be conveniently killed and Seaton, having done nothing dishonourable, would step into the dead man's shoes — as happened from time to time."

"Mr Seaton considered his goal well worth waiting for, sir." The valet nodded, understanding.

"That is what I was attempting to illustrate, yes," confirmed Smith, after drawing again on his cigarette.

"Was Mr Seaton's patience rewarded, sir?" Odways wanted to know.

"It was not. Seaton was killed near Bapaume, in August of '18, attempting to bring in the lady's husband, who was wounded and under fire. That man survived, and is now a major general, with six children."

"One can't always know when to act and when to wait, can one, sir?"

"No, one cannot, Odways," said Smith, picking up the book he had brought from London for just such a night.

A good day for hunting, thought Smith.

It was true that the air was moist, a thin coat of grey painting the sky, the sun a white disc shorn of its corona. A better day would have been dry and crisp. But Smith liked the bleak, damp days that promised rain or snow. With an experienced huntsman, a knowledgeable and controlled field, and a pack that was aware of its business, there would have been fine sport.

He was not, however, on horseback, but, rather, on foot, tramping through a wood, his booted feet falling as they habitually did, silently, expertly, as if they were guiding Smith, and not the reverse. He observed that it was a dense wood, untended by any forester for some time. The underbrush grew heavily, and trunks were decaying where they had fallen. Few birds disturbed the eerie quiet, and Smith saw and heard little else.

Through the grey verticality of bare trees and their uplifted, splayed branches, the leaves long-since fallen, a big, square object loomed. Smith's keen eyes picked out a couple of windows, and a tiled roof, with a single, slender chimney pushing up its bricks from a corner. When he realised that he was approaching a lodge, the building's camouflaged size and shape became clear to his senses.

The windows' panes were grimy, dirt crusting the glass, and there was no longer a path to the door, the blue paint of which was chipped and falling, like the leaves of the surrounding trees. The door was not locked, however, and gave way, eventually, to Smith's curiosity, and affection for things ignored or abandoned.

Within, the tiny house was dusty but not filthy. Smith estimated that it had been suffering neglect for about a year, to judge from the debris inside. The ground floor was occupied by a sitting room, its table and few chairs shrouded to keep them unsoiled. An open hearth filled one corner, while opposite, was a tightly coiled and narrow staircase.

The first floor was a bedchamber, a chest of drawers, wash-stand and bed hidden by sheets, like the furniture below. It was not so much Sleeping Beauty's castle but her woodman's cottage, unused, then forgotten. There was even a pile of wood, cut and stacked by the upper level's grate.

Smith closed the door when he departed minutes later. The historian in him thrilled to find such relics. One of his earliest memories was of his family home, where he had come upon an old marble statue, secreted among some trees in the park. Other children might have been frightened by the unmoving, lichen-dappled stone image, but little Linus Smith had been fascinated by its obvious antiquity and pastoral setting. He had wondered who it was of, and how it had come to be lost in its leafy glade.

Ruscote was not a mile from the small building Smith had found, and it did not take him long to return from his stroll. He had been through much of the village that morning and, disappointed with the results of his survey, had taken a meandering route home. The people of Marlton had had little to tell him about Colonel Coutts-Grogan. He was a stranger, he and his wife, to a community in which half a century's residence might still have left a person to be considered a newcomer by the other inhabitants. The colonel was a gentleman, they described, that was plain; polite and correct, too. His wife was friendly, and just as obviously a lady. But, as a villager put it, one could not have expected them to have socialised much when the only other gentry about, since the old squire had died, were the vicar and a Mrs Woolmer. Smith was given the impression that the clergyman was the most boring person in the parish, and Mrs Woolmer not far behind.

But as he approached his temporary home, Smith espied someone who could no doubt impart much more information regarding Coutts-Grogan, whether she would know she was doing it or not. The colonel's wife had taken the short path from Fellings to Ruscote, carrying a small burden covered in a cloth. As Diana neared the gate that debouched into Smith's back garden, she was greeted by her guest of the previous night, and smiled.

"Good afternoon, Major."

"Good day, Mrs Coutts-Grogan," he greeted, lifting his hat. "I hope you received my note of gratitude for such a pleasant evening."

"I did, though writing it was unnecessary." Nonetheless, Diana seemed happy that Smith had enjoyed himself. "And seeing how much you liked the strawberries we had for dessert, I thought I'd bring you a few more."

Smith had indeed found the fruit tasty, though he had been surprised at being served some at the peak of their ripeness after the season. He suspected that they had come from a hothouse, which would have cost Diana dear. He took the basket that she was offering and pulled back the cloth covering it. The aroma of plump, fresh strawberries teased his nostrils, and misled his brain, just instantaneously, into fancying that it was high summer once more.

"Surely you and your husband will want these," he said.

"You may have noticed, Major, that Philip ate his portion last night sparingly. He has never really cared for strawberries. As for myself..." she lowered her eyes, a little embarrassed "...too many cause me to suffer from blemishes that usually trouble adolescents, not, um, older women."

Smith smiled and said, "It's difficult to conceive of you with anything but a perfect complexion, Mrs Coutts-Grogan."

Diana's pale face reddened somewhat, making her brown eyes darker, but she was not displeased with the compliment. Though her age was probably not debatable, her skin was indeed smooth and creamy, even in the brittle air of the autumn day.

"I was looking forward to being warmed by a pot of tea," Smith stated. "Would you care to join me?"

"Oh, well, I..." Diana hesitated for a moment, but Smith had the sensibilities of a true Victorian, and if he had suggested something, few others could have found it improper. The woman smiled again, almost shyly, and gave an exaggerated shiver. "That would be most welcome, Major."

The speed with which Odways could set a pot of scalding tea before his employer sometimes made Smith wonder if he might have learned a lesson from Persian caravanserais, and kept a great kettle of water continuously on the boil. However the valet managed it, Smith and Diana had barely enough time to sit in the small parlour before a tray of refreshments was delivered.

Smith thought that his guest was more attractive now than when their roles had been reversed the other night. But then, he had always held forth that too much preparation spoiled a woman's natural appeal. The increased use of cosmetics these days did not help. Diana was garbed rather simply in a plain pink dress of wool, with fashionably padded hips, and skirts falling to just below the ankles. Her hair was gathered at the nape of the neck by a pink ribbon tied in a bow, then allowed to fall free again. It was clear to Smith that she had not intended to visit anyone in this attire, and was the more fetching for it.

"Herefordshire must be quite a contrast to Tangier," Smith said, from the depths of his easy chair on one side of the fire.

"From the very foreign to the very English," replied Diana, blowing gently on the surface of the tea in her cup. Her chair faced the fire and was at an angle to Smith's, with a little pie-crust table between them. "But we didn't come here directly from north Africa."

Smith had guessed this. The couple had settled in Marlton in 1919, but had left Morocco in 1918.

"I imagine you lived elsewhere while the colonel was on active service."

"I lived with Philip's mother, in Lincolnshire..." The manner with which Diana added nothing to the bald statement implied a great deal. Smith remained tactfully silent, and his visitor, a mischievous look in her eyes, asked, "Are you sure you've never been married, Major? You don't seem to need the notion of in-laws explained to you."

"I have two good friends, both married," Smith responded sagely.

"A man who learns from others, clearly." Diana drank some of her beverage.

"At least going first to Lincolnshire must have smoothed the otherwise jarring transition from Tangier to Herefordshire," Smith suggested. Diana started laughing, and hastily put a napkin to her mouth.

"Oh, yes," she said at last, "the Fens are a perfect mean between the two." Her cheeks were rosy with mirth and embarrassment.

"Did you like Tangier?" Smith was slightly more serious. "I understand that it can be dangerous."

Diana raised her thin eyebrows, as she accepted a biscuit from the platter Smith offered, and responded, "Yes, that's true, if one doesn't use common sense. For instance, the sea-bathing is excellent, as long as you choose a beach some distance from town. The shore fronting Tangier is a rubbish tip." Smith frowned melodramatically and Diana, laughing again, asserted, "But Tangier can be very exotic and fun."

"I expect the two of you would have had little time to enjoy it. The colonel's work must have kept him busy."

"Oh, it did, Major, especially after the War began. As you can imagine, after that things became very complicated for importing and exporting, even in a neutral port."

"I'm sure you were a tremendous asset to him," Smith said.

"Not as much as I should have been." Diana's expression seemed suddenly sad. But it vanished as she smiled once more. "I was no help with his actual business: I'm hopeless at sums."

"Your presence was undoubtedly a marvellous tonic to the stress of his duties."

Again, Diana's face reflected an unspoken disagreement with Smith's words, and she escaped a direct answer by drinking more tea.

"I think socially I proved of some value. I was hostess, of course, for the many entertainments that were held. Much of Philip's work depended on meeting people and keeping in their good graces. There were parties at our residence, nights at the Club Diplomatique, dances on the verandah of the Hotel

Valentina, dinners at the Casino..." Warm memories made her face glow. Again, the expression was momentary. "Not that I went there often. Philip took me to the Casino for our anniversary, the first year we were in Tangier. I recall thinking that it had the most beautiful views, even when there was no moon. But when there was... Oh, Major! It was breathtaking! Sitting on the tiled patio, I could look out over the bay and the straits to the cliffs of Andalusia, all so clear in perfect white light..." Diana glanced at Smith, and shook her head. "What a bore I must be, going on like this."

"Not at all," Smith assured her. "The place obviously made a deep impression upon you."

"I never tired of that prospect, especially at night..." The woman breathed in, suddenly, as if in remembrance. "I really must be going; I'm afraid I've overstayed my welcome."

"Nonsense," responded Smith, hoping to persuade Diana to stay. But as she rose to her feet, he saw that she was determined to leave. Smith stood and called Odways to bring the visitor's hat and coat. "Thank you for the strawberries, Mrs Coutts-Grogan, and please let your husband know that I plan to reciprocate your invitation to dinner soon."

Smith stood at the sitting room window and watched Diana walk out of his back garden and retrace her steps through the thin wood separating Ruscote from Fellings. He wore a ruminatory frown on his face as his valet removed the tea things.

"What do you think of her, Odways?" he asked, turning.

"Mrs Coutts-Grogan appears to miss Tangier, sir," the servant said, as he quietly placed dirty cups and saucers on a tray. "Do you believe that she was aware of the colonel's real employment, his work for the Secret Service?"

"Oh, yes," answered Smith, unhesitatingly. He sat in the chair his guest had vacated. The room was growing dim again, though the afternoon still had a couple of hours remaining. Daylight did not last long in December. "It's customary for married station officers to inform their spouses of their activities on behalf of the Service. It makes sense. In this line of work, especially when serving abroad, one might receive visitors of a definitely mysterious nature, get telephone calls from strangers, have to leave for unexplained meetings at odd hours... Under those conditions, a wife would be less than human if she didn't begin to harbour suspicions. Imagine the damage to an operation a jealous woman could inflict if she decided to look into these occurrences. Much better just to tell her the truth. She can even help keep her husband's secrets."

"I see your point, sir." Odways, having paused to listen to his question's answer, returned to his chores. "Does that policy extend to staff, sir?"

Smith chuckled and said, "It can. My trust in you, Odways, is of course without qualification. But, to be honest, I think my superiors simply like the idea that you are almost another operator — but one they don't have to pay."

"If I may reduce the expenditure of the Treasury, while providing satisfactory personal service, sir, then I am most gratified." Odways, picking up his tray, inclined his head in a dignified, if truncated, bow, and departed for the kitchen with his burden.

"But you must let us give you a ride, Major."

Diana Coutts-Grogan gestured out the open window of the Austin her husband was driving, urging Smith into the rear seat. It was two days since Smith had last seen the woman, leaving Ruscote after her delivery of the delicious strawberries. This day had been even shorter than that one, but still as grey. The sun had set behind the featureless clouds two hours before. The darkness through which Smith had to walk did not trouble him, nor did the cold. But the Coutts-Grogans, pulling to a halt beside him after their vehicle's head lamps had picked him out on the side of the road, thought it quite wrong that he should be travelling the deep, lonely country lane on foot.

"Thank you," Smith said, settling into the motor-car's rear seat, "but the Mill House is less than a mile from my cottage."

"It must be very chilly for you, nonetheless," Diana said.

The colonel, behind the steering wheel, turned slightly to regard Smith. His visage, distant and apathetic in repose, suddenly became familiar and friendly, as if Smith were party to a private joke, and he grinned. Smith understood that Grogan thought his wife's concerns kind but silly. However, everyone realised that it would have been rude for the couple not to have offered Smith a ride, once they had seen him, and ridiculous for Smith to have refused it, since all three were destined for the same place.

Coutts-Grogan directed the automobile back into the centre of the lane, and spoke over his shoulder to his new passenger.

"I hope you appreciate local gossip, Smith."

"Why is that?"

"Mrs Woolmer is the principal collector and dispenser of it in Marlton. Nothing malicious, mind you," said the colonel, sounding a trifle bored, "but nothing very interesting, either."

"She does prattle a bit, the dear," agreed Diana.

" 'A bit'?" chuckled her husband. "As we would have said back in my old regimental mess, 'She's such a bore, her head could be served at Christmas'."

"Really, Philip," Diana responded, a little angrily. "I think she's simply lonely. She's dreadfully old-fashioned and won't associate with anyone who isn't of her station in society."

Inductions Dangerous

"Do you remember last year, when she invited us and 'Major' Thomson to dinner?" Coutts-Grogan asked his wife, though the question was rhetorical. Turning his head again, he explained to Smith: "Thomson ended up being a *sergeant*-major, retired, and certainly not pretending to be anything else. He was staying at the Ullington Arms until he could move into the farm he had rented." He laughed heavily. "The look on Mrs Woolmer's face when she heard the poor fellow speak! It was pure Manchester!"

Smith assumed his acquaintance was describing Thomson's accent, and not the lady's expression in reaction to it.

"But Mr Thomson turned out to be very interesting. You told me so yourself, Philip." Diana paused, thoughtfully. "You know, we haven't seen him since then. Perhaps we could invite him to the house one evening." She peered at her husband.

"Perhaps..." was all that he said.

"You do play bridge, don't you, Major?"

Beatrice Woolmer lived in a house converted from a large mill. Smith had seen it during one of his rambles about the village, and had admired both it and its location. It was on the river, of course, just outside Marlton, a solid and strong building of stone, almost hidden among willows. Smith guessed that it had not fulfilled its original purpose for at least a generation, as the water wheel had been removed, and trees grew in its place.

"I believe I do, Mrs Woolmer, though there are those with whom I've been partnered who would disagree."

"Oh, really? But can't they see you playing at the time?"

Smith conceded that the Mill House's owner may have possessed a sense of humour, but it was probably rudimentary, and held no place for word-play. This opinion was shared by the Coutts-Grogans, to judge from their faces.

Mrs Woolmer was, Smith decided, trying to be the grand dame of Marlton, but seemed to have neither the taste nor the resources to achieve that ambition. The Mill House was big, with spacious rooms within, but filled with cheap furniture and decorations, as if purchased for their cost by the pound. The interior seemed to be a kind of pastiche of Edwardian art nouveau, arranged by someone who had no knowledge or sympathy for the style.

The lady herself was in her seventies, and had laden herself with garish jewellery, all suspect. Mrs Woolmer had dressed as for a minor levée at a palace instead of an evening of dinner and cards with acquaintances.

Nevertheless, Smith felt a warmth for the elderly woman who, despite her tastes, was cheery and friendly. As the four of them sat in the drawing room on unpleasantly designed and gaudily-hued furniture, he thought she reminded him of a slightly unbalanced old aunt.

"Now, I can tell right away that you are a *true* major," Mrs Woolmer said, leaning forward and patting Smith's sleeve. The weight of the many rings on her bony hands made her fingers feel like lead.

"True major?" Smith repeated, thinking that the phrase made his rank sound like an ancient religion, practised by only a few devoted fanatics.

"Yes, an officer — and a gentleman!"

Smith drank some of his coffee. The two ladies had, at Mrs Woolmer's insistence, left the men with their glasses of port in the dining room, next door, immediately after the meal. Smith favoured this time-honoured custom, but thought it unnecessary in such a small party. He and Coutts-Grogan had, consequently, waited for about fifteen minutes only, before joining the women.

"There was a man last year..." Mrs Woolmer recalled, her eyes rolling upward, as if unsure that her tiara was still in place among her abundant grey curls. It indeed seemed transfixed there by an immense yellow feather that made Smith think of that of the cockie-ollie bird worn in the slouch hats of South African militiamen. "Thornton? Tompkins? He claimed to be a major but was nothing of the sort. He was only a sergeant or a corporal, or some such thing. And the way he talked!" Mrs Woolmer threw up her hands with the long, drawn-out pronunciation of the final word. "And he gambles, from what I've heard."

Smith finished his coffee and set the empty cup on the metal-faced wooden table that almost glittered next to him, dazzling his eyes. One hesitated, he thought, to wonder what future historians of civilisation would deduce if they excavated intact this unfortunate collection of furniture. He caught Diana regarding him with a smile, and realised that she was musing along similar lines.

She was dressed more elegantly than on the previous two occasions on which they had met. She was attractive in spite of this. Prevalent fashions made women's clothes long and formless; they added to the wearer's height, and to the draw of Diana's face in particular. The black and white scheme of the dress did not help her colour. But with a smile, much was forgiven.

"Now, Colonel Coutts-Grogan does not like to gamble, Major," Mrs Woolmer was saying, tapping him on the arm with the force of a cosh. The folds in her neck wobbled as she nodded sagaciously and she leaned forward again, as if to impart a secret, even though Grogan was sitting two feet away.

"A wise policy, I've no doubt," remarked Smith.

"As wise a man as the colonel is, I don't believe it has anything to do with wisdom," the old woman said, smiling in good humour at the subject of the gossip. "It's simply that he is so terrible at keeping score that he is bound to cheat someone, however inadvertently!" Mrs Woolmer let loose a loud whoop, which evidently was a form of laughter, and poked Coutts-Grogan in the shoulder. "Come now, Colonel, confess!"

"Who shall partner whom tonight, Mrs Woolmer?" Diana put her empty cup and saucer down on the table with a rattle of porcelain. "Shall we see if the fair sex can defeat the gentlemen this time?"

The first day of winter was, appropriately, the coldest Smith had so far experienced in Marlton. The air smelled like snow, though none had yet fallen, and the attraction of a steady fire beckoned through the windows of Ruscote's parlour. Smith was not inside, however, but, rather, was walking noiselessly through the wood where he had found the stone lodge. He had learned that the wooded tract was known as Prior's Coppice, though it had obviously been a good while since anyone had harvested branches from its trees. The previous evening, he had played host to Colonel and Mrs Coutts-Grogan, which, Diana claimed, had shown that he forgave them for delivering him to Mrs Woolmer a couple of nights before.

Smith and the colonel had had an enjoyable argument over the extent of Scandinavian-influenced place-names in England. The former had eventually tried to broaden the subjects under discussion so as to include Diana, but her husband seemed apathetic to the attempts and she, apparently accustomed to such an attitude, had sat by indulgently. Fortunately, the meal itself was faultless, for which Odways had to be thanked.

Knowing what to look for now, Smith recognised the lodge at a distance, even through the heavy camouflage of brown and grey trees. But before his keen eyes saw it, his keener nose smelled it, or at least the smoke emanating from its chimney.

The shabby blue door on the far side was not quite ajar, but neither was it fully shut, and opening it required little of the force used by Smith on his previous visit. As the door swung haltingly inward, Diana Coutts-Grogan rose quickly from her seat by the small rectangular table, where she had been waiting.

"I'm glad you came," she said, after swallowing nervously.

"Your note this morning made me curious," admitted Smith, stepping over the threshold.

"When you mentioned last night at dinner that you would be leaving soon, I knew that there was something I needed to do before then." Diana moved closer.

"What is that?"

"This..." She put her hands to Smith's chest, lifted her head and kissed him on the mouth.

It was snowing now. The dull, mid-morning sky beyond the grimy bedroom windows was full of flakes, light and formless, blown about easily by the breath-like wind. They were accumulating fast, wherever they landed, and by late afternoon, Marlton would be smooth and white.

"I've always loved this little house..."

Diana stirred for the first time in a quarter-hour. Smith had thought that she had drifted off to sleep. Her brown eyes had been closed, the dark lashes against her pale cheeks, and her mussed chestnut hair fragrant against his face. He had felt the warmth of her naked body next to his under the sheets of the bed, and it was as though she had slumbered. Perhaps she had.

"It belonged to a woodman of Lord Ullington's, I think. When the manor house was closed up the servants who didn't go with Ullington to the south of France were let go. He still owns the estate, but no one takes care of it." Diana snuggled further down under the covers. It was chilly in the little room, in spite of the fire she had started in the corner grate before Smith's arrival. "I've always thought of it as my secret house."

Smith smiled and, his head on the pillow that still smelled slightly of dust, however much it had been cleaned, gazed upward. The ceiling was plain, the only decoration being the cobwebs tucked into the angles, and even they had been abandoned long before. The lodge was neglected and forgotten; indeed, it was secret.

"Somewhere away from your husband?" he asked.

Diana sighed quietly, and replied, "He's not cruel to me, not at all... And I still do love him, despite what this may indicate." She glanced up at Smith's eyes, but her cheeks glowed pink and she nuzzled his neck instead. "But he's cut me out of his life, out of our life..."

Smith did not want to say anything more, but knew that he must. He smoothed her brown hair.

"Is it because of the gambling?"

He could feel the woman's breathing stop for a moment. She raised herself on an elbow, instinctively gathering a blanket to her chest.

"How—? How did you know?" she stammered. Her eyes were very big and her countenance had drained of colour.

"I observed," Smith answered simply. He had not realised that he had been seeking clues to a gambler's peculiar behaviour, but he had found them nonetheless and, together, they explained everything.

"What do you mean?" Diana pushed herself into a sitting position on the bed, between Smith and the dull plaster of the wall. Smith sat up as well, propping himself with a pillow.

"The first thing I noticed was on the night we met," he said. "You surrendered to your husband all the money you'd brought back with you from Hereford. He didn't strike me as a miser, and I wondered why he wanted to have the cash back."

"Philip handles the finances in the family," Diana responded uncomfortably. "I told you that I'm hopeless with sums."

"Yet according to Mrs Woolmer, so is your husband. She may not be very reliable as informants go, but on the other hand, it's hardly so serious a claim that she would make it up."

"She's a malicious old harpy," Diana stated angrily. She climbed over Smith's legs, no longer concerned about concealing her nudity, and started picking her scattered garments from where they lay strewn on the musty floor.

"Surely not malicious." Smith shook his head. "You yourself didn't think so when you defended her during the drive to the Mill House. She also mentioned Thomson, late a sergeant-major of His Majesty's Regiments and Garrisons. He gambles, she thought. Is that why the colonel hasn't invited him to Fellings? Perhaps, as a former officer, he may feel that socialising with an erstwhile nco would be awkward, but also, as a gambler, Thomson may be a bad influence on you."

Diana was dressing, with little regard to neatness. She struggled into her stockings with difficulty.

"Then, there was your description of the Casino at Tangier." Smith caressed the woman's bare back and she fiercely shrugged off his hand. "You informed me that you and your husband went there once, for an anniversary dinner, and though you may have gone at other times, it was 'not often'. Yet you 'never tired' of its views."

As she attempted to pull on her dress, Diana found that she could not see well, her eyes full of tears. At length, she sat on the edge of the bed, her face in her hands.

"Do you know how much money I lost there, Linus?" she asked, sniffling. "More than £15,000..."

"Good Lord," Smith exhaled quietly, pretending to be shocked; indeed, hearing it from the woman's lips gave it a startling resonance. "Was it a family legacy?"

"No... No, it was worse than that..." Diana brushed at her eyes with a hand. "It wasn't even our money. It belonged to Philip's...employers..."

Smith leaned over and put his arms around Diana, expecting to be rebuffed again. She melted into his embrace.

"Your husband really is terrible at sums, isn't he?" he whispered. "You kept the company accounts in Tangier, and had at least some funds at hand whenever you wanted them." The woman nodded wretchedly. "Yes, it seemed unlikely that *both* you and he were inept at sums. Given the other facts, it made sense that you knew finances, but something had gone wrong with them."

"He trusted me to manage those accounts," confessed Diana miserably, crying once more. "He shouldn't have done it, but I am so good at things like that, you see. He didn't know about my thefts until I told him. He decided to get me away from Tangier as quickly as possible. He wrote to his company directors, claiming that agents for another firm trading with the Germans were trying to harm him, and asking to be replaced. Since then, he hasn't trusted me with money, not even with pennies..." She sniffed. "He doesn't care about the money."

"He cares that you would use it for gambling," Smith finished the thought.

"I can't control the urge, you see," she explained, "only my surroundings. If there is no temptation, there is no giving in to it. But...it's killed our marriage. When I gambled away his company's money, I gambled away Philip's honour. He doesn't trust me... I might as well have been unfaithful to him, which I've never been..." She stroked one of the arms that held her. "...Until now." Slowly, she allowed Smith to lay her back on the bed. She searched his face. "You won't tell anyone, will you?"

Smith was uncertain if Diana was referring to her gambling or to her infidelity, though, practically, it did not matter. His answer spoke to either concern.

"Your secret is safe," he promised.

Smith had uttered the truth. What had happened in the lodge would be revealed to no one, and though Diana's wagering, over several years, of £15,000 of the Government's money was explained in Smith's report, her secret would be as secure as if she had not told a soul.

"All gone to enrich a casino's owners..."

Arthur Pearson shook his bony head with regret. He squinted into his cup thoughtfully before tipping its contents into his mouth. The little tea shop, on Holland Park Road, not far from Secret Service Headquarters, seemed dreary to Smith, resembling the canteen of a large factory whose manager thought of his workers only in the most utilitarian terms. Smith raised a half-eaten biscuit to his lips, then remembered the taste of the initial bite, and replaced it on his plate.

"Such a waste," Pearson muttered, "and naturally there can be no prosecution."

The other tables were empty, and the young, unenthusiastic waitress was involved in a desultory conversation with a colleague behind the counter. There was no one to overhear the gentlemen's dialogue.

"Would such an action serve a purpose, if there could be?" asked Smith.

"No, no," Pearson agreed, "I suppose not. Still, Major, it's very impressive how you discovered all this, and in a very short time, too. I think C is very pleased."

"You can tell?"

Pearson peered at Smith short-sightedly across the table to determine if he were serious. Then the accountant chuckled, bearing his crooked teeth in amusement.

"I don't suppose you'd care to share how you accomplished this solution..." The financial officer raised an eyebrow, then lowered it, so that he could see through his spectacles again.

"Well," responded Smith, with good humour, after finishing his own tea, "let's simply say that you have your secret house, Pearson, and I have mine."

Under the Willows

"You are English?"

Linus Smith glanced up at the uniformed speaker with an expression of detached politeness. The sergeant of the Frontier Surveillance Corps, which doubled as Poland's customs guard, looked from Smith to Odways, seated opposite each other in the train compartment.

"You are both English?"

The questions were not quite official. After all, the passports that the sergeant held explained the nationality of their owners, as well as such bland facts as height and hair colour, weight and religion. Even if, as seemed to be the case, the Pole had not seen many natives of the United Kingdom, the small booklets would have satisfied any curiosity over political jurisdiction. The man's queries were for his personal interest.

"British subjects, yes," confirmed Smith. As this phrase, in the French that he was using, did not convey quite the correct response, he added, "Englishmen, yes."

The sergeant's face, middle-aged, with a strong chin and a weak brow that disappeared under the cap that he wore, changed from one of bored routine to respect, even admiration. His eyes, previously dull, brightened, and they rose to the suitcases in the racks above the passengers' seats. He handed the documents back.

"Thank you, gentlemen," he said, with a smile. "Welcome to Poland."

The door to the compartment slid shut behind the exiting sergeant, leaving Smith and his valet once more the only occupants of the compartment. Odways slipped his passport back into an inner pocket of his black coat from which it had been taken for bureaucratic inspection. He was a little puzzled.

"He did not examine the bags, sir. He did not even ask us if we had anything to declare," he stated. "He and his colleagues were almost zealous in searching the belongings of the party in the first compartment."

"That party is, I believe I overheard, German," Smith informed his servant.

"Ah, yes sir." Odways pursed his lips, as if understanding something that should have been obvious to him. The Poles, he knew, had little more reason to like their western neighbours than they did their eastern.

"Besides, there is still some of the old pre-War attitude in Europe toward the

English," said Smith, exchanging his passport for his cigarette case. "In those days, every subject of His Majesty was 'milord', and rich." He offered a cigarette to his employee, who accepted, though only because the pair were alone, and there was no one to mistake the gesture for an implication of equality.

"Such feelings toward our race must have been influenced by more than money, sir. People may envy a man with wealth and enjoy his presence if he is liberal with his cash, but largesse itself rarely commands respect."

One of the characteristics that Smith liked in Odways was his thoughtfulness, his readiness to question, in order to comprehend. His intelligence was no less sharp for being unspectacular.

"True," agreed Smith, conceding the point. He exhaled smoke. "I think it was our fondness for fair play that garnered us respect. It helped that we were by and large unconcerned with events on the Continent over the past century, as long as peace was maintained. We had no bias to serve in disputes between this group or that. Impartiality, born of circumstance, became a habit, and then a trait."

"And may be the cause of our presence here, sir?" ventured Odways, dropping ash into the small metal tray provided in the compartment.

"Just so." Smith smiled.

He peered out the window. The hour was a late one, chronologically almost night. But, as the month was August, the sun sat, as if suspended, behind the train, throwing an orange light over all. This sultry glow was almost the only entertaining sight to be viewed. Some border towns were unique, some unusual. Zbaszyń was neither. The uniforms of the two countries' officials provided some interest for Smith in a professional capacity; otherwise, the bland little town slipped by without regard from the train's passengers.

The last time Smith had been in Poland, it had been winter. He had travelled through a number of its provinces and wondered now if he would have a similar opportunity in the high summer. Poland, in its current incarnation, was a nation of contrasts, from almost primeval forests to vast marshes, from rolling plains to steep mountains. Smith's itinerary, however, would not be of his choosing, nor even, really, of his superiors'. Once given to him, his assignments often dictated their own terms.

Smith sat back again, and enjoyed the last of his cigarette. As was frequently the case, the mission he was on had come to him at short notice, having found him a member of a country house party in Hertfordshire. He had immediately caught an evening train back to London. C was surprised by his sudden materialisation.

"What the devil are you doing here at this hour?"

Under the Willows

The chief of the Secret Service was not as angry as his outburst may have made him seem. Smith's appearance in C's morning room was, however, unexpected, and not entirely welcome.

"I did go to Headquarters first, sir, but Production informed me that you wished to brief me yourself for this assignment."

C stared at his subordinate with his single eye. Smith was not disturbed by such attention, as were many. The new chief, who had succeeded the Service's founder earlier in the year, was of a different stamp than his predecessor, and when he growled, he expected submission.

"I have guests, you know, Smith..."

"Yes sir. I assume that is why I was shown to the morning room, rather than the drawing room."

Smith's unruffled attitude may have alleviated C's annoyance somewhat. The latter may also have simply decided to cope with the situation as it was. He exhaled slowly, audibly, and gestured to a chair. Smith thanked his host and sat, facing at an angle a window, the glass of which merely reflected the room's interior.

Like Smith, C was attired in evening wear, though the Secret Service chief preferred the tailless jacket to the longer and older-fashioned coat. Entitled to a uniform — few if any would have mistaken him for anything but a high-ranking army officer — C habitually dressed as a civilian, though he was just as commanding as if he had been in military garb. He sat near Smith, and deftly retrieved a cigarette from his case, lighting it and tossing the spent match into the cold grate, all with his one remaining hand. As an after-thought, he offered his guest the same refreshment.

"You were out for the night?" C indicated with his cigarette Smith's black and white clothes.

"Yes sir. Lord Mansborough had some people over for a Saturday-to-Monday," the visitor replied, nonchalantly.

No one who could go elsewhere remained in the Metropolis beyond the twelfth of August. Some, however, even the most powerful and important, had to remain, perhaps because they *were* powerful and important. C, like most British gentlemen, was a devotee of country pursuits, and remained in London through the autumn from duty.

"I'm sorry to drag you away from your recreation..." C nearly sounded apologetic.

"That's quite all right, sir." Smith smiled complacently. "My appointment book is filled until the spring. There will always be next week."

C growled, as if he had been tricked into feeling sorry for his subordinate, and snapped, "You've been to Poland." It may have been an accusation of a crime.

"Yes sir."

C's stare relaxed a little, and he tossed away his cigarette, almost unsmoked. He stood and indicated a well-stocked sideboard.

"Port, of course."

"Thank you, sir. Lord Mansborough is rather modern, and enjoys cocktails."

"Good God..." muttered the chief, disgusted. He filled a small glass with dark wine and brought it to his guest. "There's a three year old mystery in Poland that needs solving."

"Indeed?" Smith considered this introduction. "Then I suppose there was no need to bother you tonight, sir. Tomorrow would have done."

C paused as he poured some more port for himself, then continued.

"It's unofficial as far as we're concerned. It's more in the way of a favour."

"To the Poles?" Smith had set aside his cigarette, and now sipped from his glass. C's cellar contained many bottles from his family's property of Knockreagh, in Ulster, and that was recommendation enough. "You were in charge of the military mission to Poland in 1920, weren't you, sir?"

"That's right. I made a number of friends there, especially in their army." C's eye seemed to be focussed on something in the past, something exotic and foreign, but not unpleasant. "An unusual lot, but gentlemen, all of them. Do you know what the situation was like, three years ago?"

"Yes sir, I think so. Poland had just regained its independence after a century of being parts of neighbouring empires. After four years of serving as a battleground, the country was invaded by the Bolsheviks, hoping to export their revolution from Russia."

C stared at his visitor impolitely but characteristically, for several seconds.

"The Poles were in a bad way, with Warsaw itself under threat. But they saved themselves."

"The 'Miracle of the Vistula'," said Smith.

"There was no divine intervention," C scoffed. "It was good strategy, perseverance, staff work and guts. It was Pilsudski and his lot who drove back the Bolos, not Weygand and his frogs."

The indignation in C's voice reflected the fact that the world credited the French military mission, headed by General Weygand with reversing the effects of the Russian offensive. It was assumed by many that a people as flighty as the Poles lacked the professionalism and experience to achieve success. In imitation of the 'Miracle of the Marne', the French victory that had turned the Germans back and saved Paris in 1914, journalists named the Russian defeat after Warsaw's river.

"Still," added C fiercely, "they were lucky they weren't fighting the Huns."

"I suppose the common perception that the French were the Poles' saviours was almost inevitable, given the number of Frenchmen in their mission at the time, and the influence France has there."

"Then and now." C tilted his glass under his moustache and finished his wine. "That's why your mission must be as discreet as possible. The Poles don't want the French finding out that they've requested our help."

"I understand." Smith was attempting to eke out his own small portion of port, but it was too good to last. "What is my assignment?"

C inhaled and said, "Before the Poles launched their counteroffensive in 1920, their army's Second Department discovered what they thought was a Russian spy on their General Staff."

It was odd for Smith to hear a member of his profession use the word 'spy'. To someone who had spent his entire adult life in the field of intelligence, much of it in secret service, 'spy' was a very broad term, associated with thriller-writers, yellow-journalists and politicians, people who had little notion of the definition. But C knew what he meant.

"What followed took a heavy toll on Polish military intelligence," continued the chief. "The original investigator was killed, as were two of his successors."

Smith raised his eyebrows at this unconventional string of casualties, and asked, "Was the Russian agent caught?"

"Not only was he never caught, there was never any real evidence that he existed." C sounded disgusted, but with what aspect of the matter, Smith did not know. "A fellow named Szerbinski was chief of the General Staff at the time, and looked into the matter, with French help, but nothing useful was learned."

"The French aren't being asked for assistance this time, sir?" Smith frowned. "Is it because of the fear of communist sympathisers in their ranks?"

"That's it exactly," C confirmed, his chin thrust forward. "Szerbinski doesn't fully trust them."

"I assume I'm to contact General Szerbinski directly?"

"Yes. He's still CGS, and very influential. He'll provide you with everything you need to investigate the matter, including all the details."

If the chief of the Secret Service intended to talk further, he was prevented. A discreet knock on the room's closed door drew C's barked permission to enter. The interruption was a handsome middle-aged lady in attractive evening dress.

"I'm sorry, Francis, but I wanted to see if you are going to be much longer. Your guests are wondering where you've gotten to."

The tone in the feminine voice was one of mild rebuke, but was directed only to C. The lady turned to Smith with sincere sweetness on her face, and apologised to the visitor, giving the impression of a shared exasperation with the other gentleman.

"We're finished, Eileen," stated C, almost subdued. "I'll be in presently."

Smith was surprised by the meekness of his superior's response. The lady was, he guessed, C's sister, a spinster who acted as her bachelor brother's social hostess.

"Will your friend be joining us?" she asked, smiling.

"No. He's leaving."

Lady Eileen Sanction displayed no reaction to her sibling's failure to introduce Smith. Though her brother had been appointed to head the Secret Service only a few months before, she had evidently already accustomed herself to curbing any curiosity she may have had about his associates.

"Another time perhaps, Mr Smith," she remarked. "Or is it Jones?"

"Smith tonight, my lady," the visitor replied, with a smile of his own. After the door had shut once more, he resumed his seat and looked to his chief. "Am I to be Mr Smith in Poland, sir?"

"Yes." C stood and prepared to walk his subordinate to the exit. "There won't be a need for an alias this time. But stop at Headquarters in the morning; Production will give you your travel plans and tickets." Outside the flat, in the carpeted corridor, C nodded toward Smith's attire and told him, "Take that with you. The Poles are maniacs about entertaining. They may give even *you* a surfeit."

Smith and Odways had been reserved rooms at the Grande Europa Hotel, on Jerozolimska Avenue. To be more accurate, Smith had been reserved a room. The British tax-payer, quite rightly, was not expected to finance the transporting, lodging and feeding of a Secret Service operator's manservant, no matter how useful he may have been to his master's mission. Smith had amended the booking himself.

He liked hotels and inns that were, if not typical of their locales, then possessing characteristics of them, and did not care for the big establishments that may have been in London, New York or Shanghai for all their individuality. Fortunately, the flavour of Poland was strong, even in the larger hotels, such as the Bristol and the Polonia Palace. The Grand Europa was not as grand as its name may have indicated, but its porters were efficient, contrary to what some travellers viewed as the national norm, and the manager himself visited Smith as he was settling in, to make sure any complaints he may have had were addressed. There was even an elderly concierge who sat at the end of the corridor and rose to bow whenever a guest walked by.

"Most encouraging, sir."

Odways's opinion of the hotel was delivered with some surprise. His views of foreigners and their habits were often much lower than those he held of Englishmen, especially when he was in eastern Europe. He had been in the country previously, and his hopes for Poland were ambiguous.

Smith was leaning out the window, peering into the street below. Unlike London, Warsaw in August was alive with social functions. As C had implied, the Poles were mad about enjoying themselves. This trait, which the entire race seemed to share, from the lowest peasant to the noblest aristocrat, frequently obscured the lesser known but equally strong propensity for working hard. The Polish people were good at devoting parts of their day to one activity and parts to another, without being distracted by the first during the second.

"Warsaw is an historic city," Smith said, drawing his head in from the cool night air, "and with beautiful architecture. The residents are quite friendly, too, as I recall."

"I shall take some time tomorrow for exploration, sir," the servant promised, as he transferred his employer's clothes from their suitcases to the drawers of the bedroom's dressers.

"My appointment with General Szerbinski is not until the evening; I shan't need you for most of the day, so take your time in your ramblings." Smith again looked out the window. "I'll have some time to explore, as well."

Smith had been invited to dine at the Klub Mysliwiski at eight o'clock the following day. He arrived on time, to be greeted warmly by his host — and no one else. His fellow guests did not appear until later, in some cases not until after nine, when those present sat down at a long table in a private dining room. In fact, gentlemen did not seem to stop materialising throughout the night. At some point, Smith believed, there had been thirteen eating, but could not confirm it, as the number of his fellow diners kept fluctuating, even as he counted them.

"I must apologise again, Major. I know that to an Englishman, eight o'clock means eight o'clock. My countrymen are not familiar with your habits, and unpunctuality is deeply ingrained in them."

Zenon Szerbinski shrugged, in an almost Gallic manner. Indeed, he could have been mistaken for a native of France, from the style of his dark, oiled hair, to the trim of his tiny moustache, resembling nothing more than a couple of pencil lines, to the cut of his evening suit. And of course he spoke the language as fluently and knowledgeably as a member of the *Academie Français*.

Smith felt that the Pole had done nothing for which he had to be sorry. Szerbinski had admirably acquitted himself as host. The constant comings and goings of the other guests had not ruined Smith's evening and, though confusing and mildly disruptive, had proved as entertaining as the conversation, which had ranged widely and freely. He theorised that this sort of dinner-party had the potential of perpetual motion, continuing night and day, with new shifts forever replacing the tired and sated.

During the meal, Smith had not felt its effects. Now that he and Szerbinski were alone in the private parlour next to the dining room, he sensed the lateness of the hour, and observed that the ornate clock on the mantelpiece over the empty fireplace reported the time to be after two. He stifled a yawn; it would not have done to show signs of fatigue just as he was coming to the point of the visit.

"Now, we can talk," announced Szerbinski, pleased. He accepted a large glass of brandy from a waiter, while another brought him a selection of cigars. Another pair of servants repeated the process for Smith. "How much has General Sanction told you about the reason you are here?"

Smith said nothing, his eyes on the club staff still in the room. The general expressed annoyance at the waiters and barked an order in his own language. The servants quickly departed, closing the double doors to the dining room behind them. The quiet clinking of dishes and utensils being cleared from the table beyond the walls continued.

"I was told little of the situation, sir, and heard no details," Smith informed his host; "practically only that I was to help you."

"Sanction isn't the sort to waste time explaining something that will be repeated later." Szerbinski smiled, and drew on his cigar. "I will start at the beginning."

Smith settled more comfortably in his chair. He had set aside his own cigar. He preferred cigarettes, but the seemingly limitless number of them smoked between the courses of the recent meal had provided him with sufficient tobacco for the night. As for alcohol, vodka — never his first choice of beverage — had been just as plentiful as cigarettes and, though he had not consumed anything near the amount his fellow guests had, he was satisfied in that respect, as well. He would have paid a substantial sum for a cup of Odways's tea at that moment.

"It started in mid-July of 1920, as I recall," Szerbinski commenced, his voice a little raspy from hours of talk in the dining room. "A Red Army officer of Polish origin deserted to us during the retreat to the Vistula. He immediately made some claims regarding a Russian agent working on our General Staff. Since he had been posted to the Russians' own high command, he was considered both valuable and reliable. Major Tejma, a member of my Counterintelligence Section, was the one who had interviewed the deserter at the front, and proceeded to bring him by motor-car to Warsaw for detailed questioning. En route, they were both killed in an artillery barrage."

"That was very bad luck," commented Smith, though he distrusted the coincidence involved.

"It was, yes," agreed the general, waving cigar smoke away from his half-closed eyes. "Jerzy Tejma was very good at his job, and was the man to get to the bottom of the deserter's claims. He had a suspicion that there was a traitor at headquarters, even before this time."

"What was his evidence?" asked Smith, interested.

"He had none," Szerbinski responded, neither defensively nor incredulously. "His theory was based on knowledge the enemy seemed to have of our forces, including strengths and weaknesses, and on inferences from deciphered Russian wireless traffic."

"I understand that Tejma's successor shared his fate."

"That's right. Captain Josef Krzak was appointed to fill Tejma's position, but then he disappeared."

"Disappeared..." The Englishman glanced up from his brandy. "Under what circumstances?"

"Ambiguous circumstances, Major. Krzak's automobile was found...August 13th, I think it was, a few miles south of the East Prussian border. It was in a ditch alongside the road. The driver was dead behind the steering wheel, shot several times; Krzak was gone."

Smith frowned. He was less tired than he had been, or, to be more accurate, he was feeling his fatigue less. An intriguing problem was one of his most potent stimulants.

"What was Krzak doing so close to the German frontier?"

"I don't know," stated Szerbinski, with the expression of a man defeated by a mystery. "His superior, Colonel Jenowski, last saw him two days previously. Krzak explained to him that he had information pertaining to the possible Russian agent, and was going to follow where it led."

"And Colonel Jenowski," said Smith thoughtfully, tasting his brandy for the first time, "inquired no further at the time into what Krzak's information may have been?"

The Pole shook his head regretfully, and said, "The pair had known each other since before the Great War. They were best friends and trusted each other completely. Jenowski consequently gave Krzak his head."

"This matter of the alleged traitor seems to have had an ill effect on your intelligence department, General. Two of its officers gone, and both after they had begun a search for an enemy agent." Smith shrugged his eyebrows. "The events needn't have a sinister connotation, however."

"Very true, Major." Szerbinski seemed both annoyed that his guest did not immediately think the worst, and relieved that his reasoning was clear and independent. "Tejma was killed in an active battle-zone; he ran a risk driving within range of enemy artillery. And Krzak vanished in an area through which the Reds' III Cavalry Corps had just penetrated. In fact," he added, a little smugly despite the topic under discussion, "that formation had ridden so deep into our territory that we had them surrounded."

Smith sipped more of his brandy and said, "Both officers could have been killed by legitimate enemy action."

"Exactly." Szerbinski seemed quite ready to concede the point, But he sighed. "Then we suffered a third loss."

Smith regarded his host. If the situation did not involve death and possible treason, it would have been comic.

"Who was it this time?" he queried. "Krzak's replacement?"

"His superior, Colonel Jenowski, the director of the Second Bureau. He told me that he wanted to get to the truth behind the alleged Russian agent, so he proposed to investigate the matter himself. He did not put much stock in the theory, no more than I did. But Krzak's death had upset him, beyond the fact that he had lost a dear friend. There was something more. Then, on August 21st, he was found dead on his estate."

"How did *he* die?"

"A bullet to the heart, at close range, so close that the cloth of his uniform's tunic was burned by the muzzle-blast."

"That would have had to have been close indeed," Smith concurred. "It was unlikely to have been random enemy action; specific enemy action, perhaps. His assassin must have been someone whom he trusted, or someone accustomed to approaching him, unless... Were there any signs of restraint on the body?"

"No," replied Szerbinski. "The colonel had not been tied up." The general sighed. He had reduced his cigar to a stump, though he did not seem to have enjoyed it, and set its remains in the ashtray he had been using. He held his large, globular brandy glass in two hands.

"Colonel Jenowski had been working very hard; not just on this matter of the Russian agent; that took up a very small amount of his time, though it was on his mind. He had of course been fully occupied with collating and distributing intelligence for the offensive. I don't think he had had a good night's sleep since planning for it had commenced on August 6th. Then there was the loss of his friend, Krzak. When it became clear that our attack would succeed, I ordered Jenowski to take a week's rest-leave. I gave him no choice." Szerbinski was now a contrast to the ebullient host of the dinner-party hours earlier. He seemed as worn out as Jenowski must have been.

"And you would like the mystery of his death solved after three years," said Smith. He had sufficiently recovered from the vodka to appreciate the superior drink he had been given. "What of the enemy agent?"

Szerbinski smiled, almost guiltily.

"As I told you, Major, I did not believe the notion of a Russian operator in our midst," he responded. "Jenowski's death did not make me change that opinion. Lately, however, the press has picked up the old story, to be followed by politicians, opponents of the government. It has been decided discreetly to investigate." The general lowered his eyes demurely. "I have been offered advice in this matter but have determined that, if the truth is to be discovered, it will be done by an unbiased party."

"I'll do my best," promised the Englishman. He set down his glass. "By what authority will I be conducting my investigation?"

"By the army's, and by the government's," stated Szerbinski. He put aside his own drink and, leaning forward, removed a brown envelope from his dinner jacket. "These letters should facilitate your inquiry, no matter what direction it takes."

The two gentlemen stood and Smith accepted the package. As he pocketed it, Smith regarded the Pole once more.

"It may be that the investigation will lead nowhere. On the other hand, it may be that it will lead somewhere…somewhere unpleasant for your country. If there was, or is, a Russian agent on your army's General Staff—"

"It must be faced, Major," insisted Szerbinski, with rather more resignation than courage. "I am a romantic, as all my compatriots are, but I am a realist, as all soldiers must be. Discover the truth. That is all."

Smith shook his host's hand, and wondered if he could indeed solve this mystery, when a trio of native investigators had not. And, he added mentally, could he avoid their fates?

Smith liked to know the settings of his assignments. It served a dual purpose. Practically, it gave him some familiarity, however superficial, with the location, and ensured that he was not entirely ignorant of streets and buildings, amenities and neighbourhoods. Less tangibly but, perhaps, not less important, learning something of his surroundings gave him a sense of the place. A bustling market with plenty of commerce meant a good economy; empty restaurants and quiet cafés indicated a tense civil situation. These signs may have meant success or failure in a mission, life or death to a secret operator.

Considering that the country of which it was the capital had been a battleground for six years, and that every state Poland bordered was unfriendly to it, Warsaw possessed a remarkably carefree air. The August morning through which Smith strolled was warm and would not be uncomfortably hot later. The people who thronged the pavements, milled about in the shops and passed their time eating and drinking at outdoor tables were pleasant and gregarious. The traffic in the streets, both automotive and equine-powered, was heavy, and the police trying to direct its movements were seemingly resigned to ineffectiveness.

In addition to viewing the sights this morning, Smith had appointments, the next items on his mission's agenda. He stopped at the War Ministry and, with a letter from the chief of the Polish Army's Personnel Bureau, asked to see Colonel Jenowski's file. The co-operation of the officers and NCOs who attended on him did not, however, result in Smith's immediate success, as it took some time for the correct file to be found.

Soon thereafter, though, Smith was on his way to the Rynek, Warsaw's old market square. It was a location that was easy to find and, indeed, was a point of departure for tours of the city.

The Englishman could understand the attraction. The square and the streets leading into it boasted tall, narrow houses, each a distinctive design and colour. Their presence gave the Rynek a medieval appearance, accentuated by the many peasant carts that rumbled across the cobblestones, the long, wide, boat-like vehicles helmed by bearded men who may have come from the fifteenth century or earlier. Traversing the square, they passed gentlemen in lounge suits and tradesmen in neckties, the people providing as much variety as the buildings in the background.

"The Foreign Office... The English Foreign Office?"

Mrs Marie Rakowska glanced up with the hint of a smile on her face. She had read General Szerbinski's letter thoroughly, and admitted to being puzzled by it.

"Yes," Smith confirmed. "I've been consulted regarding the compilation of the official history of the recent war between Poland and Russia." He contrived to look diplomatic. "I think it has something to do with ensuring impartiality."

The woman's smile grew, and she said, "Ah, I see." She replaced the letter in its envelope and returned it to her guest, all with small, precise movements. "That was probably wise on the part of the government. For more than a hundred years, Poland was divided among three countries, and the people retain their old prejudices in many cases."

Marie Rakowski was beautiful, Smith decided, with porcelain skin and perfectly proportioned features. Her blonde hair was very fine, and worn shorn, bobbed in the latest fashion. Her eyes were blue, her nose small, and her pink lips neither full nor thin, though kept habitually parted. She wore a modicum of rouge on her cheeks, to give them a touch of colour, and a similar amount of paint on her lips. Her clothes were very modern, as if taken straight from the mannequins displaying them at the latest Parisian show and sent by the swiftest train to Warsaw. The lady's figure was slender, so the tubular garb did not prove unflattering on her.

"You yourself are Austrian, madam?" Smith asked. His hostess' eyes widened, briefly, then adopted a look that was almost jaded.

"You have been reading about me, Major," she stated, as she may have done about someone who had stretched, but not broken, the rules of a game.

"No, but I have been reading of your late husband, Colonel Jan Jenowski," Smith confessed. "He served in the army of the Austrian Empire, one of the 'three countries' you just mentioned. Your English has a Viennese accent, and you referred just now to the 'people' of Poland, rather than 'my people' or 'we'."

Again, the woman's eyes enlarged. Then they collapsed into slits as she laughed with amusement and surprise.

"You are quite correct, Major," she confirmed. "I was born a Baroness von Hilfstein, and met Jan during the War, when he was on leave." She gestured to the photographs that were displayed on the surface of a large, black piano. They depicted boys and girls, men and women; a slightly younger Marie Rakowska on horseback, and in bathing attire on a beach; a gentleman in the service uniform of an Austrian Army captain. Smith stood and walked to the piano.

"Are these your children?" he inquired.

The photos were framed in steel, giving them an appearance in contrasts — modern settings for dated images. The whole room, in fact, had the streamlined effect of the most recent styles, functionalism, serving as décor. It was not a fashion to which Smith was sympathetic, though it was clearly favoured by Mrs Rakowska.

"They are mine, but not Jan's," she said, joining her visitor at the piano. She touched the corners of the frames gently, then brought another to the fore from where it had stood behind the others. "I was married before Jan, very young, to a dashing cavalry officer. He was killed in the first month of the War, but left me with four precious gifts…"

She replaced the photograph, that of a boyish lieutenant of hussars. Momentarily, her gaze returned to the likenesses of her children. Then she laughed, and led the way back to the chairs on which she and Smith had been sitting.

"Mr Rakowski is as far from being a soldier as can be, Major," she explained, lightly. "I did not wish to be widowed a third time, so I made him promise to outlive me." Despite the humour in the sentence, her voice held a slight chill, as when a thin cloud passes before a summer sun. She indicated a final photograph, placed not with the others on the piano, but on a side-table near her chair. The subject was a rotund, middle-aged man, well-dressed, holding a cigar, and wearing a rather bemused expression. The lady looked up.

"I can guess only that your visit has to do with Jan, Major; it makes sense, as you are in Poland to help with the history of the war with Russia." Marie raised her eyebrows, curved, dark eyebrows, as if in some doubt. "Jan did not discuss his work with me, so I don't know how I can assist you."

"It's your permission I seek, rather than your knowledge, madam," admitted Smith. "I would like to examine Colonel Jenowski's personal papers, those dealing with, or dating from, the conflict."

"Oh, I see." Marie smiled again, confidently. "In that case, I *can* help you, though all of Jan's papers are stored at Proskiwicz, the family's country house. The estate itself passed to Jan's cousin, Paul, but the correspondence, of course, fell to me. I, or my nominated agent, can go there at any time to examine them. I'll provide you with a letter to give the steward. He understands the legal position of the estate, so you should have no trouble."

It took just two minutes for the lady to compose the note, seated at a writing table which was just as metallic and modern as the rest of the room's furniture. Smith stood in the meantime at a casement window; its panes were open to the morning air, and the sounds of the busy street below, though muted, were audible.

"Here you are, Major," Marie said, as she finished the letter with an exact but flowing signature. Folding the sheet of paper and slipping it into an envelope, she then turned in her chair and presented it to Smith. "I think—"

The door to the sitting room burst open at that moment, and a large, heavy man barged in. Sometimes a picture, even a photograph, produced an image quite unlike its real-life original, Smith had observed. But the man who lurched forward, without seeing the visitor, was easily recognisable from the image of Marie's current husband. He uttered a stream of Polish that sounded as though it combined pleading and cajoling, and stopped abruptly when he saw the Briton.

"Stanislas, this is Major Smith. Do you remember me telling you of his appointment?"

Rakowski's large head creased all over its surface with confusion, and momentarily Smith thought that the reaction had been caused by the man's wife's sudden use of English. Rakowski put a big hand to his pate, where the short, stout fingers grabbed at his wavy grey hair, almost as if thinking caused him pain. But he answered, in English nearly as good as Marie's, and Smith realised that the man's look of bewilderment was habitual.

"Oh, yes, of course…" Whether or not he really did recollect the notice of Smith's arrival, or if he had even been told, Rakowski now thrust forward toward the guest with an outstretched arm. "Major Smith, yes, of course…"

Marie introduced her husband, adding, for the latter, "The major wants to see some of Jan's things."

Under the Willows

"Oh? Well, yes, good, good..." Rakowski shook Smith's hand with a clumsiness that was the opposite of his wife's movements. "I'm very sorry to charge in, Major, but we are off to see my sister and her family for the day and, yes, we must be going..."

The last phrase was a hint, a request — not a demand — from Rakowski to his spouse, and the latter smiled once more.

"I'm afraid we must excuse ourselves, Major," she said, with some resignation. "If you have any difficulty seeing Jan's papers, please let me know."

"I'll see you out, sir," her husband offered. On their way to the front door of the townhouse, Rakowski suggested that the Englishman come to dine with them while he was in Poland. "I think we're having something on this week," he commented, sounding uncertain of his schedule. "Where are you staying? The Grande Europa? Very good. Very good value for the money. Watch for your invitation then, Major. Good day."

Smith and Odways did not leave Warsaw until the following evening. On the advice of the ever-helpful manager of his hotel, Smith reserved a sleeping-compartment on their train, ensuring that the journey to their destination would pass mostly while they were unconscious.

The distance between the Polish capital and Proskiwicz was not great, judging by the flatness of a map. But the country was still recovering from wars. Destroyed bridges and rail lines meant detours; train engines were worn, couplings and bogeys in need of repair. A slow progress was both necessary and wise.

"We didn't come this way last year, did we, sir?"

Odways stood next to his employer in the narrow corridor of the wobbling carriage, while an attendant converted their compartment's berths back into seats. The morning beyond the window's dirty pane was sunny and cloudless, and its warmth could be felt even in the moving train.

"No, we were in Galicia, in the south, and Poznania, in the west, the provinces ruled respectively by the Austrians and the Germans before the War. We are heading deeper into what once was Russian territory."

"It looks to be all woods, sir."

Indeed, the view from the train encompassed nothing but trees, coniferous and deciduous, their shades of green indiscriminately mixed. The landscape resembled a primeval forest, the sort associated with the farthest reaches of Siberia, or northern Canada. But it belied the sort of land beneath.

"These are the Pripet Marshes," said Smith, "a vast tract of wetland, with dry islands where villages were built, and now connected in many cases by rail, constructed on causeways."

"Like the Fens, sir?" asked Odways.

"Not quite. I've read that the principal ingredient here is mud, as glutinous and clinging as that in Flanders during the War. The difference is that there, it was created by the loss of vegetation and top-soil, blown away by a million artillery shells a week. This," Smith inclined his head to the passing scenery, "is how God designed it."

The valet was impressed, and responded, "It's no wonder travel is difficult here, sir. How far do the marshes go?"

Smith confessed his ignorance of the precise amount.

"Most of the Province of Polesia is included in the Pripet. When the Russians governed the area, they drained four million acres surrounding the city of Pinsk, and it barely affected the total."

Odways contemplated the immensity of such a land, even as he watched a small portion of it, itself seemingly interminable, pass by the window.

"It's well that more of the Pripet wasn't reclaimed," his master remarked. "It's a better barrier than any mountain range or river, and it's now Poland's border with Russia."

As Smith spoke, the carriage attendant emerged from the Britons' compartment, his restorative duty done. Smith tipped him, and inquired as to the remaining distance to the village of Gomlin.

"Oh, we'll be there in ten minutes, sir," replied the young man, in American-accented English. His was a fresh, freckled face, unlikely to need a shave every day. Though his white jacket was rather large for him, it was bright and spotless, and the brass buttons shone. He may have been a soldier on parade, proud of his regiment's uniform. "You must be going to Proskiwicz."

Smith was surprised, though he did not display it.

"How did you know?"

The attendant grinned, a sly, wry expression, but good humoured, and replied, "Say, there's nothing else in the place. Gomlin's the nearest village to Count Jenowski's house, though I guess we've been on his estate for hours."

"The villages here do seem rather isolated."

"I'll say," agreed the youth, enthusiastically. "I heard some government boys were going through these parts a couple years ago, setting up administration, you know? Anyway, they come across this one burg where the people never heard of the Great War. Fancy that! Years of killing and destruction just passed them by." He made a sweeping gesture with his hand. "They probably live in mud huts and eat potatoes for supper seven times a week, but never heard of the War? They seem like lucky sons o' guns to me! Oh, thanks, sir."

Under the Willows

The attendant accepted another coin from Smith, made a rudimentary kind of salute — despite not wearing a cap — and walked jauntily down the corridor.

Gomlin was not what an Englishman would have called a village. It was no more than a collection of wooden cottages; not quite the mud hovels envisioned by the carriage attendant, but rather primitive for the twentieth century. Smith had observed the communities becoming rougher and ruder the farther east he had travelled; Gomlin had neither shop nor post office, not even anything that may have been termed a street, though it did boast a small gendarmerie headquarters to one side, and a slightly bigger railway station on the other. The former looked new — perhaps the result of some 'government boys' having recently introduced civil bureaucracy — while the latter had at some time suffered a number of broken window panes, the deficiency of glass having been made good — or as good as it could have been — with oiled paper. To appearances, the cottages that comprised the hamlet had escaped battle damage, but were so simply constructed that they may have been replacements, built soon after the originals had been destroyed.

Only Smith and Odways disembarked at the station, their modest amount of luggage placed next to them on the decaying wooden platform by the American-educated attendant. Waving, and giving the erstwhile passengers a friendly grin, the young man was quick to board the train again, as if afraid that he might be left behind in this wilderness. Even the engine barely stopped, eager to gather steam once more with which to escape Gomlin.

There were no porters, and the stationmaster, if there was one, was absent. Odways glanced about warily, not caring either for the location or the predicament. Despite the warm sun in its blue sky, he viewed this lonely place in the far reaches of a strange land as somewhat sinister.

"Your revolver is in the smaller of the bags, sir, under the vests," he reminded his employer.

A strong sound of footfalls landing heavily upon wooden boards preceded the arrival of a man, who eventually turned the near corner of the station and walked directly toward the newcomers. He looked like a gentleman, dressed for a day in the country, in a tweed suit and stout boots.

"Good day, sirs. I am Antosik, Count Paul Jenowski's steward at Proskiwicz," he stated. "Do I have the honour of addressing Major Smith?"

"I'm Smith, and this is my man, Odways."

Antosik was almost thirty, of medium height and handsome, though his features, even at his age, were not as attractive as they had probably once been. Superficially, he was fit, but he held his right arm stiffly; a long, nearly invisible scar ran horizontally just below the hairline, and his voice, which spoke English with a clearer, more erudite pronunciation than had the carriage attendant's, possessed a hollow, raspy quality. Smith realised that Antosik had not survived his war unscathed.

"I received your letter enclosing Madam Rakowski's, Major," Antosik announced, leading the Britons behind the station, where an open tourer was waiting on a rutted dirt road. "Count Jan always stayed in the Forester's Lodge when he came to Proskiwicz. We will go first to the big house, then to the Lodge."

Just as the steward had had little difficulty handling suitcases, he had no trouble piloting the automobile. Smith recognised it as a Graft und Stift, during the War a popular model with the Austrian Army's General Staff. It had come through the conflict and, despite some abuse, was perfectly serviceable, like its driver.

"How long have the Jenowskis lived at Proskiwicz?" Smith inquired, his words bumping and tumbling with the vehicle's progress along the rural road. As a member of a land-owning family himself, foreign aristocracy interested him.

"Just over three centuries," replied the steward. "You will find Proskiwicz an excellent example of a Polish nobleman's estate, Major. The house is at the centre of a thousand acres of park, landscaped in the English fashion, and itself the centre of hundreds of square miles of farms and meadows, woods and lakes." Antosik spoke proudly, as if describing his own property. He had been raised a devoted retainer in an almost feudal setting, and shared, to a minor extent, the splendour enjoyed by his masters.

But the glory of Proskiwicz had suffered in the wars. The grass of the park was long and unkempt, ornamental shrubs unrecognisable; gates were missing from their crumbling piers, and the avenue leading to the mansion was flanked not by mighty limes, as it had been, but by low stumps.

Past shattered lodges, Antosik slowly drove the motor-car onto the weed-clogged gravel of an enclosed forecourt. Before them, Proskiwicz was a shell. Once fit for a king's palace, some of its walls no longer stood, while those that remained were blackened and scarred. The upper windows showed only the morning sunshine, and the lower, the debris of a collapsed roof.

"It is a terrible sight, is it not, Major?" Antosik stared at the grand ruin, sorrow compressing his weary features. "It was not just a house that was destroyed, but a work of art, a monument to taste, and a part of Poland's history." The steward's words stopped abruptly, as if he did not trust himself to utter more.

"Will it be re-built?" asked Smith.

"Oh, indeed." There was no doubt in Antosik's response. "Count Jan was

Under the Willows

intending it before he died, and now Count Paul has had plans drawn. The new house will be different than the old, but still magnificent. You will see."

The young man smiled, then nodded at Smith, as if the latter had audibly agreed with everything the former had said. The steward then stepped from the automobile and, facing a thick wooden door in the forecourt wall, called out in his native tongue. A moment later, there emerged from the doorway two grooms, each leading a pair of horses, three of them saddled and ready for riding, the fourth prepared as a beast of burden.

"From here, travel must be by other means," stated Antosik, matter-of-factly.

Smith glanced at Odways. Whatever the valet was thinking, he kept his face impassive.

"We can't drive?" questioned his employer.

"No sir." The Pole's reply was one of astonishment. "The Forester's Lodge is deep in the woods. The closest thing to a road that approaches it is an old cart-track, and even that disappears in places. We could go by water, but we have no boats. A horse is the usual method. You ride, of course?"

"Of course." Smith was unconcerned for himself. His valet, however, had never been confident in the saddle.

"I will be quite all right, sir," Odways insisted, with more determination than conviction. Antosik's countenance relaxed, as he realised that Smith's anxiety was for the servant.

"It is but seven miles to the Lodge," he said, "and it is a most comfortable house."

It was wonderful how easily nature could reclaim land that had once been so arduously tamed by man. Smith had read that the average English field metamorphosed from farm crops to wild woods in just ten years if abandoned to its fate. The trees would be neither tall nor strong, but the field would need clearing once more if wanted for agriculture. The Polish countryside was, it seemed, little different. The woods between the big house and the Lodge were thick, tangled in places; a wagon would not have succeeded in a passage, and a pedestrian could have become quickly lost. Yet at one time, Smith guessed, the vegetation had been kept in check, and the undergrowth regularly thinned.

On the other hand, the beauty of the estate was great. Smith rode beside Antosik, while the latter led the pack-horse, heavy with the Englishmen's luggage. Odways followed his master. Smith's senses took in the freshness of the air, and the verdure of the land. As dense as they were, the woods were relieved by natural glades, and the route was never far from water, running or still. Antosik described how Count Jan's father enjoyed touring the estate by boat.

As he listened, Smith kept the young steward under observation, as he did

Odways. The latter was an indifferent horseman, but was doing well. The Pole, Smith could plainly see, was at home in the saddle, yet already tired. Smith's eyes met Odways's, and the servant understood. He slowed, as though in difficulty. This was intimated to their guide who, with as much consideration and discretion as had prompted the Englishmen, diminished the pace.

"Does the count come to Proskiwicz frequently?" Smith asked conversationally, as he watched a small mammal, frightened by the humans' approach, plunge into a pond, a hundred feet away.

"Count Paul does not, though he is very interested in the estate," answered Antosik, who seemed grateful for the slacker rate. "Count Jan, before him, was much taken with all aspects of Proskiwicz, and came whenever he could."

Smith nodded. The day, now reaching its mid-point, was perfect, in his estimation. Some clouds had formed, harbingers perhaps of rain in the evening, but the sky was overwhelmingly blue. The temperature was warm but kept from rising by the omnipresent water.

"Count Jan had no more immediate family than the cousin who succeeded him?"

"He did..." The hesitation in Antosik's reply was not due to worry over what was proper to divulge but, rather, for what was fact. The steward leaned a little toward Smith, as if to make his words more comprehensible. "Yes, he did. Count Jan's mother — his father died in 1906 — his mother, brother and sister, to whom he was very close... The family moved eastward in 1915, you see, Major, to avoid the advancing Germans. Many, many Poles, high-born and low, fled east, into Russia...and most vanished there..."

"A quarter-million, is that right?"

Antosik's eyes expressed shock, as though he had never known the correct figure, and found the truth staggering. But he nodded slowly.

"I would not doubt that total, Major."

The Great War had created untold misery throughout Europe and forced countless numbers of people to become refugees. Poland suffered severely in that respect. The irony of the Poles' fate was striking; those ruled by Russia travelled further into that country for safety, but were then trapped in its revolution and subsequent civil war. The irony in the case of the Jenowskis was doubled. As a young man, Count Jan had dabbled in politics, and had been charged with sedition by the Russian authorities. He had sought sanctuary with friends who were under the milder regime of the Austrian Empire, where he had prospered.

"Count Jan had no children, I believe..."

"That's true, Major. Madam Rakowski, as she is now, was a widow, with several children. Count Jan doted upon them, but he and the countess had none of their own."

The horsemen continued through a line of trees anchored by thick undergrowth. The landscape opened before them, revealing wide meadows bordering a lake. Near the water's shore were gathered several buildings, as many as could have been boasted by the hamlet of Gomlin, but all much more substantial than the peasants' shacks. The biggest structure was a wooden house with a stone foundation. Superficially, it looked neglected, in need of paint, the grass around it uncut; flowers that had escaped the neat beds were everywhere, though Smith did not find this feature unattractive. It was an ideal retreat, a tranquil country haven.

"The Forester's Lodge," declared Antosik, adding that he would show the Englishmen their rooms. Despite the fluidity of his dismount, it was obvious that he had been fatigued by the ride, weakened. A hearty luncheon, though, would restore everyone, Smith knew.

The steward did not remain at the Lodge after the meal. Odways had found an abundant supply of food in the Lodge's kitchen, and combined this with what the riders had brought with them, to produce a repast that surprised the two gentlemen with its variety. Refreshed by this nourishment and an hour's rest, Antosik was confident when he mounted his horse for the journey back to the big house.

Colonel Jenowski's correspondence had been packed tidily, if not orderly, into boxes, and stored simply and without security in his study. According to the steward, no one had used the room since the day of the colonel's death, not even his successor, Count Paul. There was dust on the floor and furniture to prove the assertion, and grey clouds blew off the letters when they were removed from their boxes.

Smith remained awake far into the night. Odways had brought plenty of tea with him, as was his wont when he and his master crossed the Channel, and pots of it maintained Smith in his research.

By the light of oil lamps, in the comfort of the sitting room, Smith studied Jenowski's correspondence. Fighting the sensation that he was prying into someone's private affairs, he noticed that the most recent mail was dated from the dead man's last months, in the summer of 1920. It comprised neatly folded pages in unaddressed envelopes; the count's name had been written on the fronts. This was, he guessed, not unusual for the time and situation. Poland was at war, and had been fought over for years previously. Communications often failed, and letters most likely reached their proper destinations when delivered by messengers.

The missives were in French, and had been written by a woman. They began with familiar, even affectionate greetings, and continued with similar phrases, describing domestic details and mutual acquaintances. Though the calligraphy was excellent, the paper was cheap, and the quality of ink varied even within letters. They concluded over the signature of 'Mouche'; hardly a code-word, thought Smith, with a smile; probably a pet-name.

By the time he finished his chore, Smith had examined so many letters that he feared nightmarish postmen armed with sticks of sealing wax would pursue him through his dreams. But, as usual, what little sleep he had that night, was undisturbed.

"This was Count Jan's favourite spot."

It was just over twenty-four hours since Smith had come to the Forester's Lodge, and he now stood at the end of a stone quay that ran out from the shore, not far from the house's front door, and into the water of the lake. It had rained during the night, and the afternoon's sky was strongly blue, and the deep water at Smith's feet brightly green. He had heard Antosik approaching from some distance, and turned when the steward drew level with him.

"He would come to the Lodge for relaxation, when he could," Antosik continued, fondly. "He would stand here, and gaze across the lake. He told me that what he saw was Heaven."

Indeed, the vantage point was perfect, and the vista could not have been bettered. But that was only natural, Smith believed, when God was the gardener. The sparkling lake spread away from him, and was bounded by the dark green of forests. The sounds were peaceful, the fragrances sweet.

"Do you know anyone, a friend of Count Jan's perhaps, who went by the name of Mouche?"

"French for 'fly'?" The Pole regarded the other gentleman with incredulity, as if suspecting that he was the target of a joke.

"A pet-name," suggested Smith. "The count received many letters in the months before he died, a number from this woman, Mouche."

"A woman? Are you sure?"

"To judge from the handwriting, yes."

Antosik was silent. His brow knit, accentuating the artificiality of the scar at his hairline.

"Count Jan and I sometimes dined together on the results of a day's shooting and, though he called me 'friend', I cannot claim the privilege of having been an intimate. He would not have confided to me matters that were closest to his heart. And I knew the count lately, after the Great War, so the adventures of his youth, in Austria, are unknown to me." After a pause, he added, hopefully, "The letters may be from the countess, as Madam Rakowska was then."

Smith did not wish to sully the good opinion the steward had of his late master. The truth was, however, that the handwriting of the mysterious Mouche was distinct from that used by Mrs Rakowska in the letter that she had provided Smith.

"Yes, that's quite possible," he replied, sounding conclusive, as if persuaded by Antosik's theory. In a more business-like tone, Smith remarked, a moment later, "There was also a letter, from Count Jan, to 'Paul', describing the estate in some detail. That would be the present count?"

"Undoubtedly," answered Antosik, who gratefully accepted a cigarette from the case Smith held out for him. He glanced at the Briton. "You found that among the papers?"

"Yes." Smith drew in some smoke. "It was in an envelope simply marked with the single name upon it. Count Jan may not have had time to deliver it before his death."

The two men were quiet for half a minute. Then the Pole said:

"It was across the lake that Count Jan's body was discovered, in the water, under those willows, yonder." He pointed with his cigarette to tall and spreading trees, clearly visible from the quay. "We could ride over there if you like, Major."

"I think I shall, but you needn't accompany me."

The steward nodded with, Smith thought, a little relief. Antosik still had the ride back to the big house ahead of him, and that would be strenuous enough. He told Smith that a horse would be readied for him, then strode purposefully away, his boots on the stones of the quay sounding not unlike shod horses' hooves.

Afterward, all was quiet. The songs of the birds and the occasional rustle of wind-nudged leaves were the only disturbances. As regretful as Colonel Jenowski's death may have been, Smith mused, there were worse places at which to die. Many would have longed for a paradise such as Proskiwicz to be their last vision, their final memory. He dropped his cigarette end into the lake, where the slight and gentle waves carried it far from the shore. Antosik was leading a horse across a meadow. It was time to go.

Smith and Odways returned to Warsaw on that night's train. The major was reluctant to leave Proskiwicz, especially the remote Forester's Lodge, in its isolated haven. His servant was rather readier to come back to the city.

The day threatened rain, and the skies over Warsaw were grey, heavy with unfallen precipitation. This did not discourage multitudes of people from enjoying the Saturday afternoon. Krakow Boulevard was crowded with vehicles and pedestrians; farther along, where the thoroughfare became Ujazdow

Inductions Dangerous

Avenue, it was thronged all the more. There were fewer representatives of old Poland here, not as many peasants and farmers visiting the big town. These streets were modern, and most of what they sold was of no value to the rural visitor.

Smith had his taxi halt at the end of a row of well-kept, century-old terrace houses. Several of these had been occupied by the army as staff offices, as was plain from the sentries at the doors, and the ensigns draped from flagpoles. Smith, in uniform this day, entered one of the buildings to the snap of soldiers presenting arms.

It occurred to the Englishman that the guards may have considered Smith a member of their own army. Poles had fought for four different nations during the Great War and, later, had battled the Russians wearing their old uniforms, as well as those of a new, native design. No one would have been surprised even now to see a captain wearing Russian cavalry breeches, or a colonel swathed in a French topcoat.

With instructions from the clerk in the ground floor lobby, Smith ascended the winding stairs, generally ignored by those he met on them. He hoped that this was due to his innate invisibility, rather than being a sign of the security in the General Staff's intelligence headquarters.

Initially, Smith had despaired of finding anyone at work on a Saturday afternoon. Poles had, rightly or wrongly, the reputation of a less than ardent devotion to their jobs, and in any case, most of the civilised world shut down at one o'clock on Saturdays. Even if this did not apply in Poland, it was time for luncheon. But his thin hope that the Second Bureau, like a police station, would be manned when all else was closed seemed, in the end, to have been justified.

Behind an unmarked door, Smith discovered a nearly deserted office. A wooden counter with a chipped top made the room resemble a resort of those who come seeking lost luggage. Several desks were set out beyond this, though only one was occupied. A rotund young man, almost bursting the uniform of a lieutenant, looked up with undisguised annoyance at Smith's entry. Arranged on the desktop before him was a variety of filled dishes: soup, meat, boiled vegetables and pastries. The Briton had been correct both about the intelligence department being open and about it being time for luncheon. The duty officer pulled away his napkin with disgust and, after a couple of failed efforts, pushed himself from his chair, which issued a noise rather like a sigh of relief. He greeted Smith grumpily, and in Polish.

"I wish to consult some of your records," the visitor said, in French. Producing a letter from General Szerbinski, he added, "I think you will find this to be sufficient authorisation."

The lieutenant examined the letter with astonishment, then blinked at Smith,

Under the Willows

asking him politely, and in French, to wait on his side of the counter, if he would. Retreating to his desk, the lieutenant made a telephone call. He returned chastened and beaming in what he no doubt believed to be an ingratiating manner. The sickly smile threatened to split his wide face.

"Of course, Major, anything we can do for you." He returned the letter as a monk would have returned a sacred relic to a bishop, then, no longer touching the holy article, snapped his fingers profanely, and shouted a sharp order in Polish. Immediately, a small man in the uniform of an NCO hurried out from a back room, hastily brushing bread crumbs from his chin with a napkin. "This is Corporal Miskuski, sir. He will attend to you." Another angry command brought the subordinate to the counter. The officer then retired, almost bowing himself away.

Smith reiterated his request for help, this time to the corporal. Miskuski's stumbling response in French made Smith try again, this time in Russian and, finally, in German.

"Is this better?"

"Oh, yes sir!"

The Pole grinned happily. He was a youngster, no older than the century, though this meant that he may already have spent a third or more of his life experiencing war first-hand. His appearance was calculated to add maturity to his modest number of years: the red hair darkened with oil that plastered it to his scalp, the rather unsuccessful attempt to grow a moustache. The round-rimmed spectacles that he wore, though, made him look like a schoolboy.

"How may I assist you, sir?" The German that Miskuski spoke fluently was that of eastern Prussia, heavily coloured with Slavic. Nonetheless, it was clear and well-elocuted.

A few seconds later, the corporal opened the door to a large, windowless closet, and switched on a light bulb suspended from the ceiling. The pale illumination showed the room to be filled with cabinets and boxes, all neatly packed and arranged. There was, however, space for no more than one human being at a time.

"I apologise, Major, but room is at a premium for our section. What is it that you need?"

"I'm interested in the vehicular movements of a Captain Joseph Krzak. He worked in this department, but went missing three years ago this month, during the war with Russia. I would like to know how often he had the use of an automobile, and how long he retained it each time. It may be that he had the permanent allocation of a motor-car."

Miskuski nodded and dove into the closet. He was aware not only of which cabinet to search, but which drawer to open. His forefinger hovered over the reports stored within, as if divining by some sensation beyond touch which papers would be required. Then he plunged his hand into the files and pulled out a thick folder.

"Here, sir: these are the vehicle requests made by everyone in the Second Bureau in the last four years. At least half deal with the period of the Russian war. Will that do?"

"Excellent, Corporal. Would you happen to have the petrol-purchase orders or requisitions for these vehicles?" asked Smith, flipping through the pages he had been given.

Miskuski pursed his lips, as if considering a challenge, and squatted before the same cabinet, opening a lower drawer this time. After a moment's search, he stood again, holding a sheaf of papers clipped together. Smith raised his eyebrows.

"This is most impressive," he commented. "I hope you won't be offended if I say that this is the best example of efficiency I've witnessed in Poland."

The NCO adjusted his spectacles and said, "Before the War, I attended a German-run school, sir."

"Ah, I see."

"These documents, Major, cannot, regrettably, be removed from the section without explicit permission," the Pole said, reciting a formula learned long before, appending it, less officiously, with, "but I can provide you with a desk at which to study them, if you wish."

"Corporal," Smith said, "you are a credit to the new Poland."

Smith sat upright in his chair, having just tied his shoelaces. It was early evening, but looked to be later, for the clouds that had gathered previously were now lowered upon Warsaw and, in the gloom, many of the city's electric lights had been turned on. Rain was falling in a desultory manner, and its scent wafted in through the hotel room's open windows. It was mixed, though, with the smells endemic to a large, modern town: the exhaust of internal combustion engines, the odour of wet macadam and rubber tires. In the Polish capital, these were accompanied by the olfactory remnants of an earlier age: horses and straw, and axle grease. Smith thought that a scientific study of the distinctions of one metropolis from another based solely on fragrances would be a unique and interesting one.

The traffic in the streets was heavy but would not remain so for long. This was the beginning of the domestic period of the average Warsaw resident's day, when he hurried home to enjoy the advantages it offered. This did not mean that company was restricted to family and close friends, as delightful as such society may have been. Smith himself was invited to the Rakowski house for what for

Under the Willows

him would be an early dinner. For the next few hours, Poles would be entertaining at their own tables and hearths, and the streets would be largely deserted. Then, traffic would burst forth again as the restaurants and cafés experienced their most profitable hours of trade.

"Your visit to the intelligence department's headquarters was worthwhile, sir?"

Odways examined the dinner coat that he held in his hands, his eyes critical. He used a brush to apply a few more strokes before holding the garment open for his employer.

"It was," confirmed Smith. "According to the travel logs provided to me by a most capable clerk, the trip north during which Captain Krzak disappeared in August of 1920 had been his fourth since May."

He slipped on the coat and stood before the tall, oval cheval glass next to the wardrobe. Again, the valet scrutinised the clothes.

"I went over the petrol records and was able to look into the Transport Section's paper-work. Krzak used some of their Vauxhall Prince Henrys."

"A motor-vehicle, I assume, sir?"

"No, actual royal scions used as pack-animals here in eastern Europe."

"Really, sir..."

"I'm sorry, Odways."

"That's quite all right, sir. It was a most amusing riposte."

Smith, settled into his black coat, glanced at his servant. The latter's countenance had not altered through the conversation.

"I can tell you found it very droll. Sometimes I wonder who makes the most sport with whom, Odways."

"Do you, sir?" The valet handed his master his filled cigarette case. Smith smiled.

"I estimate that Krzak burned approximately the correct amount of fuel to get him to and from the East Prussian frontier with little to spare, each time. One must bear in mind, however, that my skill at maths is not among my higher accomplishments."

"I am sure your calculations were accurate, sir. You will take an umbrella?"

Smith considered the rain descending beyond the windows.

"I'll hardly have time to get wet, going from door to taxi and from taxi to door. Besides, we didn't bring one to Poland."

Odways opened the wardrobe and produced a furled umbrella from behind the skirts of hanging coats and jackets.

"I purchased it this afternoon, sir. I was directed to a small shop on Marszalkow Street. It had as much stock and variety as Moss Brothers, sir, and at lower prices."

Inductions Dangerous

"Moss Brothers?" Smith was surprised that his employee would have been acquainted with purveyors of used merchandise.

"A gentleman's gentleman must be aware of the sources to fill all needs, sir, just in case," was Odways's unassailable defence.

Smith acknowledged the valet's correctness and was handed the umbrella as he may have been written orders from a superior officer.

"If Krzak had been working for the Bolsheviks, journeys to East Prussia would have made sense," he said. "Germany was neutral in the war between Poland and Russia, yet would have preferred a victory for the latter. If Poland had been overrun, it would have fallen to the Huns to save Europe from Bolshevism, and it would have demonstrated their need for an army larger than that permitted by the peace treaty."

With his hat, coat and umbrella, Smith felt that he was equipped for a minor battle, rather than an evening out.

"What about wireless, sir?" asked Odways.

"No. I think if I get lost, I'll simply consult a policeman," answered his employer.

"Yes sir. I referred to the Polish spy's means of contacting his masters."

"It would have been too risky. The Poles were quite advanced at intercepting transmissions, even three years ago." Smith paused at the door Odways was about to open. "If you have a moment, give some thought to meeting the Rakowskis' servants; there may be something to learn there."

"I have already pondered that possibility, sir," responded the valet. There were evidently other matters that he had pondered as well, for he continued, "Why would Captain Krzak betray his country, sir? Would it be as simple a motive as money? Blackmail, perhaps?"

"I don't know," admitted Smith. "Perhaps it was ideology. The Poles aren't immune to the lure of Bolshevism. The Russian secret police were founded — and are still led — by a Pole."

"But even if Captain Krzak could turn on his homeland, how could he do the same to Colonel Jenowski, sir?" Odways had a difficult time comprehending treachery. "You mentioned that they were friends, and fought in the Great War together."

"They did. Yet that was a different war, with different enemies, and different allies." Smith stepped across the threshold as his servant at last opened the door. "As always, your points are cogent. Don't wait up; I have a feeling that I won't return until very late — or very early…"

It was indeed very early the next day when Smith came back to his room at the Grande Europa. The night had been full, very full, of food and drink, talk and activity.

He had initially been invited to the Rakowskis' townhouse for dinner, a big meal that seemed to have been prepared for many more participants than just the hosts and their half-dozen guests. It was, in fact, not a large repast by Polish standards. The big meal of the day came about four o'clock, when Englishmen would be sitting down to tea. The lavish use of butter, cream and eggs made Smith's dinner seem expansive, and he was glad that he had starved himself since breakfast. Copious amounts of vodka accompanied the food; out of politeness, Smith consumed his share.

The party then moved to a fashionable café in Electors' Street, where numerous acquaintances were encountered amid much hand-shaking and kissing. Smith observed that Stanislas Rakowski seemed alternately confused and bored with the conversation, which revolved around art and culture, politics and Society. These were obviously not the man's preferred topics, though his wife enjoyed the discussions, full as they were of repartée; Smith was able to join in, even as the languages used swirled from French to English to German to Russian and back again, throughout the evening. At the café, more food was consumed, though talking, drinking and smoking predominated.

It was after eleven, when patrons of the theatre and opera began arriving in great numbers, that Marie Rakowska and her friends — most half a generation younger than her husband — insisted on going to a night-club. Rakowski was reluctant, but could deny his spouse nothing. Smith guessed that this latest peregrination would result in dancing; he hoped that such exercise would not react badly, even disastrously, upon his digestion. On the other hand, he thought that it might reduce the weight that he had undoubtedly gained so far this evening.

The Jutro was situated in Jasna Street, and was a reputable establishment, fit for ladies as much as for gentlemen. Indeed, it seemed to Smith quite jolly, though this sensation may have come from the still greater number of acquaintances the party acquired there. The Briton had in mind the unseasonal image of a snowball growing as it rolled downhill.

By this time, Stanislas Rakowski was feeling the effects of the evening. Smith, almost the same age, was in better physical shape, and so would regret the night's excesses only in the morning. His host nevertheless seemed determined to prove that he could endure as long as any of his wife's young companions. Marie spent several hours alternating between animated conversation and even more animated dancing, her partners being found among friends and strangers alike. Smith himself was instructed by her in the tango, a new dance from South America that he found rather daring.

"I'd like to thank you for an unforgettable time, Mrs Rakowska," he said, as he, Marie and several others eventually emerged from the undimmed lights of the Jutro. The orange glow of a summer dawn was slowly spreading over Warsaw, rays of the sun, itself yet invisible behind buildings, throwing shadows. Shallow puddles, residue of nocturnal rain, reflected the new day. It was cool in the open air.

"Thank *you*, Major," the lady replied, as the Englishman followed the local custom of kissing her hand. Marie looked remarkably fresh, her blonde hair just as delicately coiffed as it had been at eight o'clock the previous evening and, except for slight reinforcements from lipstick and powder puff, her beautiful face was unchanged.

"Good day to you, sir, and thank you."

Smith bid farewell to his host, but Rakowski merely rubbed his bleary eyes. He had trouble placing the departing gentleman. When reminded, he shook his head.

"Oh, yes, Smith... I thought you had gone already..."

Another member of the party, pulling apart his black tie, hailed a passing droshky, the horse-drawn cab's driver no doubt used to night clubs emptying at this time. Smith's fellow offered to share his ride with him.

"But we'd better pay extra for a little speed," the Pole suggested, with a grin: "I have to be in church in an hour."

So it was that Smith returned to the Grande Europe just as the rest of the hotel's patrons were rising — unless they were natives of the country, in which case Smith suspected they would still be out.

"Good morning, sir." Odways, already awake and fully engaged about his duties, greeted his employer at the door. "Tea, I think, sir, and a light breakfast: fruit and toast. But a bath first."

Smith nodded, and was bereft of overcoat, hat and umbrella, still furled, as well as his dinner coat, tie and shoes.

"As much as I enjoy tea, Odways, I must ask if you've ever considered coffee on such a morning."

"Oh, no, sir; tea on all occasions, but especially these. The difference between its effects and coffee's is the difference between being woken gently and being roused with a douche of cold water." The valet, as if to illustrate his point, ran the hot water in the tub in the neighbouring bathroom. Its relaxing steam soon penetrated the bedchamber.

Smith remarked, "Your opinion, as always, carries weight."

"Thank you, sir." Odways set out his master's pyjamas. "You should have time for a satisfactory nap before meeting General Szerbinski. Shall I wake you at ten o'clock, sir?"

"An excellent scheme," commented Smith, as he sank into the depths of his bath-water.

"There is no fortress quite like Warsaw Citadel, Major. None in the world."

The rain of the previous day and night had not been heavy. It had been more in the nature of a descending mist. It had, however, been steady and had eventually deposited as much precipitation as the strongest downpour. It left the following morning and afternoon fresh and clean, everything quite bright and clear.

The people of Warsaw were taking advantage of the clement weather. After church, many had climbed to the fortress that dominated the city from its eminence above the Vistula River. Men and women strolled the lawns within the ramparts, chatting and laughing, meeting friends, relaxing on the grass, slumbering in the shade, while their children ran and played. Zenon Szerbinski had brought his family with him, and they accompanied him as he walked with Smith.

"The Russians constructed it as a punishment, Major," the general continued, "a very practical punishment, following our attempt to throw off their rule in 1831."

Szerbinski moved slowly, to keep pace with his wife, with whose arm his own was linked. Five children orbited the couple, their distance in direct relation to their ages, and their discipline in reverse proportion. Their father resembled a contented middle class gentleman, dressed in a white summer suit that contrasted starkly with the black of his hair. He used his free hand to remove his hat to the many people whom he knew.

"The cost of the Citadel was borne by the Polish tax-payer, was it not?" Smith asked, as he surreptitiously eyed a passing beauty.

"That's right, Major." Szerbinski was surprised by the Briton's knowledge. "And the stones were hewn by Polish hands. That too was a punishment. After the fortress was completed, the Russians not only had a stronghold from which they could bombard any part of the city, not only a cantonment for their garrison, not only a prison for political offenders, but a reminder, seen by everyone in Warsaw, of their domination."

Smith was a romantic at heart, and a nineteenth century romantic at that; there was none stronger. He regretted the passing of that era's world in the Great War, and he sighed for the old Russia that had vanished. He was, however, not blind to the erstwhile empire's defects, some of them brutal and ruthless, characteristics which made their distillation in the modern Bolshevik easy to explain.

"Times have changed," Szerbinski said. The sentence was in tune with

Smith's thoughts, yet the cheerfulness with which it was uttered was unsympathetic to the Englishman's opinion of the past. A smile broadened the Pole's tiny moustache. "The Citadel still belongs to an army — the Polish Army — but is no longer a place of dread."

Proof of the general's statement was everywhere. Despite the great red stone walls, the looming casemates, the protected batteries from which cannon once bristled, all was now gaiety and good humour. The most martial aspect of the day was the band, composed of brightly uniformed soldiers. Even so, the airs they played were arrangements of sentimental ballads.

"But you did not wish to meet me to hear a discourse on my country's history, Major," Szerbinski pointed out, a self-deprecating smirk on his knowing visage. "How may I help you?"

Smith hesitated to voice his request. Strangers, however friendly, surrounded the gentlemen, and the general's own wife continued to accompany them. It was true that most in this park-like setting were unlikely to overhear enough of what was said for it to make sense. It was true as well that Mrs Szerbinska's attention seemed fixed upon her offspring; at this moment in particular upon her youngest boy, whom she was chastising for striking her youngest girl. The general barked a short laugh.

"Come, Major, you needn't worry. Mrs Szerbinska has had the opportunity to be privy to many more important secrets than that for which you are in Poland. You may speak within her hearing."

The general's claim did not comfort Smith, who had an intelligence officer's appreciation of discretion. But he could hardly order the lady to be gone. He did, however, speak lowly.

"I was hoping, sir, that you could elaborate on something that you mentioned during our initial interview. You told me that Colonel Jenowski and Captain Krzak were friends."

"Oh, yes, best friends." Szerbinski paused to smile at one of his sons who, with a boy of his age, was gambolling about the grass with all the energy of childhood. "They were officers in the same regiment of the Austrian Army — the 20th, I believe — and became close, despite the discrepancy in their backgrounds."

Smith nodded. He had thought that the two Poles' surnames indicated different class origins.

"Jenowski's was a noble house," Szerbinski explained, "while Krzak's family was more humble. But they were friends enough for Jenowski to make Krzak the principal beneficiary in his will."

"Indeed?" Smith waited to continue until Szerbinski and his spouse finished greeting some of their countrymen. "I thought the estate at Proskiwicz went to a cousin, while the colonel's personal effects went to his widow."

"You are quite right, Major. Proskiwicz was bound to go to the nearest male relation. As the colonel had no children, and his brother was missing — eventually declared dead by the courts in '21 — the estate went to a cousin, Paul." Szerbinski smiled lovingly as he contemplated his sons and daughters. "There is nothing more wonderful than children. Do you agree?"

"I do, sir." The brevity of Smith's concurrence was not a measure of it. He nonetheless moved back to the former subject. "Colonel Jenowski's personal belongings...?"

"Oh, the will that left everything to Krzak was superseded when Jenowski married, during the War."

The crowd in the Citadel grounds was well-attired, as may have been expected of those who had come straight from church. Their manners, their behaviour, the very practice of strolling about to meet acquaintances or make new friends, seemed to belong to an earlier decade, or another century. They were reminiscent of Victorian Londoners walking through St James's Park, or of Parisians in the Belle Époque, taking the air in the Bois de Boulogne. The sensation was enhanced by the number of army officers in dress uniform, a sight not witnessed in England these days, except on special occasions. The brightest, least practical uniforms always looked most resplendent. The Polish officers added colour to the scene, and old-fashioned dash.

"There is one other thing, General," Smith said.

"What is that, Major?"

Szerbinski was a patient and helpful man, perhaps mindful that his questioner was in Warsaw at his request. Even so, Smith did not wish to occupy more of the Pole's leisure time.

"When we first spoke, you expressed doubt about the existence of a..." Smith glanced at the other's spouse, who was still engrossed by her brood "...of a Bolshevik agent on the General Staff. Why?" He lowered his voice still further. "Was it because of the deciphered wireless traffic you mentioned?"

Szerbinski peered at Smith sidelong, his mouth turned in a smirk.

"I will have to tell Sanction how sharp his man is. Yes, you are right. It was during the early part of our fight with Russia that a team under a Lieutenant Grzyna broke the enemy's principal code. It provided us with excellent intelligence for more than a year."

"Something it would not have done with a Bolshevik agent on the staff," reasoned Smith. "He would surely have alerted his masters to the fact that their code was worthless. The Russians should have quit using it, if they had had an agent in place." Szerbinski nodded, but the Briton continued. "The information you received in this manner was genuine...?"

The general chuckled and answered, "It was what made our final offensive successful, Major. It would have been too high a price for the Bolsheviks to pay to keep a spy hidden."

All of this made sense to Smith. He suspected, though, that such arguments would not have sufficed to dampen the ardour of those determined to find a Russian agent, whether he existed or not. He expressed this belief to Szerbinski, who grinned, bittersweetly.

"We Poles are an emotional people, Major," he stated, ceasing his wanderings at last, while his family moved on. "We are heavily influenced by the French but out-shine them in our romanticism, our sentimentality." The smile broadened, and became ironic. "That was why I was hoping a foreigner would end this spy-hunt, one way or another."

"I'm not done yet, General." Smith gave a smile of his own. "Thank you for your time today, sir. I hope I didn't take you away from your family for too long."

Szerbinski laughed, joyfully this time, and turned to view his wife and children, now approaching.

"No one can take me away from my family for long, Major."

The remainder of Sunday Smith spent combining work and leisure, though in a relaxed fashion. He toured the city, from the Opera House to the Jewish Quarter, from the cathedral at the centre to the aristocratic villas in the suburbs. Even as he observed the sights and learned more about this little metropolis between the east and the west, he reviewed his assignment so far. When he returned to the Grande Europa, he found his valet gone. Odways too was about in the city and, like his employer, was combining his roles of tourist and secret operator.

It was due to the valet's social skills and his affinity for other servants, no matter where they were found, that he was able to direct Smith to Senators' Street the next morning, specifically to a popular dress-maker's shop. There, he was told, Marie Rakowska would be finishing a fitting about ten o'clock.

"Good morning, madam! This is a pleasant surprise, meeting you here." Smith tipped his hat to the beautiful woman as he encountered her stepping in to the street. The blank look in her blue eyes was not unexpected. "It gives me another opportunity to thank you for Saturday night."

Marie's small mouth brightened in a smile, one of relief as well as cheerfulness, as she now placed the gentleman.

"It was very good of you to come, Major. I think my husband tires of seeing the same faces. He appreciated your presence."

Smith suspected that Stanislas Rakowski would not be able to recollect the

Under the Willows

Briton's participation in the evening's activities. Few ever remembered him.

"I hope that my presence was enjoyable to both of you," he said.

"It was, I assure you," insisted Marie, laughing. "You are an excellent dancer, and a quick study with the tango."

Smith thought that the minute amount of rouge that the woman wore had not disguised the brief blush that flushed her cheeks. He adjusted his position as the crowds on the pavements flowed around him.

"It's fortunate meeting you here, Mrs Rakowska. I wanted to speak to you further, if you have a few minutes. Will you join me for some refreshments?"

The day was as warm as the previous, though dryer. The sky was blue and white, with none of the clouds hinting at greyness to spoil the morning, or even the afternoon. The slightest of breezes kept the air from becoming too hot, even if the temperature was so inclined. Therefore, Marie chose an outside table at a café, and suggested coffee and pastries, to which Smith readily agreed. Referring to where they had just met, he commented upon the taste much of Warsaw had in its attire.

"If you are seeking a good gentlemen's tailor, Major, you could not do better than Lopatka's, just down the street," the lady said, as she took a chair. Even such an action was deliberate and poised. "It is a superb shop, to which I have at last persuaded my husband to go."

"That is indeed a recommendation, madam, but, alas, my heart belongs to a small establishment in Savile Row." Smith bit into the pastry that the waiter had brought. It had a slight smoky flavour that the Briton had not tasted before.

"That too is a recommendation," Marie said, her eyes quickly evaluating Smith's seated form, opposite hers, as though viewing it for the first time.

"I was, in fact, seeking a ladies' dress-maker," lied Smith. "That's why I was outside yours, considering it. I have a gift to bring back to London, when I complete my work here."

Marie licked the inside edge of her lower lip while she seemed to be in thought. It was an innocent gesture which Smith found very provocative.

"Your work on the official history, you mean…" the woman said, simply.

Smith inclined his head. Marie Rakowska struck him as an intelligent individual and, though perhaps fooled initially by his 'cover', may have become dubious of it since.

"No, not really," he confessed, after drinking some more coffee. He would have preferred tea at this time of day but, when on the Continent, he refrained from his habitual beverage, unless Odways prepared it. Europeans, he found, did not know how to produce a good cup of tea in the English style, any more than the English could reach the continental standard in coffee. "In truth, I'm looking into other matters."

Inductions Dangerous

"The Russian agent in the Polish Army," said Marie. It was not a question. Smith raised an eyebrow and the young woman smiled at him. "That rumour has circulated for years, Major, and is stronger than ever now. It seems somehow to involve my second husband; you wanted to examine his personal papers, and came with a letter of introduction from the highest general in the land. The right conclusion did not take long to draw."

Smith reclined in his chair. The surrounding tables were filled. Much of Warsaw had it in mind to enjoy the summer weather, and many of the city's residents seemed to have chosen to enjoy it at this café. Smith was as reluctant to discuss a sensitive matter here as he had been the day before at the Citadel. Nonetheless, he appeared to have been given no option.

"You're correct, madam. Correct about my reason for being in Poland, and correct about your late husband's association with the mystery. Much seems to centre upon his untimely demise."

"Yes, I thought it might…"

"Did he have any enemies?"

"Aside from the entire population of Russia?" Marie laughed, and Smith was relieved that the question had not upset her. But her mirth diminished, and she provided a serious answer. "No one person would have wanted to kill Jan, Major. I can suspect no Pole, which is what I think you meant. Poles fought each other during the Great War, it's true; they were in opposing armies. Jan was an Austrian officer, General Szerbinski served the tsar. It made no difference afterward."

Marie at last bit into a pastry, and chewed it carefully, as if she had planned each movement. After applying a napkin to her pink lips, she continued speaking.

"The Poles can believe very passionately about some things; art, for instance, and politics, certainly. But Jan was a thorough soldier, completely apolitical. I can't think of anyone who would want to kill him, and I've been asked before, so this isn't the first time I've tried."

"What do you know of the present count, the colonel's cousin?"

"Paul?" Marie was surprised by the new topic. She licked the inside of her lip again. "Very little. Do you think he was the Bolshevik spy? He couldn't have been. He was never in the army — any army."

Smith made a non-committal gesture.

"Your late husband's death was the third of someone who was investigating a possible traitor. The first two could have been caused directly by war."

"So if Jan's death had nothing to do with his duties, it could take your inquiries down a completely different path." Marie nodded. "Would Paul have murdered Jan? For the estate?"

Under the Willows

"Six hundred thousand acres could be quite a motive."

"Yes..." Marie was dubious. "There was Karel, Jan's brother. He was missing in Russia, yet Jan was very hopeful of his return some day. Paul would have been giving Proskiwicz to Karel by killing Jan."

"Karel was declared dead the next year. Paul must have done that."

"You have a devious mind, Major!" exclaimed Marie with a laugh. "But Paul couldn't have murdered Jan. He was in Paris that whole week, negotiating another loan on behalf of the government. He was, and is, a member of parliament; his whereabouts are never secret." Marie lowered her eyes. "What about another suspect? What about me?"

"You, madam?" Smith may have sounded surprised, even shocked, but the possibility that Jan Jenowski had been shot by his own wife had already occurred to the Englishman. He did, as Marie had described, have a devious mind. He smiled. "You *were* bequeathed all of your husband's personal belongings, everything that was not bound to his cousin."

"Exactly." The lady attempted to look devious herself, but on this bright, summer morning, with the sunshine on her lovely features, she failed. "Unfortunately for your—" She interrupted herself with a laugh. "Unfortunately for *my* theory, almost everything Jan left me, jewellery, clothes, paintings, was either looted or destroyed during the wars. I was able to save some photographs, but was left penniless."

Smith had suspected that something of the sort had happened.

"Then there's the fact that I loved Jan very much..." Marie added, as she drank some coffee. Smith used the statement to pose a question that had been on his mind.

"How long have you and Mr Rakowski been married?"

Marie set down her cup and, initially, kept her eyes on the square cloth that covered most of the round tabletop. She gathered her nerve and returned the Briton's gaze. "Just over two years. I married Stanislas ten months after Jan died." Marie paused. Smith remained silent, and the woman interpreted the reaction as a remark. "I know. I was not long in mourning, was I?" The lady's expression was one of mixed emotions. "Stanislas fell in love with me very quickly. For my part, Major, I look to the security that he provides my children. He treats them as if they were his own, and they like him."

"A parent must always think of her children first," commented Smith, "just as an army officer must think of his men before himself." Marie stared at him as though he were a clairvoyant who had startled her with his accuracy.

"But Stanislas is good to me, too. There is nothing that he wouldn't do for me. It's lucky for him that I'm modest in my demands." The woman covered her mouth as she laughed. "A yearly holiday at the seaside is my greatest, I think.

Inductions Dangerous

He takes a cottage on the beach in Latvia, in June or July. For those weeks, I practically live in the water."

Smith remembered the picture of Marie in swimming kit, seen on the piano in the Rakowski townhouse. He mentioned the photograph.

"My family call me a mermaid," said Marie, through her mirth. "I can dive deeper and hold my breath longer than any one I know. Even the children can't keep up."

"Which do you prefer, swimming or dancing?" Smith inquired, in the lighter spirit into which the conversation had slipped. He had finished his pastry and longed for some tea. He believed that that beverage would have complimented the food better than the dark flavour of coffee.

"Oh, my fondness for dancing was apparent Saturday night, was it?" Marie regarded her companion coyly, from under the narrow brim of her hat. "I do enjoy it very much. It's a pity that Stanislas can't last long on the floor. You, though, matched me step for step, Major, and my friends will tell you that not many can."

"Perhaps we can match steps again," suggested Smith. Upon the lady's affirmation that she would like the opportunity, he told her, "I have been invited to a number of events, balls and the like, perhaps—"

"It would hardly do for me to attend such functions without my husband, but with a stranger instead," Marie countered, before slipping the last morsel of her pastry between her lips. Smith could have told her that it was unlikely anyone would have noticed him in her company, or, if they had, remembered him afterward. But Marie was cogitating while she chewed. "There is, though, a discreet little dancing off Ujazdow Avenue. I think I can be free tomorrow evening…"

"A 'dancing'?" repeated Smith.

"The Poles have made the verb a noun, Major. It's essentially a night club solely for dancing. Some are good, some terrible. This one is both entertaining and respectable, though you needn't wear a dinner jacket. Put on your most comfortable shoes; an evening there can be exhausting."

"I look forward to exhausting myself in order to bring you pleasure, Mrs Rakowska," responded Smith. Marie blushed.

"No, I don't think a pistol will be necessary."

Smith glanced at his valet, wondering if the question he had just heard had been made in jest. Though he rarely utilised it, the servant had an arid sense of humour. But the recommendation that his employer arm himself to attend the 'dancing' the following evening had not been a joke.

"It's not a criminal environment, Odways. I don't believe that Mrs

Under the Willows

Rakowska would patronise such a place."

"No sir." Odways did not sound convinced. He set a cup of tea next to Smith's chair. "The idea that you may attend an evening event in a lounge suit denotes a certain environment."

Smith admitted to himself that he could not think of an instance in which he had appeared in public, after six o'clock, clothed so inappropriately. It would feel most abnormal, even improper.

Odways placed a small dish of biscuits beside the tea on its saucer. Smith opened a book, one of several that he had brought with him to Poland. He needed to think about his assignment, what he had learned and what he needed to learn. He did this best by relaxing his brain, and by allowing part of it to concentrate on something undemanding.

"There is still logic to the hypothesis that Captain Krzak was a Bolshevik agent," he said, a few minutes later. Odways was passing through the bedroom with some dirty linen for the hotel's laundry. He stopped.

"Yes sir?"

"Three years ago, during their war with Russia, the Poles began concentrating their forces for an offensive; that was on the sixth of August. If Krzak had been working for the enemy, it would make sense that he would attempt to deliver information about the impending attack, driving to meet his controller stationed in East Prussia before it began. He was, however, killed en route."

Odways nodded slowly, saying, "That is a plausible theory, sir, though one must question Captain Krzak's motive in betraying his country. Nor does the theory account for the shooting of Colonel Jenowski. Who killed that gentleman — and why? — if Captain Krzak was dead? Or is the colonel's demise unrelated to the possible Russian agent?"

"Your refusal to adhere to the stereotype of the slow-witted servant can sometimes be annoying, Odways." Smith sighed. "But you are quite correct: there are too many questions left unanswered by my theory."

"I am sure you will find the solutions you seek, sir," the valet informed his employer optimistically, as he returned to his duties. "General Sanction obviously felt the same, sir, otherwise he would not have despatched you to Poland."

Smith lowered his gaze to his book once more, muttering, "I feel his cyclopean eye following my every move…"

Czeslaw Madej worked from a suite of rooms in Ossolinskich Street, next to the headquarters of the Polish state travel authority. His offices, on the first floor of the building, looked little different than those of a solicitor in England

— or France, Austria or Spain, for that matter. There was the usual anteroom, occupied by a secretary, along with several comfortable chairs in which clients could wait. Beyond were the lawyer's own chambers, where he sat behind a heavy desk, the walls around him lined with shelf after shelf of uniformly-bound books, the published laws of his country.

Madej himself was unprepossessing and, except for the peculiarly national cut of his clothes, looked as nondescript as his surroundings. He was past middle age but not yet elderly, bald, short-sighted and large; competent, controlled and confident that he could not be surprised or startled. His smile was genuine but non-committal.

"I hope you do not mind me confirming your bona fides, Major," the solicitor said, as he replaced the handset of his telephone. It had been established that his English was inferior, so the conversation was conducted in German. "It is not every day that I am visited by a foreigner distinguished by introductions from cabinet ministers." He returned several sheets of folded paper to his guest, who was seated in front of the desk.

"Not at all, Mr Madej," replied Smith. "I would have been discouraged if you had not made some sort of verification."

Madej nodded, pleased, and adjusted his unflattering spectacles.

"You are interested in the will of the late Colonel Count Jan Jenowski, yes?" He lowered his head, and buried his chin in a broader, fleshier imitation.

"I am," Smith replied, "though in general the document is known to me. He bequeathed everything that he could to his wife, now Mrs Rakowska."

"True," declared Madej, as if being tested. He relaxed and elaborated. "The real estate passed to Paul Jenowski, as provided by a settlement of many years' standing; an agreement rather like your English entail, by which property goes automatically to the nearest male relative. The count's personal property, including jewellery of a not inconsiderable value, was to go to his wife, as you say. I understand," he appended sadly, "that it was all lost. The wars, you know…"

"This will was not the colonel's first, is that right?" Smith prompted.

"True," stated the lawyer once more. He explained further. "It was, however, the first that I drew up for him. It superseded an earlier, which had precisely the same provisions, made upon Count Jan's marriage. He felt that, as a document devised in the old Austrian Empire, it might have lost its validity." Madej frowned, suggesting a slight difference of opinion with his client. He pushed up his spectacles. "*That* will succeeded a still earlier one."

"A will that left everything to Josef Krzak."

"True again."

"Are you aware of any unusual characteristics in any of the documents, Mr

Madej?" Smith expected the Pole to continue in his exclamatory vein, and was rather disappointed when he did not cry 'false!'

"Oh, no, no," Madej responded, pushing his lips forward and shaking his round head. "In the will that I drew up for him, the count left small bequests to servants and charities; generous but not extraordinary." His eyebrows rose, taking his lenses with them, and he had to settle the spectacles once more before his eyes.

"Count Jan did instruct me, in the event of his death, to forward to his cousin a letter containing a great deal of information about the management of Proskiwicz." Madej spread his hands, as if to deny responsibility for so unorthodox an undertaking. "It in no way constituted a part of the will."

Smith recalled the letter to Paul Jenowski that he had discovered among the colonel's correspondence the previous week.

"You disapproved of this letter?"

"True, Major. I believed that Count Jan's heir might have found such a list of detailed instructions…presumptuous. I thought that Count Paul would wish to conduct his affairs in his own way. But," the lawyer sighed, "Count Jan thought it best for the estate. However…"

Smith waited, allowing Madej the effect of his dramatic pause.

"…Some time later, I believe it was in May — May of 1920, of course — Count Jan reversed his decision, and took the letter from my keeping."

"Why did he do that?"

"He told me plainly that he had come to agree with my point of view." The satisfaction of vindication could not be kept from the lawyer's voice, even after more than three years. "He decided that his heir should have the freedom of his inheritance without a predecessor's advice."

Though Smith could comprehend such an attitude, he could not help thinking that some assistance from those with experience may have been beneficial in the management of a property so vast as Proskiwicz.

"At the same time, no aspects of the will were changed?" he wanted to know.

"The will remained the same," Madej assured his visitor.

Smith appeared drifting in thought for a moment, then nodded and, standing, thanked his host.

"I've been of some help to you, Major?" The solicitor, rising as well, spoke in tones of curiosity, even concern, disguised with mild detachment. Madej may have been hoping that his aid would be brought to the notice of Smith's sponsors. The Briton assured him that he had been of great assistance. Satisfied, the Pole walked with his guest to the office door.

"It was a terrible tragedy, the count's death," he told Smith. "A mystery, too, almost obscured by the war, which was at its most critical stage then, I recall. Yet, in the midst of it...a death so personal... Ah, well... Good day, Major. Please let me know if I can be of further help to you at any time."

Smith loved the countryside. That of England held his affection first and foremost, but he revelled in fields and hedgerows, woods and marshes wherever he found them. He sometimes felt that, for himself, the greatest division in the world was not into east and west or rich and poor or rulers and ruled, but into urban and rural. He enjoyed the town and what it had to offer, but he could live without it; he believed that he could not survive without the countryside.

The part of Poland through which he was driving was pretty. The agricultural landscape's colours seemed more varied here than in Britain; reds, yellows and pinks, blues and purples, made the region appear a kingdom from a children's storybook, and worth the time to explore it. Alas, Smith's time was not his own.

Peasants were in the midst of their harvesting. Their machinery was no more complicated than horse-drawn engines though, more often than not, humans of both genders provided the motive power on the farms. Poland was slowly recovering from years of warfare. Road-mending gangs were busy, and Smith piloted his borrowed automobile over more than one new bridge. Rubble from destroyed cottages was piled up on the highway's verge, sometimes next to the neater stacks of material for the demolished structures' replacements. But regardless of wars and their effects, the lives of the peasants continued, and revolved around their crops in the fields.

The people of this province south of Warsaw were more advanced than their countrymen of the Pripet Marshes. As usual, the quantity of local food — or the lack of it — determined the peasants' status, their wealth and their health, their education, their society, even their humour. Smith did not pass one man among his grain who did not rest on his scythe for a moment and wave at the motor-car and its occupant.

Smith's destination was not difficult for him to find. The lofty wireless tower was a monolith, spare and grey, stripped of its skin to reveal the skeleton beneath. On a low hill, it rose above the surrounding flatness, and was visible for a great distance. It seemed almost to point to the house at its base. This building resembled nothing so much as a large and sprawling version of the farmsteads Smith had been passing all afternoon. Its tiled roof and whitewashed walls were, however, in excellent repair, not dependent upon a peasant's income for maintenance; indeed, the wooden shutters, secured against the exterior, were newly painted. In any case, the meshed spike that tried to touch the sky beside the cottage indicated that an unusual crop was being harvested here.

No fence or wall enclosed this military establishment, and only a simple turnpike, manned by a couple of sentries, barred Smith's vehicle from driving up to the house's front door. As it was, the Briton's credentials were not demanded even at this modest gate, and he was ushered through with a polite tip of the cap from each of the amicable guards.

A young soldier stood at his ease near a corner of the rambling cottage, but started as he saw Smith's motor-car approaching. He threw down the cigarette he had been smoking, as if the force of the riddance determined how little it had been seen, straightened his cap and buttoned his collar. By the time the Englishman had halted his vehicle in the adjacent dirt lot, next to the other automobiles, the Pole was rigid at attention, saluting as the visitor walked toward him.

"Lieutenant Grzyna?"

Smith's query drew a response in the native tongue. Polish was close enough to Russian for Smith to think that he understood, and distinct enough to know that he did not. He smiled, apologised and spoke again, initially in French, then in German.

"Captain Grzyna is inside, sir, at his luncheon." The statement conveyed a kind of warning.

"Stand easy, Private." Smith opened his cigarette case for the soldier. "I caused you to lose yours. Take two, one for later."

The Pole looked as though he suspected a trap, but cautiously accepted the gift, even permitting himself a friendly nod, as he slipped the cigarettes into the breast pocket of his tunic.

The front door of the house was shut but unlocked, and Smith entered without invitation. The room immediately within, once the single chamber of the original farmhouse, was now an anteroom, where a couple of military clerks worked at papers on their tables; at a third, an officer spoke on a telephone.

"Captain Grzyna?" Smith said. "I believe that I am expected," he added in German, mentioning his own name.

Upon learning that the newcomer was a major, all three of the room's occupants rose sharply to their feet. The duty officer, a lieutenant no older than the private outside, excused himself and retreated behind a closed door. He returned a moment later.

"Please go in, Major."

Captain Grzyna seemed hardly of an age to hold his rank, though knowledge and experience could accumulate rapidly under some conditions. Smith had, after all, recently been through a war in which battalion commanders were in their twenties and brigadiers in their thirties. Grzyna stood behind a table, his curly red hair and freckles those of an adolescent; the unimpressive attempt to

Inductions Dangerous

grow a moustache had not added many years.
"Welcome, Major," he said, shaking the hand that Smith extended. "I received word that you would come, but was unsure of the time. Have you eaten?" He gestured to the table-top before him, where a lean meal had been served. "Allow me to offer you something."

Grzyna spoke German with a Russian accent, but switched to Polish to bellow through a half-closed door. A harried-looking orderly burst into the room carrying a chair for the guest and, despite the fact that he had partially anticipated his officer's wishes, he was still sent away with what sounded to be a hard rebuke. He returned quickly with another set of dishes and utensils, as well as a bottle of champagne, to match that supplied to Grzyna. Every item on the table was duplicated for Smith.

"I want to ask you some questions, Captain," the Briton said, sitting opposite his host. He was rather glad of something wet with which to cut the dust of the road he had travelled, but was less keen on the boiled chicken that had been produced. He did not, however, wish to offend Grzyna, especially now that everything had been laid out.

"I will do what I can to help you, Major, but..." the Pole's mouth twisted wryly "...are you sure it is me you wish to speak to? I am only the officer in charge of this interception station."

The Polish Army's section dealing in signals intelligence was a leader in its field. The country's military command had been quick to recognise the advantages of reading their enemies' wireless traffic. But such efforts would have been pointless if the intercepted messages had remained encoded and incomprehensible. Thus, Poland's cryptanalysis capabilities were also impressive.

"You are the man who broke the Russians' code back in February of 1920?" The fowl Smith had been served was a tough old bird, and the wine indifferent.

"I and my team, yes."

"Can you recall who was made aware of your success when you deciphered the Bolshevik messages?" Smith wondered if discretion would, after all, prevent Grzyna from telling him all he knew; however, security was less important in the Polish Army than some other matters.

"I remember that, yes," replied the captain, chewing a piece of meat that he had hewn from his chicken. "Besides my team, there were three officers who knew of our success: the commander-in-chief, the chief of the General Staff, and the head of the Second Bureau."

"The last being Colonel Jenowski."

Grzyna rolled his eyes upward in recollection, then nodded, saying, "Yes, that's correct." He tasted some of the champagne, then barked for his servant again.

"Did Captain Krzak know?" asked Smith. "As the head of Counterintelligence within Colonel Jenowski's department, much of what would have been learned from intercepted and de-coded messages would have fallen into his jurisdiction."

Grzyna shook his head, and asserted that only the trio whom he had named had been told of the code's breaking. The orderly returned then, to receive a stern admonition. Smith wondered if the harshness on the captain's part came from his personality, or was a remnant of his previous military tradition: Grzyna's Russian accent marked him as an erstwhile member of the tsar's army. Smith half-expected his host to support his complaints to his man by lashing out with a knout. In any case, the servant hurried back a moment later with a third bottle of wine and a pair of clean glasses. These were filled, and all trace of the inferior beverage removed.

"I apologise for that previous bottle, Major. I bought several dozen cases at auction a month ago," the captain said. "The price was very good, but the merchandise's quality sporadic."

Smith denied the need for any regret. The Pole stood and made a small bow. Sitting again, he resumed his tale.

"The fact that the code was broken was kept a close secret," he remarked. "When traffic was intercepted, it was transcribed and brought to my unit. Our 'translations' of the material were then sent for distribution to Colonel Jenowski who presented them as coming from agents, rather than signals. This process continued after the second code was broken."

Smith sipped some of the new champagne. It was a considerable improvement over its predecessor. The action helped the Briton maintain a blank expression in the wake of surprise. There had been no previous mention to Smith of a second code.

"This is very good," he commented blandly, holding up his glass. "Yes, the second code... I was wondering about that. When was it de-ciphered?"

"That would have been...late July," answered Grzyna, cutting into the fibrous meat before him. He was more adept at the operation than Smith; the skill may have come with practice. "The Russians had started using a new code only a few days before. It gave us a bit of a fright but was, after all, quite simple, and easy to read. My theory is that it was a hasty concoction. They do not seem to have spent much time devising it. It has since been replaced in its turn, but that didn't occur for several months."

"Late July..." repeated Smith, musing. "Would that have been before or after Captain Krzak had been appointed to head Counterintelligence?"

"You are in luck there, Major," Grzyna said, grinning a little as he hacked off another piece of poultry. "I was still working in Warsaw then, of course, and I remember meeting Krzak in the corridor near his office. He introduced himself and I explained what it was I did. It was the next day that I learned about the new code being used."

"And Colonel Jenowski," Smith probed, casually, "what did he think of the new code?" The struggle against the boiled chicken in the dish before him proved too much, at least for the reward obtained. He placed his knife and fork over the fowl's remains.

"He instructed me to tell no one about it, sir, not even General Szerbinski. I thought that odd at the time, but then, the colonel was always worried about security more than most."

"What of the general?"

"He learned of the second code soon after the colonel's death, I think." Grzyna surveyed the debris of the luncheon. "Would you like some more chicken, Major?"

Still feeling the effects of having chewed, at great length, his first course, there were few things that Smith wanted less than its repetition.

"Thank you, Captain. That would be most enjoyable."

Then again, a field operator of the Secret Service had, by necessity, periodically to act like a diplomatist.

That evening, Smith sat in his hotel room smoking a cigarette. The lights were on and the windows' curtains drawn. Below, the streets of Warsaw were busy. It was the interlude between two acts in the city's vigorous night-life.

What he had theorised to Odways, Smith reasoned, remained true. Krzak could have been the Russian agent on the Polish Army's General Staff. He had been aware, in early August, of his country's impending offensive, and could have attempted to warn the Bolsheviks, only to be killed before he fulfilled that mission. It made sense.

Smith sighed, and dropped cinders from his cigarette into an ashtray. He was seated in an easy chair, absently watching the line of light beneath the bathroom door. His theory *had* made sense, he corrected mentally.

Krzak had not been among those informed that Grzyna's cryptanalysis team had broken the Russian codes; Jenowski had been his friend, but it was not likely that he had transgressed his own rule, and told him of the development. Yet if the Bolsheviks' agent in the Polish high command had not informed his masters that their initial code had been rendered obsolete, why did the Russians change it? And change it so swiftly that the replacement was no more than makeshift? Furthermore, if the Russians *had* been so informed, why had they not been informed when the second code was broken? Surely the same agent responsible for alerting the Russians as to the worthlessness of the first code would have done the same with the second. Krzak's sudden death would have accounted for that failure in communication — if he had had knowledge of the code's de-ciphering in the first place.

Smith drew on his cigarette.

The door to the bathroom opened and Marie Rakowska stepped out. She looked just as she had when Smith had met her three hours before. Her make-up, just a touch upon her lips and cheeks, had been re-applied; her hair had been brushed, every fine strand in place; her clothes were smooth and unrumpled.

"Well?" she asked, almost nervously.

"Very elegant," responded Smith, standing. "You may've just arrived from the opera."

"I hope so. It's where I told Stanislas I'd be. It's good that he has no interest in opera himself, and never questions me about it. He'll only want to know if I enjoyed myself."

"And what will you say?" Smith took the woman in his arms.

"If I can keep from turning red, I will tell him the truth. That I had a wonderful time." She kissed the Englishman, but then pulled back. "But I must be careful. This gown wasn't made to be worn twice in the same night."

Smith relented, offering her a cigarette, lighting it from his own.

"I have two questions for you, Marie," he said, setting the woman in a chair, then taking the one next to it. "Firstly, have you ever heard of anyone called 'Mouche'? A pet-name…"

Marie smiled at the sound of the word, but shook her head after a moment's thought.

"No… Where did that come from?"

"It may be nothing. This next question is more serious, and feel free to tell me to mind my own business if it suits you." The caution put puzzlement on the lady's face, along with curiosity. "Was there any expectation on Jan's part three years ago that you and he would be having a child?"

Marie raised her eyebrows, and surprise swept all other emotions from her features. But she was neither insulted nor hurt by the personal nature of the query.

"No," she insisted, "none at all."

"Nothing in May of 1920?" Smith pressed.

"Nothing ever." Marie smiled, sweetly, sadly. "When my last child was born, there were complications. He survived — thrived, thank God — but my capacity for more children did not." She leaned forward when she saw regret on Smith's countenance. "It's all right, Linus. I'm not sensitive about it. It's a private matter, but I think I can trust you not to spread stories." She glanced over her shoulder to the unmade bed against the far wall. "I hope I can…" she murmured.

"Did Jan know?" said Smith.

"Oh, yes. With the pride he took in his family, I felt that I had to be honest about it, even before he asked to marry me." Marie's eyes half-closed with recollections of her late husband. "He put the hopes of his dynasty in his brother, instead. Later, he was realistic about Karel's fate in Russia, and reconciled himself to his cousin inheriting the estate, and continuing the line." She inhaled from her cigarette, then licked the inside of her lower lip. "Do you have any more questions?"

"As a matter of fact, yes. Can you get away from Warsaw for a couple of days?"

Smith stood at the end of the quay near the Forester's Lodge at Proskiwicz. Night had begun to fall, and as the twilight faded, purple clouds gathered in the east. Now and then, a low rumbling could be heard, and Smith likened it, with accuracy if not originality, to artillery.

He was, however, unconcerned with the sky, or with the weather in general, except how it affected the lake that stretched out before him. Its waters were chilly now, and forbidding in the increasing darkness. It was already difficult to see the far shore, where Colonel Jenowski's body had been found, three years before.

Smith drew in smoke from his cigarette, and turned. The windows of the Lodge's ground floor glowed warmly, and silhouetted the man approaching from that direction. Smith swore under his breath.

"Ah, it is you, Major…"

Antosik sounded relieved as he walked up to the Englishman. He held his right arm stiffly; he, like Smith, had ridden to the Lodge and, as it had previously, the effect had taken a toll on the steward.

"Yes, I wanted to consult Colonel Jenowski's papers once more. I couldn't find you to ask permission, so I hoped that my previous admission still held good."

"Of course," the Pole said. "I noticed smoke coming from the woods…" He indicated the Lodge's chimney, just visible in the deepening sky, though its exhaust could no longer be viewed. "I was not sure who was here. There used to be transients, you see, people displaced by the wars…"

"I understand," said Smith, his attention diverted with difficulty from the lake. "I'm sorry I made you ride all this way."

"Not at all." Antosik sounded unconcerned, though he must not have been relishing the return ride to the ruins of the big house. "I still inspect the property, you see."

A splash, very near the quay, as if something had abruptly broken the surface of the water, startled the Pole.

"Are you alone, Major? I saw two horses in the Lodge stables…"

"My valet accompanied me." Smith offered Antosik a cigarette. "He started a fire in the sitting room of the Lodge, and that was probably the smoke you observed. It's not quite September, but the woods can be cool at night."

"Very true, Major." The steward nodded, satisfied, having found nothing out of order. "I will be on my way, then. If you need anything, please ask."

Antosik seemed to take an abnormally long time to disappear from sight, but at last Smith saw the burning end of his cigarette turn the corner of the house and vanish. The Briton immediately crushed his own cigarette under his shoe and knelt on the stones that made the quay.

"Good Lord, Marie, give me your hand," he whispered sharply. The dark, slender form that had been clinging to the side of the quay for the past minute raised an arm trembling so badly that it rained drops back into the water. Smith effortlessly pulled the woman up and wrapped his coat around her naked form. "I'm sorry. I had no idea Antosik would materialise."

"It-t d-d-doesn't m-matter," Marie stuttered, her words barely comprehensible through shaking teeth. "I f-f-found it…" Her voice reflected both triumph and tragedy as her hand pressed a pistol into Smith's open palm. It was a Steyr nine millimetre, the sort of weapon that had been used as a personal sidearm by officers of the Austrian Army during the Great War.

Smith had drawn two deep-seated easy-chairs side-by-side, close to the fire in the Lodge's sitting room. Marie Rakowska sat in one, her lithe body swaddled in half a dozen blankets. Nothing of her was visible but her head, the blonde hair tousled and tossed about; Smith had not tried to tidy it as he dried it vigorously with a towel. He now sat in the next chair, holding a cup of steaming black coffee to the woman's lips.

"Really, Linus, I'm not a baby. I can drink that myself," Marie protested. But she smiled, and did not seem to mind the attention. As for Smith's part, he felt relief that his companion had stopped shaking. Her colour had returned to its normal ivory hue.

"I should never have let you continue diving for so long, certainly not after dark," said Smith, upbraiding himself.

"You had no choice, my dear," responded Marie, sweetly. "I'm an adult. Besides, once I thought I spotted something on the bottom, I had to keep going until I had it, even if I could no longer see it. And I can hold my own cup now." It was a struggle for her to free a hand, but she managed it.

Inductions Dangerous

Smith relaxed somewhat. He had carried Marie at a run to the Lodge, where he had previously built a fire in anticipation of its need. He had rubbed her with soft towels and wrapped her in warm blankets, then fed her two glasses of brandy. The coffee followed at a more leisurely pace. He nonetheless regretted involving the woman in the search for the pistol, especially as its existence had been no more than a theory. He would insist upon her consulting a physician when they returned to Warsaw, just to ensure that there would be no lingering effects of her courageous swim.

When Marie finished her coffee, Smith relieved her of the cup, covering her arm once more. She was staring at the weapon she had found. It was lying on a small table a few feet away, a little pool of water having formed under it.

"It means you were right about how Jan died, doesn't it?" she asked quietly.

Smith nodded with reluctance.

"I think so. I'm sorry."

Marie laid her head on Smith's shoulder, and started to cry.

The Saxon Square was a prestigious address in Warsaw. Three of its sides were faced with elegant eighteenth century buildings, while the fourth was largely filled with the entrance front of the Hotel Central. It was a much more recent erection, only a few decades old, yet had been designed in the neo-classical style, so as to blend in with the neighbouring architecture.

From the window at which he stood, Smith overlooked the square, the attractive structures that walled it in, and the empty expanse that filled it. Until a couple of years before, the latter had been occupied by a church in the Byzantine fashion, ornate, almost oriental, and quite out of sympathy with its surroundings. When the Poles regained their independence, they removed the edifice. Some foreigners viewed this as vandalism, others as sacrilege. But Smith understood the decision. It had been a Russian Orthodox church in a Polish Catholic city; its existence had been a reminder of the country's former servitude. When the overlordship of the tsar ended, its symbols had to go.

The door to the room opened and General Szerbinski entered, followed by several of his children, all talking at once. He held another upside down in his arms, inducing in that boy a giggling fit.

"Give me one moment, Major," begged Szerbinski, laughing as he flipped the child he was carrying right-side up, and depositing him on the carpeted floor. He spoke to his brood in commanding but warm tones, and sent them off with a clap of the hands. He closed the door behind them, and quiet descended on the room once more.

"Are you married, Major?" the general asked unexpectedly. He pushed back the thick black hair that had been mussed by childish exertions, and tightened the knot of his tie. "No? That is a shame. Family is more important than anything. It is why we fight for our freedom; not for ourselves, but for our children. Do you agree?"

"Yes sir, I do," answered Smith. "Sometimes, however, families are not easy to come by."

Szerbinski regarded Smith strangely. Then he smiled, with a bit of sadness.

"Yes, it is true. Not everyone has been as lucky as I." He gestured. "I see you have been provided with coffee. Would you like some more? No? Then please, sit."

The room into which Smith had been shown upon his arrival at the general's townhouse was not a parlour or a library, but a study. Bookshelves alternated with framed maps on the walls, while the only portrait was of the famed King John III Sobieski. Weapons, helmets and other trophies of war provided the décor, and firmly established this as Szerbinski's private sanctum. There was a big leather chair behind the bigger walnut desk, and two lesser chairs in front of it. Smith settled himself in one.

"You wished to see me regarding the alleged Russian spy..."

"Yes sir. I believed that I've discovered the truth in the matter."

Szerbinski remained silent, but held himself as if expecting bad news.

"It wasn't long after I'd arrived in Poland, sir, that evidence seemed to me to point to Josef Krzak as the Bolshevik agent, though this evidence was always circumstantial," Smith said. "Even so, he had the means and the opportunity to deliver intelligence to a controller based in East Prussia. Between May and August of 1920, he took four trips by automobile which would have brought him to the German frontier, but nowhere else of significance." The Briton paused to finish his coffee. The tiny cup he had been given had held very little, but the beverage had been rich. "Though Krzak had the means to deliver the intelligence, he did not have the means of collecting it. That was done by Colonel Jenowski."

Szerbinski, who had been in the act of offering his guest a cigarette from the carved oak box on his desk, froze. A smile then played on the mouth below the pencil-thin moustache, but his shrewd eyes detected no humour on Smith's nondescript countenance, and his ears heard no joke in the words spoken.

"Surely not..." The Pole drew back his arm, as if the availability of the tobacco was contingent upon the Englishman recanting his implication.

"I'm afraid so, General," Smith insisted. "Jenowski and Krzak were fast friends, after all. Who better than the latter to take the Bolsheviks information that the former provided?"

"You are telling me that both were working for the Bolsheviks?" The incredulity in Szerbinski's tone suggested a certain pity for his visitor, for

Smith's failing mind that had conceived such a fantasy. He extended the cigarette box once more. "But what could have been the motive?"

"Krzak's was simple friendship," answered Smith, accepting the gift before it was withdrawn again. After his cigarette was lit, he continued. "Colonel Jenowski used the Forester's Lodge at Proskiwicz as a residence in the summer of 1920. I was able to examine his personal papers that are kept there. They included letters written to the colonel by a woman. All the correspondence is in French. That language, as we are demonstrating now, is used extensively by the aristocratic and educated classes in Poland. To the nobility, it is almost a second native tongue. The letters in question were hand-delivered, so that there was never a return address or postal cancellation mark to identify their origins."

Szerbinski had sat back with his own cigarette. He waited for his guest to go on.

"Jenowski had, at some point, written instructions to his cousin and heir, regarding the management of Proskiwicz. These instructions were left with Mr Madej, the colonel's solicitor, to be forwarded in the event of the colonel's demise. Madej thought that these instructions would cause resentment on the part of Paul Jenowski and, when the colonel took them back in May, 1920, attributed the decision to a sudden agreement with his views." Smith paused to exhale smoke. "It was in May that Captain Krzak began his journeys to East Prussia."

Briefly, there was silence in the study. The faint noises of children at play somewhere else in the house could then be heard. Szerbinski slowly came to a realisation.

"My God... The letter, the letters from a woman... They were from his family, his mother or sister... And the instructions for his cousin... He took them back because he found that his brother was still alive..."

"So I believe, sir. If research were to be done into Colonel Jenowski's childhood, one may discover that he called his sister 'Fly'; though I suspect it was done only when the two wrote to each other. The Bolsheviks had found the Jenowskis and were holding them as hostages," Smith said quietly, "keeping them as surety against intelligence." He shrugged his shoulders slightly. "If it's a consolation, General, Jenowski was a reluctant traitor. It was that reluctance, in fact, that caused my confusion. Three years ago, the cryptanalysis unit led by the then-Lieutenant Grzyna, broke in succession two codes that the Russians were using."

"Yes," replied Szerbinski, adding, after a pause, "you may have learned that the second code's existence was kept from me for a time." The general's attitude was one of annoyance and embarrassment combined.

"I hope you don't blame Jenowski too much for maintaining your ignorance in the matter, sir," said Smith, sympathetically. "He was very firmly fixed between the rock of his patriotic duties and the hard place in which his family had been put. He tried to limit the damage he was doing: he did not, for example, tell the Russians that their initial code had been cracked by Grzyna's team. When the Bolsheviks adopted a second, they were merely taking a sensible precaution."

Szerbinski was following the Englishman's logic closely now, and leaned forward, jabbing the air with his cigarette.

"The deserter!" he exclaimed. "The deserter who was killed with Major Tejma had been on the Red Army's staff. He must have been privy to their codes, and they altered them to be safe, guessing that he would tell us about them."

"Colonel Jenowski told the Bolsheviks only what he had to in order to guarantee the lives of his family," Smith pointed out. "If the Russians had discovered that you had deciphered their first code, they would have realised that their agent was withholding information from them."

Szerbinski was understanding the situation in which Jenowski had found himself. Sitting back in his chair once more, he nodded.

"He restricted knowledge of the breaking of the second code to an even greater extent than he did the first."

"He trusted Krzak, whom he had told about the broken codes, and he trusted you, General, but rumours can spread even in the most secure situations, and he could not take that risk." Smith extinguished his cigarette. "Part of the difficulty that I faced, sir, was finding a Russian agent who had not known about the deciphered codes and so had not been able to report them to his masters. What he turned out to be was an agent who *wouldn't* report to his superiors, rather than couldn't."

Szerbinski drew smoke from his stubby cigarette, an unthinking action. His mind was elsewhere, sifting the information he had just been given. Then he frowned, and stared across the desk at his guest.

"But who killed Jenowski?" he demanded, a little plaintively. "And why?"

"The colonel died because he failed to warn the Bolsheviks about the new offensive your army was to launch in mid-August of 1920." Smith answered the question involving motive first. "He undoubtedly hated helping the Russians, but if they had not been told of the details of the new attack, they would have taken it as a betrayal on his part; his family would likely have been murdered in retribution."

"Yet he didn't warn them," Szerbinski stated, spreading his hands. "Our offensive was a tremendous success, and we were able to negotiate peace because of it, negotiate from a position of strength."

"That's right, sir," agree Smith, "Jenowski did not warn the Russians — but he tried." The Pole frowned, and his visitor expostulated further. "Remember that Krzak, Jenowski's messenger, vanished, probably killed by the Red cavalry, in the interval between the first concentration of your forces and the launch of the offensive. For a few days, Jenowski was in suspense as to whether his friend had died before or after delivering to his controller information about the impending attack."

"But when our offensive resulted in a great defeat for the enemy, he knew." Szerbinski's voice was heavy. "The Russians would have seen his lack of a warning as treachery, and his family..." The general grew silent and, at a burst of muffled, childish laughter from somewhere in the house, turned toward the closed door. "I should despise Jenowski for the harm he did this country, *his* country, but... How would I have behaved in his place, I wonder..." After a while his clouded countenance cleared a little. "And Jenowski himself?" The question was little more than a formality, for Szerbinski had guessed the answer.

"He was discovered in the water, on the far side of the lake at Proskiwicz, as you know, sir," responded Smith, sadly. "That is where the water carried him. He died, however, at his favourite place: at the end of the stone quay by the Forester's Lodge. His country betrayed, his family lost forever, his best friend missing, likely dead — all due to his actions. The shame and guilt must have been too terrible for an honourable man to bear."

Smith removed from his jacket the pistol that Marie Rakowska had found in the lake, beneath the spot at which her husband had been killed.

"So he didn't," concluded Smith.

"I really should hate you."

Marie Rakowska stared unseeingly at the traffic below Smith's hotel room window. It was one o'clock, and the average Warsaw resident's work-day was ended. The Poles began their labours very early, and now they were retiring to their favourite restaurant or café for food and company. But Marie's thoughts were far from such mundane matters.

"You had no idea?"

Smith stepped up beside her. He, unlike most people, had little trouble concentrating on more than one thing at a time, and so observed the moving crowds below, while being keenly aware of the young woman whose body warmed the air next to him.

"No idea that my husband had committed suicide?" Her soft lips curved in a reproachful smile. "None. He left me no letter, not even a single line to tell me 'good-bye'." She swallowed and blinked, then gratefully remembered the cigarette that smouldered in her fingers. "Do you think he was too ashamed to explain things to me?"

Smith did think so, but avoided answering the question.

"Sometimes, it's difficult to know how to say good-bye. I believe that he must have thought it unnecessary. He trusted that you would know he loved you."

The woman exhaled tobacco smoke and said, " 'Trust' is an odd word to use about Jan, now that we know his secret…"

"You could trust him always to protect you, his family, your children, no matter what the cost," commented Smith. "That should be what you remember about him."

Marie smiled more freely now, and turned to regard the gentleman beside her. She put her pale hand on his arm.

"You're a generous person, Linus."

Smith grasped Marie's fingers tenderly. He could afford to be generous, he remarked mentally; he had not been betrayed by anyone. On the pavements beneath the window, people walked with delighted anticipation to meet their friends and family for luncheon.